Wilbur Smith

**The World's Greatest
and Most Popular Writer
of Epic Adventure**

The novels of Wilbur Smith

Shout at the Devil
Gold Mine

Wilbur Smith was born in Central Africa in 1933. He was educated at Michaelhouse and Rhodes University.

He became a full-time writer in 1964 after the successful publication of *When the Lion Feeds*, and has since written twenty-three novels, meticulously researched on his numerous expeditions worldwide.

He normally travels from November to February, often spending a month skiing in Switzerland, and visiting Australia and New Zealand for sea fishing. During his summer break, he visits environments as diverse as Alaska and the dwindling wilderness of the African interior. He has an abiding concern for the peoples and wildlife of his native continent, an interest strongly reflected in his novels.

He is married to Danielle, to whom his last nineteen books have been dedicated.

WILBUR SMITH

Shout at the Devil

Gold Mine

Mandarin

A Mandarin Paperback
SHOUT AT THE DEVIL
GOLD MINE

Shout at the Devil first published in Great Britain 1968
by William Heinemann Ltd
Mandarin paperback edition published 1992
Gold Mine first published in Great Britain 1970
by William Heinemann Ltd
Mandarin paperback edition published 1992
First published together in this omnibus edition 1993
by Mandarin Paperbacks
an imprint of Reed Consumer Books Ltd
Michelin House, 81 Fulham Road, London SW3 6RB
and Auckland, Melbourne, Singapore and Toronto

A CIP catalogue record for this title
is available from the British Library
ISBN 0 7493 1476 1

Phototypeset by Intype, London
Printed and bound in Great Britain
by Cox & Wyman Ltd, Reading

Shout at the Devil

Foreword

I will not deny that this story was suggested to me by the action in World War I, when the German mercantile raider *Königsberg* was sunk in the Kikunya channel of the Rufiji delta by ships of the Royal Navy.

However, I will most emphatically deny that the rogues and scoundrels depicted in my tale bear the slightest resemblance to any members of the company of men that operated to the destruction of *Königsberg*. In particular, I would strongly resist the suggestion that Flynn Patrick O'Flynn is based on the character of the gallant Colonel 'Jungle Man' Pretorius, who actually went aboard *Königsberg*, disguised as a native bearer, and paced out the ranges for the guns of His Majesty's warships *Severn* and *Mersey*.

I would like to express my thanks to Lieutenant-Commander Mathers (R.N. retired) for his assistance in my researches.

Part I

I

Flynn Patrick O'Flynn was an ivory poacher by profession, and modestly he admitted that he was the best on the east coast of Africa.

Rachid El Keb was an exporter of precious stones, of women for the harems and great houses of Arabia and India, and of illicit ivory. This he admitted only to his trusted clients; to the rest he was a rich and respectable owner of coastal shipping.

In an afternoon during the monsoon of 1912, drawn together by their mutual interest in pachyderms, Flynn and Rachid sat in the back room of El Keb's shop in the Arab quarter of Zanzibar, and drank tea from tiny brass thimbles. The hot tea made Flynn O'Flynn perspire even more than usual. It was so humid hot in the room that the flies sat in languid stupor upon the low ceiling.

'Listen, Kebby, you lend me just one of those stinking little ships of yours and I'll fill her so high with tusks, she'll damn nigh sink.'

'Ah!' replied El Keb carefully, and went on waving the palm-leaf fan in his own face – a face that resembled that of a suspicious parrot with a straggly, goatee beard.

'Have I ever let you down yet?' Flynn demanded aggressively, and a drop of sweat fell from the tip of his nose onto his already damp shirt.

'Ah!' El Keb repeated.

'This scheme has a flair. It has the touch of greatness to it. This scheme...' Flynn paused to find a suitable adjective, '... this scheme is Napoleonic. It is Caesarian!'

'Ah!' El Keb said again, and refilled his tea cup. Lifting it delicately between thumb and forefinger, he sipped before speaking. 'It is necessary only that I should risk the total destruction of a sixty-foot dhow worth...' prudently he inflated the figure, '... two thousand English pounds?'

3

'Against an almost certain recovery of twenty thousand,' Flynn cut in quickly, and El Keb smiled a little, almost dreamily.

'You'd put the profits so high?' he asked.

'That's the lowest figure. Good God, Kebby! There hasn't been a shot fired in the Rufiji basin for twenty years. You know damn well it's the Kaiser's private hunting reserve. The Jumbo are so thick in there I could round them up and drive them in like sheep.' Involuntarily Flynn's right forefinger crooked and twitched as though it were already curled around a trigger.

'Madness,' whispered El Keb, with the gold gloat softening the shape of his lips. 'You'd sail into the Rufiji river from the sea, hoist the Union Jack on one of the islands in the delta and fill the dhow with German ivory. Madness.'

'The Germans have formally annexed none of those islands. I'd be in and out again before Berlin had sent their first cable to London. With ten of my gun-boys hunting, we'd fill the dhow in two weeks.'

'The Germans would have a gunboat there in a week. They've got the *Blücher* lying at Dar es Salaam under steam, heavy cruiser with nine-inch guns.'

'We'd be under protection of the British flag. They couldn't dare touch us – not on the high seas – not with things the way they are now between England and Germany.'

'Mr O'Flynn, I was led to believe you were a citizen of the United States of America.'

'You damn right I am.' Flynn sat up a little straighter, a little more proudly.

'You'd need a British captain for the dhow,' El Keb mused, and stroked his beard thoughtfully.

'Jesus, Kebby, you didn't think I was fool enough to sail that cow in myself?' Flynn looked pained. 'I'll find someone else to do that, and to sail her out again through the Imperial German navy. Me, I'm going to walk in from my base camp in Portuguese Mozambique and go out the same way.'

'Forgive me.' El Keb smiled again. 'I underestimated you.' He stood up quickly. The splendour of the great jewelled dagger at his waist was somewhat spoiled by the unwashed white of his ankle-length robe. 'Mr O'Flynn, I think I have just the man to captain your dhow for you. But first it is necessary to alter his financial circumstances so that he might be willing to accept employment.'

2

The leather purse of gold sovereigns had been the pivot on which the gentle confusion of Sebastian Oldsmith's life turned. It had been presented to him by his father when Sebastian had announced to the family his intention of sailing to Australia to make his fortune in the wool trade. It had comforted him during the voyage from Liverpool to the Cape of Good Hope where the captain had unceremoniously deposited him after Sebastian's misalliance with the daughter of the gentleman who was proceeding to Sydney to take up his appointment as Governor of New South Wales.

In gradually dwindling quantity the sovereigns had remained with him through the series of misfortunes that ended in Zanzibar, when he awoke from heat-drugged sleep in a shoddy room to find that the leather purse and its contents were gone, and with them were gone the letters of introduction from his father to certain prominent wool-brokers of Sydney.

It occurred to Sebastian as he sat on the edge of his bed that the letters had little real value in Zanzibar, and with increasing bewilderment, he reviewed the events that had blown him so far off his intended course. Slowly his forehead creased in the effort of thought. It was the high, intelligent forehead of a philosopher crowned by a splendid mass of shiny black curls; his eyes were dark brown, his nose long and straight, his jaw firm, and his mouth sensitive. In his twenty-second year, Sebastian had the face of a young Oxford don; which proves, perhaps, how misleading looks can be. Those who knew him well would have been surprised that Sebastian, in setting out for Australia, had come as close to it as Zanzibar.

Abandoning the mental exercise that was already giving him a slight headache, Sebastian stood up from the bed and, with the skirt of his nightshirt flapping around his calves, began his third minute search of the hotel room. Although the purse had been under his mattress when he went to sleep the preceding evening, this time Sebastian emptied the water jug and peered into it hopefully. He unpacked his valise and shook out each shirt. He crawled under the bed, lifted the coconut matting and probed every hole in the rotten flooring before giving way to despair.

Shaved, the bed-bug bites on his person anointed with saliva, and dressed in the grey three-piece suit which was showing signs of travel fatigue, he brushed his derby hat and placed it carefully over his curls, picked up his cane in one hand, and lugging his valise in the other, he went down the stairs into the hot noisy lobby of the Hotel Royal.

'I say,' he greeted the little Arab at the desk with the most cheerful smile he could muster. 'I say, I seem to have lost my money.'

A silence fell upon the room. The waiters carrying trays out to the hotel veranda slowed and stopped, heads turned towards Sebastian with the same hostile curiosity as if he had announced that he was suffering from a mild attack of leprosy.

'Stolen, I should imagine,' Sebastian went on, grinning. 'Nasty bit of luck, really.'

The silence exploded as the bead curtains from the office were thrown open and the Hindu proprietor erupted into the room with a loud cry of, 'Mr Oldsmith, what about your bill?'

'Oh, the bill. Yes, well, let's not get excited. I mean, it won't help, now, will it?'

And the proprietor proceeded to become very excited indeed. His cries of anguish and indignation carried to the veranda where a dozen persons were already beginning the daily fight against heat and thirst. They crowded into the lobby to watch with interest.

'Ten days you owe. Nearly one hundred rupees.'

'Yes, it's jolly unfortunate, I know.' Sebastian was grinning desperately, when a new voice added itself to the uproar.

'Now just hold on a shake.' Together Sebastian and the Hindu turned to the big red-faced, middle-aged man with the pleasantly mixed American and Irish accent. 'Did I hear you called Mr Oldsmith?'

'That is correct, sir.' Sebastian knew instinctively that here was an ally.

'An unusual name. You wouldn't be related to Mister Francis

Oldsmith, wool merchant of Liverpool, England?' Flynn O'Flynn inquired politely. He had perused Sebastian's letters of introduction passed on to him by Rachid El Keb.

'Good Lord!' Sebastian cried with joy. 'Do you know my pater?'

'Do I know Francis Oldsmith?' Flynn laughed easily, and then checked himself. His acquaintance was limited to the letterheads. 'Well, I don't exactly know him person to person, you understand, but I think I can say I know *of* him. Used to be in the wool business myself once.' Flynn turned genially to the hotel proprietor and breathed on him a mixture of gin fumes and goodfellowship. 'One hundred rupees was the sum you mentioned.'

'That's the sum, Mr O'Flynn.' The proprietor was easily soothed.

'Mr Oldsmith and I will be having a drink on the veranda. You can bring the receipt to us there.' Flynn placed two sovereigns on the counter; sovereigns that had so recently reposed beneath Sebastian's mattress.

With his boots propped on the low veranda wall, Sebastian regarded the harbour over the rim of his glass. Sebastian was not a drinking man but in view of Flynn O'Flynn's guardianship he could not be churlish and refuse hospitality. The number of craft in the bay suddenly multiplied miraculously before his eyes. Where a moment before one stubby little dhow had been tacking in through the entrance, there were now three identical boats sailing in formation. Sebastian closed one eye and by focusing determinedly, he reduced the three back to one. Mildly elated with his success, he turned his attention to his new friend and business partner who had pressed such large quantities of gin upon him.

'Mr O'Flynn,' he said with deliberation, slurring the words slightly.

'Forget that mister, Bassie, call me Flynn. Just plain Flynn, the same as in gin.'

'Flynn,' said Sebastian. 'There isn't anything – well, there isn't anything funny about this?'

'How do you mean *funny*, boy?'

'I mean' – and Sebastian blushed slightly. 'There isn't anything illegal, is there?'

'Bassie.' Flynn shook his head sorrowfully. 'What do you take me for, Bassie? You think I'm a crook or something, boy?'

'Oh, no, of course not, Flynn,' and Sebastian blushed a shade deeper. 'I just thought – well, all these elephants we're going to shoot. They must belong to somebody. Aren't they German elephants?'

'Bassie, I want to show you something.' Flynn set down his glass and groping in the inside pocket of his wilted tropical suit, he produced an envelope. 'Read that, boy!'

The address at the head of the sheet of cheap notepaper was 'The Kaiserhof. Berlin. Dated June 10, 1912', and the body of the letter read:

> Dear Mr Flynn O'Flynn,
> I am worried about all those elephants down in the Rufiji basin eating up all the grass and smashing up all the trees and things, so if you've got time, would you go down there and shoot some of them as they're eating up all the grass and smashing up all the trees and things.
> > Yours sincerely,
> > Kaiser Willem III.
> > Emperor of Germany.

A vague uneasiness formed through the clouds of gin in Sebastian's skull. 'Why did he write to you?'

'Because he knows I'm the best goddamned elephant hunter in the world.'

'You'd expect him to use better English, wouldn't you?' Sebastian murmured.

'What's wrong with his English?' Flynn demanded truculently. He had spent some time in composing the letter.

'Well, I mean that bit about eating up all the grass – he said that twice.'

'Well, you got to remember he's a German. They don't write English too good.'

'Of course! I hadn't thought of that.' Sebastian looked relieved and lifted his glass. 'Well, good hunting!'

'I'll drink to that,' and Flynn emptied his glass.

3

Sebastian stood with both hands gripping the wooden rail of the dhow and stared out across a dozen miles of water at the loom of the African mainland. The monsoon wind had ruffled the sea to a dark indigo and it flipped spray from the white-caps into Sebastian's face. Overlaying the clean salt of the ocean was the taint of the mangrove swamps, an evil smell as though an animal had died in its own cage. Sebastian sniffed it with distaste as he searched the low, green line of the coast for the entrance to the maze of the Rufiji delta.

Frowning, he tried to reconstruct the admiralty chart in his mind. The Rufiji river came to the sea through a dozen channels spread over forty miles, and in doing so, carved fifty, maybe a hundred, islands out of the mainland.

Tidal water washed fifteen miles upstream, past the mangroves to where the vast grass swampland began. It was there in the swampland that the elephant herds had taken shelter from the guns and arrows of the ivory hunters, protected by Imperial decree and by a formidable terrain.

The murderous-looking ruffian who captained the dhow uttered a string of sing-song orders, and Sebastian turned to watch the complicated manoeuvre of tacking the ungainly craft. Half-naked seamen dropped out of the rigging like over-ripe brown fruit and swarmed around the sixty-foot teak boom. Bare feet padding on the filthy deck, they ran the boom back and forward again. The dhow creaked like an old man with arthritis, came round wearily on to the wind, and butted its nose in towards the land. The new motion, combined with the swamp smell and the smell of freshly-stirred bilges, moved something deep within Sebastian. His grip upon the rail increased, and new sweat popped out like little blisters on his brow. He leaned forward, and, to shouts of encouragement from the crew, made another sacrifice to the sea gods. He was still draped worshipfully across the rail as the dhow wallowed and slid in the turbulent waters of the entrance, and then passed into the calm of the southernmost channel of the Rufiji basin.

Four days later, Sebastian sat cross-legged with the dhow captain on a thick Bokhara carpet spread upon the deck, and they explained to each other in sign language that neither of them had the vaguest idea where they were. The dhow was anchored in a narrow water-way hemmed in by the twisted and deformed trunks of the mangroves. The sensation of being lost was not new to Sebastian and he accepted it with resignation, but the dhow captain, who could run from Aden to Calcutta and back to Zanzibar with the certainty of a man visiting his own outhouse, was not so stoical. He lifted his eyes to the heavens and called upon Allah to intercede with the djinn who guarded this stinking labyrinth, who made the waters flow in strange, unnatural ways, who changed the shape of each island, and thrust mud banks in their path. Driven on by his own eloquence, he leapt to the rail and screamed defiance into the brooding mangroves until flocks of ibis rose and milled in the heat mists above the dhow. Then he flung himself down on the carpet and fixed Sebastian with a stare of sullen malevolence.

'It's not really my fault, you know.' Sebastian wriggled with embarrassment under the stare. Then once again he produced his admiralty chart, spread it on the deck, and placed his finger on the island which Flynn O'Flynn had ringed in blue pencil as the rendezvous. 'I mean, it *is* rather your cup of tea, finding the place. After all, you *are* the navigator, aren't you?'

The captain spat fiercely on his deck, and Sebastian flushed.

'Now that sort of thing isn't going to get us anywhere. Let's try and behave like gentlemen.'

This time the captain hawked it up from deep down in his throat and spat a lump of yellow phlegm into the blue pencil circle on Sebastian's map, then he rose to his feet and stalked away to where his crew squatted in a group under the poop.

In the short dusk, while the mosquitoes whined in a thin mist about Sebastian's head, he listened to the Arabic muttering and saw the glances that were directed at him down the length of the dhow. So when the night closed over the ship like a bank of black steam, he took up a defensive position on the foredeck and waited for them to come. As a weapon he had his cane of solid ebony. He laid it across his lap and sat against the rail until the darkness was complete, then, silently, he changed his position and crouched beside one of the water barrels that was lashed to the base of the mast.

They were a long time coming. Half the night had wasted away before he heard the stealthy scuff of bare feet on the planking. The absolute blackness of the night was filled with the din of the swamp; the boom and tonk of frogs, the muted buzz of insects and the occasional snort and splash of a hippo, so that Sebastian had difficulty in deciding how many they had sent against him. Crouching by the water barrel he strained his eyes unavailingly into the utter blackness and tuned his hearing to filter out the swamp noises and catch only those soft little sounds that death made as it came down the deck towards him.

Although Sebastian had never scaled any academic heights, he had boxed light heavyweight for Rugby, and fast-bowled for Sussex the previous cricket season when he had led the county bowling averages. So, although he was afraid now, Sebastian had a sublime confidence in his own physical prowess and it was not the kind of fear that filled his belly with oily warmth, nor turned his ego to jelly, but rather, it keyed him to a point where every muscle in his body quivered on the edge of exploding. Crouching in the night he groped for the cane that he had laid on the deck beside him. His hands fell on the bulky sackful of green coconuts that made up part of the dhow's deck cargo. They were carried to supplement, with their milk, the meagre supply of fresh water on board. Quickly Sebastian tore open the fastenings of the sack and hefted one of the hard round fruits.

'Not quite as handy as a cricket ball, but – ' murmured Sebastian and came to his feet. Using the short run up he delivered the fast ball with which he had shattered the Yorkshire first innings the previous year. It had the same effect on the Arab first innings. The coconut whirred and cracked against the skull of one of the approaching assassins and the rest retired in confusion.

'Now send the men,' roared Sebastian and bowled a short lifter that hastened the retreat.

He selected another coconut and was about to deliver that also when there was a flash and a report from aft, and something howled over Sebastian's head. Hastily he ducked behind the sack of coconuts.

'My God, they've got a gun up there!' Sebastian remembered

then the ancient muzzle-loading Jezail he had seen the captain polishing lovingly on their first day out from Zanzibar, and he felt his anger rising in earnest.

He jumped to his feet and hurled his next coconut with fury. 'Fight fair, you dirty swine!' he yelled.

There was a delay while the dhow captain went through the complicated process of loading his piece. Then a cannon report, a burst of flame, and another potleg howled over Sebastian's head.

Through the dark hours before dawn the lively exchange of jeers and curses, of coconuts and potlegs continued. Sebastian more than held his own for he scored four howls of pain and a yelp, while the dhow captain succeeded only in shooting away a great deal of his own standing rigging. But as the light of the new day increased, so Sebastian's advantage waned. The Arab captain's shooting improved to such an extent that Sebastian spent most of his time crouching behind the sack of coconuts. Sebastian was nearly exhausted. His right arm and shoulder ached unmercifully, and he could hear the first stealthy advance of the Arab crew as they crept down towards his hide. In daylight they could surround him and use their numbers to drag him down.

While he rested for the final effort, Sebastian looked out at the morning. It was a red dawn, angry and beautiful through the swamp mists so the water glowed with a pink sheen and the mangroves stood very dark around the ship.

Something splashed farther up the channel, a water bird perhaps. Sebastian looked for it without interest, and heard it splash again and then again. He stirred and sat up a little straighter. The sound was too regular for that of a bird or a fish.

Then around the bend in the channel, from behind the wall of mangroves, driven on by urgent paddles, shot a dug-out canoe. Standing in the bow with a double-barrelled elephant gun under his arm and a clay pipe sticking out of his red face, was Flynn O'Flynn.

'What the hell's going on here?' he roared. 'Are you fighting a goddamned war? I've been waiting a week for you lot!'

'Look out, Flynn!' Sebastian yelled a warning. 'That swine has got a gun!'

The Arab captain had jumped to his feet and was looking around uncertainly. Long ago he had regretted his impulse to rid himself of the Englishman and escape from this evil swamp, and now his misgivings were truly justified. Having committed himself, however, there was only one course open to him. He lifted the Jezail to his shoulder and aimed at O'Flynn in the canoe. The discharge blew a long grey spurt of powder from the muzzle, and the potleg lifted a burst of spray from the surface of the water beyond the canoe. The echoes of the shot were drowned by the bellow of O'Flynn's rifle. He fired without moving the pipe from his mouth and the narrow dug-out rocked dangerously with the recoil.

The heavy bullet picked up the Arab captain's scrawny body, his robe fluttered like a piece of old paper and his turban flew from his head and unwound in mid-air as he was flung clear of the rail to drop with a tall splash alongside. He floated face down, trapped air ballooning his robe about him and then he drifted away slowly on the sluggish current. His crew, stunned and silent, stood by the rail and watched him depart.

Dismissing the neat execution as though it had never happened, O'Flynn glared up at Sebastian and roared, 'You're a week late. I haven't been able to do a goddamned thing until you got here. Now let's get the flag up and start doing some work!'

4

The formal annexation of Flynn O'Flynn's island took place in the relatively cool of the following morning. It had taken some hours for Flynn to convince Sebastian of the necessity of occupying the island for the British crown, and he succeeded only by casting Sebastian in the role of empire builder. He made some flattering comparisons between Clive of India and Sebastian Oldsmith of Liverpool.

The next problem was the choice of a name. This stirred up a little Anglo-American enmity, with Flynn O'Flynn campaigning aggressively for 'New Boston'. Sebastian was horrified, his patriotic ardour burned brightly.

'Now hold on a jiffy, old chap,' he protested.

'What's wrong with it? You just tell me what's wrong with it!'

'Well, first of all this is going to be one of His Britannic Majesty's possessions, you know.'

'New Boston,' O'Flynn repeated. 'That sounds good. That sounds real good.'

Sebastian shuddered. 'I think it would be – well, not quite suitable. I mean, Boston was the place where they had that tea thing, you know.'

The argument raged more savagely as Flynn lowered the level in the gin bottle, until finally Sebastian stood up from the carpet on the floor of the dhow cabin, his eyes blazing with patriotic outrage. 'If you would care to step outside, sir,' he enunciated with care as he stood over the older man, 'we can settle this matter.' The dignity of the challenge was spoiled by the low roof of the cabin which made it necessary for Sebastian to stoop.

'Man, I'd eat you without spitting the bones.'

'That, sir, is your opinion. But I must warn you I was highly thought of in the light heavyweight division.'

'Oh, goddamn it,' Flynn shook his head wearily and

capitulated. 'What difference does it make what we call the mother-loving place. Sit down, for God's sake. Here! Let's drink to whatever you want to call it.'

Sebastian sat on the carpet and accepted the mug that Flynn handed him. 'We shall call it – ' he paused dramatically, 'we shall call it New Liverpool,' and he lifted the mug.

'You know,' said Flynn, 'for a limey, you aren't a bad guy,' and the rest of the night was devoted to celebrating the birth of the new colony.

In the dawn the empire builders were paddled ashore in the dug-out by two of Flynn's gun-bearers.

The canoe ran aground on the narrow muddy beach of New Liverpool, and the sudden halt threw both of them off-balance. They collapsed gently together on to the floor of the dug-out, and had to be assisted ashore by the paddlers.

Sebastian was formally dressed for the occasion but had buttoned his waistcoat awry and he kept tugging at it as he peered about him.

Now at high tide, New Liverpool was about a thousand yards long and half as broad. At the highest point it rose not more than ten feet above the level of the Rufiji river. Fifteen miles from the mouth the water was only slightly tainted with salt and the mangrove trees had thinned out and given way to tall matted elephant grass and slender bottle palms.

Flynn's gun-bearers and porters had cleared a small opening above the beach, and had erected a dozen grass huts around one of the palm trees. It was a dead palm, its crown leaves long gone and Flynn pointed an unsteady finger at it.

'Flag pole,' he said indistinctly, took Sebastian's elbow and led him towards it.

Tugging at his waistcoat with one hand and clutching the bundled Union Jack that Flynn had provided in the other, Sebastian felt a surge of emotion within him as he looked up at the slender column of the palm tree.

'Leave me,' he mumbled and shook off Flynn's guiding hand. 'We got to do this right. Solemn occasion – very solemn.'

'Have a drink.' Flynn offered him the gin bottle, and when Sebastian waved it away, he lifted it to his own lips.

'Shouldn't drink on parade.' Sebastian frowned at him. 'Bad form.'

Flynn coughed at the vicious sting of the liquor and smote himself on the chest with his free hand.

'Should draw the men up in a hollow square,' Sebastian went on. 'Ready to salute the flag.'

'Jesus, man, get on with it,' grumbled Flynn.

'Got to do it right.'

'Oh, hell,' Flynn shrugged with resignation, then issued a string of orders in Swahili.

Puzzled and amused, Flynn's fifteen retainers gathered in a ragged circle about the flag pole. They were a curious band, gathered from half a dozen tribes, dressed in an assortment of cast-off western clothing, half of them armed with ancient double-barrelled elephant rifles from which Flynn had carefully filed the serial numbers so they could never be traced back to him.

'Fine body of men,' Sebastian beamed at them in alcoholic goodwill, unconsciously using the words of a Brigadier who had inspected Sebastian's cadet parade at Rugby.

'Let's get this show on the road,' Flynn suggested.

'My friends,' Sebastian obliged, 'we are gathered here today . . .' It was a longish speech but Flynn weathered it by nipping away quietly at the gin bottle, and at last Sebastian ended with his voice ringing and tears of great emotion prickling his eyelids, '. . . In the sight of God and man, I hereby declare this island part of the glorious Empire of His Majesty, George V, King of England, Emperor of India, Protector of the Faith . . .' His voice wavered as he tried to remember the correct form, and he ended lamely, '. . . and all that sort of thing.'

A silence fell on the assembly and Sebastian fidgeted with embarrassment. 'What do I do now?' he enquired of Flynn O'Flynn in a stage whisper.

'Get that goddamned flag up.'

'Ah, the flag!' Sebastian exclaimed with relief, and the uncertainly, 'How?'

Flynn considered this at length. 'I guess you have to climb up the palm tree.'

With shrill cries of encouragement from the gun-bearers, and with Flynn shoving and cursing from below, the Governor of New Liverpool managed to scale the flag pole to a height of about fifteen feet. There he secured the flag and descended again so swiftly he tore the buttons off the front of his waistcoat, and twisted his ankle. He was borne away to one of the grass huts singing, 'God save our Gracious King' in a voice broken with gin, pain and patriotism.

For the rest of their stay on the island, the Union Jack flew at half mast above the encampment.

Carried initially by two Wakamba fishermen, it took fully ten days for the word of the annexation to reach the outpost of the German Empire one hundred miles away at Mahenge.

5

Mahenge was in the bush country above the coastal lowlands. It consisted, in its entirety, of four trading posts owned by Indian shopkeepers – and the German boma.

The German boma was a large stone building, thatched, set about with wide verandas over which purple bougainvillaea climbed in profusion. Behind it stood the barracks and parade ground of the African Askari, and before it a lonely flag pole from which streamed the black, red and yellow of the empire. A speck in the vastness of the African bush, seat of government for an area the size of France. An area that spread south to the Rovuma river and the border of Portuguese Mozambique, east to the Indian Ocean, and west to the uplands of Sao Hill and Mbeya.

From this stronghold the German Commissioner (Southern Province) wielded the limitless powers of a medieval robber baron. One of the Kaiser's arms, or, more realistically, one of his little fingers, he was answerable only to Governor Schee in Dar es Salaam. But Dar es Salaam was many torturous miles away, and Governor Schee was a busy man not to be troubled with trivialities. Just as long as the Herr Commissioner Herman Fleischer collected the taxes, he was free to collect them in his own sweet way; though very few of the indigenous inhabitants of the southern province would have described Herman Fleischer's ways as sweet.

At the time that the messenger, carrying the news of the British annexation of New Liverpool, trotted up over the last skyline and saw through the acacia thorn trees ahead of him the tiny clustered buildings of Mahenge, Herr Fleischer was finishing his midday meal.

A man of large appetite, his luncheon consisted of approximately two pounds of *Eisbein*, as much pickled cabbage, and a dozen potatoes, all swimming in thick gravy. Having aroused his taste-buds, he then went on to the sausage. The sausage came by weekly fast-runner from Dodoma in the north, and was manufactured by a man of genius, a Westphalian immigrant who made sausage with the taste of the Black Forest in them. The sausage, and the Hansa beer cooling in its earthernware jug, aroused in Herr Fleischer a delicious nostalgia. He ate not quietly but steadily, and, these quantities of food confined within the thick grey corduroy of his tunic and breeches, built up a pressure that squeezed the perspiration from his face and neck, forcing him to pause and mop up at regular intervals.

When he sighed at last and sagged back in his chair, the leather thongs squeaked a little under him. A bubble of trapped gas found its way up through the sausage and passed in genteel eruption between his lips. Tasting it, he sighed again in happiness and squinted out from the deep shade of the veranda into the flat shimmering glare of the sunlight.

Then he saw the messenger coming. The man reached the steps of the veranda and squatted down in the sun with his loincloth drawn up modestly between his legs. His body was washed shiny black with sweat but his legs were powdered with fine dust to the knees, and his chest swelled and subsided as he drank the thin hot air. His eyes were downcast, he could not look directly at the Bwana Mkuba until his presence was formally acknowledged.

Herman Fleischer watched him broodingly, his mood evaporating for he had been looking forward to his afternoon siesta – and the messenger had spoiled that. He looked away at the low cloud above the hills in the south and sipped his beer. Then he selected a cheroot from the box before him and lit it. The cheroot burned slowly and evenly, restoring a little of his good humour. He smoked it short before flicking the stub over the veranda wall.

'Speak,' he grunted, and the messenger lifted his eyes, and gasped with wonder and awe at the beauty and dignity of the Commissioner's person. Although this was ritual admiration, it never failed to stir a faint pleasure in Herr Fleischer.

'I see you, Bwana Mkuba – Great Lord,' and Fleischer inclined his head slightly. 'I bring you greetings from Kalani, headman of Batja, on the Rufiji. You are his father, and he crawls on his belly before you. Your hair of yellow, and the great fatness of your body, blind him with beauty.'

Herr Fleischer stirred restlessly in his chair. References to his corpulence, however well-intentioned, always annoyed him. 'Speak,' he repeated.

'Kalani says thus: "Ten suns ago, a ship came into the delta of the Rufiji, and stopped by the Island of the Dogs, Inja. On the island, the men of this ship have built houses, and above the houses, they have placed on a dead palm tree the cloth of the Insingeese which is of blue and white and red, having many crosses within crosses." '

Herr Fleischer struggled upright in his chair and stared at the messenger. The pink of his complexion slowly became cross-veined with red and purple.

'Kalani says also: "Since their coming the voices of their guns have never ceased to speak along the Rufiji river, and there has been a great killing of elephants so that in the noonday the sky is dark with the birds that come for the meat." '

Herr Fleischer was thrashing around in his chair, speech was locked in his throat and his face had swollen so it threatened to burst like an over-ripe fruit.

'Kalani says further: "Two white men are on the island. One is a man who is very thin and young and is therefore of no account. The other white man Kalani has seen only at a great distance but by the redness of this man's face, and by his bulk, he knows in his heart it is Fini." '

At the name Herr Fleischer became articulate, if not coherent – he bellowed like a bull in rut. The messenger winced, such a bellow from the Bwana Mkuba usually preceded a multiple hanging.

'Sergeant!' The next bellow had form, and Herr Fleischer was on his feet, struggling to clinch the buckle of his belt.

'Rasch!' he roared again. O'Flynn was in German territory again; O'Flynn was stealing German ivory once more – and compounding the insult by flying the Union Jack over the Kaiser's domain.

'Sergeant, where the thunder of God are you?' With incredible speed for a fat man Herr Fleischer raced down the long length of the veranda. For three years now, ever since his arrival in Mahenge, the name of Flynn O'Flynn had been enough to ruin his appetite, and produce in him a condition very close to epilepsy.

Around the corner of the veranda appeared the sergeant of the Askari, and Herr Fleischer braked just in time to avert collision.

'A storm patrol,' bellowed the Commissioner, blowing a cloud of spittle in his agitation. 'Twenty men. Full field packs, and one hundred pounds of ammunition. We leave in an hour.'

The sergeant saluted and doubled away across the parade ground. A minute later a bugle began singing with desperate urgency.

Slowly, through the black mists of rage, reason returned to Herman Fleischer. He stood with shoulders hunched, breathing heavily through his mouth, and mentally digested the full import of Kalani's message.

This was not just another of O'Flynn's will-o'-the-wisp forays across the Rovuma from Mozambique. This time he had sailed brazenly into the Rufiji delta, with a full-scale expedition, and hoisted the British flag. A queasy sensation, not attributable to the pickled pork, settled on Herr Fleischer's stomach. He knew the makings of an international incident when he saw one.

This, perhaps, was the goad that would launch the fatherland on the road to its true destiny. He gulped with excitement. They had flapped that hated flag in the Kaiser's face just once too often. This was history being made, and Herman Fleischer stood in the centre of it.

Trembling a little, he hurried into his office, and began drafting the report to Governor Schee that might plunge the world into a holocaust from which the German people would rise as the rulers of creation.

An hour later, he rode out of the boma on a white donkey with his slouch uniform hat set well forward on his head to shield his eyes from the glare. Behind him his black Askari marched with their rifles at the slope. Smart in their pillbox kepis with the backflaps hanging to the shoulder, khaki uniforms freshly pressed, and putteed legs rising and falling in unison, they made as gallant a show as any commander could wish.

A day and a half march would bring them to the confluence of the Kilombero and Rufiji rivers where the Commissioner's steam launch was moored.

As the buildings of Mahenge vanished behind him, Herr Fleischer relaxed and let his ample backside conform to the shape of the saddle.

6

'Now, have you got it straight?' Flynn asked without conviction. The past eight days of hunting together had given him no confidence in Sebastian's ability to carry out a simple set of instructions without introducing some remarkable variation of his own. 'You go down the river to the island, and you load the ivory onto the dhow. Then you come back here with all the canoes to pick up the next batch.' Flynn paused to allow his words to absorb into the spongy tissue of Sebastian's head before he went on. 'And for Chrissake don't forget the gin.'

'Right you are, old chap.' With eight days' growth of black beard, and the skin peeling from the tip of his sunburned nose, Sebastian was beginning to fit the role of ivory poacher. The wide brimmed terai hat that Flynn had loaned him came down to his ears, and the razor edges of the elephant grass had shredded his trouser legs and stripped the polish from his boots. His wrists and the soft skin behind his ears were puffy and speckled with spots of angry red where the mosquitoes had drunk deep, but he had lost a little weight in the heat and the ceaseless walking, so now he was lean and hard-looking.

They stood together under a monkey-bean tree on the bank of the Rufiji, while at the water's edge the bearers were loading the last tusks into the canoes. There was a purple-greenish smell hanging over them in the steamy heat, a smell which Sebastian hardly noticed now – for the last eight days had seen a great killing of elephant and the stink of green ivory was as familiar to him as the smell of the sea to a mariner.

'By the time you get back tomorrow morning the boys will have brought in the last of the ivory. We'll have a full dhowload and you can set off for Zanzibar.'

'What about you? Are you staying on here?'

'Not bloody likely. I'll light out for my base camp in Mozambique.'

'Wouldn't it be easier for you to come along on the dhow? It's nearly two hundred miles to walk.' Sebastian was solicitous; in these last days he had conceived a burning admiration for Flynn.

'Well, you see, it's like this . . .' Flynn hesitated. This was no time to trouble Sebastian with talk of German gunboats waiting off the mouth of the Rufiji. 'I have to get back to my camp, because . . .' Suddenly inspiration came to Flynn O'Flynn. 'Because my poor little daughter is there all alone.'

'You've got a daughter?' Sebastian was taken by surprise.

'You damn right I have.' Flynn experienced a sudden rush of paternal affection and duty. 'And the poor little thing is there all alone.'

'Well, when will I see you again?' The thought of parting from Flynn, of being left to try and find his own way to Australia saddened Sebastian.

'Well,' Flynn was tactful. 'I hadn't really given that much thought.' This was a lie. Flynn had thought about it ceaselessly for the last eight days. He was eagerly anticipating waving fare-well to Sebastian Oldsmith for all time.

'Couldn't we . . .' Sebastian blushed a little under his sun-reddened cheeks. 'Couldn't we sort of team up together. I could work for you, sort of as an apprentice?'

The idea made Flynn wince. He almost panicked at the thought of Sebastian permanently trailing along behind him and discharging his rifle at random intervals. 'Well now, Bassie boy,' he clasped a thick arm around Sebastian's shoulders, 'first you sail that old dhow back to Zanzibar and old Kebby El Keb will pay you out your share. Then you write to me, hey? How about that? You write me, and we'll work something out.'

Sebastian grinned happily. 'I'd like that, Flynn. I'd truly like that.'

'All right, then, off you go. And don't forget the gin.'

With Sebastian standing in the bows of the lead canoe, the double-barrelled rifle clutched in his hands, and the terai hat pulled down firmly over his ears, the little flotilla of heavily laden canoes pulled out from the bank and caught the current. Paddles dipped and gleamed in the evening sunlight as they arrowed away towards the first bend downstream.

Still standing unsteadily in the frail craft, Sebastian looked back and waved his rifle at Flynn on the bank.

'For Chrissake, be careful with that goddamn piece,' Flynn

bellowed too late. The rifle fired, and the recoil toppled Sebastian sprawling onto the pile of ivory behind him. The canoe rocked dangerously while the paddlers struggled to keep it from capsizing, and then disappeared around the bend.

Twelve hours later, the canoes reappeared around the same bend, and headed towards the lone monkey-bean tree on the bank. The canoes rode lightly, empty of ivory, and the paddlers were singing one of the old river chants.

Freshly shaved, wearing a clean shirt and his other pair of boots, a case of Flynn's liquor between his knees, Sebastian peered eagerly ahead for his first glimpse of the big American.

A fine blue tendril of camp-fire smoke smeared out across the river, but there were no figures waving a welcome from the bank. Suddenly Sebastian frowned as he realized that the silhouette of the monkey-bean tree had altered. He wrinkled his eyes, peering ahead uncertainly.

Behind him rang the first cry of alarm from his boatmen. 'Allemand!' And the canoe served under him.

He glanced back and saw the other canoes wheel away in tight circles aimed downstream, the boatmen jabbering in terror as they leaned forward to thrust against the paddles.

His own canoe was in swift pursuit of the others as they darted beyond the bend.

'Hey!' Sebastian shouted at the sweat-shiny backs of his paddlers. 'What do you think you're doing?'

They gave him no answer but the muscles beneath their black skins bunched and rippled in their frantic efforts to drive the canoe faster.

'Stop that immediately!' Sebastian yelled at them. 'Take me back, dash it all. Take me to the camp.'

In desperation Sebastian lifted the rifle and aimed at the nearest man. 'I'm not joking,' he yelled again. The native glanced over his shoulder into the gaping twin muzzles and his face, already twisted with fear, now convulsed into a mask of terror. They had all developed a healthy reverence for the way Sebastian handled that rifle.

The man stopped paddling, and one by one the others followed his example. Sitting frozen under the hypnotic eyes of Sebastian's rifle.

'Back!' said Sebastian and gestured eloquently upstream. Reluctantly the man nearest him dipped his paddle and the canoe turned broadside across the current. 'Back!' Sebastian repeated and the men dipped again.

Slowly, warily, the single canoe crept upstream towards the monkey-bean tree and the grotesque new fruit that hung from its branches.

The hull slid in onto the firm mud and Sebastian stepped ashore.

'Out!' he ordered the boatmen and gestured again. He wanted them well away from the canoe for he knew that, otherwise, the moment his back was turned they would set off downstream again with renewed enthusiasm. 'Out!' and he herded them up the steep bank into Flynn O'Flynn's camp.

The two bearers who had died of gunshot wounds lay beside the smouldering fire. But the four men in the monkey-bean tree had been less fortunate. The ropes had cut deeply into the flesh of their necks and their faces were swollen, mouths wide in the last breath that had never been taken. On the lolling tongues the flies crawled like metallic green bees.

'Cut them down!' Sebastian roused himself from the nausea that was bubbling queasily up from his stomach. The boatmen stood paralysed and Sebastian felt anger now mixed with his revulsion. Roughly he shoved one of the men towards the tree. 'Cut them down,' he repeated, and thrust the handle of his hunting knife into the man's hand. Sebastian turned away as the native shinned up into the fork of the tree with the knife blade clamped between his teeth. Behind him he heard the heavy meaty thuds as the dead men dropped from the tree. Again his stomach heaved, and he concentrated on his search of the trampled grass around the camp.

'Flynn!' he called softly. 'Flynn. I say Flynn! Where are you?' There were the prints of hobnailed boots in the soft earth, and at one place he stooped and picked up the shiny brass cylinder of an empty cartridge case. Stamped into the metal of the base around the detonator cap were the words *Mauser Fabriken*. 7 *mm*.

'Flynn!' more urgently now as the horror of it came home to him. 'Flynn!' and he heard the grass rustle near him. He swung towards it, half raising the rifle.

'Master!' and Sebastian felt disappointment swoop in his chest.

'Mohammed. Is that you, Mohammed?' and he recognized the

wizened little figure with the eternal fez perched on the woolly head as it emerged. Flynn's chief gun-boy, the only one with a little English.

'Mohammed,' with relief, and then quickly, 'Fini? Where is Fini?'

'They shot him, master. The Askari came in the early morning before the sun. Fini was washing. They shot him and he fell into the water.'

'Where? Show me where.'

Below the camp, a few yards from where the canoe was drawn up, they found the pathetic little bundle of Flynn's clothing. Beside it was a half-consumed cake of cheap soap and a metal hand-mirror. There were the deep imprints of naked feet in the mud, and Mohammed stooped and broke off one of the green reeds at the water's edge. Wordlessly he handed it to Sebastian. A drop of blood had dried black on the leaf, and it crumbled as Sebastian touched it with his thumb-nail.

'We must find him. He might still be alive. Call the others. We'll search the banks downstream.'

In an agony of loss, Sebastian picked up Flynn's soiled shirt and crumpled it in his fist.

7

Flynn shucked off his pants and the filthy bush-shirt. Shivering briefly in the chill of dawn, he hugged himself and massaged his upper arms while he peered into the shallow water, searching the bottom for the tell-tale chicken-wire pattern that would mean a crocodile was buried in the mud waiting for him.

His body was porcelain-white where clothing had protected it from the sun, but his arms were chocolate-brown, and a deep vee of the same brown dipped down from his throat onto his chest. Above it the battered red face was creased and puffy with sleep, and his long, greying hair was tangled and matted. He belched thunderously, and grimaced at the taste of old gin and pipe tobacco, then, satisfied that no reptile lay in ambush, he stepped into the water and lowered his massive hams to sit waist-deep. Snorting, he scooped water with his cupped hands over his head, then lumbered out onto the bank again. Sixty seconds is a long time to stay in a river like the Rifiji, for the crocodiles come quickly to the sound of splashing.

Naked, dripping, hair plastered down across his face, Flynn began to soap himself, working up a thick lather at his crotch and tenderly massaging his abundant genitalia, he washed away the sloth of sleep and his appetite stirred. He called up at the camp, 'Mohammed, beloved of Allah and son of his prophet, shake your black arse out of the sack and get the coffee brewing.' Then as an afterthought, he added, 'And put a little gin in it.'

Soapsuds filled Flynn's armpits, and coated the melancholy sag of his belly when Mohammed came down the bank to him. Mohammed was balancing a large enamel mug from which curled little wisps of aromatic steam, and Flynn grinned at him, and spoke in Swahili. 'Thou art kind and merciful; this charity will be writ against your name in the Book of Paradise.'

He reached for the mug but before his fingers touched it, there was a fusillade of gun-fire above them and a bullet hit Flynn high up in the thigh. It spun him sideways so he sprawled half in mud and half in water.

Lying stunned with the shock, he heard the rush of Askari into the camp, heard their shouted triumph as they clubbed with the gun-butt those who had survived the first volley. Flynn wriggled into a sitting position.

Mohammed was coming to him anxiously.

'Run,' grunted Flynn. 'Run, damn you.'

'Lord . . .'

'Get out of here,' savagely Flynn lashed out at him, and Mohammed recoiled. 'The rope, you fool. They'll give you the rope and wrap you in a pigskin.'

A second longer Mohammed hesitated, then he ducked and scampered into the reeds.

'Find Fini,' roared a bull voice in German. 'Find the white man.'

Flynn realized then that it was a stray bullet that had hit him – perhaps even a ricochet. His leg was numb from the hip down, but he dragged himself into the water. He could not run, so he must swim.

'Where is he? Find him!' raged the voice, and suddenly the grass on the bank burst open and Flynn looked up.

For the first time they confronted each other. These two who had played murderous hide-and-seek for three long years across ten thousand square miles of bush.

'Ja!' Fleischer's jubilant bellow as he swung and sighted the pistol at the man in the water below him. 'This time!' aiming carefully, steadying the Luger with both hands.

The brittle snapping sound of the shot, and the slap of the bullet into the water a foot from Flynn's head were followed by Fleischer's snarl of disappointment.

Filling his lungs, Flynn ducked below the surface. Frog-kicking with his good leg, trailing the wounded one, he turned with the current and swam. He swam until his trapped breath threatened to explode his chest, and coloured lights flashed and twinkled behind his clenched eyelids. Then he clawed to the surface. On the bank Fleischer was waiting for him with a dozen of his Askari. 'There he is!' as Flynn blew like a whale thirty yards downstream. Gun-fire crackled and the water whipped and leaped and creamed around Flynn's head.

'Shoot straight!' Howling in frustration and blazing wildly

with the Luger, Fleischer watched the head disappear and Flynn's fat white buttocks break the surface for an instant as he dived. Sobbing with anger and exertion, Fleischer turned his fury on the Askari around him. 'Pigs! Stupid black pig dogs!' And he swung the empty pistol against the nearest head, knocking the man to his knees. Intent on avoiding the flailing pistol, none of them were ready when Flynn surfaced for the second time. A desultory volley kicked fountains no closer than ten feet to Flynn's bobbing head, and he dived again.

'Come on! Chase him!' Herding his Askari ahead of him, Fleischer trotted along the bank in pursuit. Twenty yards of good going, then they came to the first swamp hole and waded through it to be confronted by a solid barrier of elephant grass. They plunged into it and were swallowed so they no longer had sight of the river.

'Schnell! Schnell! He'll get away,' gasped Fleischer and the thick stems wrapped his ankles so that he fell headlong in the mud. Two of his Askari dragged him up and they staggered on until the thicket of tall grass ended, and they stood on the elbow of the river bend with a clear view a thousand yards downstream.

Disturbed by the gun-fire, the birds were up, milling in confused flight above the reed-beds. Their alarm cries blended into a harsh chorus that spoiled the peace of the brooding dawn. They were the only living things in sight. From bank to far bank, the curved expanse of water was broken only be a few floating islands of papyrus grass; rafts of matted vegetation cut loose by the current and floating unhurriedly down towards the sea.

Panting, Herman Fleischer shook off the supporting hands of his two Askari and searched desperately for a glimpse of Flynn's bobbing head. 'Where did he go?' His fingers trembled as he fitted a new clip of ammunition into the Luger. 'Where did he go?' he demanded again, but none of his Askari drew attention to himself by venturing a reply.

'He must be on this side!' The Rufiji was half a mile wide here, Flynn could not have crossed it in the few minutes since they had last seen him. 'Search the bank!' Fleischer ordered. 'Find him!'

With relief the sergeant of his Askari turned on his men, quickly splitting them into two parties and sending them up and downstream to scour the water's edge.

Slowly Fleischer returned the pistol to its holster and fastened the flap, then he took a handkerchief from his pocket and mopped at his face and neck.

'Come on!' he snapped at his sergeant, and set off back towards the camp.

When he reached it, his men had already set out the folding table and chair. New life had been stirred into Flynn's campfire, and the Askari cook was preparing breakfast.

Sitting at the table with the front of his tunic open, spooning up oatmeal porridge and wild honey, Fleischer was soothed into a better humour by the food, and by the thorough manner in which the execution of the four captives was conducted.

When the last of them had stopped twitching and kicking and hung quietly with his comrades in the monkey-bean tree, Herman wiped up the bacon grease in his plate with a hunk of black bread and popped it into his mouth. The cook removed the plate and replaced it with a mug of steaming coffee at the exact moment when the two parties of searchers straggled into the clearing to report that a few drops of blood at the water's edge was the only sign they had found of Flynn O'Flynn.

'Ja,' Herman nodded, 'the crocodiles have eaten him.' He sipped appreciatively at his coffee mug before he gave his next orders. 'Sergeant, take this up to the launch.' He pointed at the stack of ivory on the edge of the clearing. 'Then we will go down to the Island of the Dogs and find this other white man with his English flag.'

8

There was only the entry wound, a dark red hole from which watery blood still oozed slowly. Flynn could have thrust his thumb into it but instead he groped gently around the back of his leg and located the lump in his flesh where the spent slug had come to rest just below the skin.

'God damn it, God damn it to hell,' he whispered in pain, and in anger, at the unlikely chance which had deflected the ricochet downwards to where he had stood below the bank, deflecting it with just sufficient velocity to lodge the bullet in his thigh instead of delivering a clean in-and-out wound.

Slowly he straightened his leg, testing it for broken bone. At the movement, the matt of drifting papyrus on which he lay rocked slightly.

'Might have touched the bone, but it's still in one piece,' he grunted with relief, and felt the first giddy swing of weakness in his head. In his ears was the faint rushing sound of a waterfall heard far off. 'Lost a bit of the old juice,' and from the wound a fresh trickle of bright blood broke and mingled with the water-drops to snake down his leg and drip into the dry matted papyrus. 'Got to stop that,' he whispered.

He was naked, his body still wet from the river. No belt or cloth to use as a tourniquet but he must staunch the bleeding. His fingers clumsy with the weakness of the wound, he tore a bunch of the long sword blade leaves from the reeds around him and began twisting them into a rope. Binding it around his leg above the wound, he pulled it tight and knotted it. The dribble of blood slowed and almost stopped before Flynn sank back and closed his eyes.

Beneath him the island swung and undulated with the eddy of the current and the wavelets pushed up by the rising morning wind. It was a soothing motion, and he was tired – terribly, achingly, tired. He slept.

The pain and the cessation of motion woke him at last. The pain was a dull persistent throb, a pulse that beat through his leg and groin and his lower belly. Groggily he pulled himself on to his elbows and looked down on his own body. The leg was swollen, bluish-looking from the constriction of the grass rope. He stared at it dully, without comprehension, for a full minute before memory flooded back.

'Gangrene!' he spoke aloud, and tore at the knot. The rope fell away and he gasped at the agony of new blood flowing into the leg, clenching his fists and grinding his teeth against it. The pain slowed and settled into a steady beat, and he breathed again, wheezy as a man with asthma.

Then the change of his circumstances came through to the conscious level of his mind and he peered around short-sightedly. The river had carried him down into the mangrove swamps again, down into the maze of little islands and water-ways of the delta. His raft of papyrus had been washed in and stranded against a mud bank by the falling tide. The mud stank of rotting vegetation and sulphur. Near him a gathering of big green river crabs were clicking and bubbling over the body of a dead fish, their little eye-stalks raised in perpetual surprise. At Flynn's movement they sidled away towards the water with their red-tipped claws raised defensively.

Water! Instantly Flynn was aware of the gummy saliva that glued his tongue to the roof of his mouth. Reddened by the harsh sunlight, heated by the first fever of his wound, his body was a furnace that craved moisture.

Flynn moved and instantly cried out in pain. His leg had stiffened while he slept. It was now a heavy anchor, shackling him helplessly to the papyrus raft. He tried again, easing himself backwards on his hands and his buttocks, dragging the leg after him. Each breath was a sob in his dry throat, each movement a white-hot lance into his thigh. But he must drink, he had to drink. Inch by inch, he worked his way to the edge of the raft and slid from it on to the mud bank.

The water had receded with the tide, and he was still fifty paces from the edge. With the motion of a man swimming on his back, he moved across the slimy evil-smelling mud, and his leg slithered after him. It was beginning to bleed again, not copiously but a bright wine-drop at a time.

He reached the water at last, and rolled onto his side with the bad leg uppermost in an attempt to keep the wound out of the mud. On one elbow he buried his face in the water, drinking greedily. The water was warm, tainted with sea salt, and musky with rotted mangroves so it tasted like animal urine. But he gulped it noisily with his mouth and his nostrils and his eyes below the surface. At last he must breathe, and he lifted his head, panting for breath, coughing so the water shot up his throat, out through his nose and dimmed his vision with tears. Gradually his breathing steadied and his eyes cleared. Before he bowed his head to drink again, he glanced out across the channel and saw it coming.

It was on the surface, still a hundred yards away but swimming fast, driving towards him with the great tail churning the water. A big one – at least fifteen feet of it – showing like the rough bark of a pine log, leaving a wide wake across the surface as it came.

And Flynn screamed, just once, but shrill and high and achingly clear. Forgetting the wound in his panic, he tried to get to his feet, pushing himself up with his hands – but the leg pinned him. He screamed again, in pain and in fear.

Belly down, he wriggled in frantic haste from the shallow water back onto the mud bank, dragging himself across the glutinous slime, clawing and threshing towards the papyrus raft where it lay stranded among the mangrove roots fifty yards away. Expecting each moment to hear the slithering rush of the huge reptile across the mud behind him, he reached the first of the mangroves and rolled on his side, looking back, coated with black mud, his face working in his terror and the sound of it spilling in an incoherent babble through his lips.

The crocodile was at the edge of the mud bank, still in the river. Only its head showed above the surface and the little piggy bright eyes watched him unwinkingly, each set on its knot of horny scale.

Desperately Flynn looked about him. The mud bank was a tiny island with this grove of a dozen mangroves set in the centre of it. The trunks of the mangroves were twice as thick as a man's chest, but without branches for the first ten feet of their height; smooth bark slimy with mud and encrusted with little colonies of fresh water mussels. Unwounded Flynn would not have been able to climb any of them – with his leg those branches above him were doubly inaccessible.

Wildly now he searched for a weapon – anything, no matter how puny – to defend himself. But there was nothing. Not a branch of driftwood, not a rock – only the thick black sheet of mud around him.

He looked back at the crocodile. It had not moved. His first feeble hope that it might not come out onto the mud bank withered almost before it was born. It would come. Cowardly, loathsome creature it was – but in time it would gather its courage. It had smelled his blood; it knew him to be wounded, helpless. It would come.

Painfully Flynn leaned his back against the roots of the mangrove, and his terror settled down to a steady, pulsing fear – as steady as the pain in his leg. During the frantic flight across the bank, stiff mud had plugged the bullet hole and stopped the bleeding. But it does not matter now, Flynn thought, nothing matters. Only the creature out there, waiting while its appetite overcomes its timidity, swamps its reluctance to leave its natural element. It might take five minutes, or half a day – but, inevitably, it will come.

There was a tiny ripple around its snout, the first sign of its movement, and the long scaly head inched in towards the edge. Flynn stiffened.

The back showed, its scales like the patterned teeth of a file, and beyond it, the tail with the coxcomb double crest. Cautiously, on its short bowed legs, it waddled through the shallows. Wet and shiny, as broad across the back as a percheron stallion, more than a ton of cold, armoured flesh, it emerged from the water. Sinking elbow-deep into the soft mud, so its belly left a slide mark behind it. Grinning savagely, but with the jagged, irregular teeth lying yellow and long on its lips, and the small eyes watching him.

It came so slowly that Flynn lay passively against the tree, mesmerized by the deliberate waddling approach.

When it was half-way across the bank, it stopped – crouching, grinning – and he smelled it. The heavy odour of stale fish and musk on the warm air.

'Get away!' Flynn yelled at it, and it stood unmoving, unblinking. 'Get away!' He snatched up a handful of mud and hurled it. It crouched a little lower on its stubby legs and the fat crested tail stiffened, arching slightly.

Sobbing now, Flynn threw another handful of mud. The long

grinning jaws opened an inch, then shut again. He heard the click as its teeth met, and it charged. Incredibly fast through the mud, grinning still, it slithered towards him.

This time Flynn's voice was a lunatic babble of horror and he writhed helplessly against the mangrove roots.

The deep booming note of the gun seemed not part of reality, but the crocodile reared up on its tail, drowning the echoes of the shot with its own hissing bellow, and above the next boom of the gun, Flynn heard the bullet strike the scaly body with a thump.

Mud sprayed as the reptile rolled in convulsions, and then, lifting itself high on its legs, it lumbered in ungainly flight towards the water. Again and again the heavy rifle fired, but the crocodile never faltered in its rush, and the surface of the water exploded like blown glass, as it launched itself from the bank and was gone in the spreading ripples.

Standing in the bows of the canoe with the smoking rifle in his hands, while the paddlers drove in towards the bank, Sebastian Oldsmith shouted anxiously, 'Flynn, Flynn – did it get you? Are you all right?'

Flynn's reply was a croak. 'Bassie. Oh, Bassie boy, for the first time in my life I'm real pleased to see you,' and he sagged only half conscious against the mangrove roots.

9

The sun burned down on the dhow where it lay at anchor off the Island of the Dogs, yet a steady breeze came down the narrow waterway between the mangroves and plucked at the furled sail on the boom.

With a rope sling under his armpits, they lifted Flynn from the canoe and swung him, legs dangling, over the bulwark. Sebastian was ready to receive him and lower him gently to the deck.

'Get that goddamn sail up, and let's get the hell out of the river,' gasped Flynn.

'I must tend to your leg.'

'That can wait. We've got to get out into the open sea. The Germans have got a steam launch. They'll be looking for us. We can expect them to drop in on us at any minute.'

'They can't touch us – we're under the protection of the flag,' Sebastian protested.

'Listen, you stupid, bloody limey,' Flynn's voice was a squawk of pain and impatience. 'That murdering Hun will give us a rope dance with or without the flag. Don't argue, get that sail up!'

They laid him on a blanket in the shadow of the high poop before Sebastian hurried forward to release the Arab crew from the hold. They came up shiny with sweat and blinking in the dazzle of the sun. It took perhaps fifteen seconds for Mohammed to explain to them the urgency of the situation, and this invoked a few seconds of paralysed horror before they scattered to their stations. Four of them were hauling ineffectively at the anchor rope, but the great lump of coral was buried in the gluey mud of the bottom. Sebastian pushed them aside impatiently and with one knife stroke, severed the rope.

The crew, with the enthusiastic assistance of Flynn's bearers and gun-boys, ran up the faded and patched old sail. The wind caught it and bellied it. The deck canted slightly and two Arabs ran back to the tiller. From under the bows came the faint giggle of water, and from the stern spread a wide oily wake. With a cluster of the Arabs and bearers calling directions in the bows to the steersman at the rudder, the ancient dhow pointed downstream and ambled towards the sea.

When Sebastian went back to Flynn, he found old Mohammed squatting anxiously beside him and watching, as Flynn drank from the square bottle. Already a quarter of its contents had disappeared.

Flynn lowered the gin bottle, and breathed heavily through his mouth. 'Tastes like honey,' he gasped.

'Let's look at that leg,' Sebastian stooped over Flynn's naked, mud-besmeared body. 'My God, what a mess! Mohammed, get a basin of water and try and find some clean cloth.'

IO

With the coming of evening, the breeze gathered strength, kicking up a chop on the widening water-ways of the delta. All afternoon the little dhow had butted against the run of the tide, but now began the ebb and it helped push her down towards the sea.

'With any luck we'll reach the mouth before sunset.' Sebastian was sitting beside Flynn's blanket-wrapped form under the poop. Flynn grunted. He was weak with pain, and groggy with gin. 'If we don't, we'll have to moor somewhere for the night. Can't risk the channel in the dark.' He received no reply from Flynn and himself fell silent.

Except for the gurgle of the bow-wave and the sing-song chant of the pilot, a lazy silence blanketed the dhow. Most of the crew and the bearers were strewn in sleep about the deck, although two of them worked quietly over the open galley as they prepared the evening meal.

The heavy miasma of the swamps blended poorly with the stench of the bilges and the cargo of green ivory in the holds. It seemed to act as a drug, increasing Sebastian's fatigue. His head sagged forward on his chest and his hands slipped from the rifle in his lap. He slept.

The magpie chatter of the crew, and Mohammed's urgent hands on his shoulder, shook him awake. He came to his feet and gazed blearily around him. 'What is it? What is the trouble, Mohammed?'

For answer, Mohammed shouted the crew into silence, and turned back to Sebastian. 'Listen, master.'

Sebastian shook the remnants of sleep from his head, then cocked it slightly. 'I can't hear . . .' He stopped, an expression of uncertainty on his face.

Very faintly in the still of the evening he heard it, a faint huffing rhythm, as though a train passed in the distance. 'Yes,' he said, still uncertain. 'What is it?'

'The toot-toot boat, she comes.'

Sebastian stared at him without comprehension.

'The Allemand. The Germans.' Mohammed's hands fluttered with agitation. 'They follow us. They chase. They catch. They . . .' He clutched his own throat with both hands and rolled his eyes. His tongue protruded from the corner of his mouth.

Flynn's entire retinue was gathered in a mob around Sebastian, and at Mohammed's graphic little charade, they burst once more into a frightened chorus. Every eye was on Sebastian, waiting for his lead, and he felt confused, uncertain. Instinctively he turned to Flynn. Flynn lay on his back, his mouth open, snoring. Quickly Sebastian knelt beside him. 'Flynn! Flynn!' Flynn opened his eyes but they were focused beyond Sebastian's face. 'The Germans are coming.'

'The Campbells are coming. Hurrah! Hurrah!' muttered Flynn and closed his eyes again. His usually red face was flushed hot-scarlet with fever.

'What must I do?' pleaded Sebastian.

'Drink it!' advised Flynn. 'Never hesitate. Drink it!' his eyes still closed, his voice slurred.

'Please, Flynn. Please tell me.'

'Tell you?' muttered Flynn in delirium. 'Sure! Have you heard the one about the camel and the missionary?'

Sebastian jumped to his feet and looked wildly about him. The sun was low, perhaps another two hours to nightfall. *If only we can hold them off until then.* 'Mohammed. Get the gun-boys up into the stern,' he snapped, and Mohammed, recognizing the new crispness in his voice, turned on the mob about him to relay the order.

The ten gun-boys scattered to gather their weapons and then crowded up on to the poop. Sebastian followed them, gazing anxiously back along the channel. He could see two thousand yards to the bend behind them and the channel was empty, but he was sure the sound of the steam engine was louder.

'Spread them along the rail,' he ordered Mohammed. He was thinking hard now; always a difficult task for Sebastian. Stubborn as a mule, his mind began to sulk as soon as he flogged it. He wrinkled his high scholar's forehead and his next thought emerged slowly. 'A barricade,' he said. The thin planking of the bulwark would offer little protection against the high-powered Mausers. 'Mohammed, get the others to carry up everything they can find, and pile it here to shield the steersmen and the gun-boys. Bring everything – water barrels, the sacks of coconuts, those old fishing-nets.'

While they hurried to obey the order, Sebastian stood in frowning concentration, prodding the mass within his skull and finding it as responsive as a lump of freshly kneaded dough. He tried to estimate the relative speeds of the dhow and a modern steam launch. Perhaps they were moving at half the speed of their pursuers. With a sliding sensation, he decided that even in this wind, sail could not hope to out-run a propeller-driven craft.

The word *propeller*, and the chance that at that moment he was forced to move aside to allow four of the men to drag an untidy bundle of old fishing-nets past, eased the next idea to the surface of his mind.

Humbled by the brilliance of his idea, he clung to it desperately, lest it somehow sink once more below the surface to be lost. 'Mohammed . . .' he stammered in his excitement. 'Mohammed, those nets . . .' He looked back again along the wide channel, and saw it still empty. He looked ahead and saw the next bend coming towards them; already the helmsman was chanting the orders preparatory to tacking the dhow. 'Those nets. I want to lay them across the channel.'

Mohammed stared at him aghast, his wizened face crinkling deeper in disbelief.

'Cut off the corks. Leave every fourth one.' Sebastian grabbed his shoulders and shook him in agitation. 'I want the net to sag. I don't want them to spot it too soon.'

They were almost up to the bend now, and Sebastian pointed ahead. 'We'll lay it just around the corner.'

'Why, master?' pleaded Mohammed. 'We must run. They are close now.'

'The propeller,' Sebastian shouted in his face. He made a churning motion with his hands. 'I want to snag the propeller.'

A moment longer Mohammed stared at him, then he began to grin, exposing his bald gums.

While they worked in frantic haste the muffled engine beat from upstream grew steadily louder, more insistent.

The dhow wallowed and balked at the efforts of the helmsman

to work her across the channel. Her head kept falling away before the wind, threatening to snarl the net in her own rudder, but slowly the line of bobbing corks spread from the mangroves on one side towards the far bank, while in grim concentration Sebastian and a group led by Mohammed paid the net out over the stern. Every few minutes they lifted their faces to glance at the bend upstream, expecting to see the German launch appear and hear the crackle of Mauser fire.

Gradually the dhow edged in towards the north bank, sowing the row of corks behind her, and abruptly Sebastian realized that the net was too short – too short by fifty yards. There would be a gap in their defence. If the launch cut the bend fine, hugging the bank as it came, then they were lost. Already the note of its engine was so close that he could hear the metallic whine of the drive shaft.

Now also there was a new problem. How to anchor the loose end of the net? To let it float free would allow the current to wash it away, and open the gap still further.

'Mohammed. Fetch one of the tusks. The biggest one you can find. Quickly. Go quickly.'

Mohammed scampered away and returned immediately, the two bearers with him staggering under the weight of the long curved shaft of ivory.

His hands clumsy with haste, Sebastian lashed the end rope of the net to the tusk. Then grunting with the effort, he and Mohammed hoisted it to the side rail, and pushed it overboard. As it splashed, Sebastian shouted at the helmsman, 'Go!' and pointed downstream. Thankfully the Arab wrenched the tiller across. The dhow spun on her heel and pointed once more towards the sea.

Silently, anxiously, Sebastian and his gun-boys lined the stern and gazed back at the bend of the channel. In the fists of each of them were clutched the short-barrelled elephant rifles, and their faces were set intently.

The chug of the steam engine rose louder and still louder.

'Shout as soon as it shows,' Sebastian ordered. 'Shoot as fast as you can. Keep them looking at us, so they don't see the net.'

And the launch came around the bend; flying a ribbon of grey smoke from its single stack and the bold red, yellow and black flag of the Empire at its bows. A neat little craft, forty-footer, low in the waist, small deck-house aft, gleaming white in the sunlight, and the white moustache of the bow wave curled about her bows.

'Shoot!' bellowed Sebastian as he saw the Askari clustered on the foredeck. 'Shoot!' and his voice was lost in the concerted blast of the heavy calibre rifles around him. One of the Askari was flung backwards against the deck-house, his arms spread wide as he hung there a moment in the attitude of crucifixion before subsiding gently on to the deck. His comrades scattered and dropped into cover behind the steel bulwark. A single figure was left alone on the deck; a massive figure in the light grey uniform of the German colonial service, with his wide-brimmed slouch hat, and gold gleaming at the shoulders of his tunic.

Sebastian took him in the notch of his rear sight, held the bead on his chest, and jerked the trigger. The rifle jumped joyously against his shoulder, and he saw a fountain of spray leap from the surface of the river a hundred yards beyond the launch. Sebastian fired again, closing his eyes in anticipation of the savage recoil of the rifle. When he opened them, the German officer was still on his feet, shooting back at Sebastian with a pistol in his outstretched right hand. He was making better practice than Sebastian. The fluting hum of his fire whipped about Sebastian's head, or smacked into the planking of the dhow.

Hastily Sebastian ducked behind the water barrel and clawed a pair of cartridges from his belt. Sharper, higher than the dull booming of the elephant rifles, climbed the brittle crackle of the Mauser fire as the Askari joined in.

Cautiously Sebastian lifted his eyes above the water barrel. The launch was cutting the bend fine, and with a sudden swoop of dismay, he knew it was going to clear the fishnet by twenty feet. He dropped his rifle on to the deck and jumped to his feet. A Mauser bullet missed his ear by so little that it nearly burst his eardrum. Instinctively he ducked, then checked the movement and instead ran to the helmsman. 'Get out of the way!' he yelled in his excitement and his fear. Roughly he shoved the man aside and, grasping the tiller, pushed it across. Perilously close to the jibe, the dhow veered across the channel, opening the angle between it and the launch. Looking back Sebastian saw the fat German officer turn and shout an order towards the wheel-house. Almost immediately the bows of the launch swung, following the dhow's manoeuvre and Sebastian felt triumph flare in his chest. Now directly in the path of the launch lay the line of tiny black dots that marked the net.

His deep-drawn breath trapped in his lungs, Sebastian watched the launch sweep over the net. His grip on the tiller tightened until his knuckles threatened to push out through the skin, and then he expelled his breath in a howl of joy and relief.

For the line of corks was suddenly plucked below the surface, leaving the small disturbance of ripples where each had stood. For ten seconds the launch sped on, then abruptly the even sound of her passage altered, a harsh clattering intruded, and her bows swung suddenly as she slowed.

The gap between the two craft widened. Sebastian saw the German officer drag a frightened Askari from the wheel-house and club him unmercifully about the head, but the squeals of Teutonic fury were muted by the swiftly increasing distance, and then drowned by the tumultuous clamour of his own crew, as they pranced and danced about the deck.

The Arab helmsman hopped up on to the water barrel and hoisted the skirts of his dirty grey robe to expose his naked posterior at the launch in calculated mockery.

I I

Long after the dhow had sailed sedately first out of rifle range, and then out of sight, Herman Fleischer gave himself over completely to the epilepsy of frustrated anger. He raved about the tiny deck, lashing out with ham-sized fists while his Askari skittled around him trying to keep out of range. Repeatedly he returned to the unconscious form of his helmsman to kick him as he lay. At last his fury burned itself down to the level where it allowed him to trundle aft and hang over the stern rail peering down at the sodden bundle of netting which was wrapped around the propeller.

'Sergeant!' His voice was hoarse with strain. 'Get two men with knives over the side to cut that away!'

And a stillness fell upon them all. Every man tried to shrink himself down into insignificance, so that the choice might not fall on him. Two volunteers were selected, divested of their uniforms and hustled to the stern, despite their terrified entreaties.

'Tell them to hurry,' grunted Herman, and went to his folding chair. His personal boy placed the evening meal with its attendant pitcher of beer on the table before him and Herman fell to.

Once from the stern there was a squeak and a splash, following by a furious burst of rifle fire. Herman frowned and looked up from his plate.

'A crocodile has taken one of the men,' his sergeant reported in agitation.

'Well, put another one over,' said Herman and returned with unabated relish to his meal. This last batch of sausage was particularly tasty.

The netting had wound so tightly about the blades and shaft of the propeller, that it was an hour after midnight when the last of it was hacked away by lantern light.

The drive shaft had twisted slightly and run one of its bearings, so even at quarter speed there was a fearsome clattering and threshing sound from the stern as the launch limped slowly down the channel towards the sea.

In the grey and pallid pink of dawn they crept past the last island of mangroves and the launch lifted her head to the sluggish thrust of the Indian Ocean. It was a windless morning of flat calm, and Herman peered without hope into the misty half light that obscured the ocean's far horizon. He had come this far only on the slight chance that the dhow might have gone aground on a mud bank during her night run down the river.

'Stop!' he shouted at his battered helmsman. Immediately the agonized clatter of the propeller ceased, and the launch rose and fell uneasily on the long oily swells.

So they had got clear away then. He could not risk his damaged launch on the open sea. He must go back, and leave the dhow and its ivory and its many candidates for the rope, to head unmolested for that pest-hole of rogues and pirates on Zanzibar island.

Moodily he looked out across the sea and mourned that cargo of ivory. There had been perhaps a million Reichsmarks of it aboard, of which his unofficial handling fee would have been considerable.

Also he mourned the departure of the Englishman. He had never hanged one before.

He sighed and tried to comfort himself with the thought of that damned American, now well digested in the maw of a crocodile, but truly it would have been more satisfying to see him kick and spin on the rope.

He sighed again. Ah, well! At least he would no longer have the perpetual worry of Flynn O'Flynn's presence on his border, nor would he have to suffer the nagging of Governor Schee and his endless demands for O'Flynn's head.

Now it was breakfast time. He was about to turn away when something out there in the lightening dawn caught his attention.

A long low shape, its outline becoming crisper as he watched. There were cries from his Askari as they saw it also, huge in the dawn. The stark square turrets with their slim gun-barrels, the tall triple stacks and the neat geometrical patterns of its rigging.

'The *Blücher*!' roared Herman in savage elation. 'The *Blücher*, by God!' He recognized the cruiser, for he had seen her not six months before, lying in Dar es Salaam harbour. 'Sergeant, bring the signal pistol!' He was capering with excitement. In reply to Herman's hasty message, Governor Schee must have sent the *Blücher* racing southwards to blockade the Rufiji mouth. 'Start the engine. Schnell! Run out to her,' he shouted at the helmsman as he slid one of the fat Verey cartridges into the gaping breech of the pistol, snapped it closed and pointed the muzzle to the sky.

Beside the tall bulk of the cruiser the launch was as tiny as a floating leaf, and Herman looked up with apprehension at the frail rope ladder he was expected to climb. His Askari assisted him across the narrow strip of water between the two vessels and he hung for a desperate minute until his feet found the rungs and he began his ponderous ascent. Sweating profusely he was helped on to the deck by two seamen and faced an honour guard of a dozen or more. Heading them was a young lieutenant in crisp, smart tropical whites.

Herman shrugged off the helping hands, drew himself to attention with a click of heels. 'Commissioner Fleischer.' His voice shaky with exertion.

'Lieutenant Kyller.' The officer clicked and saluted.

'I must see your captain immediately. A matter of extreme urgency.'

12

Kapitän zur See Count Otto von Kleine inclined his head gravely as he greeted Herman. He was a tall, thin man, who wore a neat, pointed blond beard with just a few threads of grey to give it dignity. 'The English have landed a full-scale expeditionary force in the Rufiji delta, supported by capital ships? This is correct?' he asked immediately.

'The report was exaggerated.' Herman regretted bitterly the impetuous wording of his message to the Governor; he had been fired with patriotic ardour at the time. 'In fact, it was only . . . ah,' he hesitated, 'one vessel.'

'Of what strength? What is her armament?' demanded von Kleine.

'Well, it was an unarmed vessel.'

And von Kleine frowned. 'Of what type?'

Herman flushed with embarrassment. 'An Arab dhow. Of about twenty-two metres.'

'But this is impossible. Ridiculous. The Kaiser has delivered an ultimatum to the British Consul in Berlin. He has issued mobilization orders to five divisions.' The captain spun on his heel and began to pace restlessly about his bridge, clapping his hands together in agitation. 'What was the purpose of this British invasion? Where is this . . . this dhow? What explanation must I send to Berlin?'

'I have since learned that the expedition was led by a notorious ivory poacher named O'Flynn. He was shot resisting arrest by my Askari, but his accessory, an unknown Englishman, escaped down the river last night in the dhow.'

'Where will they be headed?' The captain stopped pacing and glared at Herman.

'Zanzibar.'

'This is stupidity, utter stupidity. We will be a laughing stock! A battle cruiser to catch a pair of common criminals!'

47

'But, Captain, you must pursue them.'

'To what purpose?'

'If they escape to tell their story, the dignity of the Emperor will be lowered throughout the length of Africa. Think if the British Press were to hear of this! Also, these men are dangerous criminals.'

'But I cannot board a foreign ship on the high seas. Especially if she flies the Union Jack. It would be an act of war – an act of piracy.'

'But, Captain, if she were to sink with all hands, sink without a trace?'

And Captain von Kleine nodded thoughtfully. Then abruptly he snapped his fingers and turned to his pilot. 'Plot me a course for Zanzibar Island.'

13

They lay becalmed below a sky of brazen cobalt, and every hour of the calm allowed the Mozambique current to push the little dhow another three miles off its course. Aimlessly she swung her head to meet each of the long swells, and then let it fall away into the troughs.

For the twentieth time since dawn, Sebastian climbed up on to the poop-deck and surveyed the endless waters, searching for a ruffle on the glassy surface that would herald the wind. But there was never any sign of it. He looked towards the west, but the blue line of the coast had long since sunk below the horizon.

'I'm an old dog, *Fisi*,' bellowed Flynn from the lower deck. 'Hear me laugh,' and he imitated faithfully the yammering cry of an hyena. All day Flynn had regaled the company with snatches of song and animal imitations. Yet his delirium was interspaced with periods of lucidity. 'I reckon this time old Fleischer got me good, Bassie. There's a sack of poison forming round that bullet. I can feel it there. A fat, hot sack of it. Reckon we've got to dig for it pretty soon. Reckon if we can't make it back to Zanzibar pretty soon, we're going to have to dig for it.' Then his mind escaped once more into the hot land of delirium.

'My little girl, I'll bring you a pretty ribbon. There, don't cry. A pretty ribbon for a pretty girl.' His voice syrupy, then suddenly harsh. 'You cheeky little bitch. You're just like that goddamned mother of yours. Don't know why I don't chase you out,' this last followed immediately by the hyena imitation again.

Now Sebastian turned away from the poop rail and looked down on Flynn. Beside him the faithful Mohammed was dipping strips of cloth in a bucket of sea water, wringing them out and then laying them on Flynn's flushed forehead in a futile attempt to reduce the fever.

Sebastian sighed. His responsibilities lay heavily. The command of the expedition had devolved squarely upon him. And

49

yet, there was a sneaky sensation of pleasure, of pride in his execution of that command to the present. He went back and replayed in his mind the episode of the fish-net, remembering the quick decision that had altered the launch's course and lured it into the trap. He smiled at the memory, and the smile was not his usual self-effacing grin, but something harder. When he turned away to pace the narrow deck there was more spring in his step, and he set his shoulders square.

Again he stopped by the rail and looked towards the west. There was a cloud on the horizon, a tiny dark figure of it. And he watched it with hope that it might herald the start of the afternoon sea breeze. Yet it seemed unnatural. As he watched, it moved. He could swear it moved. Now his whole attention was fastened upon it. Realization began to flicker in him, building up until it was certainty.

A ship. By God, a ship!

He ran to the poop ladder, and slid down into the waist, across it to the mast.

The crew and the bearers watched him with awakening interest. Some of them got to their feet.

Sebastian jumped on to the boom, balancing there a moment before he started to shin up the mast. Using the mainsail hoops like the rungs of a ladder, he reached the masthead and clung there, peering eagerly into the west.

There she was – no doubt about it. He could see the tips of the triple stacks, each with its feather of dark smoke, and he began to cheer.

Below him the rail was lined with his men, all peering out in the direction they took from him. Sebastian slid down the mast, the friction burning his hands in his haste. His feet hit the deck and he ran to Flynn. 'A ship. A big ship coming up fast.' Flynn rolled his head and looked at him vaguely. 'Listen to me, Flynn. There'll be a doctor aboard. We'll get you to a port in no time.'

'That's good, Bassie.' Flynn's brain clicked back into focus. 'You've done real good.'

She came up over the horizon with astonishing rapidity, and her silhouette changed as she altered course towards them. But not before Sebastian had seen the gun turrets.

'A warship!' he shouted. To his mind this proved her British – only one nation ruled the waves. 'They've seen us!' He waved his hands above his head.

Bows on, each second growing in size, grey and big, she bore down upon the little dhow.

Gradually the cheering of the crew faltered and subsided into an uneasy silence. Magnified by the still, hot air, huge on the velvety gloss of the ocean, lifting a bow wave of pearling white, the warship came on. No check in her speed, the ensign at her masthead streaming away from them so they could not see the colours.

'What are they going to do?' Sebastian asked aloud, and was answered by Flynn's voice. Sebastian glanced around. Balancing on his good leg with one arm draped around Mohammed's neck, Flynn was hopping across the deck towards him.

'I'll tell you what they're going to do! They're going to hit us smack-bang up the arse!' Flynn roared. 'That's the *Blücher*! That's a German cruiser!'

'They can't do that!' Sebastian protested.

'You'd like to bet? She's coming straight from the Rufiji delta – and my guess is she's had a chat with Fleischer. He's probably aboard her.' Flynn swayed against Mohammed, gasping with the pain of his leg before he went on. 'They're going to ram us, and then machine-gun anyone still floating.'

'We've got to make a life raft.'

'No time, Bassie. Look at her come!'

Less than five miles away, but swiftly narrowing the distance, the *Blücher's* tall bows knifed towards them. Wildly Sebastian looked around the crowded deck, and he saw the pile of cork floats they had cut from the fish nets.

Drawing his knife, he ran to one of the sacks of coconuts and cut the twine that closed the mouth. He slipped the knife back into its sheath, stooped, and up-ended the sack, spilling coconuts on to the deck. Then with the empty sack in his hand he ran to the pile of floats and dropped on his knees. In frantic haste he shovelled them into the sack, half filling it before he looked up again. The *Blücher* was two miles away, a tall tower of murderous grey steel.

With a length of rope Sebastian tied the sack closed and dragged it to where Flynn stood supported by Mohammed.

'What are you doing?' Flynn demanded.

'Fixing you up! Lift your arms!' Flynn obeyed and Sebastian tied the free end of the rope around his chest at the level of his armpits. He paused to unlace and kick off his boots before speaking again. 'Mohammed, you stay with him. Hang on to the sack and don't let go.' He left them, trotting on bare feet to find his rifle propped against the poop. Buckling on his cartridge belt, he hurried back to the rail.

Sebastian Oldsmith was about to engage a nine-inch battle cruiser with a double-barrelled Gibbs .500.

She was close now, hanging over them like a high cliff of steel. Even Sebastian could not miss a battle cruiser at two hundred yards, and the heavy bullets clanged against the armoured hull, ringing loudly above the hissing rush of the bow wave.

While he reloaded, Sebastian looked up at the line of heads in the bows of the *Blücher*; grinning faces below the white caps with their little swallow-tailed black ribbons. 'You bloody swines,' he shouted at them. Hatred stronger than he had ever dreamed possible, choked his voice. 'You filthy, bloody swine.' He lifted the rifle and fired without effect, and the *Blücher* hit the dhow.

It struck with a crash and the crackling roar of rending timber. It crushed her side and cut through in the screaming of dying men and the squeal of planking against steel.

It trod the dhow under, breaking her back, forcing her far below the surface. At the initial shock, Sebastian was hurled overboard, the rifle thrown from his hands. He struck the armoured plate of the cruiser a glancing blow and then dropped into the sea beside her. The thrust of the bow wave tumbled him aside, else he would have been dragged along the hull and his body shredded against the steel plate.

He surfaced just in time to suck a lungful of air before the turbulence of the great screws caught him and plucked him under again, driving him deep so the pressure stabbed like red-hot needles in his eardrums. He felt himself swirled end over end, buffeted, shaken vigorously as the water tore at his body.

Colour flashed and zigzagged behind his closed eyelids. There was a suffocating pain in his chest and his lungs pumped, urgently craving air, but he sealed his lips and kicked out with his legs, clawing at the water with his hands.

The churning wake of the cruiser released its grip upon him, and he was shot to the surface with such force that he broke clear to the waist before dropping back to drink air greedily. He unbuckled the heavy cartridge belt and let it sink before he looked about him.

The surface of the sea was scattered with floating debris, and a few bobbing human heads. Near him a section of torn planking rose in a burst of trapped air bubbles. Sebastian struck out for it and clung there, his legs hanging in the clear green water.

'Flynn,' he gasped. 'Flynn, where are you?'

A quarter of a mile away, the *Blücher* was circling slowly, long and menacing and shark-like, and he stared at it in hatred and in fear.

'Master!' Mohammed's voice behind him.

Sebastian turned quickly and saw the black face and the red face beside the floating sack of corks a hundred yards away. 'Flynn!'

'Good-bye, Bassie,' Flynn called. 'The old Hun is coming back to finish us off. Look! They've got machine guns set up on the bridge. See you on the other side, boy.'

Quickly Sebastian looked back at the cruiser and saw the clusters of white uniforms on the angle of her bridge.

'Ja, there are still some of them alive.' Through borrowed binoculars, Fleischer scanned the littered area of the wreck. 'You will use the Maxims, of course, Captain? It will be quicker than picking them off with rifles.'

Captain von Kleine did not answer. He stood tall on his bridge, slightly round-shouldered, staring out at the wreckage with his hands clasped behind him. 'There is something sad in the death of a ship,' he murmured. 'Even such a dirty little one as this.' Suddenly he straightened his shoulders and turned to Fleischer. 'Your launch is waiting for you at the mouth of the Rufiji. I will take you there, Commissioner.'

'But first the business of the survivors.'

Von Kleine's expression hardened. 'Commissioner, I sank that dhow in what I believed to be my duty. But now I am not sure that my judgement was not clouded by anger. I will not trespass further on my conscience by machine-gunning swimming civilians.'

'You will then pick them up. I must arrest them and give them trial.'

'I am not a policeman,' he paused and his expression softened a little. 'That one who fired the rifle at us. I think he must be

53

a brave man. He is a criminal, perhaps, but I am not so old in the ways of the world that I do not love courage merely for its own sake. I would not like to know I have saved this man for the noose. Let the sea be the judge and the executioner.' He turned to his lieutenant. 'Kyller, prepare to drop one of the life rafts.' The lieutenant stared at him in disbelief. 'You heard me?'

'Yes, my Captain.'

'Then do it.' Ignoring Fleischer's squawks of protest, von Kleine crossed to the pilot. 'Alter course to pass the survivors at a distance of fifty metres.'

'Here she comes.' Flynn grinned tightly, without humour, and watched the cruiser swing ponderously towards them.

The cries of the swimmers around him, pleading mercy, were plaintive as the voices of sea birds – tiny on the immensity of the ocean.

'Flynn. Look at the bridge!' Sebastian's voice floated across to him. 'See him there. The grey uniform.'

Tears from the sting of sea salt in his wound, and the distortion of fever had blurred Flynn's vision, yet he could make out the spot of grey among the speckling of white uniforms on the bridge of the cruiser.

'Who is it?'

'You were right. It's Fleischer,' Sebastian shouted back, and Flynn began to curse.

'Hey, you filthy, fat butcher,' he bellowed, trying to drag himself up onto the floating sack of corks. 'Hey, you whore's chamber pot.' His voice carried above the murmur of the cruiser's engines running at dead-slow. 'Come on, you blood-smeared little pig.'

The tall hull of the cruiser was close now, so close he could see the bulky figure in grey turn to the tall white-uniformed officer beside him, gesticulating in what was clearly entreaty.

The officer turned away, and moved to the rail of the bridge. He leaned out and waved to a group of seamen on the deck below him.

'That's right. Tell them to shoot. Let's get it over with. Tell them . . .'

A large square object was lifted over the rail by the gang below the bridge. It dropped and fell with a splash alongside.

Flynn's voice dried up, and he watched in disbelief as the

white-clad officer lifted his right arm in a gesture that might have been a salute. The beat of the cruiser's engines mounted as it increased speed, and she swung away towards the west.

Flynn O'Flynn began to laugh, the cackling hysteria of relief and delirium. He rolled off the sack of corks and his head dropped forward, so the warm green water smothered his laughter. Mohammed took a handful of the grey hair and lifted his face to prevent him drowning.

14

Sebastian reached the raft, and grasped the rope that hung in loops around its sides. He paused to regain his breath before hauling himself up to lie gasping, the blood-warm sea-water streaming from his sodden clothing, and watched the shape of the battle cruiser recede into the west.

'Master! Help me!'

The voice roused him and he sat up. Mohammed was struggling, dragging Flynn and the sack through the water. Among the floating wreckage a dozen others of the crew and the bearers were flapping their way towards the raft; the weaker swimmers were already failing, their cries becoming more pitiful, and their splashing more frenzied.

There were oars roped to the slatted deck of the raft. Quickly Sebastian cut one loose with his hunting knife and began rowing towards the pair. His progress was slow, for the raft was an ungainly bitch that balked and swung away from the thrust of the oar.

An Arab crewman reached the raft and scrambled aboard, then another, and another. Each of them freed an oar and helped with the rowing. They passed the body of one of the bearers floating just below the surface, both its legs cut off above the knees and the bones sticking out of the ragged meat of the stumps. This was not the only one – there was other human flotsam among the scattered wreckage, and the pinky-brown stains that drifted away on the current attracted the sharks.

The Arab beside Sebastian saw the first one and called out, pointing with the oar.

It came hunting, its fin waggling from side to side as it tacked up against the current, so that they could sense its excitement, the cold, unthinking excitement of Euselachii hunger. Below the surface, distorted and dark, showed the tapering length of its body. Not a big one. Perhaps nine feet in length and four hundred pounds in weight, but big enough to chop a leg with one bite. No longer guided by the drift of blood-taste, picking up the vibrations of the swimmers, it straightened and came in on its first run.

'Shark!' Sebastian yelled at Flynn and Mohammed where they floundered ten yards away. And both of them panicked; no longer making for the raft, they tried to clamber on to the sack of corks. Terror has no logic. Their only concern was to lift their dangling legs from the water, but the sack was too small, too unstable and their panic attracted the shark's attention. It veered towards them, showing the full height of its curved triangular fin, each sweep of its tail breaking the surface as it drove in.

'This way,' shouted Sebastian. 'Come to the raft!' He was hacking at the water with the oar, while beside him the Arabs worked in equal dedication. 'This way, Flynn. For God's sake, this way.'

His voice penetrated their panic, and once more they struck out for the raft. But the shark was closing fast, long and dappled by sunlight through the surface ripple.

The sack was still tied to Flynn's body, and its resistance to the water slowed them as it dragged behind. The shark swerved and made its first pass; it seemed to hump up out of the water, and its mouth opened. The upper jaw bulged out, the lower jaw gaped, and the multiple rows of teeth came erect like the quills of a porcupine, *and it hit the sack*. Locking its jaws into the coarse jute material, worrying it, still humped out of the water, shaking its blunt head clumsily, scattering a spray of water drops that flew like shattered glass in the sun.

'Grab here!' commanded Sebastian, leaning out to offer the blade of the oar to the pair in the water. They clutched at it with the strength of fear, and Sebastian drew them in.

But the sack and the shark were still attached to Flynn, its threshing threatening to break Flynn's hold on the life-line around the raft.

Dropping to his knees, Sebastian fumbled the knife from its sheath and sawed at the rope. It parted. The shark, still worrying the sack, worked away from the raft and Sebastian helped the Arabs to drag first Flynn, and then Mohammed, over the side.

They were not finished yet. There were still half a dozen men in the water.

Realizing its error at last, the shark relinquished its hold on the sack. It backed away. For a moment it hung motionless, puzzled, then it circled out towards the nearest sound of splashing. One of the gun-boys, clawing at the water in exhausted dog-paddle. The shark hit him in the side, and pulled him under. Moments later he reappeared, his mouth an open pink cave as he screamed, the water about him clouded dark red-brown by his own blood. Again he was pulled under as the shark hit his legs, but again he floated. This time face down, wriggling feebly, and the shark circled him, dashing in to chop off a mouthful of his flesh, backing away to gulp it down before coming in again.

Then there was another shark, two more, ten, so many that Sebastian could not count them, as they circled and dove in ecstatic greed, until the sea around the raft trembled and swirled in agitation.

Sebastian and his Arabs managed to drag two more of the crew into the raft and they had a third half out of the water when a six-foot white-pointer shot up from the depths, and fastened on his thigh with such violence that it almost jerked all of them overboard. But they steadied themselves and held on to the man's arms, frozen in this gruesome tug-of-war, while the shark worried the leg, so dog-like in its determination that Sebastian expected it to growl.

Little Mohammed staggered to his feet, snatched up an oar and swung it against the pointed snout with all his strength. They had dragged the shark's head from the water, and the oar fell on it with a series of rubbery thumps, but the shark held on. Fresh, bright blood squirted and trickled from the leg in its jaws, running down the shark's glistening snake-like head into the open slits of its gill covers.

'Hold him!' gasped Sebastian, and drew his knife. The raft rocking crazily under him, he leaned over the man's out-stretched body and drove the knife blade into the shark's expressionless little eye. It popped in a burst of clear fluid, and the shark stiffened and trembled. Sebastian withdrew the blade and stabbed into the other eye. With a convulsive gulp the shark opened its jaws and slid back into the sea to meander blindly away.

There were no more swimmers. The little group on the raft huddled together and watched the shark pack milling hungrily, seeming to sniff at the tainted water as they gathered the last morsels of meat.

The shark victim hosed the deck with his severed femoral artery and died before any of them could rouse themselves to apply a tourniquet.

'Push him over,' grunted Flynn.

'No,' Sebastian shook his head.

'Chrissake, we're crowded enough as it is. Chuck the poor bastard over.'

'Later on, not now.' Sebastian could not stand to watch the sharks squabble over the corpse.

'Mohammed, get a couple of your lads on the oars. I want to pick up as many of those coconuts as we can.'

By the time darkness stopped them, they had retrieved fifty-two of the floating coconuts, sufficient to keep the seven of them thirst-free for a week.

It was cold that night. They crowded together for warmth and watched the underwater pyrotechnics, as the shark pack circled the raft in phosphorescent splendour.

15

'You've got to cut for it,' Flynn whispered, and he shivered with cold in the burning heat of the midday sun.

'I don't know anything about it,' Sebastian protested, yet he could see that Flynn was dying.

'No more do I. But this is certain – you've got to do it soon . . . Flynn's eyes had sunk into plum-coloured cavities and the smell of his breath was that of something long dead.

Staring at the leg, Sebastian had difficulty controlling his nausea. It was swollen fat and purple. The bullet hole was covered with a crusty black scab, but Sebastian caught a whiff of the putrefaction under it – and this time his nausea came up acid-sweet into the back of his throat. He swallowed it.

'You've got to do it, Bassie boy.'

Sebastian nodded, and tentatively laid his hand on the leg. Immediately he jerked his fingers away, surprised by the heat of the skin.

'You've got to do it,' urged Flynn. 'Feel for the slug. It's not deep. Just under the skin.'

He felt the lump. It moved under his fingers, the size of a green acorn in the taut hot flesh.

'It's going to hurt like Billy-o.' Sebastian's voice was hoarse.

The rowers were resting on their oars, watching with frank curiosity, while the raft eddied and swung in the drift of the Mozambique current. Above them the sail that Sebastian had rigged from salvaged planking and canvas, flapped wearily, throwing a shadow across the leg.

'Mohammed, you and one other to hold the master's shoulders. Two others to keep his legs still.'

Flynn lay quiescent, pinioned beneath them on the slats of the deck.

Sebastian knelt over him, gathering his resolve. The knife he had sharpened against the metal edge of the raft, and then scrubbed clean with coconut fibre and sea-water. He had sluiced the leg also, and washed his hands until the skin tingled. Beside him on the deck stood half a coconut shell containing perhaps an ounce of evaporated salt scraped from the deck and the sail, ready to pack into the open wound. 'Ready?' he whispered.

'Ready,' grunted Flynn, and Sebastian located the lump of the bullet and drew the edge of the blade across it timidly. Flynn gasped, but human skin was tougher than Sebastian allowed. It did not part.

'Goddamn you!' Flynn was sweating already. 'Don't play with it. Cut, man, cut!'

This time Sebastian slashed, and the flesh split open under the blade. He dropped the knife and drew back in horror as the infection bubbled up through the lips of the knife wound. It looked like yellow custard mixed with prune juice – and the smell of it filled his nostrils and his throat.

'Go for the slug. Go for it with your fingers.' Flynn writhed beneath the men who held him. 'Hurry. Hurry. I can't take much more.'

Steeling himself, closing his throat against the vomit that threatened to vent at any moment, Sebastian slipped his little finger into the slit. Hooking with it for the bullet, finding it, easing it up although tissue clung to it reluctantly, until it popped from the wound and dropped on to the deck. A fresh gush of warm poison followed it out, flowing over Sebastian's hand, and he crawled to the edge of the raft, choking and gagging.

16

'If only we had some red cloth.' Flynn sat against the rickety mast. He was still very weak but four days ago the fever had broken with the release of the poison.

'What would you do with it?' Sebastian asked.

'Catch me one of those dolphins. Man, I'm so goddamned hungry I'd eat it raw.'

A four-day diet of coconut pulp and milk had left all their bellies grumbling.

'Why red?'

'They go for red. Make a lure.'

'You haven't any hooks or line.'

'Tie it to a bit of twine from the sack and tease them up to the surface – then harpoon one with your knife tied to an oar.'

Sebastian was silent, peering thoughtfully over the side at the deep flashes of gold where the shoal of dolphin played under the raft. 'It's got to be red, hey?' he asked, and Flynn looked at him sharply.

'Yeah. It's got to be red.'

'Well . . .' Sebastian hesitated, and then flushed with embarrassment under his tropical sunburn.

'What's wrong with you?'

Still blushing, Sebastian stood up and loosened his belt – then, shyly as a bride on her wedding night, he drew down his pants.

'My God,' breathed Flynn in shock, as he held up his hand to shield his eyes.

'Hau! Hau!' was the chorus of admiration from the crew.

'Got them at Harrods,' said Sebastian with becoming modesty.

Red, Flynn had asked for – but Sebastian's underpants were the brightest, most beautiful red; the most vivid sunset and roses red, he could have imagined. They hung in oriental splendour to Sebastian's knees.

'Pure silk,' said Sebastian, fingering the cloth. 'Ten shillings a pair.'

'Whoa now! Come on, little fishy. Come on there,' Flynn whispered as he lay on his belly, head and shoulders over the edge of the raft. On its thread of twine, the scrap of red danced deep in the green water. A long, slithering flash of gold shot towards it, and Flynn jerked the twine away at the last instant. The dolphin swirled and darted back. Again Flynn jerked the twine. Chameleon lines and dots of excitement showed against the gold of the dolphin's body. 'That's it, fishy. Chase it.' The other fish of the shoal joined hunt, forming a sparkling planetary system of movement around the lure. 'Get ready!'

'I'm ready.' Sebastian stood over him, poised like a javelin thrower. In the excitement he had forgotten to don his pants and his shirt-tails flapped around his thighs in a most undignified manner. But his legs were long and finely muscled, the legs of an athlete. 'Get back!' he snapped at the crew who were crowded around him so that the raft was listing dangerously. 'Get back – give me room,' and he hefted the oar with the long hunting knife lashed to the tip.

'Here they come.' Flynn's voice trembled with excitement as he worked the scrap of red cloth upwards, and the shoal followed it. 'Now!' he shouted as a single fish broke the surface – four feet of flashing gold, and Sebastian lunged. The steady hand and eye that had once clean-bowled the great Frank Woolley directed the oar. Sebastian hit the dolphin an inch behind the eye, and the blade slipped through to lacerate the gills.

For a few seconds the oar came alive in his hands as the dolphin twitched and fought on the blade, but there were no barbs to hold in the flesh, and the fish slipped from the knife.

'God damn it to hell!' bellowed Flynn.

'Dash it all!' echoed Sebastian.

But ten feet down the dolphin was mortally wounded; it jigged and whipped like a golden kite in a high wind while the rest of the shoal scattered.

Sebastian dropped the oar and began stripping his shirt.

'What are you doing?' demanded Flynn.

'Going after it.'

'You're mad. Sharks!'

'I'm so hungry, I'll eat a shark also,' and he dived over the side. Thirty seconds later he surfaced, blowing like a grampus but grinning triumphantly, with the dead dolphin clasped lovingly to his bosom.

They ate strips of raw fish seasoned with evaporated salt, squatting around the mutilated carcass of the dolphin.

'Well, I've paid a guinea for worse meals than this,' said Sebastian, and belched softly. 'Oh, I beg your pardon.'

'Granted,' Flynn grunted with his mouth full of fish; and then eyeing Sebastian's nudity with a world-weary eye, 'Stop boasting and put your pants on before you trip over it.'

Flynn O'Flynn was slowly, very slowly, revising his estimate of Sebastian Oldsmith.

17

The rowers had long since lost any enthusiasm they might have had for the task. They kept at it only in response to offers of bodily violence by Flynn – and the example set by Sebastian, who worked tirelessly. The thin layer of fat that had sheathed Sebastian's muscles was long since consumed, and his sun-baked body was a Michelangelo sculpture, as he leaned and dug and pulled the oar.

Six days they had dragged the raft across the southward push of the current. Six days of sun-blazing calm, with the sea flattening, until now in the late afternoon, it looked like an endless sheet of smooth green velvet.

'No,' said Mohammed. 'That means, *The two porcupines make love under the blanket*.'

'Oh!' Sebastian repeated the phrase without interrupting the rhythm of his rowing. Sebastian was a dogged pupil of Swahili, making up in determination what he lacked in brilliance. Mohammed was proud of him, and opposed any attempt by the other members of the crew to usurp his position as chief tutor.

'That's all right about the porcupines shagging themselves to a standstill,' grunted Flynn. 'But what does this mean . . . ?' and he spoke in Swahili.

'It means, *Big winds will blow across the sea*,' interpreted Sebastian, and glowed with achievement.

'And I'm not joking either.' Flynn stood up, crouching to favour his bad leg, and shaded his eyes to peer into the east. 'You see that line of cloud?'

Laying aside the oar, Sebastian stood beside him and flexed the aching muscles of his back and shoulders. Immediately all activity ceased among the other rowers.

'Keep going, me beauties!' growled Flynn, and reluctantly they obeyed. Flynn turned back to Sebastian. 'You see it?'

'Yes.' It was drawn like a kohl line across the eyelid of a Hindu woman, smeared black along the horizon.

'Well, Bassie, there's the wind you've been griping about. But, my friend, I think it's a little more than you bargained for.'

In the darkness they heard it coming from far away, a muted sibilance in the night. One by one, the fat stars were blotted out in the east as dark cloud spread out to fill half the midnight sky.

A single gust hit the raft and flogged the makeshift sail with a clap like a shotgun, and the sleepers woke and sat up.

'Hang on to those fancy underpants,' muttered Flynn, 'or you'll get them blown right up your backside.'

Another gust, another lull, but already there was the boisterous slapping of small waves against the sides of the raft.

'I'd better get that sail down.'

'You had, and all,' agreed Flynn, 'and while you're at it, use the rope to fix life-lines for us.' In haste, spurred on by the rising hiss of the wind, they lashed themselves to the slats of the deck.

The main force of the wind spun the raft like a top, splattering them with spray; the spray was icy cold in the warm rush of the wind. The wind was steady now and the raft moved uneasily – the jerky motion of an animal restless at the prick of spurs.

'At least it will push us towards the land,' Sebastian shouted across at Flynn.

'Bassie, boy, you think of the cutest things,' and the first wave came aboard, smothering Flynn's voice, breaking over their prostrate bodies, and then streaming out through the slatted deck. The raft wallowed in dismay, then gathered itself to meet the next rush of the sea.

Under the steady fury of the wind, the sea came up more swiftly than Sebastian believed was possible. Within minutes the waves were breaking over the raft with such weight as to squeeze the breath from their lungs, submerging them completely, driving the raft under before its buoyancy reasserted itself and lifted it, canting crazily, and they could gasp for air in the smother of spray.

Waiting for the lulls, Sebastian inched his way across the deck until he reached Flynn. 'How are you bearing up?' he bellowed.

'Great, just great,' and another wave drove them under.

'Your leg?' spluttered Sebastian as they came up.

'For Chrissake, stop yapping,' and they went under again.

It was completely dark, no star, no sliver of moon, but each line of breaking water glowed in dull, phosphorescent malevolence as it dashed down upon them, warning them to suck air and cling with cramped fingers hooked into the slats.

For all eternity Sebastian lived in darkness, battered by the wind and the wild, flying water. The aching chill of his body dulled out into numbness. Slowly his mind emptied of conscious thought, so when a bigger wave scoured them, he heard the tearing sound of deck slats pulling loose, and the lost wail as one of the Arabs was washed away into the night sea – but the sound had no meaning to him.

Twice he vomited sea water that he had swallowed, but it had no taste in his mouth, and he let it run heedlessly down his chin and warm on to his chest, to be washed away by the next torrential wave.

His eyes burned without pain from the harsh rake of windflung spray, and he blinked them owlishly at each advancing wave. It seemed, in time, that he could see more clearly, and he turned his head slowly. Beside him, Flynn's face was a leprous blotch in the darkness. This puzzled him, and he lay and thought about it but no solution came, until he looked beyond the next wave, and saw the faint promise of a new day show pale through the black massed cloud-banks.

He tried to speak, but no sound came for his throat was swollen closed with the salt, and his tongue was tingling numb. Again, he tried. 'Dawn coming,' he croaked, but beside him Flynn lay like a corpse frozen in rigor mortis.

Slowly the light grew over that mad, grey sea but the scudding black cloud-banks tried desperately to oppose its coming.

Now the seas were more awesome in their raging insanity. Each mountain of glassy grey rose high above the raft, shielding it for a few seconds from the whip of the wind, its crest blowing off like the plume of an Etruscan helmet, before it slid down, collapsing upon itself in the tumbling roar of breaking water.

Each time, the men on the raft shrank flat on the deck, and waited in bovine acceptance to be smothered again beneath the white deluge.

Once, the raft rode high and clear in a freak flat of the storm, and Sebastian looked about him. The canvas and rope, the coconuts and the other pathetic accumulation of their possessions were all gone. The sea had ripped away many of the deck slats so that the metal floats of the raft were exposed; it had torn the very clothing from them so they were clad in sodden tatters. Of the seven men who had ridden the raft the previous day, only he and Flynn, Mohammed and one more, were left – the other three were gone, gobbled up by the hungry sea.

Then the storm struck again, so that the raft reeled and reared to the point of capsizing.

Sebastian sensed it first in the altered action of the waves; they were steeper, marching closer together. Then, through the clamour of the storm, a new sound, like that of a cannon fired at irregular intervals with varying charges of gunpowder. He realized suddenly that he had been hearing this sound for some time, but only now had it penetrated the stupor of his fatigue.

He lifted his head, and every nerve of his being shrieked in protest at the effort. He looked about, but the sea stood up around him like a series of grey walls that limited his vision to a circle of fifty yards. Yet that discordant boom, boom, boom, was louder now and more insistent.

In the short, choppy waves, a side-break caught the raft and tossed it high – lifting him so he could see the land; so close that the palm trees showed sharply, bending their stems to the wind and threshing their long fronds in panic. He saw the beach, grey-white in the gloom and, beyond it, far beyond it, rose the watery blue of the high ground.

These things had small comfort for him when he saw the reef. It bared its black teeth at him, snarling through the white water that burst like cannon-fire upon it before cascading on into the comparative quiet of the lagoon. The raft was riding down towards it.

'Flynn,' he croaked. 'Flynn, listen to me!' but the older man did not move, His eyes were fixed open and only the movement of his chest, as he breathed, proved him still alive. 'Flynn.' Sebastian released one of his clawed hands from its grip on the wooden slatting. 'Flynn!' he said, and struck him across the cheek.

'Flynn!' The head turned towards Sebastian, the eyes blinked, the mouth opened, but no voice spoke.

Another wave broke over the raft. This time the cold, malicious rush of it stirred Sebastian, roused a little of his failing strength. He shook the water from his head. 'Land,' he whispered. 'Land,' and Flynn stared at him dully.

Two lines of surf away, the reef showed its ragged back again. Clinging with only one hand to the slatting, Sebastian fumbled the knife from its sheath and hacked clumsily at the life-line that bound him to the deck. It parted. He reached over and cut Flynn's line, sawing frantically at the wet hemp. That done, he slid back on his belly until he reached Mohammed and freed him also. The little African stared at him with bloodshot eyes from his wrinkled monkey face.

'Swim,' whispered Sebastian. 'Must swim,' and re-sheathing the knife, he tried to crawl over Mohammed to reach the Arab but the next wave caught the raft, rearing up under it as it felt the push of the land, rearing so steeply that this time the raft was overturned and they were thrown from it into the seething turmoil of the reef.

Sebastian hit the water flat, and was hardly under, before he had surfaced again. Beside him, close enough to touch, Flynn emerged. In the strength born of the fear of death, Flynn caught at Sebastian, locking both arms around his chest. The same wave that had capsized them, had poured over the reef and covered it completely, so that where the coral fangs had been was now only a frothy area of disturbed water. In it bobbed the debris of the raft, shattered into pieces against the reef. The mutilated corpse of the Arab was still roped to a piece of the wreckage. Flynn and Sebastian were locked like lovers in each other's arms and the next wave, following close upon the first, lifted them, and shot them forward over the submerged reef.

In one great swoop that left their guts behind them, they were carried over the coral which could have minced them into jelly, and tumbled into the quiet lagoon. With them went little Mohammed, and what remained of the raft.

The lagoon was covered by a thick scum of wind spume, creamy as the head of a good beer. So when the three of them staggered waist-deep towards the beach, supporting each other with arms around shoulders, they were coated with white froth. It made them look like a party of drunken snowmen returning home after a long night out.

18

Mohammed squatted with a pile of madafu, the shiny green coconuts, beside him. The beach was littered with them, for the storm had stripped the trees. He worked in feverish haste with Sebastian's hunting knife, his face frosted with dried salt, mumbling to himself through cracked and swollen lips, shaving down through the white, fibrous material of the shell, until he exposed the hollow centre filled with its white custard and effervescent milk. At this point the madafu was snatched from his hands by either Flynn or Sebastian. His despair growing deeper, he watched for a second the two white men drinking with heads thrown back, throats pulsing as they swallowed, spilled milk trickling from the corners of their mouths, eyes closed tight in their intense pleasure; then he picked up another nut and got to work on it. He opened a dozen before he was able to satiate the other two, and he held the next nut to his own mouth and whimpered with eagerness.

Then they slept. Bellies filled with the sweet, rich milk, they sagged backwards on the sand and slept the rest of that day and that night, and when they woke, the wind had dropped, although the sea still burst like an artillery bombardment on the reef.

'Now,' said Flynn, 'where, in the name of the devil and all his angels, are we?' Neither Sebastian nor Mohammed answered him. 'We were six days on the raft. We could have drifted hundreds of miles south before the storm pushed us in.' He frowned as he considered the problem. 'We might even have reached Portuguese Mozambique. We could be as far as the Zambezi river.'

Flynn focused his attention on Mohammed. 'Go!' he said. 'Search for a river, or a mountain that you know. Better still, find a village where we can get food – and bearers.'

'I'll go also,' Sebastian volunteered.

'You wouldn't know the difference between the Zambezi and the Mississippi,' Flynn grunted impatiently. 'You'd be lost after the first hundred yards.'

Mohammed was gone for two days and a half, but Sebastian and Flynn ate well in his absence.

Under a sun shelter of palm fronds they feasted three times a day on crab and sand-clams, and big green rock-lobster which Sebastian fished from the lagoon, baking them in their shells over the fire that Flynn coaxed from two dry sticks.

On the first night the entertainment was provided by Flynn. For some years now, Flynn's intake of gin had averaged a daily two bottles. The abrupt cessation of supply resulted in a delayed but classic visitation of *delirium tremens*. He spent half the night hobbling up and down the beach brandishing a branch of driftwood and hurling obscenities at the phantoms that had come to plague him. There was one purple cobra in particular which pursued him doggedly, and it was only after Flynn had beaten it noisily to death behind a palm tree, that he allowed Sebastian to lead him back to the shelter and seat him beside the camp-fire. Then he got the shakes. He shook like a man on a jack-hammer. His teeth rattled together with such violence that Sebastian was sure they must shatter. Gradually, however, the shakes subsided and by the following noon he was able to eat three large rock-lobsters and then collapse into a death-like sleep.

He woke in the late evening, looking as well as Sebastian had ever seen him, to greet the returning Mohammed and the dozen tall Angoni tribesmen who accompanied him. They returned Flynn's greeting with respect. From Beira to Dar es Salaam, the name 'Fini' was held in universal awe by the indigenous peoples. Legend credited him with powers far above the natural order. His exploits, his skill with the rifle, his volcanic temper and his seeming immunity from death and retribution, had formed the foundation of a belief that Flynn had carefully fostered. They said in whispers around the night fires when the women and the children were not listening that 'Fini' was in truth a reincarnation of the Monomatapa. They said further that in the intervening period between his death as the Great King and his latest birth as 'Fini', he had been first a monstrous crocodile, and then *Mowana Lisa*, the most notorious man-eating lion in the history of East Africa, a predator responsible for at least three hundred human killings. The day, twenty-five years previously, that Flynn had stepped ashore at Port Amelia was the exact day that *Mowana Lisa* had been shot dead by the Portuguese Chef D'Post at Sofala. All men knew these things – and only an idiot would take chances with 'Fini' – hence the respect with which they greeted him now.

Flynn recognized one of the men. 'Luti,' he roared, 'you scab on an hyena's backside!'

Luti smiled broadly, and bobbed his head in pleasure at being singled out by Flynn.

'Mohammed,' Flynn turned to his man. 'Where did you find him? Are we near his village?'

'We are a day's march away.'

'In which direction?'

'North.'

'Then we are in Portuguese territory!' exalted Flynn. 'We must have drifted down past the Rovuma river.'

The Rovuma river was the frontier between Portuguese Mozambique and German East Africa. Once in Portuguese territory, Flynn was immune from the wrath of the Germans. All their efforts at extraditing him from the Portuguese had proved unsuccessful, for Flynn had a working agreement with the Chef D'Post, Mozambique, and through him with the Governor in Lourenco Marques. In a manner of speaking, these two officials were sleeping partners in Flynn's business, and were entitled to a quarterly financial statement of Flynn's activities, and an agreed percentage of the profits.

'You can relax, Bassie boy. Old Fleischer can't touch us now. And in three or four days we'll be home.'

The first leg of the journey took them to Luti's village. Lolling in their maschilles, hammock-like litters slung beneath a long pole and carried by four of Luti's men at a synchronized jog trot, Flynn and Sebastian were borne smoothly out of the coastal lowland into the hills and bush country.

The litter-bearers sang as they ran, and their deep melodious voices, coupled with the swinging motion of the maschille, lulled Sebastian into a mood of deep contentment. Occasionally he dozed. Where the path was wide enough to allow the maschilles to travel side by side, he lay and chatted with Flynn, at other times he watched the changing country and the animal life along the way. It was better than London Zoo.

Each time Sebastian saw something new, he called across for Flynn to identify it.

In every glade and clearing were herds of the golden brown impala; delicate little creatures that watched them in wide-eyed curiosity as they passed.

Troops of guinea-fowl, like a dark cloud shadow on the earth, scratched and chittered on the banks of every stream.

Heavy, yellow eland, with their stubby horns and swinging dewlaps, trotting in Indian file, formed a regal frieze along the edge of the bush.

Sable and roan antelope; purple-brown waterbuck, with a perfect circle of white branded on their rumps; buffalo, big and black and ugly; giraffe, dainty little klipspringer, standing like chamois on the tumbled granite boulders of a kopje. The whole land seethed and skittered with life.

There were trees so strange in shape and size and foliage that Sebastian could hardly credit them as existing. Swollen baobabs, fifty feet in circumference, standing awkwardly as prehistoric monsters, fat pods filled with cream of tartar hanging from their deformed branches. There were forests of msasa trees, leaves not green as leaves should be, but rose and chocolate and red. Fever trees sixty feet high, with bright yellow trunks, shedding their bark like the brittle parchment of a snake's skin. Groves of mopani, whose massed foliage glittered a shiny, metallic green in the sun; and in the jungle growth along the river banks, the lianas climbed up like long, grey worms and hung in loops and festoons among the wild fig and the buffalo-bean vines and the tree ferns.

'Why haven't we seen any sign of elephant?' Sebastian asked.

'Me and my boys worked this territory over about six months ago,' Flynn explained. 'I guess they just moved on a little – probably up north across the Rovuma.'

In the late afternoon they descended a stony path into a valley, and for the first time Sebastian saw the permanent habitations of man. In irregular shaped plots, the bottom land of the valley was cultivated, and the rich black soil threw up lush green stands of millet, while on the banks of the little stream stood Luti's village; shaggy grass huts, shaped like beehives, each with a circular mud-walled granary standing on stilts beside it. The huts were arranged in a rough circle around an open space where the earth was packed hard by the passage of bare feet.

The entire population turned out to welcome Flynn: three hundred souls, from hobbling old white heads with grinning toothless gums, down to infants held on mothers' naked hip, who did not interrupt their feeding but clung like fat black limpets with hands and mouth to the breast.

Through the crowd that ululated and clapped hands in welcome, Flynn and Sebastian were carried to the chief's hut and there they descended from the maschilles.

Flynn and the old chief greeted each other affectionately; Flynn because of favours received and because of future favours yet to be asked for, and the chief because of Flynn's reputation and the fact that wherever Flynn travelled, he usually left behind him large quantities of good, red meat.

'You come to hunt elephant?' the chief asked, looking hopefully for Flynn's rifle.

'No.' Flynn shook his head. 'I return from a journey to a far place.'

'From where?'

In answer, Flynn looked significantly at the sky and repeated, 'From a far place.'

There was an awed murmur from the crowd and the chief nodded sagely. It was clear to all of them that 'Fini' must have been to visit and commune with his *alter ego*, Monomatapa.

'Will you stay long at our village?' again hopefully.

'I will stay tonight only. I leave again in the dawn.'

'Ah!' Disappointment. 'We had hoped to welcome you with a dance. Since we heard of your coming, we have prepared.'

'No,' Flynn repeated. He knew a dance could last three or four days.

'There is a great brewing of palm wine which is only now ready for drinking,' the chief tried again, and this time his argument hit Flynn like a charging rhinoceros. Flynn had been many days without liquor.

'My friend,' said Flynn, and he could feel the saliva spurting out from under his tongue in anticipation. 'I cannot stay to dance with you but I will drink a small gourd of palm wine to show my love for you and your village.' Then turning to Sebastian he warned, 'I wouldn't touch this stuff, Bassie, if I were you – it's real poison.'

'Right,' agreed Sebastian. 'I'm going down to the river to wash.'

74

'You do that,' and Flynn lifted the first gourd of palm wine lovingly to his lips.

Sebastian's progress to the river resembled a Roman triumph. The entire village lined the bank to watch his necessarily limited ablutions with avid interest, and a buzz of awe went up when he disrobed to his underpants.

'Bwana Manali,' they chorused. 'Lord of the Red Cloth,' and the name stuck.

As a farewell gift the headman presented Flynn with four gourds of palm wine, and begged him to return soon – bringing his rifle with him.

They marched hard all that day and when they camped at nightfall, Flynn was semi-paralysed with palm wine, while Sebastian shivered and his teeth chattered uncontrollably.

From the swamps of the Rufiji delta, Sebastian had brought with him a souvenir of his visit – his first full go of malaria.

They reached Lalapanzi the following day, a few hours before the crisis of Sebastian's fever. Lalapanzi was Flynn's base camp and the name meant 'Lie Down', or more accurately, 'The Place of Rest'.

It was in the hills on a tiny tributary of the great Rovuma river, a hundred miles from the Indian Ocean, but only ten miles from German territory across the river. Flynn believed in living close to his principle place of business.

Had Sebastian been in full possession of his senses, and not wandering in the hot shadow land of malaria, he would have been surprised by the camp at Lalapanzi. It was not what anybody who knew Flynn O'Flynn would have expected.

Behind a palisade of split bamboo to protect the lawns and gardens from the attentions of the duiker and steenbok and kudu, it glowed like a green jewel in the sombre brown of the hills. Much hard work and patience must have gone into damming the stream, and digging the irrigation furrows, which suckled the lawns and flower-beds and the vegetable garden. Three indigenous fig trees dwarfed the buildings, crimson frangipani burst like fireworks against the green kikuyu grass, beds of bright barberton daisies ringed the gentle terraces that fell away to the stream, and a bougainvillaea creeper smothered the main building in a profusion of dark green and purple.

Behind the long bungalow, with its wide, open veranda, stood half a dozen circular rondavels, all neatly capped with golden thatch and gleaming painfully white, with burned limestone paint, in the sunlight.

The whole had about it an air of feminine order and neatness. Only a woman, and a determined one at that, could have devoted so much time and pain to building up such a speck of prettiness in the midst of brown rock and harsh thorn veld.

She stood on the veranda in the shade like a valkyrie, tall and sun-browned and angry. The full-length dress of faded blue was crisp with new ironing, and the neat mends in the fabric invisible except at close range. Gathered close about her waist, her skirt ballooned out over her woman's hips and fell to her ankles, slyly concealing the long straight legs beneath. Folded across her stomach, her arms were an amber brown frame for the proud double bulge of her bosom, and the thick braid of black hair that hung to her waist twitched like the tail of an angry lioness. A face too young for the marks of hardship and loneliness that were chiselled into it, was harder now by the expression of distaste it wore as she watched Flynn and Sebastian arriving.

They lolled in their maschilles, unshaven, dressed in filthy rags, hair matted with sweat and dust; Flynn full of palm wine, and Sebastian full of fever – although it was impossible to distinguish the symptoms of their separate disorders.

'May I ask where you've been these last two months, Flynn Patrick O'Flynn?' Although she tried to speak like a man, yet her voice had a lift and a ring to it.

'You may not ask, daughter!' Flynn shouted back defiantly.

'You're drunk again!'

'And if I am?' roared Flynn. 'You're as bad as that mother of yours (may her soul rest in peace), always going on and on. Never a civil word of welcome for your old Daddy, who's been away trying to earn an honest crust.'

The girl's eyes switched to the maschille that carried Sebastian, and narrowed in mounting outrage. 'Sweet merciful heavens, and what's this you've brought home with you now?'

Sebastian grinned inanely, and tried valiantly to sit up as Flynn introduced him. 'That is Sebastian Oldsmith. My very dear friend, Sebastian Oldsmith.'

'He's also drunk!'

'Listen, Rosa. You show some respect.' Flynn struggled to climb from his maschille.

'He's drunk,' Rosa repeated grimly. 'Drunk as a pig. You can take him straight back and leave him where you found him. He's not coming in this house.' She turned away, pausing only a moment at the front door to add, 'That goes for you also, Flynn O'Flynn. I'll be waiting with the shotgun. You just put one foot on the veranda before you're sober – and I'll blow it clean off.'

'Rosa – wait – he isn't drunk, please,' wailed Flynn, but the fly-screen door had slammed closed behind her.

Flynn teetered uncertainly at the foot of the veranda stairs, for a moment it looked as though he might be foolhardy enough to put his daughter's threat to the test, but he was not that drunk.

'Women,' he mourned. 'The good Lord protect us,' and he led his little caravan around the back of the bungalow to the farthest of the rondavel huts. This room was sparsely furnished in anticipation of Flynn's regular periods of exile from the main building.

19

Rosa O'Flynn closed the front door behind her and leaned back against it wearily. Slowly her chin sagged down to her chest, and she closed her eyes to imprison the itchy tears beneath the lids, but one of them squeezed through and quivered like a fat, glistening grape on her lashes, before falling to splash on the stone floor.

'Oh, Daddy, Daddy,' she whispered. It was an expression of those months of aching loneliness. The long, slow slide of days when she had searched desperately for work to fill her hands and her mind. The nights when, locked alone in her room with a loaded shotgun beside the bed, she had lain and listened to the sounds of the African bush beyond the window, afraid then of everything, even the four devoted African servants sleeping soundly with their families in their little compound behind the bungalow.

Waiting, waiting for Flynn to return. Lifting her head in the noonday and standing listening, hoping to hear the singing of his bearers as they came down the valley. And each hour the fear and the resentment building up within her. Fear that he might not come, and resentment that he left her for so long.

Now he had come. He had come drunk and filthy, with some oafish ruffian as a companion, and all her loneliness and fear had vented itself in that shrewish outburst. She straightened and pushed herself away from the door. Listlessly she walked through the shady cool rooms of the bungalow, spread with a rich profusion of animal skins and rough native-made furniture, until she reached her own room and sank down on the bed.

Beneath her unhappiness was a restlessness, a formless, undirected longing for something she did not understand. It was a new thing; only in these last few years had she become aware of it. Before that she had gloried in the companionship of her father, never having experienced and, therefore, never missing the society of others. She had taken it as the natural order of things that much of her time must be spent completely alone with only the wife of old Mohammed to replace her natural mother – the young Portuguese girl who had died in the struggle to give life to Rosa.

She knew the land as a slum child knows the city. It was her land and she loved it.

Now all of it was changing, she was uncertain, without bearings in this sea of new emotion. Lonely, irritable – and afraid.

A timid knocking on the back door of the bungalow roused her, and she felt a leap of hope within her. Her anger at Flynn had long ago abated – now he had made the first overture she would welcome him to the bungalow without sacrifice of pride.

Quickly she bathed her face in the china wash-basin beside her bed, and patted her hair into order before the mirror, before going through to answer the knock.

Old Mohammed stood outside, shuffling his feet and grinning ingratiatingly. He stood in almost as great an awe of Rosa's temper as that of Flynn himself. It was with relief, therefore, that he saw her smile.

'Mohammed, you old rascal,' and he bobbed his head with pleasure.

'You are well, Little Long Hair?'

'I am well, Mohammed – and I can see you are also.'

'The Lord Fini asks that you send blankets and quinine.'

'Why?' Rosa frowned quickly. 'Is the fever on him?'

'Not on him, but on Manali, his friend.'

'Is he bad?'

'He is very bad.'

The rich hostility that her first glimpse of Sebastian had invoked in Rosa, wavered a little. She felt the woman in her irresistibly drawn towards anything wounded or sick, even such an uncouth and filthy specimen as she had seen Sebastian to be.

'I will come,' she decided aloud, while silently qualifying her surrender by deciding that under no circumstances would she let him in the house. Sick or healthy, he would stay out there in the rondavel.

Armed with a pitcher of boiled drinking water, and a bottle of quinine tablets, closely attended by Mohammed carrying an armful of cheap trade blankets, she crossed to the rondavel and entered.

She entered it at an unpropitious moment. For Flynn had spent the last ten minutes exhuming the bottle he had so carefully buried some months before beneath the earthen floor of the rondavel. Being a man of foresight, he had caches of gin scattered in unlikely places around the camp, and now, in delicious anticipation, he was carefully wiping damp earth from the neck of the bottle with the the tail of his shirt. So engrossed with this labour he was not aware of Rosa's presence until the bottle was snatched from his hands, and thrown through the open side window to pop and tinkle as it burst.

'Now what did you do that for?' Flynn was hurt as deeply as a mother deprived of her infant.

'For the good of your soul.' Icily Rosa turned from him to the inert figure on the bed, and her nose wrinkled as she caught the whiff of unwashed body and fever. 'Where did you find this one?' she asked without expecting an answer.

20

Five grains of quinine washed down Sebastian's throat with scalding tea, heated stones were packed around his body, and half a dozen blankets swaddled him to begin the sweat.

The malarial parasite has a thirty-six hour life cycle, and now at the crisis, Rosa was attempting to raise his body temperature sufficiently to interrupt the cycle and break the fever. Heat radiated from the bed, filling the single room of the rondavel as though it were a kitchen. Only Sebastian's head showed from the pile of blankets, and his face was flushed a dusky brick colour. Although sweat spurted from every pore of his skin and ran back in heavy drops to soak his hair and his pillow, yet his teeth rattled together and he shivered so that the camp-bed shook.

Rosa sat beside his bed and watched him. Occasionally she leaned forward with a cloth in her hand and wiped the perspiration from his eyes and upper lip. Her expression had softened and become almost broody. One of Sebastian's curls had plastered itself wetly across his forehead, and, with her finger-tips, Rosa combed it back. She repeated the gesture, and then did it again, stroking her fingers through his damp hair, instinctively gentling and soothing him.

He opened his eyes, and Rosa snatched her hand away guiltily. His eyes were misty grey, unfocused as a new-born puppy's, and Rosa felt something squirm in her stomach.

'Please don't stop.' His voice was slurred with the fever, but even so Rosa was surprised at the timbre and inflection. It was the first time she had heard him speak and it was not the voice of a ruffian. Hesitating a moment, she glanced at the door of the hut to make sure they were alone before she reached forward to touch his face.

'You are kind – good and kind.'

'Sshh!' she admonished him.

'Thank you.'

'Sshh! Close your eyes.'

His eyes flickered down and he sighed, a gusty, broken sound.

The crisis came like a big wind and shook him as though he were a tree in its path. His body temperature rocketed, and he tossed and writhed in the camp-bed, trying to throw off the weight of blankets upon him, so that Rosa called for Mohammed's wife to help her restrain him. His perspiration soaked through the thin mattress and dripped to form a puddle on the earth floor beneath the bed, and he cried out in the fantasy of his fever.

Then, miraculously, the crisis was past, and he slumped into relaxation. He lay still and exhausted so that only the shallow flutter of his breathing showed there was life in him. Rosa could feel his skin cooling under her hand, and she saw the yellowish tinge with which the fever had coloured it.

'The first time it is always bad,' Mohammed's wife released her grip on the blanket-wrapped legs.

'Yes,' said Rosa. 'Now bring the basin. We must wash him and change his blankets, Nanny.'

She had worked many times with men who were sick or badly hurt; the servants and the bearers and the gun-boys, and, of course, with her father. But now, as Nanny peeled back the blankets and Rosa swabbed Sebastian's unconscious body with the moist cloth, she felt an inexplicable tension within her – a sense of dread mingled with tight excitement. She could feel new blood warming her cheeks, and she leaned forward, so that Nanny could not see her face as she worked.

The skin of his chest and upper arms was creamy-smooth as polished alabaster, where the sun had not stained it. Beneath her fingers it had an elastic hardness, a rubbery sensuality and warmth that disturbed her. When she realized suddenly that she was no longer wiping with the flannel but using it to caress the shape of hard muscle beneath the pale skin, she checked herself and made her actions brusque and businesslike.

They dried his upper body, and Nanny reached to jerk the blankets down below Sebastian's waist.

'Wait!' It came out of Rosa as a cry, and Nanny paused with her hand on the bedclothes and her head held at an angle, quizzical, birdlike. Her wizened old features crinkling in sly amusement.

'Wait,' Rosa repeated in confusion. 'First help me get the night-shirt on him,' and she snatched up one of Flynn's freshly ironed but threadbare old night-shirts from the chair beside the bed.

'It cannot bite you, Little Long Hair,' the old woman teased her gently. 'It has no teeth.'

'You just stop that kind of talk,' snapped Rosa with unnecessary violence. 'Help me sit him up.'

Between them they lifted Sebastian and slipped the night-shirt down over his head, before lowering him to the pillow again.

'And now?' Nanny asked innocently. For answer, Rosa handed her the flannel, and turned to stare fixedly out of the rondavel window. Behind her she heard the rustle of blankets and then Nanny's voice.

'Hau! Hau!' The age-old expression of deep admiration, followed by a cackle of delighted laughter, as Nanny saw the back of Rosa's neck turning bright pink with embarrassment.

Nanny had smuggled Flynn's cut-throat razor out of the bungalow, and was supervising critically as Rosa stroked it gingerly over Sebastian's soapy cheeks. There was no sound medical reason why a malaria patient should be shaved immediately after emerging from the crisis, but Rosa had advanced the theory that it would make him feel more comfortable and Nanny had agreed enthusiastically. Both of them were enjoying themselves with all the sober delight of two small girls playing with a doll.

Despite Nanny's cautionary clucks and sharp hisses of indrawn breath, Rosa succeeded in removing the hair that covered Sebastian's face like the black pelt of an otter without inflicting any serious wounds. There was a nick on the chin and another below the left nostril, but neither of these bled more than a drop or two.

Rosa rinsed the razor and then narrowed her eyes thoughtfully as she surveyed her handiwork, and that thing squirmed in her stomach again. 'I think,' she muttered, 'we should move him into the main bungalow. It will be more comfortable.'

'I will call the servants to carry him,' said Nanny.

21

Flynn O'Flynn was a busy man during the period of Sebastian's convalescence. His band of followers had been seriously depleted during the recent exchange with Herman Fleischer on the Rufiji, so to replace his losses, he press-ganged all the maschille-bearers who had carried them home from Luti's village. These he put through a preliminary course of training and at the end of four days selected a dozen of the most promising, to become gun-boys. The remainder he despatched homeward despite their pro-tests; they would dearly have loved to stay for the glamour and reward that they were certain would be heaped upon their more fortunate fellows.

Thereafter the chosen few were entered upon the second part of their training. Securely locked in one of the rondavels behind the bungalow, Flynn kept the tools of his trade. It was an impress-ive arsenal.

Rack upon rack of cheap Martini Henry .450 rifles, a score of W. D. Lee-Metfords that had survived the Anglo-Boer war, a lesser number of German Mausers salvaged from his encounters with Askari across the Rovuma, and a very few of the expensive hand-made doubles by Gibbs and Messrs Greener of London. Not a single weapon had a serial number on it. Above these, neatly stacked on the wooden shelves, were bulk packages of cartridges, wrapped and soldered in lead foil – enough of them to fight a small battle.

The room reeked with the slick, mineral smell of gun oil.

Flynn issued his recruits with Mausers, and set about instruct-ing them in the art of handling a rifle. Again he weeded out those who showed no aptitude and he was left finally with eight men who could hit an elephant at fifty paces. This group passed into the third and last period of training.

Many years previously, Mohammed had been recruited into the German Askari. He had even won a medal during the Salito rebellion of 1904, and from there had risen to the rank of sergeant and overseer of the officers' mess. During a visit by the army auditor to Mbeya, where Mohammed was at that time stationed, there had been discovered a stock discrepancy of some twenty dozen bottles of schnapps, and a hole in the mess funds amounting to a little over a thousand Reichsmarks. This was a hanging matter, and Mohammed had resigned without ceremony from the Imperial army and reached the Portuguese border by a series of forced marches. In Portuguese territory he had met Flynn, and solicited and received employment from him. However, he was still an authority on German army drill procedure and retained a command of the language.

The recruits were handed over to him, for it was part of Flynn's plans that they be able to masquerade as a squad of German Askari. For days thereafter the camp at Lalapanzi reverberated to Mohammed's Teutonic cries, as he goose-stepped about the lawns at the head of his band of nearly naked troopers, with his fez set squarely on the grey wool of his head.

This left Flynn free to make further preparations. Seated on the stoep of the bungalow, he pored sweatily over his correspondence for many days. First there was a letter to:

His Excellency, The Governor,
   German Administration of East Africa,
      Dar Es Salaam.

Sir,
   I enclose my account for damages, as follows, herewith:

1 Dhow (Market value)	£1,500.—.—.
10 Rifles	£200.—.—.
Various stores and provisions etcetera (too numerous to list)	£100.—.—.
Injury, suffering and hardships (estimated)	£200.—.—.
TOTAL	£2,000.—.—.

This claim arises from the sinking of the above-said dhow off the mouth of the Rufiji, 10th July, 1912, which was an act of piracy by your gunboat, the *Blücher*.

I would appreciate payment in gold, on or before 25th

September, 1912, otherwise I will take the necessary steps to collect same personally.

Yours sincerely,

    Flynn Patrick O'Flynn, Esq.,

      (Citizen of The United States of America).

After much heavy thought, Flynn had decided not to include a claim for the ivory as he was not too certain of its legality. Best not to mention it.

He had considered signing himself 'United States Ambassador to Africa,' but had discarded the idea on the grounds that Governor Schee knew damned well that he was no such thing. However, there was no harm in reminding him of Flynn's nationality – it might make the old rogue hesitate before hanging Flynn out of hand if ever he got his hooks into him.

Satisfied that the only response to his demands would be a significant increase in Governor Schee's blood pressure, Flynn proceeded with his preparations to make good his threat of collecting the debt *personally*.

Flynn used this word lightly – he had long ago selected a representative debt collector in the form of Sebastian Oldsmith. It now remained to have him suitably outfitted for the occasion, and, armed with a tape-measure from Rosa's work-basket, Flynn visited Sebastian's sick bed. These days, visiting Sebastian was much like trying to arrange an interview with the Pope. Sebastian was securely under the maternal protection of Rosa O'Flynn.

Flynn knocked discreetly on the door of the guest bedroom, paused for a count of five, and entered.

'What do you want?' Rosa greeted him affectionately. She was sitting on the foot of Sebastian's bed.

'Hello, hello,' said Flynn, and then again lamely, 'Hello.'

'I suppose you're looking for a drinking companion,' accused Rosa.

'Good Lord, no!' Flynn was genuinely horrified by the accusation. What with Rosa's depredations his stock of gin was running perilously low, and he had no intention of sharing it with anyone. 'I just called in to see how he was doing.' Flynn transferred his attention to Sebastian. 'How you feeling, old Bassie boy?'

'Much better, thank you.' In fact, Sebastian was looking very chirpy indeed. Freshly shaved, dressed in one of Flynn's best night-shirts, he lay like a Roman emperor on clean sheets. On the low table beside his bed stood a vase of frangipani blooms, and there were other floral tributes standing about the room – all of them cut and carefully arranged by Rosa O'Flynn.

He was steadily putting on weight again as Rosa and Nanny stuffed food into him and colour was starting to drive the yellowish fever stains from his skin. Flynn felt a prickle of irritation at the way Sebastian was being pampered like a stud stallion, while Flynn himself was barely tolerated in his own home.

The metaphor which had come naturally into Flynn's mind, now sparked a further train of thought, and a sharper prickle of irritation. *Stud stallion!* Flynn looked at Rosa with attention, and noticed that the dress she wore was the white one with gauzy sleeves, that had belonged to her mother – a garment that Rosa usually kept securely locked away, a garment she had worn perhaps twice before in her life. Furthermore, her feet, which were usually bare about the house, were now neatly clad in store-bought patent leather, and, by Jesus, she was wearing a sprig of bougainvillaea tucked into the shiny black slick of her hair. The tip of her long braid, which was usually tied carelessly with a thong of leather, flaunted a silk ribbon.

Now, Flynn O'Flynn was not a sentimental man but suddenly he recognized in his daughter a strange new glow, and a demure air that had never been there before, and within himself he became aware of an unusual sensation, so unfamiliar that he did not recognize it as paternal jealousy. He did, however, recognize that the sooner he sent Sebastian on his way, the safer it would be.

'Well, that's fine, Bassie,' he boomed genially. 'That's just fine. Now, I'm sending bearers down to Beira to pick up supplies, and I just thought they might as well get some clothes for you while they were there.'

'Well, thank you very much, Flynn.' Sebastian was touched by the kindness of his friend.

'Might as well do it properly.' Flynn produced his tape-measure with a flourish. 'We'll send your measurements down to old Parbhoo and he can tailor-make some stuff for you.'

'I say, that *is* jolly decent of you.'

And completely out of character, thought Rosa O'Flynn as she watched her father carefully noting the length of Sebastian's legs and arms, and the girth of his neck, chest and waist.

'The boots and the hat will be a problem,' Flynn mused aloud when he had finished. 'But I'll find something.'

'And what do you mean by that, Flynn O'Flynn?' Rosa demanded suspiciously.

'Nothing, just nothing at all.' Hurriedly Flynn gathered his notes and his tape, and fled from further interrogation.

Some time later, Mohammed and the bearers returned from the shopping expedition to Beira, and he and Flynn immediately closeted themselves in secret conclave in the arsenal.

'Did you get it?' demanded Flynn eagerly.

'Five boxes of gin I left in the cave behind the waterfall at the top of the valley,' whispered Mohammed, and Flynn sighed with relief. 'But one bottle I brought with me.' Mohammed produced it from under his tunic. Flynn took it from him and drew the cork with his teeth, before spilling a little into the enamel mug that was standing ready.

'And the other purchases?'

'It was difficult – especially the hat.'

'But did you get it?' Flynn demanded.

'It was a direct intervention of Allah.' Mohammed refused to be hurried. 'In the harbour was a German ship, stopped at Beira on its way north to Dar es Salaam. On the boat were three German officers. I saw them walking upon the deck.' Mohammed paused and cleared his throat portentously. 'That night a man who is my friend rowed me out to the ship, and I visited the cabin of one of the soldiers.'

'Where is it?' Flynn could not hold his patience. Mohammed stood up, went to the door of the rondavel and called to one of the bearers. He returned and set a bundle on the table in front of Flynn. Grinning proudly, he waited while Flynn unwrapped the bundle.

'Good God Almighty,' breathed Flynn.

'Is it not beautiful?'

'Call Manali. Tell him to come here immediately.'

Ten minutes later Sebastian, whom Rosa had at last reluctantly placed on the list of walking wounded, entered the rondavel, to be greeted effusively by Flynn. 'Sit down, Bassie boy. I've got a present for you.'

Reluctantly, Sebastian obeyed, eyeing the covered object on

the table. Flynn stood over it and whisked away the cloth. Then, with the same ceremony as the Archbishop of Canterbury placing the crown, he lifted the helmet above Sebastian's head and lowered it reverently.

On the summit a golden eagle cocked its wings on the point of flight and opened its beak in a silent squawk of menace, the black enamel of the helmet shone with a polished gloss, and the golden chain drooped heavily under Sebastian's chin.

It was indeed a thing of beauty. A thing of such presence that it completely overwhelmed Sebastian, enveloping his head to the bridge of his nose so that his eyes were just visible below the jutting brim.

'A few sizes too large,' Flynn conceded. 'But we can stuff some cloth into the crown to keep it up.' He backed away a few paces and cocked his head on one side as he examined the effect. 'Bassie boy, you'll slay them.'

'What's this for?' Sebastian asked in concern from under the steel helmet.

'You'll see. Just hold on a shake.' Flynn turned to Mohammed who was cooing with admiration in the doorway. 'The clothes?' he asked, and Mohammed beckoned imperiously to the bearers to bring in the boxes they had carried all the way from Beira.

Parbhoo, the Indian tailor, had obviously laboured with dedication and enthusiasm. The task set him by Flynn had touched the soul of the creative artist in him.

Ten minutes later, Sebastian stood self-consciously in the centre of the rondavel while Flynn and Mohammed circled him slowly, exclaiming with delight and self-congratulation.

Below the massive helmet, which was now propped high with a wad of cloth between steel and scalp, Sebastian was dressed in the sky-blue tunic and riding breeches. The cuffs of the jacket were ringed with yellow silk – a stripe of the same material ran down the outside of the breeches – and the high collar was covered with embroidered metal thread. Complete with spurs, the tall black boots pinched his toes so painfully that Sebastian stood pigeon-toed and blushed with bewilderment. 'I say, Flynn,' he pleaded, 'what's all this about?'

'Bassie boy.' Flynn laid a hand fondly on his shoulder. 'You're going to go in there and collect hut tax for . . .' he almost said *me*, but altered it quickly to '. . . us.'

'What is hut tax?'

'Hut tax is the annual sum of five shillings, paid by the headmen to the German Governor for each hut in his village.' Flynn led Sebastian to the chair and seated him as gently as though he were pregnant. He lifted a hand to still Sebastian's further enquiries and protests. 'Yes, I know you don't understand. But I'll explain it to you carefully. Just keep your mouth shut and listen.' He sat down opposite Sebastian and leaned forward earnestly. 'Now! The Germans owe us for the dhow and that, like we agreed – right?'

Sebastian nodded, and the helmet slid forward over his eyes. He pushed it back.

'Well, you are going to go across the river with the gun-bearers dressed as Askari. You are going to visit each of the villages before the real tax-collector gets there and picks up the money that they owe us. Do you follow me so far?'

'Are you coming with me?'

'Now, how can I do that? Me with my leg not properly healed yet?' Flynn protested impatiently. 'Besides that, every headman on the other side knows who I am. Not one of them has ever laid eyes on you before. You just tell them you're a new officer – straight out from Germany. One look at that uniform, and they'll pay up sharpish.'

'What happens if the real tax-inspector has already been?'

'They don't start collecting until September usually – and then they start in the north and work down this way. You'll have plenty of time.'

Frowning below the rim of the helmet, Sebastian brought forward a series of objections – each one progressively weaker than its predecessor, and, one by one, Flynn annihilated them. Finally there was a long silence while Sebastian's brain ground to a standstill.

'Well?' Flynn asked. 'Are you going to do it?'

And the question was answered from an unexpected quarter in feminine, but not dulcet tones. 'He is certainly *not* going to do it!'

Guiltily as small boys caught smoking in the school latrines, Flynn and Sebastian wheeled to face the door which had carelessly been left ajar.

Rosa's suspicions had been aroused by all the surreptitious activity around the rondavel, and when she had seen Sebastian join in, she had not the slightest qualms about listening outside the window. Her active intervention was not on ethical grounds. Rosa O'Flynn had acquired a rather elastic definition of honesty from her father. Like him, she believed that German property belonged to anybody who could get their hands on it. The fact that Sebastian was involved in a scheme based on dubious moral foundations in no way lowered her opinion of him – rather, in a sneaking sort of way, it heightened her estimate of him as a potential breadwinner. To date, this was the only area in which she had held misgivings about Sebastian Oldsmith.

From experience she knew that those of her father's business enterprises in which Flynn was not eager to participate personally always involved a great deal of risk. The thought of Sebastian Oldsmith dressed in a sky-blue uniform, marching across the Rovuma and never coming back – roused in her the same instincts as those of a lioness shortly to be deprived of her cubs.

'He is certainly *not* going to do it,' she repeated, and then to Sebastian. 'Do you hear me? I forbid it. I forbid it absolutely.'

This was the wrong approach.

Sebastian had, in turn, acquired from his father very Victorian views on the rights and privileges of women. Mr Oldsmith, the senior, was a courteous domestic tyrant, a man whose infallibility had never been challenged by his wife. A man who regarded sex deviates, Bolsheviks, trade union organizers, and suffragettes, in that descending order of repugnance.

Sebastian's mother, a meek little lady with a perpetually harassed expression, would no more have contemplated *absolutely forbidding* Mr Oldsmith a course of action, than she would have contemplated denying the existence of God. Her belief in the divine rights of man had extended to her sons. From a very tender age Sebastian had grown accustomed to worshipful obedience, not only from his mother, but also from his large flock of sisters.

Rosa's present attitude and manner of speech came as a shock. It took him but a few seconds to recover and then he rose to his feet and adjusted the helmet. 'I beg your pardon?' he asked coldly.

'You heard me,' snapped Rosa. 'I'm not going to allow this.'

Sebastian nodded thoughtfully, and then hastily grabbed at the helmet as it threatened to spoil his dignity by blind-folding him again. Ignoring Rosa he turned to Flynn. 'I will leave as soon as possible – tomorrow?'

'It will take a couple more days to get organized,' Flynn demurred.

'Very well then.' Sebastian stalked from the room, and the sunlight lit his uniform with dazzling splendour.

With a triumphant guffaw, Flynn reached for the enamel mug at his elbow. 'You made a mess of that one,' he gloated, and then his expression changed to unease.

Standing in the doorway, Rosa O'Flynn's shoulders had sagged, the angry line of her lips drooped.

'Oh, come on now!' gruffed Flynn.

'He won't come back. You know what you are doing to him. You're sending him in there to die.'

'Don't talk silly. He's a big boy, he can look after himself.'

'Oh, I hate you. Both of you – I hate you both!' and she was gone, running across the yard to the bungalow.

22

In a red dawn Flynn and Sebastian stood together on the stoep of the bungalow, talking together quietly.

'Now listen, Bassie. I reckon the best thing you can do is send back the collection from each village, as you make it. No sense in carrying all that money round with you.' Tactfully Flynn refrained from pointing out that by following this procedure, in the event of Sebastian running into trouble half-way through the expedition, the profits to that time would be safeguarded.

Sebastian was not really listening – he was more preoccupied with the whereabouts of Rosa O'Flynn. He had seen very little of her in the last few days.

'Now you listen to old Mohammed. He knows which are the biggest villages. Let him do the talking – those headmen are the biggest bunch of rogues you'll ever meet. They'll all plead poverty and famine, so you've got to be tough. Do you hear me? Tough, Bassie, tough!!'

'Tough,' agreed Sebastian absent-mindedly, glancing surreptitiously into the windows of the bungalow for a glimpse of Rosa.

'Now another thing,' Flynn went on. 'Remember to keep moving fast. March until nightfall. Make your cooking fire, eat, and then march again in the dark before you camp. Never sleep at your first camp, that's asking for trouble. Then get away again before first light in the morning.' There were many other instructions, and Sebastian listened to them without attention. 'Remember the sound of gun-fire carries for miles. Don't use your rifle except in emergency, and if you do fire a shot, then don't hang about afterwards. Now the route I've planned for you will never take you more than twenty miles beyond the Rovuma. At the first sign of trouble, you run for the river. If any of your men get hurt, leave them. Don't play hero, leave them and run like hell for the river.'

'Very well,' muttered Sebastian unhappily. The prospect of leaving Lalapanzi was becoming less attractive each minute. Where on earth was she?

'Now remember, don't let those headmen talk you out of anything. You might even have to . . .' Here Flynn paused to find the least offensive phraseology, '. . . you might even have to hang one or two of them.'

'Good God, Flynn. You're not serious.' Sebastian's full attention jerked back to Flynn.

'Ha! Ha!' Flynn laughed away the suggestion. 'I was joking, of course. But . . .' he went on wistfully, 'the Germans do it, and it gets results, you know.'

'Well, I'd better be on my way.' Sebastian changed the subject ostentatiously and picked up his helmet. He placed it upon his head and descended the steps to where his Askari, with rifles at the slope, were drawn up on the lawn. All of them, including Mohammed, were dressed in authentic uniform, complete with puttees and the little pillbox kepis. Sebastian had prudently refrained from asking Flynn how he had obtained these uniforms. The answer was evident in the neatly patched circular punctures in most of the tunics, and the faint brownish stain around each mend.

In single file, the blazing eagle on Sebastian's head-piece leading like a beacon, they marched past the massive solitary figure of Flynn O'Flynn on the veranda. Mohammed called for a salute and the response was enthusiastic, but ragged. Sebastian tripped on his spurs and with an effort, regained his equilibrium and plodded on gamely.

Shading his eyes against the glare, Flynn watched the gallant little column wind away down the valley towards the Rovuma river. Flynn's voice was without conviction as he spoke aloud, 'I hope to God he doesn't mess this one up.'

23

Once out of sight of the bungalow, Sebastian halted the column. Sitting beside the footpath, he sighed with relief as he removed the weight of the metal helmet from his head and replaced it with a sombrero of plaited grass, then he eased the spurred boots from his already aching feet, and slipped on a pair of rawhide sandals. He handed the discarded equipment to his personal bearer, stood up, and in his best Swahili ordered the march to continue.

Three miles down the valley the footpath crossed the stream above a tiny waterfall. It was a place of shade where great trees reached out towards each other across the narrow watercourse. Clear water trickled and gurgled between a tumble of lichen-covered boulders, before jumping like white lace in the sunlight down the slippery black slope of the falls.

Sebastian paused on the bank and allowed his men to proceed. He watched them hop from boulder to boulder, the bearers balancing their loads without effort, and then scramble up the far bank and disappear into the dense river bush. He listened to their voices becoming fainter with distance, and suddenly he was sad and alone.

Instinctively he turned and looked back up the valley towards Lalapanzi, and the sense of loss was a great emptiness inside him. The urge to return burned up so strongly, that he took a step back along the path before he could check himself.

He stood irresolute. The voices of his men were very faint now, muted by the dense vegetation, overlaid by the drowsy droning of insects, the wind murmur in the top branches of the trees, and the purl of falling water.

Then the soft rustle beside him, and he turned to it quickly. She stood near him and the sunlight through the leaves threw a golden dapple on her, giving a sense of unreality, a fairy quality, to her presence.

'I wanted to give you something to take with you, a farewell present for you to remember,' she said softly. 'But there was nothing I could think of,' and she came forward, reached up to him with her arms and her mouth, and she kissed him.

24

Sebastian Oldsmith crossed the Rovuma river in a mood of dreamy goodwill towards all men.

Mohammed was worried about him. He suspected that Sebastian had suffered a malarial relapse and he watched him carefully for evidence of further symptoms.

Mohammed at the head of the column of Askari and bearers had reached the crossing place on the Rovuma, before he realized that Sebastian was missing. In wild concern he had taken two armed Askari with him and hurried back along the path through the thorn scrub and broken rock – expecting at any moment to find a pride of lions growling over Sebastian's dismembered corpse. They had almost reached the waterfall when they met Sebastian ambling benignly along the path towards them, an expression of ethereal contentment lighting his classic features. His magnificent uniform was not a little rumpled; there were fresh grass stains on the knees and elbows, and dead leaves and bits of dried grass clung to the expensive material. From this Mohammed deduced that Sebastian had either fallen, or in sickness had lain down to rest.

'Manali,' Mohammed cried in concern. 'Are you well?'

'Never better – never in all my life,' Sebastian assured him.

'You have been lying down,' Mohammed accused.

'Son of a gun,' Sebastian borrowed from the vocabulary of Flynn O'Flynn. 'Son of a gun, you can say that again – and then repeat it!' and he clapped Mohammed between the shoulder blades with such well-intentioned violence that it almost floored him. Since then, Sebastian had not spoken again, but every few minutes he would smile and shake his head in wonder. Mohammed was truly worried.

They crossed the Rovuma in hired canoes and camped that night on the far bank. Twice during the night Mohammed awoke, slipped out of his blanket, and crept across to Sebastian to check his condition. Each time Sebastian was sleeping easily and the silver moonlight showed just a suggestion of a smile on his lips.

In the middle of the next morning, Mohammed halted the column in thick cover and came back from the head to confer with Sebastian. 'The village of M'topo lies just beyond,' he pointed ahead. 'You can see the smoke from the fires.'

There was a greyish smear of it above the trees, and faintly a dog began yapping.

'Good. Let's go.' Sebastian had donned his eagle helmet and was struggling into his boots.

'First I will send the Askari to surround the village.'

'Why?' Sebastian looked up in surprise.

'Otherwise there will be nobody there when we arrive.' During his service with the German Imperial army, Mohammed had been on tax expeditions before.

'Well – if you think it necessary,' Sebastian agreed dubiously.

Half an hour later Sebastian swaggered in burlesque of a German officer into the village of M'topo, and was dismayed by the reception he received. The lamentations of two hundred human beings made a hideous chorus for his entry. Some of them were on their knees and all of them were wringing their hands, smiting their breasts or showing other signs of deep distress. At the far end of the village M'topo, the headman, waited under guard by Mohammed and two of his Askari.

M'topo was an old man, with a cap of pure white wool, and an emaciated body covered with a parchment of dry skin. One eye was glazed over with tropical opthalmia, and he was clearly very agitated. 'I crawl on my belly before you, Splendid and Merciful Lord,' he greeted Sebastian, and prostrated himself in the dust.

'I say, that isn't necessary, you know,' murmured Sebastian.

'My poor village welcomes you,' whimpered M'topo. Bitterly he recriminated himself for thus being taken unawares. He had not expected the tax expedition for another two months, and had taken no pains with the disposal of his wealth. Buried under the earthen floor of his hut was nearly a thousand silver Portuguese escudos and half again as many golden Deutsche Marks. The traffic of his villagers in dried fish, netted in the Rovuma river, was highly organized and lucrative.

Now he dragged himself pitifully to his old knees and signalled two of his wives to bring forward stools and gourds of palm wine.

'It has been a year of great pestilence, disease and famine,' M'topo began his prepared speech, when Sebastian was seated and refreshed. The rest of it took fifteen minutes to deliver, and Sebastian's Swahili was now strong enough for him to follow the argument. He was deeply touched. Under the spell of palm wine and his new rosy outlook on life, he felt his heart going out to the old man.

While M'topo spoke, the other villagers had dispersed quietly and barricaded themselves in their huts. It was best not to draw attention to oneself when candidates for the rope were being selected. Now a mournful silence hung over the village, broken only by the mewling of an infant and the squabbling of a pair of mangy mongrels, contesting the ownership of a piece of offal.

'Manali,' impatiently Mohammed interrupted the old man's catalogue of misfortune. 'Let me search his hut.'

'Wait,' Sebastian stopped him. He had been looking about, and beneath the single baobab tree in the centre of the village he had noticed a dozen or so crude litters. Now he stood up and walked across to them.

When he saw what they contained, his throat contracted with horror. In each litter lay a human skeleton, the bones still covered with a thin layer of living flesh and skin. Naked men and women mixed indiscriminately, but their bodies so wasted that it was almost impossible to tell their sex. The pelvic girdles were gaunt basins of bone, elbows and knees great deformed knobs distorting the stick-like limbs, each rib standing out in clear definition, the faces were skulls whose lips had shrunk to expose the teeth in a perpetual sardonic grin. But the real horror was contained in the sunken eye cavities; the lids were fixed wide open – and the eyeballs glared like red marbles. There was no pupil nor iris, just those polished orbs the colour of blood.

Sebastian stepped back hurriedly, feeling his belly heave and the taste of it in his throat. Not trusting himself to speak, he beckoned for M'topo to come to him, and pointed at the bodies in the litters.

M'topo glanced at them without interest. They were so much part of the ordinary scene that for many days he had not consciously been aware of their existence. The village was situated on the edge of a tsetse fly belt, and since his childhood there had always been the sleeping sickness cases lying under the baobab tree, deep in the coma which precedes death. He could not understand Sebastian's concern.

'When . . . ?' Sebastian's voice faltered, and he swallowed before going on. 'When did these people last eat?' he asked.

'Not for a long time.' M'topo was puzzled by the question. Everybody knew that once the sleeping time came they never ate again.

Sebastian had heard of people dying of starvation. It happened in places like India, but here he was confronted with the actual fact. A revulsion of feeling swept over him. This was irrefutable proof that all M'topo had told him was true. This was famine as he had not believed really could exist – and he had been trying to extort money from these people!

Sebastian walked slowly back to his stool and sank down upon it. He removed the heavy helmet from his head, held it in his lap and sat staring miserably at his own feet. He was helpless with guilt and compassion.

Flynn O'Flynn had reluctantly provided Sebastian with one hundred escudos as travelling expenses to meet any emergency that might arise before he could make his first collection. Some of this had been expended on the hire of canoes to cross the Rovuma, but there was still eighty escudos left.

From his hip-pocket, Sebastian produced the tobacco pouch containing the money and counted out half of it. 'M'topo,' his voice was subdued. 'Take this money. Buy food for them.'

'Manali,' screeched Mohammed in protest. 'Manali. Do not do it.'

'Shut up!' Sebastian snapped at him, and prodded the handful of coins towards M'topo. 'Take it!'

M'topo stared at him as though he offered a live scorpion. It was as unnatural as though a man-eating lion had walked up and rubbed itself against his leg.

'Take it,' Sebastian insisted impatiently, and in disbelief, M'topo extended his cupped hands.

'Mohammed,' Sebastian stood up and replaced his helmet, 'we'll move on immediately to the next village.'

Long after Sebastian's column had disappeared into the bush again, old M'topo squatted alone, clutching the coins, too stunned to move. At last he roused himself and shouted for one of his sons.

'Go quickly to the village of Saali, who is my brother. Tell him that a madman comes to him. A German lord who comes to collect the hut tax and stays to offer gifts. Tell him . . .' here his voice broke as though he could not believe what he was about to say, '. . . tell him that this lord should be shown the ones who sleep, and that the madness will then come upon him, and he will give you forty escudos of the Portuguese. And, furthermore, there will be no hangings.'

'Saali, my uncle, will not believe these things.'

'No,' M'topo admitted. 'It is true that he will not believe. But tell him anyway.'

25

Saali received the message from his elder brother, and it induced in him a state of terror bordering on paralysis. M'topo, he knew, had a vicious sense of humour – and there was between them that matter of the woman Gita, a luscious little fourteen-year-old who had deserted the village of M'topo within two days of taking up her duties as M'topo's junior wife, on the grounds that he was impotent and smelled like an hyena. She was now a notable addition to Saali's household. Saali was convinced that the true interpretation of his brother's message was that the new German commissioner was a rampaging lion who would not be content with merely hanging a few of the old men but who might extend his attentions to Saali himself. Even should he escape the noose, he would be left destitute; his carefully accumulated hoard of silver, his six fine tusks of ivory, his goat herd, his dozen bags of white salt, the bar of copper, his two European-made axes, the bolts of trade cloth – all of his treasures gone! It required an heroic effort to rouse himself from the stupor of despair and make his few futile preparations for flight.

Mohammed's Askari caught him as he was heading for the bush at a trot, and when they led him back to meet Sebastian Oldsmith, the tears that coursed freely down his cheeks and dripped on to his chest were genuine.

Sebastian was very susceptible to tears. Despite the protests of Mohammed, Sebastian pressed upon Saali twenty silver escudos. It took Saali about twenty minutes to recover from the shock, at the end of which time he, in turn, shocked Sebastian profoundly by offering him on a temporary basis the unrestricted services of the girl, Gita. This young lady was witness to the offer made by her husband, and was obviously wholeheartedly in favour of it.

Sebastian set off again hurriedly, with his retinue straggling along behind him in a state of deep depression. Mohammed now had a bad case of the mutters.

Drums tap-tap-tapped, runners scurried along the network of footpaths that crossed and criss-crossed the bush; from hilltop to hilltop men called one to the other in the high-pitched wail that carries for miles. The news spread. Village after village buzzed with incredulous excitement, and then the inhabitants flocked out to meet the mad German commissioner.

By this time Sebastian was thoroughly enjoying himself. He was carried away with the pleasure of giving, delighted with these simple lovable people who welcomed him sincerely and pressed humble little gifts upon him. Here a scrawny fowl, there a dozen half-incubated eggs, a basin of sweet potatoes, a gourd of palm wine.

But Santa Claus's bag, or, more accurately, his tobacco pouch, was soon empty – and Sebastian was at a loss for some way to help alleviate the misery and poverty he saw in each village. He considered issuing indulgences from future tax . . . *the bearer is hereby excused from the payment of hut tax for five years* . . . but realized that this was a lethal gift. He shuddered at what Herman Fleischer might do to anybody he caught in possession of one of these.

Finally he struck on the solution. These people were starving. He would give them food. He would give them meat.

In fact, this was one of the most desirable commodities Sebastian could have offered. Despite the abundance of wild life, the great herds of game that spread across the plains and hills, these people were starved for protein. The primitive hunting methods they employed were so ineffectual, that the killing of a single animal was an event that happened infrequently, and then almost by accident. When the carcass was shared out among two or three hundred hungry mouths, there was only a few ounces of meat for each. Men and women would risk their lives in attempting to drive a pride of lions from their kill, for just a few mouthfuls of this precious stuff.

Sebastian's Askari joined in the sport with delight. Even old Mohammed perked up a little. Unfortunately, their marksmanship was about the same standard as Sebastian's own, and a day's hunting usually resulted in the expenditure of thirty or forty rounds of Mauser ammunition, and a bag of sometimes as little as one half-grown zebra. But there were good days also, like the memorable occasion when a herd of buffalo virtually committed suicide by running down on the line of Askari. In the resulting chaos one of Sebastian's men was shot dead by his comrades, but eight full-grown buffalo followed him to the happy hunting grounds.

So Sebastian's tax tour proceeded triumphantly, leaving behind a trail of empty cartridge cases, racks of meat drying in the sun, full bellies, and smiling faces.

26

Three months after crossing the Rovuma river, Sebastian found himself back at the village of his good friend, M'topo. He had by-passed Saali's in order to avoid the offended Gita.

Sitting alone in the night within the hut that M'topo placed at his disposal, Sebastian was having his first misgivings. On the morrow, he would begin the return to Lalapanzi, where Flynn O'Flynn was waiting for him. Sebastian was acutely aware that from Flynn's point of view the expedition had not been a success – and Flynn would have a great deal to say on the subject. Once more Sebastian puzzled on the fates which took his best intentions, and manipulated them in such a manner that they became completely unrecognizable from the original.

Then his thoughts kicked off at a tangent. Soon, the day after tomorrow, if all went well, he would be back with Rosa. The deep yearning that had been his constant companion these last three months throbbed through Sebastian's whole body. Staring into the wood-fire on the hearth of the hut, it seemed as though the embers formed a picture of her face, and in his memory he heard her voice again.

'Come back, Sebastian. Come back soon.'

And he whispered the words aloud, watching her face in the fire. Gloating on each detail of it. He saw her smile, and her nose wrinkled a little, the dark eyes slanted upwards at the corners.

'Come back, Sebastian.'

The need of her was a physical pain so intense that he could hardly breathe, and his imagination reconstructed every detail of their parting beside the waterfall. Each subtle change and inflection of her voice, the very sound of her breathing, and the bitter salt taste of her tears upon his lips. He felt again the touch of her hands, her mouth – and through the woodsmoke that filled the hut, his nostrils flared at the warm woman smell of her body.

'I'm coming, Rosa. I'm coming back,' he whispered, and stood up restlessly from beside the fire. At that moment his attention was jerked back to the present by a soft scratching at the door of the hut.

'Lord. Lord.' He recognized old M'topo's hoarse croaking.

'What is it?'

'We seek your protection.'

'What is the trouble?' Sebastian crossed to the door and lifted the cross-bar. 'What is it?'

In the moonlight M'topo stood with a skin blanket draped around his frail shoulders. Behind him a dozen of the villagers huddled in trepidation.

'The elephant are in our gardens. They will destroy them before morning. There will be nothing, not a single stalk of millet left standing.' He swung away and stood with his head cocked. 'Listen, you may hear them now.'

It was an eerie sound in the night, the high-pitched elephant squeal, and Sebastian's skin crawled. He could feel the hair on his forearms become erect.

'There are two of them.' M'topo's voice was a scratchy whisper. 'Two old bulls. We know them well. They came last season and laid waste our corn. They killed one of my sons who tried to drive them off.' In entreaty, the old man clawed hold of Sebastian's arm and tugged at it. 'Avenge my son, lord. Avenge my son for me, and save our millet that the children will not go hungry again this year.'

Sebastian responded to the appeal in the same manner that St George would have done.

In haste he buttoned his tunic and went to fetch his rifle. On his return he found his entire command armed to the teeth, and as eager for the hunt as a pack of foxhounds. Mohammed waited at their head.

'Lord Manali, we are ready.'

'Now, steady on, old chap.' Sebastian had no intention of sharing the glory. 'This is my shauri. Too many cooks, what?'

M'topo stood by, wringing his hands with impatience, listening alternately first to the distant sounds of the garden raiders feeding contentedly in his lands, and then to the undignified wrangling between Sebastian and his Askari, until at last he could bear it no longer. 'Lord, already half the millet is eaten. In an hour it will all be gone.'

'You're right,' Sebastian agreed, and turned angrily on his men. 'Shut up, all of you. Shut up!'

They were unaccustomed to this tone of command from Sebastian, and it surprised them into silence.

'Only Mohammed shall accompany me. The rest of you go to your huts and stay there.'

It was a working compromise, Sebastian now had Mohammed as an ally. Mohammed turned on his comrades and scattered them before falling in beside Sebastian.

'Let us go.'

At the head of the main gardens, high on its stilts of poles, stood a rickety platform. This was the watch-tower from which, night and day, a guard was kept over the ripening millet. It was now deserted, the two young guards had left hurriedly at the first sight of the garden raiders. Kudu or waterbuck were one thing, a pair of bad-tempered old elephant bulls were another matter entirely.

Sebastian and Mohammed reached the watch-tower and paused beneath it. Quite clearly now they could hear the rustling and ripping sound of the millet stalks being torn up and trampled.

'Wait here,' whispered Sebastian, slinging his rifle over his shoulder, as he turned to the ladder beside him. He climbed slowly and silently to the platform, and from it, looked out over the gardens.

The moon was so brilliant as to throw sharply defined shadows below the tower and the trees. Its light was a soft silver that distorted distance and size, reducing all things to a cold, homogeneous grey.

Beyond the clearing the forest rose like frozen smoke clouds, while the field of standing millet moved in the small night wind, rippling like the surface of a lake.

Humped big and darker grey, standing high above the millet, two great islands in the soft sea of vegetation, the old bulls grazed slowly. Although the nearest elephant was two hundred paces from the tower, the moon was so bright that Sebastian could see clearly as he reached forward with his trunk, coiled it about a clump of the leafy stalks and plucked them easily. Then swaying gently, rocking his massive bulk lazily from side to side, he beat the millet against his lifted foreleg to shake the clinging earth from the roots before lifting it and stuffing it into his mouth. The tattered banners of his ears flapped gently, an untidy tangle of millet leaves hanging from his lips between the long curved shafts of ivory, he moved on, feeding and trampling so that behind him he left a wide path of devastation.

On the open platform of the tower, Sebastian felt his stomach contracting, convulsing itself into a hard ball, and his hands on the rifle were unsteady; his breathing whistled softly in his own ears as the elephant thrill came upon him. Watching those two huge beasts, he found himself held motionless with an almost mystic sense of awe; a realization of his own insignificance, his presumption in going out against them, armed with this puny weapon of steel and wood. But beneath his reluctance was the tingle of tight nerves – that strange blend of fear and eagerness – the age-old lust of the hunter. He roused himself and climbed down to where Mohammed waited.

Through the standing corn that reached above their heads, stepping with care between the rows so that they disturb not a single leaf, they moved in towards the centre of the garden. Ears and eyes tuned to their finest limit, breathing controlled so that it did not match the wild pump of his heart, Sebastian homed in on the crackle and rustle made by the nearest bull.

Even though the millet screened him, he could feel the weak wash of the wind move his hair softly, and the first whiff of elephant smell hit him like an open-handed blow in the face. He stooped so suddenly that Mohammed almost bumped into him from behind. They stood crouching, peering ahead into the moving wall of vegetation. Sebastian felt Mohammed lean forward beside him, and heard his whisper breathed softer than the sound of the wind. 'Very close now.'

Sebastian nodded, and then swallowed jerkily. He could hear clearly the soft slithering scrape of leaves brushing against the rough hide of the old bull. It was feeding down towards them. They were standing directly in the path of its leisurely approach, at any moment now – at any moment!

Standing with the rifle lifted protectively, sweat starting to prickle his forehead and upper lip in the cool of the night, his eyes watering with the intensity of his gaze, Sebastian was suddenly aware of massive movement ahead of him. A solid shape through the bank of dancing leaves, and he looked up. High above him it loomed, black and big so that the night sky was blotted out by the spread of its ears, so near that he stood beneath the forward thrust of its tusks, and he could see the trunk uncoil like a fat grey python and grope forward blindly towards him; and beneath it the mouth gaped a little, spilling leaves at the corners.

He lifted the rifle, pointing it upwards without aiming, almost touching the elephant's hanging lower lip with the muzzle, and he fired. The shot was a blunt burst of sound in the night.

The bullet angled up through the pink palate of the animal's mouth, up through the spongy bone of the skull; mushrooming and exploding, it tore into the fist-sized cell that contained the brain, and burst it into a grey jelly.

Had it passed four inches to either side; had it been deflected by one of the larger bones, Sebastian would have died before he had time to work the bolt of the Mauser, for he stood directly below the outstretched tusks and trunk. But the old bull reeled backwards from the shot, his trunk falling flabbily against his chest, his forelegs spreading, and his head unbalanced by long tusks sagged forwards, knees collapsed suddenly under him, and he fell so heavily that they heard the thump in the village half a mile away.

'Son of a gun!' gasped Sebastian, staring in disbelief at the dead mountain of flesh. 'I did it. Son of a gun, I did it!' Jubilation, a delirious release from fear and tension, mounted giddily within him. He lifted an arm to hit Mohammed across the back, but he froze in that attitude.

Like the shriek of steam escaping from a burst boiler, the other bull squealed in the moonlight nearby. And they heard the crackling rush of his run in the corn.

'He's coming!' Sebastian looked frantically about him for the sound had no direction.

'No,' squawked Mohammed. 'He turns against the wind. First he seeks for the smell of us, and then he will come.' He grabbed Sebastian's arm and clung to him, while they listened to the elephant circling to get down-wind of them.

'Perhaps he will run,' whispered Sebastian.

'Not this one. He is old and evil-tempered, and he has killed men before. Now he will hunt us.' Mohammed pulled at Sebastian's arm. 'We must get out into the open. In this stuff we will have no chance, he will be on top of us before we see him.'

They started to run. There is no more piquant sauce for fear than flying feet. Once he starts to run, even a brave man becomes a coward. Within twenty paces, both of them were in headlong flight towards the village. They ran without regard for stealth, fighting their way through the tangle of leaves and stalks, panting wildly. The noise of their flight blanketed the sounds made by the elephant, so they lost all idea of his whereabouts. This sharpened the spurs of terror that drove them, for at any moment he might loom over them.

At last they stumbled out into the open, and paused, panting, sweating heavily, heads swinging from side to side as they tried to place the second bull.

'There!' shouted Mohammed. 'He comes,' and they heard the shrill pig-squealing, the noisy rush of his charge through the millet.

'Run!' yelled Sebastian, still in the grip of panic, and they ran.

Around a freshly lit bonfire at the edge of the village, waited the rejected Askari and a hundred of M'topo's men. They waited in anxiety for they had heard the shot and the fall of the first bull – but since then, the squealing and shouting and crashing had left them in some doubt as to what was happening in the gardens.

This doubt was quickly dispelled as Mohammed, closely followed by Sebastian, came down the path towards them, giving a fair imitation of two dogs whose backsides had been dipped in turpentine. A hundred yards behind them the bank of standing millet burst open, and the second bull came out in full charge.

Immense in the great light, hump-back, shambling in the deceptive speed of his run, streaming his huge ears, each squeal of rage enough to burst the eardrums – he bore down on the village.

'Get out! Run!' Sebastian's shouted warning was as wheezy as it was unnecessary. The waiting crowd was no longer waiting, it scattered like a shoal of sardines at the approach of a barracuda.

Men threw aside their blankets and ran naked; they fell over each other and ran headlong into trees. Two of them ran straight through the middle of the bonfire and emerged on the other side trailing sparks with live coals sticking to their feet. In a wailing hubbub they swept back through the village, and from each hut women with infants bundled under their arms, or slung over their backs, scurried out to join the terrified torrent of humanity.

Still making good time, Sebastian and Mohammed were passing the weaker runners among the villagers, while from behind, the elephant was gaining rapidly on all of them.

With the force and velocity of a great boulder rolling down a steep hillside, the bull reached the first hut of the village and ran into it. The flimsy structure of grass and light poles exploded, bursting asunder without diminishing the fury of the animal's charge. A second hut disintegrated, then a third, before the elephant caught the first human straggler.

She was an old woman, tottering on thin legs, the empty pouches of her breasts flopping against her wrinkled belly, a long monotonous wail of fear keening from the toothless pit of her mouth as she ran.

The bull uncoiled his trunk from his chest, lifted it high above the woman and struck her across the shoulder. The force of the blow crumpled her, bones snapped in her chest like old dry sticks, and she died before she hit the ground.

The next was a girl. Groggy with sleep, yet her naked body was silver-smooth and graceful in the moonlight, as she emerged from a hut into the path of the bull's charge. Lightly the thick trunk enfolded her, and then with an effortless flick threw her forty feet into the air.

She screamed, and the sound of the scream knifed through Sebastian's panic. He glanced over his shoulder in time to see the girl thrown high in the night sky. Her limbs were spread-eagled and she spun in the air like a cartwheel before she dropped back to earth – falling heavily so that the scream was cut off abruptly. Sebastian stopped running.

Deliberately the elephant knelt over the girl's feebly squirming body, and driving down with his tusks, impaled her through the chest. She hung from the shaft of ivory, squashed and broken, no longer recognizable as human, until the elephant shook his head irritably and threw her off.

It needed a sight as horrible as this to rally Sebastian's shattered nerves – to summon the reserves of his manhood from the far places that fear had scattered them. The rifle was still in his hands, but he was shaking with fear and exertion; sweat had drenched his tunic and plastered his curly hair on to his forehead, and his breath sawed hoarsely in his throat. He stood irresolute, fighting the driving urge to run again.

The bull came on, and now his one tusk was painted glistening black with the girl's blood, and gouts of the same stuff were splattered across his bulging forehead and the bridge of his trunk. It was this that changed Sebastian's fear first to disgust, and then to anger.

He lifted the rifle and it weaved unsteadily in his hands. He sighted along the barrel and suddenly his vision snapped into sharp focus and his nerves stilled their clamour. He was a man again.

Coldly he moved the blob of the foresight on to the bull's head, holding it on the deep lateral crease at the root of the trunk, and he squeezed the trigger. The butt jumped solidly into his shoulder, the report stung his eardrums, but he saw the bullet strike exactly where he had aimed it – a spurt of dust from the crust of dried mud that caked the animal's head and the skin around it, twitched, the eyelids quivered shut for an instant, then blinked open again.

Without lowering the rifle Sebastian jerked the bolt open, and the empty case ejected crisply, pinging away into the dust. He levered another cartridge into the breech and held his aim into the massive head. Again he fired and the elephant staggered drunkenly. The ears which had been cocked half back, now fanned open and the head swung vaguely in his direction.

He fired again, and the bull winced as the bullet lanced into the bone and gristle of his head, then he turned and came for Sebastian – but there was a slackness, a lack of determination in his charge. Aiming now for the chest, handling the rifle with cold method, Sebastian fired again and again, leaning forward against the recoil of the rifle, sighting every shot with care, knowing that each of them was raking the chest cavity, tearing through lung and heart and liver.

And the bull broke his run into a shuffling, uncertain walk, losing direction, turning away from Sebastian to stand broadside, the barrel of his chest heaving against the agony of his torn vitals.

Sebastian lowered the rifle and with steady fingers pressed fresh cartridges down into the empty magazine. The bull groaned softly and from the tip of his trunk, blood hosed up from the haemorrhaging lungs.

Without pity, cold in his anger, Sebastian lifted the reloaded rifle, and aimed for the dark cavity that nestled in the centre of the huge ear. The bullet struck with the sharp thwack of an axe swung against a tree trunk, and the elephant sagged and fell forward to the brain shot. His weight drove his tusks into the earth, burying them to the lip.

Four tons of meat delivered fresh to the very centre of the village was good value. The price paid was not exorbitant, M'topo decided. Three huts could be rebuilt in two days, and only four acres of millet had been destroyed. Furthermore, of the women who had died, one was very old and the other, although she was almost eighteen years old, had never conceived. There was good reason, therefore, to believe she was barren and not a great loss to the community.

Warmed by the early sun, M'topo was a satisfied man. With Sebastian beside him, he sat on his carved wooden stool and grinned widely as he watched the fun.

Two dozen of his men, armed with short-handled, long-bladed spears, and divested of all clothing, were to act as butchers. They were gathered beside the mountainous carcass arguing good-naturedly as they waited for Mohammed and his four assistants to remove the tusks. Around them, in a wider circle, waited the rest of the villagers, and while they waited, they sang. A drum hammered out the rhythm for them, and the clap of hands and the stamp of feet confirmed it. The masculine bass was a foundation from which the clear, sweet soprano of the women soared, and sank, and soared again.

Beneath Mohammed's patiently chipping axe, first the one tusk and then the other were freed from the bone that held them, and, with two Askari staggering under the weight, they were carried to where Sebastian sat, and laid with ceremony at his feet.

It occurred to Sebastian that four big tusks carried home to Lalapanzi might in some measure mollify Flynn O'Flynn. They would at least cover the costs of the expedition. The thought cheered him up considerably, and he turned to M'topo. 'Old one, you may take the meat.'

'Lord.' In gratitude, M'topo clapped his hands at the level of his chest, and then turned to squawk an order at the waiting butchers.

A roar of excitement and meat hunger went up from the crowd as one of them scrambled up on to the carcass, and drove his spear though the thick grey hide behind the last rib. Then walking backwards, he drew it down towards the haunch and the razor steel sliced deep. Two others made the lateral incisions, opening a square flap – a trapdoor into the belly cavity from which the fat coils of the viscera bulged, pink and blue and glossy wet in the early morning sunlight. In mounting eagerness, four others dragged from the square hole the contents of the belly, and then, while Sebastian stared in disbelief, they wriggled into the opening and disappeared. He could hear their muffled shouts reverberating within the carcass as they competed for the prize of the liver. Within minutes one of them reappeared, clutching against his chest a slippery lump of tattered, purple liver. Like a maggot, he came squirming out of the wound, painted over-all with a thick coating of dark red blood. It had matted in the woolly cap of his hair, and turned his face into a gruesome mask from which only his teeth and his eyes gleamed white. Carrying the mutilated liver, laughing in triumph, he ran through the crowd to where Sebastian sat.

The offering embarrassed Sebastian. More than that, it made his gorge rise, and he felt his stomach heave as it was thrust almost into his lap.

'Eat,' M'topo encouraged him. 'It will make you strong. It will sharpen the spear of your manhood. Ten, twenty women will not tire you.'

It was M'topo's opinion that Sebastian needed this type of tonic. He had heard from his brother Saali, and from the chiefs along the river, about Sebastian's lack of initiative.

'Like this.' M'topo cut a hunk of the liver and popped it into his mouth. He chewed heartily, and the juice wet his lips as he grinned in appreciation. 'Very good.' He thrust a piece into Sebastian's face. 'Eat.'

'No.' Sebastian's gorge pressed heavily on the back of his throat, and he stood up hurriedly. M'topo shrugged, and ate it himself. Then he shouted to the butchers to continue their work.

In a miraculously short space of time the huge carcass disintegrated under the blades of the spears and machetes. It was a labour in which the entire village joined. With a dozen strokes of the knife, a butcher would free a large hunk of flesh and throw it down to one of the women. She, in turn, would hack it into smaller pieces and pass these on to the children. Squealing with excitement, they would run with them to the hastily erected drying racks, deposit them and come scampering back for more.

Sebastian had recovered from his initial revulsion and now he laughed to see how every mouth was busy, chewing as they worked and yet at the same time managing to emit a surprising volume of noise.

Among the milling feet the dogs snarled and yipped, and gulped the scraps. Without interrupting their feeding, they dodged the casual kicks and blows that were aimed at them.

Into the midst of this cosy, domestic scene entered Commissioner Herman Fleischer with ten armed Askari.

28

Herman Fleischer was tired and there were blisters on his feet from the series of forced marches that had brought him to M'topo's village.

A month before he had left his headquarters at Mahenge to begin the annual tax tour of his area. As was his custom, he had started in the northern province, and it had been an unusually successful expedition. The wooden chest with the rampant black eagle painted on its lid had grown heavier with each day's journey. Herman had amused himself by calculating how many more years service in Africa would be necessary before he could resign and return home to Plaven and settle down on the estate he planned to buy. Three more years as fruitful as this, he decided, would be sufficient. It was a bitter shame that he had not been able to capture O'Flynn's dhow on the Rufiji thirteen months previously – that would have advanced his date of departure by a full twelve months. Thinking about it stirred his residual anger at that episode, and he placated it by doubling the hut tax on the next village he visited. This raised such a howl of protest from the village headman that Herman nodded at his sergeant of Askari, who began ostentatiously to unpack the rope from his saddlebag.

'O fat and beautiful bull elephant,' the headman changed his mind hastily. 'If you will wait but a little while, I will bring the money to you. There is a new hut, without lice or fleas, in which you may rest your lovely body, and I will send a young girl to you with beer for your thirst.'

'Good,' agreed Herman. 'While I rest, my Askari will stay with you.' He nodded at the sergeant to bind the chief, then waddled away to the hut.

The headman sent two of his sons to dig beneath a certain tree in the forest, and they returned an hour later with mournful faces, carrying a heavy skin bag.

Contentedly Herman Fleischer signed an official receipt for ninety per cent of the contents of the bag – Fleischer allowed himself a ten per cent handling fee – and the headman, who could not read a word of German, accepted it with relief.

'I will stay tonight in your village,' Herman announced. 'Send the same girl to cook my food.'

The runner from the south arrived in the night, and disturbed Herman Fleischer at a most inopportune moment. The news he carried was even more disturbing. From his description of the new German commissioner who was doing Herman's job for him in the southern province, and shooting up the countryside in the process, Herman immediately recognized the young Englishman whom he had last seen on the deck of a dhow in the Rufiji delta.

Leaving the bulk of his retinue, including the bearers of the tax chest, to follow him at their best speed, Herman mounted at midnight on his white donkey and, taking ten Askari with him, he rode southwards on a storm patrol.

Five nights later, in those still dark hours that precede the dawn, Herman was camped near the Rovuma river when he was awakened by his sergeant.

'What is it?' Grumpy with fatigue, Herman sat up and lifted the side of his mosquito net.

'We heard the sound of gun-fire. A single shot.'

'Where?' He was instantly awake, and reaching for his boots.

'From the south, towards the village of M'topo on the Rovuma.'

Fully dressed now, Herman waited anxiously, straining his ears against the small sounds of the African night.' Are you sure . . . ?' he began as he turned to his sergeant, but he did not finish. Faintly, but unmistakable in the darkness, they heard the pop, pop, pop, of a distant rifle – a pause and then another shot.

'Break camp,' bellowed Herman. 'Rasch! You black heathen. Rasch!'

The sun was well up by the time they reached M'topo's village. They came upon it suddenly through the gardens of tall millet that screened their approach. Herman Fleischer paused to throw out his Askari in a line of skirmishers before closing in on the cluster of huts, but when he reached the fringe, he stopped once more in surprise at the extraordinary spectacle which was being enacted in the open square of the village.

The dense knot of half-naked black people that swarmed over the remains of the elephant was perfectly oblivious of Herman's presence until at last he filled his lungs, and then emptied them again in a roar that carried over the hubbub of shouts and laughter. Instantly a vast silence fell upon the gathering, every head turned towards Herman and from each head eyes bulged in horrific disbelief.

'Bwana Intambu,' a small voice broke the silence at last. 'Lord of the rope.' They knew him well.

'What . . . ?' Herman began, and then gasped in outrage as he noticed in the crowd a black man he had never seen before, dressed in the full uniform of German Askari. 'You!' he shouted, pointing an accusing finger, but the man whirled and ducked away behind the screen of blood-smeared black bodies. 'Stop him!' Herman fumbled with the flap of his holster.

Movement caught his eye and he turned to see another pseudo-Askari running away between the huts. 'There's another one! Stop him! Sergeant, Sergeant, get your men here!'

The initial shock that had held them frozen was now past, and the crowd broke and scattered. Once again, Herman Fleischer gasped in outrage as he saw, for the first time, a figure sitting on a carved native stool on the far side of the square. A figure in an outlandish uniform of bright but travel-stained blue, frogged with gold, his legs clad in high jackboots, and on his head the dress helmet of an illustrious Prussian regiment.

'Englishman!' Despite the disguise, Herman recognized him. He had finally succeeded in unbuttoning the flap of his holster, and now he withdrew his Luger. 'Englishman!' He repeated the insult and lifted the pistol.

With the quickness of mind for which he was noted, Sebastian sat bewildered by this unforeseen turn of events, but when Herman showed him the working end of the Luger, he realized that it was time to take his leave, and he attempted to leap nimbly to his feet. However, the spurs on his boots became entangled once more and he went backwards over the stool. The bullet hissed harmlessly through the empty space where he would have been standing.

'God damn!' Herman fired again, and the bullet kicked a burst of splinters out of the heavy wooden stool behind which Sebastian was lying. This second failure aroused in Herman Fleischer the blinding rage which spoiled his aim for the next two shots he fired, as Sebastian went on hands and knees around the corner of the nearest hut.

Behind the hut, Sebastian jumped to his feet and set off at a run. His main concern was to get out of the village and into the bush. In his ears echoed Flynn O'Flynn's advice.

'Make for the river. Go straight for the river.'

And he was so occupied with it that, when he charged around the side of the next hut, he could not check himself in time to avoid collision with one of Herman Fleischer's Askari, who was coming in the opposite direction. Both of them went down together in an untidy heap, and the steel helmet fell forward over Sebastian's eyes. As he struggled into a sitting position, he removed the helmet and found the man's woolly black head in front of him. It was ideally placed and Sebastian was holding the heavy helmet above it. With the strength of both his arms, he brought the helmet down again, and it clanged loudly against the Askari's skull. With a grunt the Askari sagged backwards and lay quietly in the dust. Sebastian placed the helmet over his sleeping face, picked up the man's rifle from beside him and got to his feet once more.

He stood crouching in the shelter of the hut while he tried to make sense of the chaos around him. Through the pandemonium set up by the panic-stricken villagers, who were milling about with all the purpose of a flock of sheep attacked by wolves, Sebastian could hear the bellowed commands of Herman Fleischer, and the answering shouts of the German Askari. Rifle-fire cracked and whined, to be answered by renewed outbursts of screaming.

Sebastian's first impulse was to hide in one of the huts but he realized this would be futile. At the best it would only delay his capture.

No, he must get out of the village. But the thought of covering the hundred yards of open ground to the shelter of the nearest trees, while a dozen Askari shot at him, was most unattractive.

At this moment Sebastian became aware of an unpleasant warmth in his feet, and he looked down to find that he was standing in the live ashes of a cooking fire. The leather of his jackboots was already beginning to char and smoke. He stepped back hurriedly, and the smell of burning leather acted as a laxative for the constipation of his brain.

From the hut beside him he snatched a handful of thatch and

stooped to thrust it into the fire. The dry grass burst into flame, and Sebastian held the torch to the wall of the hut. Instantly fire bloomed and shot upwards. With the torch in his hand, Sebastian ducked across the narrow opening to the next hut and set fire to that also.

'Son of a gun!' exulted Sebastian as great oily billows of smoke obscured the sun and limited his field of vision to ten paces.

Slowly he moved forward in the rolling cloud of smoke, setting fire to each hut he passed, and delighted in the frustrated bellows of Germanic rage he heard behind him. Occasionally ghostly figures scampered past him in the acrid half-darkness but none of them paid him the slightest attention, and each time Sebastian relaxed the pressure of his forefinger on the trigger of the Mauser, and moved on.

He reached the last hut and paused there to gather himself for the final sprint across open ground to the edge of the millet garden. Through the eddying bank of smoke, the mass of dark green vegetation from which he had fled in terror not many hours before, now seemed as welcoming as the arms of his mother.

Movement near him in the smoke, and he swung the Mauser to cover it; he saw the square outline of a kepi and the sparkle of metal buttons, and his finger tightened on the trigger.

'Manali!'

'Mohammed! Good God, I nearly killed you.' Sebastian threw up the rifle barrel as he recognized him.

'Quickly! They are close behind me.' Mohammed snatched at his arm and dragged him forward. The jackboots pinched his toes and thumped like the hooves of a galloping buffalo as Sebastian ran. From the huts behind them a voice shouted urgently and, immediately afterwards, came the vicious crack of a Mauser and the shrill whinny of the ricochet.

Sebastian had a lead of ten paces on Mohammed as he plunged into the bank of leaves and millet stalks.

29

'What should we do now, Manali?' Mohammed asked, and the expression on the faces of the two other men echoed the question with pathetic trust. A benevolent chance had reunited Sebastian with the remnants of his command. During the flight through the millet gardens, with random rifle-fire clipping the leaves about their heads, Sebastian had literally fallen over these two. At the time they were engaged in pressing their bellies and their faces hard against the earth, and it had taken a number of lusty kicks with the jackboot to get them up and moving.

Since then Sebastian, mindful of Flynn's advice, had cautiously and circuitously led them down to the landing-place on the bank of the Rovuma. He arrived to find that Fleisher's Askari, by using the direct route and without the necessity of concealing themselves, had arrived before him. From the cover of the reed-banks Sebastian watched dejectedly, as they used an axe to knock the bottoms out of the dug-out canoes that were drawn up on the little white beach.

'Can we swim across?' he asked Mohammed in a whisper, and Mohammed's face crumpled with horror, as he considered the suggestion. Both of them peered out through the reeds across a quarter of a mile of deep water that flowed so fast, its surface was dimpled with tiny whirlpools.

'No,' said Mohammed with finality.

'Too far?' asked Sebastian hopelessly.

'Too far. Too fast. Too deep. Too many crocodiles,' agreed Mohammed, and in an unspoken, but mutual desire to get away from the river and the Askari, they crawled out of the reed-bank and crept away inland.

In the late afternoon they were lying up in a bushy gully about two miles from the river and an equal distance from M'topo's village.

'What should we do now, Manali?' Mohammed repeated his question, and Sebastian cleared his throat before answering.

'Well . . .' he said and paused while his wide brow wrinkled in the agony of creative thought. Then it came to him with all the splendour of a sunrise. 'We'll just jolly well have to find some other way of getting across the river.' He said it with the air of a man well pleased with his own perspicacity. 'What do you suggest, Mohammed.'

A little surprised to find the ball returned so neatly into his own court, Mohammed remained silent.

'A raft?' hazarded Sebastian. The lack of tools, material and opportunity to build one was so obvious, that Mohammed did not deign to reply. He shook his head.

'No,' agreed Sebastian. 'Perhaps you are right.' Again the classic beauty of his features was marred by a scowl of concentration. At last he demanded, 'There are other villages along the river?'

'Yes,' Mohammed conceded. 'But the Askari will visit each of them and destroy the canoes. Also they will tell the headmen who we are, and threaten them with the rope.'

'But they cannot cover the whole river. It has a frontier of five or six hundred miles. We'll just keep walking until we find a canoe. It may take us a long time but we'll find one eventually.'

'If the Askari don't catch us first.'

'They'll expect us to stay close to the border. We'll make a detour well inland, and march for five or six days before we come back to the river again. We'll rest now and move tonight.'

Heading on a diagonal line of march away from the Rovuma and deeper into German territory, moving north-west along a well defined footpath, the four of them kept walking all that night. As the slow hours passed so the pace flagged and twice Sebastian noticed one or other of his men wander off the path at an angle until suddenly they started and looked about in surprise, before hurrying back to join the others. It puzzled him and he meant to ask them what they were doing, but he was tired and the effort of speech was too great. An hour later he found the reason for their behaviour.

Plodding along with the movement of his legs became completely automatic, Sebastian was slowly overcome by a state of gentle well-being. He surrendered to it and let the warm, dark mists of oblivion wash over his mind.

The sting of a thorn branch across his cheek jerked him back to consciousness and he looked about in bewilderment. Ten yards away on his flank, Mohammed and the two gun-boys walked along the path in single file, their faces turned towards him with expressions of mild interest in the moonlight. It took some moments for Sebastian to realize that he had fallen asleep on his feet. Feeling a complete ass, he trotted back to take his place at the head of the line.

When the fat silver moon sank below the trees, they kept going by the faint glow of reflected light, but slowly that waned until the footpath hardly showed at their feet. Sebastian decided that dawn could be only an hour away and it was time to halt. He stopped and was about to speak when Mohammed's clutching hand on his shoulder prevented him.

'Manali!' There was a tone in Mohammed's whisper that cautioned him, and Sebastian felt his nerves jerk taut.

'What is it?' he breathed, protectively unslinging the Mauser.

'Look. There – ahead of us.'

Screwing up his eyes Sebastian searched the blackness ahead, and it was a long time before the faint ruddiness in the solid blanket of darkness registered itself upon the exhausted retinas of his eyes. 'Yes!' he whispered. 'What is it?'

'A fire,' breathed Mohammed. 'There is someone camped across the path in front of us.'

'Askari?' asked Sebastian.

'Perhaps.'

Peering at the ruby puddle of dying coals, Sebastian felt the hair on the back of his neck stir and come erect with alarm. He was fully awake now. 'We must go around them.'

'No. They will see our spoor in the dust of the path and they will follow us,' Mohammed demurred.

'What then?'

'First let me see how many there are.'

Without waiting for Sebastian's permission, Mohammed slipped away and disappeared into the night like a leopard. Five anxious minutes Sebastian waited. Once he thought he heard a scuffling sound but he was not certain. Mohammed's shape materialized again beside him. 'Ten of them,' he reported. 'Two

Askari and eight bearers. One of the Askari sat guard by the fire. He saw me, so I killed him.'

'Good God!' Sebastian's voice rose higher. 'You did what?'

'I killed him. But do not speak so loud.'

'How?'

'With my knife.'

'Why?'

'Lest he kill me first.'

'And the other?'

'Him also.'

'You killed both of them?' Sebastian was appalled.

'Yes, and took their rifles. Now it is safe to go on. But the bearers have with them many cases. It comes to me that this party follows after Bwana Intambu, the German commissioner, and that they carry with them all his goods.'

'But you shouldn't have killed them,' protested Sebastian. 'You could have just tied them up or something.'

'Manali, you argue like a woman,' Mohammed snapped impatiently, and then went on with his original line of thought. 'Among the cases is one that by its size I think is the box for the tax money. The one Askari slept with his back against it as though to give it special care.'

'The tax money?'

'Yes.'

'Well, son of a gun!' Sebastian's scruples dissolved and in the darkness his expression was suddenly transformed into that of a small boy on Christmas morning.

They woke the German bearers by standing over them and prodding them with the rifle barrels. Then they hustled them out of their blankets and herded them into a small group, bewildered and shivering miserably in the chill of dawn. Wood was heaped on the fire; it burned up brightly, and by its light Sebastian examined the booty.

The one Askari had bled profusely from the throat on to the small wooden chest. Mohammed took him by the heels and dragged him out of the way, then used his blanket to wipe the chest clean.

'Manali,' he said with reverence. 'See the big lock. See the bird of the Kaiser painted on the lid . . .' He stooped over the chest and took a grip on the handles, '... but most of all, feel the weight of it!'

Amongst the other equipment around the fire, Mohammed found a thick coil of one-inch manila rope. A commodity which was essential equipment on any of Herman Fleischer's safaris. With it, Mohammed roped the bearers together, at waist level, allowing enough line between each of them to make concerted movement possible but preventing individual flight.

'Why are you doing that?' Sebastian asked with interest, through a mouthful of blood sausage and black bread. Most of the other boxes were filled with food, and Sebastian was breakfasting well and heartily.

'So they cannot escape.'

'We're not taking them with us – are we?'

'Who else will carry all this?' Mohammed asked patiently.

Five days later Sebastian was seated in the bows of a long dugout canoe, with the charred soles of his boots set firmly on the chest that lay in the bilges. He was eating with relish a thick sandwich of polony and picked onions, wearing a change of clean underwear and socks that were a few sizes too large, and there was clutched in his left hand an open bottle of Hansa beer – all these with the courtesy of Commissioner Fleischer.

The paddlers were singing with unforced gaiety, for the hiring fee that Sebastian had paid them would buy each of them a new wife at least.

Hugging the bank of the Rovuma on the Portuguese side, driven on by willing paddles and the eager current, in twelve hours they covered the distance that it had taken Sebastian and his heavily-laden bearers five days on foot.

The canoe deposited Sebastian's party at the landing opposite M'topo's village, only ten miles from Lalapanzi. They walked that distance without resting and arrived after nightfall.

30

The windows of the bungalow were darkened, and the whole camp slept. After cautioning them to silence, Sebastian drew his depleted band up on the front lawn with the tax chest set prominently in front of them. He was proud of his success and wanted to achieve the appropriate mood for his home-coming. Having set the stage, he went up on to the stoep of the bungalow and tip-toed towards the front door with the intention of awakening the household by hammering upon it dramatically.

However, there was a chair on the stoep, and Sebastian tripped over it. He fell heavily. The chair clattered and the rifle slipped from his shoulder and rang on the stone flags.

Before Sebastian could recover his feet, the door was flung open and through it appeared Flynn O'Flynn in his night-shirt and armed with a double-barrelled shotgun. 'Caught you, you bastard!' he roared and lifted the shotgun.

Sebastian heard the click of the safety-catch and scrambled to his knees. 'Don't shoot! Flynn, it's me.'

The shotgun wavered a little. 'Who are you – and what do you want?'

'It's me – Sebastian.'

'Bassie?' Flynn lowered the shotgun uncertainly. 'It can't be. Stand up, let's have a look at you.'

Sebastian obeyed with alacrity.

'Good God,' Flynn swore in amazement. 'It *is* you. Good God! We heard that Fleischer caught you at M'topo's village a week ago. We heard he'd nobbled you for keeps!' He came forward with his right hand extended in welcome. 'You made it, did you? Well done, Bassie boy.'

Before Sebastian could accept Flynn's hand, Rosa came through the doorway, brushed past Flynn, and almost knocked Sebastian down again. With her arms locked around his chest and her cheek pressed to his unshaven cheek, she kept repeating, 'You're safe! Oh Sebastian, you're safe.'

Acutely aware of the fact that Rosa wore nothing under the thin night-gown, and that everywhere he put his hands they came in contact with thinly-veiled warm flesh, Sebastian grinned sheepishly at Flynn over her shoulder.

'Excuse me,' he said.

His first two kisses were off target for she was moving around a lot. One caught her on the ear, the next on her eyebrow, but the third was right between the lips.

When at last they were forced to separate or suffocate, Rosa gasped, 'I thought you were dead.'

'All right, missie,' growled Flynn. 'You can go and put some clothes on now.'

Breakfast at Lalapanzi that morning was a festive affair. Flynn took advantage of his daughter's weakened condition and brought a bottle of gin to the table. Her protests were half-hearted, and later with her own hands she poured a little into Sebastian's tea to brace it.

They ate on the stoep in golden sunshine that filtered through the bougainvillaea creeper. A flock of glossy starlings hopped and chirruped on the lawns, and an oriel sang from the wild fig-trees. All nature conspired to make Sebastian's victory feast a success, while Rosa and Nanny did their best from the kitchen – drawing upon the remains of Herman Fleischer's supplies that Sebastian had brought home with him.

Flynn O'Flynn's eyes were bloodshot and underhung with plum-coloured pouches, for he had been up all night counting the contents of the German tax chest and working out his accounts by the light of a hurricane lamp. Nevertheless, he was in a merry mood made merrier by the cups of fortified tea on which he was breakfasting. He joined warmly in the chorus of praise and felicitation to Sebastian Oldsmith that was being sung by Rosa O'Flynn.

'You turned up one for the book, so help me, Bassie,' he chortled at the end of the meal. 'I'd just love to hear how Fleischer is going to explain this one to Governor Schee. Oh, I'd love to be there when he tells him about the tax money – son of a gun, it'll nigh kill them both.'

'While you're on the subject of money,' Rosa smiled at Flynn, 'have you worked out how much Sebastian's share comes to, Daddy?' Rosa only used Flynn's paternal title when she was extremely well-disposed towards him.

'That I have,' admitted Flynn, and the sudden shiftiness of his eyes aroused Rosa's suspicions. Her lips pursed a little.

'And how much is it?' she asked in the syrupy tone which Flynn recognized as the equivalent of the blood roar of a wounded lioness.

'Sure now, and who wants to be spoiling a lovely day with the talking of business?' Under pressure, Flynn exaggerated the brogue in his voice in the hope that Rosa would find it beguiling. A forlorn hope.

'How much?' demanded Rosa, and he told her.

There was a sickly silence. Sebastian paled under his sunburn and opened his mouth to protest. On the strength of his half share, he had the previous night made to Rosa O'Flynn a serious proposal, which she had accepted.

'Leave this to me, Sebastian,' she whispered and laid a restraining hand on his knee as she turned back to her father. 'You'll let us have a look at the accounts, won't you?' Still syrupy sweet.

'Sure and I will. They're all straight and square.'

The document that Flynn O'Flynn produced under the main heading, 'Joint Venture Between F. O'Flynn, Esq., S. Oldsmith, Esq., and Others. German East Africa. Period May 15, 1913, to August 21, 1913,' showed that he belonged to an unorthodox school of accountancy.

The contents of the tax chest had been converted to English sterling at the rates laid down by Pear's Almanac for 1893. Flynn set great store by this particular publication.

From the gross proceeds of £4,652. 18s. 6d., Flynn had deducted his own fifty per cent share and the ten per cent of the other partners – the Portuguese Chef D'Post and the Governor of Mozambique. From the balance he had then deducted the losses incurred on the Rufiji expedition (for which see separate account addressed to German East African Administration). From there he had gone on to charge the expenses of the second expedition, not forgetting such items as:

To L. Parbhoo (Tailor)	£15.10. —.
To One German Dress Helmet (say)	£ 5.10. —.
To Five Uniforms (Askari)	
£ 2.10. —. each	£12.10. —.
To Five Mauser Rifles £10. —. —.	
each	£50. —. —.
To Six Hundred and Twenty-Five	
Rounds 7mm Ammunition	£22.10. —.
To Advance re travelling expenses,	
One Hundred Escudos made to S.	
Oldsmith, Esq.	£ 1. 5. —.

Finally, Sebastian's half share of the net losses amounted to a little under twenty pounds.

'Don't worry,' Flynn assured him magnanimously. 'I don't expect you to pay it now – we'll just deduct it from your share of the profits of the next expedition.'

'But, Flynn, I thought you said – well, I mean, you told me I had a half share.'

'And so you have, Bassie, and so you have.'

'You said we were equal partners.'

'You must have misunderstood me, boy. I said a half share – and that means after expenses. It's just a great pity there was such a large accumulated loss to bring forward.'

While they discussed this, Rosa was busy with a stub of indelible pencil on the reverse side of Flynn's account. Two minutes later she thrust the result across the breakfast table at Flynn. She said, 'And that's the way I work it out.'

Rosa O'Flynn was a student of the 'One-for-you-one-for-me' school, and her reckonings were much simpler than those of her father.

With a cry of anguish, Flynn O'Flynn lodged objection. 'You don't understand business.'

'But I recognize crookery when I see it,' Rosa flashed back.

'You'd call your old father a crook?'

'Yes.'

'I've a damn good mind to take the kiboko to you. You're not too big and uppity that I can't warm your tail up good.'

'You just try it!' said Rosa, and Flynn backpedalled.

'Anyway, what would Bassie do with all that money? It's not good for a youngster. It would spoil him.'

'He'd marry me with it. That's what he'd do with it.'

Flynn made a noise as though there were a fish-bone stuck in his throat, his face mottled over with emotion and he swung ominously in Sebastian's direction. 'So!' he rasped. 'I thought so!'

'Now steady on, old chap,' Sebastian tried to soothe him.

'You come into my home and act like the king of bloody England. You try to fraudulently embezzle my money – but that's not enough! Oh no! That's not a bloody 'nough. You've also got to start tampering with my daughter just to round things off.'

'Don't be coarse,' said Rosa.

'That's rich – *don't be coarse*, she says, and just what exactly have you two been up to behind my back?'

Sebastian stood up from the breakfast table with dignity. 'I will not have you speak so of a lady in my presence, sir. Especially of the lady who has done me the great honour of consenting to become my wife.' He begun unbuttoning his jacket. 'Will you step into the garden with me, and give me satisfaction?'

'Come along, then.' As Flynn lumbered out of his chair he made as if to pass Sebastian, but at the moment Sebastian's arms were behind him, still bound by the sleeves of his jacket as he attempted to shrug it off. Flynn side-stepped swiftly, paused a moment as he took his aim, and the drove his left fist into Sebastian's stomach.

'Oof!' said Sebastian, and leaned forward involuntarily to meet Flynn's other fist as it came up from the level of his knees. It took Sebastian between the eyes, and he changed direction abruptly and ran backwards across the veranda. The low wooden railing caught him behind the knees and he toppled slowly into the flower-beds below the stoep.

'You've killed him,' wailed Rosa, and picked up the heavy china tea-pot.

'I hope so,' said Flynn, and ducked as the pot flew towards his head, passed over it and burst against the wall of the stoep, spraying tea and steam.

There was an ominous stirring among Rosa's flowers, and presently Sebastian's head emerged with blue hydrangea petals festively strewn in his hair and the skin around both eyes fast swelling and chameleoning to a creditable match with the petals. 'I say, Flynn. That wasn't fair,' he announced.

'He wasn't looking,' Rosa accused. 'You hit him before he was ready.'

'Well, he's looking now,' roared Flynn and went down the veranda stairs like a charging hippopotamus. From the hydrangeas, Sebastian rose to meet him and took up the classic stance of the ring fighter. 'Marquis of Queensberry rules?' he cautioned as Flynn closed in.

Flynn signified his rejection of the Marquis's code by kicking Sebastian on the shin. Sebastian yelped and hopped one-legged out of the flower-bed, while Flynn pursued him with a further series of lusty kicks. Placing his boot twice in succession into Sebastian's posterior, the third kick, however, missed and the force behind it was sufficient to throw Flynn on to his back. He sprawled on the lawn, and the pause while he scrambled to his knees, gave Sebastian respite to ready himself for the next round.

Both his eyes had puffed and he was experiencing discomfort from his rear end; nevertheless, he stood once again with his left arm extended and the right crossed over his chest. Glancing beyond Flynn, Sebastian saw his fiancée descending from the veranda. She was armed with a bread-knife.

'Rosa!' Sebastian was alarmed. It was clear that Rosa would not stop at patricide to protect her love. 'Rosa! What are you doing with that knife?'

'I'm going to stick him with it!'

'You'll do no such thing,' said Sebastian, but Flynn did not have the same faith in his daughter's restraint. Very hurriedly, he moved into a defensive position behind Sebastian. From there he listened with attention to the argument between Sebastian and Rosa. It took a full minute for Sebastian to persuade Rosa that her assistance was not necessary and that he was capable of handling the situation on his own. Reluctantly, Rosa retreated to the veranda.

'Thanks, Bassie,' said Flynn, and kicked him in his already bruised behind. It was extremely painful.

Very few people had ever seen Sebastian Oldsmith lose his temper. the last time it had happened was eight years previously; the two sixth-formers who had invoked it by forcing Sebastian's head into a toilet bowl and flushing the cistern, were both hospitalized for a short period.

This time there were more witnesses. Attracted by the cries and crash of breaking crockery, Flynn's entire following, including Mohammed and his Askari, had arrived from the compound and were assembled at the top of the lawn. They watched in breathless wonder.

From the grandstand of the veranda, Rosa, her eyes sparkling with the strange feminine ferocity that arises in even the mildest women when their man fights for them, exhorted Sebastian to even greater violence.

Like all great storms, it did not last long, and when it was over the silence was appalling. Flynn lay stretched full-length on the lawn. His eyes closed and his breathing snoring softly in his throat, and bursting from his nose in a froth of red bubbles.

Mohammed and five of his men carried him towards the bungalow. He lay massive on their shoulders with the bulge of his belly rising and falling softly, and an expression of unusual peace on his bloody face.

Standing alone on the lawn, Sebastian's features were contorted with savagery and his whole body shook as though he was in high fever. Then, watching them carry the huge, inert body, suddenly Sebastian's mood was past. His expression changed first to concern, and then to gentle dismay. 'I say . . .' his voice was husky and he took a pace after them. 'You shouldn't have kicked me.' His hands opened helplessly, and he lifted them in a gesture of appeal. 'You shouldn't have done it.'

Rosa came down from the veranda and walked slowly towards him. She stopped and looked up at him, half in awe, half in glowing pride. 'You were magnificent,' she whispered. 'Like a lion.' She reached up with both arms around his neck, and before she kissed him she spoke again. 'I love you,' she said.

Sebastian had very little luggage to take with him. He was wearing everything he possessed. Rosa on the other hand, had boxes of it, enough to give full employment to the dozen bearers that were assembled on the lawn in front of the bungalow.

'Well,' murmured Sebastian, 'I suppose we should start moving.'

'Yes,' whispered Rosa, and looked at the gardens of Lalapanzi. Although she had suggested this departure, now that the time had come she was uncertain. This place had been her home since childhood. Here she had spun a cocoon that had shielded and protected her, and now that the time had come to emerge from it, she was afraid. She took Sebastian's arm, drawing strength from him.

'Don't you want to say good-bye to your father?' Sebastian looked down at her with the tender protectiveness that was such a new and delightful sensation for him.

Rosa hesitated a moment, and then realized that it would take very little to weaken her resolve. Her dutiful affection for Flynn, which at the moment was submerged beneath the tide of anger and resentment, could easily re-emerge should Flynn employ a little of his celebrated blarney. 'No,' she said.

'I suppose it's best,' Sebastian agreed. He glanced guiltily towards the bungalow where Flynn was, presumably, still lying in state – attended by the faithful Mohammed. 'But do you think he'll be all right? I mean, I did hit him rather hard, you know.'

'He'll be all right,' Rosa said without conviction, and tugged at his sleeve. Together they moved to take their places at the head of the little column of bearers.

Kneeling on the floor of the bedroom, below the window sill, peering with one swollen eye through a slit in the curtain, Flynn saw this decisive move. 'My God,' he whispered in concern. 'The young idiots are really leaving.'

Rosa O'Flynn was his last link with that frail little Portuguese girl. The one person in his life that Flynn had truly loved. Now that he was about to lose her also, Flynn was suddenly aware of his feeling for his daughter. The prospect of never seeing her again filled him with dismay.

As for Sebastian Oldsmith, here no sentiment clouded his reasoning. Sebastian was a valuable business asset. Through him, Flynn could put into operation a number of schemes that he had shelved as involving disproportionate personal risk. In these last few years Flynn had become increasingly aware of the depreciation that time and large quantities of raw spirit had wrought in his eyes and legs and nerves. Sebastian Oldsmith had eyes like a fish eagle, legs like a prize fighter, and no nerves at all that Flynn could discern. Flynn needed him.

Flynn opened his mouth and groaned. It was the throaty death rattle of an old bull buffalo. Peering through the curtain, Flynn grinned as he saw the young couple freeze, and stand tense and still in the sunlight. Their faces were turned towards the bungalow, and in spite of himself, Flynn had to admit they made a handsome pair; Sebastian tall above her with the body of a gladiator and the face of a poet; Rosa small beside him but with the full bosom and wide hips of womanhood. The slippery black cascade of her hair glowed in the sun, and her dark eyes were big with concern.

Flynn groaned again but softly this time. A breathless, husky sound, the last breath of a dying man, and instantly Rosa and Sebastian were running towards the bungalow. Her skirts gathered up above her knees, long legs flying, Rosa led Sebastian up onto the veranda.

Flynn had just sufficient time to return to his bed and compose his limbs and his face into the attitude of one fast sinking towards the abyss.

'Daddy!' Rosa leaned over him, and Flynn opened his eyes uncertainly. For a moment he did not seem to recognize her, then he whispered, 'My little girl,' so faintly she hardly caught the words.

'Oh, Daddy, what is it?' She knelt beside him.

'My heart.' His hand crawled up like a hairy spider across his belly and clutched weakly at his hairy chest. 'Like a knife. A hot knife.'

There was a terrible silence in the room, and then Flynn spoke again. 'I wanted to . . . give you my . . . my blessing. I wish happiness for you . . . wherever you go.' The effort of speech was too much, and for a while he lay gasping. 'Think of your old Daddy sometimes. Say a prayer for him.'

A fat, tiny tear broke from the corner of Rosa's eye and slid down her cheek.

'Bassie, my boy.' Slowly Flynn's eyes sought him, found him, and focused with difficulty. 'Don't blame yourself for this. I was an old man anyway – I've had my life.' He panted a little and then went on painfully. 'Look after her. Look after my little Rosa. You are my son now. I've never had a son.'

'I didn't know . . . I had no idea that your heart . . . Flynn, I'm dreadfully sorry. Forgive me.'

Flynn smiled, a brave little smile that just touched his lips. He lifted his hand weakly and held it out towards Sebastian. While Sebastian clasped his hand, Flynn considered offering him the money that had been the cause of the dispute as a dying man's gift but he manfully restrained himself from such extravagance. Instead he whispered, 'I would like to have seen my grandson, but no matter. Good-bye, my boy.'

'You'll see him, Flynn. I promise you that. We'll stay, won't we, Rosa? We'll stay with him.'

'Yes, we'll stay,' said Rosa. 'We won't leave you, Daddy.'

'My children.' Flynn sank back and closed his eyes. Thank God, he hadn't offered the money. A peaceful little smile hovered around his mouth. 'You've made an old man very happy.'

31

Flynn made a strong come-back from the edge of death, so strong, in fact, that it aroused Rosa's suspicions. However, she let it pass for she was happy to have avoided the necessity of leaving Lalapanzi. In addition, there was another matter which was taking up a lot of her attention.

Since she had said good-bye to Sebastian at the start of his tax tour, Rosa had been aware of the cessation of certain womanly functions of her body. She consulted Nanny who, in turn, consulted the local nungane who, in his turn, opened the belly of a chicken, and consulted its entrails. His findings were conclusive, and Nanny reported back to Rosa, without disclosing the source of her information, for Little Long Hair had an almost blasphemous lack of faith in the occult.

Delighted, Rosa took Sebastian for a walk down the valley, and when they reached the waterfall where it had all begun, she stood on top-toe, put both arms around his neck and whispered in his ear. She had to repeat herself for her voice was muffled with breathless laughter.

'You're joking,' gasped Sebastian, and then blushed bright crimson.

'I'm not, you know.'

'Good grief,' said Sebastian; and then, groping for something more expressive, 'Son of a gun!'

'Aren't you pleased?' Rosa pouted playfully. 'I did it for you.'

'But we aren't even married.'

'That can be arranged.'

'And quickly, too,' agreed Sebastian. He grabbed her wrist. 'Come on!'

'Sebastian, remember my condition.'

'Good grief, I'm sorry.'

He took her back to Lalapanzi, handing her over the rough

ground with as much care as though she was a case of sweating gelignite.

'What's the big hurry?' asked Flynn jovially at dinner that evening. 'I've got a little job for Bassie first. I want him to slip across the river . . .'

'No, you don't,' said Rosa. 'We are going to see the priest at Beira.'

'It would only take Bassie a couple of weeks. Then we could talk about it when he gets back.'

'We are going to Beira – tomorrow!'

'What's the rush?' Flynn asked again.

'Well, the truth is, Flynn, old boy . . .' Wriggling in his chair, colouring up vividly, Sebastian relapsed into silence.

'The truth is I'm going to have a baby,' Rosa finished for him.

'You're *what*?!' Flynn stared at her in horror.

'You said that you wanted to see your grandchild,' Rosa pointed out.

'But I didn't mean you to start work on it right away,' roared Flynn, and he rounded on Sebastian. 'You dirty young bugger!'

'Father, your heart!' Rosa restrained him. 'Anyway, don't pick on Sebastian, I did my share as well.'

'You shameless . . . You brazen little . . .'

Rosa reached behind the seat cushion where Flynn had hidden the gin bottle. 'Have a little of this – it will help calm you.'

They left for Beira the following morning. Rosa was carried in a maschille with Sebastian trotting beside it in anxious attendance, ready to help ease the litter over the fords and rough places, and to curse any of the bearers who stumbled.

When they left Lalapanzi, Flynn O'Flynn brought up the rear of the column, lying in his maschille with a square-faced bottle for company, scowling and muttering darkly about 'fornication' and 'sin'.

But both Rosa and Sebastian ignored him, and when they camped that night the two of them sat across the camp-fire from him, and whispered and laughed secretly together. They pitched their voices at such a tantalizing level that even by straining his ears, Flynn could not overhear their conversation. It infuriated him to such an extent that finally he made a loud remark about '. . . beating the hell out of the person who had repaid his hospitality by violating his daughter.'

Rosa said that she would give anything to see him try it *again*. In her opinion it would be better than a visit to the circus. And Flynn gathered his dignity and his gin bottle and stalked away to where Mohammed had laid out his bedding under a lean-to of thorn bushes.

During the dark hours before dawn they were visited by an old lion. He came with a rush from the darkness beyond the fire-light, grunting like an angry boar, the great black bush of his mane erect, snaking with incredible speed towards the huddle of blanket-wrapped figures about the fire.

Flynn was the only one not asleep. He had waited all night, watching Sebastian's reclining figure, just waiting for him to move across to the temporary thorn-bush shelter that gave Rosa privacy. Lying beside Flynn was his shotgun, double-loaded with big loopers, lion shot, and he had every intention of using it.

When the lion charged into the camp, Flynn sat up quickly and fired both barrels of the shotgun at point-blank range into the man-eater's head and chest, killing it instantly. But the momentum of its rush bowled it forward, sent it sliding full into Sebastian, and both of them rolled into the camp-fire.

Sebastian awoke to lion noises, and gun-fire, and the violent collision of a big body into his, and red-hot coals sticking to various parts of his anatomy. With a single bound, and a wild cry, he threw off his blanket, came to his feet, and went into such a lively song and dance routine, yodelling and high-kicking, and striking out at his imaginary assailants that Flynn was reduced to a jelly of helpless laughter.

The laughter, and the praise and thanks showered on him by Sebastian, Rosa, and the bearers, cleared the air.

'You saved my life,' said Sebastian soulfully.

'Oh Daddy, you're wonderful,' said Rosa. 'Thank you. Thank you,' and she hugged him.

The mantle of the hero felt snug and comfortable on Flynn's shoulders. He became almost human – and the improvement continued as each day's march brought them closer to the little Portuguese port of Beira, for Flynn greatly enjoyed his rare visits to civilization.

The last night they camped a mile from the outskirts of the town, and after a private conference with Flynn, old Mohammed went ahead armed with a small purse of escudos to make the arrangements for Flynn's formal entry on the morrow.

Flynn was up with the dawn, and while he shaved with care, and dressed in clean moleskin jacket and trousers, one of the bearers polished his boots with hippo fat, and two others scaled the tall bottle palm tree near the camp and cut fronds from its head.

All things being ready, Flynn ascended his maschille and lay back elegantly on the leopard-skin rugs. On each side of Flynn a bearer took his position, armed with a palm-frond, and began to fan him gently. Behind Flynn, in single file, followed other servants bearing tusks of ivory and the still-green lion skin. Behind this, with instructions from Flynn not to draw undue attention to themselves, followed Sebastian and Rosa, and the baggage bearers.

With a languid gesture such as might have been used by Nero to signal the start of a Roman circus, Flynn gave the order to move.

Along the rough road through the thick coastal bush, they came at last to Beira and entered the main street in procession.

'Good Lord,' Sebastian expressed his surprise when he saw the reception that awaited them, 'where did they all come from?'

Both sides of the street were lined with cheering crowds, mainly natives, but with here and there a Portuguese or an Indian trader come out of his shop to find the cause of the disturbance.

'Fini!' chanted the crowd, clapping their hands in unison. 'Bwana Mkuba! Great Lord! Slayer of elephant. Killer of lions!'

'I didn't realize that Flynn was so well regarded.' Sebastian was impressed.

'Most of them have never heard of him,' Rosa disillusioned him. 'He sent Mohammed in last night to gather a claque of about a hundred or so. Pays them one escudo each to come and cheer – they make so much noise that the entire population turns out to see what is going on. They fall for it every time.'

'What on earth does he go to so much trouble for?'

'Because he enjoys it. Just look at him!'

Lying in his maschille, graciously acknowledging the applause, Flynn was very obviously loving every minute of it.

The head of the procession reached the only hotel in Beira and halted. Madame da Souza, the portly, well-moustached widow who was the proprietress of the hotel, rushed down to welcome Flynn with a smacking kiss and usher him ceremoniously through the shabby portals. Flynn was the kind of customer she had always dreamed about.

When Rosa and Sebastian at last fought their way through the crowd into the hotel, Flynn was already seated at the bar counter and half way through a tall glass of Laurentia beer. The man sitting on the stool beside his was the Governor of Mozambique's aide-de-camp, who had come to deliver His Excellency's invitation for Flynn O'Flynn to dine at Government House that evening. It was settlement day in the partnership of 'Flynn O'Flynn and Others'. His Excellency José De Clare Don Felezardo da Silva Marques had received from Governor Schee, in Dar es Salaam, an agitated report, in the form of an official protest and an extradition demand, of the success of the partnership's operations during the last few months – and His Excellency was delighted to see Flynn.

In fact, so pleased was His Excellency with the progress of the partnership's affairs, that he exercised his authority to waive the formalities required by law to precede a marriage under Portuguese jurisdiction. This saved a week, and the afternoon after their arrival in Beira, Rosa and Sebastian stood before the altar in the stucco and thatch cathedral, while Sebastian tried with little success to remember enough of his schoolroom Latin to understand just what he was getting himself into.

The wedding veil, that had belonged to Rosa's mother, was yellowed by many years of storage under tropical conditions, but it served well enough to keep off the flies which were always bad during the hot season in Beira.

Towards the end of the long ceremony, Flynn was so overcome by the heat, the gin he had taken at lunch, and an unusually fine flood of Irish feeling, that he began snuffling loudly. While he mopped at his eyes and nose with a grubby handkerchief, the Governor's aide-de-camp patted his shoulder soothingly and murmured encouragement.

The priest declared them husband and wife, and the congregation launched into a faltering rendition of the *Te Deum*. His voice quivering with emotion and alcohol, Flynn kept repeating, 'My little girl, my poor little girl.' Rosa lifted her veil and turned to Sebastian who immediately forgot his misgivings as to the form of the ceremony, and enfolded her enthusiastically in his arms.

Still maintaining his chorus of 'My little girl,' Flynn was led away by the aide-de-camp to the hotel where the proprietress had prepared the wedding feast. In deference to Flynn O'Flynn's mood this started on a sombre note but as the champagne, which Madame da Souza had specially bottled the previous evening, started to do its work, so the tempo changed. Among his other actions, Flynn gave Sebastian a wedding present of ten pounds and poured a full glass of beer over the aide-de-camp's head.

When, later that evening, Rosa and Sebastian slipped away to the bridal suite above the bar, Flynn was giving lusty tongue in the chorus of 'They are jolly good fellows', Madame da Souza was seated on his lap, and over-flowing it in all directions. Every time Flynn pinched her posterior, great gusts of laughter made her shake like a stranded jellyfish.

Later the pleasure of Rosa and Sebastian's wedding-bed was disturbed by the fact that, in the bar-room directly below them, Flynn O'Flynn was shooting the bottles off the shelves with a double-barrelled elephant rifle. Every direct hit was greeted by thunderous applause from the other guests. Madame da Souza, still palpitating with laughter, sat in a corner of the bar-room dutifully making such entries in her notebook as, 'One bottle of Grandio London Dry Gin 14.50 escudos; one bottle Grandio French Cognac Five Star 14.50 escudos; one bottle Grandio Scotch whisky 30.00 escudos; I magnum Grandio French Champagne 75.90 escudos.' 'Grandio' was the brand-name of the house, and signified that the liquor each bottle contained had been brewed and bottled on the premises under the personal supervision of Madame da Souza.

Once the newly-wed couple realized that the uproar from the room below was sufficient to mask the protests of their rickety brass bedstead, they no longer grudged Flynn his amusements.

For everyone involved it was a night of great pleasure, a night to be looked back upon with nostalgia and wistful smiles.

Even at Flynn's prodigious rate of expenditure, his share of the profits from Sebastian's tax expedition lasted another two weeks.

During this period Rosa and Sebastian spent a little of their time wandering hand in hand through the streets and bazaars of Beira, or sitting, still hand in hand, on the beach and watching the sea. Their happiness radiated from them so strongly that it affected anyone who came within fifty feet of them. A worried stranger hurrying towards them along the narrow little street with his face creased in a frown would come under the spell; his pace would slacken, his step losing its urgency, the frown would smooth away to be replaced by an indulgent grin as he passed them. But mostly they remained closeted in the bridal suite above the bar – entering it in the early afternoon and not reappearing until nearly noon the following day.

Neither Rosa nor Sebastian had imagined such happiness could exist.

At the expiry of the two weeks Flynn was waiting for them in the bar-room as they came down to lunch. He hurried out to join them as they passed the door. 'Greetings! Greetings!' He threw an arm around each of their shoulders. 'And how are you this morning?' He listened without attention as Sebastian replied at length on how well he felt, how well Rosa was, and how well both of them had slept. 'Sure! Sure!' Flynn interrupted his rhapsodizing. 'Listen, Bassie, my boy, you remember that £10 I gave you?'

'Yes.' Sebastian was immediately wary.

'Let me have it back, will you?'

'I've spent it, Flynn.'

'You've *what*?' bellowed Flynn.

'I've spent it.'

'Good God Almighty! All of it? You've squandered ten pounds

in as many days?' Flynn was horrified by his son-in-law's extravagance and Sebastian, who had honestly believed the money was his to do with as he wished, was very apologetic.

They left for Lalapanzi that afternoon. Madame da Souza had accepted Flynn's note of hand for the balance outstanding on her bill.

At the head of the column Flynn, broke to the wide, and nursing a burning hangover, was in evil temper. The line of bearers behind him, bedraggled and billious from two weeks spent in the flesh-pots, were in similar straits. At the rear of the doleful little caravan, Rosa and Sebastian chirruped and cooed together – an island of sunshine in the sea of gloom.

The months passed quickly at Lalapanzi during the monsoon of 1913. Gradually, as its girth increased, Rosa's belly became the centre of Lalapanzi. The pivot upon which the whole community turned. The debates in the servants' quarters, led by Nanny, the accepted authority, dealt almost exclusively with the contents thereof. All of them were hot for a man-child, although secretly Nanny cherished a treacherous hope that it might be another Little Long Hair.

Even Flynn, during the long months of enforced inactivity while the driving monsoon rains turned the land into a quagmire and the rivers into seething brown torrents, felt his grandpaternal instincts stirred. Unlike Nanny, he had no doubts as to the unborn child's sex, and he decided to name it Patrick Flynn O'Flynn Oldsmith.

He conveyed his decision to Sebastian while the two of them were hunting for the pot in the kopjes above the homestead.

By dint of diligent application and practice, Sebastian's marksmanship had improved beyond all reasonable expectation. He had just demonstrated it. They were jump-shooting in thick cat-bush among the broken rock and twisted ravines of the kopjes. Constant rain had softened the ground and enabled them to move silently down-wind along one of the ravines. Flynn was fifty yards out on Sebastian's right, moving heavily but deceptively fast through the sodden grass and undergrowth.

The kudu were lying in dense cover below the lip of the ravine. Two young bulls, bluish-gold in colour, striped with thin chalk lines across the body, pendulent dewlaps heavily fringed with yellow hair, two and a half twists in each of the corkscrew horns

– big as polo ponies but heavier. They broke left across the ravine when Flynn jumped them from their hide, and the intervening bush denied him a shot.

'Breaking your way, Bassie,' Flynn shouted and Sebastian took two swift paces around the bush in front of him, shook the clinging raindrops from his lashes, and slipped the safety-catch. He heard the tap of big horn against a branch, and the first bull came out of the ravine at full run across his front. Yet it seemed to float, unreal, intangible, through the blue-grey rain mist. It blended ghostlike into the background of dark rain-soaked vegetation, and the clumps of bush and the tree trunks between them made it an almost impossible shot. In the instant that the bull flashed across a gap between two clumps of buffalo thorn, Sebastian's bullet broke its neck a hand's width in front of the shoulder.

At the sound of the shot, the second bull swerved in dead run, gathered its forelegs beneath its chest and went up in a high, driving leap over the thorn bush that stood in its path. Sebastian traversed his rifle smoothly without taking the butt from his shoulder, his right hand flicked the bolt open and closed, and he fired as a continuation of the movement.

The heavy bullet caught the kudu in mid-air and threw it sideways. Kicking and thrashing, it struck the ground and rolled down the bank of the ravine.

Whooping like a red indian, Mohammed galloped past Sebastian, brandishing a long knife, racing to reach the second bull and cut its throat before it died so that the dictates of the Koran might be observed.

Flynn ambled across to Sebastian. 'Nice shooting, Bassie boy. Salted and dried and pickled, there's meat there for a month.'

And Sebastian grinned in modest recognition of the compliment. Together they walked across to watch Mohammed and his gang begin paunching and quartering the big animals.

With the skill of a master tactician, Flynn chose this moment to inform Sebastian of the name he had selected for his grandson. He was not prepared for the fierce opposition he encountered from Sebastian. It seemed that Sebastian had expected to name the child Francis Sebastian Oldsmith. Flynn laughed easily, and then in his most reasonable and persuasive brogue he started pointing out to Sebastian just how cruel it would be to saddle the child with a name like that.

It was a lance in the pride of the Oldsmiths, and Sebastian rose to the defence. By the time they returned to Lalapanzi, the discussion needed about six hot words to reach the stage of single combat.

Rosa heard them coming. Flynn's bellow carried across the lawns. 'I'll no have my grandson called a pewling, milksop name like that!'

'Francis is the name of kings and warriors and gentlemen!' cried Sebastian.

'My aching buttocks, it is!'

Rosa came out on to the wide veranda and stood there with her arms folded over the beautiful bulge that housed the cause of the controversy.

They saw her and started an undignified race across the lawns, each trying to reach her first to enlist her support for their respective causes.

She listened to the pleadings, a small and secret smile upon her lips, and then said with finality, 'Her name will be Maria Rosa Oldsmith.'

Some time later Flynn and Sebastian were together on the veranda.

Ten days before the last rains of the season had come roaring in from the Indian Ocean and broken upon the unyielding shield of the continent. Now the land was drying out; the rivers regaining their sanity and returning, chastened to the confines of their banks. New grass lifted from the red earth to welcome the return of the sun. For this brief period the whole land was alive and green; even the gnarled and crabbed thorn trees wore a pale fuzz of tender leaves. Behind each pair of guinea-fowl that clinked and scratched on the bottom lawns of Lalapanzi, there paraded a file of dappled chicks. Early that morning a herd of eland had moved along the skyline across the valley, and beside each cow had trotted a calf. Everywhere was new life, or the expectation of new life.

'Now, stop worrying!' said Flynn, as his impatient pacing brought him level with Sebastian's chair.

'I'm not worrying,' Sebastian said mildly. 'Everything will be all right.'

'How do you know that?' challenged Flynn.

'Well . . .'

'You know the child could be stillborn, or something.' Flynn shook his finger in Sebastian's face. 'It could have six fingers on each hand – how about that? I heard about one that was born with . . .'

While Flynn related a long list of horrors, Sebastian's expression of proud and eager anticipation crumbled slowly. He rose from his chair and fell into step beside Flynn. 'Have you got any gin left?' he asked hoarsely, glancing at the shuttered windows of Rosa's bedroom. Flynn produced the bottle from the inside pocket of his jacket.

An hour later, Sebastian was hunched forward in his chair, clutching a half-full tumbler of gin with both hands. He stared into it miserably. 'I don't know what I'd do if it was born with . . .' He could not go on. He shuddered and lifted the tumbler to his lips. At that instant a long, petulant wail issued from the closed bedroom. Sebastian leapt as though he had been bayoneted from behind, and spilled the gin down his shirt. His next leap was in the direction of the bedroom, a direction Flynn had also chosen. They collided heavily and then set off together at a gallop along the veranda. They reached the locked door and hammered upon it for admission. But Nanny, who had evicted them in the first instance, still adamantly refused to lift the locking bar or to give them any information as to the progress of the birthing. Her decision was endorsed by Rosa.

'Don't you dare let them in until everything is ready,' she whispered huskily, and roused herself from the stupor of exhaustion, to help Nanny with washing and wrapping the infant.

When at last everything was ready, she lay propped on the pillows with her child held against her chest, and nodded to Nanny. 'Open the door,' she said.

The delay had confirmed Flynn's worst suspicions. The door flew open, and he and Sebastian fell into the room, wild with anxiety.

'Oh, thank God, Rosa. You're still alive!' Sebastian reached the bed and fell on his knees beside it.

'You check his feet,' instructed Flynn. 'I'll do his hands and head,' and before Rosa could prevent him, he had lifted the infant out of her arms.

'His fingers are all right. Two arms, one head,' Flynn muttered above Rosa's protests and the infant's muffled squawls of indignation.

'This end is fine. Just fine!' Sebastian spoke in rising relief and delight. 'He's beautiful, Flynn!' And he lifted the shawl that swaddled the child's body. His expression cracked and his voice choked. 'Oh, my God!'

'What's wrong?' Flynn asked sharply.

'You were right, Flynn. He's deformed.'

'What? Where?'

'There!' Sebastian pointed. 'He hasn't got a what-ye-ma-call-it,' and they both stared in horror.

It was many long seconds before they realized simultaneously that the tiny cleft was no deformity but very much as nature had intended it.

'It's a girl!' said Flynn in dismay.

'A girl!' echoed Sebastian, and quickly pulled down the shawl to preserve his daughter's modesty.

'It's a girl,' Rosa smiled, wan and happy.

'It's a girl,' cackled Nanny in triumph.

Maria Rosa Oldsmith had arrived without fuss and with the minimum of inconvenience to her mother, so that Rosa was on her feet again within twenty-four hours. All her other activities were conducted with the same consideration and dispatch. She cried once every four hours; a single angry howl which was cut off the instant the breast was thrust into her mouth. Her bowel movements were equally regular and of the correct volume and consistency, and the rest of her days and nights were devoted almost entirely to sleeping.

She was beautiful; without the parboiled, purple look of most new-borns; without the squashed-in pug features or the vague, squinty eyes.

From the curly cap of silk hair to the tips of her pink toes, she was perfection.

It took Flynn two days to recover from the disappointment of having been cheated out of a grandson. He sulked in the arsenal or sat solitary at the end of the veranda. On the second evening Rosa pitched her voice just high enough to carry the length of the veranda.

'Don't you think Maria looks just like Daddy – the same mouth and nose? Look at her eyes.'

Sebastian opened his mouth to deny the resemblance emphatically but closed it again, as Rosa kicked him painfully on the ankle.

'She is the image of him. There's no doubting who her grandfather is.'

'Well, I suppose. . . . If you look closely,' Sebastian agreed unhappily.

At the end of the veranda, Flynn sat with his head cocked in an attitude of attention. Half an hour later Flynn had sidled up to the cradle and was studying the contents thoughtfully. By the following evening he had moved his chair alongside and was leading the discussion with such remarks as, 'There is quite a strong family resemblance. Look at those eyes – no doubt who her Granddaddy is!'

Interspersing his observations with warnings and instructions, 'Don't get so close, Bassie. You're breathing germs all over her.' 'Rosa, this child needs another blanket. When did she have her last feed?'

It was not long before he started bringing pressure to bear on Sebastian.

'You've got responsibilities now. Have you thought about that?'

'How do you mean, Flynn?'

'Just answer me this. What have you got in this world?'

'Rosa and Maria,' Sebastian answered promptly.

'Fine. That's just great! And how are you going to feed them and clothe them and . . . and look after them?'

Sebastian expressed himself well satisfied with the existing arrangements.

'I bet you are! It isn't costing you a thing. But I reckon it's about time you got up off your bum and did something.'

'Like what?'

'Like going and shooting some ivory.'

Three days later, armed and equipped for a full-scale poaching expedition, Sebastian led a column of gun-boys and bearers down the valley towards the Rovuma river.

Fourteen hours later, in the dusk of evening, he led them back.

'What in the name of all that's holy, are you doing back here?' Flynn demanded.

'I had this premonition,' Sebastian was sheepish.

'What premonition?'

'That I should come back,' muttered Sebastian.

He left again two days later. This time he actually crossed the Rovuma before the premonition overpowered him once more, and he came back to Rosa and Maria.

'Well,' Flynn sighed with resignation. 'I reckon I'll just have to go along with you and make sure you do it.' He shook his head. 'You've been a big disappointment to me, Bassie.' The biggest disappointment being the fact that he had hoped to have his granddaughter to himself for a few weeks.

'Mohammed,' he bellowed. 'Get my gear packed.'

33

Flynn sent his scouts across the river and when they reported back that the far bank was clear of German patrols, Flynn made the crossing.

This expedition was a far cry from Sebastian's amiable and aimless wandering in German territory. Flynn was a professional. They crossed in the night. They crossed in strictest silence and landed two miles downstream from M'topo's village. There was no lingering on the beach, but an urgent night march that began immediately and went on in grim silence until an hour before dawn; a march that took them fifteen miles inland from the river, and ended in a grove of elephant thorn, carefully chosen for the kopjes and ravines around it that afforded multiple avenues of escape in each direction.

Sebastian was impressed by the elaborate precautions that Flynn took before going into camp; the jinking and countermarching, the careful sweeping of their spoor with brushes of dry grass, and the placing of sentries on the kopje above the camp.

During the ten days they waited there, not a single branch was broken from a tree, not a single axe-stroke swung to leave a tell-tale white blaze on the dark bush. The tiny night fire fed with dry trash and dead wood was carefully screened, and before dawn was smothered with sand so that not a wisp of smoke was left to mark them in the day.

Voices were never raised above conversational tones, and even the clatter of a bucket brought such a swift and ferocious reprimand from Flynn, that on all of them was a nervous awareness, an expectancy of danger, a tuning of the minds and bodies to action.

On the eighth night the scouts that Flynn had thrown out began drifting back to the camp. They came in with all the stealth and secrecy of night animals and huddled over the fire to tell what they had seen.

'. . . Last night three old bulls drank at the water-hole of the sick hyena. They carried teeth so, and so, and so . . .' showing the arm to measure the length of ivory, '. . . apart from them, ten cows left their feet in the mud, six of them young with calves. Yesterday, at the place where the hill of Inhosana breaks and turns its arms, I saw where another herd had crossed, moving towards the dawn; five young bulls, twenty-three cows and . . .'

The reports were jumbled, unintelligible to Sebastian who did not carry a map of the land in his head. But Flynn, sitting beside the fire listening, fitted the fragments together and built them into an exact picture of how the game was moving. He saw that the big bulls were still separated from the breeding herds – that they lingered on the high ground while the cows had started moving back towards the swamps from which the floods had driven them, anxious to take their young away from the dangers that the savannah forests would offer once the dry season set in.

He noted the estimates of thickness and length of tusk. Immature ivory was hardly worth carrying home, good only for carving into billiard balls and piano keys. The market was glutted with it.

But on the other hand, a prime tusk, over one hundred pounds in weight, seven foot long and twice the thickness of a fat woman's thigh, would fetch fifty shillings a pound avoirdupois.

An animal carrying such a tusk in each side of his face was worth four or five hundred pounds in good, gold sovereigns.

One by one Flynn discarded the possible areas in which he would hunt. This year there were no elephant in the M'bahora hills. There was good reason for this; thirty piles of great sun-bleached bones lay scattered along the ridge, marking the path that Flynn's rifles had followed two years before. The memory of gun-fire was too fresh and the herds shunned that place.

There were no elephant on the Tabora escarpment. A blight had struck the groves of mapundu trees, and withered the fruit before it could ripen. Dearly the elephant loved mapundu berries and they had gone elsewhere to find them.

They had gone up to the Sania Heights, to Kilombera, and to the Salito hills.

Salito was an easy day's march from the German boma at Mahenge. Flynn struck it from his mental list.

As each of the scouts finished his report, Flynn asked the question which would influence his final decision.

'What of *Plough the Earth*?'

And they said, 'We saw nothing. We heard nothing.'

The last scout came in two days after the others. He looked sheepish and more than a little guilty.

'Where the hell have you been?' Flynn demanded, and the gun-boy had his excuse ready.

'Knowing that the great Lord Fini would ask of certain matters, I turned aside in my journey to the village of Yetu, who is my uncle. My uncle is a fundi. No wild thing walks, no lion kills, no elephant breaks a branch from a tree but my uncle knows of it. Thus I went to ask him of these things.'

'Thy uncle is a famous fundi, he is also a famous breeder of daughters,' Flynn remarked drily. 'He breeds daughters the way the moon breeds stars.'

'Indeed, my uncle Yetu is a man of fame.' Hurriedly the scout went on to turn Flynn aside from this line of discussion. 'My uncle sends his greetings to the Lord Fini and bids me speak thus: "This season there are many fine elephants on the Sania Heights. They walk by twos and threes. With my own eyes I have seen twelve which show ivory as long as the shaft of a throwing spear, and I have seen signs of as many more." My uncle bids me speak further: "There is one among them of which the Lord Fini knows for he has asked of him many times. This one is a bull among great bulls. One who moves in such majesty that men have named him *Plough the Earth*." '

'You do not bring a story from the honey-bird to cool my anger against you?' Flynn demanded harshly. 'Did you dream of *Plough the Earth* while you were ploughing the bellies of your uncle's many daughters?' His eagerness was soured by scepticism. Too many times he had followed wild stories in his pursuit of the great bull. He leaned forward across the fire to watch the gun-bearer's eyes as he replied, 'It is true, lord.' Flynn watched him carefully but found no hint of guile in his face. Flynn grunted, rocked back on his hams, and lowered his gaze to the small flames of the camp-fire.

For his first ten years in Africa, Flynn had heard the legend of the elephant whose tusks were of such length that their points touched the ground and left a double furrow along his spoor. He had smiled at this story as he had at the story of the rhinoceros who fifty years before had killed an Arab slaver, and now wore around his horn a massive gold bangle studded with precious stones. They said the bangle had lodged there as he gored the Arab. There were a thousand other romantic tales come out of Africa; from Solomon's treasure to the legend of the elephants' graveyard, and Flynn believed none of them.

Then he saw a myth come alive. One evening, camped near the Zambezi in Portuguese territory, he had taken a bird-gun and walked along the bank hoping for a brace of sand-grouse. Two miles from the camp he had seen a flight of birds coming in to the water, fly fast as racing pigeons, whistling in on backswept wings, and he had ducked into a thick bank of reeds and watched them come.

As they banked steeply overhead, dropping towards the sand-banks of the river, Flynn jumped to his feet and fired left and right, folding the lead bird and the second, so they crumpled in mid-air and tumbled, leaving a pale flurry of feathers to mark their fall.

But Flynn never saw the birds hit the ground. For, while the double blast of the shotgun still echoed along the river, the reed-bed below where he stood swayed and crashed and burst open, then an elephant came out into the open.

It was a bull elephant that stood fourteen feet high at the shoulder. An elephant so old that his ears were shredded to half their original size. The hide that covered his body hung in folds and deep wrinkles, baggy at the knees and the throat. The tuft of his tail long ago worn bald. The rheumy tears of great age staining his seared and dusty cheeks.

He came out of the reed-bed in a shambling, hump-backed run, and his head was tilted at an awkward, unnatural angle.

Flynn could hardly credit his vision when he saw the reason why the old bull cocked his head back in that fashion. From each side of the head extended two identical shafts of ivory, perfectly matched, straight as the columns of a Greek temple, with not an inch of taper from lip to bluntly rounded tip. They were stained to the colour of tobacco juice, fourteen long feet of ivory that would have touched the ground, if the elephant had carried his head relaxed.

As Flynn stood frozen in disbelief, the bull passed him by a mere fifty yards and lumbered on into the forest.

It took Flynn thirty minutes to get back to camp and exchange the bird-gun for the double-barrelled Gibbs, snatch up a water bottle, shout for his gun-boys, and return to the river.

He put Mohammed to the spoor. At first there were only the round pad marks in the dusty earth, smooth pad marks the size of a dustbin lid; the graining on the old bull's hooves had long been worn away. Then after five miles of flight there were other marks to follow. On each side of the spoor a double line scuffed through dead leaves and grass and soft earth where the tips of the tusks touched, and Flynn learned why the old bull was called *Plough the Earth*.

They lost the spoor on the third day in the rain, but a dozen times in the years since then, Flynn had followed and lost those double furrows, and once, through his binoculars, he had seen the old bull again, standing dozing beneath a grove of marula trees at a distance of three miles, his eroded old head propped up by the mythical tusks. When Flynn reached the spot on which he had seen the bull, it was deserted.

In all his life Flynn had never wanted anything with such obsessive passion as he wanted those tusks.

Now he sat silently staring into the camp-fire, remembering all these things, and the lust within him was tighter and more compelling than he had ever felt for a woman.

At last he looked up at the scout and said huskily, 'Tomorrow, with the first light, we will go to the village of Yetu, at Sania.'

A fly settled on Herman Fleischer's cheek and rubbed its front feet together in delight, as it savoured the prospect of drinking from the droplet of sweat that quivered precariously at the level of his ear lobe.

The Askari standing behind Herman's chair flicked the zebra tail switch with such skill, that not one of the long black hairs touched the Commissioner's face, and the fly darted away to take its place in the circuit that orbited around Herman's head.

Herman hardly noticed the interruption. He was sunk down in the chair, glowering at the two old men who squatted on the dusty parade ground below the veranda. The silence was a blanket that lay on them all in the stupefying heat. The two headmen waited patiently. They had spoken, and now they waited for the Bwana Mkuba to reply.

'How many have been killed?' Herman asked at last, and the senior of the two headmen answered.

'Lord, as many as the fingers of both your hands. But these are the ones of which we are certain, there may be others.'

Herman's concern was not for the dead, but their numbers would be a measure of the seriousness of the situation. Ritual murder was the first stage on the road to rebellion. It started with a dozen men meeting in the moonlight, dressed in cloaks of leopard skin, with designs of white clay painted on their faces. With the crude iron claws strapped to their hands, they would ceremoniously mutilate a young girl, and then devour certain parts of her body. This was harmless entertainment in Herman's view, but when it happened more frequently, it generated in the district a mood of abject terror. This was the climate of revolt. Then the leopard priests would walk through the villages in the night, walk openly in procession with the torches burning, and the men who lay shivering within the barricaded huts would listen to the chanted instructions from the macabre little procession – and they would obey.

It had happened ten years earlier at Salito. The priests had ordered them to resist the tax expedition that year. They had slaughtered the visiting Commissioner and twenty of his Askari, and they cut the bodies into small pieces with which they festooned the thorn trees.

Three months later a battalion of German infantry had disembarked at Dar es Salaam and marched to Salito. They burned the villages and they shot everything – men, women, children, chickens, dogs and goats. The final casualty list could only be estimated, but the officer commanding the battalion boasted that they had killed two thousand human beings. He was probably exaggerating. Nevertheless, the Salito hills were still devoid of human life and habitation to this day. The whole episode was irritating and costly – and Herman Fleischer wanted no repetition of it during his term of office.

On the principle that prevention was better than cure, he decided to go down and conduct a few ritual sacrifices of his own. He humped himself forward in his chair, and spoke to his sergeant of Askari.

'Twenty men. We will leave for the village of Yetu, at Sania, tomorrow before dawn. Do not forget the ropes.'

34

On the Sania Heights, in the heat of the day, an elephant stood under the wide branches of a wild fig-tree. He was asleep on his feet but his head was propped up by two long columns of stained ivory. He slept as an old man sleeps, fitfully, never sinking very deep below the level of consciousness. Occasionally the tattered grey ears flapped, and each time a fine haze of flies rose around his head. They hung in the hot air and then settled again. The rims of the elephant's ears were raw where the flies had eaten down through the thick skin. The flies were everywhere. The humid green shade beneath the wild fig was murmurous with the sound of their wings.

Across the divide of the Sania Heights, four miles from the spot where the old bull slept, three men were moving up one of the bush-choked gulleys towards the ridge.

Mohammed was leading. He moved fast, half-crouched to peer at the ground, glancing up occasionally to anticipate the run of the spoor he was following. He stopped at a place where a grove of mapundu trees had carpeted the ground beneath them with a stinking, jellified mass of rotten berries. He looked back at the two white men and indicated the marks in the earth, and the pyramid of bright yellow dung that lay upon it. 'He stopped here for the first time in the heat, but it was not to his liking, and he has gone on.'

Flynn was sweating. It ran down his flushed jowls and dripped on to his already sodden shirt. 'Yes,' he nodded and a small cloud-burst of sweat scattered from his head at the movement. 'He will have crossed the ridge.'

'What makes you so certain?' Sebastian spoke in the same sepulchral whisper as the others.

'The cool evening breeze will come from the east – he will cross to the other side of the ridge to wait for it.' Flynn spoke with irritation and wiped his face on the short sleeve of his shirt. 'Now, you just remember, Bassie. This is my elephant, you understand that? You try for it and, so help me God, I'll shoot you dead.'

Flynn nodded to Mohammed and they moved on up the slope, following the spoor that meandered between outcrops of grey granite and scrub.

The crest of the ridge was well defined, sharp as the spine of a starving ox. They paused below it, squatting to rest in the coarse brown grass. Flynn opened the binocular case that hung on his chest, lifted out the instrument and began to polish the lens with a scrap of cloth.

'Stay here!' Flynn ordered the other two, then on his belly he wriggled up towards the skyline. Using the cover of a tree stump, he lifted his head cautiously and peered over.

Below him the Sania Heights fell away at a gentle slope, fifteen hundred feet and ten miles to the plain below. The slope was broken and crenellated, riven into a thousand gulleys and ravines, covered over-all with a mantle of coarse brown scrub and dotted with clumps of bigger trees.

Flynn settled himself comfortably on his elbows and lifted the binoculars to his eyes. Systematically he began to examine each of the groves below him.

'Yes!' he whispered aloud, wriggling a little on his belly, staring at the picture puzzle beneath the spread branches of the tree, a mile away. In the shade there were shapes that made no sense, a mass too diffuse to be the trunk of the tree.

He lowered the glasses and wiped away the sweat that clung in his eyebrows. He closed his eyes to rest them from the glare, then he opened them again and lifted the glasses.

For two long minutes he stared before suddenly the puzzle made sense. The bull was standing half away from him, merging with the trunk of the wild fig, the head and half the body obscured by the lower branches of the tree – and what he had taken to be the stem of a lesser tree was, in fact, a tusk of ivory.

A spasm of excitement closed on his chest.

'Yes!' he said. 'Yes!'

Flynn planned his stalk with care, taking every precaution against the intervention of fate that twenty years of elephant hunting had taught him.

He had gone back to where Sebastian and Mohammed waited.

'He's there,' he told them.

'Can I come with you?' Sebastian pleaded.

'In a barrel you can,' snarled Flynn as he sat and pulled off his heavy boots to replace them with the light sandals that Mohammed produced from the pack. 'You stay here until you hear my shot. You so much as stick your nose over the ridge before that – and, so help me God, I'll shoot it off.'

While Mohammed knelt in front of Flynn and strapped the leather pads to his knees to protect them as he crawled over rock and thorn, Flynn fortified himself from the gin bottle. As he recorked it, he glowered at Sebastian again. 'That's a promise!' he said.

At the top of the ridge Flynn paused again with only his eyes lifted over the skyline, while he plotted his stalk, fixing in his memory a procession of landmarks – an ant-hill, an outcrop of white quartz, a tree festooned with weaver birds' nests – so that as he reached each of these he would know his exact position in relation to that of the elephant.

Then with the rifle cradled across the crook of his elbows he slid on his belly to begin the stalk.

Now, an hour after he had left the ridge, he saw before him through the grass a slab of granite like a headstone in an ancient cemetery. It stood square and weathered brown, and it was the end of the stalk.

He had marked it from the ridge as the point from which he would fire. It stood fifty yards from the wild fig-tree, at a right angle from the old bull's position. It would give him cover as he rose to his knees to make the shot.

Anxious now, suddenly overcome with a premonition of disaster – sensing that somehow the cup would be dashed from his lips, the maid plucked from under him before the moment of fulfillment, Flynn started forward. Slithering towards the granite headstone, his face set hard in nervous anticipation, he reached the rock.

He rolled carefully on to his side and, holding the heavy rifle against his chest, he slipped the catch across and eased the rifle open, so that the click of the mechanism was muted. From the belt around his waist he selected two fat cartridges and examined the brass casings for tarnish or denting; with relief he saw the fingers that held them were steadier. He slipped the cartridges into the blank eyes of the breeches, and they slid home against the seatings with a soft metallic plong. And now his breathing was faintly ragged at the end of each inhalation. He closed the rifle, and with his thumb pushed the safety-catch forward into the 'fire' position.

His shoulder against the rough, sun-heated granite, he drew up his legs against his belly and rolled gently on to his knees. With his head bowed low and the rifle in his lap, he knelt behind the rock, and for the first time in an hour he lifted his head. He brought it up with inching deliberation. Slowly the crystalline texture of the granite passed before his eyes, then suddenly he looked across fifty yards of open ground at his elephant.

It stood broadside to him but the head was hidden by the leaves and branches of the wild fig. The brain shot was impossible from here. His eyes moved down on to the shoulder and he saw the outline of the bone beneath the thick grey skin. He picked out the point of the elbow and his eyes moved back into the barrel of the chest. He could visualize the heart pulsing softly there beneath the ribs, pink and soft and vital, throbbing like a giant sea anemone.

He lifted the rifle, and laid it across the rock in front of him. He looked along the barrels, and saw the blade of dry grass that was wound around the bead of the foresight, obscuring it. He lowered the rifle and with his thumb-nail picked away the shred of grass. Again he lifted and sighted.

The black blob of the foresight lay snugly in the deep, wide vee of the backsight, he moved the gun, riding the bead down across the old bull's shoulder then back on to the chest. It lay there ready to kill, and he took up the slack in the trigger, gently, lovingly, with his forefinger.

The shout was faint, a tiny sound in the drowsy immensity of the hot African air. It came from the high ground above him.

'Flynn!' and again, 'Flynn!'

In an explosive burst of movement under the wild fig-tree, the old bull swung his body with unbelievable speed, his great tusks riding high, he went away from Flynn at an awkward shambling run, his flight covered by the trunk of the fig-tree.

For stunned seconds, Flynn crouched behind the boulder, and with each second the chances of a shot dwindled. Flynn jumped to his feet and ran out to one side of the fig-tree, opening his field of fire for a snap shot at the bull as he fled, a try for the spine where it curved down between the massive haunches to the tuftless tail.

Spiked agony stabbed up through the ball of his lightly shod foot, as he trod squarely on a three-inch buffalo thorn. Red-tipped, wickedly barbed, it buried its full length in his flesh, and he stumbled to his knees crying a protest at the pain.

Two hundred yards away, the old bull disappeared into one of the wooded ravines, and was gone.

'Flynn! Flynn!'

Sobbing in pain and frustration, his injured foot twisted up into his lap, Flynn sat in the grass and waited for Sebastian Oldsmith to come down to him.

'I'll let him get real close,' Flynn told himself. Sebastian was approaching with the long awkward strides of a man running downhill. He had lost his hat and the black tangled curls danced on his head at each stride. He was still shouting.

'I'll give it to him in the belly,' Flynn decided. 'Both barrels!' and he groped for the rifle that lay beside him.

Sebastian saw him and swerved in his run.

Flynn hefted the rifle. 'I warned him. I said I'd do it,' and his right hand settled around the pistol grip of the rifle, his forefinger instinctively hooking forward for the trigger.

'Flynn! Germans! A whole army of them. Just over the hill. Coming this way.'

'Christ!' said Flynn, immediately abandoning his homicidal intentions.

35

Lifting himself in the stirrups, Herman Fleischer reached behind to massage himself. His buttocks were of a plump, almost feminine, quantity and quality. After five hours in the saddle Herman longed to rest them. He had just crossed the ridge of the Sania Heights on his donkey, and it was cool here beneath the outspread branches of the wild fig-tree. He flirted with the temptation, decided to indulge himself, and turned to give the order to the troop of twenty Askari who stood behind him. All of them were watching him avidly, anticipating the order that would allow them to throw themselves down and relax.

'Lazy dogs!' thought Herman as he scowled at them. He turned away from them, settled his aching posterior gently on to the saddle and growled. 'Akwende! Let us go!' His heels thumped against the flanks of his donkey and it started forward at a trot.

From a crotch in the trunk of the fig-tree ten feet above Herman's head, Flynn O'Flynn viewed his departure over the double barrels of his rifle. He watched the patrol wind away down the slope and drop from sight over a fold in the ground before he put up the gun.

'Phew! That was close.' Sebastian's voice came from the leafy mass above Flynn.

'If he'd touched one foot to the ground, I'd have blown his bloody head off,' said Flynn. He sounded as though he regretted missing the opportunity. 'All right, Bassie, get me down out of this frigging tree.'

Fully dressed, except for his boots, Flynn sat against the base of the fig-tree and proffered his right foot to Sebastian. '. . . I had him right there in my sights.'

'Who?' asked Sebastian.

'The elephant, you idiot. For the first time I had him cold. And then . . . Yeow! What the hell are you doing?'

'I'm trying to get the thorn out, Flynn.'

'Feels like you're trying to knock it in with a hammer.'

'I can't get a grip on it.'

'Use your teeth. That's the only way,' Flynn instructed, and Sebastian paled a little at the thought. He considered Flynn's foot. It was a large foot; corns on the toes, flakes of loose skin and other darker matter between them. Sebastian could smell it at a range of three feet. 'Couldn't you reach it with your own teeth, Flynn?' he hedged.

'You think I'm a goddamned contortionist?'

'Mohammed?' Sebastian's eyes lit up with relief as he turned on the little gun-bearer. In answer to the question Mohammed drew back his lips in a death's head grin, exposing his smooth, pink toothless gums. 'Yes,' agreed Sebastian. 'I see what you mean.' He returned his gaze to the foot, and studied it with sickened fascination. His adam's apple bobbed as he swallowed.

'Get on with it,' said Flynn, and Sebastian stooped. There was a howl from Flynn, and Sebastian straightened up with the wet thorn gripped in his teeth. He spat it out explosively, and Mohammed handed him the gin bottle. Sebastian gargled from it loudly but when he lifted the bottle to his lips again, Flynn laid a restraining hand on his forearm. 'Now don't overdo it, Bassie boy,' he remonstrated mildly, retrieved the bottle and placed it to his own mouth. It seemed to refuel Flynn's anger, for when he removed the bottle his voice had fire in it. 'That goddamn sneaking, sausage-eating slug. He spoiled the only chance I've ever had at that elephant.' He paused to breathe heavily. 'I'd like to do something really nasty to him, like . . . like . . .' he searched for some atrocity to commit upon Herman Fleischer, and suddenly he found one. 'My God!' he said, and his scowl changed to a lovely smile. 'That's it!'

'What?' Sebastian was alarmed. He was certain that he would be selected as the vehicle of Flynn's revenge. 'What?' he repeated.

'We will go . . .' said Flynn, '. . . to Mahenge!'

'Good Lord, that's the German headquarters!'

'Yes,' said Flynn. 'With no Commissioner and no Askari to guard it! They've just passed us, heading in the opposite direction.'

36

They hit Mahenge two hours before dawn, in that time of utter darkness when mankind's vitality is at its lowest ebb. The defence put up by the corporal and five Askari whom Fleischer had left to guard his headquarters was hardly heroic. In fact, they were only half awakened by the lusty and indiscriminate use of Flynn's boot, and by the time they were fully conscious, they found themselves securely locked behind the bars of the jail-house. There was only one casualty. It was, of course, Sebastian Oldsmith, who, in the excitement, ran into a half-open door. It was fortunate, as Flynn pointed out, that he struck the door with his head, otherwise he may have done himself injury. But as it was, he had recovered sufficiently by sunrise to watch the orgy of looting and vandalism in which Flynn and his gun-bearers indulged themselves.

They began in the office of the Commissioner. Built into the thick adobe wall of the room was an enormous iron safe.

'We will open that first,' decreed Flynn as he eyed it greedily. 'See if you can find some tools.'

Sebastian remembered the blacksmith shop at the end of the parade ground. He returned from there laden with sledge-hammers and crow-bars.

Two hours later they were sweating and swearing in an atmosphere heavy with plaster dust. They had torn the safe from the wall, and it lay in the centre of the floor. Three of Flynn's gun-boys were beating on it with sledge-hammers in a steadily diminishing display of enthusiasm, while Sebastian worked with a crow-bar at the hinge joints. He had succeeded in inflicting a few bright scratches upon the metal. Flynn was seated on the Commissioner's desk, steadily working himself into a fury of frustration; for the last hour his contribution to the assault on the safe had been limited to consuming half a bottle of schnapps that he had found in a drawer of the desk.

'It's no use, Flynn.' Sebastian's curls were slick with perspiration, and he licked at the blisters on the palms of his hands. 'We will just have to forget about it.'

'Stand back!' roared Flynn. 'I'll shoot the goddamned thing open.' He rose from the desk wild-eyed, his double-barrelled Gibbs clutched in his hands.

'Wait!' shouted Sebastian and he and the gun-bearers scattered for cover.

The detonations of the heavy rifle were thunderous in the confined space of the office; gun-smoke mingled with the plaster dust, and the bullets ricocheted off the metal of the safe, leaving long smears of lead upon it, before whining away to embed themselves in the floor, wall and furniture.

This act of violence seemed to placate Flynn. He lost interest in the safe. 'Let's go and find something to eat,' he said mildly, and they trooped through to the kitchens.

Once Flynn had shot away the lock, Herman Fleischer's larder proved to be an Aladdin's cave of delight. The roof was hung with hams and polonies and sausages, there were barrels of pickled meats, stacks of fat round cheeses, cases of Hansa beer, cases of cognac, pyramids of canned truffles, asparagus tips, pâté, shrimps, mushrooms, olives in oil, and other rarities.

They stared at this profusion in awe, and then moved forward together. Each man to his own particular tastes, they fell upon Herman Fleischer's treasure house. The gun-boys rolled out a cask of pickled pork, Sebastian started with his hunting knife on the cans, while Flynn devoted himself on the case of Steinhager in the corner.

It took two hours of dedicated eating and drinking for them to reach saturation point.

'We'd better get ready to move on now,' Sebastian belched softly, and Flynn nodded owlish agreement, the movement spilling a little Steinhager down his bush jacket. He wiped at it with his hand and then licked his fingers.

'Yep! Best we are gone before Fleischer gets home.' He looked at Mohammed. 'Make up full loads of food for each of the bearers. What you can't carry away we'll dump in the latrine buckets.' He stood up carefully. 'I'll just have a look round, and make sure we haven't missed anything important,' and he went out through the door with unsteady dignity.

In Fleischer's office he stood for a minute regarding the

invulnerable safe balefully. It was certainly much too heavy to carry away, and abandoning the notion with regret, he looked around for some outlet for his frustration.

There was a portrait of the Kaiser on the entrance wall, a colour print showing the Emperor in full dress, mounted on a magnificent cavalry charger. Flynn picked up an indelible pencil from the desk and walked across to the picture. With a dozen strokes of the pencil he drastically altered the relationship between horse and rider. Then, beginning to chuckle, he printed on the whitewashed wall below the picture, 'The Kaiser loves horses.'

This struck him as being such a pearl of wit, that he had to summon Sebastian and show it to him. 'That's what you call being subtle Bassie, boy. All good jokes are subtle.'

It seemed to Sebastian that Flynn's graffiti were as subtle as the charge of an enraged rhinoceros but he laughed dutifully. This encouraged Flynn to a further essay in humour. He had two of the gun bearers carry in a bucket from the latrines, and under his supervision, they propped it above the half-open door of Herman Fleischer's bedroom.

An hour later, heavily laden with booty, the raiding party left Mahenge and began the first of a series of forced marches aimed at the Rovuma river.

37

In a state of mental confusion induced by a superfluity of adrenalin in the bloodstream, Herman Fleischer wandered through his ransacked boma. As he discovered each new outrage he regarded it with slitted eyes and laboured breathing. But first it was necessary to effect a jail-break in reverse in order to free his own captive Askari. When they emerged through the hole in the prison wall, Herman curtly ordered his sergeant to administer twenty strokes of the kiboko to each of them, as a token rebuke for their inefficiency. He stood by and drew a little comfort from the solid slap of the kiboko on bare flesh and the shrieks of the recipient.

However, the calming effect of the floggings evaporated when Herman entered the kitchen area of his establishment, and found that his larder of painstakingly accumulated foodstuffs was now empty. This nearly broke his spirit. His jowls quivered with self-pity, and from under his tongue saliva oozed in melancholic nostalgia. It would take a month to replace the sausages alone, heaven knew how long to replace the cheeses imported from the fatherland.

From the larder he went through to his office and found Flynn's subtleties. Herman's sense of humour was not equal to the occasion.

'Pig-swine, English bastard,' he muttered dejectedly, and a dark wave of despair and fatigue washed over him as he realized the futility of setting out in pursuit of the raiders. With two days start he could never hope to catch them before they reached the Rovuma. If only Governor Schee, who was so forthcoming with criticism, would allow him to cross the river one night with his Askari and visit the community at Lalapanzi. There would be no one left the following morning to make complaint to the Portuguese Government about breach of sovereignty.

Herman sighed. He was tired and depressed. He would go to

his bed now and rest a while before supervising the tidying up of his headquarters. He left the office and plodded heavily along the stoep to his private quarters, and pushed open the door of his bedroom.

His bedroom temporarily uninhabitable, Herman reposed that night on the open stoep. But his sleep was disturbed by a dream in which he pursued Flynn O'Flynn across an endless plain without ever narrowing the gap between them, while above him circled two huge birds – one with the austere face of Governor Schee, and the other with the face of the young English bandit – at regular intervals these two voided their bowels on him. After the previous afternoon's experience the olfactory hallucinations which formed part of the dream were horribly realistic.

He was tactfully awakened by one of his household servants, and struggled up in bed with an ache behind his eyes and a foul taste in his mouth.

'What is it?' he growled.

'There is a bearer from Dodoma who brings a book with the red mark of the Bwana Mkuba upon it.'

Herman groaned. An envelope with Governor Schee's seal affixed to it usually meant trouble. Surely he could not so speedily have learned about Flynn O'Flynn's latest escapade.

'Bring coffee!'

'Lord, there is no coffee. It was all stolen,' and Herman groaned again.

'Very well. Bring the messenger.' He would have to endure the ordeal of Governor Schee's rebukes without the fortifying therapy of a cup of coffee. He broke the seal and began to read:

> 4th August, 1914.
> The Residency,
> Dar es Salaam.

To The Commissioner (Southern Province)

At: Mahenge.

Sir,

It is my duty to inform you that a state of war now exists between the Empire and the Governments of England, France, Russia, and Portugal.

You are hereby appointed temporary Military Commander of the Southern Province of German East Africa, with orders to take whatever steps you deem necessary for the protection of our borders, and the confusion of the enemy.

In due course a military force, now being assembled at Dar es Salaam, will be despatched to your area. But I fear that there will be a delay before this can be achieved.

In the meantime, you must operate with the force presently at your disposal.

There was more, much more, but Herman Fleischer read the detailed instructions with perfunctory attention. His headache was forgotten, the taste in his mouth unnoticed in the fierce surge of warrior passions that arose within him.

His chubby features puckered with smiles, he looked up from the letter and spoke aloud. 'Ja, O'Flynn, now I will pay you for the bucket.'

He turned back to the first page of the letter, and his mouth formed the words as he read '. . . whatever steps you deem necessary for the protection of our borders, and the confusion of the enemy.'

At last. At last he had the order for which he had pleaded so many times. He shouted for his sergeant.

38

'Perhaps they will come home tonight.' Rosa Oldsmith looked up from the child's smock she was embroidering.

'Tonight, or tomorrow, or the next day,' Nanny replied philosophically. 'There is no profit in guessing at the coming or going of men. They all have worms in their heads,' and she began again to rock the cradle, squatting beside it on the leopard-skin rugs like an animated mummy. The child snuffled a little in its sleep.

'I'm sure it will be tonight. I can feel it – something good is going to happen.' Rosa laid aside her sewing and crossed to the door that led out on to the stoep. In the last few minutes the sun had gone down below the trees, and the land was ghostly quiet in the brief African dusk.

Rosa went out on to the stoep, and hugging her arms across her chest at the chill of evening, she stared out down the darkening length of the valley. She stood there, waiting restlessly, and as the day passed swiftly into darkness, so her mood changed from anticipation to a formless foreboding.

Quietly, but with an edge to her voice, she called back into the room, 'Light the lamps please, Nanny.'

Behind her she heard the sounds of metal on glass, then the flare of a sulphur match, and a feeble yellow square of light was thrown out on to the veranda to fall around her feet.

The first puff of the night wind was cold on her bare arms. She felt the prickle of goose-flesh and she shivered unexpectedly.

'Come inside, Little Long Hair,' Nanny ordered. 'The night is for mosquitoes and leopards – and other things.'

But Rosa lingered, straining her eyes into the darkness until she could no longer see the shape of the fig-trees at the bottom of the lawn. Then abruptly she turned away and went into the bungalow. She closed the door and slid the bolt across.

Later she woke. There was no moon outside and the room

was dark. Beside her bed she could hear the soft, piglet sounds that little Maria made in her sleep.

Again the disquieting mood of the early evening returned to her and she lay still in her bed, waiting and listening in the utter blackness, and the darkness bore down upon her so that she felt herself shrinking, receding, becoming remote from reality, small and lonely in the night.

In fear then she lifted the mosquito netting and groped for the cradle. The baby whimpered as she lifted her and brought her into the bed beside her, but Rosa's arms quietened her and soon she slept against the breast, and the warmth of the tiny body stilled Rosa's own agitation.

The shouting woke her, and she opened her eyes with a surge of joy, for the shouts would be Sebastian's bearers. Before she was fully awake she had thrown aside the bedclothes, struggled out from under the mosquito netting, and was standing in her night-dress with the baby clasped to her chest.

It was then that she realized that the room was no longer in darkness. From the window into the yard it was lit by a red-gold glow that flared, and flickered, and faded.

The last tarnish of sleep was cleaned from her brain, so she could hear that the shouts from outside were not those of welcome, and on a lower key, there were other sounds – a whispering, rustling, and popping, that she could not identify.

She crossed to the window, moving slowly, with dread for what she might find, but before she reached it a scream froze her. It came from the kitchen yard, a scream that quivered on the air long after it had ended, a scream of terror and of pain.

'Merciful God!' she whispered, and forced herself to peer out.

The servants' quarters and the outhouses were on fire. From the thatch of each the flames stood up in writhing yellow columns, lighting the darkness.

There were men in the yard, many men, and all of them wore the khaki uniform of German Askari. Each of them carried a rifle, and the bayonet blades glittered in the glare of the flames.

'They have crossed the river – No, oh please God, no!' and Rosa hugged the baby to her, crouching down below the window sill.

The scream rang out again, but weaker now, and she saw a knot of four Askari crowded around something that squirmed in the dust of the yard. She heard their laughter, the excited laughter of men who kill for fun, as they stabbed down on the squirming thing with their bayonets.

At that moment another of the servants broke from the burning outbuildings and ran for the darkness beyond the circle of the flames. Shouting again, the Askari left the dying man and chased the other. They turned him like a pack of trained greyhounds coursing a gazelle, laughing and shouting in their excitation, and drove him back into the daylight glare of the flames.

Bewildered, surrounded, the servant stopped and looked wildly about him, his face convulsed with terror. Then the Askari swarmed over him, clubbing and hacking with their rifles.

'Oh, oh God, no,' Rosa's whisper sobbed in her throat, but she could not drag her eyes away.

Suddenly in the uproar she heard a new voice, a bull-bellow of authority. She could not understand the words for they were shouted in German but from around the angle of the bungalow appeared a white man, a massive figure in the blue corduroy uniform of the German Colonial Service, with a slouch hat pulled low down on his head, and a pistol brandished in one hand. From the description that Sebastian had given her, she recognized the German Commissioner.

'Stop them!' Rosa did not speak aloud, the appeal was in her mind only. 'Please, stop them burning and killing.'

The white man was railing at his Askari, his face turned towards where Rosa crouched and she saw it was round and pink like that of an overweight baby. In the fire-light it glistened with a fine sheen of sweat.

'Stop them. Please stop them,' Rosa pleaded silently, but under the Commissioner's direction three of the Askari ran to where, in the excitement of the chase, they had dropped their torches of dry grass. While they lit them from the flaming outbuildings, the other Askari left the corpses of the two servants and spread out in a circle around the bungalow, facing inwards, with their rifles held at high port. Most of the bayonets were dulled with blood.

'I want Fini and the Singese – not bearers and gun-boys – I want the white men! Burn them out!' shouted Fleischer, but Rosa recognized only her father's name. She wanted to cry out that he was not here, that it was only her and the child.

The three Askari were running in towards the bungalow now, sparks and fire smeared back from the torches they carried. In turn each man checked his run, poised himself like a javelin thrower, then hurled his torch in a high, smoking arc towards the bungalow. Rosa heard them thump, thump, thump, on to the thatched roof above her.

'I must get my baby away, before the fire catches,' and she hurried across the room, out into the passage. It was dark here and she groped along the wall until she found the entrance to the main room. At the front door she fumbled with the bolts, and opened it a crack. Peering through to the fire-lit lawns beyond the stoep, she saw the dark forms of Askari waiting there also, and she drew back.

'The side windows of the kitchen,' she told herself. 'They're closest to the bush. That's the best chance,' and she stumbled back into the passage.

Above her now there was a sound like high wind and water, a rushing sound blending with the crackle of burning thatch, and the first taint of smoke stung her nostrils.

'If only I can reach the bush,' she whispered desperately, and the child in her arms began to cry.

'Hush, my darling, hush now,' but her voice was scratchy with fear. Maria seemed to sense it; her petulant whimperings changed to lusty high-pitched yells and she struggled in Rosa's grasp.

From the side windows of the kitchen Rosa saw the familiar waiting figures of the Askari hovering at the edge of the firelight. She felt despair catch her stomach in a cold grip and squeeze the resolve from her. Suddenly her legs were weak under her and her whole body was shaking.

From within the bungalow behind her there came a thunderous roar as part of the burning roof collapsed. A blast of scalding air blew through the kitchen and the tall column of sparks and flames thrown up by the collapse lit the surroundings even more vividly. It showed another figure beyond the line of Askari, scampering in from the edge of the bush like a little black monkey, and Rosa heard Nanny's voice.

'Little Long Hair! Little Long Hair.' A plaintive, ancient wail.

Nanny had escaped into the bush during the first minutes of the attack. She had lain there watching until the roof of the bungalow fell in – then she could no longer contain herself. Insensible of her own danger, caring for nothing except her precious charges, she was coming back.

The Askari saw her also. Their rigid, well-spaced line crumpled as all of them ran to head her off. Suddenly the ground between Rosa and the edge of the bush was clear. Now there was a chance – just the smallest chance that she could get the child away. She flung the window open and dropped through it to the earth.

One moment she hesitated and glanced towards the confusion of running men away on her right hand. In that moment she saw one of the Askari catch up with the old woman and lunge forward with his bayonet. Nanny reeled from the force of the blow in her back. Involuntarily her arms were flung wide open, and for a fleeting second Rosa saw the point of the bayonet appear miraculously from the centre of her chest, as it impaled her.

Then Rosa was running towards the wall of bush and scrub fifty yards ahead of her, while Maria howled in her arms. The sound attracted the attention of the Askari. One of them shouted a warning, and then the whole pack was after her in full tongue.

Rosa's senses were overwrought by her terror, so finely tuned that it seemed the passage of time was lagging. Weighed down by the child, each pace she took dragged on for ever, as though she waded through waist-deep water. The long night-dress around her legs hampered her, and there was rough stone and thorn beneath her bare feet. The wall of bush ahead of her seemed to come no closer, and she ran with the cold hand of fear squeezing her chest and cramping her breathing.

Then into her line of vision from the side came a man, an Askari, a big man bounding towards her with the long loping gallop of a bull baboon, cutting across her line of flight, his open mouth, an obscene pink pit in the shiny black of his face.

Rosa screamed and swung away from him. Now she was running parallel to the edge of the bush and behind her she heard the slap of feet upon the earth, closing fast, and the babbling chorus of the pursuit.

A hand snatched at her shoulder, and she twisted away from it, feeling the stuff of her night-gown tear beneath the clutching fingers.

Blind with terror she stumbled a dozen paces back towards the burning homestead. She felt the vast waves of heat from it in her face and through her thin clothing – and then a rifle butt struck her in the small of the back, and a bright burst of agony paralysed her legs. She dropped to her knees, still holding Maria.

They ringed her in, a palisade of human bodies and gloating, blood-crazed faces.

The big one who had felled her with the rifle butt stooped over her and before she recognized his intention, he had snatched Maria from her arms and stepped back again.

He stood laughing, holding the child by her ankles, letting her swing head downwards, so her tiny face was suffused with blood, scarlet in the light of the flames.

'No, please, no!' Rosa crawled painfully towards the man. 'Give her back to me. My baby. Please give her back,' and she lifted her arms towards him.

The Askari dangled the child tantalizingly in front of her, retreating slowly as she crawled towards him. The others were laughing, hoarse sensual laughter, crowding around her, faces contorted with enjoyment, and polished ebony black with the sweat of excitement, as they jostled each other for a better view of the sport.

Then with a wild yell, the Askari swung Maria high, whirled her twice above his head as he pivoted to face the bungalow – and threw Maria up towards the burning roof.

The tiny body flew with the looseness of a rag doll through the air, her night-dress fluttered as she dropped and struck the roof, rolled awkwardly down the slope of it with her clothing blooming into instant flame, until she reached a weak spot in the burning thatch. It sucked Maria in like a fiery mouth and blew a belch of sparks as it swallowed her. At that instant Rosa heard the voice of her child for the last time. It was a sound she was never to forget.

For a moment the men about her were hushed, and then as though wind blew through trees, they moved a little with a sound that was half sigh, half moan.

Still kneeling, facing the burning building which was now a pyre, Rosa slumped forward and lifted her hands to cover her face as though in prayer.

The Askari who had thrown the child snatched up his rifle from where it lay at his feet and stood over her. He lifted it above his head the way a harpooner holds his steel with the point of the bayonet aimed at the base of Rosa's neck where her hair had fallen open to expose the pale skin.

In the moment that the Askari paused to take his aim, Herman Fleischer shot him in the back of the head with the Luger.

'Mad dog!' the Commissioner shouted at the Askari's corpse. 'I told you to take them alive.'

Then, breathing like an asthma case from the exertion of his run to intervene, he turned to Rosa.

'Fräulein, my apologies,' he doffed the slouch hat with ponderous courtesy, and spoke in German that Rosa did not understand. 'We do not make war on women and babies.'

She did not look up at him. She was crying quietly into her cupped hands.

39

'Early in the year for a bush fire,' Flynn muttered. He sat with an enamel mug cupped in his hands and blew steam from the hot coffee. His blanket had slid down to his waist.

Across the camp-fire from him Sebastian was also sitting in a muddle of bedding, and cooling his own pre-dawn mug of coffee. At Flynn's words he looked up from his labour, and out into the dark south.

False dawn had paled the sky just enough to define the hills below it as an undulating mass that seemed much closer than it was. That way lay Lalapanzi – and Rosa and Maria.

Without real interest Sebastian saw the radiated glow at one point along the spine of the ridge; a fan of pink light no larger than a thumb-nail.

'Not a very big one,' he said.

'No,' agreed Flynn. 'Hope she doesn't spread though,' and he gulped noisily at his mug.

As Sebastian watched it idly, the glow diminished, shrinking into insignificance at the coming of the sun, and above it the stars paled out also.

'We'd best get moving. It's a long day's march and we've wasted enough time on this trip already.'

'You're a regular bloody fire-eater when it comes to getting your home comforts.' Flynn feigned disinterest, yet secretly the thought of returning to his granddaughter had strong appeal. He hurried the coffee a little and scalded his tongue.

Sebastian was right. They had wasted a lot of time on the return trip from the Mahenge raid.

First, there was a detour to avoid a party of German Askari that one of the native headmen had warned them was at M'topo's village. They had trekked upstream for three days before finding a safe crossing, and a village willing to hire canoes.

Then there was the brush with the hippo which had cost them

almost a week. As was usual practice, the four hired canoes, loaded to within a few inches of free-board with Flynn, Sebastian, their retinue and loot, had slipped across the Rovuma and were hugging the Portuguese bank as they headed downstream towards the landing opposite M'topo's village when the hippo had disputed their passage.

She was an old cow hippo who a few hours earlier had given birth to her calf in a tiny island of reeds, separated from the south bank by twenty feet of lily-padded water. When the four canoes entered this channel in line astern with the paddlers chanting happily, she took it as a direct threat to her offspring and she threw a tantrum.

Two tons of hippo in a tantrum has the destructive force of a localized hurricane. Surfacing violently from under the leading canoe, she had thrown Sebastian, two gun-boys, four paddlers, and all their equipment, ten feet in the air. The canoe, rotted with beetle, had snapped in half and sunk immediately.

The mother hippo had then treated the three following canoes with the same consideration, and within the space of a few minutes, the canal was clogged with floating debris, and struggling, panic-stricken men. Fortunately they were no more than ten feet from the bank. Sebastian was first ashore. None of them, however, was very far behind him, and they all took off like the start of a cross-country race over the veld, when the hippo emerged from the river and signified that, not satisfied with wrecking the flotilla, she intended chopping a few of them in half with her guillotine jaws.

A hundred yards later she abandoned the pursuit, and trotted back to the water, wiggling her little ears and snorting in triumph. Half a mile farther on the survivors had stopped running.

They camped there that night without food, bedding or weapons, and the following morning, after a heated council of war, Sebastian was elected to return to the river and ascertain whether the hippo was still in control of the channel. He came back at high speed to report that she was.

Three more days they waited for the hippo and her calf to move away. During this time they suffered the miseries of cold nights and hungry days, but the greatest misery was inflicted on Flynn O'Flynn whose case of gin was under eight feet of water – and by the third morning he was threatening *delirium tremens* again. Just before Sebastian set off for his morning reconnaissance of the channel, Flynn informed him agitatedly that there were three blue scorpions sitting on his head. After the initial alarm, Sebastian went through the motions of removing the imaginary scorpions and stamping them to death, and Flynn was satisfied.

Sebastian returned from the river with the news that the hippo and her calf had evacuated the island, and it was now possible to begin salvage operations.

Protesting mildly and talking about crocodiles, Sebastian was stripped naked and coaxed into the water. On his first dive, he retrieved the precious case of gin.

'Bless you, my boy,' Flynn murmured fervently as he eased the cork out of a bottle.

By the following morning Sebastian had recovered nearly all their equipment and booty, without being eaten by crocodiles, and they set off for Lalapanzi on foot.

Now they were in their last camp before Lalapanzi, and Sebastian felt his impatience rising. He wanted to get home to Rosa and baby Maria. He should be home by evening.

'Come on, Flynn. Let's go.' He flicked the coffee grounds from his mug, threw aside his blanket, and shouted to Mohammed and the bearers who were huddled around the other fire.

'Safari! Let us march.'

Nine hours later, with the daylight dying around him, he breasted the last rise and paused at the top.

All that day eagerness had lengthened his stride, and he had left Flynn and the column of heavily laden bearers far behind.

Now he stood alone, and stared without comprehension at the smoke-blackened ruins of Lalapanzi from which a few thin tendrils of smoke still drifted.

'Rosa!' Her name was a harsh bellow of fear, and he ran wildly.

'Rosa!' he shouted as he crossed the scorched and trampled lawns.

'Rosa! Rosa! Rosa!' the echo from the kopje above the homestead shouted back.

'Rosa!' He saw something amongst the bushes at the edge of the lawn, and he ran to it. Old Nanny lying dead with the blood dried black on the floral stuff of her night-gown.

'Rosa!' He ran back towards the bungalow. The ash swirled in a warm mist around his legs as he crossed the stoep.

'Rosa!' His voice rang hollowly through the roofless shell of the house, as he stumbled over the fallen beams that littered the main room. The reek of burned cloth and hair and wood almost choked him, so that his voice was husky as he called again.

'Rosa!'

He found her in the burnt-out kitchen block and he thought she was dead. She was slumped against the cracked and blackened wall. Her night-gown was torn and scorched, and the snarled skeins of hair, that hid her face, were powdered with white wood ash.

'My darling. Oh, my darling.' He knelt beside her, and timidly touched her shoulder. Her flesh was warm and alive beneath his fingers, and he felt relief leap up into his throat, blocking it so he could not speak again. Instead, he brushed the tangle of hair from her face and looked at it.

Beneath the charcoal smears of dirt her skin was pale as grey marble. Her eyes, tight closed, were heavily underscored with blue, and rimmed with crusty red.

He touched her lips with the tips of his fingers, and she opened her eyes, But they looked beyond him; unseeing, dead eyes. They frightened him. He did not want to look into them, and he drew her head towards his shoulder.

There was no resistance in her. She lay against him quietly, and he pressed his face into her hair. Her hair was impregnated with the smell of smoke.

'Are you hurt?' he asked her in a whisper, not wanting to hear the answer. But she made no answer, lying inert in his arms.

'Tell me, Rosa. Speak to me. Where is Maria?'

At the mention of the child's name, she reacted for the first time. She began to tremble.

'Where is she?' more urgency in his voice now.

She rolled her head against his shoulder and looked across the floor of the room. He followed the direction of her gaze.

Near the far wall an area of the floor had been swept clear of debris and ash. Rosa had done it with her bare hands while the ash was still hot. Her fingers were blistered and burned raw in places, and her arms were black to the elbows. Lying in the centre of this cleared space was a small, charred thing.

'Maria?' Sebastian whispered, and Rosa shuddered against him.

'Oh, God,' he said, and lifted Rosa. Carrying her against his chest, he staggered from the ruins of the bungalow out into the cool, sweet evening air, but in his nostrils lingered the smell of smoke and burned flesh. He wanted to escape from it. He ran blindly along the path and Rosa lay unresisting in his arms.

The following day Flynn buried their dead on the kopje above Lalapanzi. He placed a thick slab of granite over the small grave that stood apart from the others, and when it was done he sent a bearer to the camp to fetch Rosa and Sebastian.

When they came, they found him standing alone by Maria's grave under the marula trees. His face was puffy and purply red. The thinning grey hair hung limply over his ears and forehead, like the wet feathers of an old rooster. His body looked as though it was melting. It sagged at the shoulders and the belly. Sweat had soaked through his clothing across the shoulders, and at the armpits and crotch. He was sick with drink and sorrow.

Sebastian stood beside Rosa, and the three of them took their silent farewell of the child.

'There is nothing else to do now,' Sebastian spoke huskily.

'Yes,' said Flynn. He stooped slowly and took a handful of the new earth from the grave. 'Yes, there is.' He crumbled the earth between his fingers. 'We still have to find the man who did this – and kill him.'

Beside Sebastian, Rosa straightened up. She turned to Sebastian, lifted her chin, and spoke for the first time since he had come home.

'Kill him!' she repeated softly.

Part 2

41

With his hands clasped behind his back, and his chin thrust forward aggressively, Rear-Admiral Sir Percy Howe sucked in his lower lip and nibbled it reflectively. 'What was our last substantiated sighting on *Blücher*?' he asked at last.

'A month ago, sir. Two days before the outbreak of war. Sighting reported by *S.S. Tygerberg*. Latitude 0°27'N. Longitude 52°16'E. Headed south-west; estimated speed, eighteen knots.'

'And a hell of a lot of good that does us,' Sir Percy interrupted his flag-captain and glared at the vast Admiralty plot of the Indian Ocean. 'She could be back in Bremerhaven by now.'

'She could be, sir,' the flag-captain nodded, and Sir Percy glanced at him and permitted himself a wintry smile.

'But you don't believe that, do you, Henry?'

'No, sir, I don't. During the last thirty days, eight merchantmen have disappeared between Aden and Lourenco Marques. Nearly a quarter of a million tons of shipping. That's the *Blücher*'s work.'

'Yes, it's the *Blücher*, all right,' agreed the Admiral, and reached across the plot to pick up the black counter labelled '*Blücher*', that lay on the wide green expanse of the Indian Ocean.

A respectful silence held the personnel of the plotting room South Atlantic and Indian Oceans while they waited for the great man to reach his decision. It was a long time coming. He stood bouncing the '*Blücher*' in the palm of his right hand, his grey eyebrows erect like the spines of a hedgehog's back, as his forehead creased in thought. A full minute they waited.

'Refresh my memory of her class and commission.' Like most successful men Sir Percy would not hurry a decision when there was time to think, and the duty lieutenant who had anticipated his request, stepped forward with the German Imperial Navy list open at the correct page.

' "*Blücher*. Commissioned August 16, 1905. 'B' Class heavy cruiser. Main armament, eight nine-inch guns. Secondary armament, six six-inch guns." '

The lieutenant finished his reading and waited quietly.

'Who is her captain?' Sir Percy asked, and the lieutenant consulted an addendum to the list.

' "Otto von Kleine (Count). Previously commanded the light cruiser *Sturm Vogel*." '

'Yes,' said Sir Percy. 'I've heard of him,' and he replaced the counter on the plot, keeping his hand on it. 'A dangerous man to have here, south of Suez,' and he pushed the counter up towards the Red Sea and the entrance to the canal, where the tiny red shipping lanes amalgamated into a thick artery, ' – or here,' and he pushed it down towards the Cape of Good Hope, around which were curved the same red threads that joined London to Australia and India. Sir Percy lifted his hand from the black counter and left it sitting menacingly upon the shipping lanes.

'What force have we deployed against him so far?' and in answer the flag-captain picked up a wooden pointer and touched in turn the red counters that were scattered about the Indian Ocean.

'*Pegasus* and *Renounce* in the north. *Eagle* and *Plunger* sweeping the southern waters, sir.'

'What further force can we spare, Henry?'

'Well, sir, *Orion* and *Bloodhound* are at Simonstown,' and he touched the nose of the African continent with the pointer.

'*Orion* – that's Manderson, isn't it?'

'Yes, sir.'

'And who has *Bloodhound*?'

'Little, sir.'

'Good,' Sir Percy nodded with satisfaction. 'A six-inch cruiser and a destroyer should be able to deal with *Blücher*', and he smiled again. 'Especially with a hellion like Charles Little handling the *Bloodhound*. I played golf with him last summer – he damn nigh drove the sixteenth green at St Andrews!'

The flag-captain glanced at the Admiral and, on the strength of the destroyer captain's reputation, decided to permit himself an inanity. 'The young ladies of Cape Town will mourn his departure, sir.'

'We must hope that Kapitän zur See Otto von Kleine will mourn his arrival,' chuckled Sir Percy.

'Daddy likes you very much.'

'Your father is a man of exquisite good taste,' Commander the Honourable Charles Little conceded gallantly, and rolled his head to smile at the young lady who lay beside him on a rug, in the dappled shade beneath the pine trees.

'Can't you ever be serious?'

'Helen, my sweet, at times I can be deadly serious.'

'Oh, you!' and his companion blushed prettily as she remembered certain of Charles's recent actions, which would make her father hastily revise his judgement.

'I value your father's good opinion, but my chief concern is that you endorse it.'

The girl sat up slowly and while she stared at him her hands were busy, brushing the pine needles from the glorious tangle of her hair, readjusting the fastenings of her blouse, spreading the skirts of her riding-habit to cover sweet legs clad in dark, tall polished leather boots.

She stared at Charles Little and ached with the strength of her want. It was not a sensual need she felt, but an over-powering obsession to have this man as her very own. To own him in the same way as she already owned diamonds, and furs, and silk, and horses, and peacocks, and other beautiful things.

His body sprawled out on the rug with all the unconscious grace of a reclining leopard. A secret little smile tugged at the corners of his lips and his eyelids drooped to mask the sparkle of his eyes. His recent exertions had dampened the hair that flopped forward onto his forehead.

There was something satanical about him, an air of wickedness, and Helen decided it was the slant of the eyebrows and the way his ears lay flat against his temples, but were pointed like those of a satyr, yet they were pink and smooth as those of an infant.

'I think you have devil's ears,' she said, and then she blushed again, and scrambled to her feet avoiding Charles' arm that reached out for her. 'Enough of that!' she giggled and ran to the thoroughbred hunter that was tied near them in the forest. 'Come on,' she called as she mounted.

Charles stood up lazily and stretched. He tucked the tail of his shirt into his breeches, folded the rug on which they had lain, and went to his own horse.

At the edge of the pine forest, they checked their mounts and sat looking down over the Constantia valley.

'Isn't it beautiful?' she said.

'It is indeed,' he agreed.

'I meant the view.'

'And so did I.' Twice in the six days he had known her, she had led him up this mountain and subjected him to the temptation. Below them lay six thousand acres of the richest land in all of Africa.

'When my brother Hubert was killed there was no one left to carry it on. Just my sister and I – and we are only girls. Poor Daddy isn't so well any more – he finds it such a strain.'

Charles let his eyes move lazily from the great squat buttress of Table Mountain on their left, across the lush basin of vine-yards below them, and then on to where the glittering wedge of False Bay drove into the mountains.

'Doesn't the homestead look lovely from here?' Helen drew his attention to the massive Dutch-gabled residence with its attendant outbuildings, grouped in servility behind it.

'I am truly impressed by the magnificence of the stud fee,' Charles murmured, purposefully slurring the last two words, and the girl glanced at him in surprise, beginning to bridle.

'I beg your pardon?'

'It is truly magnificent scenery,' he amended. Her persistent efforts at ensnaring him were beginning to bore Charles. He had teased and avoided more artful huntresses.

'Charles,' she whispered. 'How would you like to live here. I mean, forever?'

And Charles was shocked. This little provincial had no under-standing whatsoever of the rules governing the game of flir-tation. He was so shocked that he threw back his head and laughed.

When Charles laughed it sent shivers of delight through every woman within a hundred yards. It was a merry sound with underlying tones of sensuality. His teeth were very white against the sea-tan of his face, and the muscles of his chest and upper arms tensed into bold relief beneath the silk shirt he wore.

Helen was the only witness of this particular performance, and she was helpless as a sparrow in a hurricane. Eagerly she leaned across the space between their horses and touched his arm. 'You would like it, Charles. Wouldn't you?'

She did not know that Charles Little had a private income of twenty thousand pounds a year, that when his father died he would inherit the title Viscount Sutherton and the estates that went with it. She did not know that one of those estates would swallow her father's own three times over; nor did she know that Charles had passed by willing young ladies with twice her looks, ten times her fortune, and a hundred times her breeding.

'You would, Charles. I know you would!'

So young, so vulnerable, that he stopped the flippant reply before it reached his lips.

'Helen,' he took her hand. 'I am a sea creature. We move with the wind and the waves,' and he lifted her hand to his lips.

A while she sat, feeling the warm pressure of his lips upon her flesh, and the burn of tears behind her eyes. Then she snatched her hand away, and wheeled her horse. She lifted the leather riding-crop and slashed the glossy black shoulder between her knees. Startled, the stallion jumped forward into a dead run back along the road towards the Constantia valley.

Charles shook his head and grimaced with regret. He had not meant to hurt her. It had been an escapade, something to fill the waiting days while *Bloodhound* went through the final stages of her refit. But Charles had learned to harden himself to the ending of his adventures – to the tears and tragedy.

'Shame on you, you heartless cad,' he said aloud, and touching his mount with his heels ambled in pursuit of the galloping stallion.

He caught up with the stallion in the stable yards. A groom was walking it, and there were darker sweat patches on its coat, and the barrel of its chest still heaved with laboured breathing.

Helen was nowhere in sight, but her father stood at the stable gates – a big man, with a square-cut black beard picked out with grey.

'Enjoy your ride?'

'Thank you, Mr Uys.' Charles was noncommittal, and the older man glanced significantly at the blown stallion before going on.

'There's one of your sailors been waiting for you for an hour.'

'Where is he?' Charles's manner altered abruptly, became instantly businesslike.

'Here, sir.' From the deep shade of the stable doorway, a young seaman stepped out into the bright sunlight.

'What is it, man?' Impatiently Charles acknowledged his salute.

'Captain Manderson's compliments, sir, and you're to report aboard H.M.S. *Orion* with all possible speed. There's a motor car waiting to take you to the base, sir.'

'An untimely summons, Commander.' Uys gave his opinion lounging against the worked stone gateway. 'I fear we will see no more of you for a long time.'

But Charles was not listening. His body seemed to quiver with suppressed excitement, the way a good gun-dog reacts to the scent of the bird. 'Sailing orders,' he whispered, ' — at last. At last!'

There was a heavy south-east swell battering Cape Point, so the sea spray wreathed the beam of the lighthouse on the cliffs above. A flight of malgas came in so high towards the land that they caught the last of the sun, and glowed pink above the dark water.

Bloodhound cleared Cape Hangklip and took the press of the South Atlantic on her shoulder, staggered from it with a welter of white water running waist-deep past her foredeck gun-turrets. Then in retaliation she hurled herself at the next swell, and Charles Little on her bridge exulted at the vital movement of the deck beneath his feet.

'Bring her round to oh-five-oh.'

'Oh-five-oh, sir,' repeated his navigating lieutenant.

'Revolutions for seventeen knots, pilot.'

Almost immediately the beat of the engines changed, and her action through the water became more abandoned.

Charles crossed to the angle of the flimsy little bridge and looked back into the dark, mountain-lined maw of False Bay. Two miles astern the shape of H.M.S. *Orion* melted into the dying light.

'Come along, old girl. Do try and keep up,' murmured Charles Little with the scorn that a destroyer man feels for any vessel that cannot cruise at twenty knots. Then he looked beyond *Orion* at the land. Below the massif of Table Mountain, near the head of the Constantia valley a single pin prick of light showed.

'There'll be fog tonight, sir,' the pilot spoke at Charles's elbow, and Charles turned without regret to peer over the bows into the gathering night.

'Yes, a good night for pirates.'

42

The fog condensed on the gray metal of the bridge, so the foot-plates were slippery underfoot. It soaked into the overcoats of the men huddled against the rail, and it dewed in minute pearls on the eyebrows and the beard of Kapitän zur See Otto von Kleine. It gave him an air of derring-do, the reckless look of a scholarly pirate.

Every few seconds Lieutenant Kyller glanced anxiously at his captain, wondering when the order to turn would come. He hated this business of creeping inshore in the fog, with a flood tide pushing them towards a hostile coast.

'Stop all engines,' said von Kleine, and Kyller repeated the order to the helm with alacrity. The muted throbbing died beneath their feet, and afterwards the fog-blanketed air was heavy with a sepulchral hush.

'Ask masthead what he makes of the land.' Von Kleine spoke without turning his head, and after a pause Kyller reported back.

'Masthead is in the fog. No visibility,' he paused. 'Foredeck reports fifty fathoms shoaling rapidly.'

And von Kleine nodded. The sounding tended to confirm his estimate that they were sitting five miles off the breakwater of Durban harbour. When the morning wind swept the fog aside he hoped to see the low coastal hills of Natal ahead of him, terraced with gardens and whitewashed buildings – but most of all he hoped to see at least six British merchantmen anchored off the beach waiting their turn to enter the congested harbour, plump and sleepy under the protection of the shore batteries; unaware just how feeble was the protection afforded by half a dozen obsolete ten-pounders manned by old men and boys of the militia.

German naval intelligence had submitted a very detailed report of the defences and conditions prevailing in Durban. After careful perusal of this report, von Kleine had decided that he could trade certain betrayal of his exact position to the English for such a rich prize. There was little actual risk involved. One pass across the entrance of the harbour at high speed, a single broadside for each of the anchored merchantmen, and he could be over the horizon again before the shore gunners had loaded their weapons.

The risk, of course, was in showing *Blücher* to the entire population of Durban city and thereby supplying the Royal Navy with its first accurate sighting since the declaration of war. Within minutes of his first broadside, the British squadrons, which were hunting him, would be racing in from all directions to block each of his escape routes. He hoped to counter this by swinging away towards the south, down into that watery wilderness of wind and ice below latitude 40°, to the rendezvous with *Esther*, his supply ship. Then on to Australia or South America, as the opportunity arose.

He turned to glance at the chronometer above the ship's compass. Sunrise in three minutes, then they could expect the morning wind.

'Masthead reports the fog dispersing, sir.'

Von Kleine aroused himself, and looked out into the fog banks. They were moving now, twisting upon themselves in agitation at the warmth of the sun. 'All engines slow ahead together,' he said.

'Masthead,' warbled one of the voice-pipes in the battery in front of Kyller. 'Land bearing green four-oh. Range, ten thousand metres. A big headland.'

That would be the bluff above Durban, that massive whale-backed mountain that sheltered the harbour. But in the fog von Kleine had misjudged his approach; he was twice as far from the shore as he had intended.

'All engines full ahead together. New course. Oh-oh-six.' He waited for the order to be relayed to the helm before strolling across to the voice-pipes. 'Guns. Captain.'

'Guns,' the voice from far away acknowledged.

'I will be opening fire with high explosives in about ten minutes. The target will be massed merchant shipping on an approximate mark of three hundred degrees. Range, five thousand metres. You may fire as soon as you bear.'

'Mark three hundred degrees. Range, five thousand metres. Sir,' repeated the pipe, and von Kleine snapped the voice-tube cover shut and returned to his original position, facing forward with his hands clasped loosely behind his back.

Below him the gun-turrets revolved ponderously and the long barrels lifted slightly, pointing out into the mist with impassive menace.

A burst of dazzling sunshine struck the bridge so fiercely that Kyller lifted his hand to shield his eyes, but it was gone instantly as the *Blücher* dashed into another clammy cold bank of fog. Then as though they had passed through a curtain on to a brilliantly lit stage, they came out into a gay summer's morning.

Behind them the fog rolled away in a sodden grey wall from horizon to horizon. Ahead rose the green hills of Africa, rimmed with white beach and surf and speckled with thousands of whiter flecks that were the buildings of Durban town. The scaffolding of the cranes along the harbour wall looked like derelict sets of gallows.

Humped on the smooth green mirror of water between them and the shore, lay four ungainly shapes looking like a troop of basking hippo. The British merchantmen.

'Four only,' muttered von Kleine in chagrin. 'I had hoped for more.'

The forty-foot barrels of the nine-inch guns moved restlessly, seeming to sniff for their prey, and the *Blücher* raced on, lifting a hissing white wave at her bows, vibrating and shuddering to the thrust of her engines as they built up to full speed.

'Masthead,' the voice-tube beside Kyller squawked urgently.

'Bridge,' said Kyller but the reply was lost in the deafening detonation of the first broadside, the long thunderous roll of heavy gun-fire. He jumped involuntarily, taken unawares, and then quickly lifted the binoculars from his chest to train them on the British merchantmen.

All attention, every eye on the bridge was concentrated ahead, waiting for the fall of shot upon the doomed vessels.

In the comparative silence that followed the bellow of the broadside, a shriek from the masthead voice-pipe carried clearly.

'Warships! Enemy warships dead astern!'

'Starboard ten.' Von Kleine raised his voice a little louder than was his wont, and still under full power, *Blücher* swerved away from the land, leaning out from the turn, with her wake curved like an ostrich plume on the surface of the sea behind her, and ran for the shelter of the fog banks, leaving the rich prize of cargo shipping unscathed. On her bridge von Kleine and his officers were staring aft, the merchantmen forgotten as they searched for this new threat.

'Two warships.' The masthead look-out was elaborating his sighting report. 'A destroyer and a cruiser. Bearing ninety degrees. Range, five-oh-seven-oh. Destroyer leading.'

In the spherical field of von Kleine's binoculars the neat little triangle of the leading destroyer's superstructure popped up above the horizon. The cruiser was not yet in sight from the bridge.

'If they'd been an hour later,' lamented Kyller, 'we'd have finished the business and...'

'What does masthead see of the cruiser?' von Kleine interrupted him impatiently. He had no time to mourn this chance of fate – his only concern was to evaluate the force that was pursuing him, and then make the decision whether to run, or to turn back and engage them immediately.

'Cruiser is a medium, six or nine-inch. Either "O" class, or an "R". She's four miles behind her escort. Both ships still out of range.'

The destroyer was of no consequence; he could run down on her and blast her into a burning wreck, before her feeble little 4.7-inch guns were able to drop a shell within a mile of *Blücher*, but the cruiser was another matter entirely. To tackle her, *Blücher* would be engaging with her own class; victory would only be won after a severe mauling, and she was six thousand miles from the nearest friendly port where she could effect major repairs.

There was a further consideration. These two British ships might be the vanguard of a battle squadron. If he turned now and challenged action, engaged the cruiser in a single ship action, he might suddenly find himself pitted against imponderable odds. There could very well be another cruiser, or two, or three – even a battleship, below the southern horizon.

His duty and his orders dictated instant flight, avoiding action, and so prolonging *Blücher*'s fighting life.

'Enemy are streaming their colours, sir,' Kyller reported.

Von Kleine lifted his binoculars again. At the destroyer's masthead flew the tiny spots of white and red. This time he must leave the challenge to combat unanswered. 'Very well,' he said, and turned away to his stool in the corner of the bridge. He slumped into it and hunched his shoulders in thought. There were many interesting problems to occupy him, not least of them was how long he could run at full speed towards the north while his boilers devoured coal ravenously, and each minute widened the gap between *Blücher* and *Esther*.

He swivelled his stool and looked back over his stern. The destroyer was visible to the unaided eye now, and von Kleine frowned at it in irritation. She would yap at his heels like a terrier, clinging to him and shouting his course and speed across the ether to the hungry British squadrons, that must even now be closing with him from every direction. For days now he could expect to see her sitting in his wake.

43

'Come on! Come on!' Charles Little slapped his hand impatiently against the padded arm of his stool as he watched *Orion*.

For a night and a day he had watched her gaining on *Blücher* but so infinitesimally slowly that it required his range finder to confirm the gain every thirty minutes.

Orion's bows were unnaturally high, and the waves she lifted with the passage of her hull through the water were the white wings of a seagull in the tropical sunlight; for Manderson, her captain, had pumped out her forward fresh-water tanks and fired away half the shell and explosive propellent from her forward magazines. Every man whose presence in the front half of the ship was not essential to her operation had been ordered aft to stand on the open deck as human ballast – all this in an effort to lift *Orion*'s bows and to coax another inch of speed from the cruiser.

Now she faced the most dangerous hour of her life, for she was creeping within extreme range of *Blücher*'s terrible nine-inch armament, and, taking into account the discrepancy in their speeds, it would be another hour before she could bring her own six-inch guns to bear. During that time she would be under fire from *Blücher*'s after turrets and would have no answer to them.

It was heart-breaking for Charles to watch the chase, for *Bloodhound* had not once been asked to extend herself. Below there was a reserve of speed that would allow her to close with *Blücher* in fifty minutes of steaming – always provided she was not smashed into a fiery shambles long before.

Thus the three vessels fled towards the ever-receding northern horizon. The two long shapes of the cruisers flying arrow straight, solid columns of reeking smoke pouring from the triple funnels to besmear the gay, glittering surface of the sea with a long double bank of black that dispersed only slowly on the easterly breeze; while, like a water beetle, the diminutive *Bloodhound* circled out to the side of *Blücher* from where, when the time came, she could spot the fall of *Orion*'s shells more accurately and signal the corrections to her. But always *Bloodhound* tactfully kept outside the fifteen mile radius which marked the length of *Blücher*'s talons.

'We can expect *Blücher* to open fire at any moment now, sir,' the navigating lieutenant commented as he straightened up from the sextant, over which he had been measuring the angle subtended by the two cruisers.

Charles nodded in agreement. 'Yes. Von Kleine must try for a few lucky hits, even at that range.'

'This isn't going to be very pretty to watch.'

'We'll just have to sit tight, keep our fingers crossed, and hope old *Orion* can – ' He stopped abruptly, and then jumped up from his stool. 'Hello! *Blücher*'s up to something!'

The silhouette of the German cruiser had altered drastically in the last few seconds. The gap between her funnels widened and now Charles could see the humped menace of her forward turrets.

'By God, she's altering course! The bloody bastard is bringing all his turrets to bear!'

Lieutenant Kyller studied his captain's face. In sleep there was an air of serenity about the man. It reminded Kyller of a painting he had seen in the cathedral at Nürnberg, a portrait of Saint Luke by Holbein. The same fine bone structure, the golden blond beard and moustache that framed the mobile and sensitive lips. He pushed the idea aside and leaned forward. Gently he touched von Kleine's shoulder.

'Captain. My Captain,' and von Kleine opened his eyes. They were smoky blue with sleep but his voice was crisp.

'What is it, Kyller?'

'The gunnery officer reports the enemy will be within range in fifteen minutes.'

Von Kleine swivelled his stool and looked quickly about his ship. Above him the smoke poured from every funnel, and from the mouth of each stack a volcano of sparks and shimmering heat blew steadily. The paint had blistered and peeled from the metal of the funnels and they glowed red hot, even in the sunlight. *Blücher* was straining herself far beyond the limits her makers had set. God alone knew what injury this constant running at full speed was doing her, and von Kleine winced as he felt her tremble in protest beneath him.

He turned his eyes astern. The British cruiser was hull up on the horizon now. The difference in their speeds must be a small fraction of a knot, but *Blücher*'s superiority in fire power was enormous.

For a moment he allowed himself to ponder the arrogance of a nation that constantly, almost by choice, matched their men and ships against unnatural odds. Always they sent terriers to fight against wolfhounds. Then he smiled, you had to be English or mad, to understand the English.

He glanced out to starboard. The British destroyer had worked out on to his flank. It could do little harm from there.

'Very well, Kyller . . .' He stood as he spoke.

'Bridge – Engine Room,' the voice-tube squealed.

'Engine Room – Bridge.' Kyller turned to it.

'Our port main bearing is running red hot. I must shut down our port engine!'

The words struck von Kleine like a bucket of iced water thrown down his back. He leaped to the voice-tube.

'This is the Captain. I must have full power for another hour!'

'I can't do it, sir. Another fifteen minutes and the main drive shaft will seize up. God knows what damage it will do.'

For five seconds von Kleine hunched silently over the voice-tube. His mind raced. On one engine *Blücher* would lose ten knots on her speed. The enemy would be able to manoeuvre about him freely – possibly hold off until nightfall and then. . . . He must attack immediately; turn on them and press his attack home with all his armament.

'Give me full power for as long as you can,' he snapped, and then turning to the gunnery officer's tube. 'This is the Captain. I am turning four points to starboard, and will keep the enemy directly on our starboard beam for the next fifteen minutes. After that I will be forced to reduce speed. Open fire when you bear.' Von Kleine snapped the cover closed and turned to his yeoman of signals. 'Hoist the battle ensign!'

He spoke softly, without heat, but there were lights in his eyes like those in a blue sapphire.

44

'There she goes!' whispered Charles Little without lowering his glasses. Upon the black turrets of *Blücher* the gun-fire gleamed and sparkled without sound. Quickly he traversed his glasses across the surface of the sea until he found *Orion*. She was plunging in eagerly, narrowing the gap very rapidly between herself and *Blücher*. In another seven minutes she would be able to return the German's fire.

Suddenly, a quarter of a mile ahead of her, there rose from the sea a series of tall columns, stately as the columns of a Greek temple, slender and beautiful, shining like white marble in the sun. Then slowly they dropped back.

'Short,' grunted the navigating lieutenant.

'Her guns are still cold,' Charles commented. 'Please God let old *Orion* get within range.'

Again *Blücher*'s shells fell short, and short again, but each time they were closer to the low bulk of *Orion*, and the next broadside dropped all around her, partially screening her with spray, and *Orion* started to zigzag.

'Another three minutes,' the navigating lieutenant spoke with tension making his voice husky.

At regular intervals of fifteen seconds the German salvos fell around *Orion* – once within fifty feet of her bows so that as she tore into the standing columns of spray, they blew back over her and mingled with the black smoke of her funnels.

'Come on, old girl! Go in and get her. Go on! Go on!' Charles was gripping the rail in front of him and cheering like a maniac, all the dignity of his rank and his thirty-five years gone in the tense excitement of the battle. It had infected all of them on the bridge of the destroyer, and they capered and shouted with him.

'There she blows!' howled the lieutenant.

'She's opened fire!'

'Go it, *Orion*, go it!'

On *Orion*'s forward turrets gun-fire sparkled, then again and again. The harsh roll of the broadsides carried to them against the light wind.

'Short,' groaned Charles. 'She's still out of range.'

'Short again!'

'Still short.'

Each time the call of shot was signalled by the chief yeoman at the Aldis lamp, and briefly acknowledged from *Orion*'s bridge-works.

'Oh my God,' moaned Charles.

'She's hit!' echoed his lieutenant.

A flat yellow glare, like sheet lightning on a summer's day, lit *Orion*'s afterdeck, and almost immediately a ball of yellowish grey smoke enveloped her. Through it Charles saw her after-funnel sag drunkenly and hang back at an unnatural angle.

'She's holding on!'

Orion emerged from the shell smoke and dragged it after her like a funeral cloak, but her speed seemed unabated, and the regular salvos burned briefly and brightly on her forward turrets.

'Now she's hitting,' exulted the lieutenant, and Charles turned quickly to see shell-fire burst on *Blücher*, and his wide grin split his face.

'Kill her! Kill her!' he roared, knowing that though *Blücher* was better armed yet she was as vulnerable as *Orion*. Her plating was egg-shell thin and the six-inch shells that crashed through it would be doing her terrible damage.

Now the two cruisers were pounding each other. The range was closing so rapidly that soon they must hit with every broadside. This was a contest from which only one ship, or neither of them, would emerge.

Charles was trying to estimate the damage that had been inflicted upon *Blücher* during the last few minutes. She was on fire forward. Sulphur-yellow flames poured from her, her upperworks were riven into a grotesque sculpture of destruction, and a pall of smoke enveloped her, so her profile was shadowy and vague, yet every fifteen seconds her turrets lit with those deadly little flashes.

Charles turned to assess the relative damage that *Orion* had suffered. He found and held her with his binoculars – and at that moment *Orion* ceased to exist.

Her boilers, pierced by high explosive shell, burst and tore her in half. A cloud of white steam spurted five hundred feet into the air, completely blanketing her. The steam hung for thirty seconds then sagged wearily, and rolled aside. *Orion* was gone. A wide circle of oil slick and floating debris marked her grave. The speed of her charge had run her clean under.

On the bridge of *Bloodhound*, the cheering strangled into deathly silence. The silence was not spoiled but rather accentuated by the mournful note of the wind in her rigging and the muted throb of her engines.

45

For eight long hours Charles Little had ridden his anger and his hatred, using the curb to hold it on the right side of madness, resisting the consuming and suicidal urge to hurl his ship at the German cruiser and die as *Orion* had died.

Immediately after the sinking of *Orion*, the *Blücher* had reduced speed sharply and turned due south. With her fires still raging, she had limped along like a gun-shot lion. The battle ensigns at her masthead were tattered by shrapnel and blackened by smoke.

As seen as she had passed, *Bloodhound* altered course and cruised slowly over the area of water that was still rainbowed by floating oil and speckled with wreckage. There were no survivors from *Orion*; all of them had died with her.

Bloodhound turned and trailed after the crippled German cruiser, and the hatred that emanated from the destroyer was of such strength that it should have reached out across the sea as a physical force and destroyed *Blücher*.

But as Charles Little stood at the rail of his bridge, he saw the smoke and flame upon *Blücher*'s decks reduce perceptibly every minute as her damage control teams fought it to a standstill. The last wisp of smoke from her shrivelled.

'Fire's out,' said the pilot, and Charles made no answer. He had hoped that the flames would eat their way into one of *Blücher*'s magazines and blow her into the same oblivion into which she had sent *Orion*.

'But she isn't making more than six knots. *Orion* must have hit her in the engine room.' Hopefully the navigating lieutenant went on, 'My bet is that she's got major damage below. At this speed we can expect *Pegasus* and *Renounce* to catch up with us by midday tomorrow. Then *Blücher* will stand no chance!'

'Yes,' agreed Charles softly.

Summoned by *Bloodhound*'s frantic radio transmissions,

Pegasus and *Renounce*, the two heavy cruisers of the northern squadron, were racing down the East African coast, cutting through the five hundred miles of water that separated them.

46

'Kyller. Ask the chief how he's making out.' Von Kleine was fretting beneath the calm set of his features. Night was closing, and in the darkness, even the frail little English destroyer was a danger to him. There was danger all around, danger must each minute be approaching from every quarter of the sea. He must have power on his port side engine before nightfall; it was a matter of survival; he must have speed to carry him south through the hunting packs of the British – south to where *Esther* waited to give him succour, to replace the shell he had fired away, to replenish his coal bunkers which were now dangerously depleted. Then once more *Blücher* would be a force to reckon with. But first he must have speed.

'Captain.' Kyller was beside him again. 'Commander Lochtkamper reports they have cleared the oil line to the main bearing. They have stripped the bearing and there is no damage to the shaft. He is fitting new half shells. The work is well advanced, sir.'

The words conjured up for von Kleine a picture of half-naked men, smeared to the elbows with black grease, sweating in the confined heat of the drive shaft tunnel as they worked. 'How much longer?' he asked.

'He promised full power on both engines within two hours, sir.'

Von Kleine sighed with relief, and glanced over his stern at the British destroyer that was shadowing him. He began to smile.

'I hope, my friend, that you are a brave man. I hope that when you see me increase speed, you will not be able to control your disappointment. I hope tonight you will try with your torpedoes, so that I can crush you, for your eyes always on me are a dangerous embarrassment.' He spoke so softly that his lips barely moved, then he turned back to Kyller. 'I want all the battle lights checked and reported.'

'Aye, aye, sir.'

Von Kleine crossed to the voice-tubes. 'Gunnery officer,' he said. 'I want "X" turret guns loaded with star shell and trained to maximum elevation . . .' He went on listing his preparations for night action and then he ended, '. . . stand all your gun crews down. Let them eat and rest. From dusk action stations onwards they will be held in the first degree of readiness.'

'Commander, sir!'

The urgent call startled Commander Charles Little, and he spilled his mug of cocoa. This was the first period of rest he had allowed himself all day, and now it was interrupted within ten minutes. 'What is it?' He flung open the door of the chart room, and ran out on to the bridge.

'*Blücher* is increasing speed rapidly.'

'No!' It was too cruel a blow, and the exclamation of protest was wrung from Charles. He darted to the voice-pipe.

'Gunnery officer. Report your target.'

A moment's delay, and then the reply. 'Bearing mark, green oh-oh. Range, one-five-oh-five-oh. Speed, seventeen knots.'

It was true. *Blücher* was under full power again, with all her guns still operable. *Orion* had died in vain.

Charles wiped his mouth with the open palm of his hand, and felt the brittle stubble of his new beard rasp under his fingers. Beneath the tan, his face was sickly pale with strain and fatigue. There were smears of dark blue beneath his eyes, and in their corners were tiny lumps of yellow mucus. His eyes were bloodshot, and the wisp of hair that escaped from under the brim of his cap was matted on to his forehead by the salt spray, as he peered into the gathering dusk.

The fighting madness which had threatened all that day to overwhelm him, rose slowly from the depth of his belly and his loins. He no longer struggled to suppress it.

'Turn two points to starboard, pilot. All engines full ahead together.' The engine telegraph clanged, and *Bloodhound* pivoted like a polo pony. It would take her thirty minutes to work up to full speed, and by that time it would be dark.

'Sound action stations.' Charles wanted to attack in the hour of darkness before the moon came up. Through the ship the alarm bells thrilled, and without taking his eyes from the dark dot on the darkening horizon, Charles listened to the reports coming into the bridge, until the one for which he waited, 'Torpedo party closed up, sir!'

Now he turned and went to the voice-tube. 'Torps,' he said, 'I hope to give you a chance at *Blücher* with both port and starboard tubes. I am going to take you in as close as possible.'

The men grouped around Charles on the bridge listened to him say 'as close as possible', and knew that he had pronounced sentence of death upon them.

Henry Sargent, the navigating lieutenant, was afraid. Stealthily he groped in the pocket of his overcoat until he found the little silver crucifix that Lynette had given him. It was warm from his own body heat. He held it tightly.

He remembered it hanging between her breasts on its silver chain, and the way she had lifted both hands to the back of her neck as she unclasped it. The chain had caught in the shiny cascade of hair as she had tried to free it, kneeling on the bed facing him. He had leaned forward to help her, and she had clung to him, pressing the warm smooth bulge of her pregnant stomach against him.

'God protect you, my darling husband,' she had whispered. 'Please God bring you back safely to us.'

And now he was afraid for her and the daughter he had never seen.

'Hold your course, damn you!' he snapped at Herbert Cryer, the helmsman.

'Aye, aye, sir,' Herbert Cryer replied with just a trace of injured innocence in his tone. No man could hold *Bloodhound* true when she hurled herself from swell to swell with such abandoned violence, she must yaw and throw her head that fraction before the helm could correct her. The reprimand was unjustified, uttered in fear and tension. 'Give it a flipping break, mate,' Herbert retorted silently. 'You're not the only one who is going to catch it. Tighten up the old arsehole like a bloody officer and a ruddy gentleman.'

In these wordless exchanges of repartee with his officers, Herbert Cryer was never bested. They were wonderful release for resentments and pent-up emotion, and now because he was also afraid, he became silently lyrical.

'Climb-aboard-Romeo's one way express to flipping glory.' Commander Little's reputation with the ladies had resulted in him being irreverently but affectionately baptized by his crew.

'Come along with us. We're off to shout at the devil, while Charlie kisses his daughter.'

Herbert glanced sideways at his commander and grinned. Fear made the grin wolfish, and Charles Little saw it and misinterpreted it. He read it as a mark of the same berserk fury that possessed him. The two of them grinned at each other for an instant in complete misunderstanding, before Herbert refocused his attention on *Bloodhound*'s next wild crabbing lunge.

Charles was afraid as well. He was afraid of finding a weakness in himself – but this was the fear that had walked at his right hand all his life, close beside him, whispering to him, 'Harder, try harder. You must do it better, you must do it quicker, or bigger than they do, or they'll laugh at you. You mustn't fail – not in one thing, not for one moment, you mustn't fail. You mustn't fail!' This fear was the eternal companion and partner in every venture on which he embarked.

It had stood beside the thirteen-year-old Charles in a duck blind, while he fired a twelve gauge shotgun, and wept slow fat tears of agony every time the recoil smashed into his bruised bicep and shoulder.

It had stooped over him as he lay in the mud hugging a broken collar bone. 'Get up!' it hissed at him. 'Get up!' It had forced him to his feet and led him back to the unbroken colt to mount again, and again, and again.

So conditioned was he to respond to its voice that when it crouched beside him now, twisted and misshapen on the footplates of the bridge, its presence almost tangible, and croaked so Charles alone could hear it, 'Prove it! Prove it!' there was only one course open to Charles Little; a peregrine stooping at a golden eagle, he took his ship in against the *Blücher*.

'The turn to starboard was a feint.' Otto von Kleine spoke with certainty, staring out to where the dusk had obliterated the frail silhouette of the English destroyer. 'Even now he is turning again to cross our stern. He will attack on our port side.'

'Captain, it could be the double bluff,' Kyller answered dubiously.

'No.' Von Kleine shook his golden beard. 'He must try to outline us against the last of the light from the sunset. He will attack from the east.' A moment longer he frowned in thought, as he anticipated his opponent's moves across the chessboard of the ocean. 'Kyller, plot me his course, assuming a speed of twenty-five knots, a turn four points to port three minutes after our last sighting, a run of fifteen miles across our stern, and then a turn of four points to starboard. If we hold our present course and speed, where will he be in relation to us, in ninety minutes' time?'

Working quickly, Kyller completed the problem. Von Kleine had been mentally checking every step of the calculation. 'Yes,' he agreed with Kyller's solution, and already he had formulated the orders for change of course and speed to place *Bloodhound* in ambush.

48

Under full power, *Bloodhound* threw a bow-wave ten feet high, and a wake that boiled out for a quarter of a mile behind her, a long, faintly phosphorescent smear in the darkness.

Aboard *Blücher* a hundred pairs of eyes were straining out into the night, watching for that phosphorescence. Behind the battle lights on her upperworks men waited, in the dimly-lit turrets men waited, on the open bridge, at the masthead, deep in her belly, the crew of *Blücher* waited.

Von Kleine had reduced speed to lessen his own wake, and turned away from the land at an angle of forty-five degrees. He wanted to catch the Englishman on his starboard beam, out of torpedo range.

He stood peering out across the dark sea, with the fur-lined collar of his overcoat drawn up to his ears. The night was cool. The sea was a black immensity, vast as the sky that was lined in glowing ivory by the whorls and smears of the star patterns.

A dozen men saw it at the same instant; pale, ethereal, seeming to float upon the darkness of the sea like a plume of iridescent mist – the wake of the Englishman.

'Star shell!' Von Kleine snapped the order to the waiting guns. He was alarmed by the English destroyer's proximity. He had hoped to spot her at greater range.

High above the ocean, the star shells burst blue-white, so intensely bright as to sear the retina of the eye that looked directly at them. Beneath them the surface of the sea was polished ebony, sculptured and scooped with the pattern of the swells. The two ships were starkly and crisply lit, steaming on converging courses, already so close to each other that the mile-long, solid white beams of their battle lights jumped out to join, fumbling together like the hands of hesitant lovers.

In almost the same second both ships opened fire, but the

banging of *Bloodhound*'s little 4.7-inch guns were lost in the bellow of the cruiser's broadside.

Blücher was firing over open sights with her guns depressed until the long barrels were horizontal to the surface of the sea. Her first salvo was aimed a fraction high, and the huge shells howled over *Bloodhound*'s open bridge.

The wind of their passage, the fierce draught of disrupted air they threw out, caught Charles Little and sent him reeling against the compass pinnacle. He felt the ribs below his armpit crack.

The command he shouted at the helm was hoarse with pain. 'Turn four points to port! Steer for the enemy!' and *Bloodhound* spun like a ballet dancer, and charged straight at *Blücher*.

The cruiser's next broadside was high again but now her secondary armament had joined in, and a four-pound shell from one of the quick-firing pom-poms burst on the director tower above *Bloodhound*'s bridge. It swept the exposed area with a buzzing hailstorm of shrapnel.

It killed the navigating lieutenant instantly, cutting away the top of his head as though it were the shell of a soft-boiled egg. He fell on the deck and splattered the footplates with the warm custard of his brains.

A piece of the red hot shell casing, the size of a thumb-nail entered the point of Herbert Cryer's right elbow and shattered the bone to splinters. He gasped at the shock and sprawled against the wheel.

'Hold her. Hold her true!' The order from Commander Little was blurred as the speech of a spastic. Herbert Cryer pulled himself up and with his left hand spun the wheel to meet *Bloodhound*'s wild swing, but with his right arm hanging useless, his steering was clumsy and awkward.

'Steady her, man. Hold her steady!' Again that thick slurring voice, and Cryer was aware of Charles Little beside him, his hands on the helm, helping to hold *Bloodhound*'s frantic head.

'Aye, aye, sir.' Cryer glanced at his commander and gasped again. This time in horror. Razor-sharp steel had sliced off Charles Little's ear, then gone on to cut his cheek away, and expose the bone of his jaw and the white teeth that lined it. A flap of tattered flesh hung down on to his chest, and from a dozen severed blood vessels dark blood dripped and spurted and dribbled.

The two of them crouched wounded over the wheel, with the dead men at their feet, and aimed *Bloodhound* at the long low bulk of the German cruiser.

Now in the daylight glare of the star shells, the sea around them was thrashed and whipped into seething life by the cacophony of *Blücher*'s guns. Tall towers of white water rose briefly and majestically about them, then dropped back to leave the surface troubled and restless with foam.

And *Bloodhound* drove on until suddenly it seemed she had run into a cliff of solid granite. Beneath their feet, she jarred and bucked violently. A nine-inch shell had taken her full in the bows.

'Port full rudder.' Charles Little's voice was sloshy sounding, wet with the blood that filled his mouth, and together they spun the wheel to full left lock.

But *Bloodhound* was dying. The shell had split her bows wide open, torn her plating and fanned it open like the petals of a macabre orchid. The black night sea rushed through her. Already her bows were sinking, slumping wearily, lifting her stern so the rudder no longer had full purchase. But even in death she was trying desperately to obey. Slowly she swung, inchingly, achingly, she swung.

Charles Little left the helm and tottered towards the starboard rail. His legs were numb and heavy under him, and the weakness of his lost blood drummed in his ears. He reached the rail and clung there, peering down on the torpedo tubes that stood on the deck below him.

The tubes looked like a rack of fat cigars, and with weary jubilation Charles saw that there were men still tending them, crouching behind the sheet of armour plate, waiting for *Bloodhound* to turn and bring *Blücher* on to her starboard beam.

'Turn, old girl. Come on! That's it! Turn!' Charles croaked through the blood.

Another shell struck *Bloodhound*, and she heaved in mortal agony. Perhaps this movement, combined with a chance push of the sea swell, was enough to swing her those last few degrees.

There, full in the track of the torpedo tubes, lit by her own star shells and the gun-fire from her turrets, a scant thousand yards across the black water, lay the German cruiser.

Charles heard the whoosh, whoosh, whoosh, whoosh, of the tubes as they fired. He saw the long sharklike shapes of the torpedoes leap out from the deck and strike the water, saw the four white wakes arrowing away in formation, and behind him he heard the torpedo officer's triumphant shout, distorted by the voice-pipe.

'All four fired, and running true!'

Charles never saw his torpedoes strike, for one of *Blücher's* nine-inch shells hit the bridgework three feet below him. For one brief unholy instant, he stood in the centre of a furnace as hot as the flames of the sun.

49

Otto von Kleine watched the English destroyer explode. Towering orange flames erupted from her, and a solid ball of black smoke spun upon itself, blooming on the dark ocean like a flower from the gardens of hell. The surface of the sea around her was dimpled by the fall of thrown debris and the cruiser's shells – for all of *Blücher*'s guns were still blazing.

'Cease fire,' he said, without taking his eyes from the awesome pageant of destruction that he had created.

Another salvo of star shell burst above, and von Kleine lifted his hand to his eyes and pressed his thumb and forefinger into the closed lids, shielding them from the stabbing brilliance of the light. It was finished, and he was tired.

He was tired, drained of nervous and physical energy, overwhelmed by the backwash of fatigue that followed these last two days and nights of ceaseless strain. And he was sad – sad for the brave men he had killed, and the terrible destruction he had wrought.

Still holding his eyes, he opened his mouth to give the order that would send *Blücher* once more thrashing southward, but before the words reached his lips, a wild shout from the lookout interrupted him.

'Torpedoes! Close on the starboard beam!'

Long seconds von Kleine hesitated. He had let his brain relax, let the numbness wash over it. The battle was over, and he had dropped back from the high pinnacle of alertness on which he had balanced these last desperate hours. It needed a conscious physical effort to call up his reserves, and during those seconds, the torpedoes fired by *Bloodhound* in her death throes were knifing in to revenge her.

At last von Kleine snapped the bonds of inertia that bound his mind. He leaped to the starboard rail of the bridge, and saw in the light of the star shells the pale phosphorescent trails of the four torpedoes. Against the dark water they looked like the tails of meteors on a night sky.

'Full port rudder. All engines full astern together!' he shouted, his voice pitched high with consternation.

He felt his ship swerve beneath him, thrown violently over as the great propellers clawed at the sea to hold her from crossing the path of the torpedoes.

Hopelessly he stood and reviled himself. *I should have anticipated this. I should have known the destroyer had fired.*

Helplessly he stood and watched the four white lines drawn swiftly across the surface towards him.

In the last moments he felt a fierce upward surge of hope. Three of the English torpedoes would miss. That was certain. They would cross *Blücher*'s bows as she side-stepped. And the fourth torpedo it was just possible would miss also.

His fingers upon the bridge rail clenched, until it felt as though they must press into the metal. His breath jammed in his throat and choked him.

Ponderously, *Blücher* swung her bows away. If he had given the order for the turn only five seconds earlier . . .

The torpedo struck *Blücher* five feet below the surface, on the very tip of her curved keel.

The explosion shot a mountain of white water one hundred and fifty feet into the air. It slammed *Blücher* back onto her haunches with such violence that Otto von Kleine and his officers were thrown heavily to the steel deck.

Von Kleine scrabbled to his knees and looked forward. A fine veil of spray, like pearl dust in the light of the star shells, hung over *Blücher*. As he watched, it subsided slowly.

All that night they struggled to keep *Blücher* afloat.

They sealed off her bows with the five-inch steel doors in the watertight bulkhead, and behind those doors they locked thirty German seamen whose battle stations were in the bows. At intervals during the frenzied activity of the night, von Kleine had visions of those men floating face-down in the flooded compartments.

While the pumps clanged throughout the ship to free her of the hundreds of tons of sea-water that washed through her, von Kleine left the bridge and, with his engineer commander and damage control officer, they listed the injuries that *Blücher* had received.

In the dawn they assembled grimly in the chart-room behind the bridge, and assessed their plight.

'What power can you give me, Lochtkamper?' von Kleine demanded of his engineer.

'I can give you as much as you ask.' A reddish-purple bruise covered half the engineer's face where he had been thrown against a steam cock-valve when the torpedo struck. 'But anything over five knots will carry away the watertight bulkheads forward. They will take the full brunt of the sea.'

Von Kleine swivelled his stool, and looked at the damage control officer. 'What repairs can you effect at sea?'

'None, sir. We have braced and propped the watertight bulkhead. We have patched and jammed the holes made by the British cruiser's guns. But I can do nothing about the underwater damage without a dry dock – or calm water where I can put divers over the side. We must enter a port.'

Von Kleine leaned back in his stool and closed his eyes to think.

The only friendly port within six thousand miles was Dar es Salaam, the capital of German East Africa, but he knew the British were blockading it. He discarded it from his list of possible refuges.

An island? Zanzibar? – The Seychelles? – Mauritius? – All hostile territories with no anchorage safe from bombardment by a British squadron.

A river mouth? The Zambezi? No, that was in Portuguese territory, navigable for only the first few miles of its length.

Suddenly he opened his eyes. There was one ideal haven situated in German territory, navigable even by a ship of *Blücher*'s tonnage for twenty miles. It was guarded from overland approach by formidable terrain, yet he could call upon the German Commissioner for stores and labour and protection.

'Kyller,' he said. 'Plot me a course for the Kikunya mouth of the Rufiji delta.'

Five days later the *Blücher* crawled painfully as a crippled centipede into the northernmost channel of the Rufiji delta. She was blackened with battle smoke, her rigging hung in tatters, and at a thousand places shell splinters had pierced her upperworks.

Her bows were swollen and distorted, and the sea washed through her forward compartments and then boiled and spilled out of the ghastly rents in her plating.

As she passed between the forests of mangroves that lined the channel, they seemed to enfold her like welcoming arms.

Overside she lowered two picket boats and these darted ahead of her like busy little water beetles as they sounded the channel, and searched for a secure anchorage. Gradually *Blücher* wriggled and twisted her way deeper and deeper into the wilderness of the delta. At a place where the flood waters of the Rufiji had cut a deep bay between two islands, and formed a natural jetty on both sides, the *Blücher* came to rest.

50

Herman Fleischer wiped his face and neck with a hand towel and then looked at the sodden material. God, how he hated the Rufiji basin. As soon as he entered its humid and malodorous heat, a thousand tiny taps opened under his skin and out gushed the juices of his body.

The prospect of an extended stay aroused in him a dark resentment to all things, but especially to this young snob who stood beside him on the foredeck of the steam launch. Herman darted a glance at him now. Cool he looked, as though he were sauntering down Unter den Linden in June. The shimmering white of his tropical uniform was unwrinkled and dry, not like the thick corduroy that bunched damply at Herman's armpits and crotch. Mother of a dog, it would start the rash again; he could feel it beginning to itch and he scratched at it moodily, then checked his hand as he saw the lieutenant smile.

'How far are we from *Blücher*?' and then as an afterthought he used the lieutenant's surname without rank, 'How far, Kyller?' It was as well to keep reminding the man that as the equivalent of a full colonel, he far outranked him.

'Around the next bend, Commissioner.' Kyller's voice carried the lazy inflection that made Fleischer think of champagne and opera houses, of skiing parties, and boar hunts.

'I hope that Captain von Kleine has made adequate preparation to defend her against enemy attack?'

'She is safe.' For the first time there was a brittle undertone to Kyller's reply, and Fleischer pounced on it. He sensed an advantage. For the last two days, ever since Kyller had met him at the confluence of the Ruhaha river, Herman had been needling him to find a weakness.

'Tell me, Kyller,' he dropped his voice to an intimate, confidential level. 'This is in strict confidence, of course, but do you really feel that Captain von Kleine is able to handle this situation? I mean, do you feel that someone else may have been able to reach a more satisfactory result?' Ah! Yes! That was it! Look at him flush, look at the anger stain those cool brown cheeks. For the first time the advantage was with Herman Fleischer.

'Commissioner Fleischer,' Kyller spoke softly but Herman exulted to hear his tone. 'Captain von Kleine is the most skilful, efficient, and courageous officer under which I have had the honour to serve. He is, furthermore, a gentleman.'

'So?' Herman grunted. 'Then why is this paragon hiding in the Rufiji basin with his buttocks shot full of holes?' Then he threw back his head and guffawed in triumph.

'At another time, sir, and in different circumstances, I would ask you to withdraw those words.' Kyller turned from him and walked to the forward rail. He stood there staring ahead, while the launch chugged around another bend in the river, opening the same dreary vista of dark water and mangrove forest. Kyller spoke without turning his head. 'There is the *Blücher*,' he said.

There was nothing but the sweep of water and the massed fuzzy heads of the mangroves below a hump of higher ground upon the bank. The laughter faded from Herman's chubby face as he searched, then a small scowl replaced it as he realized that the lieutenant was baiting him. There was certainly no battle cruiser anchored in the water-way. 'Lieutenant . . .' he began angrily, then checked himself. The high ground was divided by a narrow channel, not more than a hundred yards wide, fenced in by the mangrove forest, but the channel was blocked by a shapeless and ungainly mound of vegetation. He stared at it uncomprehendingly until suddenly beneath the netting that was festooned with branches of mangroves, he saw the blurred outline of turrets and superstructure.

The camouflage had been laid with fascinating ingenuity. From a distance of three hundred yards the *Blücher* was invisible.

51

The bubbles came up slowly through the dark water as though it had the same viscosity as warm honey. They burst on the surface in a boiling white rash.

Captain von Kleine leaned across the foredeck rail of the *Blücher* and peered at the disturbance below him, with the absorption of a man attempting to read his own future in the murky mirror of the Rufiji waters. For almost two hours he had waited like this, drawing quietly on a succession of little black cheroots, occasionally easing his body into a more comfortable position.

Although his body was at rest, his brain was busy, endlessly reviewing his preparations and his plans. His preparations were complete, he had mentally listed them and found no omissions.

A party of six seamen had been despatched fifteen miles downstream by picket boat to the entrance of the delta. They were encamped on a hummock of high ground above the channel to watch the sea for the British blockade squadron.

As *Blücher* crept up the channel she had sown the last of her globular multi-horned mines behind her. No British ship could follow her.

Remote as the chances of overland attack seemed, yet von Kleine had set up a system of defence around the *Blücher*. Half his seamen were ashore now, spread in a network to guard each of the possible approaches. Fields of fire had been cut through the mangroves for his Maxim guns. Crude fortifications of log and earth had been built and manned, communication lines set up, and he was ready.

After long discussions with his medical officer, von Kleine had issued orders to protect the health of his men. Orders for the purification of water, the disposal of sanitation and waste, for the issue of five grains of quinine daily to each man, and fifty other safeguards to health and morale.

He had ordered an inventory made of stocks of food and supplies, and he was satisfied that with care he could subsist for a further four months. Thereafter he would be reduced to fishing and hunting, and foraging.

He had despatched Kyller upstream to make contact with the German Commissioner, and solicit his full co-operation.

Four days had been spent in hiding the *Blücher* under her camouflage, in setting up a complete workshop on the foredeck under sun awnings, so that the engineers could work in comparative comfort.

Now at last they had begun a full underwater appraisal of *Blücher*'s wounds.

Behind him he heard the petty officer pass an order to the team at the winch. 'Bring him up – slowly.'

The donkey engine spluttered into life, and the winch clattered and whined shrilly. Von Kleine stirred against the rail and focused his full attention on the water below him.

The heavy line and airpipe reeled in smoothly, then suddenly the surface bulged and the body of the diver was lifted dangling on the line. Black in shiny wet rubber, the three brass-bound cyclopean eyes of his helmet glaring, grotesque as a sea monster, he was swung inboard and lowered to the deck.

Two seamen hurried forward and unscrewed the bolts at the neck, lifted off the heavy helmet, and exposed the head of the engineering commander, Lochtkamper. The heavy face, flat and lined as that of a mastiff, was made heavier than usual by the thoughtful frown it now wore. He looked across at his captain and shook his head slightly.

'Come to my cabin when you are ready, Commander,' said von Kleine, and walked away.

'A small glass of cognac?' von Kleine suggested.

'I'd like that, sir.' Commander Lochtkamper looked out of place in the elegance of the cabin. The hands that accepted the glass were big, knuckles scarred and enlarged by constant violent contact with metal, the skin etched deeply with oil and engine filth. When he sank into the chair at his captain's invitation, his legs seemed to have too many knees.

'Well?' asked von Kleine, and Lochtkamper launched into his report. He spoke for ten minutes and von Kleine followed him slowly through the maze of technicalities where strange and irrelevant obscenities grew along the way. In moments of deep concentration such as these Lochtkamper fell back on the gutter idiom of his native Hamburg, and von Kleine was unable to suppress a smile when he learned that the copulatory torpedo had committed a perversion on one of the main frames, springing the plating whose morals were definitely suspect. The damage sounded like that suffered in a brothel during a Saturday night brawl.

'Can you repair it?' von Kleine asked at last.

'It will mean cutting away all the obscenely damaged plating, lifting it to the deck, recutting it, welding and shaping it. But we will still be short of at least eight hundred obscene square feet of plate, sir.'

'A commodity not readily obtainable in the delta of the Rufiji river,' von Kleine mused.

'No, sir.'

'How long will it take you – if I can get the plating for you?'

'Two months, perhaps.'

'When can you start?'

'Now, sir.'

'Do it then,' said von Kleine, and Lochtkamper drained his glass, smacked his lips, and stood up. 'Very good cognac, sir,' he complimented his captain, and shambled out of the cabin.

52

Staring upward at the massive warship, Herman Fleischer surveyed the battle damage with the uncomprehending curiosity of a landsman. He saw the gaping ulcers where *Orion*'s shells had struck, the black blight where the flames had raged through her, the irregular rash with which the splinters had pierced and peppered her upperworks, and then he dropped his eyes to the bows. Work cradles were suspended a few feet above the water, and upon them clutters of seamen were illuminated by the crackling blue glare of the welding torches.

'God in heaven, what a beating!' He spoke with sadistic relish.

Kyller ignored the remark. He was directing the native helmsman of the launch to the landing ladder that had been rigged down the side of *Blücher*. Not even the presence of this sweaty peasant, Fleischer, could spoil his pleasure in this moment of homecoming. To Ernst Kyller, the *Blücher* was home in the deep sense of the word; it contained all that he valued in life, including the man for whom he bore a devotion surpassing the natural duty of a son to his father. He was savouring the anticipation of von Kleine's smile and words of commendation for another task well done.

'Ah, Kyller!' Von Kleine rose from behind his desk and moved around it to greet his lieutenant.

'Back so soon? Did you find Fleischer?'

'He is waiting outside, sir.'

'Good, good. Bring him in.'

Herman Fleischer paused in the companion-way and blinked suspiciously around the cabin. His mind was automatically converting the furnishings into Reichsmarks, the rugs were silk Teheran in blue and gold and red, the chairs were in dark buttoned leather, all the heavy furniture, including the panelling, was polished mahogany. The light fittings were worked in brass, the glasses in the liquor cabinet were sparkling diamond crystal flanked by a platoon of bottles that wore the uniforms of the great houses of Champagne and Alsace and the Rhine. There was a portrait in oils opposite the desk of two women, both beautiful golden women, clearly mother and daughter. The portholes were curtained with forest green velvet, corded and tasselled in gold.

Herman decided that the Count must be a rich man. He had a proper respect for wealth, and it showed in the way he stepped forward, drew himself up, brought his heels together sharply, and then creased his bulging belly in a bow.

'Captain. I came as soon as I received your message.'

'I am grateful, Commissioner.' Von Kleine returned the salutation. 'You will take refreshment?'

'A glass of beer, and...' Herman hesitated, he was certain that somewhere aboard *Blücher* there must be a treasure trove of rare foods, '...a bite to eat. I have not eaten since noon.'

It was now the middle of the afternoon. Von Kleine saw nothing unusual in a two-hour period of abstinence, yet he passed the word for his steward while he opened a bottle of beer for his guest.

'I must congratulate you on your victory over the two English warships, Captain. Magnificent, truly magnificent!'

Lying back in one of the leather chairs Fleischer was engaged in mopping his face and neck, and Kyller grinned cynically as he listened to this new tune.

'A victory that was dearly bought,' murmured von Kleine, bringing the glass to Fleischer's chair. 'And now I need your help.'

'Of course! You need only ask.'

Von Kleine went to his desk, sat down and drew towards him a sheaf of notes. From their chamois leather case, he produced a pair of gold-rimmed spectacles and placed them on his nose.

'Commissioner...' he started, but at that moment he completely lost Fleischer's attention. For with a discreet knock the Captain's steward returned with a large, heavily laden carving-plate. He placed it on the table beside Fleischer's chair.

'Sweet Mother of God!' whispered Herman, his eyes glittering, and a fresh sweat of excitement breaking out on his upper lip.

'Smoked salmon!'

Neither von Kleine nor Kyller had ever been privileged to watch Herman eat before. They did so now in awed silence.

This was a specialist working with skill and dedication. After a while von Kleine made another effort to attract Herman's attention by coughing and rustling his sheaf of notes, but the Commissioner's snufflings and small moans of sensual pleasure continued. Von Kleine glanced at his lieutenant and lifted a golden eyebrow, Kyller half smiled in embarrassment. It was like watching a man in orgasm, so intimate that von Kleine was obliged to light a cheroot and concentrate his attention on the portrait of his wife and daughter across the cabin.

A gusty sigh signalled Herman's climax, and von Kleine looked at him again. He sagged back in the chair, a vague and dreamy smile playing over the ruddy curves of his face. The plate was empty, and with the sweet sorrow of a man remembering a lost love, Herman dabbed a forefinger on to the last shred of pink flesh and lifted it to his mouth.

'That was the best salmon I have ever tasted.'

'I am pleased that you found it so.' Von Kleine's voice crackled a little. He felt slightly nauseated by the exhibition.

'I wonder if I might trouble you for another glass of beer, Captain.'

Von Kleine nodded at Kyller, and the lieutenant went to refill Fleischer's glass.

'Commissioner. I need at least eight hundred square feet of $1\frac{1}{2}$-inch steel plate delivered to me here. I want it within six weeks,' von Kleine said, and Herman Fleischer laughed. He laughed the way a man laughs at a children's tale of fairies and witches, then suddenly he noticed von Kleine's eyes . . . and he stopped abruptly.

'Lying in Dar es Salaam harbour under British blockade is the steamer *Rheinlander*.' Von Kleine went on speaking softly and clearly. 'You will proceed there as fast as you can. I will send one of my engineers with you. He will beach the *Rheinlander* and dismantle her hull. You will then arrange to convey the plating to me here.'

'Dar es Salaam is one hundred kilometres away.' Herman was aghast.

'According to the admiralty chart it is seventy-five kilometres,' von Kleine corrected him.

'The plating will weigh many tons!' he cried.

'In German East Africa there are many hundreds of thousands

of indigenes. I doubt not that you will be able to persuade them to serve as porters.'

'The route is impossible . . . and what is more, there is a band of enemy guerrillas operating in the area north of here. Guerrillas led by those same bandits that you allowed to escape from the dhow, off the mouth of this river.' In agitation Fleischer had risen from his chair and now he pointed a fat accusing forefinger at von Kleine. 'You allowed them to escape. Now they are ravaging the whole province. If I try to bring a heavily laden, slow moving caravan of porters down from Dar es Salaam, word will reach them before I have marched five kilometres. It's madness – I won't do it!'

'It seems then, that you have a choice.' Von Kleine smiled with his mouth only. 'The English marauders, or a firing party on the afterdeck of this ship.'

'What do you mean?' howled Fleischer.

'I mean that my request is no longer a request, it is now an order. If you defy it, I will immediately convene a court martial.'

Von Kleine drew his gold watch and checked the time.

'We should be able to dispose of the formalities and shoot you before dark. What do you think, Kyller?'

'It will be cutting things fine, sir. But I think we could manage it.'

53

When the Governor of Mozambique had offered Flynn a captaincy in the army of Portugal, there had been an ugly scene. Flynn felt strongly that he deserved at least the rank of colonel. He had suggested terminating their business relationship. The Governor had countered with an offer of major – and signalled to his aide-de-camp to refill Flynn's glass. Flynn had accepted both offers, but the one under protest. That was seven months ago, a few short weeks after the massacre at Lalapanzi.

Since then Flynn's army, a mixed bag of a hundred native troops, officered by himself, Sebastian and Rosa Oldsmith, had been operating almost continually in German territory.

There had been a raid on the Songea railway siding where Flynn had burned five hundred tons of sugar, and nearly a thousand of millet that was in the warehouses awaiting shipment to Dar es Salaam, supplies badly needed by Governor Schee and Colonel Lettow von Vorbeck who were assembling an army in the coastal area.

There had been another brilliant success when they had ambushed and wiped out a band of thirty Askari at a river crossing. Flynn released the three hundred native recruits that the Askari were escorting, and advised them to get the hell back to their villages and forsake any ambitions of military glory – using the corpses of the Askari that littered the banks of the ford as tangible argument.

Apart from cutting every telegraph line, and blowing up the railway tracks they came across, three other raids had met with mixed results. Twice they had captured supply columns of bearers carrying in provisions to the massing German forces. Each time they had been forced to run as German reinforcements came up to drive them off. The third effort had been an abject failure, the ignominy of it being compounded by the fact that they had almost had the person of Commissioner Fleischer in their grasp.

Carried on the swift feet of the runners who were part of Flynn's intelligence system came the news that Herman Fleischer and a party of Askari had left Mahenge boma and marched to the confluence of the Ruhaha and Rufiji rivers. There they had gone aboard the steam launch and disappeared into the fastness of the Rufiji delta on a mysterious errand.

'What goes up must come down,' Flynn pointed out to Sebastian. 'And what goes down the Rufiji must come up again. We will go to the Ruhaha and wait for Herr Fleischer to return.'

For once there was no argument from either Sebastian or Rosa. Between the three of them it was understood without discussion that Flynn's army existed chiefly to act as the vehicle of retribution. They had made a vow over the grave of the child, and now they fought not so much from a sense of duty or patriotism, but from a burning desire for revenge. They wanted the life of Herman Fleischer in part payment for that of Maria Oldsmith.

They set out for the Ruhaha river. As happened so often these days, Rosa marched at the head of the column. There was only the long braid of dark hair hanging down her back to show she was a woman, for she was dressed in bush jacket and long khaki cotton trousers that concealed the feminine fullness of her hips. She stepped out long-legged, and from her shoulder the loaded Mauser hung on its strap and bumped lightly against her flank at each pace.

The change in her was so startling as to leave Sebastian bewildered. The new hard line of her mouth, her eyes that gave off the dark hot glow of a fanatic, the voice that had lost the underlying ripple of laughter. She spoke seldom, but when she did, both Flynn and Sebastian were forced to hear her with respect. Sometimes listening to that flat deadly tone Sebastian could feel a prickle of horror under his skin.

They reached the landing-place and the jetty on the Ruhaha river and waited for the launch to return. It came three days later, heralding its approach by the soft chugging of its engine. When it came round the river bend, pushing briskly against the current, headed for the wooden jetty, they were lying in wait for it.

'There he is!' Sebastian's voice was thick with emotion as he recognized the plump grey-clad figure in the bows.

'The swine, oh, the bloody swine!' and he jerked the bolt of his rifle open then snapped it shut.

'Wait!' Rosa's hand closed on his wrist before he could lift the butt to his shoulder.

'I can get him from here!' protested Sebastian.

'No. I want him to see us. I want to tell him first. I want him to know why he must die.'

The launch swung in broadside to the current, losing its way, until it came in gently to nudge the jetty. Two of the Askari jumped ashore, laying back on the lines to hold her while the Commissioner disembarked.

Fleischer stood on the jetty for a minute, looking back down the river. This action should have warned Flynn, but he did not see its significance. Then the Commissioner shrugged slightly and trudged up the jetty towards the boat-house.

'Tell your men to drop their weapons into the river,' said Flynn in his best German as he stood up from the patch of reeds beside the jetty.

Herman Fleischer froze in mid-stride, but his belly quivered and his head turned slowly towards Flynn. His blue eyes seemed to spread until they filled his face, and he made a clucking noise in his throat.

'Tell them quickly, or I will shoot you through the stomach,' said Flynn, and Fleischer found his voice. He relayed Flynn's order to the Askari, and there were a series of splashes around the launch as it was obeyed.

Movement in the corner of his eye made Fleischer swing his head, and he was face to face with Rosa Oldsmith. Beyond her in a half circle stood Sebastian and a dozen armed Africans, but some instinct warned Fleischer that the woman was the danger. There was a merciless quality about her, some undefinable air of deadly purpose. It was to her he addressed his question.

'What do you want?' His voice was husky with apprehension.

'What did he say?' Rosa asked her father.

'He wants to know what you want.'

'Ask him if he remembers me.'

As he heard the question, Fleischer remembered her in her night-dress, kneeling in the fire-light, and with the memory came real fear.

'It was a mistake,' he whispered. 'The child! I did not order it.'

'Tell him . . .' said Rosa, 'tell him that I am going to kill him.'
And her hands moved deliberately on the Mauser, slipping the
safety-catch across, but her eyes never left his face.

'It was a mistake,' Herman repeated and he stepped backwards,
lifting his hands to ward off the bullet that he knew must come.

At that moment Sebastian shouted behind Rosa, just one
word.

'Look!'

Around the bend of the Ruhaha river, only two hundred yards
from where they stood, another launch swept into view. It came
silently, swiftly and at its stubby masthead flew the ensign of
the German navy. There were men in crisp white uniforms
clustered around the Maxim machine gun in its bows.

Flynn's party stared at it in complete disbelief. Its presence
was as unbelievable as that of the Loch Ness monster in the
Serpentine or a man-eating lion in St Paul's Cathedral, and in
the long seconds that they stood paralysed the launch closed in
quickly on the jetty.

Herman Fleischer broke the spell. He opened his mouth and
from the barrel of his chest issued a bellow that rang clearly
across the water.

'Kyller, they are Englishmen!'

Then he moved, with three light steps he danced sideways,
incredibly quickly he moved his gross body from under the
threatening muzzle of Rosa's rifle and dived from the jetty into
the dark green swirl of water below the boards.

The splash of his dive was immediately followed by the tack,
tack, tack of the launch's machine gun – and the air was filled
with the swishing crack of a hundred whips. The launch drove
straight in towards them with the Maxim blazing on its prow.
Around Flynn, and Rosa and Sebastian the earth erupted in a
rapid series of dust fountains, a ricochet howled dementedly,
one of the gun-boys spun on his heels in a brief dervish dance
and then sprawled down the bank, with his rifle clattering on
the wooden boards of the jetty, and the frozen party on the bank
exploded into violent movement. Flynn and his black troopers
ducked and dodged away up the bank, but Rosa ran forward. She
reached the edge of the jetty unscathed through the hailstorm
of Maxim fire, there she checked and aimed the Mauser at the
wallowing body of Herman Fleischer in the water below her.

'You killed my baby!' Rosa shrieked, and Fleischer looked up at her and knew he was about to die. A Maxim bullet struck the metal of the rifle, tearing it from Rosa's hands, and she staggered off balance, her arms windmilling as she tottered on the edge of the jetty.

Sebastian reached her as she fell. He caught her and swung her up on to his shoulder, whirled with her and bounded away up the bank, running with all the reserves of his strength unlocked by the key of his terror.

With ten of the gun-boys Sebastian took the rearguard; for that day and the next they skirmished back along the line of the retreat, briefly holding each natural defensive point until the Germans brought up the Maxim gun. Then they dropped back, retreating slowly while Flynn and Rosa made a straight run of it. In the second night Sebastian broke contact with the pursuers and fled north towards the rendezvous at the stream below the ruins of Lalapanzi.

Forty-eight hours later he reached it. In the moonlight he staggered into the camp, and Rosa threw off her blankets and came running to him with a low joyous cry of greeting. She knelt before him, unlaced and gently drew off each of his boots. While Sebastian gulped the mug of coffee and hot gin that Flynn brewed for him, Rosa bathed and tended the blisters that had burst on his feet. Then she dried her hands, stood and picked up her blankets.

'Come,' she said, and together they walked away along the bank of the stream. Behind a curtain of hanging creepers, on a nest of dry grass and blankets, while the jewelled night sky glowed above them, they gave each other the comfort of their bodies for the first time since the death of the child. Afterwards they slept entwined until the low sun woke them. Then they rose and went down the bank together naked into the stream. The water was cold when she splashed him, and she giggled like a little girl and ran through the shallows across the sandbank with the water bursting in a sparkling spray around her legs, drops of it glittering like sequins on her skin, her waist was the neck of a Venetian vase flaring down into full double rounds on her lower body.

He chased and caught her and they fell together and knelt facing each other, spluttering and laughing, and with each gust of laughter her bosom jumped and bounced. Sebastian leaned forward with the laughter drying in his throat and cupped them in his hands.

Instantly her own laughter ceased, she looked at him a moment, then suddenly her face hardened and she struck his hands away.

'No!' she hissed at him, and jumping to her feet she waded to where her clothing lay on the bank. Swiftly she covered her femininity, and as she strapped the heavy bandolier of ammunition around her body the last soft memory of their loving was gone from her face.

54

It was that stinking Rufiji water, Herman Fleischer decided, and moved painfully in his maschille as another cramp took him.

The hot hand of dysentery that closed on his stomach added to his mood of dark resentment. His present discomfort was directly linked to the arrival of *Blücher* in his territory, the indignities he had experienced at the hands of her captain, the danger he had run into in his brush with the English bandits at the start of this expedition, and since then the constant gruelling work and ever-present fear of another attack, the nagging of the engineer whom von Kleine had placed over him – he hated everything to do with that cursed warship, he hated every man aboard her.

The jogging motion of the maschille bearers stirred the contents of his belly, making it gurgle and squeak. He would have to stop again, and he looked ahead for a suitable place in which to find privacy.

Ahead of him the caravan of porters was toiling along the shallow bottom of a valley between two sparsely wooded ridges of shale and broken rock.

The column was spread out in an untidy straggle half a mile long, for it comprised just under a thousand men.

In the van a hundred of them, stripped to loin-cloths and shiny with sweat, were wielding their long pangas on the scrub. The blades glinting as they rose and fell, the thudding of the blows muted in the lazy heat of afternoon. Working under the supervision of Gunther Raube, the young engineering officer from *Blücher*, they were cutting out the narrow track, widening it for the passage of the bulky objects that followed.

Dwarfing the men that swarmed around them, these four objects rolled slowly along, rocking and swaying over patches of uneven ground. Now and then halting as they came up against a tree stump or an outcrop of rock, before the animal exertions of two hundred black men could get them rolling again.

Three weeks previously they had beached the freighter *Rheinlander* in Dar es Salaam harbour and dismantled eight slabs of her plating. Then from the metal frames of her hull, Raube had shaped eight enormous wheel rims, fourteen feet in diameter, into each of these he had welded a sheet of 1½-inch plating ten foot square. Using the freighter's bollards as axles, he had linked these eight discs in four pairs. Thus each of these contraptions looked like the wheel and axle assembly of a gigantic Roman chariot.

Herman Fleischer had made a swift recruitment tour, and secured nine hundred able-bodied volunteers from the town of Dar es Salaam and its outlying villages. These nine hundred were now engaged in trundling the four sets of wheels southward towards the Rufiji delta. While they worked, Herman's Askari stood by with loaded Mausers to discourage any of the volunteers from succumbing to an attack of homesickness; a malady which was fast reaching epidemic proportions, aggravated as it was by shoulders rubbed raw by contact with harsh sun-heated metal, and by palms whose outer layers of skin had been smeared away on the rough hemp ropes. They had been two weeks at their labours and they were still thirty torturous miles from the river.

Herman Fleischer squirmed again in his maschille as the amoebic dysentery gnawed at his guts.

'Mother of a pig!' he moaned, and then shouted at the bearers, 'Quickly, take me to those trees.' He pointed to a clump of wild ebony that smothered one of the side draws of the valley.

With alacrity, the maschille bearers swung off the path and trotted up the draw. Within the screen of wild ebony they paused while the Commissioner alighted from the hammock and hurried into the deepest recess of the bush to be alone. Then they drew themselves down with a communal sigh and gave themselves up to a session of African callisthenics.

When the Commissioner came out of retreat he was hungry. It was cool and restful in the shade, an ideal place to take his mid-afternoon snack. Raube would have to fend for himself for an hour or so. Herman nodded to his personal servant to set up the camp table and open the food box. His mouth was full of sausage when the first rifle shot clapped dully in the dusty dry air.

55

'Where is he? He must be here. The scouts said he was here. Can you see him?' Rosa Oldsmith spoke through lips that were chapped dry by sun and wind, white flakes of skin had come loose from the raw red patches of sunburn on her nose, and her eyes were bloodshot from the dust and the glare.

She lay on her stomach behind a bank of shale and coarse grass with the Mauser probing out in front of her.

'Can you see him?' she demanded again impatiently, turning her head towards her father.

Flynn grunted noncommittally, holding the binoculars to his eyes, panning them slowly down the length of the valley then back again to the head of the strange caravan.

'There is a white man there,' he said.

'Is it Fleischer, is it?'

'No,' doubtfully Flynn gave the negative.

'No, I don't think so.'

'Look for him. He must be there somewhere.'

'I wonder what the hell those things are.'

Flynn concentrated on the four huge sets of wheels. The lens of the binoculars magnified the heat distortion through the still air, making them change shape and size so that one second they were insignificant and the next they were monstrous.

'Look for Fleischer. Damn those things, look for Fleischer,' Rosa snapped at him.

'He's not with them.'

'He must be. He must be there.' Rosa rolled on her side and reached out to snatch the binoculars from Flynn's hands. Eagerly she scanned the long column that moved slowly towards them up the valley.

'He must be there. Please God, he must be there,' she whispered her hatred through cracked dry lips.

'We will have to attack soon. They are nearly in position now.'

'We must find Fleischer.' Desperately Rosa searched, her knuckles showing white through sun-brown skin as she clutched the binoculars.

'We can't let it go much longer. Sebastian is in position, he will be expecting my signal.'

'Wait! You must wait.'

'No. We can't let them get closer.' Flynn half lifted his body, and called softly.

'Mohammed! Are you ready?'

'We are ready.' The reply came from farther down the slope where the line of riflemen lay.

'Remember my words, oh, thou chosen of Allah. Kill the Askari first and the others will run.'

'Your words ring in my ears with the brightness and the beauty of golden bells,' Mohammed replied.

'Up yours!' said Flynn and unbuttoned the pocket flap of his tunic. He fumbled out the hand-mirror and held it slanted to catch the sun, deflecting a bright splinter of light towards the far slope of the valley. From the jumble of rock and bush there was an immediate answering flash as Sebastian acknowledged the signal.

'Ah!' Flynn breathed theatrical relief, 'I was afraid our Bassie might have fallen asleep over there.' And he picked up the Mauser from the rock in front of him.

'Wait,' pleaded Rosa. 'Please wait.'

'We can't. You know we can't – if Fleischer is down there then we'll get him. If he isn't, then waiting any longer isn't going to help us.'

'You don't care,' she accused. 'You have forgotten about Maria already.'

'No,' said Flynn. 'No, I haven't forgotten,' and he cuddled the Mauser into his shoulder. There was an Askari he had been watching. A big man who moved ahead of the column. Even at this range Flynn sensed that this man was dangerous. He moved with a leopard's slouching awareness, head cocked and alert.

Flynn picked him up in the notch of the rear sight and rode the pip down his body, aiming low to compensate for the down-hill shot, taking him in the belly. He gathered the slack in the trigger, squeezing it up gently. The Mauser cracked viciously and the recoil jumped back into his shoulder.

Incredulously Flynn saw the bullet throw a jump of dust from the slope below the Askari. A clean miss at four hundred yards from a carefully aimed shot – By Christ, he was getting old.

Frantically he worked the bolt of the rifle, but already the Askari had ducked for cover, unslinging his rifle as he disappeared into a bank of grey thorn bush, and Flynn's next shot ripped ineffectively into the coarse dry vegetation.

'Damn it to hell!' howled Flynn, and his voice was small in the storm of gun-fire that blew around him. From both slopes all his riflemen were shooting down into the solid pack of humanity that clogged the valley floor.

For startled seconds the mass of native bearers stood quiescent under the lash of the Mausers, each man frozen in the attitude in which the attack had caught him; bent to the giant wheels, leaning forward against the ropes, panga raised to strike at a branch, or merely standing watching while others worked. Every head lifted to stare up at the slopes from which Flynn's hidden rifles menaced them, then with a sound like a rising wind a single voice climbed in a wail of terror, to be lost almost instantly in the babble from a thousand throats.

Without regard for Flynn's orders to single out only the armed Askari, his men were firing blindly into the mass of men around the wheels, bullets striking with a meaty thump, thump, thump, or whining from rock to inflict the ghastly secondary wounds of a ricochet.

Then the bearers broke. Flowing back like flood water along the valley, carrying the Askari whose khaki uniforms bobbed with them like driftwood in the torrent.

Beside Flynn in the donga, Rosa was firing also. Her hands on the rifle incongruously feminine, fingers long and sensitive working the bolt as though it were the shuttle of a loom, weaving death, her eyes slitted behind the gunsight, her lips barely moving as they formed the name which had become her battle hymn.

'Maria! Maria!' With each shot she said it softly.

As he fumbled a fresh clip of cartridges from his bandolier, Flynn glanced sideways at her. Even in this moment of hot excitement Flynn felt the prickle of disquiet as he saw his daughter's face. There was a madness in her eyes, the madness of grief too long sustained, the madness of hatred too carefully nourished.

His rifle was loaded and he switched his attention back to the valley. The scene had changed. From the rush of fear-crazed bearers, the German, whom Flynn had earlier watched through the binoculars, was rallying a defence. With him was the big Askari, the one that Flynn had missed with his first shot. These two stood to hold the guards who were being carried away on the rush of panic-stricken bearers, stopping them, turning them back, pushing and shoving them into defensive cover around the four huge wheels. Now they were returning the fire of Flynn's men.

'Mohammed! Get that man! The white man – get him!' roared Flynn, and fired twice, missing with each shot. But his bullets passed so close that the German dodged back behind the metal shield of the nearest wheel.

'That's done it,' lamented Flynn, as his hopes of quick success faded. 'They're getting settled in down there. We are going to have to prise them loose.'

The prospect was unattractive. Flynn had found from experience that while every man in his motley band was a hero when firing from ambush, and a master in the art of strategic retreat, yet their weak suit was frontal assault, or any other manoeuvre that involved exposure to the enemy. Of the hundred under his command, there were a dozen whom he could rely on to obey an order to attack. Flynn was understandably reluctant to issue such an order, for there are few situations more humiliating than bellowing, 'Charge!' – then having everybody look at you with a 'Who, me? You must be joking!' expression.

Now he steeled himself to do it, aware that with every second the battle madness of his men was cooling and being replaced by sanity and caution. He filled his lungs and opened his mouth, but Rosa saved him.

She rolled and lifted her knees, coming on to her feet with one fluid motion whose continuation was a catlike leap that carried her over the shale bank and into the open. Boyish, big hipped, but graceful – the rifle across her hip, firing. Long hair streaming, long legs flying, she went down the slope.

'Rosa!' roared Flynn in consternation, and jumped up to chase her in an ungainly lumbering run like the charge of an old bull buffalo.

'Fini!' shouted Mohammed, and scampered after his master.

'My goodness!' Sebastian gasped where he lay on the opposite side of the valley. 'It's Rosa!' and in a completely reflex response he found himself on his feet and bounding down the rocky slope.

'Akwende!' yelled the man beside him, carried away in his excitement, and before any of them had time to think, fifty of them were up and following. After the first half-dozen paces they were committed, for once they had started to run down the steep incline they could not stop without falling flat on their faces, they could only accelerate.

Down both slopes of the valley, scrambling, sliding on loose stone, pell-mell through thorn bush, screaming, shouting, they poured down on the cluster of Askari around the wheels.

From opposite sides, Rosa and Sebastian were first to reach the perimeter of the German position. Their momentum carried them unscathed through the first line of the defenders, and then with the empty rifle in her hands Rosa ran chest to chest against the big Askari who rose from behind a boulder to meet her. She shrieked as he caught her, and the sound exploded within Sebastian's brain in a red burst of fury.

Twenty yards away Rosa struggled with the man, but she was helpless as a baby in his arms. He lifted her, changing his grip on her body, snatching her up above his head, steadying himself to hurl her down on to the pointed rock behind which he had hidden. There was such animal power in the bunched muscles of his arms, in the thick sweat-slimy neck, in the muscular straddled legs, that Sebastian knew that when he dashed Rosa against the rock he would kill her. Her spine, her ribs must shatter with the force of it; the soft vital organs within her trunk must bruise or burst.

Sebastian went for him. Brushing from his path two lesser men of the bewildered defenders, clubbing the Mauser in his hands because he could not fire for fear of hitting Rosa, silently saving his breath for physical effort, he crossed the distance that separated them and reached them in the moment that the Askari began the first downward movement of his arms.

'Aah!' A gusty grunt was forced up Sebastian's throat by the force with which he swung the rifle, he used it like an axe, swinging it low with the full weight of his body behind it. The blade of the butt hit the Askari across the small of his back, and within his body cavity the kidneys popped like overripe satsuma plums. He was dying as he toppled backwards. As he hit the ground Rosa fell on top of him, his body cushioning her fall.

Sebastian dropped the rifle and stooped to gather her in his arms, crouching over her protectively.

Around them Flynn led his men boiling over the defenders, swamping them, knocking the rifles from their hands and dragging them to their feet, laughing in awe of their own courageous assault, chattering in excitement and relief.

Sebastian was on the point of straightening up and lifting Rosa to her feet, he glanced around quickly to assure himself that all danger was past – and his breathing jammed in his throat.

Ten paces away, kneeling in the shadow of one of the huge steel wheels was the white officer. He was a young man, swarthy for a German, but with pale green eyes. The tropical white of his uniform was patchy with damp sweat stains, and smeared with dust; his cap was pushed back, the gold braid on its peak sparkling with incongruous gaiety, for beneath it the face was taut and angry, the mouth pulled tight by the clenched jaws.

There was a Luger pistol clutched in his right hand. He lifted it and aimed.

'No!' croaked Sebastian, clumsily trying to shield Rosa with his own body, but he knew the German was going to fire.

'Mädchen!' cried Sebastian in his schoolboy German. 'Nein shutzen dis ein Mädchen!' and he saw the change in the young officer's expression, the pale green glitter of his eyes softening as he responded automatically to the appeal to his chivalry. Yet still the Luger was levelled, and over it Sebastian and the officer stared at each other. All this in seconds, but the delay was enough. While the officer still hesitated, suddenly it was too late, for Flynn stood over him and pressed the muzzle of his rifle into the back of the German's neck.

'Drop it, me beauty. Else I'll shoot your tonsils clean out through your Adam's apple.'

56

Strewn along the floor of the valley were the loads dropped by the native bearers, in their anxiety to leave for far places and fairer climes. Many of the packs had burst open and all had been trampled in the rush, so the contents littered the ground and discarded clothing flapped in the lower branches of the thorn trees.

Flynn's men were looting, a pastime in which they demonstrated a marked aptitude and industry. Busy as jackals around a lion's kill they gleaned the spoils and bickered over them.

The German officer sat quietly against the metal wheel. In front of him stood Rosa; she had in her hand the Luger pistol. The two of them watched each other steadily and expressionlessly. To one side Flynn squatted and pored over the contents of the German's pockets. Beside him Sebastian was ready to give his assistance.

'He's a naval officer,' said Sebastian, looking at the German with interest. 'He's got an anchor on his cap badge.'

'Do me a favour, Bassie,' pleaded Flynn.

'Of course.' Sebastian was ever anxious to please.

'Shut up!' said Flynn, without looking up from the contents of the officer's wallet which he had piled on the ground in front of him. In his dealings with Flynn, Sebastian had built up a thick layer of scar tissue around his sensitivity. He went on without a change of tone or expression.

'I wonder what on earth a naval officer is doing in the middle of the bush – pushing these funny contraptions around.' Sebastian examined the wheel with interest, before addressing himself to the German. 'Bitte, was it das?' He pointed at the wheel. The young officer did not even glance at him. He was watching Rosa with almost hypnotic concentration.

Sebastian repeated his question and when he found that he

was again ignored he shrugged slightly, and leaned across to lift a sheet of paper from the small pile in front of Flynn.

'Leave it,' Flynn slapped his hand away. 'I'm reading.'

'Can I look at this, then?' He touched a photograph.

'Don't lose it,' cautioned Flynn, and Sebastian held it in his lap and examined it. It showed three young men in white overalls and naval peaked caps. They were smiling broadly into the camera with their arms linked together. In the background loomed the superstructure of a warship, the gun-turrets showed clearly. One of the men in the photograph was their prisoner who now sat against the wheel.

Sebastian reversed the square of heavy cardboard and read the inscription on the back of it.

' "Bremerhaven. 6 Aug. 1911." '

Both Flynn and Sebastian were absorbed in their studies, and Rosa and the German were alone. Completely alone, isolated by an intimate relationship.

Gunther Raube was fascinated. Staring into the girl's face, he had never known this sensation of mingled dread and elation which she invoked within him. Though her expression was flat and neutral, he could sense in her a hunger and a promise. He knew that they were bound together by something he did not understand, between them there was something very important to happen. It excited him, he felt it crawling like a living thing in his loins, ghost-walking along his spine, and his breathing was cramped and painful. Yet there was fear with it, fear that was as cloying as warm olive oil in his belly.

'What is it?' he whispered huskily as a lover. 'I do not understand. Tell me.'

And he sensed that she could not understand his language, but his tone made something move in her eyes. They darkened like cloud shadow on a green sea, and he saw she was beautiful. With a pang he thought how close he had been to firing the Luger she now held in her hand.

I might have killed her, and he wanted to reach out and touch her. Slowly he leaned forward, and Rosa shot him in the centre of his chest. The impact of the bullet threw him back against the metal frame of the wheel. He lay there looking at her.

Deliberately, each shot spaced, she emptied the magazine of the pistol. The Luger jumped and steadied and jumped again in her hand. Each blurt of gun-fire shockingly loud, and the wounds appeared like magic on the white front of his shirt, beginning to weep blood as he slumped sideways, and he lay with his eyes still fastened on her face as he died.

The pistol clicked empty and she let it drop from her hand.

57

Sir Percy held the square of cardboard at arm's length to read the inscription on the back of it.

'"Bremerhaven. 6 Aug. 1911," ' he said. Across the desk from him his flag-captain sat uncomfortably on the edge of the hard-backed H.M. issue chair. His right hand reached for his pocket, checked, then withdrew guiltily.

'For God's sake, Henry. Smoke that damned thing if you must,' grunted Sir Percy.

'Thank you, sir.' Gratefully Captain Henry Green completed the reach for his pocket, brought out a gnarled briar and began stuffing it with tobacco.

Laying aside the photograph, Sir Percy took up the bedraggled sheet of paper and studied the crude hand-drawn circles upon it, reading the descriptions that were linked by arrows to the circles. This sample of primitive art had been laboriously drawn by Flynn Patrick O'Flynn as an addendum to his report.

'You say this lot came in the diplomatic bag from the Embassy in Lourenco Marques?'

'That's right, sir.'

'Who is this fellow . . .' Sir Percy checked the name, 'Flynn Patrick O'Flynn?'

'It seems that he is a major in the Portuguese army, sir.'

'With a name like that?'

'You find these Irishmen everywhere, sir.' The captain smiled. 'He commands a group of scouts who raid across the border into German territory. They have built up something of a reputation for derring-do.'

Sir Percy grunted again, dropped the paper, clasped his hands behind his head and stared across the room at the portrait of Lord Nelson.

'All right, Henry. Let's hear what you make of it.'

The captain held a flaring match to the bowl of his pipe and sucked noisily, waved the match to extinguish it, and spoke through wreaths of smoke.

'The photograph first. It shows three German engineering officers on the foredeck of a cruiser. The one in the centre was the man killed by the scouts.' He puffed again. 'Intelligence reports that the cruiser is a "B" class. Nine-inch guns in raked turrets.'

' "B" class?' asked Sir Percy. 'They only launched two vessels of that class.'

'*Battenberg* and *Blücher*, sir.'

'*Blücher*!' said Sir Percy softly.

'*Blücher*!' agreed Henry Green. 'Presumed destroyed in a surface action with His Majesty's ships *Bloodhound* and *Orion* off the east coast of Africa between 16 and 20 September.'

'Go on.'

'Well, this officer could have been a survivor from *Blücher* who was lucky enough to come ashore in German East Africa – and is now serving with von Vorbeck's army.'

'Still dressed in full naval uniform, trundling strange round objects about the continent?' asked Sir Percy sceptically.

'An unusual duty, I agree, sir.'

'Now what do you make of these things?' With one finger Sir Percy prodded Flynn's diagram in front of him.

'Wheels,' said Green.

'For what?'

'Transporting material.'

'What material?'

'Steel plate.'

'Now who would want steel plate on the east coast of Africa?' mused Sir Percy.

'Perhaps the captain of a damaged battle cruiser.'

'Let's go down into the plotting room.' Sir Percy heaved his bulk out of the chair, and headed for the door.

His shoulders hunched, massive jaw jutting, Admiral Howe brooded over the plot of the Indian Ocean.

'Where was this column intercepted?' he asked.

'Here, sir.' Green touched the vast map with the pointer. 'About fifteen miles south-east of Kibiti. It was moving southwards towards . . .' He did not finish the statement but let the tip of the marker slide down on to the complexity of islands that clustered about the mouth of the long black snake that was the Rufiji river.

'Admiralty plot for East Africa, please.' Sir Percy turned to the lieutenant in charge of the plot, and the lieutenant selected Volume II of the blue-jacketed books that lined the shelf on the far wall.

'What are the sailing directions for the Rufiji mouth?' demanded the Admiral, and the lieutenant began to read.

'*Ras Pombwe to Kikunya mouth, including Mto Rufiji and Rufiji delta (Latitude 8° 17' S, Longitude 39° 20' E).* For fifty miles the coast is a maze of low, swampy, mangrove-covered islands, intersected by creeks comprising the delta of Mto Rufiji. During the rainy season the whole area of the delta is frequently inundated.

'The coast of the delta is broken by ten large mouths, eight of which are connected at all times with Mto Rufiji.'

Sir Percy interrupted peevishly, 'What is all this *Mto* business?'

'Arabic word for "river", sir.'

'Well, why don't they say so? Carry on.'

'With the exception of *Simba Uranga mouth* and *Kikunya mouth*, all other entrances are heavily shoaled and navigable only by craft drawing one metre or less.'

'Concentrate on those two then,' grunted Sir Percy, and the lieutenant turned the page.

'*Simba Uranga mouth.* Used by coasting vessels engaged in the timber trade. There is no defined bar and, in 1911, the channel was reported by the German Admiralty as having a low river level mean of ten fathoms.

'The channel is bifurcated by a wedge-shaped island, *Rufiji-ya-wake*, and both arms afford secure anchorage to vessels of large burden. However, holding ground is bad and securing to trees on the bank is more satisfactory. Floating islands of grass and weed are common.'

'All right!' Sir Percy halted the recitation, and every person in the plotting room looked expectantly at him. Sir Percy was glowering at the plot, breathing heavily through his nose. 'Where is *Blücher*'s plaque?' he demanded harshly.

The lieutenant went to the locker behind him, and came back with the black wooden disc he had removed from the plot two months previously. Sir Percy took it from him, and rubbed it slowly between thumb and forefinger. There was complete silence in the room.

Slowly Sir Percy leaned forward across the map and placed the disc with a click upon the glass top. They all stared at it. It sat sinister as a black cancer where the green land met the blue ocean.

'Communications!' grunted Sir Percy and the yeoman of signals stepped forward with his pad ready.

'Despatch to Commodore Commanding Indian Ocean. Captain Joyce. H.M.S. *Renounce*. Maximum Priority. Message reads: Intelligence reports indicate high probability . . .'

58

'You know something, Captain Joyce, this is bloody good gin.' Flynn O'Flynn pointed the base of the glass at the ceiling, and in his eagerness to engulf the liquid, he did the same for the slice of lemon that the steward had placed in his glass. He gurgled like an air-locked geyser, his face changed swiftly to a deeper shade of red, then he expelled the lemon and with it a fine spray of gin and Indian tonic in a burst of explosive coughing.

'Are you all right?' Anxiously Captain Joyce leapt across the cabin and begun pounding Flynn between the shoulder-blades. He had visions of his key tool in the coming operation being asphyxiated before they had started.

'Pips!' gasped Flynn. 'Goddamned lemon pips.'

'Steward!' Captain Joyce called over his shoulder without interrupting the tattoo he was playing on Flynn's back. 'Bring the major a glass of water. Hurry!'

'Water?' wheezed Flynn in horror and the shock was sufficient to diminish the strength of his paroxysm.

The steward, who from experience could recognize a drinking man when he saw one, rose nobly to the occasion. He hurried across the cabin with a glass in his hand. A mouthful of the raw spirit effected a near miraculous cure, Flynn lay back in his chair his face still bright purple but his breathing easing, and Joyce withdrew to the far side of the cabin to inhale with relief the moist warm tropical air that oozed sluggishly through the open porthole. After a close range whiff of Flynn's body smell, it was as sweet as a bunch of tulips.

Flynn had been in the field for six weeks, and during that time it had not occurred to him to change his clothing. He smelled like a Roquefort cheese.

There was a pause while everybody recovered their breath, then Joyce picked up where he had left off.

'I was saying, Major, how good it was of you to return so promptly to meet me here.'

'I came the moment I received your message. The runner was waiting for us in M'topo's village. I left my command camped south of the Rovuma, and pushed through in forced marches. A hundred and fifty miles in three days! Not bad going, hey?'

'Damn good show!' agreed Joyce, and looked across at the other two men in the cabin for confirmation. With the Portuguese Governor's aide-de-camp was a young army lieutenant. Neither of them could understand a word of English. The aide-de-camp was wearing a politely non-committal expression, and the lieutenant had loosened the top button of his tunic and was lolling on the cabin's day couch with a little black cigarette drooping from his lips. Yet he contrived to look as gracefully insolent as a matador.

'The English captain asks that you recommend me to the Governor for the Star of St Peter.' Flynn translated Captain Joyce's speech to the aide-de-camp. Flynn wanted a medal. He had been hounding the Governor for one these last six months.

'Will you please tell the English captain that I would be delighted to convey his written citation to the Governor.' The aide-de-camp smiled blandly. Through their business association he knew better than to take Flynn's translation literally. Flynn scowled at him, and Joyce sensed the strain in the cabin. He went on quickly.

'I asked you to meet me here to discuss a matter of very great importance.' He paused. 'Two months ago your scouts attacked a German supply column near the village of Kibiti.'

'That's right.' Flynn sat up in his chair. 'A hell of a fight. We fought like madmen. Hand-to-hand stuff.'

'Quite,' Joyce agreed quickly. 'Quite so. With this column was a German naval officer . . .'

'I didn't do it,' interjected Flynn with alarm. 'It wasn't me. He was trying to escape. You can't pin that one on me.'

Joyce looked startled.

'I beg your pardon.'

'He was shot trying to escape – and you try and prove different,' Flynn challenged him hotly.

'Yes, I know. I have a copy of your report. A pity. A great pity. We would dearly have liked to interrogate the man.'

'You calling me a liar?'

'Good Lord, Major O'Flynn. Nothing is further from my mind.' Joyce was finding that conversation with Flynn O'Flynn was similar to feeling your way blindfolded through a hawthorn bush. 'Your glass is empty, may I offer you a drink?'

Flynn's mouth was open to emit further truculent denials, but the offer of hospitality took him unawares and he subsided.

'Thank you. It's damn good gin, haven't tasted anything like it in years. I don't suppose you could spare a case or two?'

Again Joyce was startled.

'I'm sure the wardroom secretary will be able to arrange something for you.'

'Bloody good stuff,' said Flynn, and sipped at his recharged glass. Joyce decided on a different approach.

'Major O'Flynn, have you heard of a German warship, a cruiser, named *Blücher*?'

'Have I, hell!' bellowed Flynn with such vehemence that Joyce was left in no doubt that he had struck another jarring note. 'The bastard sank me!'

These words conjured up in the eye of Captain Joyce's mind a brief but macabre picture of a Flynn floating on his back, while a battle cruiser fired on him with nine-inch guns.

'Sank you?' asked Joyce.

'Rammed me! There I was sailing along in this dhow peaceful as anything when up she comes and – bang, right up the arse.'

'I see,' murmured Joyce. 'Was it intentional?'

'You bloody tooting it was.'

'Why?'

'Well . . .' started Flynn, and then changed his mind. 'It's a long story.'

'Where did this happen?'

'About fifty miles off the mouth of the Rufiji river.'

'The Rufiji?' Joyce leaned forward eagerly. 'Do you know it? Do you know the Rufiji delta?'

'Do I know the Rufiji delta?' chucked Flynn. 'I know it like you know the way to your own Thunder Box. I used to do a lot of business there before the war.'

'Excellent! Wonderful!' Joyce could not restrain himself from pursing his lips and whistling the first two bars of 'Tipperary'. From him this was expression of unadulterated joy.

'Yeah? What's so wonderful about that?' Flynn was immediately suspicious.

'Major O'Flynn. On the basis of your report, Naval Intelligence considers it highly probable that the *Blücher* is anchored somewhere in the Rufiji delta.'

'Who are you kidding? The *Blücher* was sunk months ago – everybody knows that.'

'Presumed sunk. She, and the two British warships that pursued her, disappeared off the face of the earth – or more correctly the ocean. Certain pieces of floating wreckage were recovered that indicated that a battle had been fought by the three ships. It was thought that all three had gone down.' Joyce paused and smoothed the grey wings of hair along his temples. 'But now it seems certain that *Blücher* was badly damaged during the engagement, and that she was holed up in the delta.'

'Those wheels! Steel plating for repairs!'

'Precisely, Major, precisely. But . . .' Joyce smiled at Flynn, '. . . thanks to you, they did not get the plating through.'

'Yes, they did.' Flynn growled a denial.

'They did?' demanded Joyce harshly.

'Yeah. We left them lying in the veld. My spies told me that after we had gone the Germans sent another party of bearers up and took them away.'

'Why didn't you prevent it?'

'What the hell for? They've got no value,' Flynn retorted.

'The enemy's insistence must have demonstrated their value.'

'Yeah. The enemy were so insistent they sent up a couple of Maxim guns with the second party. In my book the more Maxims there are guarding something, the less value it is.'

'Well, why didn't you destroy them while you had the chance?'

'Listen, friend, how do you reckon to destroy twenty tons of steel – swallow it perhaps?'

'Do you realize just what a threat this ship will be once it is seaworthy?' Joyce hesitated. 'I tell you now in strict confidence that there will be an invasion of German East Africa in the very near future. Can you imagine the havoc if *Blücher* were to slip out of the Rufiji and get among the troop convoys.'

'Yeah – all of us have got troubles.'

'Major.' The captain's voice was hoarse with the effort of checking his temper. 'Major. I want you to do a reconnaissance and locate the *Blücher* for us.'

'Is that so?' boomed Flynn. 'You want me to go galloping round in the delta when there's a Maxim behind every mangrove tree. It might take a year to search that delta, you've got no idea what it's like in there.'

'That won't be necessary.' Joyce swivelled his chair, he nodded at the Portuguese lieutenant. 'This officer is an aviator.'

'What's that mean?'

'He is a flyer.'

'Yeah? Is that so good? I did a bit of sleeping around when I was young – still get it up now and then.'

Joyce coughed.

'He flies an aircraft. A flying-machine.'

'Oh!' said Flynn. He was impressed. 'Jeez! is that so?' He looked at the Portuguese lieutenant with respect.

'With the co-operation of the Portuguese army I intend conducting an aerial reconnaissance of the Rufiji delta.'

'You mean flying over it in a flying-machine?'

'Precisely.'

'That's a bloody good idea.' Flynn was enthusiastic.

'When can you be ready?'

'What for?'

'For the reconnaissance.'

'Now just hold on a shake, friend!' Flynn was aghast. 'You not getting me into one of those flying things.'

Two hours later they were still arguing on the bridge of H.M.S. *Renounce*, as Joyce conned her back towards the land to deposit Flynn and the two Portuguese on the beach from which his launch had picked them up that morning. The British cruiser steamed over a sea that was oil-slick calm and purple blue, and the land lay as a dark irregular line on the horizon.

'It is essential that someone who knows the delta flies with the pilot. He has just arrived from Portugal, besides which he will be fully occupied in piloting the machine. He must have an observer.' Joyce was trying again.

Flynn had lost all interest in the discussion, he was now occupied with weightier matters.

'Captain,' he started, and Joyce recognized the new tone of his voice and turned to him hopefully.

'Captain, that other business. What about it?'

'I'm sorry – I don't follow you.'

'That gin you promised me, what about it?'

Captain Arthur Joyce R.N was a man of gentle mien. His face was smooth and unlined, his mouth full but grave, his eyes thoughtful, the streaks of silver grey at his temples gave him dignity. There was only one pointer to his true temperament, his eyebrows grew in one solid continuous line across his face; they were as thick and furry across the bridge of his nose as they were above his eyes. Despite his appearance he was a man of dark and violent temper. Ten years on his own bridge, wielding the limitless power and authority of a Royal Naval Captain had not mellowed him, but had taught him how to use the curb on his temper. Since early that morning when he had first shaken Flynn O'Flynn's large hairy paw, Arthur Joyce had been exercising every bit of restraint he possessed – now he had exhausted it all.

Flynn found himself standing speechless beneath the full blaze of Captain Joyce's anger. In a staccato, low-pitched speech, Arthur Joyce told him his opinion of Flynn's courage, character, reliability, drinking habits and sense of personal hygiene.

Flynn was shocked and deeply hurt.

'Listen . . .' he said.

'*YOU* listen,' said Joyce. 'Nothing will give me more pleasure than to see you leave this ship. And when you do so you can rest content in the knowledge that a full report of your conduct will go to my superiors – with copies to the Governor of Mozambique, and the Portuguese War Office.'

'Hold on!' cried Flynn. Not only was he going to leave the cruiser without the gin, but he could imagine that the wording of Joyce's report would ensure that he never got that medal. They might even withdraw his commission. In this moment of terrible stress the solution came to him.

'There is one man. *Only* one man who knows the delta better than I do. He's young, plenty of guts – and he's got eyes like a hawk.'

Joyce glared at him, breathing hard as he fought to check the headlong run of his rage.

'Who?' he demanded.

'My own son,' intoned Flynn, it sounded better than son-in-law.

'Will he do it?'

'He'll do it. I'll see to that,' Flynn assured him.

59

'It's as safe as a horse and cart,' boomed Flynn, he liked the simile, and repeated it.

'How safe is a horse and cart when it's up in the clouds?' asked Sebastian, without lowering his eyes from the sky.

'I'm disappointed in you, Bassie. Most young fellows would jump at this chance.' Flynn was literally in excellent spirits. Joyce had come through with three cases of best Beefeater gin. He sat on one of the gasoline drums that lay beneath the shade of the palm trees above the beach, around him in various attitudes of relaxation lay twenty of his scouts, for it was a drowsy, warm and windless morning. A bright sun burned down from a clear sky, and the white sand was dazzling against the dark green of the sea. The low surf sighed softly against the beach, and half a mile out, a cloud of seabirds were milling and diving on a shoal of bait-fish. Their cries blending with the sound of the sea.

Even though they were a hundred miles north of the Rovuma mouth, deep in German territory, a holiday atmosphere prevailed. Heightened by anticipation of the imminent arrival of the flying-machine they were enjoying themselves – all of them except Sebastian and Rosa. They were holding each other's hands and looking into the southern sky.

'You must find it for us.' Rosa's voice was low, but not low enough to cover her intensity. For the last ten days, since Flynn had returned from his meeting with Joyce on board the *Renounce*, she had spoken of little else but the German warship. It had become another cup to catch the hatred that overflowed from her.

'I'll try,' said Sebastian.

'You must,' she said. 'You must.'

'Should be able to get a good view from up there. Like standing on a mountain – only with no mountain under you,' said Sebastian and he felt his skin crawl at the thought.

'Listen!' said Rosa.

'What?'

'Ssh!'

And he heard it, an insect drone that swelled and sank and swelled again. They heard it under the trees also, and some of them came out into the sun and stood peering towards the south.

Suddenly in the sky there was a flash of reflected sunlight off metal or glass, and a shout went up from the watchers.

It came in towards them, low on wobbly wings, the clatter of its engine rising to a crescendo, its shadow racing ahead of it along the white beach. The group of native scouts exploded in panic-stricken retreat, Sebastian dropped on his face in the sand, only Rosa stood unmoving as it roared a few feet over her head, and then rose and banked away in a curve out over the sea.

Sebastian stood up and sheepishly brushed sand from his bush-jacket, as the aircraft levelled in and sank down on to the hard-packed sand near the water's edge. The beat of its engine faded to a spluttering burble, and it waddled slowly towards them, the backwash of the propeller sending a misty plume of sand scudding out behind. The wings looked as though they were about to fall off.

'All right,' bellowed Flynn at his men who were standing well back in the palm grove. 'Get these drums down there.'

The pilot switched off the motor, and the silence was stunning. He climbed stiffly out of the cockpit on to the lower wing, dumpy and awkward in his thick leather jacket, helmet and goggles. He jumped down on to the beach and shrugged out of the jacket, pulled off the helmet and was revealed as the suave young Portuguese lieutenant.

'Da Silva,' he said offering his right hand as Sebastian ran forward to greet him. 'Hernandez da Silva.'

While Flynn and Sebastian supervised the refuelling of the aircraft, Rosa sat with the pilot under the palms, while he breakfasted on garlic polony and a bottle of white wine that he had brought with him – suitably exotic food for a dashing knight of the air.

Although his mouth was busy, the pilot's eyes were free and he used them on Rosa. Even at a distance of fifty yards Sebastian became aware with mounting disquiet that Rosa was suddenly a woman again. Where before there had been a lifted chin and the straightforward masculine gaze; now there were downcast eyes broken with quick bright glances and secret smiles, now there were soft rose colours that glowed and faded beneath the sun-browned skin of her cheeks and neck. She touched her hair with a finger, pushing a strand back behind her ear. She tugged at the front of her bush-jacket to straighten it, then drew her long khaki-clad legs up sideways beneath her as she sat in the sand. The pilot's eyes followed the movement. He wiped the neck of the wine bottle on his sleeve, and then with a flourish offered it to Rosa.

Rosa murmured her thanks and accepted the bottle to sip at it delicately. With the freckles across her cheeks and the skin peeling from her nose she looked as fresh and as innocent as a little girl, Sebastian thought.

The Portuguese lieutenant on the other hand looked neither fresh nor innocent. He was handsome, if you liked the slimy continental type with that slightly jaded tom cat look. Sebastian decided that there was something obscenely erotic about that little black moustache, that lay upon his upper lip and accentuated the cherry-pink lips beneath.

Watching him take the bottle back from Rosa and lift it towards her in salutation before drinking, Sebastian was overcome with two strong desires. One was to take the wine bottle and thrust it down the lieutenant's throat, the other was to get him into the flying-machine and away from Rosa just as quickly as was possible.

'Paci. Paci,' he growled at Mohammed's gang who were slopping gasoline into the funnel on the upper wing. 'Get a move on, for cat's sake!'

'Get your clobber into this thing, Bassie, and stop giving orders – you know it just confuses everybody.'

'I don't know where to put it – you'd better tell that greaser to come and show me. I can't speak his language.'

'Put it in the front cockpit – the observer's cockpit.'

'Tell that damned Portuguese to come here.' Sebastian dug in stubbornly. 'Tell him to leave Rosa alone and come here.'

Rosa followed the pilot to the aircraft and the expression of awed respect on her face, as she listened to him throwing out orders in Portuguese, infuriated Sebastian. The ritual of starting the aircraft completed, it stood clattering and quivering on the beach, and the pilot waved imperiously at Sebastian from the cockpit to come aboard.

Instead he went to Rosa and took her possessively in his arms.

'Do you love me?' he asked.

'What?' she shouted above the bellow of the engine.

'Do you love me?' he roared.

'Of course I do, you fool,' she shouted back and smiled up into his face before going up on tip-toe to kiss him while the slipstream of the propeller howled around them. Her embrace had passion in it that had not been there these many months, and Sebastian wondered sickly how much of it had been engendered by an outside agency.

'You can do that when you get back.' Flynn prised him loose from Rosa's grip, and boosted him up into the cockpit. The machine jerked forward and Sebastian clutched desperately to retain his balance, then glanced back. Rosa was waving and smiling, he was not certain if the smile was directed at him or at the helmeted head in the cockpit behind him, but his jealousy was swamped by the primeval instinct of survival.

Clutching with both hands at the sides of the cockpit, even his toes curling in their boots as though to grip the floorboards of the cockpit, Sebastian stared ahead.

The beach disappeared beneath the fuselage in a solid white blur; the palm trees whipped past on one side, the sea on the other; the wind tore at his face and tears streamed back along his cheeks, the machine bumped and bucked and jounced, and then leaped upwards under him, dropped back to bounce once more and then was airborne. The earth fell away gently beneath them as they soared, and Sebastian's spirits soared with them. His misgivings melted away.

Sebastian remembered at last to pull the goggles down over his eyes to protect them from the stinging wind, and godlike he looked down through them at a world that was small and tranquil.

When at last he looked back over his shoulder at the pilot, this strange and wonderful shared experience of immortality had lifted him above the petty passions of mere men, and they smiled at each other.

The pilot pointed out over the right wing tip, and Sebastian followed the direction of his arm.

Far, far out on the crenellated blue blanket of the sea, tiny beneath vast fluffy piles of thunderhead cloud, he saw the grey shape of the British cruiser *Renounce* with the pale white feather of its wake fanning on the surface of the ocean behind it.

He nodded and smiled at his companion. Again the pilot pointed, this time ahead.

Still misty in the blue haze of distance, haphazard as the unfitted pieces of a jigsaw puzzle, the islands of the Rufiji delta were spilled and scattered between ocean and mainland.

In the rackety little cockpit, Sebastian squatted over his pack and took from it binoculars, pencil and map-case.

60

It was hot. Moist itchy hot. Even in the shade beneath the festooned camouflage-nets the decks of *Blücher* were smothered with hot sticky waves of swamp air. The sweat that oozed and trickled down the glistening bodies of the half-naked men who slaved on her foredeck gave them no relief, for the air was too humid to evaporate the moisture. They moved like sleep-walkers, with slow mechanical determination, manhandling the thick sheet of steel plate into its slings beneath the high arm of the crane.

Even the flow of obscenity from the lips of Lochtkamper, the engineering commander, had dried up like a spring in drought season. He worked with his men, like them stripped to the waist, and the tattoos on his upper arms and across his chest heaved and bulged as they rode on an undulating sea of muscles.

'Rest,' he grunted; and they straightened up from their labour, mouths gaping as they sucked in the stale air, massaging aching backs, glowering at the sheet of steel with true hatred.

'Captain.' Lochtkamper became aware of von Kleine for the first time. He stood against the forward gun-turret, tall in full whites, the blond beard half concealing the cross of black enamel and silver that hung at his throat. Lochtkamper crossed to him.

'It goes well?' von Kleine asked, and the engineer shook his head.

'Not as well as I had hoped.' He wiped one huge hand across his forehead, leaving a smudge of grease and rust scale on his own face. 'Slow,' he said. 'Too slow.'

'You have encountered difficulties?'

'Everywhere,' growled the engineer, and he looked around at the heat mist and the mangroves, at the sluggish black waters and the mud banks. 'Nothing works here – the welding equipment, the winch engines, even the men – everything sickens in this obscene heat.'

'How much longer?'

'I do not know, Captain. I truly do not know.'

Von Kleine would not press him. If any man could get *Blücher* seaworthy, it would be this man. When Lochtkamper slept at all, it was here on the foredeck, curled like a dog on a mattress thrown on the planking. He slept a few exhausted hours amid the whine and groan of the winches, the blue hissing glare of the welding torches and the drum splitting hammering of the riveters, then he was up again bullying, leading, coaxing and threatening.

'Another three weeks,' Lochtkamper estimated reluctantly. 'A month at the most – if all goes as it does now.'

They were both silent, standing together, two men from different worlds drawn together by a common goal, united by respect for each other's ability.

A mile up the channel, movement caught their attention. It was one of the launches returning to the cruiser, yet it looked like a hayrick under its bulky cargo. It came slowly against the sluggish current, sitting so low in the water that only a few inches of freeboard showed, while its load was a great shaggy hump on which sat a dozen black men.

Von Kleine and Lochtkamper watched it approaching.

'I still do not know about that obscene wood, Captain.' Lochtkamper shook his big untidy head again. 'It is so soft, so much ash, it could clog the furnace.'

'There is nothing else we can do,' von Kleine reminded him.

When *Blücher* entered the Rufiji, her coal-bunkers were almost empty. There was enough fuel for perhaps four thousand miles of steaming. Hardly enough to carry her in a straight run down into latitude 45° south, where her mother ship, *Esther*, waited to refuel her, and fill her magazines with shell.

There was not the faintest chance of obtaining coal. Instead von Kleine had set Commissioner Fleischer and his thousand native porters to cutting cordwood from the forests, that grew at the apex of the delta. It was a duty that Commissioner Fleischer had opposed with every argument and excuse he could muster. He felt that in delivering safely to Captain von Kleine the steel plating from Dar es Salaam, he had discharged any obligation that he might have towards the *Blücher*. His eloquence availed him not at all – Lochtkamper had fashioned two hundred primitive axe heads from the steel plate, and von Kleine had sent Lieutenant Kyller up-river with Fleischer to help him keep his enthusiasm for wood-cutting burning brightly.

For three weeks now, the *Blücher*'s launches had been plying steadily back and forth. Up to the present they had delivered some five hundred tons of timber. The problem was finding storage for this unwieldy cargo once the coal-bunkers were filled.

'We will have to begin deck loading the cordwood soon,' von Kleine muttered, and Lochtkamper opened his mouth to reply when the alarm bells began to clamour an emergency, and the loudhailer boomed.

'Captain to the bridge. Captain to the bridge.'

Von Kleine turned and ran.

On the companion ladder he collided with one of his lieutenants. They caught at each other for balance and the lieutenant shouted into von Kleine's face.

'Captain – an aircraft. Flying low. Coming this way. Portuguese markings.'

'Damn it to hell!' Von Kleine pushed past him, and bounded up the ladder. He burst on to the bridge, panting.

'Where is it?' he shouted.

The officer of the watch dropped his binoculars and turned to von Kleine with relief.

'There it is, sir!' He pointed through a hole in the tangled screen of camouflage that hung like a veranda roof over the bridge.

Von Kleine snatched the binoculars from him and, as he trained them on the distant winged shape in the mist haze above the mangroves, he issued his orders.

'Warn the men ashore. Everybody under cover,' he barked. 'All guns trained to maximum elevation. Pom-poms loaded with shrapnel. Machine gun crews closed up – but no firing until my orders.'

He held the aircraft in the round field of the field glasses.

'Portuguese, all right,' he grunted; the green and red insignia showed clearly against the brown body of the aircraft.

'She's searching . . .' The aircraft was sweeping back and forth, banking over and turning back at the end of each leg of her search pattern, like a farmer ploughing a field. Von Kleine could make out the head and shoulders of a man crouched forward in the squat round nose of the aircraft. '. . . Now we'll find out how effective is our camouflage.'

So the enemy have guessed at last. They must have reported the convoy of steel plate – or perhaps the chopping of the cordwood has alerted them, he thought, watching the aircraft tacking slowly towards him. *We could not hope to go undetected for ever – but I did not expect them to send an aircraft.*

Then suddenly the thought struck him so hard that he gasped with the danger of it. He whirled and ran to the forward rail of the bridge and peered out through the camouflage net.

Still half a mile distant, trundling slowly down the centre of the channel with the wide rippling V of her wake spread on the current behind her, clumsy as a pregnant hippo with her load of cordwood, the launch was aimed straight at *Blücher*. From the air she would be as conspicuous as a fat tick on a white sheet.

'The launch . . .' shouted von Kleine, '. . . hail her. Order her to run for the bank – get her under cover.'

But he knew it was useless. By the time she was within hail, it would be too late. He thought of ordering his forward turrets to fire on the launch and sink her – but discarded the idea immediately, the fall of shell would immediately draw the enemy's attention.

Impatiently he stood gripping the rail of the bridge, and mouthing his anger and his frustration at the approaching launch.

61

Sebastian hung over the edge of the cockpit. The wind buffeted him, flapping his jacket wildly about his body, whipping his hair into a black tangle. With his usual dexterity Sebastian had managed to drop the binoculars overboard. They were the property of Flynn Patrick O'Flynn, and Sebastian knew that he would be expected to pay for them. This spoiled Sebastian's enjoyment of the flight to some extent, he already owed Flynn a little over three hundred pounds. Rosa would have something to say also. However, the loss of the binoculars was no handicap, the aircraft was flying too low and was so unstable that the unaided eye was much more effective.

From a height of five hundred feet the mangrove forest looked like a fluffy overstuffed mattress, a sickly fever green in colour, with the channels and the water-ways between them dark gunmetal veins that flashed the sunlight back like a heliograph. The clouds of white egrets that rose in alarm as the aircraft approached looked like drifts of torn paper scraps. A fish eagle hung suspended in silent flight ahead of them, the wide span of its wings flared at the tips like the fingers of a hand. It dipped away, sliding past the aircraft's wing tip so close, that Sebastian saw the fierce yellow eyes in its white hooded head.

Sebastian laughed with delight, and then grabbed at the side of the cockpit to steady himself, as the machine rocked violently under him. This was the pilot's method of attracting Sebastian's attention, and Sebastian wished he would think up some other way of doing it.

He looked back angrily shouting in the howl of wind and engine.

'Watch it! You stupid dago.'

Da Silva was gesticulating wildly, his pink mouth working under the black moustache, his eyes wild behind the panes of his goggles, his right hand stabbing urgently out over the star-board wing.

Sebastian saw it immediately on the wide water-way, the launch was so glaringly conspicuous that he wondered why he had not seen it before, then he recalled that his attention had been concentrated on the terrain directly beneath the aircraft – and he excused himself.

Yet there was little to justify da Silva's excitement, he thought. This was no battle cruiser, it was a tiny vessel of perhaps twenty-five feet. Quickly he ran his eyes down the channel, following it to the open sea in the blue distance. It was empty.

He glanced back at the pilot and shook his head. But da Silva's excitement had, if anything, increased. He was making another frenzied hand-signal that Sebastian could not understand. To save argument Sebastian nodded in agreement, and instantly the machine dropped away under him so that Sebastian's belly was left behind and he clutched desperately at the side of the cockpit once more.

In a shallow turning dive, da Silva took the machine down and then levelled out with the landing-wheels almost brushing the tops of the mangroves. They rushed towards the channel, and as the last mangroves whipped away under them da Silva eased the nose down still farther and they dropped to within a few feet of the surface of the water. It was a display of fine flying that was completely wasted on Sebastian. He was cursing da Silva quietly, his eyes starting from their sockets.

A mile ahead of them across the open water bobbed the overladen launch. It was only a few feet below their own level, and they raced towards it with the wash of the propeller blowing a squall of ripples across the surface behind them.

'My God!' The blasphemy was wrung from Sebastian in his distress. 'He's going to fly right into it!'

It was an opinion that seemed to be shared by the crew of the launch. As the machine roared in on them, they began to abandon ship. Sebastian saw two men leap from the high piled load of timber and hit the water with small white splashes.

At the last second da Silva lifted the plane and they hopped over the launch. For a fleeting instant Sebastian stared at a range of fifteen feet into the face of the German naval officer who crouched down over the tiller bar at the stern of the launch.

They were then past and climbing sharply, banking and turning back.

Sebastian saw the launch had rounded to, and that her crew were clambering aboard and splashing around her sides. Once more the aircraft dropped towards the channel, but da Silva had throttled back and the engine was burbling under half power. He leveled out fifty feet above the water, and flew sedately, keeping away from the launch and well towards the northern side of the channel.

'What are you doing?' Sebastian mouthed the question at da Silva. In reply the pilot made a sweeping gesture with his right hand at the thick bank of mangroves alongside.

Puzzled, Sebastian stared into the mangroves. What was the fool doing, surely he didn't think that . . .

There was a hump of high ground on the bank, a hump that rose perhaps one hundred and fifty feet above the level of the river. They came up to it.

Like a hunter following a wounded buffalo, moving carelessly through thin scattered bush which could not possibly give cover to such a large animal, and then suddenly coming face to face with it – so close, that he sees the minute detail of crenellation on the massive bosses of the horns, sees the blood dripping from moist black nostrils, and the dull furnace glare of the piggy little eyes – in the same fashion Sebastian found the *Blücher*.

She was so close he could see the pattern of rivets on her plating, the joints in the planking of her foredeck, the individual strands of the canopy of camouflage netting spread over her. He saw the men on her bridge, and the gun-crews behind the pom-poms and the Maxim machine guns on the balconies of her upperworks. From her squatting turrets her big guns gaped at him with hungry mouths, revolving to follow the flight of the machine.

She was monstrous, grey and sinister among the mangroves, crouching in her lair, and Sebastian cried aloud in surprise and alarm, a sound without shape or coherence, and at the same moment the engine of the aeroplane bellowed in full power, as da Silva thrust the throttle wide and hauled the joystick back into his crotch.

As the aircraft rocketed upwards, the deck of the *Blücher* erupted in a thunderous volcano of flame. Flame flew in great bell-shaped ejaculations from the muzzles of her nine-inch guns.

Flame spat viciously from the multi-barrelled pom-poms and the machine guns on her upperworks.

Around the little aircraft the air boiled and hissed, disrupted, churned into violent turbulence by the passage of the big shells.

Something struck the plane, and she was whirled upwards like a burning leaf from a garden bonfire. Wing over wing she rolled, her engine surging wildly, her rigging groaning and creaking at the strain.

Sebastian was flung forward, the bridge of his nose cracked against the edge of the cockpit and instantly twin jets of blood spurted from his nostrils to douse the front of his jacket.

The machine stood on her tail, propeller clawing ineffectively at the air, engine wailing in over rev. Then she dropped away on one wing and one side swooped sickeningly downwards.

Da Silva fought her, feeling the sloppiness of the stall in her controls come alive again as she regained air-speed. The fluffy tops of the mangroves rushed up to meet him, and desperately he tried to ease her off. She was trying to respond, the fabric wrinkling along her wings as they flexed to the enormous pressure. He felt her lurch again as she touched the top branches, heard above the howl of the engine the faint crackling brush of the vegetation against her belly. Then suddenly, miraculously, she was clear; flying straight and level, climbing slowly up and away from the hungry swamp.

She was sluggish and heavy, and there was something loose under her. It banged and thumped and slapped in the slipstream, jarring the whole fuselage. Da Silva could not dare to manoeuvre her. He held her on the course she had chosen, easing her nose slightly upwards, slowly gaining precious altitude.

At a thousand feet he brought her round in a wide gentle turn to the south, and banging and thumping, one wing heavy, she staggered drunkenly through the sky towards her rendezvous with Flynn O'Flynn.

62

Flynn stood up with slow dignity from where he had been leaning against the bole of the palm tree.

'Where are you going?' Rosa opened her eyes and looked up at him.

'To do something you can't do for me.'

'That's the third time in an hour!' Rosa was suspicious.

'That's why they call it the East African quickstep,' said Flynn, and moved off ponderously into the undergrowth. He reached the lantana bush, and looked around carefully. He couldn't trust Rosa not to follow him. Satisfied, he dropped to his knees and dug with his hands in the loose sand.

With the air of an old-time pirate unearthing a chest of doubloons, he lifted the bottle from its grave, and withdrew the cork.

The neck of the bottle was in his mouth, when he heard the muted beat of the returning aircraft. The bottle stayed there a while longer, Flynn's Adam's apple pulsing up and down his throat as he swallowed, but his eyes swivelled upwards and creased in concentration.

With a sigh of intense pleasure he recorked, and laid the bottle once more to rest, kicked sand over it, and set course for the beach.

'Can you see them?' he shouted the question at Rosa as he came down through the palms. She was standing out in the open. Her head was thrown back so that the long braid of her hair hung down to her waist behind. She did not answer him, but the set of her expression was hard and strained with anxiety. The men standing about her were silent also, held by an expectant dread.

Flynn looked up and saw it coming in like a wounded bird, the engine stuttering and surging irregularly, streaming a long bluish streak of oily smoke from the exhaust manifold, the wings rocking crazily, and a loose tangle of wreckage hanging and swinging under the belly where one of the landing-wheels had been shot away.

It sagged wearily towards the beach, the broken beat of the engine failing so they could hear the whisper of the wind in her rigging.

The single landing-wheel touched down on the hard sand and for fifty yards she ran true, then with a jerk she toppled sideways. The port wing bit into the sand, slewing her towards the edge of the sea, the tail came up and over. There was a crackling, ripping, tearing sound; and in a dust storm of flying sand she cartwheeled, stern over stem.

The propeller tore into the beach, disintegrating in a blur of flying splinters, and from the forward cockpit a human body was flung clear, spinning in the air so that the outflung limbs were the spokes of a wheel. It fell with a splash in the shallow water at the edge of the beach, while the aircraft careened onwards, tearing herself to pieces. A lower wing broke off – the guy wires snapping with a sound like a volley of musketry. The body of the machine slowed as it hit the water, skidding to a standstill on its back, with the surf washing around it. Da Silva hung motionless in the back cockpit, suspended upside down by his safety-straps, his arms dangling.

The next few seconds of silence were appalling.

'Help the pilot! I'll get Sebastian.' Rosa broke it at last. Mohammed and two other Askari ran with her towards where Sebastian was lying awash, a piece of flotsam at the water's edge.

'Come on!' Flynn shouted at the men near him, and lumbered through the soft fluffy sand towards the wreck. They never reached it.

There was a concussion, a vast disturbance in the air that sucked at their eardrums, as the gasoline ignited in explosive combustion. The machine and the surface of the sea about it was instantly transformed into a roaring, raging sheet of flame.

They backed away from the heat. The flames were dark red laced with satanic black smoke, and they ate the canvas skin from the body of the aircraft, exposing the wooden framework beneath.

In the heart of the flames da Silva still hung in his cockpit, a blackened monkey-like shape as his clothing burned. Then the fire ate through the straps of his harness and he dropped heavily into the shallow water, hissing and sizzling as the flames were quenched.

The fire was still smouldering by the time Sebastian regained consciousness, and was able to lift himself on one elbow. Muzzily he stared down the beach at the smoking wreckage. The shadows of the palms lay like the stripes of a tiger on the sand that the low evening sun had softened to a dull gold.

'Da Silva?' Sebastian's voice was thick and slurred. His nose was broken and squashed across his face. Although Rosa had wiped most of the blood away, there were still little black crusts of it in his nostrils and at the corners of his mouth. Both his eyes were slits in the swollen plum-coloured bruises that bulged from the sockets.

'No!' Flynn shook his head. 'He didn't make it.'

'Dead?' whispered Sebastian.

'We buried him back in the bush.'

'What happened?' asked Rosa. 'What on earth happened out there?' She sat close beside him, protective as a mother over her child. Slowly Sebastian turned his head to look at her.

'We found the *Blücher*,' he said.

63

Captain Arthur Joyce, R.N., was a happy man. He stooped over his cabin desk, his hands placed open and flat on either side of the spread admiralty chart. He glowed with satisfaction as he looked down at the hand-drawn circle in crude blue pencil as though it were the signature of the President of the Bank of England on a cheque for a million sterling.

'Good!' he said. 'Oh, very good,' and he pursed his lips as though he were about to whistle 'Tipperary'. Instead he made a sucking sound, and smiled across at Sebastian. Behind his flattened nose and blue-ringed eyes, Sebastian smiled back at him.

'A damn good show, Oldsmith!' Joyce's expression changed, the little lights of recognition sparkled suddenly in his eyes. 'Oldsmith?' he repeated. 'I say, didn't you open the bowling for Sussex in the 1911 cricket season?'

'That's right, sir.'

'Good Lord!' Joyce beamed at him. 'I'll never forget your opening over to Yorkshire in the first match of the season. You dismissed Graham and Penridge for two runs – two for two, hey?'

'Two for two, it was,' Sebastian liked this man.

'Fiery stuff! And then you made fifty-five runs?'

'Sixty-five,' Sebastian corrected him. 'A record ninth wicket partnership with Clifford Dumont of – one hundred and eighty-six!'

'Yes! Yes! I remember it well. Fiery stuff! You were damned unlucky not to play for England.'

'Oh, I don't know about that,' said Sebastian in modest agreement.

'Yes, you were.' Joyce pursed his lips again. 'Damned unlucky.'

Flynn O'Flynn had not understood a word of this. He was thrashing around in his chair like an old buffalo in a trap, bored to the point of pain. Rosa Oldsmith had understood no more than he had, but she was fascinated. It was clear that Captain Joyce knew of some outstanding accomplishment of Sebastian's, and if a man like Joyce knew of it – then Sebastian was famous. She felt pride swell in her chest and she smiled on Sebastian also.

'I didn't know, Sebastian. Why didn't you tell me?' She glowed warmly at him.

'Some other time,' Joyce interrupted quickly. 'Now we must get on with this other business.' And he returned his attention to the chart on the desk.

'Now I want you to cast your mind back. Shut your eyes and try to see it again. Every detail you can remember, every little detail – it might be important. Did you see any signs of damage?'

Obediently Sebastian closed his eyes, and was surprised at how vividly the acid of fear had engraved the picture of *Blücher* on his mind.

'Yes,' he said. 'There were holes in her. Hundreds of holes, little black ones. And at the front end – the bows – there were trapezes hanging down on ropes, near the water. You know the kind that they use when they paint a high building . . .'

Joyce nodded at his secretary to record every word of it.

64

The single fan suspended over the table in the wardroom hummed quietly, the blades stirred the air that was moist and warm as the bedding of a malarial patient.

Except for the soft clink of cutlery on china, the only other sound was that of Commissioner Fleischer drinking his soup. It was thick, green pea soup, scalding hot, so that Fleischer found it necessary to blow heavily on each spoonful before ingesting it with a noise, not of the same volume as, but with the delicate tonal quality, of a flushing water closet. During the pause while he crumbled a slice of black bread into his soup, Fleischer looked across the board at Lieutenant Kyller.

'So you did not find the enemy flying-machine, then?'

'No.' Kyller went on fiddling with his wine glass without looking up. For forty-eight hours he and his patrols had searched the swamps and channels and mangrove forests for the wreckage of the aircraft. He was exhausted and covered with insect bites.

'Ja,' Fleischer nodded solemnly. 'It fell only a short way, but it did not hit the trees. I was sure of that. I have seen sandgrouse do the same thing sometimes when you shoot them with a shot-gun. Pow! They come trumbling down like this . . .' He fluttered his hand in the air, letting it fall towards his soup, '. . . then suddenly they do this.' The hand took flight again in the direction of Commander (Engineering) Lochtkamper's rugged Neanderthal face. They all watched it.

'The little bird flies away home. It was bad shooting from so close,' said Fleischer, and ended the demonstration by picking up his soup spoon, and the moist warm silence once more gripped the wardroom.

Commander Lochtkamper stoked his mouth as though it were one of his furnaces. The knuckles of both his hands were knocked raw by contact with steel plate and wire rope. Even when Fleischer's hand had flown into his face, he had not been distracted from his thoughts. His mind was wholly occupied with steel and machinery, weights and points of balance. He wanted to achieve twenty degrees of starboard list on *Blücher*, so that a greater area of her bottom would be exposed to his welders. This meant displacing one thousand tons of dead weight. It seemed an impossibility – unless we flood the port magazines, he thought, and take the guns from their turrets and move them. Then we could rig camels under her . . .

'It was not bad shooting,' said the gunnery lieutenant. 'She was flying too close, the rate of track was . . .' He broke off, wiped the side of his long pointed nose with his forefinger, and regarded balefully the sweat that came away on it. This fat peasant would not understand, he would not waste energy in explaining the technicalities. He contented himself with repeating, 'It was not bad shooting.'

'I think we must accept that the enemy machine has returned safely to her base,' said Lieutenant Kyller. 'Therefore we can expect the enemy to mount some form of offensive action against us in the very near future.' Kyller enjoyed a position of privilege in the wardroom. No other of the junior officers would have dared to express his opinions so freely. Yet none of them would have made as much sense as Kyller. When he spoke his senior officers listened, if not respectfully, at least attentively. Kyller had passed out sword of honour cadet from Bremerhaven Naval Academy in 1910. His father was a Baron, a personal friend of the Kaiser's, and an Admiral of the Imperial Fleet. Kyller was wardroom favourite, not only because of his dark good looks and courteous manner – but also because of his appetite for hard work, his meticulous attention to detail, and his ready mind. He was a good officer to have aboard – a credit to the ship.

'What can the enemy do?' Fleischer asked with scorn. He did not share the general opinion of Ernst Kyller. 'We are safe here – what can he do?'

'A superficial study of naval history will reveal, sir, that the English can be expected to do what you least expect them to do. And that they will do it, quickly, efficiently and with iron purpose.' Kyller scratched the lumpy red insect bites behind his left ear.

'Bah!' said Fleischer, and sprayed a little pea soup with the violence of his disgust. 'The English are fools and cowards – at the worst, they will skulk off the mouth of the river. They would not dare come in here after us.'

'I have no doubt that time will prove you correct, sir.' This was Kyller's phrase of violent disagreement with a senior officer, and from experience Captain von Kleine and his commanders recognized it. They smiled a little.

'This soup is bitter,' said Fleischer, satisfied that he had carried the argument. 'The cook has used sea-water in it.'

The accusation was so outrageous, that even von Kleine looked up from his plate.

'Please do not let our humble hospitality delay you, Herr Commissioner. You must be anxious to return up-river to your wood-cutting duties.'

And Fleischer subsided quickly, hunching over his food. Von Kleine transferred his gaze to Kyller.

'Kyller, you will not be returning with the Herr Commissioner. I am sending Ensign Proust with him this trip. You will be in command of the first line of defence that I plan to place at the mouth of the delta, in readiness for the English attack. You will attend the conference in my cabin after this meal, please.'

'Thank you, sir.' His voice was husky with gratitude for the honour his captain was conferring upon him. Von Kleine looked from him to his gunnery lieutenant.

'You also, please, Guns. I want to relieve you of your beloved upper deck pom-poms.'

'You mean to take them off their mountings, sir?' The gunnery lieutenant asked, looking at von Kleine dolefully over his long doleful nose.

'I regret the necessity,' von Kleine told him sympathetically.

65

'Well, Henry. We were right. *Blücher*'s there.'

'Unfortunately, sir.'

'Two heavy cruisers tied up indefinitely on blockade service.'
Admiral Sir Percy thrust out his lower lip lugubriously as he
regarded the plaques of *Renounce* and *Pegasus* on the Indian
Ocean plot. 'There is work for them elsewhere.'

'There is, at that,' agreed Henry Green.

'That request of Joyce's for two motor torpedo-boats . . .'

'Yes, sir?'

'We must suppose he intends mounting a torpedo attack into
the delta.'

'It looks like it, sir.'

'It might work – worth a try anyway. What can we scratch
together for him?'

'There is a full squadron at Bombay, and another at Aden, sir.'
For five seconds, Sir Percy Howe reviewed the meagre forces
with which he was expected to guard two oceans. With this new
submarine menace, he could not detach a single ship from the
approaches to the Suez Canal – it would have to be Bombay.
'Send him an M. T. B. from the Bombay squadron.'

'He asked for two, sir.'

'Joyce knows full well that I only let him have half of anything
he requests. He always doubles up.'

'What about this recommendation for a decoration, sir?'

'The fellow who spotted the *Blücher*?'

'Yes, sir.'

'A bit tricky – Portuguese irregular and all that sort of thing.'

'He's a British subject, sir.'

'Then he shouldn't be with the dagos,' said Sir Percy. 'Leave
it over until the operation is completed. We'll think about it
after we've sunk the *Blücher*.'

66

The sunset was blood and roses, nude pink and tarnished gold as the British blockade squadron stood in towards the land.

Renounce led with the commodore's penant flying at her mast-head. In the smooth wide road of her wake, *Pegasus* slid over the water. Their silhouettes were crisp and black against the garish colours of the sunset. There was something prim and old-maidish about the lines of a heavy cruiser – none of the solid majesty of a battle-ship, nor the jaunty devil-may-care rake of a destroyer.

Close in under *Pegasus*'s beam, screened by her hull from the land, like a signet swimming beside the swan, rode the motor torpedo-boat.

Even in this light surface chop she was taking in water. Each wave puffed up over her bows and then streamed back greenish and cream along her decks. The spray rattled against the thin canvas that screened the open bridge.

Flynn O'Flynn crouched behind the screen and cursed the vaunting ambition that had led him to volunteer as pilot for this expedition. He glanced across at Sebastian who stood in the open wing of the bridge, behind the canvas-shrouded batteries of Lewis guns. Sebastian was grinning as the warm spray flew back into his face and trickled down his cheeks.

Joyce had recommended Sebastian for a Distinguished Service Order. This was almost more than Flynn could bear. He wanted one also. He had decided to go along now for that reason alone. Therefore Sebastian was directly to blame for Flynn's present discomfort, and Flynn felt a small warmth of satisfaction as he looked at the flattened, almost negroid contours of Sebastian's new nose. The young bastard deserved it, and he found himself wishing further punishment on his son-in-law.

'Distinguished Service Order and all . . .' he grunted. 'A half-trained chimpanzee could have done what he did. Yet who was it who found the wheels in the first place? No, Flynn Patrick, there just ain't no justice in this world, but we'll show the sons of bitches this time . . .'

His thoughts were interrupted by the small bustle of activity on the bridge around him. An Aldis lamp was winking from the high dark bulk of *Renounce* ahead of them.

The lieutenant commanding the torpedo-boat spelled the message aloud.

'Flag to YN2. D . . . P departure point. Good luck.' He was a dumpy amorphous figure in his duffle coat with the collar turned up. 'Thanks a lot, old chap – and one up your pipe also. No, Signaller, don't make that.' He went on quickly, 'YN2 to Flag. Acknowledged! Then turning to the engine voice-pipe. 'Both engines stop,' he said.

The beat of her engines faded away, and she wallowed in the trough of the next wave. *Renounce* and *Pegasus* sailed on sedately, leaving the tiny vessel rolling crazily in the turbulence of their wakes. A lonely speck five miles off the mouth of the Rufiji delta, too far off for the shorewatchers to see her in the fading evening light.

Lieutenant Ernst Kyller watched through his binoculars as the two British cruisers turned in succession away from the land and coalesced with the darkness that fell so swiftly over the ocean and the land. They were gone.

'Every day it is the same.' Kyller let the binoculars fall against his chest and pulled his watch from the pocket of his tunic. 'Fifteen minutes before sunset, and again fifteen minutes before sun-up they sail past to show us that they are still waiting.'

'Yes, sir,' agreed the seaman who was squeezed into the crow's-nest beside Kyller.

'I will go down now. Moon comes up at 11.44 tonight – keep awake.'

'Yes, sir.'

Kyller swung his legs over the side and groped with his feet for the rungs of the rope ladder. Then he climbed down the palm tree to the beach fifty feet below. By the time he reached it the light had gone, and the beach was a vague white blur down to the green lights of phosphorus in the surf.

The sand crunched like sugar under his boots as he set off to where the launch was moored. As he walked, his mind was wholly absorbed with the details of his defence system.

There were only two of the many mouths of the Rufiji, up which the English could attack. They were separated by a low wedge-shaped island of sand and mud and mangrove. It was on the seaward side of this island that Kyller had sited the four-pounder pom-poms taken from their mountings on *Blucher*'s upper deck.

He had sunk a raft of logs into the soft mud to give them a firm foundation on which to stand, and he had cut out the mangroves so they commanded an arc of fire across both channels. His search-lights he sited with equal care – so they could sweep left or right without blinding his gunners.

From Commander Lochtkamper he had solicited a length of four-inch steel hawser. This was rather like an unrehabilitated insolvent raising an unsecured loan from a money-lender, for Commander Locktkamper was not easily parted from his stores. Far up river Ensign Proust had diverted some of his axe-men to felling fifty giant African mahogany trees. They had floated the trunks down on the tide; logs the size of the columns of a Greek temple. With these and the cable Kyller had fashioned a boom that stretched across both channels, an obstacle so formidable that it would rip the belly out of even a heavy cruiser coming down on it at speed.

Not satisfied with this, for Kyller had highly developed the Teutonic capacity for taking infinite pains, he lifted the fat globular mines with their sinister horns that *Blücher* had sown haphazardly behind her on her journey up-river. These he rearranged into neat geometrical ranks behind his log boom, a labour that left his men almost prostrated with nervous exhaustion.

This work had taken ten days to complete, and immediately Kyller had begun building observation posts. He placed them on every hump of high ground that commanded a view of the ocean, he built them in the tops of the palm trees, and on the smaller islands that stood out at sea. He arranged a system of signals with his observers – flags and heliographs for the day, sky-rockets for the night.

During the hours of darkness, two whale boats rowed steadily back and forth along the log boom, manned by seamen who slapped steadily and sulkily at the light cloud of mosquitoes that haloed their heads, and made occasional brief but vitriolic statements about Lieutenant Kyller's ancestry, present worth and future prospects.

At 2200 hours on the moonless night of 16 June 1915, the British motor torpedo-boat YN2 crept with both engines running dead slow into the centre of Lieutenant Kyller's elaborate reception arrangements.

68

After the clean cool air on the open sea, the smell was like entering the monkey-house of London Zoo. The land masked the breeze, and the frolic of the surface chop died away. As the torpedo-boat groped its way into the delta, the miasma of the swamps spread out to meet her.

'My God, that smell,' Sebastian twitched his flattened nose. 'It brings back pleasant memories.'

'Lovely, isn't it?' agreed Flynn.

'We must be almost into the channel.' Sebastian peered into the night, sensing rather than seeing the loom of the mangroves ahead and on either hand.

'I don't know what the hell I'm doing on this barge,' grunted Flynn. 'This is raving bloody madness. We've got more chance of catching a clap than finding our way up to where *Blücher* is anchored.'

'Faith! Major O'Flynn, and shame on ye!' The commander of the torpedo-boat exclaimed in his best music-hall brogue. 'We put our trust in you and the Lord.' His tone changed and he spoke crisply to the helmsman beside him. 'Lay her off a point to starboard.'

The long nose of the boat, with the torpedo tubes lying like a rack of gigantic champagne bottles on her foredeck, swung fractionally. The commander cocked his head to listen to the whispered soundings relayed from the leadsman in the bows.

'Twelve fathoms,' he repeated thoughtfully. 'So far so good.' Then he turned back to Flynn.

'Now, Major, I heard you shooting the blarney to Captain Joyce about how well you know this river, I think your exact words were, "Like you know the way to your own Thunder Box." You don't seem so certain about it any longer. Why is that?'

'It's dark,' said Flynn sulkily.

'My, so it is. But that shouldn't fluster an old river pilot like you.'

'Well, it sure as hell does.'

'If we get into the channel and lay up until the moon rises, would that help?'

'It wouldn't do any harm.'

That exchange seemed to exhaust the subject and for a further fifteen minutes the tense silence on the bridge was spoiled only by the commander's quiet orders to the helm, as he kept his ship within the ten fathom line of the channel.

Then Sebastian made a contribution.

'I say, there's something dead ahead of us.'

A patch of deeper darkness in the night; a low blurred shape that showed against the faint sheen of the star reflections on the surface. A reef perhaps? No, there was a splash alongside it as an oar dipped and pulled.

'Guard boat!' said the commander, and stooped to the voice-pipe. 'Both engines full ahead together.'

The deck canted sharply under their feet as the bows lifted, the whisper of the engines rose to a dull bellow and the torpedo-boat plunged forward like a bull at the cape.

'Hold on! I'm going to ram it.' The commander's voice was pitched at conversational level, and a hubbub of shouts broke out ahead, oars splashed frantically as the guard boat tried to pull out of their line of charge.

'Steer for them,' said the commander pleasantly, and the helmsman put her over a little.

Flash and crack, flash and crack, someone in the guard boat fired a rifle just as the torpedo-boat struck her. It was a glancing blow, taken on her shoulder, that spun the little whale boat aside, shearing off the protruding oars with a crackling popping sound.

She scraped down the gunwhale of the torpedo-boat, and then was left astern bobbing and rocking wildly as the larger vessel surged ahead.

Then abruptly it was no longer dark. From all around them sparkling trails of fire shot into the sky and burst in balls of blue, that lit it all with an eerie flickering glow.

'Sky rockets, be Jesus. Guy Fawkes, Guy,' said the commander.

They could see the banks of mangrove massed on either hand, and ahead of them the double mouths of the two channels.

'Steer for the southern channel.' This time the commander lifted his voice a little, and the ship plunged onward, throwing out white wings of water from under her bows, bucking and jarring as she leapt over the low swells pushed up by the out-flowing tide, so the men on the bridge hung on to the hand rail to steady themselves.

Then all of them gasped together in the pain of seared eyeballs as a solid shaft of dazzling white light struck them. It leapt out from the dark wedge of land that divided the two channels, and almost immediately two other searchlights on the outer banks of the channels joined in the hunt. Their beams fastened on the ship like the tentacles of a squid on the carcass of a flying fish.

'Get those lights!' This time the commander shouted the order at the gunners behind the Lewis guns at the corners of the bridge. The tracer that hosed out in a gentle arc towards the base of the searchlight beams was anaemic and pinkly pale, in contrast to the brilliance they were trying to quench.

The torpedo-boat roared on into the channel.

Then there was another sound. A regular thump, thump, thump like the working of a distant water pump. Lieutenant Kyller had opened up with his quick firing pom-pom.

The four-pound tracer emanated from the dark blob of the island. Seeming to float slowly towards the torpedo-boat, but gaining speed as it approached, until it flashed past with the whirr of a rocketing pheasant.

'Jesus!' said Flynn as though he meant it. He sat down hurriedly on the deck and began to unlace his boots.

Still held in the cold white grip of the searchlights, the torpedo-boat roared on with four-pounder shell streaking around her, and bursting in flurries of spray on the surface near her. The long dotted tendrils of tracer from her own lewis guns still arched out in delicate lines towards the shore, and suddenly they had effect.

The beam of one of the searchlights snapped off as a bullet shattered the glass, for a few seconds the filaments continued to glow dull red as they burned themselves out.

In the relief from the blinding glare, Sebastian could see ahead, and he saw a sea serpent. It lay across the channel, undulating in the swells, bellied from bank to bank by the push of the tide, showing its back at the top of the swells and then ducking into the troughs; long and sinuous and menacing, Lieutenant Kyller's log boom waited to welcome them.

'Good God, what's that?'

'Full port rudder!' the commander bellowed. 'Both engines full astern together.'

And before the ship could answer her helm or the drag of her propellers, she ran into a log four feet thick and a hundred feet long. A log as unyielding as a reef of solid granite that stopped her dead in the water and crunched in her bows.

The men in the well of her bridge were thrown into a heap of tangled bodies on the deck. A heap from which the bull figure of Flynn Patrick O'Flynn was the first to emerge. On stockinged feet he made for the side of the ship.

'Flynn, where are you going?' Sebastian shouted after him.

'Home,' said Flynn.

'Wait for me.' Sebastian scrambled to his knees.

The engines roaring in reverse pulled the torpedo-boat back off the log-boom, her plywood hull crackling and squeaking, but she was mortally wounded. She was sinking with a rapidity that amazed Sebastian. Already her cockpit was flooding.

'Abandon ship,' shouted the commander.

'You damned tooting,' said Flynn O'Flynn and leaped in an untidy tangle of arms and legs into the water.

Like a playful seal the torpedo-boat rolled over on its side, and Sebastian jumped. Drawing his breath while he was in the air, steeling himself against the cold of the water.

He was surprised at how warm it was.

69

From the bridge of H.M.S. *Renounce*, the survivors looked like a cluster of bedraggled water rats. In the dawn they floundered and splashed around the edge of the balloon of stained and filthy water where the Rufiji had washed them out, like the effluent from the sewer outlet of a city. *Renounce* found them before the sharks did, for there was no blood. There was one broken leg, a fractured collar bone and a few cracked ribs – but miraculously there was no blood. So from a crew of fourteen, *Renounce* recovered every man – including the two pilots.

They came aboard with their hair matted, their faces streaked, and their eyes swollen and inflamed with engine oil. With a man on either hand to guide them, leaving a trail of malodorous Rufiji water across the deck, they shuffled down to the sick-bay, a sodden and sorrowful-looking assembly of humanity.

'Well,' said Flynn O'Flynn, 'if we don't get a medal for *that*, then I'm going back to my old job – and the hell with them.'

'That,' said Captain Arthur Joyce, sitting hunched behind his desk, 'was not a roaring success.' He showed no inclination to whistle 'Tipperary'.

'It wasn't even a good try, sir,' agreed the torpedo-boat commander. 'The Boche had everything ready to throw at our heads.'

'A log boom — ' Joyce shook his head, ' — good Lord, they went out with the Napoleonic War!' He said it in a tone that implied that he was a victim of unfair play.

'It was extraordinarily effective, sir.'

'Yes, it must have been.' Joyce sighed. 'Well, at the very least we have established that an attack up the channel is not practical.'

'During the few minutes before the tide swept us away from the boom I looked beyond it, and I saw what I took to be a mine.

I think it certain that the Boche have laid a minefield beyond the boom, sir.'

'Thank you, Commander,' Joyce nodded. 'I will see to it that their Lordships receive a full account of your conduct. I consider it excellent.' Then he went on, 'I would value your opinion of Major O'Flynn and his son – do you think they are reliable men?'

'Well . . .' the commander hesitated, he did not want to be unfair, ' – they can both swim and the young one seems to have good eyesight. Apart from that I am not really in a position to give a judgement.'

'No, I don't suppose you are. Still I wish I knew more about them. For the next phase in this operation I am going to rely quite heavily on them.' He stood up. 'I think I will talk to them now.'

'You mean you actually want someone to go on board *Blücher*!' Flynn was appalled.

'I have explained to you, Major, how important it is for me to know exactly what state she is in. I must be able to estimate when she is likely to break out of the delta. I must know how much time I have.'

'Madness,' whispered Flynn. 'Stark raving bloody madness.' He stared at Joyce in disbelief.

'You have told me how well organized is your intelligence system ashore, of the reliable men who work for you. Indeed it is through you that we know that the Germans are cutting cordwood and taking it aboard. We know that they have recruited an army of native labourers and are using them not only for wood-cutting, but also for heavy work aboard the *Blücher*.'

'So?' Into that single word Flynn put a wealth of caution.

'One of your men could infiltrate the labour gangs and get aboard *Blücher*.'

And Flynn perked up immediately; he had anticipated that Joyce would suggest that Flynn Patrick O'Flynn should personally conduct a survey of *Blücher*'s damage.

'It might be done.' There was a lengthy pause while Flynn

considered every aspect of the business. 'Of course, Captain, my men aren't fighting patriots like you and I. They work for money. They are . . .' Flynn searched for the word. 'They are . . .'

'Mercenaries?'

'Yes,' said Flynn. 'That's exactly what they are.'

'Hmm,' said Joyce. 'You mean they would want payment?'

'They'd want a big dollop of lolly – and you can't blame them, can you?'

'The person you send would have to be a first-class man.'

'He would be,' Flynn assured him.

'On behalf of His Majesty's Government, I could undertake to purchase a complete and competent report on the disposition of the German cruiser *Blücher*, for the sum of . . .' he thought about it a moment, '. . . one thousand pounds.'

'Gold?'

'Gold,' agreed Joyce.

'That would cover it nicely.' Flynn nodded, then allowed his eyes to move across the cabin to where Sebastian and Rosa sat side by side on the day couch. They were holding hands, and showing more interest in each other than in the bargainings of Flynn and Captain Joyce.

It was a good thing, Flynn decided, that the Wakamba tribe from which Commissioner Fleischer had recruited the majority of his labour force, effected clean-shaven pates. It would be impossible for a person of European descent to dress his straight hair to resemble the woollen cap of an African.

It was also a good thing about the M'senga tree. From the bark of the M'senga tree the fishermen of Central Africa decocted a liquid in which they soaked their nets. It toughened the fibres of the netting and it also stained the skin. Once Flynn had dipped his finger into a basin of the stuff, and despite constant scrubbing, it was fifteen days before the black stain faded.

It was finally a good thing about Sebastian's nose. Its new contours were decidedly negroid.

70

'A thousand pounds!' said Flynn O'Flynn as though it were a benediction, and he scooped another mugful of the black liquid and poured it over Sebastian Oldsmith's clean-shaven scalp. 'Think of it, Bassie, me lad, a thousand pounds! Your half share of that is five hundred. Why! You'll be in a position to pay me back every penny you owe me. You'll be out of debt at last.'

They were camped on the Abati river, one of the tributaries of the Rufiji. Six miles downstream was Commissioner Fleischer's wood-cutting camp.

'It's money for jam,' opined Flynn. He was sitting comfortably in a riempie chair beside the galvanized iron tub, in which Sebastian Oldsmith squatted with his knees drawn up under his chin, Sebastian had the dejected look of a spaniel taking a bath in flea shampoo. The liquid in which he sat was the colour and viscosity of strong Turkish coffee and already his face and body were a dark purply chocolate colour.

'Sebastian isn't interested in the money,' said Rosa Oldsmith. She knelt beside the tub and, tenderly as a mother bathing her infant, she was ladling the M'senga juice over Sebastian's shoulders and back.

'I know, I know!' Flynn agreed quickly. 'We are all doing our duty. We all remember little Maria – may the Lord bless and keep her tiny soul. But the money won't hurt us either.'

Sebastian closed his eyes as another mugful cascaded over his head.

'Rub it into the creases round your eyes – and under your chin,' said Flynn, and Sebastian obeyed. 'Now, let's go over it again, Bassie, so you don't get it all balled up. One of Mohammed's cousins is boss-boy of the gang loading the timber into the launches. They are camped on the bank of the Rufiji. Mohammed will slip you in tonight, and tomorrow his cousin will get you on to one of the launches going down with a load for

Blücher. All you've got to do is keep your eyes open. Joyce just wants to know what work they are doing to repair her; whether or not they've got the boilers fired; things like that. You understand?'

Sebastian nodded glumly.

'You'll come back up-river tomorrow evening, slip out of camp soon as it's dark and meet us here. Simple as a pimple, right?'

'Right,' murmured Sebastian.

'Right then. Out you get and dry off.'

As the dry wind from the uplands blew over his naked body, the purply tint of the dye faded into a matt chocolate. Rosa had modestly moved away into the grove of Marula trees behind the camp. Every few minutes Flynn came across to Sebastian and touched his skin.

'Coming along nicely,' he said, and, 'Nearly done,' and, 'Jeez, you look better than real.' Then finally in Swahili, 'Right, Mohammed, mark his face.'

Mohammed squatted in front of Sebastian with a tiny gourd of cosmetics; a mixture of animal fat and ash and ochre. With his fingers he daubed Sebastian's cheeks and nose and forehead with the tribal patterns. His head held on one side in artistic concentration, making soft clucking sounds of concentration as he worked, until at last Mohammed was satisfied.

'He is ready.'

'Get the clothes,' said Flynn. This was an exaggeration. Sebastian's attire could hardly be called clothing.

A string of bark around his neck from which was suspended a plugged duiker horn filled with snuff, a cloak of animal skin that smelled of woodsmoke and man-sweat, draped over his shoulders.

'It stinks!' said Sebastian cringing from contact with the garment. 'And it's probably got lice.'

'The real thing,' agreed Flynn jovially. 'All right, Mohammed. show him how to fit the istopo – the hat.'

'I don't have to wear that also,' Sebastian protested, staring in horror as Mohammed came towards him, grinning.

'Of course you've got to wear it.' Impatiently Flynn brushed aside his protest.

The hat was a hollow six-inch length cut from the neck of a calabash gourd. An anthropologist would have called it a penis-sheath. It had two purposes; firstly to protect the wearer from the scratches of thorns and the bites of insect pests, and secondly as a boost to his masculinity.

Once in position it looked impressive, enhancing Sebastian's already considerable muscular development.

Rosa said nothing when she returned. She took one long startled look at the hat and then quickly averted her gaze, but her cheeks and neck flared bright scarlet.

'For God's sake, Bassie. Act like you proud of it. Stand up straight and take your hands away.' Flynn coached his son-in-law.

Mohammed knelt to slip the rawhide sandals on to Sebastian's feet, and then hand him the small blanket roll tied with a bark string. Sebastian slung it over one shoulder then picked up the long-handled throwing-spear.

Automatically he grounded the butt and leaned his weight on the shaft; lifting his left leg and placing the sole of his foot against the calf of his right leg, he stood in the stork posture of rest.

In every detail he was a Wakamba tribesman.

'You'll do,' said Flynn.

71

In the dawn, little wisps of river mist swirled around Commissioner Fleischer's legs as he came down the bank and on to the improvised jetty of logs.

He ran his eyes over the two launches, checking the ropes that held down the cargoes of timber. The launches sat low in the water, their exhausts puttering and blowing pale blue smoke that drifted away across the slick surface of the river.

'Are you ready?' he called to his sergeant of Askari.

'The men are eating, Bwana Mkuba.'

'Tell them to hurry,' growled Fleischer. It was a futile order and he stepped to the edge of the jetty, unbuttoning his trousers. He urinated noisily into the river, and the circle of men who squatted around the three-legged pot on the jetty watched him with interest, but without interrupting their breakfast.

With leather cloaks folded around their shoulders against the chill air off the water, they reached in turn into the pot and took a handful of the thick white maize porridge, moulding it into a mouth-size ball and then with the thumb forming a cup in the ball, dipping the ball into the smaller enamel dish and filling the depression with the creamy yellow gravy it contained, a tantalizing mixture of stewed catfish and tree caterpillars.

It was the first time that Sebastian had tasted this delicacy. He sat with the others and imitated their eating routine, forcing himself to place a lump of the spiced maize meal in his mouth. His gorge rose and gagged him, it tasted like fish oil and new-mown grass, not really offensive – it was just the thought of those fat yellow caterpillars. But had he been eating ham sandwiches, his appetite would not have been hearty.

His stomach was cramped with apprehension. He was a spy. A word from one of his companions, and Commissioner Fleischer would shout for the hanging ropes. Sebastian remembered the men he had seen in the monkey-bean tree on the bank of this same river, he remembered the flies clustered on their swollen, lolling tongues. It was not a mental picture conducive to enjoyment of breakfast.

Now, pretending to eat, he watched Commissioner Fleischer instead. It was the first time he had done so at leisure. The bulky figure in grey corduroy uniform, the pink-boiled face with pale golden eyelashes, the full petulant lips, the big freckled hands, all these revolted him. He felt his uneasiness swamped by a revival of the emotions that had possessed him as he stood beside the newly filled grave of his daughter on the heights above Lalapanzi.

'Black pig-animals,' shouted Herman Fleischer in Swahili, as he rebuttoned his clothing. 'That is enough! You do nothing but eat and sleep. It is time now for work.' He waddled across the logs of the jetty, into the little circle of porters. His first kick sent the three-legged pot clattering, his second kick caught Sebastian in the back and threw him forward on to his knees.

'Rasch!' He aimed another kick at one of them, but it was dodged, and the porters scattered to the launches.

Sebastian scrambled up. He had been kicked only once before in his life, and Flynn O'Flynn had learned not to do it again. For Sebastian there was nothing so humiliating as the contact of another man's foot against his person, also it had hurt.

Herman Fleischer had turned away to chivvy the others, so he did not see the hatred nor the way that Sebastian snarled at him, crouching like a leopard. Another second and he would have been on him. He might have killed Fleischer before the Askari shot him down – but he never made the attempt.

A hand on his arm. Mohammed's cousin beside him, his voice very low.

'Come! Let it pass. They will kill us also.'

And when Fleischer turned back the two of them had gone to the launch.

On the run down-river, Sebastian huddled with the others. Like them, drawing his cloak over his head to keep off the sun, but unlike them, he did not sleep. Through half-hooded eyes he was still watching Herman Fleischer, and his thoughts were hate-ugly.

Even with the current, the run in the deep-laden launches took almost four hours, and it was noon before they chugged around the last bend in the channel and turned in towards the mangrove forests.

Sebastian saw Herman Fleischer swallow the last bite of sausage and carefully repack the remainder into his haversack. He stood up and spoke to the man at the rudder, and both of them peered ahead.

'We have arrived,' said Mohammed's cousin, and removed his cloak from over his head. The little huddle of porters stirred into wakefulness and Sebastian stood up with them.

This time he knew what to look for, and he saw the muzzy silhouette of the *Blücher* skulking under her camouflage. From low down on the water she looked mountainous, and Sebastian's spine tingled as he remembered when last he had seen her from this angle, driving down to ram them with those axe-sharp blows. But now she floated awry, listing heavily.

'The boat leans over to one side.'

'Yes,' agreed Mohammed's cousin. 'The Allemand wanted it so. There has been a great carrying of goods within her, they have moved everything to make the boat lean over.'

'Why?'

The man shrugged and pointed with his chin. 'They have lifted her belly from the water, see how they work with fire on the holes in her skin.'

Tiny as beetles, men swarmed on the exposed hull, and even in the bright glare of midday, the welding torches flared and sparkled with blue-white flame. The new plating was conspicuous in its coat of dull brown zinc oxide paint, against the battleship-grey of the original hull.

As the launch approached, Sebastian studied the work carefully. He could see that it was nearing completion, the welders were running closed the last seams in the new plating. Already there were painters covering the oxide red with the matt grey final coat.

The pock marks of the shell splinters in her upperworks had been closed, and here again men hung on the flimsy trapezes of rope and planks, their arms lifting and falling as they plied the paint brushes.

An air of bustle and intent activity gripped the *Blücher*. Everywhere men moved about fifty different tasks, while the uniforms of the officers were restless white spots roving about her decks.

'They have closed all the holes in her belly?' Sebastian asked.

'All of them,' Mohammed's cousin confirmed. 'See how she spits out the water that was in her womb.' And he pointed again with his chin. From a dozen outlet vents, *Blücher*'s pumps were expelling solid streams of brown water as she emptied the flooded compartments.

'There is smoke from her chimneys,' Sebastian exclaimed, as he noticed for the first time the faint shimmer of heat at the mouths of her stacks.

'Yes. They have built fire in the iron boxes deep inside her. My brother Walaka works there now. He is helping to tend the fires. At first the fires were small, but each day they feed them higher.'

Sebastian nodded thoughtfully, he knew it took time to heat cold furnaces without cracking the linings of fireclay.

The launch nosed in and bumped against the cliff-high side of the cruiser.

'Come,' said Mohammed's cousin. 'We will climb up and work with the gangs carrying the wood down into her. You will see more up there.'

A new wave of dread flooded over Sebastian. He didn't want to go up there among the enemy. But already his guide was scrambling up the catwalk that hung down *Blücher*'s flank.

Sebastian adjusted his penis-sheath, hitched up his cloak, took a deep breath and followed him.

'Sometimes it goes like that. In the beginning everything is an obscene shambles; nothing but snags and accidents and delays. Then suddenly everything drops into place and the job is finished.' Standing under the awning on the foredeck, Commander (Engineering) Lochtkamper was a satisfied man, as he looked around the ship. 'Two weeks ago it looked as though we would still be messing around when the war was over – but now!'

'You have done well,' von Kleine understated the facts. 'Again you have justified my confidence. But now I have another task to add to your burdens.'

'What is it, Captain?' Lochtkamper kept his voice noncommittal, but there was a wariness in his eyes.

'I want to alter the ship's profile – change it to resemble that of a British heavy cruiser.'

'How?'

'A dummy stack abaft the radio office. Canvas on a wooden frame. Then mask "X" turret, and block in the dip of our waist. If we run into the British blockade squadron in the night, it may give us the few extra minutes that will make the difference between success or failure.' Von Kleine spoke again as he turned away, 'Come, I will show you what I mean.'

Lochtkamper fell in beside him and they started aft, an incongruous pair; the engineer swaddled in soiled overalls, long arms dangling, shambling along beside his captain like a trained ape. Von Kleine tall over him, his tropical whites crisp and sterile, hands clasped behind his back and golden beard bowed forward on to his chest, leaning slightly against the steeply canted angle of the deck.

He spoke carefully. 'When can I sail, Commander? I must know precisely. Is the work so far advanced that you can say with certainty?'

Lochtkamper was silent, considering his reply as they picked their way side by side through the milling jostle of seamen and native porters.

'I will have full pressure on my boilers by tomorrow night, another day after that to complete the work on the hull, two more days to adjust the trim of the ship and to make the alterations to the superstructure,' he mused aloud. Then he looked up. Von Kleine was watching him. 'Four days,' he said. 'I will be ready in four days.'

'Four days. You are certain of that?'

'Yes.'

'Four days,' repeated von Kleine, and he stopped in mid-stride to think. This morning he had received a message from Governor Schee in Dar es Salaam, a message relayed from the Admiralty in Berlin. Naval Intelligence reported that three days ago a convoy of twelve troop ships, carrying Indian and South African infantry, had left Durban harbour. Their destination was not known, but it was an educated guess that the British were about to open a new theatre of war. The campaign in German West Africa had been brought to a swift and decisive conclusion by the South Africans. Botha and Smuts had launched a double-pronged offensive, driving in along the railroads to the German capital of Windhoek. The capitulation of the German West African army had released the South African forces for work elsewhere. It was almost certain that those troopships were trundling up the east coast at this very moment, intent on a landing at one of the little harbours that dotted the coast of East Africa. Tanga perhaps, or Kilwa Kvinje – possibly even Dar as Salaam itself.

He must have his ship seaworthy and battle-ready to break out through the blockade squadron, and destroy that convoy.

'The big job will be readjusting the ship's trim. There is much to be done. Stores to be manhandled, shell from the magazines, the guns remounted . . .' Lochtkamper interrupted his thoughts, 'We will need labour.'

'I will order Fleischer to bring all his forced labour down to assist with the work,' von Kleine muttered. 'But we must sail in four days. The moon will be right on the night of the thirtieth, we must break out then.' The saintly face was ruffled by the force of his concentration, he paced slowly, the golden beard sunk on his chest as he formulated his plans, speaking aloud.

'Kyller has buoyed the channel. He must start clearing the mine-field at the entrance. We can cut the boom at the last moment – and the current will sweep it aside.'

They had reached the waist of the cruiser. Von Kleine was so deep in his thoughts that it took Lochtkamper's restraining hand on his arm, to return him to reality.

'Careful, sir.'

With a start von Kleine looked up. They had walked into a knot of African porters. Wild tribesmen, naked beneath their filthy leather cloaks, faces daubed with yellow ochre. They were man-handling the faggots of cordwood that were coming aboard from the launch that lay alongside *Blücher*. One of the heavy bundles was suspended from the boom of the derrick, it was swaying twenty feet above the deck and von Kleine had been about to walk under it. Lochtkamper's warning stopped him.

While he waited for them to clear away the faggot, von Kleine idly watched the native gang of workers.

One of the porters caught his attention. He was taller than his companions, his body sleeker, lacking the bunched and knotty muscle. His legs also were sturdier and finely moulded. The man lifted his head from his labours, and von Kleine looked into his face. The features were delicate; the lips not as full as, the forehead broader and deeper than, the typical African.

But it was the eyes that jerked von Kleine's attention back from the troop convoy. They were brown, dark brown and shifty. Von Kleine had learned to recognize guilt in the faces of his subordinates, it showed in the eyes. This man was guilty. It was only an instant that von Kleine saw it, then the porter dropped his gaze and stooped to take a grip on the bundle of timber. The man worried him, left him feeling vaguely uneasy, he wanted to speak with him – question him. He started towards him.

'Captain! Captain!' Commissioner Fleischer had come puffing up the catwalk from the launch, plump and sweaty he was pawing von Kleine's arm.

'I must speak with you, Captain.'

'Ah, Commissioner,' von Kleine greeted him coolly, trying to avoid the damp paw. 'One moment, please. I wish to . . .'

'It is a matter of the utmost importance. Ensign Proust . . .'

'In a moment, Commissioner.' Von Kleine pulled away, but Fleischer was determined. He stepped in front of von Kleine, blocking his path.

'Ensign Proust, the cowardly little prig...' and von Kleine found himself embroiled in a long report about Ensign Proust's lack of respect for the dignity of the Commissioner. He had been insubordinate, he had argued with Herr Fleischer, and further he had told Herr Fleischer that he considered him 'fat'.

'I will speak to Proust,' said von Kleine. It was a trivial matter and he wanted no part of it. Then Commander Lochtkamper was beside them. Would the Captain speak to the Herr Commissioner about labour for the handling of ballast? They fell into a long discussion and while they talked, the gang of porters lugged the bundle of timber aft and were absorbed by the bustling hordes of workmen.

Sebastian was sweating with fright, trembling, giddy with fright. Clearly he had sensed the German officer's suspicions. Those cold blue eyes had burned like dry ice. Now he stooped under his load, trying to shrink himself into insignificance, trying to overcome the grey clammy sense of dread that threatened to crush him.

'He saw you,' wheezed Mohammed's cousin, shuffling along beside Sebastian.

'Yes.' Sebastian bent lower. 'Is he still watching?'

The old man glanced back over his shoulder.

'No. He speaks with Mafuta, the fat one.'

'Good.' Sebastian felt a lift of relief. 'We must get back on the launch.'

'The loading is almost finished, but we must first speak with my brother. He waits for us.'

They turned the corner of the aft gun-turrets. On the deck was a mountain of cordwood. Stacked neatly and lashed down with rope. Black men swarmed over it, between them spreading a huge green tarpaulin over the wood pile.

They reached the wood pile and added the faggots they carried to the stack. Then, in the custom of Africa, they paused to rest and talk. A man clambered down from the wood pile to join them, a sprightly old gentleman with woolly grey hair, impeccably turned out in cloak and penis-sheath. Mohammed's cousin greeted him with courteous affection, and they took snuff together.

'This man is my brother,' he told Sebastian. 'His name is Walaka. When he was a young man he killed a lion with a spear. It was a big lion with a black mane.' To Sebastian this information seemed to be slightly irrelevant, his fear of discovery was making him nervously impatient. There were Germans all around them, big blond Germans bellowing orders as they chivvied on the labour gangs, Germans looking down on them from the tall superstructure above them, Germans elbowing them aside as they passed. Sebastian found it difficult to concentrate.

His two accomplices were involved in a family discussion. It seemed that Walaka's youngest daughter had given birth to a fine son, but that during his absence a leopard had raided Walaka's village and killed three of his goats. The new grandson did not seem to compensate Walaka for the loss of his goats. He was distressed.

'Leopards are the excrement of dead lepers,' he said, and would have enlarged on the subject but Sebastian interrupted him.

'Tell me of the things you have seen on this canoe. Say swiftly, there is little time. I must go before the Allemand comes for all of us with the ropes.'

Mention of the ropes brought the meeting to order, and Walaka launched into his report.

There were fires burning in the iron boxes in the belly of the canoe. Fires of such heat that they pained the eye when the door of the box was opened, fires with a breath like that of a hundred bush fires, fires that consumed . . .

'Yes, yes.' Sebastian cut short the lyrical description. 'What else?'

There had been a great carrying of goods, moving of them to one side of the canoe to make it lean in the water. They had carried boxes and bales, unbolted machinery and guns. See how they had been moved. They had taken from the rooms under her roof a great quantity of the huge bullets, also the white bags of powder for the guns and placed them in other rooms on the far side.

'What else?'

There was more, much more to tell. Walaka enthused about meat which came out of little tins, of lanterns that burned without wick, flame or oil, of great wheels that spun, and boxes of steel that screamed and hummed, of clean fresh water that gushed from the mouths of long rubber snakes, sometimes cold and at other times hot as though it had been boiled over a fire. There were marvels so numerous that it confused a man.

'These things I know. Is there nothing else that you have seen?'

Indeed there was. The Allemand had shot three native porters, lining them up and covering their eyes with strips of white cloth. The men had jumped and wriggled and fallen in a most comical fashion, and afterwards the Germans had washed the blood from the deck with water from the long snakes. Since then none of the other porters had helped themselves to blankets and buckets and other small moveables – the price was exorbitant.

Walaka's description of the execution had a chilling effect on Sebastian. He had done what he had come to do and now his urge to leave *Blücher* became overpowering. It was helped on by a German petty officer who joined the group uninvited.

'You lazy black baboons,' he bellowed. 'This is not a bloody Sunday-school outing – move, you swine, move!' And his boots flew. Led by Mohammed's cousin they left Walaka without farewell and scampered back along the deck. Just before they reached the entry port, Sebastian checked. The two German officers stood where he had left them, but now they were looking up at the high smoke stacks. The tall officer with the golden beard was describing sweeping motions with his outstretched hand, talking while the stocky one listened intently.

Mohammed's cousin scurried past them and disappeared over the side into the launch, leaving Sebastian hesitant and reluctant to run the gauntlet of those pale blue eyes.

'Manali, come quickly. The boat swims, you will be left!' Mohammed's cousin called from down below, his voice faint but urgent above the chug of the launch's engine.

Sebastian started forward again, his stomach a cold lump under his ribs. A dozen paces and he had reached the entry port.

The German officer turned and saw him. He challenged with raised voice, and came towards Sebastian, one arm outstretched as though to hold him.

Sebastian whirled and dived down the catwalk. Below him the launch was casting off her lines, water churning back from her propeller.

Sebastian reached the grating at the bottom of the catwalk. There was a gap of ten feet between him and the launch. He jumped, hung for a moment in the air, then hit the gunwale of the launch. His clutching fingers found a grip while his legs dangled in the warm water.

Mohammed's cousin caught his shoulder and dragged him aboard. They tumbled together in a heap on the deck of the launch.

'Bloody kaffir,' said Herman Fleischer and stooped to cuff them both heavily around the ears. Then he went back to his seat in the stern, and Sebastian smiled at him with something close to affection. After those deadly blue eyes, Herman Fleischer seemed as dangerous as a teddy-bear.

Then he looked back at *Blücher*. The German officer stood at the top of the catwalk, watching them as they drew away, and set a course upstream. Then he turned away from the rail and disappeared.

73

Sebastian sat on the day couch in the master cabin of H.M.S. *Renounce*, he sagged against the arm-rest and fought off the grey waves of exhaustion that washed over his mind.

He had not slept in thirty hours. After his escape from *Blücher* there had been the long launch journey up-river during which he had remained awake and jittery with the after-effects of tension.

After disembarking he had sneaked out of Fleischer's camp, avoiding the Askari guards, and trotted through the moonlight to meet Flynn and Rosa.

A hurried meal, and then all three of them had mounted on bicycles supplied with the compliments of the Royal Navy, and ridden all night along a rough elephant path to where they had left a canoe hidden among the reeds on the bank of one of the Rufiji tributaries.

In the dawn they had paddled out of one of the unguarded channels of the delta and made their rendezvous with the little whaler from H.M.S. *Renounce*.

Two long days of activity without rest, and Sebastian was groggy. Rosa sat beside him on the couch. She leaned across and touched his arm, her eyes dark with concern. Neither of them were taking any part in the conference in which the other persons in the crowded cabin were deeply involved.

Joyce sat as chairman, and beside him an older heavier man with bushy grey eyebrows and a truculent jaw, hair brushed in streaks across his pate in an ineffectual attempt to conceal his baldness. This was Armstrong, Captain of H.M.S. *Pegasus*, the other cruiser of the blockade squadron.

'Well, it looks as though *Blücher* has made good her damage, then. If she has fired her boilers, we can expect her to break out any day now – von Kleine would not burn up good fuel to keep his stokers warm.' He said it with relish, a fighting man anticipating a good hard fight. 'There's a message I'd like to give her from *Bloodhound* and *Orion* – an old account to settle.'

But Joyce also had a message, one that had its origin at the desk of Admiral Sir Percy Howe, Commander-in-Chief, South Atlantic and Indian Oceans. In part this message read:

'The safety of your squadron considered secondary to containing *Blücher*. Risk involved in delaying until *Blücher* leaves the delta before engaging her is too high. Absolutely imperative that she be either destroyed or blocked at her present anchorage. Consequences of *Blücher* running blockade and attacking the troop convoy conveying landing forces to invasion of Tanga will be catastrophic. Efforts being made to send you two tramp steamers to act as block ships, but failing their arrival, and failing also effective offensive action against *Blücher* before 30 July 1915, you are hereby ordered to scuttle *Renounce* and *Pegasus* in the channel of the Rufiji to block *Blücher*'s exit.'

It was a command that left Captain Arthur Joyce sick with dread. To scuttle his splendid ships – a thought as repulsive and loathsome as that of incest, of patricide, of human sacrifice. Today was 26 July, he had four days in which to find an alternative before the order became effective,

'She'll come out at night, of course, bound to!' Armstrong's voice was thick with battle lust. 'This time she'll not have an old girl and a baby like *Orion* and *Bloodhound* to deal with.' His tone changed slightly. 'We'll have to look lively. New moon in three days so *Blücher* will have dark nights. There could be a change in the weather...' Armstrong was looking a little worried now, '... we'll have to tighten up...'

'Read this,' said Joyce, and passed the flimsy to Armstrong. He read it.

'My God!' he gasped. 'Scuttle. Oh, my God!'

'There are two channels that *Blücher* could use.' Joyce spoke softly. 'We would have to block both of them – *Renounce* and *Pegasus*!'

'Jesus God!' swore Armstrong in horror. 'There must be another way.'

'I think there is,' said Joyce, and looked across at Sebastian. 'Mr Oldsmith,' he spoke gently, 'would it be possible for you to get on board the German cruiser once again?'

There were tiny lumps of yellow mucus in the corner of

Sebastian's bloodshot eyes, but the stain that darkened his skin concealed the rings of fatigue under them.

'I'd rather not, old chap.' He ran his hand thoughtfully over his shaven scalp and the stubble of new hair rasped under his fingers. 'It was one of the most unpleasant hours of my life.'

'Quite,' said Captain Joyce. 'Quite so! I wouldn't have asked you, had I not considered it to be of prime importance.' Joyce paused and pursed his lips to whistle softly the first bar of Chopin's 'Funeral March', then he sighed and shook his head. 'If I were to tell you that you alone have it in your power to save both the cruisers of this squadron from destruction and to protect the lives of fifteen thousand British soldiers and seamen – how would you answer then?'

Glumly, Sebastian sagged back against the couch and closed his eyes.

'Can I have a few hours sleep first?'

74

It was exactly the size of a box of twenty-four Monte Cristo Havana Cigars, for that had been its contents before *Renounce's* chief engine room artificer and the gunnery lieutenant had set to work on it.

It lay on the centre of Captain Joyce's desk, while the artificer explained its purpose to the respectful audience that stood around him.

'It's verra simple,' started the artificer in an accent that was as bracing as the fragrance of heather and highland whisky.

'It would have to be . . .' commented Flynn O'Flynn, '. . . for Bassie to understand it.'

'All you do is lift the lid.' The artificer suited action to the words, and even Flynn craned forward to examine the contents of the cigar box. Packed neatly into it were six yellow sticks of gelignite, looking like candles wrapped in grease-proof paper. There was also the flat dry cell battery from a bull's eye lantern, and a travelling-clock in a pigskin case. All of these were connected by loops and twists of fine copper wire. Engraved into the metal of the clock base were the words:

> 'To my dear husband Arthur,
> With love,
> Iris.
> Christmas 1914.'

Captain Arthur Joyce stilled a sentimental pang of regret with the thought that Iris would understand.

'Then . . .' said the artificer, clearly enjoying the hold he had on his audience, '. . . you wind the knob on the clock.' He touched it with his forefinger, '. . . close the lid,' he closed it, '. . . wait twelve hours, and – Boom!' The enthusiasm with which the Scotsman simulated an explosion blew a fine spray of spittle across the desk, and Flynn withdrew hurriedly out of range.

'Wait twelve hours?' asked Flynn, dabbing at the droplets on his cheeks. 'Why so long?'

'I ordered a twelve-hour delay on the fusing of the charge.' Joyce answered the question. 'If Mr Oldsmith is to gain access to the *Blücher*'s magazines, he will have to infiltrate the native labour gangs engaged in transferring the explosives. Once he is a member of the gang he might find difficulty in extricating himself and getting away from the ship after he has placed the charge. I am sure that Mr Oldsmith would be reluctant to make this attempt unless we could ensure that there is time for him to escape from *Blücher*, when his efforts . . . ah,' he sought the correct phraseology, '. . . ah . . . come to fruition.' Joyce was pleased with this speech, and he turned to Sebastian for endorsement. 'Am I correct in my assumption, Mr Oldsmith?'

Not to be outdone in verbosity, Sebastian pondered his reply for a second. Five hours of deathlike sleep curled in Rosa'a arms had refreshed his body and sharpened his wit to the edge of a Toledo steel blade.

'Indubitably,' he replied, and beamed in triumph.

75

They sat together in the time when the sun was dying and bleeding on the clouds. They sat together on a kaross of monkey skin in a thicket of wild ebony, at the head of one of the draws that wrinkled down into the valley of the Rufiji. They sat in silence. Rosa bent forward over her needlework, as she stitched a concealed pocket into the filthy cloak of leather that lay across her lap. The pocket would hold the cigar box. Sebastian watched her, and his eyes upon her were a caress. She pulled the last stitch tight, knotted it, then leaned forward to bite the thread.

'There!' she said. 'It's finished.' And looked up into his eyes.

'Thank you,' said Sebastian. They sat together quietly and Rosa reached out to touch his shoulder. The muscle under the black stained skin was rubber hard, and warm.

'Come,' she said and drew his head down to her so that their cheeks touched, and they held each other while the last light faded. The African dusk thickened the shadows in the wild ebony, and down the draw a jackal yipped plaintively.

'Are you ready?' Flynn stood near them, a dark bulky figure, with Mohammed beside him.

'Yes.' Sebastian looked up at him.

'Kiss me,' whispered Rosa, 'and come back safely.'

Gently Sebastian broke from her embrace. He stood tall above her, and draped the cloak over his naked body. The cigar box hung heavily between his shoulder blades.

'Wait for me,' he said, and walked away.

Flynn Patrick O'Flynn moved restlessly under his single blanket and belched. Heartburn moved acid sour in his throat, and he was cold. The earth under him had long since lost the warmth it had sucked from yesterday's sun. A small slice of the old moon gave a little silver light to the night.

Unsleeping he lay and listened to the soft sound of Rosa

sleeping near him. The sound irritated him, he lacked only an excuse to waken her and make her talk to him. Instead he reached into the haversack that served as his pillow and his fingers closed round the cold smooth glass of the bottle.

A night-bird hooted softly down the draw, and Flynn released the bottle and sat up quickly. He placed two fingers between his lips and repeated the night-bird's cry.

Minutes later Mohammed drifted like a small black ghost into camp and came to squat beside Flynn's bed.

'I see you, Fini.'

'You I see also, Mohammed. It went well?'

'It went well.'

'Manali has entered the camp of the Allemand?'

'He sleeps now beside the man who is my cousin, and in the dawn they will go down the Rufiji, to the big boat of the Allemand once again.'

'Good!' grunted Flynn. 'You have done well.'

Mohammed coughed softly to signify that there was more to tell.

'What is it?' Flynn demanded.

'When I had seen Manali safely into the care of my cousin, I came back along the valley and . . .' he hesitated, '. . . perhaps it is not fitting to speak of such matters at a time when our Lord Manali goes unarmed and alone into the camp of the Allemand.'

'Speak,' said Flynn.

'As I walked without sound, I came to a place where this valley falls down to the little river called Abati. You know the place?'

'Yes, about a mile down the draw from here.'

'That is the place.' Mohammed nodded. 'It was here that I saw something move in the night. It was as though a mountain walked.'

A sliver of ice was thrust down Flynn's spine, and his breathing snagged painfully in his throat.

'Yes?' he breathed.

'It was a mountain armed with teeth of ivory that grew from its face to touch the ground as it walked.'

'*Plough the Earth*.' Flynn whispered the name, and his hand fell on to the rifle that lay loaded beside his bed.

'It was that one.' Mohammed nodded again. 'He feeds quietly, moving towards the Rufiji. But the voice of a rifle would carry down to the ears of the Allemand.'

'I won't fire,' whispered Flynn. 'I just want to have a look at him. I just want to see him again.' And the hand on the rifle shook like that of a man in high fever.

76

The sun pushed up and sat fat and fiery as molten gold, on the hills of the Rufiji basin. Its warmth lifted streamers of mist from the swamps and reed-beds that bounded the Abati river, and they smoked like the ashes of a dying fire.

Under the fever trees the air was still cool with the memory of the night, but the sun sent long yellow shafts of light probing through the branches to disperse and warm it.

Three old eland bulls came up from the river, bigger than domestic cattle, light bluey-brown in colour with faint chalk stripes across the barrel of their bodies, they walked in single file, heavy dewlaps swinging, thick stubby horns held erect, and the tuft of darker hair on their foreheads standing out clearly. They reached the grove of fever trees and the lead bull stopped, suddenly alert. For long seconds they stood absolutely still, staring into the open palisade of fever tree trunks where the light was still vague beneath the canopy of interlaced leaves and branches.

The lead bull blew softly through his nostrils, and swung off the game path that led into the grove. Stepping lightly for such large animals, the three eland skirted the grove and moved away to blend into the dry thorn scrub higher up the slope.

'He is in there,' whispered Mohammed. 'The eland saw him, and turned aside.'

'Yes,' agreed Flynn. 'It is such a place as he would choose to lie up for the day.' He sat in the crotch of a M'banga tree, wedged securely ten feet above the ground, and peered across three hundred yards of open grassland at the dense stand of fever trees. The hands that held the binoculars to his eyes were unsteady with gin and excitement, and he was sweating, a droplet broke from his hair-line and slid down his cheek, tickling like an insect. He brushed it away.

'A wise man would leave him, and walk away even as the

eland did.' Mohammed gave his opinion. He leaned against the base of the tree, holding Flynn's rifle across his chest. Flynn did not reply. He peered through the binoculars, swinging them slowly in an arc as he searched.

'He must be deep among the trees, I cannot see him from here.' And he loosened his leg grip from the crotch and clambered down to where Mohammed waited. He took his rifle and checked the load.

'Leave him, Fini,' Mohammed urged softly. 'There is no profit in it. We cannot carry the teeth away.'

'Stay here,' said Flynn.

'Fini, the Allemand will hear you. They are close – very close.'

'I will not shoot,' said Flynn. 'I must see him again – that is all. I will not shoot.'

Mohammed took the gin bottle from the haversack and handed it to him. Flynn drank.

'Stay here,' he repeated, his voice husky from the burn of the raw spirit.

'Be careful, Fini. He is an old one of evil temper – be careful.' Mohammed watched Flynn start out across the clearing. He walked with the slow deliberation of a man who goes in good time to a meeting that has long been prearranged. He reached the grove of fever trees and walked on into them without checking.

Plough the Earth was sleeping on his feet. His little eyes closed tightly in their wrinkled pouches. Tears had oozed in a long dark stain down his cheeks, and a fine haze of midges hovered about them. Tattered as battle-riven banners on a windless day, his ears lay back against his shoulders. His tusks were crutches that propped up the gnarled old head, and his trunk hung down between them, grey and slack and heavy.

Flynn saw him, and picked his way towards him between the trunks of the fever trees. The setting had an unreal quality, for the light effect of the low sun through the branches was golden beams reflected in shimmering misty green from the leaves of the fever trees. The grove was resonant with the whine of cicada beetles.

Flynn circled out until he was head on to the sleeping elephant, and then he moved in again. Twenty paces from him Flynn stopped. He stood with his feet set apart, the rifle held ready across one hip, and his head thrown back as he looked up at the unbelievable bulk of the old bull.

Up to this moment Flynn still believed that he would not shoot. He had come only to look at him once more, but it was as futile as an alcoholic who promised himself just one taste. He felt the madness begin at the base of his spine, hot and hard it poured into his body, filling him as though he were a container. The level rose to his throat and he tried to check it there, but the rifle was coming up. He felt the butt in his shoulder. Then he heard with surprise a voice, a voice that rang clearly through the grove and instantly stilled the whine of the cicadas. It was his own voice, crying out in defiance of his conscious resolve.

'Come on, then,' he shouted. And the old elephant burst from massive quiescence into full charge. It came down on him like a dynamited cliff of black rock. He saw it over the open rear sight of his rifle, saw it beyond the minute pip of the foresight that rode unwaveringly in the centre of the old bull's bulging brow – between the eyes, where the crease of skin at the base of its trunk was a deep lateral line.

The shot was thunderous, shattering into a thousand echoes against the boles of the fever trees. The elephant died in the fullness of his run. Legs buckled, and he came toppling forward, carried by his own momentum, a loose avalanche of flesh and bone and long ivory.

Flynn turned aside like a matador from the run of the bull, three quick dancing steps and then one of the tusks hit him. It took him across the hip with a force that hurled him twenty feet, the rifle spinning from his hands so that as he fell and rolled in the soft bed of loose trash and leaf mould, his lower body twisted away from his trunk at an impossible angle. His brittle old bones had broken like china; the ball of the femur snapping off in its socket, his pelvis fracturing clean through.

Lying face down, Flynn was mildly surprised that there was no pain. He could feel the jagged edges of bone rasping together deep in his flesh at his slightest movement, but there was no pain.

Slowly, pulling himself forward on his elbows so that his legs slithered uselessly after him, he crawled towards the carcass of the old bull.

He reached it, and with one hand stroked the yellowed shaft of ivory that had crippled him.

'Now,' he whispered, fondling the smoothly polished tusk the

313

way a man might touch his firstborn son. 'Now, at last you are mine.'

And then the pain started, and he closed his eyes and cowered down, huddled beneath the hillock of dead and cooling flesh that had been *Plough the Earth*. The pain buzzed in his ears like cicada beetles, but through it he heard Mohammed's voice.

'Fini. It was not wise.'

He opened his eyes and saw Mohammed's monkey face puckered with concern.

'Call Rosa,' he croaked. 'Call Little Long Hair. Tell her to come.'

Then he closed his eyes again, and rode the pain. The tempo of the pain changed constantly – first it was drums, tom-toms that throbbed and beat within him. Then it was the sea, long undulating swells of agony. Then again it was night, cold black night that chilled him so he shivered and moaned – and the night gave way to the sun. A great fiery ball of pain that burned and shot out lances of blinding light that burst against his clenched eyelids. Then the drums began again.

Time was of no significance. He rode the pain for a minute and a million years, then through the beat of the drums of agony he heard movement near him. The shuffle of feet through the dead leaves, the murmur of voices that were not part of his consuming anguish.

'Rosa,' Flynn whispered, 'you have come!'

He rolled his head and forced his eyelids open.

Herman Fleischer stood over him. He was grinning. His face flushed as a rose petal, fresh sweat clinging in his pale eyebrows, breathing quickly and heavily with exertion as though he had been running, but he was grinning.

'So!' he wheezed. 'So!'

The shock of his presence was muted for Flynn by the haze of pain in which he lay. There were smears of dust dulling the gloss of Fleischer's jackboots, and dark patches of sweat had soaked through the thick grey corduroy tunic at the armpits. He held a Luger pistol in his right hand and with his left hand he pushed the slouch hat to the back of his head.

'Herr Flynn!' he said and chuckled. It was the fat infectious chuckle of a healthy baby.

Mildly Flynn wondered how Fleischer had found him so quickly in the broken terrain and thick bush. The shot would have alerted him, but what had led him directly to the grove of fever trees?

Then he heard a rustling fluting rush in the air above him, and he looked upwards. Through the lacework of branches he saw the vultures spiralling against the aching blue of the sky. They turned and dipped on spread black wings, cocking their heads sideways in flight to look down with bright beady eyes on the elephant carcass.

'Ja! The birds. We followed the birds.'

'Jackals always follow the birds,' whispered Flynn, and Fleischer laughed. He threw back his head and laughed with genuine delight.

'Good. Oh, ja. That is good.' And he kicked Flynn. He swung the jackboot lazily into Flynn's body, and Flynn shrieked. The laughter dried instantly in Fleischer's throat, and he bent quickly to examine Flynn.

He noticed for the first time how his lower body was grotesquely twisted and distorted. And he dropped to his knees beside him. Gently he touched Flynn's forehead, and deep concern flashed across his chubby features at the clammy cold feeling of the skin.

'Sergeant!' There was a desperate edge to his voice now. 'This man is badly injured. He will not last long. Be quick! Get the rope! We must hang him before he loses consciousness.'

Rosa awoke in the dawn and found that she was alone. Beside Flynn's personal pack, his discarded blanket had been carelessly flung aside. His rifle was gone.

She was not alarmed, not at first. She guessed that he had gone into the bush on one of his regular excursions to be alone while he drank his breakfast. But an hour later when he had not returned she grew anxious. She sat with her rifle across her lap, and every bird noise or animal scuffle in the ebony thicket jarred her nerves.

Another hour and she was fretting. Every few minutes she stood up and walked to the edge of the clearing to listen. Then she went back to sit and worry.

Where on earth was Flynn? Why had Mohammed not returned? What had happened to Sebastian? Was he safe, or had he been discovered? Had Flynn gone to assist him? Should she wait here, or follow them down the draw?

Her eyes haunted, her mouth hard set with doubts, she sat and twisted the braid of her hair around one finger in a nervously restless gesture.

Then Mohammed came. Suddenly he appeared out of the thicket beside her, and Rosa jumped up with a low cry of relief. The cry died in her throat as she saw his face.

'Fini!' he said. 'He is hurt. The great elephant has broken his bones and he lies in pain. He asks for you.'

Rosa stared at him, appalled, not understanding.

'An elephant?'

'He followed *Plough the Earth*, the great elephant, and killed him. But in dying the elephant struck him, breaking him.'

'The fool. Oh, the fool!' Rosa whispered. 'Now of all times. With Sebastian in danger, he must . . .' And then she caught herself and broke off her futile lament. 'Where is he, Mohammed? Take me to him.'

Mohammed led along one of the game paths, Rosa ran behind him. There was no time for caution, no thought of it as they hurried to find Flynn. They came to the stream of the Abati, and swung off the path, staying on the near bank. They plunged through a field of arrow grass, skirted around a tiny swamp and ran on into a stand of buffalo thorn. As they emerged on the far side Mohammed stopped abruptly and looked at the sky.

The vultures turned in a high wheel against the blue, like debris in a lazy whirlwind. The spot above which they circled lay half a mile ahead.

'Daddy!' Rosa choked on the word. In an instant all the hardness accumulated since that night at Lalapanzi disappeared from her face.

'Daddy!' she said again, and then she ran in earnest. Brushing past Mohammed, throwing her rifle aside so it clattered on the earth, she darted out of the buffalo thorn and into the open.

'Wait, Little Long Hair. Be careful.' Mohammed started after her. In his agitation he stepped carelessly, full on to a fallen twig from the buffalo thorn. There was a worn spot on the sole of his sandal, and three inches of cruel red-tipped thorn drove up through it and buried in his foot.

For a dozen paces he struggled on after Rosa, hopping on one leg, flapping his arms to maintain his balance and calling, but not too loudly.

'Wait! Be careful, Little Long Hair.'

But she took not the least heed, and went away from him, leaving him at last to sink down and tend to his wounded foot.

She crossed the open ground before the fever tree grove with the slack, blundering steps of exhaustion. Running silently, saving her breath for the effort of reaching her father. She ran into the grove, and a drop of perspiration fell into her eye, blurring her vision so she staggered against one of the trunks. She recovered her balance and ran on into the midst of them.

She recognized Herman Fleischer instantly. She had run almost against his chest, and his huge body towered over her. She screamed with shock and twisted away from the bear-like arms outspread to clutch her.

Two of the native Askari who were working over the crude litter on which lay Flynn O'Flynn, jumped up. As she ran they closed on her from either side, the way a pair of trained greyhounds will course a hare. They caught her between them, and dragged her struggling and screaming to where Herman Fleischer waited.

'Ah, so!' Fleischer nodded pleasantly in greeting. 'You have come in time for the fun.' Then he turned to his sergeant. 'Have them tie the woman.'

Rosa's screams penetrated the light mists of insensibility that screened Flynn's brain. He stirred on the litter, muttering incoherently, rolling his head from side to side, then he opened his eyes and focused them with difficulty. He saw her struggling between the Askari and he snapped back into full consciousness.

'Leave her!' he roared. 'Call those bloody animals off her. Leave her, your murderous bloody German bastard.'

'Good!' said Herman Fleischer. 'You are awake now.' Then he lifted his voice above Flynn's bellows. 'Hurry, Sergeant, tie the woman – and get the rope up.'

While they secured Rosa, one of the Askari shinned up the smooth yellow trunk of a fever tree. With his bayonet he hacked the twigs from the thick horizontal branch above their heads. The sergeant threw the end of the rope up to him, and at the second attempt the Askari caught it and passed it over the branch. Then he dropped back to earth.

There was a hangman's knot fixed in the rope, ready for use.

'Set the knot,' said Fleischer, and the sergeant went to where Flynn lay. With poles cut from a small tree they had rigged a combination litter and splints. The poles had been laid down Flynn's flanks from ankle to armpit, with bark strips they had bound them firmly so that Flynn's body was held rigidly as that of an Egyptian mummy, only his head and neck were free.

The sergeant stooped over him, and Flynn fell silent, watching him venomously. As his hands came down with the noose to loop it over Flynn's head, Flynn moved suddenly. He darted his head forward like a striking adder and fastened his teeth in the man's wrist. With a howl the sergeant tried to pull away, but Flynn held on, his head jerking and wrenching as the man struggled.

'Fool,' grunted Fleischer, and strode over to the litter. He lifted his foot and placed it on Flynn's lower body. As he brought his weight down on it Flynn stiffened and gasped with pain, releasing the Askari's wrist.

'Do it this way.' Fleischer lunged forward and took a handful of Flynn's hair, roughly he yanked Flynn's head forward. 'Now, the rope, quickly.'

The Askari dropped the noose over Flynn's head and drew the slip-knot tight until it lay snugly under Flynn's ear.

'Good.' Fleischer stepped back. 'Four men on the rope,' he ordered. 'Gently. Do not jerk the rope. Walk away with it slowly. I don't want to break his neck.'

Rosa's hysteria had stilled into cold horror as she watched the preparations for the execution, and now she found her voice again.

'Please,' she whispered. 'He's my father. Please don't. Oh, no, please don't.'

'Hush, girl,' roared Flynn. 'You'd not shame me now by pleading with this fat bag of pus.' He swivelled his head, his eyes rolled towards the four Askari who stood ready with the rope end. 'Pull! You black sons of bitches. Pull! And damn you. I'll beat you to hell, and speak to the devil so he'll have you castrated and smeared with pig's fat.'

'You heard what Fini told you,' smiled Fleischer at his Askari. 'Pull!'

And they walked backwards in single file, shuffling through the dead leaves, leaning against the rope.

The litter lifted slowly at one end, came upright and then left the ground.

Rosa turned away and clenched her eyelids tight closed, but her hands were bound so she could not stop her ears, she could not keep out the sounds that Flynn Patrick O'Flynn made as he died.

When at last there was silence, Rosa was shivering. Hard spasms that shuddered through her whole body.

'All right,' said Herman Fleischer. 'That's it. Bring the woman. We can get back to camp in time for lunch if we hurry.'

When they were gone, the litter and its contents still hung in the fever tree. Swinging a little and turning slowly on the end of the rope. Near it lay the carcass of the elephant, and a vulture planed down slowly and made a flapping ungainly landing in the top branches of the fever tree. It sat hunched and suspicious, then suddenly squawked and launched again into noisy flight, for it had seen the man coming.

The little old man limped slowly into the grove. He stopped

beside the dead elephant and looked up at the man who had been his master and his friend.

'Go in peace, Fini!' said Mohammed.

78

The alleyway was a narrow low-roofed corridor, the bulkheads were painted a pale grey that glistened in the harsh light of the electric globes set in small wire cages at regular intervals along the roof.

At the end of the corridor, a guard stood outside the heavy watertight door in the bulkhead that led through into the handling room of the forward magazine. The guard wore only a thin white singlet and white flannel trousers, but his waist was belted in a blancoed webbing from which hung a sheathed bayonet, and there was a Mauser rifle slung from his shoulder.

From his position he could look into the handling room, and he could keep the full length of the alleyway under surveillance.

A double file of Wakamba tribesmen filled the alleyway, living chains along one of which passed the cordite charges; along the other the nine-inch shells.

The Africans worked with the stoical indifference of draught animals, turning to grip the ugly cylindro-conical shells, hugging a hundred and twenty pounds' weight of steel and explosive to their chests while they moved it on to the next man in the chain.

The cordite charges, each wrapped in thick paper, were not so weighty and moved more swiftly along their line. Each man bobbed and swung as he handled his load, so it seemed that the two ranks were sets in a complicated dance pattern.

From this mass of moving humanity rose clouds of warm body odour, that filled the alleyway and defeated the efforts of the air-conditioning fans.

Sebastian felt sweat trickling down his chest and back under the leather cloak, he felt also the tug of weight within the folds of the cloak each time he swung to receive a fresh cordite charge from his neighbour.

He stood just outside the door of the handling room, and each time he passed a charge through, he looked into the interior of the magazine where another gang was at work, packing the charges into the shelves that lined the bulkheads, and easing the nine-inch shells into their steel racks. Here there was another armed guard.

The work had been in progress since early that morning, with a half-hour's break at noon, so the German guards had relaxed their vigilance. They were restless in anticipation of relief. The one in the magazine was a fat middle-aged man who at intervals during the day had broken the monotony by releasing sudden ear-splitting posterior discharges of gas. With each salvo he had clapped the nearest African porter on the back and shouted happily.

'Have a bite at that one!' or, 'Cheer up – it doesn't smell.'

But at last he also was deflated. He slouched across the handling room, and leaned against the angle of the door to address his colleague in the alleyway.

'It's hot as hell, and smells like a zoo. These savages stink.'

'You've been doing your share.'

'I'll be glad when it's finished.'

'It's cooler in the magazine with the fans running – you are all right.'

'Jesus, I'd like to sit down for a few minutes.'

'Better not, Lieutenant Kyller is on the prowl.'

This exchange was taking place within a few feet of Sebastian. He followed the German conversation with more ease now that he had been able to exercise his rusty vocabulary, but he kept his head down in a renewed burst of energy. He was worried. In a short while the day's shift would end and the African porters would be herded on deck and into the launches to be transported to their camp on one of the islands. None of the native labour force were allowed to spend the night aboard *Blücher*.

He had waited since noon for an opportunity to enter the magazine and place the time charge. But he had been frustrated by the activities of the two German guards. It must be nearly seven o'clock in the evening now. It would have to be soon, very soon. He glanced once more into the magazine, and he caught the eye of Walaka, Mohammed's cousin. Walaka stood by the cordite shelves, supervising the packing, and now he shrugged at Sebastian in eloquent helplessness.

Suddenly there was a thud of a heavy object being dropped to the deck, and a commotion of shouts in the alleyway behind Sebastian. He glanced round quickly. One of the bearers had fainted in the heat and fallen with a shell in his arms, the shell had rolled and knocked down another man. Now there was a milling confusion clogging the alleyway. The two guards moved forward, forcing their way into the press of black bodies, shouting hoarsely and clubbing with the rifle butts. It was the opportunity for which Sebastian had waited.

He stepped over the threshold of the magazine, and went to Walaka beside the cordite shelves.

'Send one of your men to take my place,' he whispered, and reaching up into the folds of his cloak he brought out the cigar box.

With his back towards the door of the magazine, using the cloak as a screen to hide his movements, he slipped the catch of the box and opened the lid.

His hands trembled with haste and nervous agitation as he fumbled with the winder of the travelling-clock. It clicked, and he saw the second hand begin its endless circuit of the dial. Even over the shouts and scuffling in the alleyway, the muted ticking of its mechanism seemed offensively loud to Sebastian. Hastily he shut the lid and glanced guiltily over his shoulder at the doorway. Walaka stood there, and his face was sickly grey with the tension of imminent discovery, but he nodded to Sebastian, a signal that the guards were still occupied without.

Reaching up to the nearest shelf, Sebastian wedged the cigar box between two of the paper-wrapped cylinders of cordite. Then he packed others over it, covering it completely.

He stood back and found with surprise that he was panting, his breathing whistling in his throat. He could feel the little drops of sweat prickling on his shaven head. In the white electric light they shone like glass beads on his velvety, black-stained skin.

'Is it done?' Walaka croaked beside him.

'It is done,' Sebastian croaked back at him, and suddenly he was overcome with a driving compulsion to be out of this steel room, out of this box-packed room with the ingredients of violent death and destruction; out of the stifling press of bodies that had surrounded him all day. A dreadful thought seized his imagination, suppose the artificer had erred in his assembly of the time charge, suppose that even now the battery was heating the wires of the detonator and bringing them to explosion point. He felt panic as he looked around wildly at the tons of cordite and shell around him. He wanted to run, to fight his way out and up into the open air. He made the first move, and then froze.

The commotion in the alleyway had subsided miraculously, and now only one voice was raised. It came from just outside the doorway, using the curt inflection of authority. Sebastian had heard that voice repeatedly during that long day, and he had come to dread it. It heralded danger.

'Get them back to work immediately,' snapped Lieutenant Kyller as he stepped over the threshold into the magazine. He drew a gold watch from the pocket of his tunic and read the time. 'It is five minutes after seven. There is still almost half an hour before you knock off.' He tucked the watch away, and swept the magazine with a gaze that missed no detail. He was a tall young man, immaculate in his tropical whites. Behind him the two guards were hurriedly straightening their dishevelled uniforms and trying to look efficient and intelligent.

'Yes, sir,' they said in unison.

For a moment Kyller's eyes rested on Sebastian. It was probably because Sebastian was the finest physical specimen among the bearers, he stood taller than the rest of them – as tall as Kyller himself. But Sebastian felt his interest was deeper. He felt that Kyller was searching beneath the stain on his skin, that he was naked of disguise beneath those eyes. He felt that Kyller would remember him, had marked him down in his memory.

'That shelf.' Kyller turned away from Sebastian and crossed the magazine. He went directly to the shelf on which Sebastian had placed his time charge, and he patted the cordite cylinders that Sebastian had handled. They were slightly awry. 'Have it repacked immediately,' said Kyller.

'Right away, sir,' said the fat guard.

Again Kyller's eyes rested on Sebastian. It seemed that he was about to speak, then he changed his mind. He stooped through the doorway and disappeared.

Sebastian stood stony still, appalled by the order that Kyller had given. The fat guard grimaced sulkily.

'Christ, that one is a busy bastard.' And he glared at the cordite shelf. 'There's nothing wrong there.' He crossed to it and fiddled ineffectually. After a moment he asked the guard at the door. 'Has Kyller gone yet?'

'Yes. He's gone down the companion-way into the sick-bay.'

'Good!' grunted the fat one. 'I'm damned if I'm going to waste half an hour repacking this whole batch.' He hunched his shoulders, and screwed up his face with effort. There was a bagpipe squeal, and the guard relaxed and grinned. 'That one was for Lieutenant Kyller, God bless him!'

Darkness was falling, and with it the temperature dropped a few degrees into the high eighties and created an illusion that the faint evening breeze was chilly. Sebastian hugged his cloak around his body, and shuffled along in the slow column of native labourers that dribbled over the side of the German battle cruiser into the waiting launches.

He was exhausted both in body and in mind from the strain of the day's labour in the magazine, so that he went down the catwalk and took his place in the whaler, moving in a state of stupor. When the boat shoved off and puttered up the channel towards the labour camp on the nearest island, Sebastian looked back at *Blücher* with the same dumb stare as the men who squatted beside him on the floorboards of the whaler. Mechanically he registered the fact that Commissioner Fleischer's steam launch was tied up alongside the cruiser.

'Perhaps the fat swine will be aboard when the whole lot blows to hell,' he thought wearily. 'I can at least hope for that.'

He had no way of knowing who else Herman Fleischer had taken aboard the cruiser with him. Sebastian had been below decks toiling in the handling room of the magazine when the launch arrived from up-river, and Rosa Oldsmith had been ushered up the catwalk by the Commissioner in person.

'Come along, Mädchen. We will take you to see the gallant captain of this fine ship.' Fleischer puffed jovially as he mounted the steps behind her. 'I am sure there are many interesting things that you can tell him.'

Bedraggled and exhausted with grief, pale with the horror of her father's death, and with cold hatred for the man who had engineered it, Rosa stumbled as she stepped from the catwalk on to the deck. Her hands were still bound in front of her so she could not check herself. She fell forward, letting herself fall uncaring, and with mild surprise felt hands hold and steady her.

She looked up at the man who had caught her, and in her confusion of mind she thought it was Sebastian. He was tall and dark and his hands were strong. Then she saw the peaked uniform cap with its golden insignia, and she jerked away from him in revulsion.

'Ah! Lieutenant Kyller.' Commissioner Fleischer spoke behind her. 'I have brought you a visitor – a lovely lady.'

'Who is she?' Kyller was appraising Rosa. Rosa could not understand a word that was spoken. She stood in quiet acceptance, her whole body drooping.

'This . . .' answered Fleischer proudly, '. . . is the most dangerous young lady in the whole of Africa. She is one of the leaders of the gang of English bandits that raided the column bringing down the steel plate from Dar es Salaam. It was she who shot and killed your engineer. I captured her and her father this morning. Her father was the notorious O'Flynn.'

'Where is he?' Kyller snapped.

'I hanged him.'

'You hanged him?' demanded Kyller. 'Without trial?'

'No trial was necessary.'

'Without interrogating him?'

'I brought in the woman for interrogation.'

Kyller was angry now, his voice crackled with it.

'I will leave it to Captain von Kleine to judge the wisdom of your actions,' and he turned to Rosa; his eyes dropped to her hands, and, with an exclamation of concern, he took her by the wrist.

'Commissioner Fleischer, how long has this woman been bound?'

Fleischer shrugged. 'I could take no chances on her escaping.'

'Look at this!' Kyller indicated Rosa's hands. They were swollen, the fingers puffy and blue, sticking out stiffly, dead-looking and useless.

'I could take no chances.' Fleischer bridled at the implied criticism.

'Give me your knife,' Kyller snapped at the petty officer in charge of the gangway, and the man produced a large clasp knife. He opened it and handed it to the lieutenant.

Carefully Kyller ran the blade between Rosa's wrists and sawed at the rope. As her bonds dropped away Rosa cried out in pain of fresh blood flowing into her hands.

'You will be lucky if you have not done her permanent damage,' Kyller muttered furiously as he massaged Rosa's bloated hands.

'She is a criminal. A dangerous criminal,' growled Fleischer.

'She is a woman, and therefore deserving of your consideration. Not of this barbarous treatment.'

'She will hang.'

'Her crimes she will answer for, in due course – but until she has stood trial she will be treated as a woman.'

Rosa did not understand the harsh German argument that raged around her. She stood quietly and her eyes were fastened on the knife in Lieutenant Kyller's hand. The hilt brushed her fingers as he worked to restore the circulation of her blood. The blade was long and silver bright, she had seen how keen was its edge by the way in which it had cut through the rope. As she stared at it, it seemed to her fevered fancy that there were two names engraved in the steel of the blade. The names of the two persons she had loved. The names of her father and her child.

With an effort she tore her gaze from the knife and looked at the man she hated. Fleischer had come close up to her, as though to take her away from Lieutenant Kyller's attention. His face was flushed with anger and the fold of flesh under his chin wobbled flabbily as he argued.

Rosa flexed her fingers. They were still numb and stiff, but she could feel the strength flowing back into them. She let her gaze drop down to Fleischer's belly.

It jutted out round and full, soft-looking under the grey corduroy tunic, and again her fevered imagination formed a picture of the blade going into that belly. Slipping in silently, smoothly, burying itself to the hilt and then drawing upwards to open the flesh like a pouch. The picture was so vivid that Rosa shuddered with the intense sensual pleasure of it.

Kyller was completely occupied with Fleischer. He felt the girl's fingers slide into the cupped palm of his right hand, but before he could pull away she had scooped the knife deftly from his grip. He lunged at her, but she pirouetted lightly away from him. Her knife hand dropped and then darted forward, driven by the full weight of her body at the bulging belly of Herman Fleischer.

Rosa thought that because he was fat he would be slow. She

expected him to be stunned by the unexpected attack, to stand and take the knife in his vitals.

Herman Fleischer was fully alert before she even started her thrust. He was fast as a striking mamba, and strong beyond credibility. He did not make the mistake of intercepting the knife with his bare hands. Instead he struck her right shoulder with a clenched fist the size of a carpenter's mallet. The force of the blow knocked her sideways, deflecting the blade from its target. Her arm from the shoulder downwards was paralysed, and the knife flew from her hand and slithered away across the deck.

'Ja!' roared Fleischer triumphantly. 'Ja! So! Now you see how I was right to tie the bitch. She is vicious, dangerous.'

And he lifted the huge fist again to smash it into Rosa's face as she crouched, hugging her hurt shoulder and sobbing with pain and disappointment.

'Enough!' Kyller stepped between them. 'Leave her.'

'She must be tied up like an animal – she is dangerous,' bellowed Fleischer, but Kyller put a protective arm around Rosa's bowed shoulders.

'Petty Officer,' he said. 'Take this woman to the sick-bay. Have Surgeon Commander Buchholz see to her. Guard her carefully, but be gentle with her. Do you hear me?' And they took her away below.

'I must see Captain von Kleine,' Fleischer demanded. 'I must make a full report to him.'

'Come,' said Kyller, 'I will take you to him.'

80

Sebastian lay on his side beside the smoky little fire with his cloak draped over him. Outside he heard the night sounds of the swamp, the faint splash of a fish or a crocodile in the channel, the clink and boom of the tree frogs, the singing of insects, and the lap and sigh of wavelets on the mud bank below the hut.

The hut was one of twenty crude open-sided shelters that housed the native labour force. The earth floor was thickly strewn with sleeping bodies. The sound of their breathing was a restless murmur, broken by the cough and stir of dreamers.

Despite his fatigue, Sebastian was not sleeping, he could not relax from the state of tension in which he had been held all that day. He thought of the little travelling-clock ticking away in its nest of high explosive, measuring out the minutes and the hours, and then his mind side-stepped and went to Rosa. The muscles of his arms tightened with longing. Tomorrow, he thought, tomorrow I will see her and we will go away from this stinking river. Up into the sweet air of the highlands. Again his mind jumped. Seven o'clock, seven o'clock tomorrow morning and it will be over. He remembered Lieutenant Kyller's voice as he stood in the doorway of the magazine with the gold watch in his hand. '. . . The time is five minutes past seven . . .' he had said. So that Sebastian knew to within a few minutes when the time fuse would explode.

He must stop the porters going aboard *Blücher* in the morning. He had impressed on old Walaka that they must refuse to turn out for the next day's shift. They must . . .

'Manali! Manali!' his name was whispered close by in the gloom, and Sebastian lifted himself on one elbow. In the flickering light from the fire there was a shadowy figure, crawling on hands and knees across the earthen floor, and searching the faces of the sleeping men.

'Manali, where are you?'

'Who is it?' Sebastian answered softly, and the man jumped up and scurried to where he lay.

'It is I, Mohammed.'

'Mohammed?' Sebastian was startled. 'Why are you here? You should be with Fini at the camp on the Abati.'

'Fini is dead.' Mohammed's whisper was low with sorrow, so low that Sebastian thought he had misunderstood.

'What? What did you say?'

'Fini is dead. The Allemand came with the ropes. They hung him in the fever trees beside the Abati, and when he was dead they left him for the birds.'

'What talk is this?' Sebastian demanded.

'It is true,' mourned Mohammed. 'I saw it, and when the Allemand had gone, I cut the rope and brought him down. I wrapped him in my own blanket and buried him in an ant-bear hole.'

'Dead? Flynn dead? It isn't true!'

'It is true, Manali.' In the red glow of the camp-fire Mohammed's face was old and raddled and gaunt. He licked his lips. 'There is more, Manali. There is more to tell.'

But Sebastian was not listening. He was trying to force his mind to accept the reality of Flynn's death, but it balked. It would not accept the picture of Flynn swinging at the rope's end, Flynn with the rope burns at his throat and his face swollen and empurpled, Flynn wrapped in a dirty blanket and crammed into an ant-bear hole. Flynn dead? No! Flynn was too big, too vital – they could not kill Flynn.

'Manali, hear me.'

Sebastian shook his head, bemused, denying it. It could not be true.

'Manali, the Allemand, they have taken Little Long Hair. They have bound her with ropes and taken her.'

Sebastian winced, and jerked away as though he had been struck open-handed across the face.

'No!' He tried to close his mind against the words.

'They caught her this morning early as she went to Fini. They took her down-river in the small boat, and she is now on the great ship of the Allemand.'

'*Blücher*? Rosa is aboard the *Blücher*?'

'Yes. She is there.'

'No. Oh, God, *no*!'

In five hours *Blücher* would blow up. In five hours Rosa would die. Sebastian swung his head and looked out into the night, he looked through the open side of the hut, down the channel to where *Blücher* lay at her moorings half a mile away. There was a dim glow of light across the water from the hooded lanterns on *Blücher*'s main deck. But her form was indistinguishable against the dark mass of the mangroves. Between her and the island, the channel was a smooth expanse of velvety blackness on which the reflection of the stars were scattered sequins of light.

'I must go to her,' said Sebastian. 'I cannot let her die there alone.' His voice gathered strength and resolve. 'I cannot let her die. I'll tell the Germans where to find the charge – I'll tell them . . .' Then he faltered. 'I can't. No, I can't. I'd be a traitor then, but, but . . .'

He threw aside his cloak.

'Mohammed, how did you come here? Did you bring the canoe? Where is it?'

Mohammed shook his head. 'No. I swam. My cousin brought me close to the island in the canoe, but he has gone away. We could not leave the canoe here, lest the Askari find it. They would have seen the canoe.'

'There isn't a boat on the island – nothing,' muttered Sebastian. The Germans were careful to guard against desertion. Each night the labour force was marooned on the island – and the Askari patrolled the mud banks.

'Mohammed, hear me now,' Sebastian reached across and laid his hand on the old man's shoulder. 'You are my friend. I thank you that you have come to tell me these things.'

'You are going to Little Long Hair?'

'Yes.'

'Go in peace, Manali.'

'Take my place here, Mohammed. When the guards count tomorrow morning, you will stand for me.' Sebastian tightened his grip on the bony shoulder. 'Stay in peace, Mohammed.'

His blackened body blending into the darkness, Sebastian crouched beneath the spread branches of a clump of pampa scrub, and the Askari guard almost brushed against him as he passed. The Askari slouched along with his rifle slung so that the barrel stood up behind his shoulder. The constant patrolling had beaten a path around the circumference of the island, the guard followed it mechanically. Half asleep on his feet, completely unaware of Sebastian's presence. He stumbled in the darkness and swore sleepily, and moved on.

Sebastian crossed the path on his hands and knees, then stretched out on his belly into a reptilian slither as he reached the mud bank. Had he tried to walk across it, the glutinous mud would have sucked so loudly around his feet that every guard within a hundred yards would have heard him.

The mud coated his chest and belly and legs with its coldly loathsome, clinging oiliness, and the reek of it filled his nostrils so he gagged. Then he was into the water. The water was blood warm, he felt the tug of the current and the bottom dropped away beneath him. He swam on his side, careful that neither legs nor arms should break the surface. His head alone showed, like the head of a swimming otter, and he felt the mud washing off his body.

He swam across the current, guided by the distant glimmer of *Blücher*'s deck lights. He swam slowly, husbanding his strength, for he knew he would need all of it later.

His mind was filled with layers of awareness. The lowest layer was a lurking undirected terror of the dark water in which he swam, his dangling legs were vulnerable to the scaly predators which infested the Rufiji river. The current must be carrying his scent down to them. Soon they would come hunting up to find him. But he kept up the easy stroke of arms and legs. It was a chance, one chance of the many he was taking and he tried to ignore it and grapple with the practical problems of his attempt. When he reached *Blücher*, how was he to get aboard her? Her sides were fifty feet high, and the catwalks were the only means of access. These were both heavily guarded. It was a problem without solution, and yet he harried it.

Over this was a thick layer of hopeless sorrow. Sorrow for Flynn.

But the uppermost layer was thickest, strongest. Rosa, Rosa and Rosa.

He found with surprise that he was saying it aloud.

'Rosa!' with each forward thrust of his body through the water.

'Rosa!' each time he drew breath.

'Rosa!' as his legs kicked out and pushed him towards the *Blücher*.

He did not know what he would do if he reached her. Perhaps

there was some half-formed idea of escaping with her, of fighting his way out of *Blücher* with his woman. Getting her away before that moment when the ship would vanish in a holocaust of flame. He did not know, but he swam on quietly.

Then he was under *Blücher*'s side. The towering mass of steel blotted out the starry night sky, and he stopped swimming and hung in the warm water looking up at her.

There were small sounds. The hum of machinery within her, the faint clang of metal struck against metal, the low guttural murmur of voices at her gangway, the thump of a rifle butt against the wooden deck, the soft wash of water around the hull – and then a closer, clearer sound, a regular creak and tap, creak and tap.

He swam in towards the hull, searching for the source of this new sound. It came from near the bows, creak and tap. The creak of rope, and the tap of wood against the steel hull. He saw it then, just above his head. He almost cried out with joy.

The cradles! The platforms still suspended above the water on which the welders and the painters had worked.

He reached up and gripped the wooden edge and drew himself on to the platform. He rested a few seconds and then began to climb the rope. Hand over hand, gripping the rope between the insides of his bare feet, he went up.

His head came level with the deck and he hung there, searching carefully. Fifty yards away he saw two seamen at the gangway. Neither was looking his way.

At intervals the hooded lanterns threw puddles of yellow light upon the deck, but there were concealing shadows beyond them. It was dark around the base of the forward gun-turrets, and there were piles of material, abandoned welding equipment, heaps of rope and canvas in the shadows which would hide him when he had crossed the deck.

Once more he checked the two guards at the gangway, their backs were turned to him.

Sebastian filled his lungs and steeled himself to act. Then with one fluid movement he drew himself up and rolled over the side. He landed lightly on his feet and darted across the exposed deck into the shadows. He ducked down behind a pile of canvas and rope netting, and struggled to control his breathing. He could feel his legs trembling violently under him, so he sat down on the planking and huddled against the protecting pile of canvas. River water trickled from his shaven pate over his forehead and into his eyes. He wiped it away.

'Now what?' He was aboard *Blücher*, but what should he do next?

Where would they hold Rosa? Was there some sort of guard-room for prisoners? Would they put her in one of the officer's cabins? The sick-bay?

He knew roughly where the sick-bay was located. While he was working in the magazine he had heard the one German guard say, 'He has gone down the companion-way to the sick-bay.'

It must be somewhere just below the forward magazine – oh, God! If they had her there she would be almost at the centre of the explosion.

He came up on his knees, and peered over the pile of canvas. It was lighter now. Through the screen of camouflage netting, he could see the night sky had paled a little in the east. Dawn was not far off. The night had passed so swiftly, morning was on its way and there were but a few scant hours before the hands of the travelling-clock completed their journey, and made the electrical connection that would seal the *Blücher*'s fate, and the fate of all those aboard her.

He must move. He rose slowly and then froze. The guards at the gangway had come to attention. They stood stiffly with their rifles at the slope, and into the light stepped a tall, white-clad figure.

There was no mistaking him. It was the officer that Sebastian had last seen in the forward magazine. Kyller, they had called him, Lieutenant Kyller.

Kyller acknowledged the salutes of the two guards, and he spoke with them a while. Their voices were low and indistinct. Kyller saluted again, and then left them. He came down the deck towards the bows; he walked briskly, and his face below the peak of his cap was in darkness.

Sebastian crouched down again, only his eyes lifted above the piled canvas. He watched the officer and he was afraid.

Kyller stopped in mid-stride. He half stooped to look at the deck at his feet, and then in the same movement, straightened with his right hand dropping to the holstered pistol on his belt.

'Guard!' he bellowed. 'Here! At the double!'

On the holystoned white planking, the wet footprints that

Sebastian had left behind him glittered in the lantern light. Kyller stared in the direction that they led, coming directly towards Sebastian's hiding-place.

The boots of the two guards pounded heavily along the deck. They had unslung their rifles as they ran to join Kyller.

'Someone has come aboard here. Spread out and search...' Kyller shouted at them, as he closed in on Sebastian.

Sebastian panicked. He jumped up and ran, trying to reach the corner of the gun-turret.

'There he is!' Kyller's voice. 'Stop! Stop or I'll fire.'

Sebastian ran. His legs driving powerfully, his elbows pumping, head down, bare feet slapping on the planking, he raced through shadow.

'Stop!' Kyller was balanced on the balls of his feet, legs braced, right shoulder thrust forward and right arm outflung in the classic stance of the pistol marksman. The arm dropped slowly and then kicked up violently, as the shot spouted from the Luger in a bell of yellow flame. The bullet spanged against the plating of the turret and then glanced off in whining ricochet.

Sebastian felt the wind of the bullet pass his head and he jinked his run. The corner of the turret was very close, and he dodged towards it.

Then Kyller's next shot blurted loudly in the night, and simultaneously something struck Sebastian a heavy blow under his left shoulder-blade. It threw him forward off balance and he reeled against the turret, his hands scrabbled at the smooth steel without finding purchase. His body flattened against the side of the turret, so that the blood from the exit hole that the bullet had torn in his breast sprayed on to the pale grey, painted turret.

His legs buckled and he slid down, slowly, still trying to find purchase with the hooked claws of his fingers, so that as his knees touched the deck he was in the attitude of devout prayer. Forehead pressed against the turret, kneeling, arms spread high and wide.

Then the arms sank down, and he slid sideways, collapsed onto the deck and rolled on to his back.

Kyller came and stood over him. The pistol hanging slackly in the hand at his side.

'Oh, my God,' there was genuine regret in Kyller's voice. 'It's only one of the porters. Why did the fool run! I wouldn't have fired if he had stood.'

Sebastian wanted to ask him where Rosa was. He wanted to explain that Rosa was his wife, that he loved her, and that he had come to find her.

He concentrated his vision on Kyller's face as it hung over him, and he summoned his school-boy German, marshalling the sentences in his mind.

But as he opened his mouth the blood welled up in his throat and choked him. He coughed, racking, and the blood bubbled through his lips in a pink froth.

'Lung shot!' said Kyller, and then to the guards as they came up, 'Get a stretcher. Hurry. We must take him down to the sick-bay.'

81

There were twelve bunks in *Blücher*'s sick-bay, six down each side of the narrow cabin. In eight of them lay German seamen; five malaria cases and three men injured in the work of repairing her bows.

Rosa Oldsmith was in the bunk farthest from the door. She lay behind a movable screen, and a guard sat outside the screen. He wore a pistol at his belt and was wholly absorbed in a year-old variety magazine, the cover of which depicted a buxom blonde woman in a black corset and high boots, with a horse whip in one hand.

The cabin was brightly lit and smelled of antiseptic. One of the malarial cases was in delirium, and he laughed and shouted. The medical orderly moved along the rows of bunks carrying a metal tray from which he administered the morning dosages of quinine. The time was 5 a.m.

Rosa had slept only intermittently during the night. She lay on top of the blankets and she wore a striped towelling dressing-gown over the blue flannel night-gown. The gown was many sizes too large and she had rolled back the cuffs of the sleeves. Her hair was loose on the pillows, and damp at the temples with sweat. Her face was pale and drawn, with bluish smudges of fatigue under her eyes, and her shoulder ached dully where Fleischer had struck her.

She was awake now. She lay staring up at the low roof of the cabin, playing over in her mind fragments from the happenings of the last twenty-four hours.

She recalled the interrogation with Captain von Kleine. He had sat opposite her in his luxuriously furnished cabin, and his manner had been kindly, his voice gentle, pronouncing the English words with blurring of the consonants and a hardening of the vowel sounds. His English was good.

'When did you last eat?' he asked her.

'I am not hungry,' she replied, making no attempt to conceal her hatred. Hating them all – this handsome, gentle man, the tall lieutenant who stood beside him, and Herman Fleischer who sat across the cabin from her, with his knees spread apart to accommodate the full hang of his belly.

'I will send for food.' Von Kleine ignored her protest and rang for his steward. When the food came, she could not deny the demands of her body and she ate, trying to show no enjoyment. The sausage and pickles were delicious, for she had not eaten since the previous noon.

Courteously von Kleine turned his attention to a discussion with Lieutenant Kyller until she had finished, but when the steward removed the empty tray he came back to her.

'Herr Fleischer tells me you are the daughter of Major O'Flynn, the commander of the Portuguese irregulars operating in German territory?'

'I was until he was hanged, murdered! He was injured and helpless. They tied him to a stretcher . . .' Rosa flared at him, tears starting in her eyes.

'Yes,' von Kleine stopped her, 'I know. I am not pleased. That is now a matter between myself and Commissioner Fleischer. I can only say that I am sorry. I offer you my condolence.' He paused and glanced at Herman Fleischer. Rosa could see by the angry blue of his eyes that he meant what he said.

'But now there are some questions I must ask you . . .'

Rosa had planned her replies, for she knew what he would ask. She replied frankly and truthfully to anything that did not jeopardize Sebastian's attempt to place the time fuse aboard *Blücher.*

What were she and Flynn doing when they were captured? Keeping the *Blücher* under surveillance. Waiting to signal her departure to the blockading cruisers.

How did the British know that Blücher was in the Rufiji? The steel plate, of course. Then confirmation by aerial reconnaissance.

Were they contemplating offensive action against Blücher? No, they would wait until she sailed.

What was the strength of the blockade squadron? Two cruisers that she had seen, she did not know if there were other warships waiting over the horizon.

Von Kleine phrased his questions carefully, and listened attentively to her replies. For an hour the interrogation continued, until Rosa was yawning openly, and her voice was slurred with exhaustion. Von Kleine realized that there was nothing to be learned from her, all she had told him he already knew or had guessed.

'Thank you,' he finished. 'I am keeping you aboard my ship. There will be danger here, for soon I will be going out to meet the British warships. But I believe that it will be better for you than if I handed you over to the German administration ashore.' He hesitated a moment and glanced at Commissioner Fleischer. 'In every nation there are evil men, fools and barbarians. Do not judge us all by one man.'

With distaste at her own treachery, Rosa found that she could not hate this man. A weary smile tugged her mouth and she answered him.

'You are kind.'

'Lieutenant Kyller will see you to the hospital. I am sorry I can offer you no better quarters, but this is a crowded vessel.'

When she had gone, von Kleine lit a cheroot and while he tasted its comforting fragrance, he allowed his eyes to rest on the portrait of the two golden women across the cabin. Then he sat up in his chair and his voice had lost its gentleness as he spoke to the man who lolled on the couch.

'Herr Fleischer, I find it difficult to express fully my extreme displeasure at your handling of this affair . . .'

After a night of fitful sleep, Rosa lay on her hospital bunk behind the screen and she thought of her husband. If things had gone well Sebastian must by now have placed the time charge and escaped from *Blücher*. Perhaps he was already on his way to the rendezvous on the Abati river. If this were so, then she would not see him again. It was her one regret. She imagined him in his ludicrous disguise, and she smiled a little. Dear lovable Sebastian. Would he ever know what had happened to her? Would he know that she had died with those whom she hated? She hoped that he would never know – that he would never torture himself with the knowledge that he had placed the instrument of her death with his own hands.

I wish I could see him just once more to tell him that my death is unimportant beside the death of Herman Fleischer, beside the destruction of this German warship. I wish only that when the time comes, I could see it. I wish there were some way I could know the exact time of the explosion so I could tell Herman Fleischer a minute before, when it is too late for him to escape, and watch him. Perhaps he would blubber, perhaps he would scream with fear. I would like that. I would like that very much.

The strength of her hatred was such that she could no longer lie still. She sat up and tied the belt of her gown around her waist. She was filled with a restless itchy exhilaration. It would be today – she felt sure – sometime today she would slake this burning thirst for vengeance that had tormented her for so long.

She threw her legs over the side of the bunk and pulled open the screen. The guard dropped his magazine and started up from his chair, his hand dropping to the pistol at his hip.

'I will not harm you . . .' Rosa smiled at him, '. . . . not yet!'

She pointed to the door which led into the tiny shower cabinet and toilet. The guard relaxed and nodded acquiescence. He followed her as she crossed the cabin.

Rosa walked slowly between the bunks, looking at the sick men that lay in them.

'All of you,' she thought happily. 'All of you!'

She slid the tongue of the lock across, and was alone in the bathroom. She undressed, and leaned across the wash-basin to the small mirror set above it. She could see the reflection of her head and shoulders. There was a purple and red bruise spreading down from her neck and staining the white swell of her right breast. She touched it tenderly with her finger-tips.

'Herman Fleischer,' she said the name gloatingly, 'it will be today – I promise you that. Today you will die.'

And then suddenly she was crying.

'I only wish you could burn as my baby burned – I wish you could choke and swing on the rope as my father did.' And the tears fell fat and slow, sliding down her cheeks to drop into the basin. She started to sob, dry convulsive gasps of grief and hatred. She turned blindly to the shower cabinet, and turned both taps full on so that the rush of the water would cover the sound of her weeping. She did not want them to hear it.

Later, when she had bathed her face and body and combed her hair and dressed again, she unlocked the door and stepped through it. She stopped abruptly and through puffy reddened eyes tried to make sense of what was happening in the sick-bay.

It was crowded. The surgeon was there, two orderlies, four German seamen, and the young lieutenant. All of them hovered about the stretcher that was being manoeuvred between the bunks. There was a man on the stretcher, she could see his form under the single grey blanket that covered him, but Lieutenant Kyller's back obscured her view of the man's face. There was blood on the blanket, and a brown smear of blood on the sleeve of Kyller's white tunic.

She moved along the bulkhead of the cabin and craned her head to see around Kyller, but at that moment one of the orderlies leaned across to swab the mouth of the man on the stretcher with a white cloth. The cloth obscured the wounded man's face. Bright frothy blood soaked through the material, and the sight of it nauseated Rosa. She averted her gaze and slipped away towards her own bunk at the end of the cabin. She reached the screen, and behind her somebody groaned. It was a low delirious groan, but the sound of it stopped Rosa instantly. She felt as though something within her chest was swelling to stifle her. Slowly, fearfully, she turned back.

They were lifting the man from the stretcher to lay him on an empty bunk. The head lolled sideways, and beneath its stain of bark juice Rosa saw that dear, well loved face.

'Sebastian!' she cried, and she ran to him, pushing past Kyller, throwing herself on to the blanket-draped body, trying to get her arms around him to hug him.

'Sebastian! What have they done to you!'

82

'Sebastian! Sebastian!' Rosa leaned across him and held her mouth to his ear.

'Sebastian!' She called his name quietly but urgently, then brushed his forehead with her lips. The skin was cold and damp.

He lay on his back with the bed clothes turned back to his waist. His chest was swathed in bandages, and his breathing sawed and gurgled.

'Sebastian. It's Rosa. It's Rosa. Wake up, Sebastian. Wake up, it's Rosa.'

'Rosa?' At last her name had reached him. He whispered it painfully, wetly, and fresh blood stained his lips.

Rosa had been on the edge of despair. Two hours she had been sitting beside him. Since the surgeon had finished dressing the wound, she had sat with him – touching him, calling to him. This was the first sign of recognition he had given her.

'Yes! Yes! It's Rosa. Wake up, Sebastian.' Her voice lifted with relief.

'Rosa?' His eyelashes trembled.

'Wake up.' She pinched his cold cheek and he winced. His eyelids fluttered open.

'Rosa?' on a shallow, sawing breath.

'Here, Sebastian. I'm here.' His eyes rolled in their sockets, searching, trying desperately to focus.

'Here,' she said, leaning over him and taking his face between her hands. She looked into his eyes.

'Here, my darling, here.'

'Rosa!' His lips convulsed into a dreadful parody of a smile.

'Sebastian, did you set the bomb?'

His breathing changed, hoarser, and his mouth twitched with the effort.

'Tell them,' he whispered.

'Tell them what?'

'Seven. Must stop it.'

'Seven o'clock?'

'Don't – want – you – '

'Will it explode at seven o'clock?'

'You – ' It was too much and he coughed.

'Seven o'clock? Is that it, Sebastian?'

'You will . . .' He squeezed his eyes closed, putting all his strength into the effort of speaking. 'Please. Don't die. Stop it.'

'Did you set it for seven o'clock?' In her impatience she tugged his head towards her. 'Tell me, for God's sake, tell me!'

'Seven o'clock. Tell them – tell them.'

Still holding him, she looked at the clock set high up on the bulkhead of the sick-bay.

On the white dial, the ornate black hands stood at fifteen minutes before the hour.

'Don't die, please don't die,' mumbled Sebastian.

She hardly heard the pain-muted pleading. A fierce surge of triumph lifted her – she knew the hour. The exact minute. Now she could send for Herman Fleischer, and have him with her.

Gently she laid Sebastian's head back on the pillow. On the table below the clock she had seen a pad and pencil among the bottles and jars, and trays of instruments. She went to it, and while the guard watched her suspiciously she scribbled a note.

'Captain,

My husband is conscious. He has a message of vital importance for Commissioner Fleischer. He will speak to no one but Commissioner Fleischer. The message could save your ship.

Rosa Oldsmith.'

She folded the sheet of paper and pushed it into the guard's hand.

'For the Captain. Captain.'

'Kapitän,' repeated the guard. 'Jawohl.' And he went to the door of the sick-bay. She saw him speak with the second guard outside the door, and then pass him the note.

Rosa sank down on the edge of Sebastian's bunk. She ran her hand tenderly over his shaven head. The new hair was stiff and bristly under her fingers.

'Wait for me. I'm coming with you, my darling. Wait for me.'

But he had lapsed back into unconsciousness. Crooning softly, she gentled him. Smiling to herself, happily, she waited for the minute hand of the clock to creep up to the zenith of the dial.

83

Captain Arthur Joyce had personally supervised the placing of the scuttling charges. Perhaps, long ago, another man had felt the way he did – hearing the command spoken from the burning bush, and knowing he must obey.

The charges were small, but laid in twenty places against the bare plating, they would rip *Renounce*'s belly out of her cleanly. The watertight bulkhead had been opened to let the water rush through her. The magazines had all of them been flooded to minimize the danger of explosion. The furnaces had been damped down, and he had blown the pressure on his boilers – retaining a head of steam, just sufficient to take *Renounce* in on her last run into the channel of the Rufiji.

The cruiser had been stripped of her crew. Twenty men left aboard her to handle the ship. The rest of them trans-shipped aboard *Pegasus*.

Joyce was going to attempt to force the log boom, take *Renounce* through the minefield, and sink her higher up, where the double mouth of the channel merged into a single thoroughfare.

If he succeeded he would effectively have blocked *Blücher*, and sacrificed a single ship.

If he failed, if *Renounce* sank in the minefield before she reached the confluence of the two channels, then Armstrong would have to take *Pegasus* in and scuttle her also. On his bridge Joyce sat hunched in his canvas deck chair, looking out at the land; the green line of Africa which the morning sun lit in harsh golden brilliance.

Renounce was running parallel to the coast, five miles off shore. Behind her *Pegasus* trailed like a mourner at a funeral.

'06.45 hours, sir.' The officer of the watch saluted.

'Very well.' Joyce roused himself. Until this moment he had hoped. Now the time had come and *Renounce* must die.

'Yeoman of Signals,' he spoke quietly, 'make this signal with *Pegasus* number "Plan A Effective".' This was the code that *Renounce* was to stand in for the channel. 'Stand by to pick up survivors.'

'*Pegasus* acknowledges, sir.'

Joyce was glad that Armstrong had not sent some inane message such as 'Good luck'. A curt acknowledgement, that was as it should be.

'All right, Pilot,' he said, 'take us in, please.'

It was a beautiful morning and a flat sea. The captain of the escort destroyer wished it were not, he would have forfeited a year's seniority for a week of fog and rain.

As his ship tore down the line of transports to administer a rebuke to the steamer at the end of the column for not keeping proper station, he looked out at the western horizon. Visibility was perfect, a German masthead would be able to pick out this convoy of fat sluggish transports at a distance of thirty miles.

Twelve ships, fifteen thousand men – and *Blücher* could be out. At any moment she could come hurtling up over the horizon, with those long nine-inch guns blazing. The thought gave him the creeps. He jumped up from his stool, and crossed to the port rail of his bridge to glower at the convoy.

Close alongside wallowed one of the transports. They were playing cricket on her afterdeck. As he watched, a sun-bronzed giant of a South African clad only in short khaki pants swung the bat and clearly he heard the crack as it struck the ball. The ball soared up and dropped into the sea with a tiny splash.

'Oh, good shot, sir!' applauded the lieutenant who stood beside the captain.

'This is not the members' enclosure at Lords, Mr Parkinson,' snarled the destroyer captain. 'If you have nothing to occupy you, I can find duties for you.'

The lieutenant retired hurt, and the captain glanced along the line of troopships.

'Oh, no!' he groaned. Number Three was making smoke again. Ever since leaving Durban harbour Number Three had been giving periodic impersonations of Mount Vesuvius. It would be a give-away to the look-out at *Blücher*'s masthead.

He reached for his megaphone, ready to hurl the most scathing reprimand he could muster at Number Three as he passed her.

'This is worse than being a teacher in a kindergarten. They'll break me yet.' Ane he lifted the megaphone to his lips as Number Three came abreast.

The infantrymen that lined the troopship's rail cheered his eloquence to the echo.

'The fools. Let them cheer *Blücher* when she comes,' growled the captain and crossed the bridge to gaze apprehensively into the west where Africa lay just below the horizon.

'Strength to *Renounce* and *Pegasus*.' He made the wish fervently. 'God grant they hold *Blücher*. If she gets through . . .'

85

'It's no use, Bwana. They won't move,' the sergeant of Askari reported to Ensign Proust.

'What is the trouble?' demanded Proust.

'They say there is a bad magic on the ship. They will not go to her today.'

Proust looked over the mass of black humanity. They squatted sullenly among the huts and palm trees, rank upon rank of them, huddled in their cloaks, faces closed and secretive.

Drawn up on the mud bank of the island were the two motor launches, ready to ferry the bearers downstream to the day's labour aboard *Blücher*. The German seamen tending the launches were watching with interest this charade of dumb rebellion, and Ensign Proust was very conscious of their attention.

Proust was at the age where he had an iron-clad faith in his own sagacity, the dignity of a patriarch, and pimples.

He was, in other words, nineteen years of age.

It was clear to him that these native tribesmen had embarked on their present course of action for no other reason than to embarrass Ensign Proust. It was a direct and personal attack on his standing and authority.

He lifted his right hand to his mouth and began to feed thoughtfully on his fingernails. His rather prominent Adam's apple moved in sympathy with the working of his jaws. Suddenly he realized what he was doing. It was a habit he was trying to cure, and he jerked his hand away and linked it with its mate behind his back, in a faithful imitation of Captain Otto von Kleine, a man whom he held in high admiration. It had hurt him deeply when Lieutenant Kyller had greeted his request for permission to grow a beard like Captain von Kleine's with ribald laughter.

Now he sank his bare chin on to his chest and began to pace solemnly up and down the small clearing above the mud bank.

The sergeant of Askari waited respectfully with his men drawn up behind him for Ensign Proust to reach a decision.

He could send one of the launches back to *Blücher*, to fetch Commissioner Fleischer. After all, this was really the Herr Commissioner's shauri (Proust had taken to using odd Swahili words like an old Africa hand). Yet he realized that to call for Fleischer would be an admission that he was unable to handle the situation. Commissioner Fleischer would jeer at him, Commissioner Fleischer had shown an increasing tendency to jeer at Ensign Proust.

'No,' he thought, flushing so that the red spots on his skin were less noticeable, 'I will not send for that fat peasant.' He stopped pacing and addressed himself to the sergeant of Askari.

'Tell them . . .' he started, and his voice squeaked alarmingly. He adjusted the timbre to a deep throaty rumble, 'Tell them I take a very serious view of this matter.'

The sergeant saluted, did a showy about-face with much feet stamping, and passed on Ensign Proust's message in loud Swahili. From the dark ranks of bearers there was no reaction whatsoever, not so much as a raised eyebrow. The crews of the launches were more responsive. One of them laughed.

Ensign Proust's Adam's apple bobbed, and his ears chameleoned to the colour of a good burgundy.

'Tell them that it is *mutiny*!' The last word squeaked again, and the sergeant hesitated while he groped for the Swahili equivalent. Finally he settled for:

'Bwana Heron is very angry.' Proust had been nicknamed for his pointed nose and long thin legs. The tribesmen bore up valiantly under this intelligence.

'Tell them I will take drastic steps.'

Now, thought the sergeant, he is making sense. He allowed himself literary licence in his translation.

'Bwana Heron says that there are trees on this island for all of you – and he has sufficient rope.'

A sigh blew through them, soft and restless as a small wind in a field of wheat. Heads turned slowly until they were all looking at Walaka.

Reluctantly Walaka stood up to reply. He realized that it was foolhardy to draw attention to himself when there was talk of ropes in the air, but the damage had already been done. The hundreds of eyes upon him had singled him out to the Allemand.

Bwana Intambu always hanged the man that everyone looked at.

Walaka began to speak. His voice had the soothing quality of a rusty gate squeaking in the wind. It went on and on, as Walaka attempted a one-man filibust.

'What is he talking about?' demanded Ensign Proust.

'He is talking about leopards,' the sergeant told him.

'What is he saying about them?'

'He says, among other things, that they are the excrement of dead lepers.'

Proust looked stunned, he had expected Walaka's speech to have at least some bearing on the business in hand. He rallied gamely.

'Tell him that he is a wise old man, and that I look to him to lead the others to their duties.'

And the sergeant gazed upon Walaka sternly.

'Bwana Heron says that you, Walaka, are the son of a diseased porcupine and that you feed on offal with the vultures. He says further that you he has chosen to lead the others in the dance of the rope.'

Walaka stopped talking. He sighed in resignation and started down towards the waiting launch. Five hundred men stood up and followed him.

The two vessels chugged sedately down to *Blücher*'s moorings. Standing in the bows of the leading launch with his hands on his hips, Ensign Proust had the proud bearing of a Viking returning from a successful raid.

'I understand these people,' he would tell Lieutenant Kyller. 'You must pick out their leader and appeal to his sense of duty.'

He took his watch from his breast pocket.

'Fifteen minutes to seven,' he murmured. 'I'll have them aboard on the hour.' He turned and smiled fondly at Walaka who squatted miserably beside the wheel-house.

'Good man, that! I'll bring his conduct to Lieutenant Kyller's attention.'

Lieutenant Ernst Kyller shrugged out of his tunic and sat down on his bunk. He held the tunic in his lap and fingered the sleeve. The smear of blood had dried, and as he rubbed the material between thumb and forefinger, the blood crumbled and flaked.

'He should not have run. I had to shoot.'

He stood up and hung the tunic in the little cupboard at the head of his bunk. Then he took his watch from the pocket and sat down again to wind it.

'Fifteen minutes to seven.' He noted the time mechanically, and laid the gold hunter on the flap table beside the bunk. Then he lay back and arranged the pillows under his head, he crossed his still-booted feet and regarded them dispassionately.

'He came aboard to try and rescue his wife. It was the natural thing to do. But that disguise – the shaven head, and stained skin – that must have been carefully thought out. It must have taken time to arrange.'

Kyller closed his eyes. He was tired. It had been a long and eventful watch. Yet there was something nagging him, a feeling that there was an important detail that he had overlooked, a detail of vital – no, of deadly importance.

Within two minutes of the girl's recognition of the wounded man, Kyller and the surgeon commander had established that he was not a native, but a white man disguised as one.

Kyller's English was sketchy, but he had understood the girl's cries of love and concern and accusation.

'You've killed him also. You've killed them all. My baby, my father – and now my husband. You murderers, you filthy murdering swines!'

Kyller grimaced and pressed his knuckles into his aching eyes. Yes, he had understood her.

When he had reported to Captain von Kleine, the captain had placed little importance on the incident.

'Is the man conscious?'

'No, sir.'

'What does the surgeon say his chances are?'

'He will die. Probably before midday.'

'You did the right thing, Kyller.' Von Kleine touched his shoulder in a show of understanding. 'Do not reproach yourself. It was your duty.'

'Thank you, sir.'

'You are off watch now. Go to your cabin and rest – that is an order. I want you fresh and alert by nightfall.'

'Is it tonight then, sir?'

'Yes. Tonight we sail. The minefield has been cleared and I have given the order for the boom to be destroyed. The new moon sets at 11.47. We will sail at midnight.'

But Kyller could not rest. The girl's face, pale, smeared with her tears, haunted him. The strangled breathing of the dying man echoed in his ears, and that nagging doubt scratched against his nerves.

There was something he must remember. He flogged his tired brain, and it balked.

Why was the man disguised? If he came as soon as he had heard that his wife was a prisoner he would not have had time to effect the disguise.

Where had the man been when Fleischer had captured his wife? He had not been there to protect her. Where had he been? It must have been somewhere near at hand.

Kyller rolled on to his stomach and pressed his face into the pillow. He must rest. He must sleep now for tonight they would go out to break through the blockading English warships.

A single ship against a squadron. Their chances of slipping through unchallenged were small. There would be a night action. His imagination was heightened by fatigue, and behind his closed eyelids he saw the English cruisers, lit by the flashes of their own broadsides as they closed with *Blücher*. The enemy intent on vengeance. The enemy in overwhelming strength. The enemy strong and freshly provisioned, their coalbunkers glutted, their magazines crammed with shell, their crews uncontaminated by the fever miasma of the Rufiji.

Against them a single ship with her battle damage hastily patched, half her men sick with malaria, burning green cordwood in her furnaces, her fire-power hampered by the desperate shortage of shell.

He remembered the tiers of empty shell racks, the depleted cordite shelves in the forward magazine.

The magazine? That was it! The magazine! It was something about the magazine that he must remember. That was the thing that had been nagging him. The magazine!

'Oh, my God!' he shouted in horror. In one abrupt movement he had leapt from his prone position on the bunk to stand in the centre of the cabin.

The skin on his bare upper arms prickled with goose-flesh.

That was where he had seen the Englishman before. He had been with the labour party – in the forward magazine.

He would have been there for one reason only – sabotage.

Kyller burst from his cabin, and raced, half dressed, along the corridor.

'I must get hold of Commander Lochtkamper. We'll need a dozen men – strong men – stokers. There are tons of explosive to move, we'll have to handle it all to find whatever the Englishman placed there. Please, God, give us time. Give us time!'

87

Captain Otto von Kleine bit the tip from the end of his cheroot, and removed a flake of black tobacco from the tip of his tongue with thumb and forefinger. His steward held a match for him and von Kleine lit the cheroot. At the wardroom table, the chairs of Lochtkamper, Kyller, Proust and one other were empty.

'Thank you, Schmidt,' he said through the smoke. He pushed his chair back and stretched out his legs, crossing his ankles and laying his shoulders against the padded back-rest. The breakfast had not been of gourmet standard; bread without butter, fish taken from the river and strong with the taste of the mud, washed down with black unsweetened coffee. Nevertheless, Herr Fleischer seemed to be enjoying it. He was beginning his third plateful.

Von Kleine found his appreciative snuffling distracting. This would be the last period of relaxation that von Kleine could anticipate in the next many days. He wanted to savour it along with his cheroot, the wardroom was not the place to do so. Apart from the gusto with which the Herr Commissioner was demolishing his breakfast, and the smell of fish – there was a mood among his officers that was almost tangible. This was the last day and it was heavy with the prospect of what the night might bring. They were all of them edgy and tense. They ate in silence, keeping their attention on their plates, and it was obvious that most of them had slept badly. Von Kleine decided to finish his cheroot alone in his cabin. He stood up.

'Excuse me please, gentlemen.'

A polite murmur, and von Kleine turned to leave.

'Yes, Schmidt. What is it?' His steward was standing deferentially in his path.

'For you, sir.'

Von Kleine clamped the cheroot between his teeth and took

the note in both hands, screwing up his eyes against the blue spiral of tobacco smoke. He frowned.

This woman, and the man she claimed was her husband, worried him. They were a drain on the attention which he should be devoting entirely to the problem of getting *Blücher* ready for tonight. Now this message – what could she mean by 'could save your ship'? He felt a prickle of apprehension.

He swung around.

'Herr Commissioner, a moment of your time, please.'

Fleischer looked up from his food with a smear of grease on his chin.

'Ja?'

'Come with me.'

'I will just finish . . .'

'Immediately, please.' And to avert argument von Kleine stooped out of the wardroom, leaving Herman Fleischer in terrible indecision, but he was a man for the occasion, he took the remaining piece of fish on his plate and put it in his mouth. It was a tight fit, but he still found space for the half cup of coffee as well. Then he scooped up a slice of bread and wiped his plate hurriedly. With the bread in his hand he lumbered after von Kleine.

He was still masticating as he entered the sick-bay behind von Kleine. He stopped in surprise.

The woman sat on one of the bunks. She had a cloth in her hand and with it she wiped the mouth of a black man who lay there. There was blood on the cloth. She looked up at Fleischer. Her expression was soft with compassion and sorrow, but it changed the moment she saw Fleischer. She stood up quickly.

'Oh, thank God, you've come,' she cried with joy as though she were greeting a dear friend. Then incongruously she looked up at the clock.

Keeping warily away from her, Fleischer worked his way around to the opposite side of the bunk by which she stood. He leaned over and studied the face of the dying man. There was something very familiar about it. He chewed stolidly as he puzzled over it. It was the association with the woman that triggered his memory.

He made a choking sound, and bits of half chewed bread flew from his mouth.

'Captain!' he shouted, 'this is one of them – one of the English bandits.'

'I know,' said von Kleine.

'Why wasn't I told? This man must be executed immediately. Even now it might be too late. Justice will be cheated.'

'Please, Herr Commissioner. The woman has an important message for you.'

'This is monstrous. I should have been told . . .'

'Be still,' snapped von Kleine. Then to Rosa, 'You sent for me? What is it you have to tell us?'

With one hand Rosa was stroking Sebastian's head, but she was looking up at the clock.

'You must tell Herr Fleischer that the time is one minute before seven.'

'I beg your pardon?'

'Tell him exactly as I say it.'

'Is this a joke?'

'Tell him, quickly. There is very little time.'

'She says the time is one minute to seven,' von Kleine rattled out the translation. Then in English, 'I have told him.'

'Tell him that at seven o'clock he will die.'

'What is the meaning of that?'

'Tell him first. Tell him!' insisted Rosa.

'She says that you will die at seven o'clock.' And Fleischer interrupted his impatient gobbling over the prone form of Sebastian. He stared at the woman for a moment, then he giggled uncertainly.

'Tell her I feel very well,' he said, and laughed again, 'better than this one here.' He prodded Sebastian. 'Ja, much better.' And his laughter came full and strong, booming in the confined space of the sick-bay.

'Tell him my husband has placed a bomb in this ship, and it will explode at seven o'clock.'

'Where?' demanded von Kleine.

'Tell him first.'

'If this is true you are in danger also – where is it?'

'Tell Fleischer what I said.'

'There is a bomb in the ship.' And Fleischer stopped laughing. 'She is lying,' he spluttered. 'English lies.'

'Where is the bomb?' von Kleine had grasped Rosa's arm.

'It is too late,' Rosa smiled complacently. 'Look at the clock.'

358

'Where is it?' Von Kleine shook her wildly in his agitation.

'In the magazine. The forward magazine.'

'In the *magazine*! Sweet merciful Jesus!' von Kleine swore in German, and turned for the door.

'The magazine?' shouted Fleischer and started after him. 'It is impossible – it can't be:' But he was running, wildly, desperately, and behind him he heard Rosa Oldsmith's triumphant laughter.

'You are dead. Like my baby – dead, like my father. It is too late to run, much too late!'

88

Von Kleine went up the companion-way steps three at a time. He came out into the alleyway that led to the magazine, and stopped abruptly.

The alleyway was almost blocked by a mountain of cordite charges thrown haphazard from the magazine by a knot of frantically busy stokers.

'What are you doing?' he shouted.

'Lieutenant Kyller is looking for a bomb.'

'Has he found it?' von Kleine demanded as he brushed past them.

'Not yet, sir.'

Von Kleine paused again in the entrance to the magazine. It was a shambles. Led by Kyller, men were tearing at the stacks of cordite, sweeping them from the shelves, ransacking the magazine.

Von Kleine jumped forward to help.

'Why didn't you send for me?' he asked as he reached up to the racks above his head.

'No time, sir,' grunted Kyller beside him.

'How did you know about the bomb?'

'It's a guess – I could be wrong, sir.'

'You're right! The woman told us. It's set for seven o'clock.'

'Help us God! Help us!' pleaded Kyller, and hurled himself at the next shelf.

'It could be anywhere – anywhere!' Captain von Kleine worked like a stevedore, knee-deep in spilled cylinders of cordite.

'We should clear the ship. Get the men off.' Kyller attacked the next rack.

'No time. We've got to find it.'

Then in the uproar there was a small sound, a muffled tinny buzz. The alarm bell of a travelling-clock.

'There!' shouted Kyller. 'That's it!' And he dived across the magazine at the same moment as von Kleine did. They collided and fell, but Kyller was up instantly, dragging himself on to his feet with hands clawing at the orderly rack of cordite cylinders.

The buzz of the alarm clock seemed to roar in his ears. He reached out and his hands fell on the smoothly paper wrapped parcels of death, and at that instant the two copper terminals within the leather case of the clock that had been creeping infinitesimally slowly towards each other for the past twelve hours, made contact.

Electricity stored in the dry cell battery flowed through the circuit, reached the hair-thin filament in the detonator cap, and heated it white-hot. The detonator fired, transferring its energy into the sticks of gelignite that were packed into the cigar box. The wave of explosion leapt from molecule to molecule with the speed of light so that the entire contents of *Blücher's* magazine were consumed in one hundredth part of a second. With it were consumed Lieutenant Kyller and Captain von Kleine and the men about them.

In the centre of that fiery holocaust they burned to vapour.

The blast swept through *Blücher*. Downwards through two decks with a force that blew the belly out of her as easily as popping a paper bag, down through ten fathoms of water to strike the bottom of the river and the shock wave bounced up to raise fifteen-foot waves along the surface.

It blew sideways through *Blücher's* watertight bulkheads, crumpling and tearing them like silver paper.

It caught Rosa Oldsmith as she lay across Sebastian's chest, hugging him. She did not even hear it come.

It caught Herman Fleischer just as he reached the deck, and shredded him to nothingness.

It swept through the engine room and burst the great boilers, releasing millions of cubic feet of scalding steam to race through the ship.

It blew upwards through the deck, lifting the forward gun-turret off its seating, tossing the hundreds of tons of steel high in a cloud of steam and smoke and debris.

It killed every single human being aboard. It did more than merely kill them, it reduced them to gas and minute particles of flesh or bone. Then still unsatisfied, its fury unabated, it blew outwards from *Blücher's* shattered hulk, a mighty wind that tore the branches from the mangrove forest and stripped it of leaves.

It lifted a column of smoke and flame writhing and twisting into the bright morning sky above the Rufiji delta, and the waves swept out across the river as though from the eye of a hurricane.

They overwhelmed the two launches that were approaching *Blücher*, pouring over them and capsizing them, swirling them over and over and spilling their human cargo into the frightened frothing water.

And the shock waves rolled on across the delta to burst thunderously against the far hills, or to dissipate out on the vastness of the Indian Ocean.

They passed over the British cruiser *Renounce* as she entered the channel between the mangroves. They rolled overhead like giant cannon-balls across the roof of the sky.

Captain Arthur Joyce leapt to the rail of his bridge, and he saw the column of agonized smoke rise from the swamps ahead of him. A grotesque living thing, unbelievable in its size, black and silver and shot through with flame.

'They've done it!' shouted Arthur Joyce. 'By Jove, they've done it!'

He was shaking; his whole body juddering, his face white as ice, and his eyes which he could not drag from that spinning column of destruction that rose into the sky, filled slowly with tears. He let them overflow his eyelids and run unashamedly down his cheeks.

Two old men walked into a grove of fever trees that stood on the south bank of the Abati river. They stopped beside a pile of gargantuan bones from which the scavengers had picked the flesh, leaving them scattered and white.

'The tusks are gone,' said Walaka.

'Yes,' agreed Mohammed, 'the Askari came back and stole them.'

Together they walked on through the fever trees and then they stopped again. There was a low mound of earth at the edge of the grove. Already it had settled and new grass was growing upon it.

'He was a man,' said Walaka.

'Leave me, my cousin. I will stay here a while.'

'Stay in peace, then,' said Walaka, and settled the string of his blanket roll more comfortably over his shoulder before he walked on.

Mohammed squatted down beside the grave. He sat there unmoving all that day. Then in the evening Mohammed stood up and walked away towards the south.

Gold Mine

This book is for Danielle

I

It began in the time when the world was young, in the time before man, in the time before life itself had evolved upon this planet.

The crust of the earth was still thin and soft, distorted and riven by the enormous pressures from within.

What is now the flat, compacted shield of the African continent, stable and unchanging, was a series of alps. It was range upon range of mountains, thrown up and tumbled down by the movements of the magma at great depth. These were mountains such as man has never seen, so massive as to dwarf the Himalayas, mountains of steaming rock from whose clefts and gaping wounds the molten magma trickled.

It came up from the earth's centre along the fissures and weak places in the crust, bubbling and boiling, yet cooling steadily as it neared the surface so that the least volatile minerals were deposited deeper down, but those with a lower melting point were carried to the surface.

At one point in the measureless passage of time, another series of these fissures opened upon one of the nameless mountain ranges, but from them gushed rivers of molten gold. Some natural freak of temperature and chemical change had resulted in a crude but effective process of refinement during the journey to the earth's surface. The gold was in high concentration in the matrix, and it cooled and solidified at the surface.

If the mountains of that time were so massive as to challenge the imagination of man, then the storms of wind and rain that blew around them were of equal magnitude.

It was a hellish landscape in which the gold field was conceived, cruel mountains reaching stark and sheer in the clouds. Cloud banks dark with the sulphurous gases of the belching earth, so thick that the rays of the sun never penetrated them.

The atmosphere was laden with all the moisture that was to

become the seas, so heavy with it that it rained in one perpetual wind-lashed storm upon the hot rock of the cooling earth, then the moisture rose in steam to condense and fall again.

As the years passed by their millions, so the wind and the rain whittled away at the nameless mountain range with its coating of gold-rich ore, grinding it loose and carrying it down in freshets and rivers and rushes of mud and rock into the valley between this range and the next.

Now as the country rock cooled, so the waters lay longer upon the earth before evaporating, and they accumulated in this valley to form a lake the size of an inland sea.

Into this lake poured the storm waters from the golden mountains, carrying with them tiny particles of the yellow metal which settled with other sand and quartz gravel upon the lake bed, to be compacted into a solid sheet.

In time all the gold was scoured from the mountains, transported and laid down upon the lake beds.

Then, as happened every ten million years or so, the earth entered another period of intense seismic activity. The earth shuddered and heaved as earthquake after mammoth earthquake convulsed it.

One fearsome paroxysm cracked the bed of the lake from end to end draining it and fracturing the sedimentary beds, scattering fragments haphazardly so that great sheets of rock many miles across tilted and reared on end.

Again and again the earthquakes gripped and shook the earth. The mountains tottered and collapsed, filling the valley where the lake had stood, burying some of the sheets of gold-rich rock, pulverizing others.

That cycle of seismic activity passed, and the ages wheeled on in their majesty. The floods and the great droughts came and receded. The miraculous spark of life was struck and burned up brightly, through the time of the monstrous reptiles, on through countless twists and turns of evolution until near the middle of the pleistocene age a man-ape – australopithecus – picked up the thigh bone of a buffalo from beside an outcrop of rock to use it as a weapon, a tool.

Australopithecus stood at the centre of a flat, sun-seared plateau that reached five hundred miles in each direction to the sea, for the mountains and the lake beds had long ago been flattened and buried.

Eight hundred thousand years later, one of the australopithecus' distant but direct line stood at the same spot with a tool in his hand. The man's name was Harrison and the tool was more sophisticated than that of his ancestor, it was a prospector's pick of wood and metal.

Harrison stooped and chipped at the outcrop of rock that protruded from the dry brown African earth. He freed a piece of the stone and straightened with it in his hand.

He held it to catch the sun and grunted with disgust. It was a most uninteresting piece of stone, conglomerate, marbled black and grey. Without hope he held it to his mouth and licked it, wetting the surface before again holding it to the sun, an old prospectors' trick to highlight the metal in the ore.

His eyes narrowed in surprise as the tiny golden flecks in the rock sparkled back at him.

History remembers only his name, not his age nor his antecedents, not the colour of his eyes nor how he died, for within a month he had sold his claim for £10 and disappeared – in search, perhaps, of a really big strike.

He might have done better to retain his title to those claims.

In the eighty years since then an estimated five hundred million ounces of fine gold have been recovered from the fields of the Transvaal and Orange Free State. This is a fraction of that which remains, and which in time will be taken from the earth. For the men who mine the South African fields are the most patiently persistent, inventive and pig-headed of all Vulcan's brood.

This mass of precious metal is the foundation on which the prosperity of a vigorous young nation of eighteen million souls is based.

Yet the earth yields her treasure reluctantly – men must coax and wrest it from her.

2

Even with the electric fan blowing up a gale from the corner it was stinking hot in Rod Ironsides' office.

He reached for the silver Thermos of iced water at the edge of his desk, and arrested the movement as the jug began to dance before his finger tips touched it. The metal bottle skittered across the polished wooden surface; the desk itself shuddered, rustling the papers upon it. The walls of the room shook, so that the windows rattled in their frames. Four seconds the tremor lasted, and then it was still again.

'Christ!' said Rod, and snatched up one of the three telephones on his desk.

'This is the Underground Manager. Get me the rock mechanic's lab, honey, and snap it up, please.'

He drummed his fingers on the desk impatiently as he waited to be connected. The interleading door of his office opened and Dimitri put his head around the jamb.

'You feel that one, Rod? That was a bad one.'

'I felt it.' Then the telephone spoke into his ear.

'Dr Wessels here.'

'Peter, it's Rod. Did you read that one?'

'I haven't got a fix on it yet – can you hold on a minute?'

'I'll wait.' Rod curbed his impatience. He knew that Peter Wessels was the only person who could read the mass of complicated electronic equipment that filled the instrument room of the rock mechanic's laboratory. The laboratory was a joint research project by four of the major gold-mining companies; between them they had put up a quarter of a million Rand to finance an authoritative investigation of rock and seismic activity under stress. They had selected the Sonder Ditch Gold Mining Company's lease area as the site for the laboratory. Now Peter Wessels had his microphones sited thousands of feet down in the earth, and his tape recorders and stylus graphs ready to pin-point any underground disturbance.

Another minute ticked by, and Rod swivelled his chair and stared out of the plate glass window at the monstrous head gear of No. 1 shaft, tall as a ten-storey building.

'Come on, Peter, come on, boy,' he muttered to himself. 'I've got twelve thousand of my boys down there.'

With the telephone still pressed to his ear, he glanced at his watch.

'Two-thirty,' he muttered. 'The worst possible time. They'll still be in the stopes.'

He heard the receiver picked up on the other end, and Peter Wessels' voice was almost apologetic.

'Rod?'

'Yes.'

'I'm sorry, Rod, you've had a force seven pressure burst at 9,500 feet in sector Sugar seven Charlie two.'

'Christ!' said Rod and slammed down the receiver. He was up from his desk in one movement, his face set and angry.

'Dimitri,' he snapped at his assistant still in the doorway. 'We won't wait for them to call us, it's a top sequence emergency. That was a force seven bump, with its source plumb in the middle of our eastern longwall at 95 level.'

'Sweet Mary Mother,' said Dimitri, and darted back into his own office. He bent his glossy black head of curls over the telephone and Rod heard him start his top sequence calls.

'Mine hospital ... emergency team ... Chief Ventilation Officer ... General Manager's office.'

Rod turned away, as the outer door of his office opened and Jimmy Paterson, his electrical engineer, came in.

'I felt it, Rod. How's it look?'

'Bad,' said Rod, then there were the other line managers crowding into his office talking quietly, lighting cigarettes, coughing and shuffling their feet, but all of them watching the white telephone on Rod's desk. The minutes crawled by like crippled insects.

'Dimitri,' Rod called out to break the tension. 'Have you got a cage held at the shaft head?'

'They're holding the Mary Anne for us.'

'I've got five men checking the high tension cable on 95 level,' said Jimmy Paterson, and they ignored him. They were watching the white phone.

'Have you located the boss yet, Dimitri?' Rod asked again, he was pacing in front of his desk. It was only when he stood close to other men that you saw how tall he was.

'He's underground, Rod. He went down at twelve-thirty.'

'Put in an all-stations call for him to contact me here.'

'I've done that already.'

The white phone rang.

Only once, a shrill note that ripped along Rod's nerve ends. Then he had the receiver up to his ear.

'Underground Manager,' he said. There was a long silence and he could hear the man breathing on the other end.

'Speak, man, what is it?'

'The whole bloody thing has come down,' said the voice. It was husky, rough with fear and dust.

'Where are you speaking from?' Rod asked.

'They're still in there,' said the voice. 'They're screaming in there. Under the rock. They're screaming.'

'What is your station?' Rod made his voice cold, hard, trying to reach the man through his shock.

'The whole stope fell in on them. The whole bloody thing.'

'God damn you! You stupid bastard!' Rod bellowed into the phone. 'Give me your station!'

There was stunned silence for a moment. Then the man's voice came back, steadier now, angry from the insult.

'95 level main haulage. Section 43. Eastern longwall.'

'We're coming.' Rod hung up, picked up his yellow fibreglass hard helmet and lamp from the desk.

'43 section. The hanging wall has come down,' he said to Dimitri.

'Fatals?' the little Greek asked.

'For sure. They've got squealers under the rock.'

Rod clapped on his hat.

'Take over on surface, Dimitri.'

3

Rod was still buttoning the front of his white overalls as he reached the shaft head. Automatically he read the sign above the entrance:

STAY ALERT.   STAY ALIVE.
WITH YOUR CO-OPERATION THIS MINE HAS WORKED
16 FATALITY FREE DAYS.

'We'll have to change the number again,' Rod thought with grim humour.

The Mary Anne was waiting. Into its heavily wired confines were crowded the first aid team and emergency squad. The Mary Anne was the small cage used for lowering and hoisting personnel, there were two much larger cages that could carry one hundred and twenty men at one trip, while the Mary Anne could handle only forty. But that was sufficient for now.

'Let's go,' said Rod as he stepped into the cage, and the onsetter slammed the steel roller doors closed. The bell rang once, twice, and the floor dropped away from under him as the Mary Anne started down. Rod's belly came up to press against his ribs. They went down in one long continuous rush in the darkness. The cage jarring and racketing, the air changing in smell and taste, becoming chemical and processed, the heat building up rapidly.

Rod stood hunch-shouldered, leaning against the metal screen of the cage. The head room was a mere six foot three, and with his helmet on Rod stood taller than that. *So today we get another butcher's bill*, he thought angrily.

He was always angry when the earth took its payment in mangled flesh and snapping bones. All the ingenuity of man and the experience gained in sixty years of deep mining on the Witwatersrand were used in trying to keep the price in blood as low as possible. But when you go down into the ultra-deep levels below eight thousand feet and from those depths you remove a quarter of a million tons of rock each month, mining on an inclined sheet of reef that leaves a vast low-roofed chamber thousands of feet across, then you must pay, for the stress builds up in the rock as the focal points of pressure change until the moment when it reaches breaking point and she bumps. That is when men die.

Rod's knees flexed under him as the cage braked and then yoyoed to a halt at the brightly lit station on 66 level.

Here they must trans-ship to the sub-main shaft. The door rattled up and Rod left the cage, striding out down the main haulage the size of a railway tunnel; concreted and whitewashed, brightly lit by the bulbs that lined the roof, it curved gently away.

The emergency team followed Rod. Not running, but walking with the suppressed nervous energy of men going into danger. Rod led them towards the sub-main shaft.

There is a limit to the depth which you can sink a shaft into the earth and then equip it to carry men suspended on a steel cable in a tiny wire cage. The limit is about seven thousand feet.

At this depth you must start again, blast out a new headgear chamber from the living rock and below it sink your new shaft, the sub-main.

The sub-main Mary Anne was waiting for them, and Rod led them into it. They stood shoulder to shoulder, and the door rattled shut and again the stomach-swooping rush down into darkness.

Down, down, down.

Rod switched on his head lamp. Now there were tiny motes in the air – air that had been sterilely clean before.

Dust! One of the deadly enemies of the miner. Dust from the burst. As yet the ventilation system had been unable to clear it.

Endlessly they fell in darkness and now it was very hot, the humidity building up so the faces about him, both black and white, were shiny with sweat in the light of his head lamp.

The dust was thicker now, someone coughed. The brightly lit stations flashed past them – 76, 77, 78 – down, down. The dust was a fine mist now. 85, 86, 87. No one had spoken since entering the cage. 93, 94, 95. The deceleration and stop.

The door rattled up. They were 9,500 feet below the surface of the earth.

'Come on,' said Rod.

4

There were men cluttering the lobby of 95 station, a hundred and fifty, perhaps two hundred of them. Still filthy from their work in the stopes, clothing sodden with sweat, they were laughing and chattering with the abandon of men freshly released from frightful danger.

In a clear space in the centre of the lobby lay five stretchers, on two of them the bright red blankets were pulled up to cover the faces of the men upon them. The faces of the other three men looked as though they had been dusted with flour.

'Two' – grunted Rod – 'so far.'

The station was a shambles, with men milling aimlessly, each minute more of them came back down the haulages as they were pulled out of the undamaged stopes, which were now suspect.

Quickly Rod looked about him, recognizing the face of one of his mine captains.

'McGee,' he shouted. 'Take over here. Get them sitting down in lines ready to load. We'll start hauling the shift out immediately. Get onto the hoist room, tell them I want the stretcher cases out first.'

He paused long enough to watch McGee take control. He glanced at his watch. Two fifty-six. He realized with astonishment that only twenty-six minutes had passed since he felt the pressure burst in his office.

McGee had the station under a semblance of control. He was shouting into the hoist room telephone, on Rod's authority demanding priority to clear 95 station.

'Right,' said Rod. 'Come on.' And he led into the haulage.

The dust was thick. He coughed. The hanging wall was lower here. As he trudged on once more, Rod pondered the unfortunate choice of mining terminology that had named the roof of an excavation 'the hanging wall'. It made one think of a gallows, or at the best it emphasized the fact that there were millions of tons of rock *hanging* overhead.

The haulage branched, and unerringly Rod took the right fork. In his head he carried an accurate three-dimensional map of the entire 176 miles of tunnels that comprised the Sonder Ditch's workings. The haulage came to a 'T' junction and the arms were lower and narrower. Right to 42 section, left to 43 section. The dust was so thick that visibility was down to ten feet. The dust hung in the air, sinking almost imperceptibly.

'Ventilations knocked out here,' he called over his shoulder. 'Van den Bergh!'

'Yes, sir.' The leader of the emergency squad came up behind him.

'I want air in this drive. Get it on. Use canvas piping if you have to.'

'Right.'

'Then I want pressure on the water hoses to lay this dust.'

'Right.'

Rod turned into the drive. Here the foot wall – the floor – was rough and the going slower. They came upon a line of steel trolleys filled with gold reef abandoned in the centre of the drive.

'Get these the hell out of the way,' ordered Rod, and went on.

Fifty paces and he stopped abruptly. He felt the hair on his forearms stand on end. He could never accustom himself to the sound, no matter how often he heard it.

In the deliberately callous slang of the miner they called them 'squealers'. It was the sound of a grown man, with his legs crushed under hundreds of tons of rock, perhaps his spine broken, dust suffocating him, his mind unhinged by the mortal horror of the situation in which he was trapped, calling for help, calling to his God, calling for his wife, his children, or his mother.

Rod started forward again, with the sound of it becoming louder, a terrifying sound, hardly human, sobbing and babbling into silence, only to start again with a blood-chilling scream.

Suddenly there were men ahead of Rod in the tunnel, dark shapes looming in the dust mist, their head lamps throwing shafts of yellow light, grotesque, distorted.

'Who is that?' Rod called, and they recognized his voice.

'Thank God. Thank God you've come, Mr Ironsides.'

'Who is that?'

'Barnard.' The 43 section shift boss.

'What's the damage?'

'The whole hanging wall of the stope came down.'

'How many men in the stope?'

'Forty-two.'

'How many still in?'

'So far we've got out sixteen unhurt, twelve slightly hurt, three stretcher cases and two dead 'uns.'

The squealer started again, but his voice was much weaker.

'Him?' asked Rod.

'He's got twenty ton of rock lying across his pelvis. I've hit him with two shots of morphine, but it won't stop him.'

'Can you get into the stope?'

'Yes, there is a crawling hole.' Barnard flashed his lamp over the pile of fractured blue quartzite that jammed the drive like a collapsed garden wall. On it was an aperture big enough for a fox terrier to run through. Reflected light showed from the hole, and faintly from within came the grating sounds of movement over loose rock and the muffled voices of men.

'How many men have you got working in there, Barnard?'

'I' – Barnard hesitated, 'I think about ten or twelve.'

And Rod grabbed a handful of his overall front and jerked him almost off his feet.

'You think!' In the head lamps Rod's face was white with fury. 'You've put men in there without recording their numbers? You've put twelve of my boys against the wall to try and save nine?' With a heave Rod lifted the shift boss off his feet and swung him against the side wall of the drive, pinning him there.

'You bastard, you know that most of those nine are chopped already. You know that stope is a bloody killing ground, and you send in *twelve* more to get the chop *and* you don't record their numbers. How the hell would we ever know who to look for if the hanging fell again?' He let the shift boss free, and stood back. 'Get them out of here, clear that stope.'

'But, Mr Ironsides, the General Manager is in there, Mr Lemmer is in there. He was doing an inspection in the stope.'

For a moment Rod was taken aback, then he snarled. 'I don't give a good damn if the State President is in there, clear the stope. We'll start again and this time we'll do it properly.'

Within minutes the rescuers had been recalled, they came

squirming out of the aperture, white with dust like maggots wriggling from rotten cheese.

'Right,' said Rod, 'I'll risk four men at a time.'

Quickly he picked four of the floury figures, among them an enormous man on whose right shoulder was the brass badge of a boss boy.

'Big King – you here?' Rod spoke in fanikalo, the lingua franca of the mines which enabled men from a dozen ethnic groups to communicate.

'I am here,' answered Big King.

'You looking for more awards?' A month before, Big King had been lowered on a rope two hundred feet down a vertical orepass to retrieve the body of a white miner. The bravery award by the company had been 100 Rand.

'Who speaks of awards when the earth has eaten the flesh of men?' Big King rebuked Rod softly. 'But today is children's play only. Is the Nkosi coming into the stope?' It was a challenge.

Rod's place was not in the stope. He was the organizer, the co-ordinator. Yet, he could not ignore the challenge, no Bantu would believe that he had not stood back in fear and sent other men in to die.

'Yes,' said Rod, 'I'm coming into the stope.'

He led them in. The hole was only just big enough to admit the bulk of Rod's body. He found himself in a chamber, the size of an average room, but the roof was only three and a half feet high. He played his lamp quickly across the hanging wall, and it was wicked. The rock was cracked and ugly, 'a bunch of grapes' was the term.

'Very pretty,' he said, and dropped the beam of his lamp.

The squealer was within an arm's length of Rod. His body from the waist up protruded from under a piece of rock the size of a Cadillac. Someone had wrapped a red blanket around his upper body. He was quiet now, lying still. But as the beam of Rod's lamp fell upon him, he lifted his head. His eyes were crazed, unseeing, his face running with the sweat of terror and insanity. His mouth snapped open, wide and pink in the shiny blackness of his face. He began to scream, but suddenly the sound was drowned by a great red-black gout of blood that came gushing up his throat, and spurted from his mouth.

As Rod watched in horror, the Bantu posed like that, his head thrown back, his mouth gaping as though he were a gargoyle, the life blood pouring from him. Then slowly the head sagged forward, and flopped face downwards. Rod crawled to him, lifted his head and pillowed it on the red blanket.

There was blood on his hands and he wiped it on the front of his overalls.

'Three,' he said, 'so far.' And leaving the dying man he crawled on towards the broken face of the fall.

Big King crawled up beside him with two pinch bars. He handed one to Rod.

Within an hour it had become a contest, a trial of strength between two men. Behind them the other three men were shoring up and passing back the rock that Rod and Big King loosened from the face. Rod knew he was being childish, he should have been back in the main haulage, not only directing the rescue, but also making all the other decisions and alternative arrangements that were needed now. The company paid him for his brains and his experience, not for his muscle.

'The hell with it,' he thought. 'Even if we miss the blast this evening, I'm staying here.' He glanced at Big King, and reached forward to get his hands onto a bigger piece of rock in the jam. He strained, using his arms first, then bringing the power of his whole body into it, the rock was solid. Big King placed huge black hands on the rock, and they pulled together. In a rush of smaller rock it came away, and they shoved it back between them, grinning at each other.

At seven o'clock Rod and Big King withdrew from the stope to rest and eat sandwiches, and drink Thermos coffee while Rod spoke to Dimitri over the field telephone that had been laid up to the face.

'We've pulled shift on both shafts, Rod, the workings are clear to blast. Except for your lot, there are fifty-eight men in your 43 section.' Dimitri's voice was reedy over the field telephone.

'Hold on.' Rod revolved the situation in his mind. He worked it out slower than usual, for he was tired, emotionally and physically drained. If he stopped the blast on both shafts for fear of bringing down more rock in 43 section, it would cost the Company a day's production, ten thousand tons of gold reef worth sixteen Rand a ton, the formidable sum of R160,000 or £80,000 or $200,000 whichever way you looked at it.

It was highly probable that every man in the stope was already dead, and the original pressure burst had de-stressed the rock above and around the 95 level, so there was little danger of further bumps.

And yet there might be someone alive in there, someone lying pinned in the womb-warm darkness of the stope with a bunch of loose grapes hanging over his unprotected body. When they hit all the blast buttons on the Sonder Ditch Mine, they fired eighteen tons of Dynagel. The kick was considerable, it would bring down those grapes.

'Dimitri,' Rod made his decision, 'burn all longwalls on No. 2 shaft at seven-thirty exactly.' No. 2 shaft was three miles away. That would save the Company R80,000. 'Then at precisely five minute intervals burn south, north and west longwalls here on No. 1 shaft.' Spreading the blast would reduce the disturbance, and that put another R60,000 in the shareholders' pockets. The total monetary loss inflicted by the disaster was around R20,000. Not too bad really, Rod thought sardonically, blood was cheap. You could buy it at three Rand a pint from the Central Blood Transfusion Service.

'All right,' he stood up, and flexed his aching shoulders, 'I'm pulling everybody back into the safety of the shaft pillar while we blast.'

5

After the successive earth tremors of the blast, Rod put them back into the stope, and at nine o'clock they uncovered the bodies of two machine boys crushed against the metal of their own rock drill. Ten feet further on they found the white miner, his body was unmarked, but his head was flattened.

At eleven o'clock they found two more machine boys. Rod was in the haulage when they dragged them out through the small opening. Neither of them were recognizable as human, they looked more like lumps of raw meat that had been rubbed in dirt.

A little after midnight Rod and Big King went into the stope again to take over from the team at the face, and twenty minutes later they holed through the wall of loose rock into another chamber that had been miraculously left standing.

The air in here was steamy with heat. Rod recoiled instinctively from the filthy moist gush of it against his face. Then he forced himself to crawl forward and peer into the opening.

Ten feet away lay Frank Lemmer, the General Manager of the Sonder Ditch Mine. He lay on his back. His helmet had been knocked from his head, and a deep gash split the skin above his eye. Blood from the gash had run back into his silver hair and clotted black. He opened his eyes and blinked owlishly in the dazzle of Rod's lamp. Quickly Rod averted the beam.

'Mr Lemmer,' he said.

'What the bloody hell are you doing with the rescue team?' growled Frank Lemmer. 'It's not your job. Haven't you learned a single goddamned thing in twenty years of mining?'

'Are you all right, sir?'

'Get a doctor in here,' replied Frank Lemmer. 'You're going to have to cut me loose from this lot.'

Rod wriggled up to where he lay, and then he saw what Frank Lemmer meant. From the elbow his arm was pinned under a solid slab of rock. Rod ran his hands over the slab, feeling it. Only explosive would shift that rock. As always Frank Lemmer was right.

Rod wriggled out of the opening and called over his shoulder. 'Get the telephone up here.'

After a few minutes delay he had the receiver, and was through to the station at 95 level which had been set up as an advance aid post and rest station for the rescuers.

'This is Ironsides, get me Doctor Stander.'

'Hold on.'

Then moments later, 'Hello, Rod, it's Dan.'

'Dan, we've found the old man.'

'How is he, conscious?'

'Yes, but he's pinned – you'll have to cut.'

'Are you sure?' Dan Stander asked.

'Of course I'm bloody well sure,' snapped Rod.

'Whoa, boy!' admonished Dan.

'Sorry.'

'Okay, where's he caught?'

'Arm. You'll have to cut above the elbow.'

'Charming!' said Dan.

'I'll wait here for you.'

'Right. I'll be up in five minutes.'

6

'It's funny, you see them chopped time and again, but you know it will never happen to you.' Frank Lemmer's voice was steady and even, the arm must be numb, Rod thought as he lay beside him in the stope.

Frank Lemmer rolled his head towards Rod. 'Why don't you go farming, boy?'

'You know why,' said Rod.

'Yes.' Lemmer smiled a little, just a twitching of the lips. With his free hand he wiped his mouth. 'You know, I had just three months more before I went on pension. I nearly made it. You'll end like this, boy, in the dirt with your bones crunched up.'

'It's not the end,' said Rod.

'Isn't it?' asked Frank Lemmer, and this time he chuckled. 'Isn't it?'

'What's the joke?' asked Dan Stander, poking his head into the tiny chamber.

'Christ, it took you long enough to get here,' growled Frank Lemmer.

'Give me a hand, Rod.' Dan passed his bag through, then as he crawled forward he spoke to Frank Lemmer.

'Union Steel closed at 98 cents tonight. I told you to buy.'

'Over-priced, over-capitalized,' snorted Frank Lemmer. Dan lay on his side in the dirt and laid out his instruments, and they argued stocks and shares. When Dan had the syringe full of pentathol and was swabbing Frank Lemmer's stringy old arm, Lemmer rolled his head towards Rod again.

'We made a good dig here, Rodney, you and I. I wish they'd give it to you now, but they won't. You're still too young. But whoever they put in my place, you keep an eye on him, you know the ground – don't let him balls it up.'

And the needle went in.

Dan cut through the arm in four and a half minutes, and

twenty-seven minutes later Frank Lemmer died of shock and exposure in the Mary Anne on his way to the surface.

7

Once he had paid Patti's alimony there was not too much of Rod's salary left for extravagances, but one of these was the big cream Maserati. Although it was a 1967 model, and had done nearly thirty thousand miles when he bought it, yet the instalments still took a healthy bite out of his monthly pay cheque.

On mornings like this he reckoned the expense worthwhile. He came twisting down from the Kraalkop ridge, and when the national road flattened and straightened for the final run into Johannesburg he let the Maserati go. The car seemed to flatten against the ground like a running lion, and the exhaust note changed subtly, becoming deeper, more urgent.

Ordinarily, it was an hour's run from the Sonder Ditch Mine into the city of Johannesburg, but Rod could clip twenty minutes off that time.

It was Saturday morning, and Rod's mood was light and expectant.

Since the divorce Rod had lived a Jekyll and Hyde existence. Five days of the week he was the company man in top-line management, but on the last two days of the week he went into Johannesburg with his golf clubs in the boot of the Maserati, the keys to his luxury Hillbrow apartment in his pocket, and a chuckle on his lips.

Today the anticipation was keener than ever for, in addition to the twenty-two-year-old blonde model who was prepared to devote her evening to entertaining Rodney Ironsides, there was the mysterious summons from Dr Manfred Steyner to answer.

The summons had been delivered by a nameless female caller describing herself as 'Dr Steyner's Secretary'. It had come the day after Frank Lemmer's funeral, and was for Saturday at 11 a.m.

Rod had never met Manfred Steyner, but he had, of course, heard of him. Anyone who worked for any of the fifty or sixty companies that comprised the Central Rand Consolidation Group must have heard of Manfred Steyner, and the Sonder Ditch Gold Company was just one of the Group.

Manfred Steyner had a bachelor's degree in Economics from Berlin University, and a Doctor's degree in Business Administration from Cornell. He had joined C.R.C. a mere twelve years previously at the age of thirty, and now he was the front runner. Hurry Hirschfeld could not live for ever, although he gave indications of doing so, and when he went down to make a takeover bid on Hades, the word was that Manfred Steyner would succeed him as Chairman of C.R.C.

Chairmanship of C.R.C. was an enviable position, the incumbent automatically became one of the five most powerful men in Africa, and that included heads of state.

The betting favoured Dr Steyner for a number of good reasons. He had a brain that had earned him the nickname of 'The Computer'; no one had yet been able to detect in him the slightest evidence of a human weakness, and more than this he had taken the trouble ten years previously to catch Hurry Hirschfeld's only granddaughter as she emerged from Cape Town University and marry her.

Dr Steyner was in a strong position, and Rod was intrigued with the prospect of meeting him.

The Maserati was registering 125 miles an hour as he went under the over-pass of the Kloof Gold Mining Company property.

'Johannesburg, here I come!' Rod laughed aloud.

It was ten minutes before eleven o'clock when Rod found the brass plaque reading 'Dr M. K. Steyner' in a secluded lane of the lush Johannesburg suburb of Sandown. The house was not visible from the road, and Rod let the Maserati roll gently in through the tall white gates, with their imitation Cape Dutch gables.

The gates, he decided, were a display of shocking taste but the gardens beyond them were paradise. Rod knew rock, but flowers were his weak suit. He recognized the massed banks of red and yellow against the green lawns as cannas, but after that he had no names for the blazing beauty spread about him.

'Wow!' he muttered in awe. 'Someone has done a hell of a lot of work around here.'

Around a curve in the macadamized drive lay the house. It also was Cape Dutch and Rod forgave Dr Steyner his gates.

'Wow!' he said again, and involuntarily braked the Maserati to a standstill.

Cape Dutch is one of the most difficult styles to copy effectively, where one line in a hundred out of place could spoil the effect; this particular example worked perfectly. It gave the feel of timelessness, of solidarity, and mixed it subtly with a grace and finesse of line. He guessed that the shutters and beams were genuine yellow wood and the windows hand-leaded.

Rod looked at it, and felt envy prickle and burn within him. He loved fine things, like his Maserati, but this was another concept in material possessions. He was jealous of the man that owned it, knowing that his own entire year's income would not be sufficient for a down payment on the land alone.

'So I've got my flat,' he grinned ruefully, and coasted down to park in front of the line of garages.

It was not clear which was the correct entrance to use, and he chose at random from a number of paved paths that all led in the general direction of the house.

Around a bend in this path he came on another spectacle. Though smaller it had, if anything, a more profound effect on Rod than the house had. It was a feminine posterior of equal grace and finesse of line, clad in Helanka stretch ski-pants, and protruding from a large and exotic bush.

Rod was captivated. He stood and watched as the bush shook and rustled, and the bottom wriggled and heaved.

Suddenly, in ladylike tones there issued from the bush a most unladylike oath and the bottom shot backwards and its owner straightened up with her forefinger in her mouth, sucking noisily.

'It bit me!' she mumbled around the finger. 'Damned stinkbug bit me!'

'Well, you shouldn't tease them,' said Rod.

And she spun round to face him. The first thing Rod noticed were her eyes, they were enormous, completely out of proportion to the rest of her face.

'I wasn't—' she started, and then stopped. The finger came out of her mouth. Instinctively one hand went to her hair, and the other began straightening her blouse and brushing off bits of vegetation that were clinging to her.

'Who are you?' she asked, and those huge eyes swept over him. This was fairly standard reaction for any woman between the ages of sixteen and sixty viewing Rodney Ironsides for the first time, and Rodney accepted it gracefully.

'My name is Rodney Ironsides. I've an appointment to see Dr Steyner.'

'Oh.' She was hurriedly tucking her shirt-tails into her slacks. 'My husband will be in his study.'

He had known who she was. He had seen her photographs fifty times in the Group newspaper; but in them she was usually in full-length evening dress and diamonds, not in a blouse with a tear in one sleeve nor pig-tails that were coming down. In the pictures her make-up was immaculate, now she had none at all and her face was flushed and dewed with perspiration.

'I must look a mess. I've been gardening,' said Theresa Steyner unnecessarily.

'Did you do this garden yourself?'

'Only a very little of the muscle work, but I planned it,' she answered. She decided he was big and ugly – no, not really ugly, but battered-looking.

'It's beautiful,' said Rod.

'Thank you.' No, not battered-looking, she changed her mind, tough-looking, and the chest hair curled out of the vee of his open neck shirt.

'This is a protea, isn't it?' He indicated the bush from which she had recently emerged. He was guessing.

'Nutans,' she said; he must be in his late thirties, there was greying at his temples.

'Oh, I thought it was a protea.'

'It is. "Nutans" is its proper name. There are over two hundred different varieties of proteas,' she answered seriously. His voice didn't fit his appearance at all, she decided. He looked like a prize fighter but spoke like a lawyer, probably was one. It was usually lawyers or business consultants who came calling on Manfred.

'Is that so? It's very pretty.' Rod touched one of the blooms.

'Yes, isn't it? I've got over fifty varieties growing here.'

And suddenly they were smiling at each other. 'I'll take you up to the house,' said Theresa Steyner.

8

'Mr Ironsides is here, Manfred.'

'Thank you.' He sat at the stinkwood desk in a room that smelled of wax polish. He made no effort to rise from his seat.

'Would you like a cup of coffee?' Theresa asked from the doorway. 'Or tea?'

'No, thank you,' answered Manfred Steyner without consulting Rod who stood beside her.

'I'll leave you to it, then,' she said.

'Thank you, Theresa.' And she turned away. Rod went on standing where he was, he was studying this man of whom he had heard so much.

Manfred Steyner appeared younger than his forty-two years. His hair was light brown, almost blond, and brushed straight back. He wore spectacles with heavy black frames, and his face was smooth and silky-looking, soft as a girl's with no beard shadow on his chin. His hands that lay on the polished desk top were hairless, smooth, so that Rod wondered if he had used a depilatory on them.

'Come in,' he said, and Rod moved to the desk. Steyner wore a white silk shirt in which the ironing creases still showed, the cloth was snowy white and over it he wore a Royal Johannesburg Golf Club tie, with onyx cuff links. Suddenly Rod realized that neither shirt nor tie had ever been worn before, that much was true of what he had heard then. Steyner ordered his shirts hand-made by the gross and wore each once only.

'Sit down, Ironsides.' Steyner slurred his vowels slightly, just a trace of a Teutonic accent.

'Dr Steyner,' said Rod softly, 'you have a choice. You may call me Rodney or *Mr* Ironsides.'

There was no change in Steyner's voice nor expression.

'I would like to go over your background, please, Mr Ironsides, as a preliminary to our discussion. You have no objection?'

'No, Dr Steyner.'

'You were born October 16th, 1931, at Butterworth in the Transkei. Your father was a native trader, your mother died January 1939. Your father was commissioned Captain in the Durban Light Infantry and died of wounds on the Po River in Italy during the winter of 1944. You were raised by your maternal uncle in East London. Matriculating from Queen's College, Grahamstown, in 1947, you were unsuccessful in obtaining a Chamber of Mines scholarship to Witwatersrand University for a B.Sc. (Mining Engineering) degree. You enrolled in the G.M.T.S. (Government Mining Training School) and obtained your blasting ticket during 1949. At which time you joined the Blyvooruitzicht Gold Mining Company Ltd as a learner miner.'

Dr Steyner stood up from his desk and crossing to the panelled wall he pressed a concealed switch and a portion of the panelling slid back to reveal a wash basin and towel rack. As he went on talking he began very meticulously to soap and wash his hands.

'In the same year you were promoted to miner and in 1952 to shift boss, 1954 to mine captain. You successfully completed the examination for the Mine Manager's ticket in 1959, and in 1962 you came to us as an Assistant Underground Manager, and in 1968 you achieved your present position as Underground Manager.'

Dr Steyner began drying his hands on a snowy white towel.

'You've memorized my company record pretty thoroughly,' Rod admitted.

Dr Steyner crumpled the towel and dropped it into a bin below the wash basin. He pressed the button and the panelling slid closed, then he came back to the desk stepping precisely over the glossy polished wooden floor, and Rod realized that he was a small man, not more than five and a half feet tall, about the same height as his wife.

'This is something of an achievement,' Steyner went on. 'The next youngest Underground Manager in the entire Group is forty-six years of age, whereas you are not yet thirty-nine.'

Rod inclined his head in acknowledgement.

'Now,' said Dr Steyner as he reseated himself and laid his freshly washed hands on the desk top. 'I would like briefly to touch on your private life – you have no objections?'

Again Rod inclined his head.

'The reason that your application for the Chamber of Mines

scholarship was refused, despite your straight A matriculation was the recommendation of your headmaster to the selection board in effect that you were of unstable and violent disposition.'

'How the hell did you know that?' ejaculated Rod.

'I have access to the board's records. It seems that once you had received your matric you immediately assaulted your former headmaster.'

'I beat the hell out of the bastard,' Rod agreed happily.

'An expensive indulgence, Mr Ironsides. It cost you a university degree.'

And Rod was silent.

'To continue: In 1959 you married Patricia Anne Harvey. Of the union was born a girl child in the same year, to be precise, seven and a half months after the wedding.'

Rod squirmed slightly in his chair, and Dr Steyner went on quietly.

'This marriage terminated in divorce in 1964. Your wife suing you on the grounds of adultery, and receiving custody of the child, alimony and maintenance in the sum of R450.000 monthly.'

'What's all this about?' demanded Rod.

'I am attempting to establish an accurate picture of your present circumstances. It is necessary, I assure you.' Dr Steyner removed his spectacles and began polishing the lens on a clean white handkerchief. There were the marks of the frames on the bridge of his nose.

'Go on, then.' Despite himself, Rod was fascinated to learn just how much Steyner knew about him.

'In 1968 there was a paternity suit brought against you by a Miss Diane Johnson and judgement for R150.00 per month.'

Rod blinked and was silent.

'I should mention two further actions against you for assault, both unsuccessful on the grounds of justification or self-defence.'

'Is that all?' asked Rod Sarcastically.

'Almost,' admitted Dr Steyner. 'It is only necessary to note further recurrent expenditure in the form of a monthly payment of R150.00 on a continental sports car, and a further R100.00 per month rental on the premises 596 Glen Alpine Heights, Corner Lane, Hillbrow.'

Rod was furious, he had believed that no one in C.R.C. knew about the flat.

'Damn you! You've been prying into my affairs!'

'Yes,' agreed Dr Steyner levelly. 'I am guilty, but in good cause. If you bear with me, you'll see why.'

Suddenly Dr Steyner stood up from the desk, crossed the room to the concealed wash basin, and again began to wash his hands. As he dried them, he spoke again.

'Your monthly commitments are R850. Your salary, after deduction of tax, is less than one thousand Rand. You have no mining degree, and the chances of your taking the next step upwards to General Manager without it are remote. You are at your ceiling, Mr Ironsides. On your own ability you can go no further. In thirty years' time you will not be the youngest Underground Manager in the C.R.C. Group, but the oldest.' Dr Steyner paused. 'That is, provided that your rather expensive tastes have not landed you in a debtors' prison, and that neither the quickness and heat of your temper, nor the matching speed and temperature of your genitalia have gotten you into really serious trouble.'

Steyner dropped the towel in the bin and returned to his seat. They sat in absolute silence, regarding each other for a full minute.

'You got me all the way up here to tell me this?' asked Rod, his whole body was tense, his voice slightly husky, it needed only the ounce more of provocation to launch him across the desk at Steyner's throat.

'No.' Steyner shook his head. 'I got you up here to tell you that I will use all my influence, which I flatter myself is considerable, to secure your appointment – and I mean immediate appointment – to the position of General Manager of the Sonder Ditch Gold Mining Company Ltd.'

Rod recoiled in his chair as though Steyner had spat in his face. He stared at him aghast.

'Why?' he asked at last. 'What do you want in exchange?'

'Neither your friendship, nor your gratitude,' Dr Steyner told him. 'But your unquestioning obedience to my instructions. You will be my man – completely.'

Rod went on staring at him while his mind raced. Without Steyner's intervention he would wait at the very least ten years for this promotion, if it ever came. He wanted it, my God, how he wanted it. The achievement, the increase in income, the power that went with the job. His own mine! His own mine at the age of thirty-eight – and an additional ten thousand Rand per annum.

Yet Rod was not gullible enough to believe that Manfred Steyner's price would be cheap. When the instruction came that he was to follow with unquestioning obedience, he knew it would stink like a ten-day corpse. But once he had the job he could refuse the instruction. Get the job first, then decide once he received the instruction whether to follow it or not.

'I accept,' he said.

Manfred Steyner stood up from the desk.

'You will hear from me,' he said. 'Now you may go.'

9

Rod crossed the wide-flagged stoep without seeing or hearing, vaguely he wandered down across the lawns towards his car. His mind was harrying the recent conversation, tearing it to pieces like a pack of wild dogs on a carcass. He almost bumped into Theresa Steyner before he saw her, and abruptly his mind dropped the subject of the General Managership.

Theresa had changed her clothing, made up her face and eyes, and the pig-tails were concealed under a lime-coloured silk scarf, all this in the half hour since their last meeting. She was hovering over a flower bed with a flower basket on one arm, as bright and pleasing as a hummingbird.

Rod was amused and flattered, vain enough to realize that the change was in his honour, and connoisseur enough to appreciate the improvement.

'Hello.' She looked up, contriving successfully to look both surprised and artless. Her eyes were really enormous, and the make-up was designed to enhance their size.

'You are a busy little bee.' Rod ran a knowledgeable appraisal over the floral slack suit she wore, and saw the colour start in her cheeks as she felt his eyes.

'Did you have a successful meeting?'

'Very.'

'Are you a lawyer?'

'No. I work for your grandfather.'

'Doing what?'

'Mining his gold.'

'Which mine?'

'Sonder Ditch.'

'What's your position?'

'Well, if your husband is as good as his word, I'm the new General Manager.'

'You're too young,' she said.

'That's what I thought.'

'Pops will have something to say on the subject.'

'Pops?' he asked.

'My grandfather.' And Rod laughed before he could stop himself.

'What's so funny?'

'The Chairman of C.R.C. being called "Pops".'

'I'm the only one who calls him that.'

'I bet you are.' Rod laughed again. 'In fact I'd bet you'd get away with a lot of things no one else would dare.'

Suddenly the underlying sexuality of his last remark occurred to them both and they fell silent. Theresa looked down and carefully snipped the head off a flower.

'I didn't mean it that way,' apologized Rod.

'What way, Mr Ironsides?' She looked up and inquired with mischievous innocence, and they laughed together with the awkwardness gone again.

She walked beside him to the car, making it seem a completely natural thing to do, and as he slipped behind the steering-wheel she remarked:

'Manfred and I will be coming out to the Sonder Ditch next week. Manfred is to present long service and bravery awards to some of your men.' She had already refused the invitation to accompany Manfred, she must now see to it that she was re-invited. 'I shall probably see you then.'

'I look forward to it,' said Rod, and let in the clutch.

Rod glanced in the rear view mirror. She was a remarkably provocative and attractive woman. A careless man could drown in those eyes.

'Dr Manfred Steyner has got himself a big fat problem there,' he decided. 'Our Manfred is probably so busy soaping and scrubbing his equipment, that he never gets round to using it.'

IO

Through the leaded windows Dr Steyner caught a glimpse of the Maserati as it disappeared around the curve in the driveway, and he listened as the throb of the engine dwindled into silence.

He lifted the receiver of the telephone and wiped it with the white handkerchief before putting it to his ear. He dialled and while it rang he inspected the nails of his free hand minutely.

'Steyner,' he said into the mouthpiece. 'Yes – yes.' He listened. 'Yes . . . He has just left . . . Yes, it is arranged . . . No, there will be no difficulty there, I am sure.' As he spoke he was looking at the palm of his hand, he saw the tiny beads of perspiration appear on his skin and an expression of disgust tightened his lips.

'I am fully aware of the consequences. I tell you, I know.'

He closed his eyes and listened for another minute without moving as the receiver squawked and clacked, then he opened his eyes.

'It will be done in good time, I assure you. Goodbye.'

He hung up and went to wash his hands. Now, he thought, as he worked up lather, to get it past the old man.

II

He was old now, seventy-eight long hard years old. His hair and his eyebrows were creamy white. His skin was folded and creased, freckled and spotted, hanging in unexpected little pouches under his chin and eyes.

His body had dried out, so he stood gaunt and stooped like a tree that has taken a set before the prevailing winds; but there was still the underlying urgency in the way he held himself, the same urgency that had earned him the name of 'Hurry' Hirschfeld when first he bustled into the gold fields sixty years ago.

On this Monday morning he was standing before the full length windows of his penthouse office, looking down on the city of Johannesburg. Reef House stood shoulder to massive shoulder with the Schlesinger Building on the Braamfontein ridge above the city proper. From this height it seemed that Johannesburg cowered at Hurry Hirschfeld's feet, as well it should.

Long ago, even before the great depression of the 'thirties, he had ceased to measure his wealth in terms of money. He owned outright a little over a quarter of the issued share capital of Central Rand Consolidated. At the present market price of R120 per share, this was a staggering sum. In addition, through a complicated arrangement of trusts, proxy rights and interlocking directorates, he had control of a further massive block of twenty per cent of the company's voting rights.

The overhead intercom pinged softly into this room of soft fabrics and muted colours, and Hurry started slightly.

'Yes,' he said, without turning away from the window.

'Dr Steyner is here, Mr Hirschfeld,' his secretary's voice whispered, ghostly and disembodied into the luscious room.

'Send him in,' snapped Hurry. That goddamned intercom always gave him the creeps. The whole goddamned room gave him the creeps. It was, as Hurry had said often and loudly, like a fairy brothel.

For fifty-five years he had worked in a bleak uncarpeted office with a few yellowing photographs of men and machinery on its walls. Then they had moved him in here – he glanced around the room with the distaste that five years had not lulled. What did they think he was, a bloody ladies' hairdresser?

The panelling door slid noiselessly aside and Dr Manfred Steyner stepped neatly into the room.

'Good morning, Grandfather,' he said. For ten years, even since Terry had been bird-brained enough to marry him, Manfred Steyner had called Hurry Hirschfeld that, and Hurry hated it. He remembered now that Manfred Steyner was also responsible for the design and decor of Reef House, and therefore the author of his recent irritation.

'What ever it is you want – No!' he said, and he moved across to the air-conditioning controls. The thermostat was already set at 'high', now Hurry turned it to 'highest'. Within minutes the room would be at the correct temperature for growing orchids.

'How are you this morning, Grandfather?' Manfred seemed not to have heard, his expression was bland and neutral as he moved to the desk and laid out his papers.

'Bloody awful,' said Hurry. It was impossible to disconcert the little prig, he thought, you might as well shout insults at an efficiently functioning piece of machinery.

'I am sorry to hear that.' Manfred took out his handkerchief and touched his chin and forehead. 'I have the weekly reports.'

Hurry capitulated and went across to the desk. This was business. He sat down and read quickly. His questions were abrupt, cutting and instantly answered, but Manfred's handkerchief was busy now, swabbing and dabbing. Twice he removed his spectacles and wiped steam from the lens.

'Can I turn the air-conditioning down a little, Grandfather?'

'You touch it and I'll kick your arse,' said Hurry without looking up.

Another five minutes and Manfred Steyner stood up suddenly.

'Excuse me, Grandfather.' And he shot across the office and disappeared into the adjoining bathroom suite. Hurry cocked his head to listen, and when he heard the taps hiss he grinned happily. The air-conditioning was the only method he had discovered of disconcerting Manfred Steyner, and for ten years he had been experimenting with various techniques.

'Don't use all the soap,' he shouted gleefully. 'You are the one always on about office expenses!'

It did not seem ludicrous to Hurry that one of the richest and most influential men in Africa should devote so much time and energy to baiting his personal assistant.

At eleven o'clock Manfred Steyner gathered his papers and began packing them carefully in his monogrammed pigskin brief-case.

'About the appointment of a new General Manager for the Sonder Ditch to replace Mr Lemmer. You will recall my memo regarding the appointment of younger men to key positions—'

'Never read the bloody thing,' lied Hurry Hirschfeld. They both knew he read everything, and remembered it.

'Well—' Manfred went on to enlarge his thesis for a minute, then ended , 'In view of this, my department, myself concurring entirely, urges the appointment of Rodney Barry Ironsides, the present Underground Manager, to the position. I hoped that you would initial the recommendation and we can put it through at Friday's meeting.'

Dextrously Manfred slid the yellow memo in front of Hurry Hirschfeld, unscrewed the cap of his pen and offered it to him. Hurry picked the memo up between thumb and forefinger as though it were someone's dirty handkerchief and dropped it into the waste-paper bin.

'Do you wish me to tell you in detail what you and your planning department can do?' he asked.

'Grandfather,' Manfred admonished him mildly, 'you cannot run the company as though you were a robber baron. You cannot ignore the team of highly trained men who are your advisers.'

'I've run it that way for fifty years. You show me who's going to change that.' Hurry leaned back in his chair with vast satisfaction and fished a powerful-looking cigar out of his inner pocket.

'Grandfather, that cigar! The doctor said—'

'And I said Fred Plummer gets the job as Manager of the Sonder Ditch.'

'He goes on pension next year,' protested Manfred Steyner.

'Yes,' Hurry nodded. 'But how does that alter the position?'

'He's an old dodderer,' Manfred tried again, there was a desperate edge to his voice. He had not anticipated one of the old man's whims cutting across his plans.

'He's twelve years younger than I am,' growled Hurry ominously. 'How's that make him an old dodderer?'

12

Now that the weekend was over, Rod found the apartment oppressive, and he longed to get out of it.

He shaved, standing naked before the mirror, and he caught a whiff of the reeking ashtrays and half-empty glasses in the lounge. The char would have her customary Monday-morning greeting when she came in later today. From Louis Botha Avenue the traffic noise was starting to build up and he glanced at his watch – six o'clock in the morning. A good time to examine your soul, he decided, and leaned forward to watch his own eyes in the mirror.

'You're too old for this type of living,' he told himself seriously. 'You've had four years of it now, four years since the divorce, and that's about enough. It would be nice now to go to bed with the same woman on two consecutive nights.'

He rinsed his razor, and turned on the taps in the shower cabinet.

'Might even be able to afford it, if our boy Manfred delivers the goods.' Rod had not allowed himself to believe too implicitly in Manfred Steyner's promise; but during the whole of these last two days the excitement had been there beneath the cynicism.

He stepped into the shower and soaped himself, then turned the cold tap full on. Gasping he shut it off and reached for his towel. Still drying himself, he went through and stood at the foot of the bed; as he towelled himself he examined the girl who lay among the tousled sheets.

She was tanned dark toffee brown so she appeared to be dressed in white transparent bra and panties where the skin was untouched by the sun. Her hair was a blonde-gold flurry across her face and the pillow, at odds with the jet black triangle of body hair. Her lips in sleep were fixed in a soft pink pout, and she looked disquietingly young. Rod had to make a conscious effort to remember her name, she was not the companion with whom he had begun the weekend.

'Lucille,' he said, sitting down beside her. 'Wake up. Time to roll.'

She opened her eyes.

'Good morning,' he said and kissed her gently.

'Mmm.' She blinked. 'What time is it? I don't want to get fired.'

'Six,' he told her.

'Oh, good. Plenty of time.' And she rolled over and snuggled down into the sheets.

'Like hell.' He slapped her bottom lightly. 'Move, girl, can you cook?'

'No—' She lifted her head. 'What's your name again?' she asked.

'Rod,' he told her.

'That's right – Piston Rod,' she giggled 'What a way to die! Are you sure you aren't powered by steam?'

'How old are you?' he asked.

'Nineteen. How old are you?'

'Thirty-eight.'

'Daddy, you're vintage!' she told him vehemently.

'Yes, sometimes I feel that way.' He stood up. 'Let's go.'

'You go. I'll lock up when I leave.'

'No sale,' he said, the last one he had left in the flat had cleaned it out – groceries, liquor, glasses, towels, even the ashtrays. 'Five minutes to dress.'

Fortunately she lived on his way. She directed him to a run-down block of flats under the mine dumps at Booysens.

'I'm putting three blind sisters through school. You want to help?' she asked as he parked the Maserati.

'Sure.' He eased a five-Rand note out of his wallet and handed it to her.

'Ta muchly.' And she slipped out of the red leather seat, closed the door and walked away. She did not look back before she disappeared into the block, and Rod felt an unaccountable wave of loneliness wash over him. It was so intense that he sat quiescent for a full minute before he could throw it off, then he hit the gears and screeched away from the kerb.

'My little five-Rand friend,' he said. 'She really cares!'

He drove fast, so that as he topped the Kraalkop ridge the

shadows were still long, and the dew lay silver on the grass. He pulled the Maserati into a layby and climbed out. Leaning against the bonnet he lit a cigarette, grimacing at the taste, and looked down at the valley.

There was no natural surface indication of the immense treasure house that lay below. It was like any of the other countless grassy plains of the Transvaal. In the centre stood the town of Kitchenerville, which for half a century had rejoiced in the fact that Lord Kitchener had camped one night here in pursuit of the wily Boer: a collection of three dozen buildings which had expanded miraculously into three thousand, around a magnificent town hall and shopping complex. Dressed in public lawns and gardens, wide streets and bright new houses, all of it paid for by the mining houses whose lease areas converged on the town.

Out of the bleak veld surrounding the town their headgears stood like colossal monuments to the gold hunger of man. Around the headgears clustered the plants and workshops. There were fourteen headgears in the valley. The field was divided into five lease areas, following the original farm titles, and was mined by five separate companies. Thornfontein Gold Mining, Blaauberg Gold Mining, West Tweefontein Mining, Deep Gold Levels, and the Sonder Ditch Gold Mining Company.

It was to this last that Rod naturally directed his attention.

'You beauty,' he whispered, for in his eyes the mountainous dumps of blue rock beside the shafts were truly beautiful. The complex but carefully thought out pattern of the works buildings, even the sulphur-yellow acres of the slimes dam, had a functional beauty.

'Get it for me, Manfred,' he spoke aloud. 'I want it. I want it badly.'

On the twenty-eight square miles of the Sonder Ditch's property lived fourteen thousand human beings, twelve thousand of them were Bantu who had been recruited from all over Southern Africa. They lived in the multi-storied hostels near the shaft heads, and each day they went down through two small holes in the ground to depths that were scarcely credible, and came up again out of those same two holes. Twelve thousand men down, twelve thousand up. That was not all: out of those two same holes came ten thousand tons of rock daily, and down them went timber and tools and piping and explosive, ton upon ton of material and equipment. It was an undertaking that must evoke pride in the men who accomplished it.

Rod glanced at his watch, 7.35 a.m. They were down already, all twelve thousand of them. They had started going down at three-thirty that morning and now it was accomplished. The shift was in. The Sonder Ditch was breaking rock, and bringing the stuff out.

Rod grinned happily. His loneliness and depression of an hour ago were gone, swallowed up in the immensity of his involvement. He watched the massive wheels of the headgears spinning, stopping briefly, and then spinning again.

Each of those shafts had cost fifty million Rand, the surface plant and works another fifty million. The Sonder Ditch represented an investment of one hundred and fifty million Rand, two hundred and twenty million dollars. It was big, and it would be his.

Rod flicked away the butt of his cigarette. As he drove down the ridge, his eyes moved eastward down the valley. All mining activity ceased abruptly along an imaginary north-south line, drawn arbitarily across the open grassland. There was no surface indication why this should be so, but the reason was deep down.

On that line ran a geological freak, a dyke, a wall of hard serpentine rock that had been named 'the Big Dipper'. It cut through the field like an axe stroke, and beyond it was bad ground. The gold reef existed in the bad ground, they knew this; but not one of the five companies had gone after it. They had prospected it tentatively and then shied away from it, for the boreholes that they sank were frightening in their inconsistency.

A big percentage of the Sonder Ditch lease area lay on the far side of the Dipper, and there was a diamond-drilling team working there now. They had already completed five holes.

Rod could remember accurately the results:—

Borehole S.D. No. 1.	Abandoned in water at 4,000 ft.
S.D. No. 2.	Abandoned in dry hole at 5,250 ft.
S.D. No. 3.	Intersected carbon leader reef at 6,600 ft.

Assay valve	27,323 inch penny-weights.
First deflection	6,212 inch penny-weights.
Second deflection	2,114 inch penny-weights.
S.D. No. 4.	Abandoned in artesian water at 3,500 ft.
S.D. No. 5	Intersected carbon leader at 8,116 ft.
Assay valve	562 inch penny-weights.

And they were drilling the deflections on that one now.

The problem was to build up a picture from results like that. It looked like a mess of faulted and water-logged ground with the gold reef fragmented and fluky, showing unbelievably high values at one spot, and then more than likely pinching out fifty feet away.

They may mine it one day, thought Rod, but I hope to hell I'm on pension by the time they do.

In the distance beyond the slimes dam he could just make out the spidery triangle of the drilling rig against the grown grass.

'Go to it, boys,' he muttered. 'Whatever you find there won't make much difference to me.'

And he went in through the imposing gates at the entrance to the mine property, halting carefully at the stop sign where the railway line crossed the road and he forked two fingers at the traffic policeman lurking behind the gates.

The traffic cop grinned and waved, he had caught Rod the previous week, so he was still one up.

Rod drove down to his office.

13

That Monday morning Allen 'Popeye' Worth was preparing to drill his first deflection on the S.D. No. 5 borehole. Allen was a Texan – not a typical Texan. He stood five feet four inches tall, but was as tough as the steel drill with which he worked. Thirty years before he had started learning his trade on the oilfields around Odessa and he had learned it well.

Now he could start at the surface and drill a four-inch hole down thirteen thousand feet through the earth's crust, keeping the hole straight all the way, an almost impossible task if you took into account the whippiness and torque in a jointed rod of steel that long.

If, as happened occasionally, the steel snapped and broke off thousands of feet down, Allen could fit a fishing tool on the end of his rig, and patiently grope for the stump, find it, grapple it and pull it out of the borehole. When he hit the reef down there, he could purposely kick his drill off the line and pierce the reef again and again to sample it over an area of hundreds of feet. This was what was meant by deflecting.

Allen was one of the best. He could command his own salary and behave like a prima donna, and his bosses would still fawn on him, for the things he could do with a diamond drill were almost magical.

Now he was assessing the angle of his first deflection. The previous day he had lowered a long brass bottle to the end of his borehole and left it overnight. The bottle was half filled with concentrated sulphuric acid, and it had etched the brass of the bottle. By measuring the angle of the etching he knew just how his drill was branching off from his original hole.

In the tiny wood and iron building beside the drilling rig he finished his measurements and stood back from the work bench, grunting with satisfaction.

From his hip pocket he drew a corncob pipe and pouch. Once

he had stuffed tobacco into the pipe and lit it, it became very clear as to why his nickname was 'Popeye'. He was a dead ringer for the cartoon character, aggressive jaw, button eyes, battered maritime cap and all.

He puffed contentedly, watching through the single window of the shack as his gang went about the tedious business of lowering the drilling bit down into the earth. Then he took the pipe from his mouth and spat accurately through the window, replaced the pipe and stooped to minutely check his measurements.

His foreman driller interrupted him from the doorway.

'On bottom, and ready to turn, boss.'

'Huh!' Popeye checked his watch. 'Two hours forty to get down, you don't reckon to rupture a gut do you?'

'That's not bad,' protested the foreman.

'And it sure as hell isn't good either! Okay, okay, cut the cackle and let's get her turning.' He bounced out of the shed and set off for the rig, darting quick beady little glances about him. The rig was a fifty-foot high tower of steel girders and within it the drill rod hung down until it disappeared into the collar. The twin two hundred-horsepower diesel engines throbbed expectantly, waiting to provide the power, their exhausts smoking blue in the early morning sunlight. Beside the rig lay a mountainous heap of drilling rods, beyond them the ten thousand-gallon puddling reservoir to provide water for the hole. Water was pumped into the hole continuously to cool and lubricate the tool as it cut into the rock.

'Stand by to turn her,' Popeye called to his gang, and they moved to their stations. Dressed in blue overalls, coloured fibreglass helmets, and leather gloves, they stood ready and tensed. This was an anxious moment for the whole team, power had to be applied with a lover's touch to the mile and a half length of rod, or it would buckle and snap.

Popeye climbed nimbly up onto the collar, and glanced about him to make sure all was in readiness. The foreman driller was at the controls, watching Popeye with complete absorption, his hands resting on the levers.

'Power up!' shouted Popeye and made the circular motion with his right hand. The diesels bellowed harshly, and Popeye reached out to lay his left hand on the drilling rod. This was how he did it, feeling the rod with his bare hand as he brought in the power, judging the tension by ear and eye and touch.

His right hand gestured and the foreman delicately let in the clutch, the rod moved under Popeye's hand, he gestured again and it revolved slowly. He could feel it was near breaking point and he cut down the power instantly, then let it in again. His right hand moved eloquently, expressively as an orchestral conductor, and the foreman followed it, the junior member of a highly skilled team.

Slowly the tension of the gang relaxed as the revolutions of the drill built up steadily, until Popeye gave the clenched fist 'okay' and jumped down from the collar. They scattered casually to their other duties, while Popeye and the foreman strolled back to the shed, leaving the drill to grind away at a steady four hundred revolutions a minute.

'Got something for you,' said the foreman, as they entered the shed.

'What?' demanded Popeye.

'The latest *Playboy*.'

'You're kidding!' Popeye accused him delightedly, but the foreman fished the rolled magazine out of his lunch box.

'Hey, there!' Popeye snatched it from him and turned immediately to the coloured foldout.

'Isn't that something!' He whistled. 'This dolly could get a job in a stockyard beating the oxen to death with her boo-boos!'

The foreman joined the discussion of the young lady's anatomy, and so neither of them noticed the change in the sound of the drill until two minutes had passed. Then Popeye heard it through an erotic haze. He flung the magazine from him, and went through the door of the shed white-faced.

It was fifty yards from the shed to the rig, but even at that distance Popeye could see the vibration in the drilling rod. He could hear the labouring note of the diesels as they carried increased load, and he ran like a fox terrier, trying to reach the controls and shut off the engines before it happened.

He knew what it was. His drill had cut into one of the many fissures with which this badly faulted ground was criss-crossed. The puddling water from his borehole had drained away leaving the bit to run dry against dry rock. The friction head had built up, the dust from the cut was not being washed away – and in consequence the rod had jammed. It was being held tightly at one end while at the other the two big diesels were straining to turn it. The whole rig was seconds away from a twist-off.

There should have been an operator at the controls to meet just such an emergency, but he was a hundred yards away, just emerging from the wood and iron latrine beyond the puddling dam. He was desperately trying to hoist his pants, clinch the buckle of his belt and run all at the same time.

'You whore's chamberpot!' roared Popeye, as he ran. 'What the hell you goofing off—'

The words choked off in his throat, for as he reached the door of the engine room there was a report like a cannon shot as the rod snapped, and immediately the diesels screamed into over-rev as they were relieved of the load. Just too late, Popeye punched the earth buttons on the magnetos, and the engines spluttered into silence.

In that silence Popeye was sobbing with exertion and frustration and anger.

'A twist-off,' he sobbed. 'A deep one. Oh no! God, no!' It might take two weeks to fish out the broken rod, pump cement into the fissure to seal it, and then start again.

He removed the cap from his head, and with all his strength hurled it on the engine room floor. He then proceeded to jump on it with both feet. This was standard procedure. Popeye jumped on his cap at least once a week, and the foreman knew that when he had finished doing that he would then assault anybody within range.

Quietly the foreman slipped behind the wheel of the Ford truck, and the rest of the gang scrambled aboard. They all bumped away down the rutted track. There was a roadhouse on the main road where they went for coffee at times like this. When the mists of rage had dispersed sufficiently from his mind for Popeye to start seeking a human sacrifice, he looked about to find the drilling area strangely still and deserted.

'Stupid bunch of yellow-bellied baboons!' he bellowed in frustration after the retreating truck, and, as the next best thing, went into the shed to phone his Managing Director.

This gentleman sitting in the air-conditioned offices of 'Hart Drilling and Cementation' high above Rissik Street in Johannesburg was a little taken aback to learn from Popeye Worth that he, the Managing Director, was directly responsible for the twist-off of an expensive diamond drill at the Sonder Ditch No. 5 hole.

'If you used that sack of custard that passes for a brain, you'd fight shy of trying to sink holes into this bunch of knitting,' Popeye yelled into the mouthpiece. 'I'd prefer to stick my old man into a meat grinder, than put a drill into this ground. It stinks, I tell you! It's really ugly down there. God help the poor son of a bitch who tries to mine it!'

He slammed down the phone and stuffed his pipe with trembling fingers. Ten minutes later his breathing had returned to normal and his hands were steady. He picked up the phone again and dialled the number of the roadhouse. The proprietor answered.

'José, tell my boys it's okay, they can come home now,' said Popeye.

14

For Rod Ironsides there was more excitement than usual in meeting and solving the dozen paper problems that lay on his desk to welcome him back to the office. As he worked he kept remembering that Manfred Steyner might be able to do it, might just be able to do it.

The Sonder Ditch might really belong to him soon. He dispatched the last problem and lay back in his swivel chair. His mind was clear of the last cobwebs of dissipation and, as always, he felt purged and cleansed.

If I get her, I'll make her the star performer in the whole field, he thought greedily, they'll talk about the Sonder Ditch from Wall Street to the Bourse, and about the man who is running her. I know how to do it too. I'll cut the costs to the bone, I'll tighten her up solid. Frank Lemmer was a good man, he could get the stuff out of the ground, but he let it creep up on him. It cost him almost nine Rand a ton to mill it.

Well, I'll get it out as well as he did *and* I'll get it out cheaper. An operation takes its temperament from the man at the head. Frank Lemmer would talk about costs every now and then, but he didn't mean it and we knew he didn't mean it. We have become a wasteful operation because we are on a rich reef, we have become big spenders. Well, I'm going to talk costs, and I'll skin the arse of anybody who thinks I'm joking.

Last year Hamilton at Western Holdings kept his working costs per ton milled down to just a touch over six Rand. I could do the same here! I could jump our profits twelve million Rand in one year, if only they give me the job I'll shout the Sonder Ditch's name across the financial markets of the world.

The problem that Rod was pondering was the nightmare of the gold mining industry. Since the 1930s the price of gold had been fixed at \$35 a fine ounce. Each year since then the cost of mining had crept up steadily. In those days they reckoned four penny-weights of gold in a ton of ore was payable value. Now around eight penny-weights was the marginal value.

So in the interim all those millions of tons of ore whose values fell between four and eight penny-weights had been placed beyond the reach of man until such time as they increased the price of gold.

There were many mines with vast reserves of gold-bearing ore, millions in bullion, whose values lay just below the magical number eight. Those mines stood deserted and forlorn, rust reddening their headgears, and the corrugated iron roofs of the buildings collapsing wearily. Rising costs had shot the guts out of them, they were condemned by the single word 'UNPAY'.

The Sonder Ditch was running twenty to twenty-five penny-weights per ton. She was fat, but she could be fatter, Rod decided.

There was a knock at the door.

'Come in!' called Rod, and looked at his watch. It was nine o'clock already. Time for the Monday meeting of his mine captains.

They came in singly and in pairs, twelve of them. These were Rod's front-line men, his combat officers. They went down there each day, each to his own section and directed the actual assault on the rock.

While they chatted idly, waiting for the meeting to begin, Rod looked them over surreptitiously and was reminded of a remark that Herman Koch of Anglo American had made to him once.

'Mining is a hard game, and it attracts a hard breed of men.'

These were men of the hard breed, physically and mentally tough, and Rod realized with a start that he was one of them. No, more than one of them. He was their leader, and with a fierce affection and pride he opened the meeting.

'Right, let's hear your gripes. Who is going to be first to break my heart?'

There are some men with a talent for controlling, and getting the very best results out of other men. Rod was one of them. It was more than his physical size, his compelling voice and hearty chuckle. It was a special magnetism, a personal charm and unerring sense of timing. Under his Chairmanship the meeting would erupt, voices crackle and snap, then subside into chuckles and nods as Rod spoke.

They knew he was as tough as they were, and they respected that. They knew that when he spoke it made sense, so they listened. They knew that when he promised, he delivered, so they were placated. And they knew that when he made a decision or judgement, he acted upon it, so every man knew exactly where he stood.

If asked, any one of these mine captains would have admitted grudgingly that 'there was no bulldust in Ironsides'. This was the equivalent of a presidential citation.

'Very well then.' Rod terminated the meeting. 'You have spent a good two hours of the company's time beating your gums. Now, will you kindly haul arse, go down there and start sending the stuff out.'

15

As these men planned the week's operation, so their men were at work in the earth below them.

On 87 level, Kowalski moved like a great bear down the dimly-lit drive. He had switched off the lamp on his helmet, and he moved without sound, lightly for a man of such bulk. He heard their voices ahead of him in the dimly-lit tunnel, and he paused, listening intently. There was no sound of shovel crunching into loose rock, and Kowalski's Neanderthal features convulsed into a fearsome scowl.

'Bastards!' he muttered softly. 'They think I am in stopes, hey? They think it all right if they sit on fat black bum, no move da bloody rock, hey?'

He started forward again, a bear on cat's feet.

'They find plenty different from what they bloody think, soon!' he threatened.

He stepped round the angle of the drive and flashed his lamp. There were three men Kowalski had put on lashing, shovelling the loose stuff from the footwall into waiting cocopans. Two of them sat against the cocopan, smoking contentedly while the third regaled them with an account of a beer drink he had attended the previous Christmas. Their shovels and sledge hammers leaned unemployed against the side wall of the drive.

All three of them froze into rigidity as the beam of Kowalski's lamp played over them.

'So!' The word burst explosively from Kowalski, and he snatched up a fourteen-pound hammer in one massive fist, reversed it and struck the butt of the handle against the foot wall. The steel head of the hammer fell off and Kowalski was left with a four foot length of selected hickory in his hand.

'You, boss boy!' he bellowed, and his free hand shot out and fastened on the throat of the nearest Bantu. With one heave he jerked him off his feet onto his knees and began dragging him away up the drive. Even in his rage, Kowalski was making sure there were no witnesses. The other two men sat where they were, too horrified to move, while their companion's wails and cries receded into the darkness.

Then the first blow reverberated in the confined space of the drive, followed immediately by a shriek of pain.

The next blow, and another shriek.

The crack, thud, crack, thud, went on repeatedly, but the accompanying shrieks dwindled into moans and soft whimperings, then into the complete silence.

Kowalski came back down the drive alone, he was sweating heavily in the lamp light, and the handle of the hammer in his hand was black and glistening with wet blood.

He threw it at their feet.

'Work!' he growled, and was gone, big and bearlike, into the shadows.

16

On 100 level, Joseph M'Kati was hosing down and sweeping the spillings from under the giant conveyor belt. Joseph had been on this job for five years, and he was a contented and happy man.

Joseph was a Shangaan approaching sixty years of age, the first frost was touching his hair. There were laughter lines around his eyes and at the corner of his mouth. He wore his helmet pushed to the back of his head, his overalls were hand-embroidered and ornamentally patched in blue and red, and he moved with a jaunty bounce and strut.

The conveyor was many hundreds of yards long. From all the levels above the shattered gold reef was scraped from the stopes and trammed back down the haulages in the cocopans. Then from the cocopans it was tipped into the mouths of the ore-passes. These were vertical shafts that dropped down to 100 level, hundreds of feet through living rock to spew the reef out onto the conveyor belt. A system of steel doors regulated the flow of rock onto the conveyor, and the moving belt carried it down to the shaft and dumped it into enormous storage bins. From there it was fed automatically into the ore cage in fifteen-ton loads and carried at four-minute intervals to the surface.

Joseph worked on happily beneath the whining conveyor. The spillings were small, but important. Gold is strange in its behaviour, it moves downwards. Carried by its own high specific gravity it works its way down through almost any other material. It would find any crack or regularity in the floor and work its way into it. It would disappear into the solid earth itself if left long enough.

It was this behaviour of gold that accounted in some measure for Joseph M'Kati's contentment. He had worked his way to the end of the conveyor, washing and sweeping, and now he straightened, laid his bast broom aside and rubbed his kidneys with both hands, looking quickly around to make certain that there was no one else in the conveyor tunnel. Beside him was the ore storage bin into which the conveyor was emptying its load. The bin could hold many thousands of tons.

Satisfied that he was alone, Joseph dropped onto his hands and knees and crawled under the storage bin, ignoring the continuous roar of rock into the bin above him, working his way in until he reached the holes.

It had taken Joseph many months to chisel the heads off four of the rivets that held the seam in the bottom of the bin, but once he had done it, he had succeeded in constructing a simple but highly effective heavy media separator.

Free gold in the ore that was dumped into the storage bin immediately and rapidly worked its way down through the underlying rock, its journey accelerated by the vibration of the conveyor and bin as more reef was dropped. When the gold reached the floor of the bin, it sought an avenue through which to continue its downward journey, and it found Joseph's four rivet holes, beneath which he had spread a square of Polythene sheet.

The gold-rich fines made four conical piles on the sheet of polythene, looking exactly like powdered black soot.

Crouched beneath the bin, Joseph carefully transferred the black powder to his tobacco pouch, replaced the Polythene to catch the next filtering, stuffed the pouch into his hip pocket, and scrambled out from under the bin. Whistling a tribal planting tune Joseph picked up his broom and returned to the endless job of sweeping and hosing.

17

Johnny Delange was marking his shot holes. Lying on his side in the low stope of 27 section he was calculating by eye the angle and depth of a side cutter blast to straighten a slight bulge in his longwall.

In the Sonder Ditch they were on single blast. One daily, centrally fired, blast. Johnny was paid on *fathomage*, the cubic measure of rock broken and taken out of his stope. He must, therefore, position his shot holes to achieve the maximum disruption and blow-out from the face.

'So,' he grunted, and marked the position of the hole in red paint. 'And so.' With one bold stroke of the paint brush he set the angle on which his machine boy was to drill.

'Shaya, madoda!' Johnny clapped the shoulder of the black man beside him. 'Hit it, man.'

Machine boys were selected for stamina and physique, this one was a Greek sculpture in glistening ebony.

'Nkosi!' The machine boy grinned an acknowledgement, and with his assistant lugged his rock drill into position. The drill looked like a gargantuan version of a heavy calibre machine gun.

The noise as the big Bantu opened the drill was shattering in the low-roofed, constricted space of the stope. The compressed air roared and fluttered into the drill, buffeting the eardrums. Johnny made the clenched-fist gesture of approval, and for a second they smiled at each other in the companionship of shared labour. Then Johnny crawled on up the stope to mark the next shot hole.

Johnny Delange was twenty-seven years old, and he was top rock breaker on the Sonder Ditch. His gang of forty-eight men were a tightly-knit team of specialists. Men fought each other for a place on 27 section, for that's where the money was. Johnny could pick and choose, so each month when the surveyors came in and measured up, Johnny Delange was way out ahead in fathomage.

Here was the remarkable position where the man at the lowest point of authority earned more than the man at the top. Johnny Delange earned more than the General Manager of the Sonder Ditch. Last year he had paid super-tax on an income of twenty-two thousand Rand. Even a miner like Kowalski, who brutalized and bullied his gang until he was left with the dregs of the mine, would earn eight or nine thousand Rand a year, about the same salary as an official of Rod Ironsides' rank.

Johnny reached the top of his longwall and painted in the last shot holes. Down the inclined floor of the stope below him all his drills were roaring, his machine boys lying or crouching behind them. He lay there on one elbow, removed his helmet and wiped his face, resting a moment.

Johnny was an extraordinary-looking young man. His long jet black hair was swept back and tied with a leather thong at the back of his head in a curlicue. His features were those of an American Indian, gaunt and bony. He had cut the sleeves out of his overalls to expose his arms – arms as muscular and sinuous as pythons, tattooed below the elbows, immensely powerful but supple. His body was the same, long and sinewy and powerful.

On his right hand he wore eight rings, two on each finger, and it was clear from the design of the rings that they were not merely ornamental. They were heavy gold rings with skull and cross-bones, wolves' heads and other irregularities worked into them, a mass of metal that formed a permanent knuckle-duster. Of the big eyes in the one skull's head Rod Ironsides had once asked: 'Are those real rubies, Johnny?' And Johnny had replied seriously:

'If they aren't, then I've sure as hell been gypped out of three Rand fifty, Mr Ironsides.'

Johnny Delange had been a really wild youngster, until eight months ago. It was then he had met and married Hettie. Courtship and marriage occupying the space of one week. Now he was settling down very well. It was all of ten days since he had last fought anybody.

Lying in the stope he allowed himself five minutes to think about Hettie. She was almost as tall as he was, with a wondrously buxom body and chestnut red hair. Johnny adored her.

He was not the best speechmaker in Kitchenerville when it came to expressing his affection, so he bought her things.

He bought her dresses and jewellery, he bought her a deep-freezer *and* a fifteen cubic foot Frigidaire, he bought her a Chrysler Monaco with leopard-skin upholstery and a Kenwood Chef. In fact, it was becoming difficult to enter the Delange household without tripping over at least one of Johnny's gifts to Hettie. The congestion was made more acute by the fact that living with them was Johnny's brother, Davy.

'Hell, man!' Happily Johnny shook his head. 'She's a bit of all-right, hey!'

There was an eye-level oven he had spotted in a furniture store in Kitchenerville the previous Saturday.

'She'll love that, man,' he muttered, 'and it's only four hundred Rand. I'll get it for her on pay day.'

The decision made, he clapped his helmet onto his head and began crawling out of the stope. It was time now to go up to the station and collect the explosives for the day's blast.

His boss boy should have been waiting for him in the drive, and Johnny was furious to find no sign of him nor the piccanin who was his assistant.

'Bastard!' he grunted, playing the beam of his lamp up and down the drive. 'He's been acting up like hell.'

The boss boy was a pock-marked Swazi, not a big man, but powerful for his size and highly intelligent. He was also a man of mean disposition, Johnny had never seen him smile, and for an extrovert like Johnny it was galling to work with someone so sullen and taciturn. He tolerated the Swazi because of his drive and reliability, but he was the only man in the gang that Johnny disliked.

'Bastard!' The drive was deserted, the roar of the rock drills was muted.

'Where the hell is he?' Johnny scowled impatiently. 'I'll skin him when I find him.'

Then he remembered the latrine.

'That's where he is!' Johnny set off down the drive. The latrine was a rock chamber cut into the side of the drive, a flap of canvas served as a door; beyond was a regular four-holer over sanitary buckets.

Johnny pulled the canvas aside and stepped into the cubicle. The boss boy and his assistant were there. Johnny stared in surprise, for a moment not understanding what they were doing. They were so absorbed they were unaware of Johnny's presence.

Suddenly realization dawned, and Johnny's face tightened with revulsion and disgust.

'You filthy—' Johnny snarled, and catching the boss boy by the shoulders pulled him backwards and pinned him against the wall. He lifted his heavily metalled fist and drew it back ready to hurl it into the boss boy's face.

'Strike me and you know what happens,' said the boss boy softly, his expression flat and neutral, looking steadily into Johnny's eyes. Johnny hesitated. He knew the Company rules, he knew the Government labour officers' attitude, he knew what the police would do. If he hit him, they would crucify him.

'You are a pig!' Johnny hissed at him.

'You have a wife,' said the boss boy. 'My wife is in Swaziland. Two years I have not seen her.'

Johnny lowered his fist. Twelve thousand men, and no women. It was a fact. The actuality sickened him, but he understood why it happened.

'Get dressed.' He stepped back, releasing the boss boy. 'Get dressed both of you. Come to the station. I will meet you there.'

18

For a week now, since the fall of hanging in 43 section, Big King had been out of the stopes.

Rod had ordered it that way. The excuse was that Big King's white miner had been killed in the fall and now he must await an allocation to another section. In reality Rod wanted to rest him. He had seen the strain both physical and emotional that Big King had undergone during the rescue. When together they had unearthed the miner's corpse, the man with whom Big King had worked and laughed, Rod had seen the tears roll unashamedly down Big King's cheeks as he picked up the body and held it easily against his chest.

'Hamba gahle, madoda,' Big King had muttered. 'Go in peace, man.'

Big King was a legend on the Sonder Ditch. They boasted about him; how much Bantu beer he could drink in a sitting, how much rock he could lash single-handed in a shift, how he could dance any other man off his feet. He had been awarded a total of over a thousand Rand in bravery awards. Big King set the pace, others tried to equal him.

Rod had put him in charge of a transport team. For the first few days Big King had enjoyed the opportunity of showing off his strength and socializing, for the transport team moved about the workings allowing Big King to visit most of his numerous friends during a shift. But now Big King was becoming bored. He wanted to get back into the stopes.

'This,' he told his transport team contemptuously, 'is work for old men and young women.' And with one snatch and lift he picked up a forty-four gallon drum of dieseline and unaided placed it on the platform of the loco.

A forty-four gallon drum of dieseline weighs a little over eight hundred pounds avoirdupois.

19

All this fuss for that, Davy Delange paused in his labour of tamping the Dynagel into the shot holes. He leaned forward to inspect the reef. In the face of the stope it was a black line, drawn against the blue quartz rock.

The Carbon Leader Reef, it was called. A thin layer of carbon never more than a few inches thick, more often half an inch. Black soot, that's what it was. Davy shook his head thoughtfully. You could not even see the gold in it.

Davy was two years older than his brother Johnny, and there was no physical or mental resemblance between the two of them. Davy's sandy hair was cropped into a conventional 'short back and sides'. He wore no personal jewellery, and his manner was quiet and reserved.

Johnny was tall and lean, Davy squat and muscular. Johnny was extravagant, Davy careful beyond the point of meanness. Their only common trait was that they were both first-class miners. If Johnny broke more rock than Davy, it was only because Davy was more careful than Johnny; he did not take the same chances, he observed all the safety procedures which Johnny frequently flouted.

Davy earned less money than Johnny, but saved every penny he could. It was for his farm. Davy was going to buy a farm one day. Already he had saved a little over R49,000 towards it. In five more years he would have enough. Then he could get himself a farm and a wife to help run it. Johnny, on the other hand, spent every penny he earned. He was usually in debt to Davy by the end of each month.

'Lend us a hundred 'till pay day, Davy.' Disapprovingly, Davy lent him the money. Davy disapproved of Johnny, his appearance, attire and habits.

Abandoning his microscopic inspection of the Carbon Leader Reef, Davy resumed tamping in the explosive, working carefully and precisely on this highly dangerous procedure. The sticks of explosive were charged with detonators and ready to burn. By law, nobody but the miner-in-charge could perform this operation, but Davy did it automatically while he thought about Johnny's latest trespass. He had raised Davy's rent.

'A hundred Rand a month!' Davy protested aloud. 'I've got a good mind to move out and find my own digs.'

But he knew he would do no such thing. Hettie's cooking was too good, and her presence too feminine and alluring. Davy would stay on with them.

20

'Rod.' Dan Stander's voice was serious and low. 'I've got a nasty one for you.'

'Thanks for nothing.' Rod made his own voice weary and resigned as he spoke into the telephone. 'I'm just going on my underground tour. Can't it wait?'

'No,' Dan assured him. 'Anyway, it's on your way. I'm speaking from the first-aid station at the shaft head. Come across.'

'What is it?'

'Assault. White on Bantu.'

'Christ.' Rod jerked upright in his chair. 'Bad?'

'Ugly. Worked him over with the handle of a fourteen-pound hammer. I've put in forty-seven stitches, but I am worried about a fracture of the skull.'

'Who did it?'

'Miner by the name of Kowalski.'

'Him!' Rod was breathing heavily. 'All right, Dan. Can he make a statement?'

'No. Not for a day or two.'

'I'll be there in a few minutes.'

Rod hung up the phone and crossed the office.

'Dimitri.'

'Boss?'

'Pull Kowalski out of the stopes. I want him in my office soonest. Put someone in to finish his shift.'

'Okay, Rod, what's the trouble?'

'He beat up one of his boys.'

Dimitri whistled softly, and Rod went on.

'Call personnel, get them onto the police.'

'Okay, Rod.'

'Have Kowalski here when I get back from my tour.'

Dan was waiting for him in the first-aid room.

'Take a look.' He indicated the figure on the stretcher. Rod knelt beside him, his mouth tightening into a thin pale line.

The catgut stitches lay neatly across the dark swollen gashes in the man's flesh. His one ear had been torn off, and Dan had sewn it back on. There was a black gap where teeth had been behind the swollen purple lips.

'You will be all right now.' Rod spoke gently, and the Bantu's eyes swiveled towards him. 'The man who did this will be punished.'

Rod stood up. 'Let me have a written report on his injuries, Dan.'

'I'll fix it. See you for a drink at the Club after work?'

'Sure,' said Rod, but underneath he was seething with anger, and it stayed with him during the whole of his underground tour.

21

Rod dropped straight down to 100 level. His first duty was to get the stuff out, and he wanted to check the reserve in the ore storage bins. He came into the long brightly-lit tunnel beneath the ore passes, and paused. The loaded conveyor belt whined monotonously, speeding the broken reef towards the bins.

The tunnel was deserted, except for the lonely figure of the sweeper at the far end. It was one of the phenomena of a well-run gold mine that in a tour through the workings you encountered so few human beings. Mile after mile of haulage and drive were silent and devoid of life, and yet there were twelve thousand men down here.

Rod set off towards the bins at the shaft end of the tunnel.

'Joseph,' he greeted the old sweeper with a smile.

'Nkosi.' Joseph ducked and bobbed with shy pleasure.

'All is well?' Rod asked. Joseph was one of Rod's favourites, he was always so cheerful, so uncomplaining, so patently honest and without guile. Rod always made a point of stopping to chat to him.

'It is well with me, Nkosi. Is it well with you?'

Rod's smile died suddenly, he had noticed the fine white powdering of dust on Joseph's upper lip.

'You old rogue!' he scolded him. 'How often must I tell you to hose down before you sweep? Water! You must use water!'

This was part of the ceaseless battle of the miner to keep down the dust.

'The dust will eat your lungs!'

Phthisis, the dread incurable occupational disease of the miner, caused by silica particles being drawn into the lungs and there solidifying.

Joseph grinned shamefaced, shifting from one foot to the other. He was always embarrassed by Rod's childish obsession with dust. In Joseph's opinion this was one of the few flaws in Rod

430

Ironsides' character. Apart from this weird delusion that dust could hurt a man, he was a good boss.

'It is much harder to sweep wet dirt than dry dirt,' Joseph explained patiently. Rod never seemed to understand this self-evident fact, Joseph had to point it out to him every time they had this particular discussion.

'Listen to me, old man, without water the dust will enter your body.' Rod was exasperated. 'The dust will kill you!'

Joseph bobbed again, grinning at Rod to placate him.

'Very well, I will use plenty water.'

To prove it he picked up the hose and began spraying the floor with enthusiasm.

'That is good!' Rod encouraged him. 'Use plenty of water.' And Rod went on down to the storage bins.

When Rod was out of sight, Joseph turned off the hose and leaned on his broom.

'The dust will kill you!' he mimicked Rod, and chuckled merrily, shaking his head in wonder at the childishness of it.

'The dust will kill you!' he repeated, and burst into delighted laughter, slapping his thigh.

He did a few shuffling dance steps, it was so funny.

The dance steps were awkward, for under his trousers, strapped to the calves of both legs, were heavy polythene bags filled with gold fines from under the bins.

22

Rod stepped out of the Mary Anne at 85 level, and paused to watch Big King loading a baulk of timber onto the loco while his transport team stood back respectfully and watched him. Turning from his task Big King saw Rod standing on the station landing and marched up to him.

'I see you,' he greeted Rod. Big King was not one to make hasty judgements, it was only after the rescue operations in 43 section that he had decided Rod was a man. He was now ready to accept him as an equal.

'I see you also, King Nkulu.' Rod returned the greeting.

'Find me work with men. I sicken of this.'

'You will be back in the stopes before the week is ended,' Rod promised.

'You are my father,' Big King thanked him and went back to the transport team.

23

Johnny Delange saw the Underground Manager coming up the haulage towards him. There was no mistaking that tall wide-shouldered silhouette, nor the man's free swinging stride.

'Whee!' Johnny whistled with relief, grateful for the premonition that had warned him to pack the fifty-pound cardboard cartons of Dynagel into the explosives locker of the railway truck, rather than, as he usually did, pile them haphazard onto the platform in defiance of safety standards.

'Stop!' Johnny commanded the boss boy and his assistant who were pushing the truck, and it trundled to a halt beside Rod.

'Morning, Johnny.'

'Hello, Mr Ironsides.'

'How's it going?'

Johnny hesitated before replying, and immediately Rod was aware of the tension between the three men. He glanced at the two Swazis, they were sullen and apprehensive.

'There's been trouble,' he thought. 'Not like Johnny, he's too clever to let tension cut down his fathomage.'

'Well—' Johnny paused again. 'Look, Mr Ironsides, get rid of this bastard for me.' He jerked his thumb at the boss boy. 'Give me someone else.'

'What's the trouble?'

'No trouble, I just can't work with him.'

Rod raised an eyebrow in disbelief, but turned to the boss boy.

'Are you happy in this section, or do you want transfer?'

'I want transfer!' growled the boss boy.

'Right.' Rod was relieved, sometimes in a case like this the Swazi would refuse transfer. 'Tomorrow you will be told your new section.'

'Nkosi!' The boss boy glanced sideways at his assistant. 'It is the wish of my friend that he transfers with me.'

So that's it, Rod thought, the ever-present spectre which we must ignore because we can find no way to lay it. Johnny had probably caught them at it.

'Your friend shall go with you,' Rod nodded, telling himself that this was not condonation, but merely practical politics. If he separated them, the boss boy would pick on someone else who might not be receptive. Then there would be more trouble, stabbings, faction fighting.

'I'll get you a replacement,' he told Johnny, and then suddenly a thought occurred to him. My God, yes! What a team they would make!

'Johnny, how would you like Big King?'

'Big King!' Johnny's gaunt bony features split into a wide smile. 'Now you're talking, boss!'

24

At three o'clock Rod had finished his tour and was in the cage on the way to the surface. The cage was crowded, men pressed shoulder to shoulder, the stench of sweat almost overpowering. They were hauling shift now, the day's work was over, the stopes were scraped and washed down, the shot holes drilled and charged, the fuses connected into the electrical circuit.

The men were out of the stopes now, falling back in orderly companies and battalions along the haulages to the stations. There to wait patiently for their turn to enter the cages and be whisked to the surface.

Rod was mulling over the myriad problems he had encountered during the day, and the solutions he had dreamed up. He had opened a new section in the back pages of his notebook and headed it simply 'COSTS'.

Already there were two entries there. Let them give me the job, he thought fervently, just let me have it one month and I'll move the world.

'Mr Ironsides.' The man beside him spoke. Rod glanced down at him recognizing him.

'Hello, Davy.' It was remarkable how dissimilar the two brothers were.

'Mr Ironsides, my boss boy has worked his ticket. He's going home at the end of the month. Can you see that I get a good man to replace him?'

'Your brother's boss boy has asked for transfer. Will you take him?'

'Ja!' Davy Delange nodded. 'I know him, he's a good boy.'

And that takes care of one more detail, thought Rod, as he stepped out of the cage into a bright summer's afternoon and tasted the fresh sweet air with pleasure. Now there are only the butt ends of the day's work to tidy up. Then I can go and fetch the drink that Dan promised me.

Dimitri met him in the passage outside the office.

'I've got Kowalski in my office.'

'Good,' said Rod grimly. He went into his own office and sat on the edge of his desk.

'Send him in,' he called through to Dimitri.

Kowalski came through the door and stopped. He stood very still, his long arms hanging slackly at his side, his belly bulging out over his belt.

'You call me,' he muttered thickly, his English hardly intelligible. It was a peasant's face, coarse-featured, dull-eyed. He had not shaved, dirt from the stopes clung in the thick black stubble of beard.

'You beat a man today?' Rod asked softly.

'He no work,' Kowalski nodded. 'I beat him. Maybe next time his brothers they work. No bloody nonsense!'

'You're fired,' said Rod. 'Pull your time and get the hell off this property.'

'You fire?' Kowalski blinked in surprise.

'There will be criminal charges pressed against you by the company.' Rod went on. 'But in the meantime I want you off the property.'

'Police?' Kowalski growled. There was expression on his face now.

'Yes,' said Rod, 'police.'

The spade-sized hands at the end of Kowalski's arms balled slowly into massive fists.

'You call da bloody police!' He took a step towards the desk, big, menacing.

'Dimitri,' Rod called sharply, 'close the door.'

Dimitri had been listening intently, now he jumped up from his desk and closed the interleading door. He stood with his ear pressed to the panelling. For thirty seconds more there was the growl and mutter of voices, then suddenly a thud, a bellow, another thud and a shattering crash.

Dimitri winced theatrically.

'Dimitri!' Rod's voice, and he pushed the door open.

Rod sat on the edge of his desk, swinging one leg casually, he was sucking the knuckle of his right hand.

'Dimitri, tell them not to put so much polish on the floor. Our friend slipped and hit his jaw on the desk.'

Dimitri clucked sympathetically as he stood over the reclining hulk of the big Pole. Kowalski was snoring loudly through his mouth.

'Gave himself a nasty bump,' said Dimitri. 'Shame!'

25

Dr Steyner worked on quietly for the remainder of Monday morning. He favoured the use of a tape recorder, for this cut out human contact which Manfred found vaguely repellent. He disliked having to speak his thoughts to a female who sat opposite him with skirts up around her thighs, squirming her bottom and touching her hair. However, what he really could not abide was the odour. Manfred was very sensitive to smells, even his own body smell of perspiration disgusted him. Women, he found, had a peculiar cloying odour that he could detect beneath their perfume and cosmetics. It nauseated him. This was why he had insisted on separate bedrooms for Theresa and himself. Naturally he had not told her the reason, but had insisted instead that he was such a light sleeper that he could not share a room with another person.

His office was in white and ice-blue, the air clean and cold from the air-conditioning unit, his voice was crisp and impersonal, the whirr of the recorder subdued, and with the conscious portion of his mind Manfred was happily absorbed in his conjuring tricks with figures and money, past performance and future estimates, a three-dimensional structure of variables and contingencies which only a super-normal brain could visualize. But beneath it was a sense of disquiet, he was waiting, hanging in time, and the outward sign of his agitation was the way the fingers of his right hand ran up and down his thigh as he worked, a caressing narcissistic gesture.

A few minutes before noon the unlisted direct telephone on his desk rang, and the movement of his hand stilled. Only one caller could reach him here, only one caller had that number. For a few seconds he sat unmoving, delaying the moment, then deliberately he switched off the recorder and lifted the telephone.

'Dr Manfred Steyner.' He identified himself.

'You have got our man in?' the voice inquired.

'Not yet, Andrew.'

There was silence from the other end, a dangerous crackling silence.

'But there is no cause for alarm. It is nothing. A delay merely, not a setback.'

'How long?'

'Two days – at the latest by the end of the week.'

'You will be in Paris next week?'

'Yes.' Manfred was an adviser to the Government team which was to meet the French for gold price talks.

'He will meet you there. It would be best for you that your side of the bargain were completed by then. You understand?'

'I understand, Andrew.'

The discussion was ended, but Manfred interjected to prevent the caller from hanging up.

'Andrew!'

'Yes.'

'Will you ask him if—' Manfred's tone had changed almost imperceptively, there was an obsequious edge in it. 'Ask him if I may play tonight, please, Andrew.'

'Wait.'

The minutes drifted by, and then the voice came back on the line.

'Yes, you may play. Simon will inform you of your limits.'

'Thank you. Tell him, thank you.'

Manfred made no effort to conceal his relief as he cradled the receiver. He sat beaming at the ice-blue paper on the far wall of his office, even his spectacles seemed to sparkle.

26

There were five men in the opulently furnished room. One of the men was subservient to the others, he was younger than they, attentive to their moods and wishes. Clearly he was a servant. Of the remaining four, one was just as obviously the host. He was seated at the focus of all their attention. He was fat, but not excessively so, the fat of good living not of gluttony. He was speaking, addressing himself to his three guests.

'You have expressed doubts as to reliability of the tool I intend using in the coming venture. I have arranged a demonstration which I hope will convince you that your concern is groundless. That is the reason for the invitation that Andrew here conveyed to you this afternoon.'

The host turned to the younger man. 'Andrew, would you be good enough to go through and wait for Dr Steyner to arrive, as soon as that happens, please let Simon seat him while you come through and inform us.' He gave his orders with dignity and courtesy, a man accustomed to command.

'Now, gentlemen, while we wait may I offer you a drink?'

The conversation that sprang up between the four of them as they sipped their drinks was knowledgeable, and extraordinarily well informed. At its root was one subject: wealth. Mineral wealth, industrial wealth, the harvest of the land and the sea. Oil, steel, coal, fish, wheat and – gold.

There were clues to the stature of these men in the cut and quality of the cloth they wore, the sparkle of a stone on a finger, the tone of authority in a voice, the casual unaffected use of a high name.

'He is here, sir,' Andrew interrupted them from the doorway.

'Oh! Thank you, my boy.' The host stood up. 'Would you mind stepping this way, please, gentlemen.'

He crossed the room and drew aside one of the gold and maroon drapes. Behind it was a window.

The four men clustered about the window and looked through into the room beyond. It was a gaming room of an expensive gambling establishment. There were men and women sitting about a baccarat table, and none of them so much as glanced up at the window overlooking them.

'This is a one-way glass, gentlemen,' the host explained. 'So you need not worry about being seen in such a den of iniquity.'

They chuckled politely.

'What kind of profit does this place show you?' one of them asked.

'My dear Robert!' The host feigned shock. 'You don't for a moment believe that I would be in any way associated with an illegal undertaking?'

This time they chuckled with genuine amusement.

'Ha!' explained the host. 'Here he is.'

Across the gaming room Dr Manfred Steyner was being ushered to a seat at the table by a tall sallow-faced young man, who in his evening dress looked like an undertaker.

'I have asked Simon to place him so that you may watch his face as he plays.'

They were intent now, leaning forward slightly, scrutinizing the man as he arranged the plaques that Simon had stacked at his elbow.

Dr Manfred Steyner began to play. His face was completely devoid of expression, but the pallor was startling. Every few seconds the pink tip of his tongue slipped out between his lips, then disappeared again. In the intervals between each coup, there was a reptilian stillness about him, the stillness of a lizard or an iguana. Only a pulse beat steadily in his throat and his spectacles glittered like a snake's eyes.

'May I direct your attention to his right hand during the play of this coup,' the host murmured, and all their eyes flicked downwards.

Manfred's right hand lay open beside the pile of his chips, but as his card was laid before him so his fingers closed.

'*Carte.*' Soundlessly he mouthed the word, and now his hand was a fist, the knuckles whitened, the tension was so fierce that his fist trembled. Yet, still his face was neutral.

The banker flipped his card.

'*Sept!*' The croupier's mouth formed the number. He faced Manfred's card, then he swept Manfred's stake away. Manfred's hand flopped open and lay soft and hairless as a dead fish on the green baize.

'Let us leave him to his pleasures,' suggested the host and drew the curtains across the window. They returned to their chairs, and they were strangely subdued.

'Jesus,' muttered one of the guests. 'That was ugly. I felt like a peeping tom, like watching someone, you know, pulling his pudding.'

The host glanced at him quickly, surprised at his perception.

'In effect, that is exactly what you were watching,' he told him. 'You will excuse me playing the role of lecturer, but I know a little about this man. It cost me nearly four hundred Rand for an analytic report on him by one of our leading psychiatrists.'

The host paused, assuring himself of their complete attention.

'The reasons are obscure, probably arising from an event or series of events during the period in which Dr Steyner was an orphan wandering through the smoking ruins of war-torn Europe.' The host coughed, deprecating his own flight oratory. 'Be that as it may. The results are there for all to see. Dr Manfred Kurt Steyner's intelligence quotient is a genius rating of 158. He neither smokes nor drinks. He has no hobbies, plays no sport, has never made so much as an improper remark to any woman other than his wife, and there is some doubt as to just how often or to what extent she is favoured by his attentions.' The host sipped his drink conscious of their intense interest. 'Mechanically, if that is the correct term, Dr Steyner is neither impotent nor deficient in his manhood. However, he finds all bodily contact, and especially the secretions that may arise from such contact, to be utterly loathsome. For arousal he relies on the baccarat cards, for release he might endure a brief contact with a member of the opposite sex, but more likely he would – oh, what was the expression you used, Robert?'

They absorbed this in silence.

'He is to be precise, a compulsive gambler. He is also a compulsive loser.'

They stirred with disbelief.

'You mean he tries to lose?' demanded Robert incredulously.

'No.' The host shook his head. 'Not on the conscious level. He believes he is trying to win, but he lays bets against odds that, with his magnificent brain, he must realize are suicidal. It is a deep-seated sub-conscious need to lose, to be humiliated. A form of masochism.'

The host opened a black leather notebook and checked its contents.

'During the period from 1958 to 1963 Dr Steyner lost the total sum of R227,000 at this table. In 1964 he was able to arrive at an arrangement with his sole creditor to discharge the debt plus the accumulated interest.'

You could see the faces change as they rapidly searched their memories for a set of circumstances which would fit the dates and principals. Robert reached the correct deduction first. In 1964 their host had sold his majority holdings in the North Maun Copper Co. to C.R.C. at a price that could only be considered advantageous. Just prior to this De Steyner had been made head of finance and planning at C.R.C.

'North Maun Copper,' said Robert with admiration. That is how he had done it, the cunning old fox! He had forced Steyner to buy well above market value.

The host smiled softly, deferentially, neither confirming nor denying.

'Since 1964 to the present Dr Steyner has continued to patronize this establishment. His gambling losses for this further period amount to—' he consulted his notebook again, pretending surprise at the figure, 'to a touch over R300,000.'

They sighed and moved restlessly. Even to these men it was a very large sum of money.

'I think we can rely on him.' The host closed his notebook with a snap, and smiled around at them.

27

Theresa lay in the dark. The night was warm, the stillness spoiled only by the klonking of a frog down at the fishpond. The moonlight came in through the window, playing shadow pictures through the branches of the Pride of India tree onto the wall of her bedroom.

She threw back the single sheet, and swung her legs off the bed. She could not sleep, it was too warm, her nightdress kept binding under her armpits. She stood up and on a sudden reckless impulse she drew the nightdress off over her head and tossed it through the open door of her dressing-room, then, naked, she walked out onto the wide veranda. Into the moonlight, with the cool stone flags under her bare feet, and the warm night air moving like the touch of fairy hands on her skin.

She felt suddenly devilish and daring, she wanted to run down across the lawns and to have someone catch her doing it. She giggled, uncertain of this mood. It was so far removed from Manfred's conception of a good German Hausfrau's behaviour.

'He'd be furious,' she whispered with wicked delight, and then she heard the motor of the car.

She froze with horror, the headlights flicked through the trees as the car came up the driveway and she darted back into her room; in panic she dropped to her knees and searched for her nightgown, found it and ran to the bed as she dragged it on over her head.

She lay in the darkness and listened to the car door slam. There was silence until she heard him pass her door. His heels clacked on the yellow wood floor, he was almost running. Theresa knew the symptoms, the late night return, the suppressed urgency, and she lay rigid in her bed, waiting.

The minutes passed slowly, and then the interleading door from Manfred's suite swung open silently.

'Manfred, is that you?' She sat up and reached for the switch of the bedside lamp.

'Don't put the light on.' His voice was breathless, slurred as though he had been drinking but there was no trace of liquor on his breath as he stooped over her and kissed her. His lips were dry and tightly closed, as he slipped off his dressing-gown.

Two and a half minutes later he stood up from the bed, turning his back to Theresa as he quickly shrugged into the silk dressing-gown.

'Excuse me a minute, Theresa.' The breathlessness was gone from his voice. He went through the door of his own suite, and seconds later she heard the hiss of the shower and the tinkling splash of water.

She lay on her back and her fingernails cut into the palms of her hands. Her body was trembling with a mixture of revulsion and desire, it had been so fleeting a contact – enough to stir her, but so swift as to leave her with a feeling of having been used and sullied. She knew that the rest of the night would pass infinitely slowly, with restless burning tension, remorse and self-pity alternating with wild elation and half-crazed erotic fantasy.

'Damn him,' she screamed silently within her skull. 'Damn him! Damn him!'

She heard the shower stop, and then Manfred returned to her room. He smelt of 4711 Eau de Cologne, and he sat down carefully on the end of the bed.

'You may turn on the light, Theresa.'

It required a conscious effort for her to unclench her hand and reach out for the lamp switch. Manfred blinked behind his spectacles at the flood of light. His hair was damp and freshly combed, his cheeks shone like ripe apples.

'I hope you had an enjoyable day?' he asked, and listened seriously to her reply. Despite her tension, Theresa found herself falling under the almost hypnotic influence he wielded over her. His voice precise, almost monotonous. The glitter of his spectacles, the reptilian stillness of his body and features.

As she had so many times before, she thought of herself as a warm fluffy rabbit sitting tense and fascinated before the cobra.

'It is late,' he said at last and he stood up.

Looking down at her as she lay cuddled into the white silk sheets, he asked with as little emphasis as if he were requesting her to pass the sugar: 'Theresa, could you raise three hundred thousand Rand without your grandfather knowing?'

'Three hundred thousand!' She sat up startled.

'Yes. Could you?'

'Good Lord, Manfred, that's a small fortune.' She truly saw nothing unusual in her choice of adjective. 'You know it's all in the Trust Fund, well, most of it. There is the farm and the – no, I couldn't find half of that without Pops knowing.'

'Pity,' murmured Manfred.

'Manfred, you aren't in – difficulties?'

'No. Good Lord, no. It was just a thought. Forget that I asked. Good night, Theresa, I hope you sleep well.'

Involuntarily she lifted her hands towards him in invitation.

'Good night, Manfred.'

He turned and left the room, she let her hands fall to her sides. For Theresa Steyner the long night had begun.

28

'Ladies and Gentlemen, it is customary for the General Manager to introduce the distinguished guest who presents our special service awards. Last week, in tragic circumstances our General Manager, Mr Frank Lemmer, was killed in the Company's service, a loss which we all bitterly regret, and I am sure you all join me in sincere condolence to Mrs Eileen Lemmer.' Rod paused for the acknowledging murmur from his audience. There were two hundred of them packed into the mine club hall. 'It falls upon me, therefore, as Acting General Manager, to introduce to you Dr Manfred Steyner who is a senior Director of Central Rand Consolidated, our parent company. He is also head of the Departments of Finance and Planning.'

Sitting beside her husband, Theresa Steyner had noticed Manfred's irritation at Rod's mention of Frank Lemmer. It was company policy not to draw public attention to accidental death or injury inflicted on employees by the Company's operation. She liked Rod the better for his small tribute to Frank Lemmer.

Theresa was wearing sunglasses, for her eyes were swollen and red. In the dawning, after a sleepless night, she had succumbed suddenly to a fit of bitter weeping. The tears were without cause, or reason, and had left her feeling strangely lightheaded and with a brittle sense of well-being. However, her enormous eyes always showed up badly for hours after she had wept.

She sat with her legs demurely crossed, immaculate in a suit of cream shantung, a black silk scarf catching her hair and then letting it fall in dark glossy brown cascade onto her shoulders. She leaned forward in polite attention to the speaker, one elbow on her knee, her chin cupped in her palm, one long tapered finger laying against her cheek. A lady with diamonds on her fingers and pearls at her throat, smiling an acknowledgment at Rod's reference to 'the lovely granddaughter of our Chairman'.

Except for the slight incongruity of the sunglasses, she was

447

the perfect image of the young matron. Polished, poised, cosseted, secure in her unassailable virtue and duty.

However, the thoughts that we running through Theresa Steyner's head, and the flutterings and sensations that were prickling and tickling her, had they been known, would have broken up the assembly in disorder. All the formless fantasy and emotional disturbance of the previous night were now directed at one target – Rodney Ironsides. Suddenly, with a start of amusement and alarm, she was aware of a phenomenon that she had last experienced many years ago. She moved quickly, shifting her seat for the cream shantung marked so easily with any moisture.

'Terry Steyner!' she thought, deliciously shocked at herself, and found with relief that Rod had finished speaking and Manfred was standing up to reply. She joined in the applause enthusiastically to distract her errant fancy.

Manfred briefly mentioned the six gentlemen sitting in the front row of seats whose courage and devotion to duty they had come to honour, he then went on into an exploration of the prospects of an increase in the price of gold. In measured, carefully considered terms, he set out the advantages and benefits that would accrue to the industry, the nation and the world at large. It was an erudite and convincing dissertation, and there was a large contingent of newspaper men to record it. The press had been alerted by the public relations department of C.R.C. to the text of Dr Steyner's speech and all the leading dailies, weeklies, financial gazettes and journals were represented.

At intervals a photographer would come to crouch below the platform and pop a flash bulb up at Dr Steyner. On the eve of the gold price talks with France this would make good copy, for Steyner was the boy genius in the South African team.

The six heroes sat uncomfortably, forlorn in their best suits, scrubbed like schoolboys at a prize-giving ceremony, staring up at the speaker, not understanding a single word of the foreign language, but maintaining expressions of grave dignity.

Rod caught Big King's eye and winked at him. Solemnly Big King's right eyelid drooped and rose in reply, and quickly Rod averted his gaze to prevent himself laughing out loud.

He looked straight into Theresa Steyner's face, taking her completely off her guard. Not even the dark glasses could conceal her thoughts, they were as clear as if she had spoken them aloud. Before she could drop her eyes to examine the hem of her skirt, Rod knew with a stomach swoop of excitement how it could be if he chose.

With a new awareness he examined her from the corner of his eye, seeing her for the first time as an accessible woman, a highly desirable woman, but nevertheless still the granddaughter of Hurry Hirschfeld and the wife of Manfred Steyner. This made her as dangerous as a force ten pressure burst, he knew, but the desire and temptation was hard to deny, inflamed perhaps rather than dampened by the danger.

He saw that she was blushing now, her fingers picking nervously at the hem of her skirt. She was as agitated as a schoolgirl, she knew he was watching her. Rod Ironsides, who until five minutes before had been thinking of nothing but his speech, now found himself impelled into a completely new and exciting dimension.

After the awards had been made, tea had been drunk, biscuits consumed and the crowd had dispersed, Rod escorted the Steyners down across the vivid green lawns of Kikuyu grass to where the chauffeur was holding the Daimler.

'What a magnificent physique that Shangaan has, what was his name – King?' Terry was walking between the two men.

'King Nkulu. Big King, we call him.'

Rod found his speech unsteady, he had stuttered slightly. This thing between the two of them was suddenly overpowering, it hummed like a turbine, making the space between them crackle with tension. Unless he were deaf, Manfred Steyner must be aware of it.

'He is pretty special. There is nothing he can't do, and do it far and away better than his nearest rival. My God, you should see him dance.'

'Dance?' inquired Terry with interest.

'Tribal dancing, you know.'

'Of course.' Terry hoped the relief in her voice was not obvious, she had been racking her badly flustered brain for an excuse to visit the Sonder Ditch again or have Rod Ironsides come to Johannesburg. 'I have a friend who is absolutely mad keen on seeing the dances. She pesters me every time I see her.'

Quickly she selected a name from her list of friends, she must have one ready should Manfred ask.

'They dance every Saturday afternoon, bring her out any time.' Rod fielded the ball neatly.

'What about this Saturday?' Terry turned to her husband, 'Would that be all right, Manfred?'

'What's that?' Manfred looked at her vaguely, he had not been following the conversation. Manfred Steyner was a worried man, he was pondering his obligation to gain control of the management of the Sonder Ditch within two days.

'May we come out here on Saturday afternoon to watch the tribal dancing?' Terry repeated her question.

'Have you forgotten that I fly to Paris on Saturday morning, Theresa?'

'Oh, dear.' Terry bit her lip thoughtfully. 'It *had* slipped my mind. What a pity, I would have enjoyed it.'

Manfred frowned slightly, irritated.

'My dear Theresa, there is no reason why you shouldn't come out to the Sonder Ditch without me. I am sure you will be safe enough in Mr Ironsides' hands.'

His choice of words brought the colour to Terry's cheeks again.

29

After the award ceremony, Big King's first stop was the Recruiting Agency office at the entrance to the No. 1 shaft hostel. There were men clustered about the counter, but they stood aside for Big King and he acknowledged the courtesy by slapping their backs indiscriminately and greeting them with:

'Kunjane, madoda. How is it, men?'

The clerk behind the counter hurried to serve him. Up at the Mine Club Big King might be a little out of his depth, but here he was treated like a reigning monarch.

In two neat bundles Big King placed the award money on the counter.

'Twenty-five Rand you will send to my senior wife.' He instructed the clerk. 'And twenty-five Rand you will put to my book.'

Big King was scrupulously fair. Half of all his earnings was remitted to the senior of his four wives, and half was added to the substantial sum already credited in his savings bank passbook.

The agency was the procurer of labour for the insatiably man-hungry gold mines of the Witwatersrand and Orange Free State. Its representatives operated across the southern half of the continent. From the swamps and fever lagoon along the great Zambesi, from among the palm groves fringing the Indian Ocean, out of these simmering plains that the bushmen called 'the big dry', down from the mountains of Basutoland and the grasslands of Swaziland and Zululand they gathered the Bantu, the men themselves completing the first fifty or sixty miles of the journey on foot. Individuals meeting on a footpath to become pairs, arriving at a little general dealer's store in the bleak scrub desert to find three or four others already waiting, the arrival of the recruiting truck with a dozen men and their luggage aboard, the long bumping grinding progress through the bush. The stops at which more men scrambled aboard, until a full truck load of fifty or sixty disembarked at a railway siding in the wilderness.

Here the tiny trickle of humanity joined a stream, and at the first major centre they trans-shipped and became part of the great flood that washed towards 'Goldi'.

However, once they had reached Johannesburg and been allocated to one of the sixty major gold mines, the Agency's obligations towards its recruits were not yet discharged. Between them the employing mine and the Agency must provide each man with employment, training, advice and comfort, maintain contact between him and his family, for very few of them could write, reassure him when he worried that his goats were sick or his wife unfaithful. They must provide a banking and savings service with a personal involvement unknown to any commercial banking institute. They had, in short, to make certain that a man taken from an environment that had not changed in a thousand years and deposited into the midst of a sophisticated and technological society would retain his health, happiness and sanity, so that at the end of his contract he would return to the place from which he had come and tell them all how wonderful it was at 'Goldi'. He would show them his hard helmet, and his new suitcase crammed with clothes, his transistor radio and the little blue book with its printed figures, inflaming them also with the desire to make the pilgrimage, and keep the flood washing towards 'Goldi'.

Big King completed his business transactions and went in through the gates of the hostel, he was going to take advantage of the fact that he had missed the shift and would be among the first at the ablutions and dining-hall.

He went down across the lawns to his block. Despite the size of an establishment that housed six thousand men, the Company had tried to make it as attractive as possible. The result was an unusual design, half-way between a motel and an advanced penitentiary.

As a senior boss boy, Big King rated a room of his own. An ordinary labourer would share with five others.

Carefully Big King brushed down his suit and hung it in the built-in cupboard, wiped down his glossy shoes and racked them, then with a towel around his waist he set off for the ablution block and was irritated to find it already filled with new recruits up from the acclimatization centre.

Big King ran an appraising eye over their naked bodies and judged that this batch must be nearing the completion of their eight-day acclimatization. There were sleek and shiny, the muscle definition showing clearly through the skin.

You could not take a man straight out of his village, probably suffering from malnutrition, and put him down a gold mine to lash and bar and drill in a dry bulb heat of 91° Fahrenheit and 84% relative humidity, without running a serious risk of killing him with heat stroke or exhaustion.

Every recruit judged medically fit to work underground went into acclimatization. For eight days, eight hours a day, he and hundreds of others stood with only a loin cloth about his middle in a vast barn-like hall stepping up onto and down from a platform. The height of the platform was carefully matched to the man's height and body weight, the speed of his movements was regulated by a flashing panel of lights, the temperature and humidity were controlled at 91° and 84%, every ten minutes he was given water and his body temperature was registered by the half dozen trained medical assistants in charge of the room.

At the end of the eighth day he emerged as fit as an olympic athlete, and quite able to perform heavy physical labour in conditions of high temperature and humidity without discomfort or danger.

'Gwedeni!' growled Big King, and the nearest recruit, still white with soap suds, hurriedly vacated his shower with a respectful 'Keshle!' in deference to Big King's rank and standing. Big King removed his towel and stepped under the shower, revelling as always in the rush of hot water over his skin, flexing the great muscles of his arms and chest.

The messenger found him there.

'King Nkulu, I have word for thee.' The man used Shangaan, not the bastard Fanikalo.

'Speak,' Big King invited, soaping his belly and buttocks.

'The Induna bids you call at his house after you have eaten the evening meal.'

'Tell him I will attend his wishes,' said Big King and held his face up into the rush of steaming water.

Dressed in a white open-necked shirt and blue slacks, Big King sauntered down to the kitchens. Again the recruits were ahead of him, queueing with bowls in hand outside the serving hatches.

Big King walked past them through the door marked 'No Admittance – Staff only'.

The kitchens were cavernous, glistening with white porcelain tile and stainless steel cookers and bins that could serve eighteen thousand hot meals a day.

When Big King entered a room, even one as large as this, no one was unaware of his presence. One of the assistant cooks snatched up a bowl not much smaller than a baby's bath, and hurried across to the nearest stainless steel bin. He opened the lid and looked expectantly at Big King. Big King nodded and the cook ladled about two litres of steaming sugar beans into the bowl, before passing on to the next bin where he again looked for and obtained Big King's approval. He added an equal quantity of mixed vegetables to the bowl, slammed down the lid and scampered across to where a second assistant waited with a spade beside yet another bin.

The spade was the same as those used for lashing gold reef underground, but the blade of this one had been polished to gleaming cleanliness. The second cook dug into the bin and came up with a spadeful of white maize porridge, cooked stiff as cake, the smell of it as saliva-making as the smell of new bread. This was the staple of Bantu diet. He deposited the spadeful in the bowl.

'I am hungry.' Big King spoke for the first time, and the second cook dug out another spadeful and added it to the bowl. They passed on to the end of the kitchens and at their approach another cook lifted the lid on a pressure cooker the size of a washing machine. From it arose a cloud of fragrant steam.

Apologetically the cook held out his hand and Big King produced his meat ticket. Meat was the only food that was rationed. Each man was limited to one pound of meat a day; the Company had long ago discovered to its astonishment and cost that a Bantu, offered unlimited supplies of fresh meat, was quite capable of eating his own weight of it monthly.

Having ascertained that Big King was entitled to his daily pound, the cook proceeded to ladle at least five pounds of it into the bowl.

'You are my brother,' Big King thanked him, and the little procession moved on to where yet another cook was filling a half-gallon jug of thick, gruel-like, mildly alcoholic Bantu beer

454

from one of the multiple spiggots beneath the thousand-gallon tank.

The bowl and jug were ceremonially handed to Big King and he went out onto the covered terraces where benches and tables were set out for alfresco dining in mild weather.

While he ate, the terrace began to fill, for the shift was out of the mine now. Every man who passed his table greeted Big King, but only a few privileged persons took the liberty of seating themselves at the same table. One of them was Joseph M'Kati, the little old sweeper from 100 level.

'It has been a good week, King Nkulu.'

'You say so.' Big King was non-committal. 'I go now to a meeting with the Old One. Then we shall see.'

The Old One, the Shangaan Induna, lived in a Company house. A self-contained residence with lounge and dining-room, kitchen and bathroom. He was handsomely paid by the Company, provided with servants, food, furniture and all the other appurtenances of his rank and station.

He was the head of the Shangaan community on the Sonder Ditch. A chief of the blood, a greybeard and member of the tribal councils. In similar houses and with the same privileges and in equal style lived the Indunas of the other tribal groups that made up the labour force of the Sonder Ditch. They were the paternal figureheads, the tribal jurists, ruling and judging within the framework of law and custom. The Company could not hope to maintain harmony and order without the assistance of these men.

'Baba!' Big King greeted his Induna from the doorway of his house, touching the forehead in respect not only for the man but also for what he represented.

'My son.' The Induna smiled his greeting. 'Come and sit by me.' He gestured for his servants to leave the room, and Big King went to squat at the feet of the old man. 'Is it true you go now to work with the mad one?' That was Johnny Delange's nickname.

They talked, the Induna questioning him on fifty matters that affected the welfare of his people. For Big King this was a comforting and nostalgic experience, for the Induna stood in the place of his father.

At last, satisfied, the Induna went on to other matters.

'There is a parcel ready tonight. Crooked Leg waits for you.'

'I shall go for it.'

'Go in peace then, my son.'

On his way through the gates of the hostel Big King stopped to chat with the guards. These men had the right to search over any person entering or leaving the hostel. Particularly they were concerned with preventing either women disguised as men or bottles of spirits entering the premises, both of which tended to have a disruptive effect on the community. As an after-thought they were also instructed to look out for stolen property entering or leaving. Big King had to ensure that none of them would ever, under any circumstances, take it into his head to search Big King.

While he stood at the gates, the last glow of the sunset faded and the lights began to come on across the valley. The clusters of red aerial warning lights atop the headgears, the massed yellow squares of the hotels, the strings of street lamps and the isolated pinpricks of the residential areas up on the ridge.

When it was truly dark, Big King left the guards and sauntered down the main road, until a bend in the road took him out of their sight. Then Big King left the road and started up the slope. He moved like a night animal, swiftly and with certainty of the path he followed.

He passed the ranch-type split-levels of the line management officials with their wide lawns and swimming-pools, pausing only once when a dog yapped nearby, then moving on again until he was into the broken rock and rank grass of the upper ridge; he crossed the skyline and started down the far side until he made out the grass-covered mound of rubble in the moonlight. He slowed and moved cautiously forward until he found the rusty barbed wire fence that guarded the entrance. He vaulted it easily and went on into the black mouth of the tunnel.

Fifty years before, a long-defunct mining company had suspected the existence of a gold reef in this area and had driven prospecting addits into the side of the ridge, exhausting its funds in the process, and finally abandoning the network of tunnels in despair.

Big King paused long enough to draw an electric torch from his pocket before going on into the tunnel, flashing the beam ahead of him. Soon the air stank of bats and their wings swished about his head. Unperturbed, Big King went on deeper and deeper into the side of the hill, taking a turning and fork in the tunnel without hesitation. At last there was a faint glow of yellow light ahead and Big King switched off his torch.

'Crooked Leg!' he called, his voice bounced and boomed along the tunnel. There was no reply.

'It is I, Big King!' he shouted again, and immediately a shadow detached itself from the sidewall and limped towards him, sheathing a wicked-looking knife as it came.

'All is ready.' The little cripple came to greet him. 'Come, I have it here.'

Crooked Leg had earned his limp and his nickname in a rock-fall a dozen years ago. Now he owned and operated the concession photographic studio on the mine property, a flourishing enterprise, for dearly the Bantu love their own image on film. Not, however, as profitable as his nocturnal activities in the abandoned workings beyond the ridge.

He led Big King into a small rock chamber lit by a suspended hurricane lantern. Mingled with the bat stench was the acrid reek of sulphuric acid in high concentration.

On a wooden trestle table that occupied most of the chamber were earthenware jars, heavy glass bowls, polythene bags, and a variety of shoddy and very obviously second-hand laboratory equipment. In a clear space amongst all this clutter stood a large screw-topped bottle. The bottle was filled with a dirty yellow powder.

'Ha!' Big King exclaimed his pleasure. 'Plenty!'

'Yes. It has been a good week,' Crooked Leg agreed.

Big King picked up the bottle, marvelling once again at the unbelievable weight of it. This was not pure gold, for Crooked Leg's acid reduction methods were crude, but it was at least sixteen carats fine.

The bottle represented the week's collection of fines and concentrates by men like Joseph M'Kati from a dozen vulnerable points along the line of production; in some cases carried out from the company reduction works itself under the noses of the heavily armed guards.

All the men involved in this surreptitious milking off of the company's gold were Shangaans, there was only one man in whom was vested sufficient authority and prestige to prevent the greed and hostility which gold breeds from destroying the whole operation. That was the Shangaan Induna. There was only one man with the physical presence and necessary command of the Portuguese language to negotiate the disposal of the gold. That was Big King.

Big King placed the bottle in his pocket. The weight pulled his clothing out of shape.

'Run like a gazelle, Crooked Leg.' He turned back into the dark tunnel.

'Hunt like a leopard, King Nkulu,' chuckled the little cripple, as he disappeared into the moving shadows.

30

'A packet of Boxer tobacco,' said Big King. The eyes of José Almeida, the Portuguese owner of the mine concession store and the local roadhouse, narrowed slightly. He took down the yellow four-ounce packet from the shelves and handed it across the counter, accepted Big King's payment and counted the change into his palm.

He watched as the giant Bantu wandered down between the loaded shelves and racks of merchandise to disappear through the front door of the store into the night.

'Take charge,' he muttered in Portuguese to his plump little wife with her silky dark moustache, and she nodded in understanding, moving into José's place in front of the cash register. José went through into his storerooms and living quarters behind the store.

Big King was waiting in the shadows. When the back door opened he slipped through and José closed the door behind him. José led him through into a cubicle of an office, and from a cupboard he took down a jeweller's balance. Under Big King's watchful eye he began to weigh the gold.

José Almeida purchased the gold from the unofficial outlet of each of the five major mines on the Kitchenerville field, paying five Rands an ounce and selling again for sixteen. He justified the large profit margin he allowed himself by the fact that mere possession of unregistered gold was a criminal offence in South Africa, punishable by up to five years' imprisonment.

Almeida was a man in his middle thirties with lank black hair that he continually pushed back from his forehead, bright brown inquisitive eyes and dirty fingernails. Despite his grubby and well-worn clothing and unkempt hair style, he was a man of substance.

He had been able to pay in cash the forty thousand Rand demanded by the Company for the monopoly concession to trade on the mine property. He had, therefore, an exclusive clientele of twelve thousand well-paid Bantu, and had recovered his forty thousand during his first year of trading. He did not really need to run the risk of illicit gold buying, but gold is strange material. It infects most men who touch it with a reckless greed.

'Two hundred and sixteen ounces,' said José. His scale was set to record a twenty per cent error – in José's favour.

'One thousand and eighty Rand,' agreed Big King in Portuguese, and José went to the the big green safe in the corner.

31

Terry Steyner entered the 'Grape and Gable' bar of the President Hotel at 1.14 p.m. precisely, and as Hurry Hirschfeld stood to greet her he reflected that fourteen minutes was hardly late at all for a beautiful woman. Terry's grandmother would have considered herself to be early if she was only that late.

'You're late,' growled Hurry. No sense in letting her get away with it unscathed.

'And you are a big, cuddly, growly, lovable old bear,' said Terry and kissed him on the tip of his nose before he could duck. Hurry sat down quickly scowling thunderously with pleasure. He decided he didn't give a good damn if Marais and Hardy, who further down the bar were listening and trying to cover their grins, repeated the incident to the entire membership of the Rand Club.

'Good day, Mrs Steyner.' The scarlet-jacketed barman smiled his greeting. 'Can I mix you a Manhattan?'

'Don't tempt me, Thomas. I'm on a diet. I'll just have a glass of soda water.'

'Diet,' snorted Hurry. 'You're skinny enough as it is. Give her a Manhattan, Thomas, and put a cherry in it. Never was a Hirschfeld woman that looked like a boy, and you'll not be the first of them.' As an afterthought, he added: 'I've ordered your lunch also, you'll not starve yourself in my company.'

'You are a shocker, Pops,' said Terry fondly.

'Now, young lady, let's hear what you've been up to since I last saw you.'

They talked together as friends, very dear and trusted friends. The affection they felt for each other went beyond the natural duty of their blood tie. There was a kinship of the spirit as well as the flesh. They sat close, heads together, watching each other's face as they talked, completely lost in the pleasure of each other's company, the murmur of their voices interrupted by a tinkling burst of laughter or a deep chuckle.

They were so absorbed that Peter, the headwaiter, came through from the Transvaal Room to find them.

'Mr Hirschfeld, the chef is in tears.'

'Good Lord.' Hurry looked at the antique clock above the bar. 'It's almost two o'clock. Why didn't someone tell me?'

•The oysters had been flown up from Mossel Bay that morning, and Terry sighed with pleasure after each of them.

'I was out at the Sonder Ditch with Manfred on Wednesday.'

'Yes, I saw the photograph in the paper.' Hurry engulfed his twelfth and final oyster.

'I must say I like your new General Manager.'

Hurry laid down his fork and a little flush of anger started in his withered old cheeks.

'You mean Fred Plummer?'

'Don't be silly, Pops, I mean Rodney Ironsides.'

'Has that cold fish of yours been briefing you?' Hurry demanded.

'Manfred?' She was genuinely puzzled by the question, Hurry could see that. 'What's he got to do with it?'

'All right, forget it.' Hurry dismissed Manfred with a shake of his head. 'Why do you like Ironsides?'

'Have you heard him speak?'

'No.'

'He's very good. I'm sure he must be a first-class mining man.'

'He is.' Hurry nodded, watchful and non-committal.

Peter whisked Terry's plate away, giving her the respite she needed to gather her resources. In the previous few seconds she had realized that Rodney Ironsides was not, as she had believed, a certainty for the job. In fact, Pops had already chosen old plum-faced Plummer for the General Managership. It took another moment for her to decide that she would use even the dirtiest in-fighting to see that Rod was not overlooked.

Peter laid plates of cold rock lobster in front of them, and when he had withdrawn Terry looked up at Hurry. She had perfected the trick of enlarging her already enormous eyes. By holding them open like this she could flood them with tears. The effect was devastating.

'Do you know, Pops, he reminds me so much of the photographs of Daddy.'

462

Colonel Bernard Hirschfeld, Terry's father, had burned to death in his tank at Sidi Rezegh. She saw Hurry Hirschfeld's expression crack with pain, and Terry felt a sick little flutter of guilt. Had it been necessary to use such a vicious weapon to achieve her ends?

Hurry pushed at the rock lobster with his fork, his head was bowed so she could not see his face. She reached out to touch his hand.

'Pops–' she whispered, and he looked up. There was a restrained excitement in Hurry's manner.

'You know, you're bloody well right! He does look a bit like Bernie. Did I ever tell you about the time when your father and I –'

Terry felt dizzy with relief. I didn't hurt him, she told herself, he likes the idea, he really does. With a woman's instinct she had chosen the only form of persuasion that could have moved Hurry Hirschfeld from his decision.

32

Manfred Steyner fastened his safety belt and lay back in the seat of the Boeing 707, feeling slightly nauseated with relief.

Ironsides was in, and he was safe. Hurry Hirschfeld had sent for him two hours before to wish him farewell and good luck with the talks. Manfred had stood before him, trying desperately to think of some way in which he could bring up the subject naturally. Hurry saved him the trouble.

'By the way, I'm giving Ironsides the Sonder Ditch. Reckon it's about time we had some young blood in top management.'

It was as easy as that. Manfred had difficulty in persuading himself that those threats which had kept him lying awake during the past four nights were no longer of consequence. Ironsides was in. He could go to Paris and tell them. *Ironsides is in. We are ready to go.*

The note of the jets changed, and the Boeing began to roll forward. Manfred twisted his head against the neck rest and peered through the Perspex porthole. He could not distinguish Terry's figure amongst the crowd on the observation balcony of Jan Smuts Airport. They taxied past a Pan Am Boeing which cut off his view and Manfred looked straight ahead. Instantly his nostrils flared, he looked around quickly.

The passenger in the seat beside him had stripped to his shirt-sleeves. He was a big beefy individual who very obviously did not use deodorant. Almost in desperation Manfred looked about. The aircraft was full, there would be little chance of changing seats and beside him the beefy individual produced a pack of cigarettes.

'You can't smoke,' cried Manfred. 'The light's on.' The combination of body odour and cigarette smoke would be unbearable.

'I'm not smoking,' said the man, 'yet.' And placed a cigarette between his lips, his lighter ready in the other hand.

Nearly two thousand miles to Nairobi, thought Manfred, with his stomach starting to heave.

33

'Terry darling, why on earth should I go all the way out to Kitchenerville to watch a lot of savages prancing around?'

'As a favour to me, Joy,' Terry pleaded into the telephone.

'It means mucking up my whole weekend. I've got rid of the kids to their grandmother, I've got a copy of *A Small Town in Germany* and I was going to have a lovely time reading and—'

'Please, Joy, you're my last hope.'

'What time will we be home?' Joy was weakening. Terry sensed her advantage and pressed forward ruthlessly.

'You might meet a lovely man out at the mine, and he'll sweep you—'

'No, thanks.' Joy had been divorced a little over a year ago, some people took longer than others to recover. 'I've had lovely men in big fat chunks.'

'Oh, Joy, you can't sit around moping for ever. Come on, I'll pick you up in half an hour.'

Joy sighed with resignation. 'Damn you, Terry Steyner.'

'Half an hour,' said Terry and hung up before she could change her mind.

'I'm playing golf. It's Saturday, and I'm playing golf,' said Doctor Daniel Stander stubbornly.

'You remember when I drove all the way to Bloemfontein to—' Rod began, and Dan interrupted quickly.

'All right, all right, I remember. You don't have to bring that up again.'

'You owe me plenty, Stander,' Rod reminded him. 'All I am asking is one of your lousy Saturday afternoons. Is that so much?'

'I can't let the boys down. It's a long-standing date.' Dan wriggled to escape.

'I've already phoned Ben. It will be a pleasure for him to take your place.'

There was a long gloomy silence, then Dan asked, 'What's this bird like?'

'She's a beautiful, rich nymphomaniac, and she owns a brewery.'

'Yeah! Yeah!' said Dan sarcastically. 'All right, I'll do it. But I hereby declare all obligations and debts to you fully discharged.'

'I'll give you a written receipt,' Rod agreed.

Dan was still sulking when the Daimler came up the drive and parked in the front of the Mine Club. He and Rod were standing at the Ladies' Bar, watching for the arrival of their guests.

Dan had just ordered his third beer.

'Here they come,' said Rod.

'Is that them?' Dan's depression lifted magically as he peered through the coloured-glass windows. The chauffeur was letting the two ladies out of the Daimler. They were both in floral sack suits and dark glasses.

'That's them.'

'Jesus!' said Dan with rare approval. 'Which one is mine?'

'The blonde.'

'Ha!' Dan grinned for the first time since their meeting. 'Why the hell are we standing here?'

'Why indeed?' asked Rod, his stomach was tied up in knots that twisted tighter as he went down the front steps toward Terry.

'Mrs Steyner. I'm so glad you could come.' With a wild lift of elation he saw it was still there, he had not imagined it, it was there in her eyes and her smile.

'Thank you, Mr Ironsides.' She was like a schoolgirl again, uncertain of herself, flustered.

'I'd like you to meet Mrs Albright. Joy, this is Rodney Ironsides.'

'Hello.' He smiled at her as he clasped her hand. 'It's gin time, I think.'

Dan was waiting at the bar for them, and Rod made the introductions.

'Joy is so excited at the chance of watching the dancing,' said Terry as they sat down on the bar stools. 'She's been looking forward to it for days.' And for an instant Joy looked stunned.

'You'll love it,' agreed Dan moving in to take up a position at Joy's elbow. 'I wouldn't miss it for anything.'

Joy was a tall slim girl with long straight golden hair that hung to her shoulders, her eyes were cool green but her mouth when she smiled was soft and warm. She smiled now full into Dan's eyes.

'Nor would I,' she said, and with relief Rod knew he could devote all his attention to Terry Steyner. Joy Albright would be more than adequately looked after. He ordered drinks, and all four of them promptly lost further interest in tribal dancing.

At one stage Rod told Terry Steyner, 'I am going up to Johannesburg this evening. There is no point in your unfortunate chauffeur sit around all afternoon. Let him go, and I'll take you home.'

'Good,' Terry agreed immediately. 'Would you tell him, please?'

The next time Rod looked at his watch it was half past three.

'Good Lord!' he exclaimed. 'If we don't hurry, it will be all over.' Reluctantly Joy and Dan, who had their heads close together, drew apart.

The overflow from the amphitheatre pressed about them, a merry jostling throng, all inhibitions long since evaporated in the primeval excitement of the dance, much like the crowd at a bull ring.

Rod and Dan ran interference for the girls, ploughing a path through the main gateway and down to their reserved seats in the front row. All four of them were laughing and flushed by the time they were seated, the excitement about them was infectious and the liquor had heightened their sensibilities.

An expectant hum of voices.

'The Shangaans!' And the audience craned towards the entrance from which pranced a dozen drummers, their long wooden drums hung on rawhide straps about their necks, they took up stations around the circular earthen stage.

Tap, tap. Tap, tap – from one of the drummers, and silence gripped the ampitheatre.

Tap, tap. Tap, tap. Naked, except for their brief loin cloths, stooped over the drums that they clasped between their knees, they began to lay down the rhythm of the dance. It was a broken, disturbing beat, that jerked and twitched like a severed nerve. A compelling, demanding sound, the pulse of a continent and a people.

Then came the dancers, shuffling, row upon row, head-dresses dipping and rustling, the animal tail kilts swirling, war rattles at the wrists and ankles, black muscles already oiled with the sweat of excitement, coming in slowly rank upon majestic rank, moving as though the drums were pumping life into them.

A shrill blast on a duiker horn and the ranks whirled like dry leaves in a wind, they fell again into a new pattern, and through the opening in their midst came a single gigantic figure.

'Big King!' The name blew like a sigh through the audience, and immediately the drums changed their rhythm. Faster, demanding, and the dancers hissed in their throats a sound like storm surf rushing up a stony beach.

Big King flung his arms wide, braced on legs like black marble columns, his head thrown back. He sang a single word of command, shrilling it, and in instantaneous response every right knee was brought up to the level of the chest. Half a second's pause and then two hundred horny bare feet stamped down simultaneously with a crash that shook the amphitheatre to its foundations. The Shangaans began to dance, and reality was gone in the moving, charging, swirling, retreating ranks.

Once Rod tore his eyes from the spectacle. Terry Steyner was sitting forward on the bench, eyes sparkling, lips slightly parted, completely lost in the erotic turmoil and barbaric splendour of it.

Joy and Dan had a firm hold on each others' hands, their shoulders and the outside of their thighs were pressed tightly together, and Rod was stabbed by a painful thrust of envy.

Afterwards, back in the Ladies' Bar of the Club, there was very little conversation but they were all of them tensed up, restless, moved by strange undercurrents and interplays of primitive desires and social restraints.

'Well,' said Rod at last, 'if I am to get you two ladies back to Johannesburg at a decent hour—'

Dan and Joy spoke together.

'Don't worry, Rod, I'll—'

'Dan says he will—' Then they stopped and grinned at each other sheepishly.

'I take it that Dan has suddenly remembered that he has to go to Johannesburg this evening also, and he has offered to give you a lift?' asked Rod dryly, and they laughed in confirmation.

'It looks as though we are on our own, Mrs Steyner.' Rod turned to Terry.

'I'll trust you,' said Terry.

'If you do that, you're crazy,' said Dan.

Outside the Maserati, darkness was falling swiftly. The horizon blending into the black sky, isolated lights winking at them out of the surrounding veld.

Rod switched on the headlights, and the instrument panel glowed softly, turning the interior into a warm secluded place, isolating them from the world. The wind whispered, and the tyres and the engine hummed a gentle intimate refrain.

Terry Steyner sat with her legs curled up under her, cuddled into the soft maroon leather of the bucket seat. She was staring ahead down the path of the headlights, and she seemed withdrawn and yet very close. Every few minutes Rod would take his eyes from the road and study her profile briefly. He did so again, and this time she met his gaze frankly.

'You realize what is happening?' she asked.

'Yes,' he answered as frankly.

'You know how dangerous it could be for you?'

'And you.'

'No, not me. I am invulnerable. I am a Hirschfeld – but you, it could destroy you.'

Rod shrugged.

'If we counted the consequences before very action, nobody would do anything.'

'Have you thought that I might be a spoiled little rich girl amusing myself? I might do this all the time.'

'You might,' Rod agreed. They were silent for a long while, then Terry spoke again.

'Rod?' she used his given name for the first time.

'Yes?'

'I don't, you know, I really don't.'

'I guessed that.'

'Thank you.' She opened her bag. 'I need a cigarette. I feel as though I'm standing poised on the edge of a cliff and I've got this terrible compulsion to hurl myself over the edge.'

'Light me one, Terry.'

'You need one also?'

'Badly.'

They smoked in silence again, both of them staring ahead,

then Terry rolled down the window and flicked the cigarette butt away.

'You've got the job, you know.' All day she had wanted to tell him, it had been bubbling inside her. Watching his face, she saw his lips stiffen, his eyes crease into slits.

'Did you hear me?' she asked at last, and he braked the Maserati, swinging it off onto the shoulder of the road. He pulled on the hand brake and turned to face her.

'Terry, what did you say?'

'I said, you've got the job.'

'What job?' he demanded harshly.

'Pops signed the instruction this morning. You'll receive it on Monday. You're the new General Manger of the Sonder Ditch.' She wanted to go on and say – *and I got it for you. I made Pops give it to you.*

I never will, she promised, I will never spoil it for him. He must believe he won it fairly, not as my gift.

34

It was Saturday night, the big night in Dump City.

The Blaauberg Mine was the older producer on the Kitchener-ville field. There were sections of its property which had been worked out completely, and the old waste dumps were now abandoned and overgrown. Among the scrub and head-high weed in the valleys between these man-made hills had grown up a shanty town. Dump City, the inhabitants had named it. The buildings were made of discarded galvanized iron sheets and flattened oil drums, there was no sanitation or running water.

Remote from the main roads, the residential communities of the neighbouring mines or the town of Kitchenerville, hidden among the dumps, accessible only to a man on foot, never visited by members of the South African Constabulary, it was ideally suited to the purposes for which its three hundred permanent inhabitants had chosen it.

Every one of the shacks was a shebeen, a clip joint where watered liquor was sold at inflated prices, where dagga* was freely obtainable and where men from the surrounding mines gathered to carouse.

They came not so much for the liquor. Each of the mine hostels had a bar where a full range of liquor was on sale a club prices. Very few of them came for the dagga. There was little addiction amongst these well-fed, hard-worked and contented men. What they came for were the women.

Five mines in the area, each employing ten or twelve thousand men. Here at Dump City were two hundred women, the only available women within twenty miles. It was not necessary for the young ladies of Dump City to solicit custom, even the fat, the withered, the toothless, could behave like queens.

Big King came down the path that skirted the mine dump. With him were two dozen of his fellow tribesmen, big Shangaans

* Marijuana.

472

wearing their regalia, carrying their fighting sticks and still tensed up from the dancing. They came at a trot, Big King leading them. They were singing, not the gentle planting or courting melodies, not the work chant nor the song of welcome.

They were singing the fighting songs, those their forefathers had sung when they carried the spear in search of cattle and slaves. The driving inflammatory rhythm, the fiercely patriotic words wrought so mightily on the delicate susceptibilities of the average Shangaan that the company had found it necessary to ban the singing of these songs.

Like a Scot hearing the pipes, when a Shangaan began singing these warlike chants, he was ready for violence.

The song ended as Big King led them down to the nearest shanty, and pushed aside the sacking that acted as a door. He stooped through the opening, and his comrades crowded in behind him.

A brittle electric silence fell on the large room. The air was so thick with smoke, and the light from the suspended hurricane lamps so feeble, that it was impossible to see the far wall. The room was filled with men, forty or fifty of them, the smell of humanity and bad liquor was solid. Among this press of men were half a dozen bright spots of the girls' dresses, but with their curiosity aroused by the singing more girls were coming through from the interleading doorways at the back, some of them had men with them and were still shrugging into their clothing. When they saw Big King and his warriors in full war kit, they fell silent and watchful.

At Big King's shoulder one of his Shangaans whispered:

'Basutos! They are all Basutos!' He was right, Big King saw that they were all men of that mountainous little independent state.

Big King started forward, swaggering just enough to make his leopard tail kilt swing and swirl and the heron feathers of his headdress rustle. He reached the primitive bar counter.

'Flying Bird,' he told the crone who owned the house, and she placed a bottle of Eagle Brandy on the counter.

Big King half filled a tumbler, conscious that every eye was on him, and drained it.

Slowly he turned and surveyed the room.

'What is it,' he asked in a voice that carried to every corner, 'that sits on top of a mountain and scratches its fleas. Is it a baboon, or a Basuto?'

A roar of delight went up from his Shangaans.

'A Basuto!' they shouted, crowding forward to the bar, while a growl and a mutter went up from the rest of the room.

'What is it,' shouted a Basuto jumping to his feet, 'that has feathers on its head and crows from a dungheap? Is it a rooster, or a Shangaan?'

Without seeming to move, Big King picked up the bottle of Eagle Brandy and hurled it. With a crack it burst against the Basuto's forehead and he went over backwards taking two of his companions with him.

The old crone snatched up her cash register and ran as the room exploded into violent movement.

There was not enough space in which to use the fighting sticks, Big King realized, so he lifted a section of the bar counter off its trestles and holding it in front of him like the blade of a bulldozer, he charged across the room, flattening all and everything before him.

The crash of breaking furniture and the yelp and squeal of men being struck down drove Big King beyond the frontiers of sanity into the red atavistic fury of the berserker.

Basuto is also one of the fighting tribes of the N'guni group. These wiry mountaineers rushed into the conflict with the same savage joy as the Shangaans, a conflict that raged and roared out of the single room to engulf the entire population of Dump City.

One of the girls, her dress ripped from her back so she was left with only a tattered pair of bloomers, had climbed on top of the remains of the bar counter from where, with her big melon breasts swinging in the lamp light, she shrilled that peculiar ululation that Bantu women used to goad their menfolk into battle frenzy. A dozen of the other girls joined in, trilling, squealing, and the sound was too much for Big King.

With the bar top held ahead of him he charged straight through the flimsy wall of the shack, bursting it open like a paper bag, the roof sagged down wearily, and Big King raged on unchecked down the narrow dirt street, striking down any man who crossed his path, scattering chickens and yelping dogs, roaring like a bull gorilla.

He turned at the end of the encampment and came back, his frustration mounting as he found the street deserted except for a few prostrate bodies, through the gaping hole in the wall he entered the shebeen once more to find that here also the fighting had died down. A few of the participants were crawling, or moaning as they lay on the carpet of broken glass.

Big King glared about him, seeking a further outlet for his wrath.

'King Nkulu!' The girl was still on the trestle table, her eyes bright with excitement, her legs trembling with it.

Big King let out another roar, and hurled the bar top from him. It clattered against the far wall and Big King started towards her.

'You are a lion!' She shrieked encouragement at him, and she took one of her big black velvety breasts in each hand and pointed them at him, squeezing them together, shaking with excitement.

'Eat me!' she screamed, as Big King swept her off the table and lifting her high, ran with her out into the night. Carrying her into the scrub below the mine dumps, holding her easily with one arm, ripping the leopard-tail kilt from his own waist as he ran.

35

It was Saturday night in Paris also, but there were men who were still working, for there were lights burning in the upstairs rooms of one of the big Embassies in the rue Royale.

The fat man who had been the host in the gambling establishment in Johannesburg was now the guest. He sat at ease in a leather club easy, his corpulence and the steel-grey hair at his temples giving him dignity. His face heavy, tanned, intelligent. His eyes glittery and hard as the diamond on his finger.

He was listening intently to a man of about the same age as himself who stood before a projected image on a screen that covered one wall of the room. There was that in the man's bearing and manner that marked him as a scholar, he was speaking now, addressing himself directly to the listener in the easy chair, pointing with a marker to the screen beside him.

'You see here a plan of the working of the five producing gold mines of the Kitchenerville fields in relation to each other.' He touched the screen with the marker. 'Thornfontein, Blaauberg, Tweefontein, Deep Gold Levels and Sonder Ditch.'

The man in the chair nodded. 'I have seen and studied this diagram before.'

'Good, then you will know that the Sonder Ditch property sits in the centre of the field. It has common boundaries with the other four mines and here,' he tapped the screen again, 'it is intersected by the massive serpentine dyke which they call the Big Dipper.'

Again the fat man nodded.

'It is for these reasons we have selected the Sonder Ditch as the trigger point.' The lecturer touched a button on the wall panel and the image on the screen changed.

'Now, here is something you have not seen before.'

The man in the chair crouched forward.

'What is it?'

'It is an underground map based on the borehole results of the five companies who have been exploring the ground to the east of the Big Dipper. These results have been pooled and interpreted by some of the finest brains in the fields of geology and hydrophysics. You have here a carefully considered representation of exactly what lies on the far side of the Big Dipper fault.'

The big man moved uncomfortably in his chair.

'It's a monster!'

'Yes, a monster. Lying just beyond the fault is an underground lake, no, that is not the correct word. Let us call it an underground sea, the size of, say, Lake Eyrie. The water is held in a vast sponge of porous dolomite rock.'

'My God.' For the first time the fat man had lost his poise. 'If this is right, why don't the mining companies arrive at the same conclusion and keep well away from it?'

'Because,' the lecturer switched off the image and the overhead lights came on, 'because in their highly competitive attitude none of them has access to the findings of the others. It is only when all the results are studied that the picture becomes clear.'

'How did your Government come to be in possession of *all* the results?' demanded the fat man.

'That is not important.' The lecturer was brusque, impatient of the interruption. 'We are also in possession of the findings of a certain Dr Peter Wessels who is at present head of a research team in Rock Mechanics based on the Sonder Ditch mine property. It is Company classified information and consists of a paper that Dr Peter Wessels has written on the shatter patterns and stresses of rock. His researches are directly related to the Ventersdorp quartzites which comprise the country rock of the Sonder Ditch workings.'

The lecturer picked up a pamphlet from his desk.

'I will not weary you by asking you to wade through its highly technical findings. Instead I will give it to you in capsule form. Dr Wessels arrives at the conclusion that a column of Ventersdorp quartzite 120 feet thick would shatter under a side pressure of 4000 pounds per square inch.'

The lecturer dropped the pamphlet back on the desk.

'As you know, by law, the gold mining companies are bound to leave a barrier of solid rock 120 feet thick along their boundaries. That is all that separates one mine's working from another, just that wall of rock. You understand?'

'Of course. It is very simple.'

'Simple? Yes, it is simple! This Dr Steyner, over whom you have control, will instruct the new General Manager of the Sonder Ditch to drive a tunnel through the Big Dipper dyke. The drive will puncture the vast underground reservoir and the water will run back and flood the entire Sonder Ditch workings. Once they are flooded, the pressure delivered by a 6000-foot head of water at the lower levels will be in excess of 4000 pounds per square inch. That is sufficient to burst the rock walls, and flood the Thornfontein, the Blaauberg, Deep Gold Levels and Tweefontein gold mines.'

'The entire Kitchenerville gold fields would be effectively and permanently put out of production. The consequences for the economy of the Republic of South Africa would be catastrophic.'

The fat man was visibly shaken.

'Why do you want to do it?' he asked, shaking his head in awe.

'My colleague here,' the lecturer indicated a man who was sitting quietly in one corner, 'will explain that to you presently.'

'But – people!' the fat man protested. 'There will be people down there when it burst, thousands of them.'

The lecturer smiled, raising one eyebrow. 'If I were to tell you that six thousand men would drown, would you refuse to proceed, and forfeit the million-dollar payment my Government has offered you?'

The fat man looked down, embarrassed, and muttered barely audibly. 'No.'

The lecturer chuckled. 'Good! Good! However, you may salve you aching conscience by assuring yourself that we do not expect more than forty or fifty fatalities from the flooding. Naturally, those men actually working on the face will be killed. But that tremendous volume of water under immense pressure should make it a merciful death. For the rest of them, the mine can be evacuated swiftly enough to allow them excellent chances of survival. The surrounding mines will have days to evacuate before the water pressure builds up sufficiently to burst through the boundary walls.'

There was silence then in the room for nearly a minute.

'Have you any questions?'

The fat man shook his head.

'Very well, in that case I will leave it to my colleague to

478

complete the briefing. He will explain the necessity for this operation, will arrange the terms of payment and conditions upon which you will proceed.' The lecturer gathered up the pamphlet and other papers from the desk. 'It remains only for me to wish you good luck.' He chuckled again and left the room quickly.

The little man who up until them had remained silent, suddenly bounced out of his chair and began pacing up and down the wall-to-wall carpeting. He spoke rapidly, shooting occasional sideways glances at his audience, his bald head shining in the fluorescent lighting, wriggling his moustache like rabbit whiskers, puffing nervously at his cigarette.

'Reasons first. I'll make it short and sweet, right? The South Africans and the Frogs have got together. They're here in Paris now cooking up mischief. We know what they're up to, they're going to launch an all-out attack on my Government's currency. Gold price increase, you know. Very complicated and very nasty for us, right? They might just be able to do it, South Africa is the world's biggest gold producer. With the Frogs helping her, they might just be able to force an increase.'

He stopped in front of the fat man and thrust out an accusing finger.

'Are we going to sit back and let them have a free run? No, sir! We are going to throw down our own curve ball! In three months time the Syndicate will be ready to attack. At that precise moment we will kick the chair out from under the South Africans by cutting their gold production in half. We will flood the Kitchenerville goldfields and the attack will fizzle out like a damp squib, right?'

'As simple as that?' asked the fat man.

'As simple as that!' The bald head nodded vigorously. 'Now, my next duty is to make clear to you that the agreed million dollars is *all* the reward you receive. Neither you nor your agents may indulge in any financial transactions that might, in retrospect, show that this was a planned operation, right?'

'Right.' The fat man nodded.

'You give your assurance that you will not deal in any of the shares of the companies involved?'

'You have my solemn word.' The fat man told him earnestly, and not for the first time in his life reflected how easily and painlessly a promise could be given.

With the assistance of the three men who had watched Manfred Steyner that night at the gambling club in Johannesburg, he intended launching a bear offensive on the stock exchanges of the world.

On the day that they drilled into the Big Dipper dyke he and his partners would sell millions of the shares of the five mining companies for one of the biggest financial killings in the history of money.

'We are agreed then.' The bald head bobbed. 'Now, as for this Dr Steyner, we have had a screening and personality analysis and we believe that, despite the secure hold you have on his loyalties, he would jib at giving the order to drive on the Big Dipper if he were aware of the consequences. Therefore we have prepared a second geological report,' he produced from his brief case a thick manila folder, 'incorporating those figures which he will recognize. In other words the drilling results of the C.R.C. exploration teams, but the other figures are fictitious. This report purports to prove the existence of a fabulously rich gold reef beyond the fault.' He crossed to the fat man and handed him the folder. 'Take it. It will help you convince Dr Steyner, and he in turn to convince the new General Manager of the Sonder Ditch gold mine.'

'You have been thorough,' said the fat man.

'We try to give a satisfactory service to our customers,' said the bald man.

36

The game was five card stud poker, and there were two big winners at the table, Manfred Steyner and the Algerian.

Manfred had timed his arrival in Paris to ensure himself an uninterrupted weekend before the rest of the delegates came in on the Monday morning flight.

He had checked in at the Hotel George Cinq on Saturday afternoon, bathed and rested for three hours until eight in the evening, then he had set out for the Club Chat Noir by taxi.

He had been playing now for five hours, and a steady succession of strong cards had pushed his winnings up to a formidable sum. It lay piled in front of him, a fruit salad of garish French bank notes. Across the table sat the Algerian, a slim dark-skinned Arab with toffee eyes and a silky black moustache. His teeth were very white against the creamy brown skin. He wore a turtle-neck shirt in pink silk, and a linen jacket of baby blue. With long brown fingers he kept smoothing and stacking his own pile of bank notes.

A girl sat on the arm of his chair, an Arab girl in a skin-tight gold trouser suit. Her hair was shiny black and hung onto her shoulders, her eyes were disconcertingly level as she watched Manfred.

'Ten thousand.' Manfred's voice was explosive, like that of a teutonic drillmaster. He was betting on his fourth card which had just been dealt to him. He and the Algerian were the remaining players in the game. The others had folded their hands and were sitting back watching with the casual interest of men no longer involved.

The Algerian's eyes narrowed slightly and the girl leaned down to whisper softly in his ear. He shook his head, annoyed, and drew on his cigarette. He had a pair of queens and a six showing and he leaned forward to study Manfred's cards.

The dealer's voice prodded. 'The bet is ten thousand francs, from four, five, seven of clubs. Possible straight flush.'

'Bet or drop,' said one of the uncommitted players. 'You're wasting time.'

The Algerian flashed him a venomous glance.

'Bet,' he said, and counted out ten thousand-franc notes into the pool.

'*Carte.*' The dealer slid a card face down in front of each of them. Quickly the Algerian lifted one corner of his card with his thumb, glanced at it and then closed the face.

Manfred sat very still, the card lying inches from his right hand. His face was pale, calm, but he was seething internally. Far from a possible straight flush, Manfred was holding four, five, seven of clubs and the eight of hearts. A six was the only card that could improve his hand and one six was already showing among the Algerian's cards. His chances were remote.

His lower belly and loins were tight and hot with excitement, his chest constricted. He drew out the sensation, wanting it to last for ever.

'Pair of queens still to bet,' murmured the dealer.

'Ten thousand.' The Algerian pushed the notes forward.

'He has found another queen,' thought Manfred, 'but he is uncertain of my flush or straight.'

Manfred placed his smooth white hand over his fifth card, cupping it. He lifted it.

'Table,' said Manfred calmly, and there was a gasp and rustle from the watchers. The girl's hand tightened on the Algerian's sleeve, she stared with hatred into Manfred's face.

'The gentleman has made a table bet,' intoned the croupier. 'House rules. Any player may bet the entire stake he has upon the table.' He reached across and began to count the notes in front of Manfred.

Minutes later he announced the total. 'Two hundred and twelve thousand francs.' He looked across at the Algerian. 'It is now up to you to bet against the possible straight flush.'

The girl whispered urgently into the Arab's ear, but he snapped a single word at her and she recoiled. He looked about the room, as if seeking guidance, then he lifted and examined his hole cards again.

Suddenly his face hardened, and he looked steadily across at Manfred.

'Call!' he blurted, and Manfred's clenched right hand fell open upon the table.

The Arab faced his hand. Three queens. The whole room looked expectantly at Manfred.

He flicked over his last card. Two of diamonds. His hand was worthless.

With a birdlike cry of triumph the Algerian leaped from his seat and reaching across the table began raking Manfred's stake with both arms towards him.

Manfred stood up from the table, and the Arab girl grinned maliciously at him, taunting him in Arabic. He turned quickly away and almost ran down the steps that led to the cloakrooms. Twenty minutes later, feeling weak and slightly dizzy, Manfred slipped into the backseat of a Citroen taxi cab.

'George Cinq,' he told the driver. As he entered the lobby of the hotel he saw a tall figure rise from one of the leather armchairs and follow him across to the lifts. Shoulder to shoulder they stepped into the lift and as the doors slid closed the tall man spoke.

'Welcome to Paris, Dr Steyner.'

'Thank you, Andrew. I presume you have come to give me my instructions?'

'That is correct. He wishes to see you tomorrow at ten o'clock. I will call for you.'

37

It was Saturday night in Kitchenerville and in the men's bar of
the Lord Kitchener Hotel the daily-paid men from the five gold
mines were bellying up to the counter three deep.

The public dance had been in progress for three hours. At
tables along the veranda the women-folk sat primly sipping their
port and lemonade. Although they all were admirably ignoring
the absence of the men, yet a constant and merciless vigil was
kept on the door to the men's bar. Most of the wives already
had the automobile keys safely in their handbags.

In the dining-hall, cleared of its furniture and sprinkled liber-
ally with french chalk, the local four-piece band who played
under the unlikely name of the 'Wind Dogs' launched without
preliminaries into a lively rendition of 'Die Ou Kraal Liedjie',
and from the men's bar, in various stages of inebriation, answering the call to arms came the troops.

Many of them had shed their jackets, the knots of their ties
had slipped, their voices were boisterous and legs were a little
unsteady as they led their women onto the dance floor and
immediately showed to which school of the dance they
belonged.

There was the cavalry squadron which tucked partner under
one arm, very much like a lance, and charged. At the other end of
the scale were those who plodded grimly around the perimeter,
looking neither left nor right, speaking to no one, not even their
partners. Then there were the sociables who reeled about the
floor, red in the face, their movements completely unrelated to
the music, shouting to their friends and attempting to pinch any
feminine posterior that came within range. Their unpredictable
progress interfered with the evolutions of the dedicated.

The dedicated took up their positions in the centre of the floor
and twisted. A half dozen years previously the twist had swept
like an Asian 'flu epidemic through the world and then faded

out. Gone, forgotten, except in places like Kitchenerville. Here it had been taken and firmly entrenched into the social culture of the community.

Even in this stronghold of the twist, there was one master. 'Johnny Delange? Gott man, but he can twist, hey!' they murmured with awe.

With the sinuous erotic movements of an erect cobra, Johnny was twisting with Hettie. His shiny rayon suit caught the light and the lace ruffles of his shirt fluttered at this throat. There was a fierce grin of pleasure on his hawk features, and the jewelled buckles of his pointed Italian shoes twinkled as he danced.

A big girl with copper hair and creamy skin, Hettie was light on her feet. She had a tiny waist and a swelling regal bottom under the emerald-green skirt. She laughed as she danced, a full healthy laugh to match her body.

The two of them moved with the expertise of a couple who have danced together often. Hettie anticipated each of Johnny's movements, and he grinned his approval at her.

From the veranda Davy Delange watched them. He stood in the shadows, clutching a tankard of beer, a squat, lonely figure. When another dancing couple cut off his view of Hettie's luscious revolving buttocks he would exclaim with irritation and move restlessly.

The music ended and the dancers spilled out onto the veranda, laughing and breathless, mopping streaming faces; girls squealing and giggling as the men led them to their seats, deposited them and then headed for the bar.

'See you.' Johnny left Hettie reluctantly, he would have liked to stay with her, but he was sensitive about what the boys would say if he spent the whole evening with his wife.

He was absorbed into the masculine crowd, to join their banter and loud laughter. He was deeply involved in a discussion of the merits of the new Ford Mustang, which he was considering buying, when Davy nudged him.

'It's Constantine!' he whispered, and Johnny looked up quickly. Constantine was a Greek immigrant, a stoper on the Blaauberg Mine. He was a big strong black-haired individual with a broken nose. Johnny had broken his nose for him about ten months previously. As a bachelor Johnny would fight him on the average of once a month, nothing serious, just a semi-friendly punch-up.

However, Constantine could not understand that nowadays Johnny was forbidden by his brand new wife from indulging in casual exchanges of fisticuffs. He had developed the erroneous theory that Johnny Delange was afraid of him.

He was coming down the bar room now, holding his glass in his massive hairy right hand with the little finger extended genteely. On his hip rested his other hand and he minced along with a simpering smile on his blue-jowled granite-textured features. Stopping in front of the mirror to pat his hair into place, he winked at his cronies and then came on down to where Johnny stood. He paused and ogled Johnny heavily, fluttering his eyelids and wriggling his hips. His colleagues from the Blaauberg Mine were weak with laughter, gurgling merrily, hanging onto each other's shoulders.

Then with a bump and grind that raised another howl of laughter Constantine disappeared into the lavatories, to emerge minutes later and blow Johnny a kiss as he went back to join his friends. They plied liquor on the Greek in appreciation of his act. Johnny's smile was a little strained as he resumed the discussion on the Mustang's virtues.

Twenty minutes and half a dozen brandies later, Constantine repeated his little act again on the way to the latrine. His repertoire was limited.

'Hold it, Johnny,' whispered Davy. 'Let's go and sit on the veranda.'

'He's asking for it. I'm telling you!' Johnny's smile had disappeared.

'Come on, Johnny, man.'

'No, hell, they'll think I'm running. I can't go now.'

'You know what Hettie will say,' Davy warned him. For a moment longer Johnny hesitated.

'The hell with what Hettie says.' Johnny bunched his right fist with its array of gold rings as he moved down to Constantine and leaned beside him on the counter.

'Herby,' he called the barman, and when he had his attention he indicated the Greek. 'Please give the lady a port and lemonade.'

And the bystanders scattered for cover. Davy shot out of the door onto the veranda to report to Hettie.

'Johnny!' he gasped. 'He's fighting again.'

'Is he!' Hettie came to her feet like a red-headed Valkyrie. But her progress to the men's bar was delayed by the crowd of spectators that jammed the doorway and all the windows. The crowd was tiptoeing and climbing onto the chairs and tables for a better view, every thud or crash of breaking furniture was greeted with a roar of delight.

Hettie had her handbag clutched in her right hand, and like a jungle explorer hacking his way through the undergrowth with a machete, she opened a path for herself to the bar room door.

At the door she paused. The conflict had reached a critical stage. Among a litter of broken glass and shattered stools, Johnny and the Greek were circling each other warily, weaving and feinting, all their wits concentrated upon each other. Both of them were marked. The Greek was bleeding from his lip, a thin red ribbon of blood down his chin that dripped onto his shirt. Johnny had a shiny red swelling closing one eye. The crowd was silent, waiting.

'Johnny Delange!' Hettie's voice cracked like a mauser rifle fired from ambush. Johnny started guiltily, dropping his hands, half turning towards her as the Greek's fist crashed into the side of his head. Johnny spun from the blow, hit the wall and slid down quietly.

With a roar of triumph Constantine rushed forward to put the boots into Johnny's prostrate form, but he pitched forward to sprawl unconscious beside Johnny. Hettie had hit him with the water bottle snatched up from one of the table tops.

'Please help me get my husband to the car,' she appealed to the men around her, suddenly helpless and little-girlish.

She sat beside Davy in the front of the Monaco, fuming with anger.

Johnny lay at ease upon the back seat. He was snoring softly.

'Don't be angry, Hettie.' Davy was driving sedately.

'I've told him, not once, a hundred times.' Hettie's voice crackled like static. 'I told him I wouldn't put up with it.'

'It wasn't his fault. The Greek started it,' Davy explained softly and placed his hand on her leg.

'You stick up for him, just because he is your brother.'

'That's not true,' Davy soothed her, stroking her leg. 'You know how I feel about you, Hettie.'

487

'I don't believe you.' His hand was moving higher. 'You men are all the same. You all stick together.'

Her anger was fast solidifying into a burning resentment of Johnny Delange, one in which she was willing to take a calculated revenge. She knew that Davy's hand was no longer trying to comfort her and quench her anger. Before she married Johnny Delange, Hettie had had every opportunity to learn about men, and she had been an enthusiastic and receptive pupil. She placed no special importance on an act of the flesh, dispensing her favours as casually as someone might offer a cigarette-case around.

'Why not?' she thought. 'That will fix Mr Johnny Delange! Not all the way, of course, but just enough to get my own back on him.'

'No, Hettie. It's true – I tell you.' Davy's voice was husky, as he felt her knees fall apart under his hand. He touched the silky-smooth skin above her stocking top.

The Monaco slowed to almost walking pace, and it was ten minutes more before they reached the company-owned house on the outskirts of Kitchenerville.

In the back seat Johnny groaned. Immediately Davy's hand jerked back to the steering-wheel, and Hettie sat up in the seat, straightening her skirt.

'Help me get him inside,' she said, and her voice was shaky and her cheeks flushed. She was no longer angry.

38

They were both a little tipsy. They had stopped to celebrate Rod's promotion at the Sunnyside Hotel. They had sat side by side in one of the booths, drinking quickly, excitedly, laughing together, sitting close but not touching.

Terry Steyner could not remember when she had last behaved this way. It must have been all of ten years ago, her last term at Cape Town varsity, swigging draught beer in the 'Pig and Whistle' at Randall's Hotel and talking the most inane rubbish. All the matronly dignity that Manfred insisted she maintain was gone, she felt like a freshette on a first date with the captain of the rugby team.

'Let's get out of here,' Rod said suddenly, and she stood up unquestioningly. He took her arm down the stairs, and the light touch of his fingers tingled on her bare skin.

In the Maserati again she experienced the feeling of isolation from reality.

'How often do you see your daughter, Rod?' she asked as he settled into the seat beside her, and he glanced at her, surprised.

'Every Sunday.'

'Tomorrow?'

'Yes.'

'How old is she?'

'Nine next birthday.'

'What do you do with her?'

Rod pressed the starter.

'How do you mean?'

'Where do you take her, what do you do together?'

'We go rowing on Zoo Lake, or eat ice cream sundaes. If it's cold or raining we sit in the apartment and we play mah-jong.' He let in the clutch, and as they pulled away he added, 'She cheats.'

'The apartment?'

'I keep a hideaway in town.'

'Where?'

'I'll show you,' said Rod quietly.

She sat on the studio couch and looked about her with interest. She had not expected the obvious care that he had taken in furnishing the apartment. It was in wheatfield gold, chocolate brown and copper. There was a glorious glowing autumn landscape on the far wall that she recognized as a Dino Paravano.

She noticed a little ruefully how Rod stage-managed the lighting for full romantic effect, and then moved automatically to the liquor cabinet.

'Where is the bathroom?' Terry asked.

'Second left, down the passage.'

She lingered in the bathroom, opening the medicine cabinet like a thief. There were three toothbrushes hanging in the slots, and below them an aerosol can of 'Bidex'. Quickly she shut the cabinet. Feeling disturbed, not sure if it was jealousy or guilt at her own prying.

The bedroom door was open and so she could not help seeing the double bed as she went back to the lounge. She stood in front of the painting.

'I love his work,' she said.

'Not too photographic for your taste?'

'No. I love it.'

He gave her the drink and stood beside her, studying the painting. She tinkled the ice in her glass, and he turned towards her. The feeling of unreality was still holding Terry as she felt him take the glass from her hand.

She was conscious of his hands only, they were strong and very practised. They touched her shoulders, and then moved onto her back calmly. She felt a voluptuous shudder shake her whole body, and then his mouth came down over hers and the sense of unreality was complete. It was all warm and misty, and she let him take control.

She never knew how long afterwards she jerked back to complete, chilling reality. They were on the couch. She lay in his arms. The front of her slack suit was open to the waist and her bra was unhooked. His head was bowed over her and with a handful of thick springy hair she was directing his lips in their quest. His mouth was warm and sucky on her breast.

'I must be mad!' she gasped, and struggled violently from his arms. She was trembling with fright, horrified with herself. Nothing like this had ever happened to her before.

'This is madness!' Her eyes were great dark pools in her pale face, and her fingers were frantic as she buttoned her blouse. As the last button slipped into its hole, anger replaced her fright.

'How many women have you seduced on that couch, Rodney Ironsides?'

Rod stood up, reaching out a hand to reassure her.

'Don't touch me!' She stepped back. 'I want to go home!'

'I'll take you home, Terry. Just calm down. Nothing happened.'

'That's not your fault,' she blazed.

'No, it's not,' he agreed.

'If you had your way, you'd have—' she bit it off.

'Yes, I would have.' Rod nodded. 'But only if you wanted the same thing.'

She stared at him, starting to recover her temper and her control.

'I shouldn't have come up here, I know. It was asking for trouble, but please take me home now.'

39

The telephone woke Rod. He checked his wrist watch as he tottered naked and half asleep through to the lounge. Eight o'clock.

'Ironsides!' He yawned into the mouthpiece, and then came fully awake as he recognized her voice.

'Good morning, Rodney. How's your hangover?'

He had not expected to hear from her again.

'Just bearable.'

'I called to thank you for an amusing and – instructive evening.'

'Hark at the girl!' He grinned and scratched his chest. 'She changes with the wind. Last night I expected a bullet between the eyes.'

'Last night I got one big fright,' she admitted. 'It comes as a bit of a shock to discover suddenly that you are quite capable of acting the wanton. Not all the names I called you were meant.'

'I am sorry for my contribution to your distress,' Rod said.

'Don't be, you were very impressive.' Then quickly, changing the subject, 'You are picking up your daughter today?'

'Yes.'

'I'd like to meet her.'

'That could be arranged.' Rod was cautious.

'Does she like horses?'

'She's crazy about them.'

'Would you like to take her and me out to my stud farm on the Vaal river?'

Rod hesitated. 'Is it safe? I mean, being seen together?'

'It's my reputation, I'll look after it.'

'Fine!' Rod agreed. 'We'd love to visit your farm.'

'I'll meet you at your apartment. When?'

'Half past nine!'

Patti was still in her dressing-gown and she offered Rod her cheek casually to be pecked. There were curlers in her hair and from her eyes he could tell she'd had a late night.

'Hello, you're getting thin. Melly is dressing. Do you want some coffee? Your maintenance cheque was late again this month.' And she took a swipe at the spaniel pup as it squatted on the carpet. 'Damn dog pees all over the place. *Melanie.*' She raised her voice. 'Hurry up! Your Papa is here.'

'Hello, Daddy!' Melanie's voice shrieked delightedly from the interior of the apartment.

'Hello, baby.'

'You can't come in, Daddy, I haven't got any clothes on.'

'Well hurry up! I've come a million miles to see you.'

'Not a *million!*' You couldn't fool Melanie Ironsides.

'Did you say you wanted coffee? It's no trouble, it's made already.' Pattie led him through into the sitting-room.

'Thanks.'

'How are things?' she asked as she filled a cup and gave it to him.

'They've made me General Manager of the Sonder Ditch.' He could not prevent himself, it was too good. He had to boast.

Patti looked at him, startled.

'You're joking!' she accused, and then he saw her mind beginning to work like a cash register.

He almost laughed out loud. 'No. It's true.'

'God!' She sat down limply. 'It will nearly *double* your salary.'

He looked at her dispassionately, and not for the first time felt a great wash of relief as he realized he was no longer shackled to her.

'It's usual to offer congratulations,' he prompted her.

'You don't deserve it.' She was angry now. 'You are a selfish, philandering bastard, Rodney Ironsides, you don't deserve the good things that keep happening to you.' He had cheated her. She could have been the General Manager's wife, first lady of the goldfields. Now she was a divorcée, stuck with a miserable four fifty a month. It had seemed good before, but not now.

'I hope you will have enough conscience to make a suitable adjustment for Melanie and me. We are entitled to a share.'

The door burst open and Melanie Ironsides arrived at a gallop to wrap herself around Rod's neck. She had long blonde hair and green eyes.

'I got nine out of ten for spelling!'

'You're not clever, you're a genius. Also you're beautiful.'

'Will you carry me down to the car, Daddy?'

'What's wrong? Your legs in plaster?'

'Please, please, pretty please times three.'

Patti interrupted the love feast.

'Have you got your jersey, young lady?' And Melanie flew.

'I'll have her back before seven,' said Rod.

'You haven't answered my question.' Patti was surly. 'Do we get a share?'

'Yes, of course,' said Rod. 'The same big juicy four fifty you've had all along.'

They had been in Rod's apartment ten minutes when the door-bell announced Terry's arrival. She was in jeans and a checked shirt with her hair in a plait, and she greeted Rod self-consciously. When he introduced her to Melanie, she did not look much older than his daughter.

The two girls summed each other up solemnly. Melanie suddenly very demure and refined, and Rod was relieved to see that Terry had the good sense not to gush over the child.

They were in the Maserati and half way to the village of Parys on the Vaal River before Melanie had completed her microscopic scrutiny of Terry.

'Can I come up front and sit on your lap?' she asked at last.

'Yes, of course.' Terry was hard put to conceal her relief and pleasure. Melanie scrambled over the seat and settled on Terry's lap.

'You are pretty,' Melanie gave her considered opinion.

'Thank you. So are you.'

'Are you Daddy's girl friend?' Melanie demanded. Terry glanced across at Rod, then burst out laughing.

'Almost,' she gurgled, and then all three of them were laughing.

They laughed often that day. It was a day of sunshine and laughter.

Terry and Rod walked together with fingers almost touching through the green paddocks along with willow-lined bank of the Vaal. Melanie ran ahead of them shrieking with glee at the antics of the foals.

They went up to the stables where Melanie fed sugar lumps

to a winner of the Cape Metropolitan Handicap and then kissed his velvety muzzle.

They swam in the pool beside the elegant white-washed homestead, laughter mingling with the splashes, and when they drove back to Johannesburg in the evening Melanie curled in exhausted slumber on Terry's lap, her head cushioned on Terry's bosom.

Terry waited in the Maserati while Rod carried the sleeping child up to her mother, and when he returned and slipped into the driver's seat, Terry murmured, 'My car is at your apartment. You'll have to take me with you.'

Neither of them spoke until they were back in Rod's sitting-room. Then he said, 'Thank you for a wonderful day.' And he took her to his chest and kissed her.

In the darkness she lay pressed to his sleeping body, clinging to him, as though he might be taken from her. She had never felt such intensity of emotion before, it was a compound of awed wonder and gratitude. She had just been admitted to a new level of human experience she had never suspected existed.

The sheets were still damp. She felt bruised internally, aching, a slow voluptuous pulse of pain that she cherished.

Lightly she touched his body, not wanting to wake him, running her fingertips through the coarse curls that covered his chest, marvelling still at the infinity that separated this from what she had known before.

She shuddered with almost unbearable pleasure as she remembered his voice describing her body to her, making her proud of it for the first time in her life. She remembered the words he had used to tell her exactly what they were doing together, and the feel of his hands, so gentle, sure, so lovingly possessive upon her.

He was so unashamed, taking such obvious joy in her, that the reserves which the barren years of her marriage had placed in her mind were swept away and she was able to go with Rodney Ironsides beyond the storm into that tranquil state where mind and body are completely at peace.

She became aware of him awakening beside her, and she touched his face, his lips and his eyes with her fingertips.

'Thank you,' she whispered, and he seemed to understand, for he took her head and drew it gently down into the hollow of his shoulder.

'Sleep now,' he told her softly, and she closed her eyes and lay very still and quiet beside him, but she did not sleep. She would not miss one moment of this experience.

40

Rod's letter of appointment lay on his desk when he arrived at his office at seven-thirty on the Monday morning.

He sat down and lit a cigarette. Then he began to read it slowly, savouring each word.

'Duly instructed by the Board of Directors,' it began, and ended, 'it remains only to tender the congratulations of the Board, and to voice their confidence in your ability.'

Dimitri came through from his office, distracted.

'Hey! Rod! Christ what a start to the week! We've got a fault in the main high voltage cable on 90 level, and—'

'Don't come squealing to me,' Rod cut him short. 'I'm not the Underground Manager.'

Dimitri gaped at him, taken by surprise.

'What the hell, have they fired you?'

'Next best thing,' said Rod and flipped the letter across the desk. 'Look what the bastards have done to me.'

Dimitri read and then whooped;

'My God, Rod! My God!' He shot down the passage to carry the news to the other line managers. Then they were all in his office, shaking his hand. He judged most of their reactions as favourable, though occasionally he detected a false note. A twinge of envy here, one there who had recently had his ears burned by the Ironsides tongue, and an incompetent who knew his job was now in danger. The phone rang. Rod answered it, his expression changed and he cleared his office with a peremptory wave.

'Hirschfeld here.'

'Morning, Mr Hirschfeld.'

'Well, you've got your chance, Ironsides.'

'I'm grateful for it.'

'I want to see you. I'll give you today to sort yourself out. Tomorrow morning at nine o'clock, my office at Reef Buildings.'

'I'll be there.'

'Good.'

Rod hung up, and the day dissolved into a welter of activity and reorganization, constantly interrupted by a stream of well-wishers. He was still running the Underground Manager's job in addition to the General Manager's. It would be some considerable time before a new Underground Manager was transferred in from one of the other group mines. He was trying to arrange his move to the big office in the main Administrative Block up on the ridge, when he had another visitor, Frank Lemmer's secretary, Miss Lily Jordan, in a severe grey flannel suit looking like a wardress from Ravensbruck.

'Mr Ironsides, you and I have not seen eye to eye in the past.'

This was the understatement of the year. 'It is unlikely that we will in the future. Therefore, I have come to tender my resignation. I have made arrangements.'

The phone rang. Dan Stander's voice, breezy and carefree.

'Rod, I'm in love.'

'Oh Christ, no!' Rod groaned. 'Not this morning.'

'I've got to thank you for introducing me to her. She's the most wonderful—'

'Yeah, yeah!' Rod cut him short. 'Look, Dan, I'm rather busy. Some other time, all right?'

'Oh yes, I forgot. You are the new General Manager they tell me. Congratulations. You can buy me a drink at the Club. Six o'clock.'

'Right. By then I'll need one.' Rod hung up, and faced the hanging-judge expression of Miss Lily Jordan.

'Miss Jordan, in the past our interests have conflicted. In the future they will not. You are the best private secretary within a hundred miles of the Sonder Ditch. I need you, the Company needs you.'

That was the magic word. Miss Jordan had twenty-five years' service with the Company. She wavered visibly.

'Please, Miss Jordan, give me a chance.' Shamelessly Rod switched on his most engaging smile. Miss Jordan's femininity was not so completely atrophied that she could resist that smile.

'Very well, then, Mr Ironsides. I'll stay on initially until the end of the month. We'll see after that.' She stood up. 'Now, I'll get your things moved up to the new office.'

'Thank you, Miss Jordan.' With relief he let her take over, and tackled the problems that were piling up on his desk. One man, two jobs. Now he was responsible for surface operation as well as underground. The phone rang, men queued up in the passage, memos kept coming through from Dimitri's office. There was no lunch hour, and by the time she rang he was exhausted.

'Hello,' she said. 'Do I see you tonight?' Her voice was as refreshing as a wet cloth on the brow of a prizefighter between rounds.

'Terry.' He simply spoke her name in reply.

'Yes or no. If it's *no*, I intend jumping off the top of Reef Building.'

'Yes,' he said. 'Pops has summoned me to a meeting at nine tomorrow morning, so I'll be staying overnight at the apartment. I'll call you as soon as I get in.'

'Goody! Goody!' said she.

At five-thirty Dimitri stuck his head around the door.

'I'm going down to No. 1 shaft to supervise the shoot, Rod.'

'My God, what time is it?' Rod checked his watch. 'So late already.'

'It gets late early around here,' Dimitri agreed. 'I'm off.'

'Wait!' Rod stopped him. 'I'll shoot her.'

'No trouble.' Dimitri demurred. Company standard procedure laid down that each day's blast must be supervised by either the Underground Manager or his Assistant.

'I'll do it,' Rod repeated. Dimitri opened his mouth to protest further, then he saw that expression on Rod's face and changed his mind quickly.

'Okay then. See you tomorrow.' And he was gone.

Rod grinned at his own sentimentality. The Sonder Ditch was his now and, by God, he was going to shoot his own first blast on her.

They were waiting for him at the steel door of the blast control room at the shaft head. It was a small concrete room like a wartime pillbox, and there were only two keys to the door. Dimitri had one, Rod the other.

The duty mine captain and the foreman electrician added their congratulations to the hundreds he had received during the day, and Rod opened the door and they went into the tiny room.

'Check her out,' Rod instructed, and the mine captain began his calls to the shaft overseers at both No. 1 and No. 2 for

499

their confirmation that the workings of the Sonder Ditch were deserted, that every human being who had gone down that morning had come out again this evening.

Meanwhile, the foreman electrician was busy at the electrical control board. He looked up at Rod.

'Ready to close the circuits, Mr Ironsides.'

'Go ahead,' Rod nodded and the man touched a switch. A green light showed up on the board.

'No. 1 north longwall closed and green.'

'Lock her in,' Rod instructed and the electrician touched another switch.

'No. 1 east longwall closed and green.'

'Lock her in.'

The green light showed that the firing circuit was intact. A red light would indicate a fault and the faulty circuit would not be locked into the blast pattern.

Circuit after circuit was readied until finally the foreman stood back from the control board.

'All green and locked in.'

Rod glanced at the mine captain.

'All levels clear, Mr Ironsides. She's ready to burn.'

'Cheesa!' said Rod, the traditional command that had come down from the days when each fuse had been individually lit by a hand-held igniter stick.

'Cheesa' was the Bantu word for 'burn'.

The mine captain crossed to the control board and opened the cage that guarded a large red button.

'Cheesa!' echoed the mine captain and hit the button with the heel of his hand.

Immediately the row of green lights on the control board were extinguished, and in their place showed a row of red lights. Every circuit had been broken by the explosions.

The ground under their feet began to tremble. Throughout the workings the shots were firing. In the stopes the head charges fired at the top of the inclines, then in succession the other shots went off behind them. Each charge taking a ten-ton bite of rock and reef out of the face.

At the end of the development drives, a more complicated pattern was shooting. First a row of *cutters* went off down the middle of the oval face. Then the *shoulder charges* at the top corners, followed by the *knee charges* at the bottom corners. A moment's respite with the dust and nitrous fumes swirling back down the drive, then a roar as the *easers* on each side shaped the hole. Another respite and then the *lifters* along the bottom picked up the heap of broken rock and threw it back from the face.

Rod could imagine it clearly. Though no human eye had ever witnessed the blast, he knew exactly what was taking place down there.

The last tremor died away.

'That's it. A full blast,' said the mine captain.

'Thank you.' Rod felt tired suddenly. He wanted that drink, even though their brief exchange that morning had warned him that Dan would probably be insufferable. He could guess the conversation would revolve around Dan's new-found love.

Then he smiled as he thought about what waited for him in Johannesburg later that night, and suddenly he wasn't all that tired.

41

They sat facing each other.

'Only three things worry me,' Terry told Rod.

'What are they?' Rod rubbed soap into the face flannel.

'Firstly, your legs are too long for this bath.'

Rod rearranged his limbs, and Terry shot half out of the water with a squeak.

'Rodney Ironsides, would you be good enough to take a bit more care where you put your toes!'

'Forgive me.' He leaned forward to kiss her. 'Tell me what else worries you.'

'Well, the second thing that worries me is that I'm not worried.'

'What part of Ireland did you say you were from?' Rod asked. 'County Cork?'

'I mean, it's terrible but I'm not even a little conscience-stricken. Once I believed that if it ever happened to me I would never be able to look another human being in the eyes, I'd be so ashamed.' She took the flannel from his hands and began soaping his chest and shoulders. 'But, far from being ashamed, I'd like to stand in the middle of Eloff Street at rush hour and shout "Rodney Ironsides is my lover".'

'Let's drink to that.' Rodney rinsed the soap from his hands and reached over the side of the bath to pick up the two wine glasses from the floor. He gave one too Terry and they clinked them together, the sparkling Cape Burgundy glowed ruby red.

'Rodney Ironsides is my lover!' she toasted him.

'Rodney Ironsides is your lover,' he agreed and they drank.

'Now, I give *you* a toast,' he said.

'What is it?' She held her glass ready, and Rod leaned forward and poured the red wine from the crystal glass between her breasts. It ran like blood down her white skin and he intoned solemnly:

'Bless this ship and all who sail in her!'

Terry gurgled with delight.

'To her Captain. May he keep a firm hand on the rudder!'

'May her bottom never hit the reef!'

'May she be torpedoed regularly!'

'Terry Steyner, you are terrible.'

'Yes, aren't I?' And they drained their glasses.

'Now,' Rod asked, 'what is your third worry?'

'Manfred will be home on Saturday.'

They stopped laughing, Rod reached down for the Burgundy bottle and refilled the glasses.

'We still have five days,' he said.

42

It had been a week of personal triumph for Manfred Steyner. His address to the conference had been the foundation of the entire talks, all discussion had revolved upon it. He had been called upon to speak at the closing banquet which General de Gaulle had attended in person, and afterwards the General had asked Manfred to take coffee and brandy with him in one of the anterooms. The General had been gracious, had asked questions and listened attentively to the answers. Twice he had called his finance minister's attention to Manfred's replies.

Their farewells had been cordial, with a hint of state recognition for Manfred, a decoration. In common with most Germans, Manfred had a weakness for uniforms and decorations. He imagined how a star and ribbon might look on the snowy front of his dress shirt.

There had been a wonderful press both in France and at home. Even a bad-tempered quarter column in *Time* Magazine, with a picture, de Gaulle stooping over the diminutive Manfred solicitously, one hand on his shoulder. The caption read:

'The huntsman and the hawk. To catch a dollar?'

Now standing in the tiny cloakroom in the tail of the South African Airways Boeing, Manfred was whistling softly as he stripped his shirt and vest, crumpled them into a ball and dropped them into the waste bin.

Naked to the waist, he wiped his upper body with a wet cloth and then rubbed 4711 Eau de Cologne into his skin. From the briefcase he took an electric razor. The whistling stopped as he contorted his face for the razor.

Through his mind ran page after page of the report that Andrew had delivered that morning to his hotel room. Manfred had total recall when it came to written material. Although the report was in the briefcase beside him, in his mind's eye he could review it word for word, figure for figure.

It was a stupendous piece of work. How the authors had gained access to the drilling and exploration reports of the five Kitchenerville field companies he could not even guess, for the gold mining companies' security was as tight as that of any national intelligence agency. But the figures were genuine. He had checked those purporting to be from C.R.C. carefully. They were correct. So therefore the other four must also be genuine.

The names of the authors of the report were legend. They were the top men in the field. Their opinions were the best in Harley Street. The conclusion that they reached was completely convincing. In effect it was this:

If a haulage was driven from 66 level of the Sonder Ditch No. I shaft through the Big Dipper dyke, it would pass *under* the limestone water-bearing foundations, and just beyond the fault it would intersect a reef of almost unbelievable value.

It had not needed the lecture that Manfred had received from his corpulent creditor to show him the possibilities. The man who gave the order to drive through the Big Dipper would receive the credit. He would certainly be elected to the Chairmanship of the Group when that office fell vacant.

There was another possibility. A person who purchased a big packet of Sonder Ditch shares immediately before the reef was intersected would be a very rich man when he came to sell those shares later. He would be so rich that he would no longer be dependent on his wife for the means to live the kind of life he wanted, and indulge his own special tastes.

Manfred blew the hairs from his razor and returned it to his brief case. Then as he took out a fresh shirt and vest, he began to sing the words to the tune:

'Heute ist der schönste Tag
In meinem Leben.'

He would telephone Ironsides from Jan Smuts Airport as soon as he had passed through customs. Ironsides would come up to the house on Sunday morning and receive his orders.

As he knotted the silk of his tie Manfred knew that he stood at the threshold of a whole new world, the events of the next few months would lift him high above the level of ordinary men.

It was the chance for which he had worked and waited all these years.

43

Circumstances had changed completely since his last visit, Rod reflected, as he took the Maserati up the drive towards the Dutch gabled house.

He parked the car and switched off the ignition, sitting a while, reluctant to face the man who had sponsored his career and whom Rod in return had presented with a fine pair of horns.

'Courage, Ironsides!' he muttered and climbed out of the Maserati and went up the path across the lawns.

Terry was on the veranda in a gay print dress, with her hair loose, sprawled in a canvas chair with the Sunday papers scattered about her.

'Good morning, Mr Ironsides,' she greeted him as he came up the steps. 'My husband is in his study. You know the way, don't you?'

'Thank you, Mrs Steyner.' Rod kept his voice friendly but disinterested, then as he passed her chair he growled softly, 'I could eat you without salt.'

'Don't waste it, you gorgeous beast,' Terry murmured and ran the tip of her tongue over her lips.

Fifteen minutes later, Rod sat stony-faced and internally chilled before Manfred Steyner's desk. When at last he forced himself to speak, it felt as though the skin on his lips would tear with the effort.

'You want me to drive through the Big Dipper,' he croaked.

'More than that, Mr Ironsides. I want you to complete the drive within three months, and I want a complete security blanket on the development,' Manfred told him primly. Despite the fact that it was Sunday he was formally dressed, white shirt and dark suit. 'You will commence the drive from No. 1 shaft 66 level and make an intersect on reef at 6,600 feet with the S.D. No. 3 borehole 250 feet beyond the calculated extremity of the serpentine intrusion of the Big Dipper.'

'No,' Rod shook his head. 'You can't go through that. No one can take the chance. God alone knows what is on the other side, we only know that is bad ground. Stinking rotten ground.'

'How do you know that?' Manfred asked softly.

'Everybody on the Kitchenerville field knows it.'

'How?'

'Little things.' Rod found it hard to put into words. 'You get a feeling, the signs are there and when you've been in the game long enough you have a sixth sense that warns you when—'

'Nonsense,' Manfred interrupted brusquely. 'We no longer live in the days of witchcraft.'

'Not witchcraft, experience,' Rod snapped angrily. 'You've seen the drilling results from the other side of the fault?'

'Of course,' Manfred nodded. 'S.D. No. 3 found values of thousands of penny-weights.'

'And the other holes went dry and twisted off, or had water squirting out of them like a pissing horse!'

Manfred flushed fiercely. 'You will be good enough not to employ bar-room terminology in this house.'

Rod was taken off balance, and before he could answer Manfred went on.

'Would you put the considered opinions of,' Manfred named three men, 'before your own vague intuitions?'

'They are the best in the business,' Rod conceded reluctantly.

'Read that,' snapped Manfred. He tossed a manila folder onto the desk top, then stood up and went to wash his hands at the concealed basin.

Rod picked up the folder, opened it and was immediately engrossed. Ten minutes later, without looking up from the report, he fumbled a pack of cigarettes from his pocket.

'Please do not smoke!' Manfred stopped him sharply.

Three-quarters of an hour later, Rod closed the folder. During that time Manfred Steyner had sat with reptilian stillness behind his desk, with the glitter of his eyes the only signs of life.

'How the hell did you get hold of those figures and reports?' Rod asked with wonder.

'That does not concern you.' Manfred retrieved the folder from him, his first movement in forty-five minutes.

'So that's it!' muttered Rod. 'The water is in the lime stone near the surface. We go in under it!' He stood up from the chair

507

abruptly and began to pace up and down in front of Manfred's desk.

'Are you convinced?' Manfred asked, and Rod did not answer.

'I have promoted you above older and more experienced men' said Manfred softly. 'If I tear you down again, and tell the world you were not man enough for the job, then, Rodney Ironsides, you are finished. No one else would take a chance on you again, ever!'

It was true. Rod knew it.

'However, if you were to follow my instructions and we intersected this highly enriched reef, then part of the glory would rub off on you.'

That was also true. Rod stopped pacing, he stood with shoulders hunched, in an agony of indecision. Could he trust that report beyond his own deep intuition? When he thought about that ground beyond the dyke, his skin tickled with gooseflesh. He almost had the stink of it in his nostrils. Yet he could be wrong, and the weight of the opposition was heavy. The eminent names on the report, the threats which he knew Manfred would not hesitate to put into effect.

'Will you give me a written instruction?' Rod demanded harshly.

'What effect would that have?' Manfred asked mildly. 'As General Manager, the decision to work certain ground or not to work it is technically yours. In the very unlikely event that you encountered trouble beyond the fault, it would be no defence to produce a written instruction from me. Just as if you murdered my wife you could not defend yourself by producing a written instruction from me to do so.'

This again was true. Rod knew he was trapped. He could refuse, and wreck his career. Or he could comply and take the consequences whatever they may be.

'No,' said Manfred, 'I will not give you a written instruction.'

'You bastard,' Rod said softly.

Manfred answered as gently. 'I warned you that you would not be able to refuse to obey me.'

And the last twinge of remorse that Rod felt for his association with Terry Steyner faded and was gone.

'You've given me three months to hit the Big Dipper. All right, Steyner. You've got it!'

Rod turned on his heel and walked out of the room.

Terry was waiting for him among the protea plants on the bottom lawn. She saw his face and dropped all pretence. She went to meet him.

'Rod, what is it?' Her hand on his arm, looking up into his eyes.

'Careful!' he warned her, and she dropped her hand and stood back.

'What is it?'

'That bloody Gestapo bastard,' Rod snarled, and then, 'I'm sorry, Terry, he's your husband.'

'What has he done?'

'I can't tell you here. When can I see you?'

'I'll find an excuse to get away later today. Wait for me at your apartment.'

Later she sat on the couch below the Paravano painting and listened while he told her about it. All of it, the report, the threat and the order to pierce the Big Dipper.

She listened but expressed neither approval nor disapproval of his decision.

Manfred turned away from the window and went back to his desk. Even at that distance there had been no doubt about his wife's gesture. The hand outstretched, the face turned up, the lips parted in anxious inquiry, and then the guilty start and withdrawal.

He sat down at his desk, and laid his hands neatly in front of him. For the first time he was thinking of Rodney Ironsides as a man and not a tool.

He thought how big he was, tall and as wide across the shoulders as a gallow. Any reprisal on Ironsides could not be physical, and it could not be immediate. It must be after the drive to the Big Dipper.

I can wait, he thought coldly, there is time for everything in this life.

44

Johnny and Davy Delange sat in the two chairs before Rod's desk. They were both awkward and uncomfortable up here in the big office with picture windows looking out over the Kitchenerville valley.

I don't blame them, Rod thought, even I am not accustomed to it yet. Wall-to-wall carpeting, air-conditioning, original paintings on the wood-panelled walls.

'I have sent for you because you two are the best rock breakers on the Sonder Ditch,' Rod began.

'Tin Ribs wants something,' thought Davy, with all the suspicion of the union man for management.

'We will now have a few words from our sponsor,' Johnny grinned to himself. 'Before we start the programme.'

Rod looked at their faces and knew exactly what they were thinking. He had been on daily pay himself once. Cut out the compliments, Ironsides – he advised himself – these are two tough cookies and they are not impressed.

'I am pulling you out of the stopes and putting you onto a special development end. You will take it in turns to work day and night shift. You will be directly responsible to me and there will be a security blanket on your activity.'

They watched him without reaction, their expressions guarded. Johnny broke the short silence.

'One end, one blast a day?' He was thinking of his pay. Calculated on the amount of rock broken, he would earn little more than basic salary with a blast on one small face daily.

'No.' Rod shook his head. 'Ultra-fast, multi-blast, and shaft sinkers' rates.'

And both the Delange brothers sat forward in their chairs.

'Multi-blast?' Davy asked. That meant that they could shoot just as soon as they were ready. A good team could blast three – maybe four times a shift.

'Ultra-fast?' Johnny demanded. That was language Johnny understood. It was a term employed only in emergency, as when driving in to rescue trapped men after a fall. It was tacit approval from management to waive standard safety procedure in favour of speed. Christ, Johnny exulted, I can shoot her four – maybe five times a shift.

'Shaft sinkers' rates?' they asked together. That was a 20 per cent bonus on stopers' rates. It was a fortune they were being offered.

Rod nodded affirmative to their questions, and waited for the reaction which he knew would follow. It came immediately.

The Delange brothers now began to look for the catch. They sat stolidly turning the deal over in their minds, like two cautious housewives examining a tomato for blemishes because the price was too cheap.

'How long is this drive?' Johnny asked. If the drive was short, a few hundred feet, then it was worth nothing. They would hardly get into their stride before it was completed.

'Close on six thousand feet,' Rod assured him. They looked relieved.

'Where is it headed?' Davy discovered the rub.

'We are going to drive through the Big Dipper to intersect on reef at 6,000 feet.'

'Jesus!' said Johnny. 'The Big Dipper!' He was awed but unafraid. It excited him, the danger, the challenge. Had he been born earlier, Johnny Delange would have made a fine Spitfire pilot.

'The Big Dipper,' Davy murmured, his mind was racing. Nothing in this world or beyond would entice Davy Delange to drive through the Big Dipper. He had an almost religious fear of it. The name alone conjured up all sorts of hidden menace and unspeakable horror. Water. Gas. Friable ground, faults. Mudrushes. All a miner's nightmare.

There was no question of him doing it, yet the money was too good to pass up. He could net ten or eleven thousand Rand on those terms.

'All right, Mr. Ironsides,' he said. 'I'll take the first night shifts. Johnny can start the day shifts.'

Davy Delange had made his decision. He would work until his drills hit the greenish-black serpentine rock of the dyke. He would then walk out of the drive and quit. He would go up to, but not beyond the dyke.

Afterwards, any of the other mines would snap him up, he had an impeccable record and he would force Johnny to follow him.

'Hey, Davy!' Johnny was delighted, he had expected Davy to turn the deal down flat.

Now he would be able to buy the Mustang for certain – and perhaps an MGB GT for Hettie – and take a holiday to Durban over Christmas, and . . .

Rod was puzzled by Davy's easy agreement. He studied him a moment and decided that he had ferrety eyes. He's a sneaky little bastard, Rod decided, I'll have to watch him.

45

It took one shift only to prepare for the development. Rod selected the starting point. The main haulage curved away from the shaft on 66 level. Three hundred feet along this tunnel there was a chamber that had been cut out as a loco repair station but which was now out of use. Two large batwing ventilation doors were fitted to the opening of the chamber to provide privacy and behind them the chief underground surveyor set up his instruments and marked out the head of the tunnel that would fly arrow straight a mile and more through the living rock to strike through the Big Dipper into the unknown.

The area surrounding the head chamber was roped off and sign-posted with warnings.

'DANGER
INDEPENDENT BLASTING'

The mine captains were instructed to keep their men well away, and all loco traffic was rerouted through a secondary haulage.

On the doors of the chamber another notice was fixed.

'FIERY MINE PROCEDURE IN FORCE
NO NAKED LIGHTS BEYOND THIS POINT'

Owing to small deposits of coal and other organic substance in the upper stratas of rock, the Sonder Ditch was classed as a fiery mine and subject to the Government legislation covering this subject. No matches, lighters or other spark-generating devices were allowed into a new development end, because the presence of methane gas was always suspected.

Colourless, odourless, tasteless, detectable only by test with a safety lamp, it was a real and terrifying danger. A nine per cent concentration in air was highly explosive. Stringent precautions were taken against accidental triggering of methane that may have oozed out of a fissure or cavity in the rock.

From the main compressed air-pipes running down the corners of the shaft were taken leads to air tanks in the haulage, ensuring that sixty pounds per square inch of pressure was available for the rock drills. Then drills, pinchbars, hammers, shovels, and the other tools were unloaded from the cage at 66 level and stored at the shaft head.

Lastly, explosive was placed in the red lockers at the head of the development, and on the evening of October 23rd 1968, thirty minutes after the main blast, Davy Delange and his gang disembarked from the cage and went to the disused loco shop.

Davy, with the surly little Swazi boss boy beside him, stood before the rock wall on which the surveyor had marked the outline of the tunnel. Behind him his gang had fallen unbidden to their labour, each man knowing exactly what was expected of him.

Already the machine boys and their assistants were lugging their ungainly tools forward.

'You! You! You! You!' Davy indicated to each of them the hole on which he was to begin and then stepped back.

'Shaya!' he commanded. 'Hit it!' And with a fluttering bellow that buffeted the eardrums the drive began.

The drilling ceased and Davy charged the holes. The fuses hung like the tails of white mice from their holes. Each length carefully cut to ensure correct firing sequence.

'Clear the drive!' The boss boy's whistle shrilled, the tramp of heavy boots receded until silence hung heavy in the chemically cleaned air.

'Cheesa!' Davy and the boss boy, with the igniters burning like children's fireworks in their right hands, touched them to the hanging tails until the chamber was lit by the fierce blue light of the burning fuses. The shadows of the two men flickered gigantic and distorted upon the walls.

'All burning. Let's go!' And the two men walked quickly back to where the gang waited along the haulage.

The detonations sucked at their ears, and thrust against their lungs, so that afterwards the silence was stunning.

Davy checked his wristwatch. By law there was a mandatory thirty minutes' wait before anyone could go back to the face.

There may be a hang-fire waiting to blow the eyes out of some-one's head. Even if there were not, there was still the cloud of poisonous nitrous fumes that would destroy the hair follicles in a man's nostrils and render him still more vulnerable to the fine particles of rock dust that would seek to enter his lungs.

Davy waited those thirty minutes, by which time the venti-lation had sucked away the fumes and dust.

Then, alone, he went up the haulage. With him he carried his safety lamp, its tiny blue flame burning behind the screen of fine brass wire mesh. That mesh was flash proof and insulated the flame from any methane in the air.

Standing before the raw circular wound in the rock wall, Davy tested for methane gas. Watching the blue flame for the tell-tale cap. There was no sign of it, and satisfied he extinguished the lamp.

'Boss boy!' he yelled, and the Swazi came up uncoiling the hose behind him.

'Water down!'

Only when the rock face and all the loose rubble below it was glistening and dripping with water was Davy satisfied that the dust was laid sufficiently to bring up his gang.

'Bar boys!' he yelled, and they came up, carrying the twelve-foot long pinchbars, a tool like a giant crowbar.

'Bar down. Make safe!' And the bar boys attacked the bunches of loose rock that were flaking and crumbling from the hanging wall. Two of them manipulating one bar between them, with the steel point striking sparks from the rock. The dislodged fragments rained down, heavily at first and then less and less until the rock above their heads was solid and clean.

Only then did Davy scramble over the pile of rubble to reach the face and begin marking in the shot holes.

Behind him his gang were lashing the stuff into the waiting coco pans, and his machine boys were dragging the drills up to the face.

Davy's gang made three blasts that first night. As he rode up in the cage into a pink, sweet-smelling dawn, Davy was satisfied.

'Perhaps tonight we will get in four blasts,' he thought.

In the Company change house he showered, running the water steaming hot so his skin turned dull angry red, and he worked up a fat white lather of soap suds over his head and at his armpits and crotch.

He rubbed down with a rough thick towel and dressed quickly. Crossing the parking lot to his battered old Ford Anglia he felt happy and good-tired; hungry and ready for bed.

He drove into Kitchenerville at a steady forty miles an hour, and by this time the sun was just showing over the Kraalkop ridge. The dawn was misty rose, with long shadows against the earth, and he thought that this was how it would be in the early mornings on the farm.

On the outskirts of the town Johnny's Monaco roared past him going in the opposite direction. Johnny waved and blew the horn, shouting something that was lost in the howl of wind and motor.

'They'll catch him yet.' Davy shook his head in disapproval. 'The speed limit is forty-five along here.'

He parked the Anglia in the garage and let himself in through the kitchen door. The Bantu maid was busy over the stove.

'Three eggs,' he told her and went through to his bedroom. He shrugged off his jacket and threw it on the bed. Then he returned to the door and glanced quickly up and down the passage. It was deserted, and there was no sound besides the clatter of the maid in the kitchen.

Davy sidled into the passage. The door to Johnny's bedroom was ajar, and Davy moved quietly down to it. His heart was pounding in his throat, his breathing was stifled by his guilt and excitement.

He peered around the edge of the door and gasped aloud. This morning it was better than usual.

Hettie was a sound sleeper. Johnny always maintained it would take a shot of Dynagel to wake her. She never wore night clothes and she never rose before ten-thirty in the morning. She lay on her stomach, hugging a pillow to her chest, her hair a joyous tangle of flaming red against the green sheets. The morning was warm and her blankets had been kicked aside.

Davy stood in the passage. A nerve in his eyelid began to twitch, and under his shirt a drop of perspiration slid from his armpit down along his flank.

On the bed Hettie mumbled unintelligibly in her sleep, drew her knees up and rolled slowly onto her back. One arm came up and flopped limply over her face, her eyes were covered by the crook of her elbow.

She sighed deeply. The twin mounds of her bosom were pulled

out of shape by their own weight and the angle of her arm. The hair in her armpit and at the base of her belly was bright shiny red-gold. She was long and smooth and silky white, crowned and tipped with flame.

She moved her body languourously, voluptuously, and then settled once more into slumber.

'Breakfast ready, master,' the maid called from the kitchen. Davy started guiltily, then retreated down the passage.

He found with surprise that he was panting, as though he had run a long way.

46

Johnny Delange leaned against the sidewall of the haulage, his hard helmet tilted at a jaunty angle and a cigarette dangling from his lips.

Down at the face the shots began to fire. Johnny recognized each detonation, and when the last dull jar disrupted the air about them, he pushed himself away from the wall with his shoulder.

'That was the *lifters*,' he announced. 'Come on Big King!'

Not for Johnny Delange a thirty-minute waste of time. As he and Big King set off down the haulage together they were binding scarves over their noses and mouths. Ahead of them a bluey-white fog of dust and fumes filled the tunnel, and Big King had the hose going, using a fine mist spray to absorb the fumes and particles.

They pushed on up to the face, Johnny stooping over the safety lamp. Even he had a healthy respect for methane gas.

'Bar boys!' he bellowed, not waiting for Big King to finish watering down. They came up like ghosts in the fog. Hard behind them the machine boys hovered with their drills.

Taking calculated risks Johnny had his drills roaring forty-five minutes sooner than Davy Delange would have in the same circumstances.

When he came back to the face from cutting fuses and priming his explosives, he found his lashing gang struggling with a massive slab of rock that had been blown intact from the face. Five of them were beating on it with fourteen-pound hammers in an attempt to crack it into manageable pieces. As Johnny reached them, Big King was berating them mercilessly.

'You look like a bunch of virgins grinding millet.'

The hammers clanged and struck sparks from the slab. Sweat oozed from every pore of the hammer boys' skin, greasing their bodies, flying from their heads in sparkling droplets with each blow.

'Shaya!' Big King goaded them on. 'Between you all you wouldn't crack the shell of an egg. Hit it, man! Hit it!'

One by one the men fell back exhausted, their chests heaving, gulping air through gaping mouths, blinded by their own sweat.

'All right,' Johnny intervened. The rock was holding up the whole blast. It warranted drastic measures to break it up.

'I'll pop her,' he said, and any government inspector or mine safety officer would have paled at those words.

'Stand far back and turn your faces away,' Big King instructed his gang. From the forehead of one of his men he took a pair of wire mesh goggles, designed to shield the eyes from flying splinters and rock fragments. He handed them to Johnny who placed them over his eyes.

From the canvas carrying bag he took out a stick of Dynagel. It looked like a candle wrapped in yellow greased paper.

'Give me your knife.' Big King opened a large clasp knife and handed it to Johnny.

Carefully Johnny cut a coin-shaped sliver of explosive from one end of the stick, a piece twice as thick as a penny. He returned the remains of the stick to the bag and handed it to Big King.

'Get back,' he said and Big King moved away.

Johnny eyed the slab of rock thoughtfully and then placed the fragment of Dynagel in the centre of it. He adjusted the goggles over his eyes, and picked up one of the fourteen-pound hammers.

'Turn your eyes away,' he warned and took deliberate aim. Then with a smooth overhead two-handed swing he brought the hammer down on the Dynagel.

The explosion was painful in the confined space of the drive, and afterwards Johnny's ears hummed with it. A tiny drop of blood ran down his cheek from the scratch inflicted by a flying splinter. His wrists ached from the jolt of the hammer in his hands.

'Gwenyama!' grunted Big King in admiration. 'The man is a lion.'

The explosion had cracked the slab into three wedge-shaped segments. Johnny pushed the goggles onto his forehead and wiped the blood from his cheek with the back of his hand.

'Get it the hell out of here,' he grinned, then he turned to Big King.

'Come.' He jerked his head towards the end of the tunnel. 'Help me charge the holes.'

The two of them worked quickly, sliding the sticks of Dynagel into the shot holes and tamping them home with the charging sticks.

For anyone who was not in possession of a blasting licence, to charge up was an offence punishable by a fine of one hundred rand or two months' imprisonment, or both. Big King had no licence, but his assistance saved fifteen minutes on the operation.

Johnny and his gang blew the face five times that day, but as they rode up in the cage into the cool evening air he was not satisfied.

'Tomorrow we'll shoot her six times,' he told Big King.

'Maybe seven,' said Big King.

Hettie was waiting for him in the lounge when he got home. She flew to him and threw her arms about his neck.

'Did you bring me a present?' she asked with her lips against his ear, and Johnny laughed tantalizingly. It was very seldom that he did not have a gift for her.

'You did!' she exclaimed, and began to run her hands over his pockets.

'There!' She thrust her hand into the inside pocket of his jacket, and brought out the little white jeweller's box.

'Oh!' She opened it, and then her expression changed slightly.

'You don't like them?' Johnny asked anxiously.

'How much did they cost?' she inquired as she examined the porcelain and lacquer earrings, representing two vividly coloured parrots.

'Well,' Johnny looked shamefaced, 'you see, Hettie, it's the end of the month, you see, and well, like I'm a bit short till pay day, you see, so I couldn't—'

'How much?'

'Well, you see,' he took a breath, 'two Rand fifty.'

'Oh,' said Hettie, 'they're nice.' And she promptly lost interest in them. She tossed the box carelessly onto the crowded mantelpiece and set off for the kitchen.

'Hey, Hettie,' Johnny called after her. 'How about we go across to Fochville? There's a dance there tonight. We go and twist, hey?'

Hettie turned back, her expression alive again.

'Gee, yes, man!' she enthused. 'Let's do that. I'll go and change, hey!' And she ran up the passage.

Davy came out of his bedroom, on his way to work.

'Hey, Davy.' Johnny stopped him. 'You got any money on you?'

'Are you broke again?'

'Just 'till pay day.'

'Hell, man, Johnny, you got a cheque for eleven hundred the beginning of the month. You spent it all?'

'Next month,' Johnny winked, 'I'm going to get a cheque for two or three thousand. Then watch me go! Come, Davy, lend me fifty. I'm taking Hettie dancing.'

47

For Rod the days flicked past like telegraph poles viewed from a speeding automobile. Each day he gained confidence in his own ability. He had never doubted that the could handle the underground operation and now he found that he had a firm grasp on the surface as well. He knew that his campaign to reduce working costs was having effect, but its full harvest would only be apparent when the quarterly reports were drafted.

Yet he lay awake in the big Manager's residence on the ridge in which he and his few sticks of furniture seemed lost and lonely, and he worried. There were always myriad nagging little problems, but there were others more serious.

This morning Lily Jordan had come through into his office.

'Mr Innes is coming up to see you at nine.'

'What's he want?' Herbert Innes was the Manager of the Sonder Ditch Reduction works.

'He wouldn't tell me,' Lily answered. The end of the month had come and gone and Lily was still with him. Rod presumed that he had been approved.

Herby Innes, burly and red-faced, sat down and drank the cup of tea that Lily provided, while he regaled Rod with a stroke by stroke account of his Sunday afternoon golf round. Rod interrupted him after he had hit a nine-iron short at the third and shanked his chip.

'Okay, Herby. What's the problem?'

'We've got a leak, Rod.'

'Bad?'

'Bad enough,' Herby grunted. To him the loss of a single ounce of gold during the process of recovery and refinement was catastrophic.

'What do you reckon?'

'Between the wash and the pour we are losing a couple hundred ounces a week.'

'Yes,' Rod agreed. 'That is bad enough.'

Twenty thousand Rand a month, one hundred and twenty thousand and year.

'Have you any ideas?'

'It's been going on for some time, even in Frank Lemmer's day. We have tried everything.'

Rod was a little hazy about the workings of the reduction plant, not that he would admit that, but he was. He knew that the ore was weighed and sampled when it reached the surface, from this a fairly accurate estimate of gold content was made and compared with actual recovery. Any discrepancy had to be investigated and traced.

'What is your recovery rate for the last quarter?'

'Ninety-six point seven-three.'

'That's pretty good,' Rod admitted. It was impossible to recover all the gold in the ore that was surfaced but Herby was getting most of it out. 96.73 per cent of it, to be precise. Which meant that very little of the missing two hundred ounces was being lost into the dumps and the slimes dam.

'I tell you what, Herby,' Rod decided. 'I'll come down to the plant this afternoon. We'll go over it together, perhaps a fresh eye may be able to spot the trouble.'

'May do.' Herby was sceptical. 'We've tried everything else. We are pouring this afternoon. What time shall I expect you?'

'Two o'clock.'

They started at the shaft head, where the ore cage, the copie, arrived at the surface every four minutes with its cargo of rock which it dumped into a concrete shute. Each load was classified as either 'reef' or 'waste'.

The reef was dropped into the massive storage bins, while the waste was carried off on a conveyor to the wash house to be sluiced down before going to the dump. Tiny particles of gold sticking to the waste rock were gathered in this way.

Herby put his lips close to Rod's ear to make himself heard above the rumbling roar of rock rolling down the chute.

'I'm not worried about this end. It's all bulk here and very little shine.' Herby used the reduction plant slang for gold. 'The closer we get to the end, the more dangerous it is.'

Rod nodded and followed Herby down the steel ladder until they reached a door below the storage bins. They went through into a long underground tunnel very similar to the ore tunnel on 100 level.

Again there was a massive conveyor belt moving steadily along the tunnel while ore from the bins above was fed onto it. Rod and Herby walked along beside the belt until it passed under a massive electro magnet. Here they paused for a while. The magnet was extracting from the ore all those pieces of metal which had found their way into the ore passes and bins.

'How much you picking up?' Rod asked.

'Last week fourteen tons,' Herby answered, and taking Rod's arm led him through the door beside them. They were in an open yard that looked like a scrap-metal merchant's premises. A mountain of pinch bars, jumper bits, shovels, steel wire rope, snatch blocks, chains, spanners, fourteen-pound hammers, and other twisted and unrecognizable pieces of metal filled the yard. All of it was rusted, much of it unusable. It had been separated from the ore by the magnet.

Rod's mouth tightened. Here he was presented with indisputable evidence of the carelessness and it-belongs-to-the-company attitude of his men. This pile of scrap represented a waste that would total hundreds of thousands of Rand annually.

'We will see about that!' he muttered.

'If one of those hammers got into my jaw mills it would smash it to pieces,' Herby told him dolefully and led him back into the conveyor tunnel.

The belt angled upwards sharply and they followed the catwalk beside it. They climbed steadily for five minutes and Herby was puffing like a steam engine. Through the holes in the honeycomb steel plate under his feet, Rod could see that they were now a few hundred feet above ground level.

The conveyor reached the head of a tall tower and dumped its load of ore into the gaping mouths of the screeners. As the rock fell down the tower to ground level again it was sorted for size, and the larger pieces diverted to the jaw crushers which chewed it into fist-size bites.

'See anything?' Herby asked, barely concealing the sarcasm.

Rod grinned at him.

They climbed down the steel ladders that seemed endless. The screeners rattling and the crushers hammering, until Rod's eardrums pleaded for mercy.

At last they reached ground level and went through into the

mill room. This was a cavernous galvanized-iron shed the size of a large aircraft hangar. At least one hundred yards long and fifty feet high, it was filled with long rows of the cylindrical tube mills.

Forty of them in all, they were as thick as the boiler of a steam locomotive and about twice as long. Into one end of them was fed the ore which had been reduced in size by the jaw crushers. The tube mills revolved and the loose steel balls within them pounded the rock to powder.

If the noise before had been bad, it was hideous in the mill room. Rod and Herby made no effort to speak to each other until they had walked through into the comparative quiet of the first heavy-media separator room.

'Now,' Herby explained. 'This is where we start worrying.' He indicated the rows of pale blue six-inch piping that came through the wall from the mill room.

'In there is the powdered rock mixed with water to a smooth flowing paste. About forty per cent of the gold is free.'

'No one can get into those pipes and you've checked for any possible leak?' Rod asked. Herby nodded.

'But,' he said, 'have a look here!'

Along the far wall was a series of cages. They were made of heavy steel mesh, the perforations would not allow a man's finger through. The heavy steel doors were barred and locked. Outside each battery of cages stood a Bantu attendant in clean white overalls. They were all concentrating on the manipulation of the turncock that obviously regulated the flow of the powdered ore through the pipes.

Herby stopped at one of the cages.

'Shine!' he pointed. Beyond the heavy guard screen the grey paste of rock powder was flowing from a series of nozzles over an inclined black rubber sheet. The surface of the rubber sheet was deeply corrugated, and in each corrugation the free gold was collecting, held there by its own weight. The gold was thick as butter in a Dagwood sandwich, greasy yellow-looking in the folds of rubber.

Rod laid hold of the steel screen and shook it.

'No,' Herby laughed. 'No one will get in that way.'

'How do you clean the gold off that sheet? Does someone have access to the separator?' Rod asked.

'The separator cleans itself automatically,' Herby answered. 'Look!'

Rod noticed for the first time that the rubber sheet was moving very slowly, it was also an endless belt running round two rollers. As the belt inverted, so fine jets of water washed the gold from the corrugations into a collection tank.

'I'm the only one who has access. We change the collection tanks daily,' said Herby.

It looked foolproof, Rod had to admit.

Rod turned and glanced down the row of four Bantu attendants. They were all intent on their duties, and Rod knew that each of them had a high security rating. They had been carefully selected and screened before being allowed into the reduction works.

'Satisfied?' Herby asked.

'Okay,' Rod nodded, and the two of them went out through the door in the far wall. Locking it behind them.

Immediately they had gone the four Bantu attendants reacted. They straightened up, the scowls of concentration smoothed out to be replaced by grins of relief. One made a remark and they all laughed, and opened the waist bands of their tunics. From inside each trouser leg they drew a length of quarter-inch copper wire and began probing them through the steel screen.

It had taken Crooked Leg, the photographer, almost a year to work out a means of milking gold from the heavily screened and guarded separators. The method which he had discovered was, like all workable plans, extremely simple.

Mercury, quicksilver, absorbs gold the way blotting paper sucks up moisture. It will suck in any speck of gold that comes in contact with it. Mercury has a further property, it can be made to spread on copper like butter on bread. This layer of mercury on copper retains its powers of absorbing gold.

Crooked Leg had devised the idea of coating lengths of copper wire with mercury. The wire could be inserted through the apertures in the steel mesh and the wire laid across the corrugated rubber sheet, where it set about mopping up every speck of gold that flowed over it. The lengths of wire could be quickly slipped down the trouser leg at the approach of an official, and they could be smuggled in and out of the reduction works the same way.

Every evening Crooked Leg retrieved the gold-thickened wire, and issued his four accomplices with newly coated lengths. Every night in the abandoned workings beyond the ridge he boiled the mercury to make it release its gold.

'Now,' Herby could speak normally in the blessed quiet of the cyanide plant, 'we have skimmed off the free gold – and we are left with the sulphide gold.' He offered Rod a cigarette as they made their way between the massive steel tanks that spread over many acres. 'We pump this into the tanks and add cyanide. The cyanide dissolves the gold and takes it into solution. We tap it off and run it through zinc powder. The gold is deposited on the zinc, we burn away the zinc and we are left with the gold.'

Rod lit his cigarette. He knew all this but Herby was giving him a Cooks' tour for visiting V.I.P.s. He flicked his lighter for Herby. 'There is no way anyone could swipe it when it's in solution.'

Herby shook his head, exhaling smoke. 'Apart from anything else, cyanide is a deadly poison.' He glanced at his watch. 'Three-twenty, they'll be pouring now. Shall we go across to the smelt house?'

The smelt house was the only brick building among all the galvanized iron. It stood a little isolated. Its windows were high up and heavily barred.

At the steel door Herby buzzed, and a peephole opened in the door. He and Rod were immediately recognized and the door swung open. They were in a cage of bars which could only be opened once the door was closed behind them.

'Afternoon, Mr Ironsides, Mr Innes.' The guard was apologetic. 'Would you sign, please?' He was a retired policeman with a paunch and a holstered revolver on his hip.

They signed and the guard signalled to his mate on the steel catwalk high above the smelt room floor. This guard tucked his pump action shotgun under one arm, and threw the switch on the walk beside him.

The cage door opened and they went through.

Along the far wall the electric furnaces were set into the brickwork. They resembled the doors of the bread ovens in a bakery.

The concrete floor of the room was uncluttered, except for

the mechanical loader that carried the gold crucible in its steel arms, and the moulds before it. The half dozen personnel of the smelt house barely looked up as Rod and Herby approached.

The pour was well advanced, the arms of the loader tilted and a thin stream of molten gold issued from the spout of the crucible, and fell into the mould. The gold hissed and smoked and crackled, and tiny red and blue sparks twinkled on its surface as it cooled.

Already forty or fifty bars were laid out on the rubber-wheeled trolley beside the mould. Each bar was a little smaller than a cigar box. It had the knobby bumpy look of roughly cast metal.

Rod stopped and touched one of the bars. It was still hot and it had the slightly greasy feeling that new gold always has.

'How much?' he asked Herby, and Herby shrugged.

'About a million Rand's worth, perhaps a little more.'

So that's what a million Rand looks like, Rod mused, it's not very impressive.

'What's the procedure now?' Rod asked.

'We weigh it, and stamp the weight and batch number into each bar.' He pointed to a massive circular safe deposit door in the near wall. 'It's stored there over-night, and tomorrow a refinery armoured car will come out from Johannesburg and pick it up.' Herby led the way out of the smelt house. 'Anyway, that's not the trouble. Our leak is sucking off the shine before it ever reaches the smelt house.'

'Let me think about it for a few days,' Rod said. 'Then we'll get together again, try and find the solution.'

He was still thinking about it now. Lying in the darkness and smoking cigarette after cigarette.

There seemed to be only one solution. They would have to plant Bantu police in the reduction works.

It was an endless game involving all the mining companies and their reduction plant personnel. An inventive mind would devise a new system of sucking off the shine. The Company would become aware of the activity by comparison of estimated and actual recovery and they would work on the leak for a week, a month, sometimes a year. Then they would break the system. There would be prosecutions, stiff gaol sentences, and the Company would circularize its neighbours, and they would all settle back and wait for the next customer to appear.

Gold has many remarkable properties, its weight, its non-corruptiblity and, not least, the greed and lust it conjures up in the hearts of men.

Rod stubbed his cigarette, rolled onto his side and pulled the bed-clothes up over his shoulders. His last thought before sleep was for the major problem that, these days, was never very far from the surface of his mind.

The Delange brothers had driven almost fifteen hundred feet in two weeks. At this rate they would hit the Big Dipper seven weeks from now, then even the theft of gold would pale into insignificance.

48

At the time that Rod Ironsides was composing himself for sleep, Big King was taking a little wine with his business associate and tribal brother Philemon N'gabai, alias Crooked Leg.

They sat facing each other in a pair of dilapidated cane chairs with a lantern and a gallon jug of Jeripigo set between them. The bat stench of the abandoned workings did little to bring out the bouquet of the wine, which was of small concern to either man, for they were drinking not for taste but for effect.

Crooked Leg refilled the cheap glass tumbler that Big King proffered, and as the wine glug-glugged from the jar he continued his attack on the character and moral fibre of José Almeida, the Portuguese.

'For many months now I have had it in my heart to speak to you of these matters,' he told Big King, 'but I have waited until I could set a deadfall for the man. He is like a lion that preys upon our herds, we hear him roar in the night and in the dawn we see his spoor in the earth about the carcasses of our animals, but we cannot meet him face to face.'

Big King enjoyed listening to the oratory of Crooked Leg and while he listened he drank the Jeripigo as though it were water, and Crooked Leg kept refilling the tumbler for him.

'In counsel with myself I spoke thus: "Philemon N'gabai, it is not enough that thou should suspect this white man. It is necessary also that you see with your own eyes that he is eating your substance".'

'How, Crooked Leg?' Big King's voice was thickening, the level of the jug had fallen steadily and now showed less than half. 'Tell me how we shall take this man.' Big King showed a fist the size of a bunch of bananas. 'I will . . .'

'No, Big King.' Crooked Leg was scandalized. 'You must not hurt the man. How then would we sell our gold? We must prove he is cheating us and show him we know it. Then we will proceed as ever, but he will give us full measure in the future.'

Big King thought about that for some time, then at last he sighed regretfully. 'You are right, Crooked Leg. Still, I would have liked to . . .' He showed that fist again, and Crooked Leg went on hurriedly.

'Therefore, I have sent to my brother who drives a delivery van for S.A. Scale Company in Johannesburg, and he has taken from his Company a carefully measured weight of eight ounces.' Crooked Leg produced the cylindrical metal weight from his pocket and handed it to Big King who examined it with interest. 'Tonight, after the Portuguese has weighed the gold you take to him, you will say, "Now, my friend, please weigh this for me on your scale," and you will watch to see that his scale reads the correct number. Each time in the future he will weigh this on his scale before we sell our gold.'

'Hau!' Big King chuckled. 'You are a crafty one, Crooked Leg.'

Big King's eyes were smoky and blood-shot. The Jeripigo was a raw rough fortified wine, and he had drunk very nearly a gallon of it. He sat opposite the Portuguese store-keeper in the back room behind the concession store, and watched while he poured the gold dust into the pan of the jeweller's scale. It made a yellow pyramid that shone dully in the light from the single bare bulb above their heads.

'One hundred and twenty-three ounces.' Almeida looked up at Big King for confirmation, a strand of greasy black hair hung onto his forehead. His face was pale from lack of sun so that the blue stubble of beard was in heavy contrast.

'That is right,' Big King nodded. He could taste the liquor fumes in the back of his throat, and they were as strong as his distaste for the man who sat opposite him. He belched.

Almeida removed the pan from the scale and carefully poured the dust back into the screw top bottle.

'I will get the money.' He half rose from his chair.

'Wait!' said Big King, and the Portuguese looked at him in mild surprise.

Big King took the weight from the pocket of his jacket. He placed it on the desk.

'Weigh that on your scale,' he said in Portuguese.

Almeida's eyes flicked down to the weight, and then back to

Big King's face. He sank back into his seat, and pushed the strand of hair off his forehead. He began to speak, but his voice cracked and he cleared his throat.

'Why? Is there something wrong?' Suddenly he was aware of the size of the man opposite him. He could smell the liquor on his breath.

'Weigh it!' Big King's voice was flat, without rancour. His face was expressionless, but the smoky red glare of his eyes was murderous.

Suddenly Almeida was afraid, deadly, coldly afraid. He could guess what would happen once the error in his balance was disclosed.

'Very well,' he said, and his voice was forced and off key. The pistol was in the drawer beside his right knee. It was loaded, with a cartridge under the hammer. The safety-catch was on, but that would only delay him an instant. He knew it would not be necessary to fire, once he had the weapon in his hand he would have control of the situation again.

If he did have to fire, the calibre was .45 and the heavy slug would stop even a giant like this Bantu. *Self-defence*, he was working it out feverishly. *A burglar*, I surprised him and he attacked. *Self-defence*. It would work. They'd believe it.

But how to get the pistol? Try and sneak it out of the drawer, or make a grab for it?

There was a desk between them, it would take a few seconds for the Bantu to realize what he was doing, a few more for him to get around the desk. He would have plenty of time.

He snatched the handle of the drawer, and it flew open. His fingernails scrabbled against the wood work as he clawed for the big black U.S. Navy automatic, and with a surge of triumph his hand closed over the butt.

Big King came over the top of the desk like a black avalanche. The scale and the jar of gold dust was swept aside to clatter and shatter against the floor.

Still seated in his chair, with the pistol in his hand, Almeida was borne over backwards with Big King on top of him. Many years before, Big King had worked with a safari outfit in Portuguese East Africa, and he had seen the effect of gunshot wounds in the flesh of dead animals.

In the instant that he had recognized the weapon in Almeida's hand, he had been as afraid as the Portuguese. Fear had triggered the speed of his reaction, it was responsible for the savagery of his attack as he lay over the struggling body of the Portuguese.

He had Almeida's pistol hand held by the wrist and he was shaking it to force him to drop the firearm. With his right hand he had the Portuguese by the throat, and instinctively he was applying the full strength of his arms to both grips. He felt something break under his right hand, cracking like the kernel of a nut, and his fingers that were suddenly without strength, and skittered across the floor to come up against the far wall with a thump.

Only then did Big King begin to regain the sanity that fear had scattered. Suddenly he realized that the Portuguese was lying quietly under him. He released his grip and scrambled to his knees. The Portuguese was dead. His neck was twisted away from his shoulders at an impossible angle. His eyes were wide and surprised, and a smear of blood issued from one nostril over his upper lip.

Big King backed away towards the door, his gaze fixed in horror on the sprawling corpse. When he reached the door, he hesitated, fighting down the urge to run. He subdued it, and went back to kneel beside the desk. First he picked up the controversial cylindrical weight and placed it in his pocket, then he began sweeping up the scattered gold dust and the shattered fragments of the screw-topped container. He placed them into separate envelopes that he found among the papers on the desk. Ten minutes later he slipped out through the back door of the concession store, into the night.

49

At the time Big King was hurrying back towards the mine hostel, Rod Ironsides thrashed restlessly in a bed in which the sheets were already bunched and damp with sweat. He was imprisoned in his own fantasy, locked in a nightmare from which he could not break away. The nightmare was infinite and green, quivering, unearthly, translucent. He knew it was held back only by a transparent barrier of glass. He cowered before it, and he knew it was icy cold, he could see light shining through it, and he was deadly afraid.

Suddenly there was a crack in the glass wall, a hairline crack, and through it oozed a single drop. A large, pear-shaped drop, as perfect as though it had been painted by Tretchikoff. It glittered like a gemstone.

It was the most terrifying thing that Rod had ever seen in his life. He cried out in his sleep, trying to warn them, but the crack starred further, and the drop slid down the glass, to be followed by another and another. Suddenly a jagged slab of glass exploded out of the wall, and Rod screamed as the water burst through, in a frothing jet.

With a roar the entire glass wall collapsed, and a mountain high wave of green water hissed down upon him, carrying a white plume of spray at its crest.

He awoke sitting upright in his bed, a cry of horror on his lips and his body bathed in sweat. It took minutes for him to steady the wild racing of his heart. Then he went through to the bathroom. He ran a glass of water and held it up to the light. 'Water. It's there!' he muttered. 'I know it's there!' He drank from the tumbler.

Standing naked, with his sweat drying cold on his body, the tumbler held to his lips, the idea came to him. He had never heard of anyone trying it before, but then nobody he knew would be crazy enough to drive into a death trap like the Big Dipper.

'I'll drill and charge a matt of explosive into the hanging wall of the drive. I'll get the Delange boys on to it right away. Then at any time I choose I can blast the whole bloody roof in and seal off the tunnel.'

Rod was surprised at the strength of the relief that flooded over him. He knew then how it had been worrying him. He went back to the bedroom and straightened out his bedclothes. However, sleep would not come easily to him. His imagination was overheated, and a series of events and ideas kept playing through his mind, until abruptly he was presented with the image of Terry Steyner.

He had not seen her for almost two weeks, not since Manfred Steyner's return from Europe. He had spoken to her twice on the telephone, hasty, confused conversations that left him feeling dissatisfied. He was increasingly aware that he was missing her. His one attempt to find solace elsewhere had been a miserable failure. He had lost interest half way through the approach manoeuvres and had returned the young lady to the bosom of her family at the unheard of hour of eleven o'clock on a Saturday night.

Only the unremitting demands of his new job had prevented him from slipping away to Johannesburg and taking a risk.

'You know, Ironsides, you'd better start bracing up a little, don't lose your head over this woman. Remember our vow – *Never Again*!'

He punched the pillow into shape and settled into it.

Terry lay quietly, waiting for it. It was after one o'clock in the morning. It was one of those nights. He would come soon now. As never before she was filled with dread. A cold slimy feeling in the pit of her stomach. Yet she had been fortunate. He had not been near her since his return from Paris. Over two weeks, but it could not last. Tonight.

She heard the sound of the car coming up the drive and she felt physically ill. I can't do it, she decided, not any more, not ever again. It wasn't meant to be like this, I know that now. It's not dirty and furtive and horrible, it's like ... like ... it's the way Rod makes it.

She heard him in his bedroom, suddenly she sat up in bed She felt desperate, hunted.

The door of her room opened softly.

'Manfred?' she asked sharply.

'It's me. Don't worry.' He came briskly towards her bed, a dark impersonal shape and he was undoing the cord of his dressing-gown.

'Manfred,' Terry blurted. 'I'm early this month, I'm sorry.'

He stopped. She saw his hands fall back to his sides, and he stood completely still.

'Oh!' he said at last, and she heard him shuffle his feet into the thick pile of the carpet. 'I just came to tell you,' he hesitated, seeking an excuse for his visit, 'that . . . that I'll be going away for five days. Leaving on Friday. I have to go to Durban and Cape Town.'

'I'll pack for you,' she said.

'What? Oh, yes – thank you.' He shuffled his feet again. 'Well, then.' He hesitated, then stooped quickly and brushed her cheek with his lips. 'Good night, Theresa.'

'Good night, Manfred.'

Five days, she lay alone in the darkness and gloated. *Five whole days alone with Rod.*

50

Detective Inspector Hannes Grobbelaar of the South African Criminal Investigation Department sat on the edge of the office chair with his hat tipped onto the back of his head and spoke into the telephone, which he held in a handkerchief-covered hand. He was a tall man with a long sad face and a mournful looking moustache that was streaked with grey.

'Gold buying,' he said into the receiver, and then in reply to the obvious question. 'There's gold dust spilled all over the place and a jeweller's scale, and a .45 automatic with a full magazine and the safety-catch still on, dead man's prints on it.' He listened. 'Ja. Ja. All right, ja. Broken neck, looks like.' Inspector Grobbelaar swivelled his chair and looked down at the corpse that lay on the floor beside him. 'Bit of blood on his lip, but nothing else.'

One of the finger-print men came to the desk and Grobbelaar stood up to give him room to work, the receiver still held to his ear.

'Prints?' he asked in disgust. 'There are finger prints on everything, we have isolated at least forty separate sets so far.' He listened a few seconds. 'No, we will get him, all right. It must be a Bantu mine worker and we have got all the finger prints of the men from outside the Republic. It's just a matter of checking them all out and then questioning. Ja, we'll have him within a month, that's for sure! I'll be back at John Vorster Square about five o'clock, just as soon as we finish up here.' He hung up the receiver, and stood looking down at the murdered man.

'Ugly bastard,' said Sergeant Hugo beside him. 'Asked for it, buying gold. It's as bad as diamonds.' He drew attention to the large envelope he carried in his hand. 'I've got a whole lot of glass fragments. Looks like the container the gold was in. The murderer tried to clean up, but he didn't make a very good job. These were under the desk.'

'Prints?'

'Only one piece big enough. It's got a smeary print on it. Might be of use.'

'Good,' Grobbelaar nodded. 'Get cracking on that, then.'

There was a feminine wail from somewhere in the interior of the building, and Hugo grimaced.

'There she starts again. Hell, I thought she'd exhausted herself. Bloody Portuguese women are the end.'

'You should hear them having a baby,' grunted Grobbelaar.

'Where did you hear one?'

'There was one in the ward next door to my old girl at the maternity home. She nearly brought the bloody roof down.'

Grobbelaar's moustache took on a more melancholy droop as he thought about the work that lay ahead. Hours, days, weeks of questioning and checking and cross-checking, with a succession of sullen and uncooperative suspects.

He sighed and jerked a thumb at the corpse. 'All right, we've finished with him. Tell the butcher boys to come and fetch him.'

51

It had taken Rod almost two days to design his drop-blast matt. The angle and depth of the shot holes were carefully placed to achieve maximum disruption of the hanging wall. In addition he had decided to drill and charge the side walls of the drive with charges timed to explode *after* the hanging wall had collapsed. This would kick in on the rubble filling the tunnel and jam it solid.

Rod was fully aware of the power of water under pressures of 2,000 pounds per square inch and more and he had decided it was necessary to block at least three hundred feet of the tunnel. His matt blast was designed to do so, and yet he knew that this would not seal off the water completely. It would, however, reduce the flow sufficiently to allow cementation crews to get in and plug the drive solid.

The Delange brothers did not share Rod's enthusiasm for the project.

'Hey man, that's going to take three or four days to drill and charge,' Johnny protested when Rod showed him his carefully drawn plan.

'Like hell it will,' Rod growled at him. 'I want it done properly. It will take at least a week.'

'You said ultra-fast. You didn't say nothing about drilling the hanging wall with more holes than a cheese!'

'Well, I'm saying it now,' Rod told him grimly. 'And I'm also saying that you will drill, but you won't charge the holes until I come down and make sure that you've gone in as deep as I want them.'

He didn't trust either Johnny or Davy to spend time drilling in twenty feet, when he could go in six feet, charge up and nobody would know the difference. Not until it was too late.

Davy Delange spoke for the first time.

'Will you credit us bonus fathomage while we fiddle around with this?' he asked.

'Four fathoms a shift.' Rod agreed to pay them for the removal of fictitious rock.

'Eight?' said Davy.

'Hell, no!' Rod exclaimed. That was robbery.

'I don't know,' Davy murmured, watching Rod with sly ferrety little eyes. 'Maybe I should talk to Brother Duivenhage, you know, ask his advice.'

Duivenhage was No. 1 shaft shop steward for the Mine Workers' Union. He had driven Frank Lemmer to the edge of a nervous breakdown and was now starting on Rodney Ironsides. Rod was pleading with Head Office to offer Duivenhage a fat job in management to get him out of the way. The last thing in the world that Rod wanted was Brother Duivenhage snooping around his drive on the Big Dipper.

'Six,' he said.

'Well . . .' Davy hesitated.

'Six is fair, Davy,' Johnny interrupted, and Davy glared at him. Johnny had snatched complete victory from his grasp.

'Good, that's agreed.' Quickly Rod closed the negotiations. 'You'll start drilling the matt right away.'

Rod's design demanded nearly twelve hundred shot holes to be filled with two and a half tons of explosive. It was a thousand feet down the drive from the main haulage on 66 level to where the matt began.

The drive now was a spacious, well lit and freshly ventilated tunnel, with the vent piping, the compressed air pipe, and the electrical cable bolted into the hanging wall, and a set of steel railway tracks laid along the floor.

All work on the face ceased while the Delange brothers set about drilling the matt. It was light work that demanded little from the men. As each hole was drilled, Davy would insert his charging rod to check the depth and then plug the entrance with a wad of paper. There was much time for drinking Thermos coffee and for thinking.

There were three subjects that endlessly occupied Davy's mind as he sat at ease, waiting for the completion of the next shot hole. Sometimes for half an hour at a time Davy would hold the image of that fifty thousand Rand in his mind. It was his, tax paid, painstakingly accumulated over the years and lovingly deposited with the local branch of the Johannesburg Building Society. He imagined it bundled and stacked in neat green piles in the Society's vault. Each bundle was labelled 'David Delange'.

Then his imagination would pass automatically on to the farm that the money would buy. He saw how it would be in the evenings when he sat on the wide stoep, with the setting sun striking the peaks of the Swart Berg across the valley, and the cattle coming in from the paddocks towards the homestead.

Always there was a woman sitting beside him on the stoep. The woman had red hair.

On the fifth morning Davy drove home in the dawn, he was not tired. The night's labours had been easy and unexacting.

The door of Johnny and Hettie's bedroom was closed. Davy read the newspapers with his breakfast, as always the cartoon strip adventures of Modesty Blaise and Willie Garvin intrigued him completely. This morning Modesty was depicted in a bikini and Davy studied her comparing her to the big healthy body of his brother's wife. The thought of her stayed with him as he rolled onto his bed, and he lay unsleeping, daydreaming an adventure in which Modesty Blaise had become Hettie, and Willie Garvin was Davy.

An hour later he was still awake. He sat up and reached for the towel which lay across the foot of his bed. He wrapped the towel around his waist as he went down the passage to the bathroom. As he reached for the handle of the bathroom door, it opened under his hand and he was face to face with Hettie Delange.

She wore a white lace dressing-gown with ostrich-feather mules on her feet. Her face was innocent of make-up and she had brushed her hair and tied it with a ribbon.

'Oh!' she gasped with surprise. 'You gave me a fright, man.'

'I'm sorry, hey.' Davy grinned at her, holding the towel with one hand. Hettie let her eyes run quickly over his naked upper body.

Davy was muscled like a prize fighter. His chest hair was crisp and curly. On both arms the tattoos drew attention to the thickness and weight of muscle.

'Gee, you *are* built,' Hettie murmured in admiration, and Davy sucked in his belly reflexively.

'You think so?' His grin was self-conscious now.

'Yes.' Hettie leaned forward and touched his arm. 'It's hard too!'

The movement had allowed the front of her dressing-gown to gape open. Davy's face flushed as he looked down into the opening. He started to say something, but his voice had dried up on him. Hettie's fingers stroked down his arm, and she was watching the direction of his eyes. Slowly she moved closer to him.

'Do you like me, Davy?' she asked, her voice throaty and low, and with an animal cry Davy attacked her.

His hands ripping at the opening of her gown, pinning her to the wall of the bathroom with his mouth frantically hunting hers. His body pressing hard and urgent, his eyes wild, his breathing ragged.

Hettie was laughing, a breathless gasping laugh.

This was what she loved. When they lost their heads, when they went mad for her.

'Davy,' she said, jerking loose his towel. 'Davy.'

She kept wriggling away from this thrusting hips, knowing that it would inflame him further. His hands tearing at her body, his eyes were maniacal.

'Yes!' she hissed into his mouth. He threw her off balance and she slid down the wall onto the floor.

'Wait,' she panted. 'Not here – the bedroom.'

But it was too late.

Davy had spent the afternoon locked in his bedroom, lying on his bed in an agony of black all-pervading remorse and guilt.

'My brother,' he kept repeated. 'Johnny is my brother.'

Once he wept, each sob tearing something in his chest. The tears squeezed out between burning eyelids, leaving him feeling exhausted and weak.

'My *own* brother,' he shook his head slowly in horrified disbelief. 'I cannot stay here,' he decided miserably. 'I'll have to go.'

He went to the washbasin and washed his eyes. Stooping over the basin, water still dripping from his face, he decided.

'I will have to tell him.' The burden of guilt was too heavy. 'I'll write to Johnny. I'll write it all, and then I'll go away.'

Frantically he searched for pen and paper, it was almost as though he could wipe away the deed by writing it down. He sat at the table by the window and wrote slowly and laboriously. When he had finished it was three o'clock. He felt better.

He sealed the four closely written pages into an envelope and slipped it into the inside pocket of his jacket. He dressed quickly, and crept out of the house, fearful of meeting Hettie, but she was nowhere about. Her big white Monaco was not in the garage, and with relief he turned out of the driveway and took the road out to the Sonder Ditch. He wanted to reach the mine before Johnny came off shift.

Davy listened to his brother's voice, as he kidded and laughed with the other off-duty miners in the company change house. He had locked himself in one of the lavatory closets to avoid meeting his brother, and he sat disconsolately on the toilet seat. The sound of Johnny's voice brought his guilt flooding back in its full strength. His letter of confession was buttoned into the top pocket of his overalls, and he took it out, broke open the flap and reread the contents.

'So long, then.' Johnny's voice sang out gaily from the change room. 'See you bastards tomorrow.'

There was an answering chorus from the other miners, then the door slammed.

Davy went on sitting alone for another twenty minutes in the stench of stale bodies and urine, dirty socks and rank disinfections from the foot baths. At last he tucked the letter away in his pocket and opened the closet door.

Davy's gang were at their waiting place at the head of the drive. They were sitting along the bench laughing and chatting. There was a holiday spirit amongst them for they knew it would be another shift of easy going.

They greeted Davy cheerfully, as he came down the haulage. Both the Delange brothers were popular with their gangs and it was unusual that Davy did not reply to the chorused greeting. He did not even smile.

The Swazi boss boy handed him the safety lamp, and Davy grunted an acknowledgement. He set off alone down the tunnel, trudging heavily, not conscious of his surroundings, his mind encased in a padding of guilt and self-pity.

A thousand feet along the drive he reached the day's work area. Johnny's shift had left the rock drills in place, still connected to the compressed air system, ready for use. Davy came to a halt in the centre of the work area, and without a conscious command from his brain his hands began the routine process of striking the wick of the safety lamp.

The little blue flame came alight behind the protective screen of wire mesh, and Davy held the lamp at eye level before him and walked slowly along the drive. His eyes were watching the flame without seeing it.

The air in the tunnel was cool and refrigerated, scrubbed and filtered, there was no odour nor taste to it. Davy walked on somnambulantly. He was wallowing in self-pity now. He saw himself in a semi-heroic role, one of the great lovers of history caught up in tragic circumstances. His brain was fully occupied with the picture. His eyes were unseeing. Blindly he performed the ritual that a thousand times before had begun the day's shift.

Slowly in its wire mesh cage the blue flame of the safety lamp changed shape. Its crest flattened, and there formed above it a ghostly pale line. Davy's eyes saw it, but his brain refused to accept the message. He walked on in a stupor of guilt and self-pity.

That line above the flame was called 'the cap', it signified that there was at least a five per cent concentration of methane gas in the air. The last shot hole that Johnny Delange's gang had drilled before going off shift, had bored into a methane-filled fissure. For the previous three hours, gas had been blowing out of that hole. The ventilation system was unable to wash the air fast enough and now the gas had spread slowly down the drive. The air surrounding Davy's body was heavy with gas, he had breathed it into his lungs. It needed just one spark to ignite it.

Davy reached the end of the drive and snapped the snuffer over the wick, extinguishing the flame in the lamp.

'All safe,' he muttered, not realizing that he had spoken. He went back to his waiting men.

'All safe,' he repeated, and with the Swazi boss boy leading them the forty men of Davy Delange's gang trooped gaily into the mouth of the drive.

Moodily Davy followed them. As he walked he reached into

544

his hip pocket and took out a pack of Lexington filter tips. He put one between his lips, returned the pack and began patting his pockets to locate his lighter.

Davy went from team to team of his machine boys, directing them in the line and spot to be drilled. Every time he spoke, the unlit cigarette waggled between his lips. He gesticulated with the hand that held his cigarette-lighter.

It took twenty minutes for him to set all his drills to work. And he stood and looked back along the tunnel. Each machine boy and his assistant formed a separate sculpture. Most of them were stripped to the waist. Their bodes appeared to be carved and polished in oiled ebony, as they braced themselves behind the massive rock drills.

Davy lifted his cupped hands, holding the cigarette-lighter near his face and he flicked the cog wheel.

The air in the tunnel turned to flame. In a flash explosion, the flame reached the temperature of a welding torch. It seared the skin from the faces and exposed bodies of the machine boys, it burned the hair from their scalps. It turned their arms to charred stumps. It roasted their eyeballs in their sockets. It scorched their clothing, so as they fell the cloth smouldered and burned against their flesh.

In that instant, as the skin was licked from his face and hands, Davy Delange opened his mouth in a great gasp of agony. The flame shot down his throat into his gas-drenched lungs. Within the confines of his body the gas exploded and his chest popped like a paper bag, his ribs fanning outward about the massive wound like the petals of a sunflower.

Forty-one men died at the same moment. In the silence after that whooshing, sucking detonation, they lay like scorched insets along the floor of the drive. One or two of them were moving still, an arched spine relaxing, a leg straightening, charred fingers unclenching, but within a minute all was absolutely still.

Half an hour later Doctor Dan Stander and Rodney Ironsides were the first men into the drive. The smell of burned flesh was overpowering. Both of them had to swallow down their nausea as they went forward.

52

Dan Stander sat at his desk and looked out over the car park in front of the mine hospital. He appeared to have aged ten years since the previous evening. Dan envied his colleagues the detachment they could bring to their work. He had never been able to perfect the trick. He had just completed forty-one examinations for issue of death certificates.

For fifteen years he had been a mine doctor, so he was accustomed to dealing with death in its more hideous forms. This, however, was the worst he had ever encountered. Forty-one of them, all victims of severe burning and massive explosion trauma.

He felt washed out, exhausted with ugliness. He massaged his temples as he examined the tray of pathetic possessions that lay on the desk before him. This was the contents of the pockets of the man Delange. Extracting them from the scorched clothing had been a filthy business in itself. Cloth had burned into the flesh, the man had been wearing a cheap nylon shirt under his overalls. The fabric had melted in the heat and had become part of his blistered skin.

There was a bunch of keys on a brass ring, a Joseph Rogers pen-knife with a bone handle, a Ronson cigarette-lighter which had been clutched in the man's clawed and charred right hand, a springbok skin wallet, and a loose envelope with one corner burned away.

Dan had already passed on the effects of the Bantu victims to the agent of the Bantu Recruiting Agency, who would send them on to the men's families. Now he sighed with distaste and picked up the wallet. He opened it.

In one compartment there were half a dozen postage stamps, and five Rands in notes. The other flap bulged with paper. Dan glanced through salesmen's cards, dry-cleaning receipts, newspaper cuttings offering farms for sale, a folded page from the

Farmer's Weekly on the planning of a dairy herd, a J.B.S. Savings Book.

Dan opened the Savings Book and whistled when he saw the total. He fanned the remaining pages.

There was a much-fingered envelope, unsealed and tucked behind the cardboard cover of the Savings Book. Dan opened it, and pulled a face. It contained a selection of photographs of the type which one found offered for sale in the dock area of the Mozambique port of Lourenço Marques. It was for this type of material that Dan was searching.

When the man's possessions were returned to his grieving relatives, Dan wanted to spare them this evidence of human frailty. He burned the photographs and the envelope in his ash-tray and then crushed the blackened sheets to powder before spilling it into his waste-paper bin.

He went across to the window and opened it to let the smell of smoke escape. He stood at the window and searched the car park for Joy's Alfa Romeo. She had not arrived as yet and Dan returned to his desk.

The remaining envelope caught his eye and he picked it up. There was a smear of blood upon it, and the corner was burned away. Dan removed the four sheets of paper and spread them on the desk:

'Dear Johnny,

When Pa died you were still little – and I always reckoned you were more like my son, you know, than my brother.

Well, Johnny, I reckon now I've got to tell you something . . .'

Dan read slowly, and he did not hear Joy come into the room. She stood at the door watching him. Her expression fond, a small smile on her lips, shiny blonde hair hanging straight to her shoulders. Then she moved up quietly behind his chair and kissed his ear. Dan started and turned to face her.

'Darling,' Joy said and kissed him on the mouth. 'What is so interesting that you ignore my arrival?'

Dan hesitated a moment before telling her.

'There was a man killed last night in a ghastly accident. This was in his pocket.'

He handed her the letter and she read it slowly.

'He was going to send this to his brother?' she asked, and Dan nodded.

'The bitch,' Joy whispered, and Dan looked surprised.

'Who?'

'The girl – it's her fault, you know.' Joy opened her purse and took out a tissue to dab her eyes. 'Damn it, now I'm messing my make-up.' She sniffed, and then went on. 'It would serve her right if you gave that letter to her husband.'

'You mean I shouldn't give it to him?' Dan asked. 'We have no right to play God.'

'Haven't we?' asked Joy, and Dan watched quietly as she tore the letter to tiny shreds, screwed them into a ball, then dropped them into the waste bin.

'You are wonderful,' he said. 'Will you marry me?'

'I've already answered that question, Dr Stander.' And she kissed him again.

53

Hettie Delange was in a turmoil.

It had started with the phone call that had roused Johnny from their bed. He had said something about trouble at the shaft as he pulled on his clothes, but she had come only briefly awake and then drifted off again as Johnny hurried out into the night.

He had come in hours later and sat on the edge of the bed, his hands clasped between his knees and his head bowed.

'What's wrong, man,' she had snapped at him. 'Come to bed. Don't just sit there.'

'Davy's dead.' His voice had been listless.

There was a moment's shock that had convulsed the muscles of her belly, and brought her fully awake. Then, immediately she had felt a swift cleansing rush of relief.

He was dead. It was as easy as that! All day she had worried. She had been stupid to let it happen. Just that moment of weakness, that self-indulgent slip and she had been dreading the consequences all that day. She had imagined Davy trailing after her with puppy eyes, trying to touch her, making it so obvious that even Johnny would see it. She had enjoyed it but just the once was enough. She wanted no repeat performance and certainly no complications to follow the original deed.

Now it was all taken care of. He was dead.

'Are you sure?' she had asked anxiously, and Johnny heard the tone as concern.

'I saw him!' Johnny had shuddered, and wiped the back of his hand across his mouth.

'Gee, that's terrible.' Hettie had remembered her role, and sat up and put her arms about Johnny. 'That's terrible for you.'

She had not slept again that night. Somehow the thought of Davy going directly from her to his violent death was exciting. It was like in the movies, or a book, or something. Like he was an airman and he had been shot down, and she was his girl.

Perhaps she was pregnant and all alone in the world, and she would have to go to Buckingham Palace and get his medal for him. And the Queen would say . . .

The fantasies had played out in her mind until the dawn, with Johnny tossing and muttering beside her.

She woke him when it was first light in the room.

'How was he?' she asked softly. 'What did he look like, Johnny?'

Johnny shuddered again, and then he started to tell her. His voice was husky, and the sentences broken and disconnected. When he stumbled into silence, Hettie found herself trembling with excitement.

'How terrible,' she kept repeating. 'Oh, how awful!' And she pressed against him. After a while Johnny made love to her, and for Hettie it was better than she had ever known it to be.

All that morning there were phone calls, and four of her friends came over to drink coffee with her. A reporter and photographer from the *Johannesburg Star* called and asked questions. Hettie was the centre of attraction, and again and again she repeated the story with all its grisly details.

After lunch Johnny came home with a little dark-haired man in a charcoal suit and black Italian shoes, with a matching black briefcase.

'Hettie, this is Mr Boart. He was Davy's lawyer. He's got something to tell you.'

'Mrs Delange. May I convey to you my sincere condolences in the tragic bereavement you and your husband have suffered.'

'Yes, it's terrible, isn't it?' Hettie was apprehensive. Had Davy told this lawyer about them? Had this man come to make trouble?

'Your brother-in-law made a will of which I am the executor. Your brother-in-law was a wealthy man. His estate is in excess of fifty thousand Rand.' Boart paused portentously. 'And you and your husband are the sole beneficiaries.'

Hettie looked dubiously from Boart to Johnny.

'I don't – what's that mean? Beneficiary?'

'It means that you and your husband share the estate between you.'

'I get half of fifty thousand Rand?' Hettie asked in delighted disbelief.

'That's right.'

'Gee,' exulted Hettie. 'That's fabulous!' She could hardly wait for Johnny and the lawyer to go before she phoned her friends again. All four of them returned to drink more coffee, to thrill again and to envy Hettie the glamour and excitement of it.

'Twenty-five thousand,' they kept repeating the sum with relish.

'Hell, man, he must really have liked you a lot, Hettie,' one of the girls commented with heavy emphasis, and Hettie lowered her eyes and contrived to look bereft and mysterious.

Johnny came home after six, unsteady on his feet and reeking of liquor. Reluctantly Hettie's four friends left to rejoin their waiting families, and almost immediately after that a big white sports car pulled up in the driveway and Hettie's day of triumph was complete. Not one of her friends had ever had the General Manager of the Sonder Ditch Gold Mining Company call at their home.

She had the front door open the instant the doorbell rang. Her greeting had been shamelessly plagiarized from a period movie that had recently played at the local cinema.

'Mr Ironsides, how good of you to come.'

When she led Rod through into the over-furnished lounge, Johnny looked up but did not get to his feet.

'Hello, Johnny', said Rod. 'I have come to tell you that I'm sorry about Davy, and to . . .'

'Don't give me that bull dust, Tin Ribs,' said Johnny Delange.

'Johnny,' gasped Hettie, 'you can't talk to Mr Ironsides like that.' And she turned to Rod, laying a hand on his sleeve. 'He doesn't mean it, Mr Ironsides. He has been drinking.'

'Get out of here,' said Johnny. 'Get into the bloody kitchen where you belong.'

'Johnny!'

'Get out!' roared Johnny, rising from his chair, and Hettie fled from the room.

Johnny lurched across to the chrome and glass liquor cabinet that filled one corner. He sloshed whisky into two glasses and handed one to Rod.

'God speed to my brother,' he said.

'To Davy Delange, one of the best rock hounds on the Kitchenerville field,' said Rod, and tossed the drink back in one gulp.

'The best!' Johnny corrected him, and emptied his own glass.

He gasped at the sting of the whisky, then leaned forward to speak into Rod's face.

'You've come to find out if I'm game to finish your bloody drive for you, or if I'm going to quit. Davy didn't mean nothing to you and I don't mean nothing to you. Only one thing worrying you – you want to know about your bloody drive.' Johnny refilled his glass. 'Well, hear this, friend, and hear it well. Johnny Delange don't quit. That drive ate my brother but I'll beat the bastard, so you got nothing to worry about. You go home and get a good night's sleep, 'cos Johnny Delange will be on shift and breaking rock tomorrow morning first thing.'

54

A Silver Cloud Rolls-Royce was parked amongst the trees in the misty morning. Ahead was the practice track with the white-painted railings curving away towards the willow-lined river. The mist was heavier along the river and the grass was very green against it.

The uniformed chauffeur stood away from the Rolls, leaving its two occupants in privacy. They sat on the back seat with an angora wool travelling rug spread over their knees. On the folding table in front of them was a silver Thermos of coffee, shell-thin porcelain cups, and a plate of ham sandwiches.

The fat man was eating steadily, washing each mouthful down with coffee. The little bald-headed man was not eating, instead he puffed quickly and nervously at his cigarette and looked out of the window at the horses. The grooms were walking the horses in circles, nostrils streaming in the morning chill, blankets flapping. The jockeys stood looking up at the trainer. They wore hard caps and polo-necked jerseys. All of them carried whips. The trainer was speaking urgently, his hands thrust deep into the pockets of his overcoat.

'It's a very fine service,' said the little man. 'I particularly enjoyed the stop in Rio. My first visit there.'

The fat man grunted. He was annoyed. They shouldn't have sent this agent out. It was a mark of suspicion, distrust, and it would seriously hamper his market operation.

The conference between trainer and jockeys had ended. The diminutive riders scattered to their mounts, and the trainer came towards the Rolls.

'Good morning, sir.' He spoke through the open window, and the fat man grunted again.

'I'm giving him a full run,' the trainer went on. 'Emerald Isle will make pace for him to the five, Pater Noster will take over and push him to the mile, I've Tiger Shark to pace him for the run in.'

'Very well.'

'Perhaps you'd like to keep time, sir.' The trainer proferred a stop-watch, and the fat man seemed to recover his urbanity and charm.

'Thank you, Henry.' He smiled. 'He looks good, I'll say that.' The trainer was pleased by the condescension.

'Oh! He's red hot! By Saturday I'll have him sharpened down to razor edge.' He stood back from the window. 'I'll get them off, then.' He walked away.

'You have a message for me?' asked the fat man.

'Of course.' The other wriggled his moustache like a rabbit's whiskers. It was an annoying habit. 'I didn't fly all this way out here to watch a couple of mokes trotting around a race-track.'

'Would you like to give me the message?' The fat man hid his affront. What the agent had called a moke was some of the finest horseflesh in Africa.

'They want to know about this gas explosion.'

'Nothing.' The fat man dismissed the question with a wave of his hand. 'A flash explosion. Killed a few men. No damage to the workings. Negligence on the part of the miner in charge.'

'Will it affect our plans?'

'Not one iota.'

The two horses had jumped away from the start, shoulder to shoulder, with the wreaths of mist swirling in their wake. The glossy bay horse on the rails ran with an easy floating action while the grey plunged along beside it.

'My principals are very concerned.'

'Well, they have no need to be,' snapped the fat man. 'I tell you it makes no difference.'

'Was the explosion due to an error of judgement on the part of this man Ironsides?'

'No.' The fat man shook his head. 'It was negligence of the miner in charge. He should have detected the gas.'

'Pity.' The bald man shook his head regretfully. 'We had hoped it was a flaw in the Ironsides character.'

The grey horse was tiring, while the bay ran on smoothly, drawing away from him. From the side rail a third horse came in to replace the grey, and ran shoulder to shoulder with the bay.

'Why should the character of Ironsides concern you?'

'We have heard disturbing reports. This is no pawn to be moved at will. He is taking the job of general manager by the throat. Already our sources indicate that he has reduced running costs on the Sonder Ditch by a scarcely believable two per cent. He seems to be tireless, inventive – a man, in short, to reckon with.'

'Well and good,' the fat man conceded. 'But I still fail to see why your – ah, principals – are alarmed. Do they expect that this man will hold back the flood waters by the sheer force of his personality?'

The second pacemaker was faltering, but still the big bay ran on alone. A far figure in the mist, passing the mile post, joined at last by the third pacemaker.

'I know nothing about horses,' said the bald man watching the two flying forms. 'But I've just seen that one,' he pointed with his cigarette at the far-off bay. 'I've just seen him run the guts out of the other two. One after the other he has broken their hearts and left them staggering along behind him. We would call him an imponderable, one who cannot be judged by normal standards.' He puffed at his cigarette before going on. 'There are men like that also, imponderable. It seems to us that Ironsides is one of them, and we don't like it. We don't like them on the opposing team. It is just possible that he could upset the entire operation, not, as you put it, by sheer force of personality, but by suddenly doing the unexpected, by behaving in a manner for which we have not allowed.'

Both men fell silent watching the galloping horses come round the last bend and hit the straight.

'Watch this.' The fat man spoke softly, and as though in response to his words the big bay lengthened his stride, reaching out, driving strongly away from the other horse. His head was going like a hammer, twin jets of steam shot from wide flaring nostrils, and thrown turf and dirt flew from his hooves. Five lengths clear of the following horse he went slashing past the finish line and the fat man clicked his stop watch.

He scrutinized the dial of the watch anxiously and then chuckled like a healthy baby.

'And he wasn't really being extended!'

He rapped on the window beside him, and immediately the

unformed chauffeur opened the driving door and slid in behind the wheel.

'To my office,' instructed the fat man, 'and close the partition.'

When the sound-proof glass panel had slid closed between driver and passengers, the fat man turned to his guest.

'And so, my friend, you consider Ironsides to be an imponderable. What do you want me to do about him?'

'Get rid of him.'

'Do you mean what I think you mean?' The fat man lifted an eyebrow.

'No. Nothing that drastic.' The bald head bobbed agitatedly. 'You have been reading too much James Bond. Simply arrange it that Ironsides is far away and well occupied when the drive holes through the Big Dipper Dyke, otherwise there is an excellent chance that he will do something to frustrate our good intentions.'

'I think we can arrange that,' said the fat man and helped himself to another ham sandwich.

55

As he had promised, Manfred caught the Friday evening flight for Cape Town. On the Saturday night Rod and Terry took a wild chance on not being recognized and spent the evening at the Kyalami Ranch Hotel. They danced and dined in the Africa Room, but were on their way back to the apartment before midnight.

In the dawn a playful slap with the rolled-up Sunday papers which Rod delivered to Terry's naked posterior as she slept triggered off a noisy brawl in which a picture was knocked off the wall by a flying pillow, a coffee table overturned and the shrieking and laughter reached such a pitch that it called down a storm of indignant thumping from the apartment above them.

Terry made a defiant gesture at the ceiling, but they both subsided gasping with laughter back onto the bed to indulge in activity every bit as strenuous if not nearly so noisy.

Later, much later, they collected Melanie and once again spent the Sunday at the stud farm on the Vaal. Melanie actually *rode* a horse, a traumatic experience which bade fair to alter her whole existence. After lunch they launched the speedboat from the boat house on the bank of the river and water-skied down as far as the barrage, Terry and Rod taking turns at the wheel and on the skis. It occurred to Rod that Terry Steyner looked good in a white bikini. It was dark before Rod delivered his sleeping daughter to her mother.

'Who is this *Terry* that Melanie talks about all the time?' demanded Patti, she was still sulking about Rod's promotion. Patti had a memory like a tax collector.

'Terry?' Rod feigned surprise. 'I thought you knew.' And he left Patti glaring after him as he went back down the stairs.

Terry was curled up in the leather bucket seat of the Maserati, just the tip of her nose protruding from the voluminous fur coat she wore.

'I love your daughter, Mr Ironsides,' she murmured.

'It would appear that the feeling is reciprocated.'

Rod drove slowly towards the hillbrow ridge, and Terry's hand came out of the wide fur sleeve and lay on his knee.

'Wouldn't it be nice if we had a daughter of our own one day?'

'Wouldn't it,' Rod agreed dutifully, and then found to his intense amazement that he really meant it.

He was still investigating this remarkable phenomenon as he parked the Maserati in the basement garage of his apartment and went round to open Terry's door.

Manfred Steyner watched Terry climb out of the Maserati and lift her face towards Rodney Ironsides. Ironsides stooped over her and kissed her, then he slammed and locked the door of the Maserati, and arm in arm the two of them crossed to the elevator.

'Peterson Investigations always delivers the goods,' said the man at the wheel of the black Ford parked in the shadows of the garage. 'We will give them half an hour to get settled in comfortably, then we will go up and knock on the door of his apartment.'

Manfred Steyner sat very still and unblinking on the seat beside the private detective. He had arrived back in Johannesburg three hours previously in answer to the summons from the investigation bureau.

'You will leave me here. Drive the Ford out and park at the corner of Clarendon Circle. Wait for me there,' said Manfred.

'Hey? Aren't you going to . . .?' The detective was taken aback.

'Do as I tell you.' Manfred's voice stung like thrown vitriol, but the detective persisted.

'You will need evidence for the court, you need me as a witness . . .'

'Get out,' Manfred snapped, and opening the door of the Ford he climbed out and closed the door behind him. The detective hesitated a moment longer, then started the engine and drove out of the garage leaving Manfred alone.

Manfred moved slowly towards the big shiny sports car. From his pocket he took a gold-plated pen-knife and opened the large blade.

He had recognized that the car was of special significance to the man. It was the only form of retaliation he could make at the moment. Until Rodney Ironsides completed the drive on the

Big Dipper Dyke, he could not confront him nor Theresa Steyner. He could not let them know he even suspected them.

Such human emotions as love and hate and jealousy Manfred Steyner seldom experienced, except in their mildest manifestations. Theresa Hirschfield he had never loved, as he had never loved any woman. He had married her for her wealth and station in life. The emotion that gripped him was neither hatred nor jealousy. It was affront. He was affronted that these two insignificant persons should conspire to cheat him.

He would not rush in blindly now with threats of physical violence and divorce. No, he would administer an anonymous punishment that would hurt the man deeply. This would be part payment. Later, when he had served his purpose, Manfred would crush him as coldly as though he were stepping on an ant.

As for the woman, he was aware of a mild relief. Her irresponsible behaviour had placed her completely at his mercy, both legally and morally. As soon as the strike beyond the Big Dipper had made him financially secure and independent, he could throw her aside. She would have served her purpose admirably.

The journey which he had interrupted by this hurried return to Johannesburg was connected with the purchase of Sonder Ditch shares. He was touring the major centres arranging with various firms of stock brokers that on a given date they would commence to purchase every available scrap of Sonder Ditch script.

As soon as he had completed this business he would tell the private detective to drive him out to Jan Smuts Airport where he had a reservation on the night plane to Durban where he would continue his preparations.

It had all worked out very well, he thought, as he slipped the knife blade through the rubber buffer of the triangular side window of the Maserati. With a quick twist he lifted the window catch, and pushed the window open. He reached through and turned the door handle. The door clicked open and Manfred climbed into the driver's seat.

The blade of the pen-knife was razor sharp. He started on the passenger seat and then the driver's seat, ripping the leather upholstery to shreds before moving to the back seat and repeating the process there. He slid the panel that concealed the tray of tools each in their separate foam rubber padded compartment, and selected a tyre lever.

With this he smashed all the dials on the dashboard, broken glass tinkling and falling to the carpeted floor. With the point of the tyre lever he dug into the rosewood panelling and tore out a section, splintering and cracking the woodwork into complete ruin.

He climbed out of the Maserati and struck the windshield with the tyre lever. The glass starred. He rained blows on it, unable to shatter it but reducing it to a sagging opaque sheet.

Then he dropped the tyre lever and groped for his pen-knife again. On his knees he slashed at the front offside tyre. The rubber was tougher than he had allowed. Annoyed, he slashed again. The knife turned in his hand, the blade folding against the blow. It sliced the ball of his thumb, a deep stinging cut. Manfred came to his feet with a cry, clutching his injured thumb. Blood spurted from the wound.

'Mein Gott! Mein Gott!' Manfred gasped, horrified by his own blood. As he staggered wildly from the basement garage, he was wrapping a handkerchief around his thumb.

He reached the waiting Ford, hauled the door open and fell into the front seat beside the detective.

'A Doctor! For God's sake, get me to a Doctor. I'm badly hurt. Quickly! Drive quickly!'

56

Terry's husband is due back in town today, Rod thought, as he sat down at his desk. It was not a thought that gave him strength to work through a day he knew would be filled with hectic activity.

The quarterly reports were due at Head Office tomorrow morning. In consequence the entire administration was in its usual late-minute panic. Already there was a mob in the waiting-room outside his office that Lily Jordan would soon need a stock whip to control. At three o'clock he was due at a consultants' meeting at Head Office, but before that he wanted to go underground to check the drop-blast matt that Johnny Delange had now completed and charged up.

The phone went as Lily led in his first visitor, a tall, thin, sorrowful-looking man with a droopy moustache.

'Mr Ironsides?' said the voice on the phone.

'Yes.'

'Porters Motors here. I've got an estimate on the repairs to your Maserati.'

'How much?' Rod cross his fingers.

'Twelve hundred Rand.'

'Wow!' Rod gasped.

'Do you want us to go ahead?'

'No, I'll have to contact my insurance company first. I'll call you.' He hung up. That act of unaccountable vandalism still irked him terribly. He realised that he would be reduced to the Company Volkswagen for a further indefinite period.

He turned his attention to his visitor.

'Detective Inspector Grobbelaar,' the tall man introduced himself. 'I am investigating officer in the murder of José Almeida, the concession store proprietor on this mine.'

They shook hands.

'Have you any ideas on who did it?' Rod asked.

'We have always got ideas,' said the Inspector, so sadly that for a moment Rod had the impression that his name was on the list of suspects. 'We believe that the murderer is employed by one of the mines in the district, probably the Sonder Ditch. I have called on you to ask for your co-operation in the investigation.'

'Of course.'

'I will be conducting a great number of interrogations amongst your Bantu employees. I hoped you might find a room for me to use on the premises.'

Rod lifted his phone and while he dialled he told Grobbelaar, 'I'm calling our Compound Manager.' Then he transferred his attention to the mouthpiece. 'Ironsides here. I am sending an Inspector Grobbelaar down to see you. Please see that an office is placed at his disposal and that he receives full co-operation.'

Grobbelaar stood up and extended his hand.

'I won't take up more of your time. Thank you, Mr Ironsides.'

His next visitor was Van der Bergh, his Personnel Officer, brandishing his departmental reports as though they were a winning lottery ticket.

'All finished,' he announced triumphantly. 'All we need is your signature.'

As Rod uncapped his pen, the telephone squealed again.

'My God,' he muttered with pen in one hand and telephone in the other. 'Is it worth it?'

It was well after one o'clock when Rod fled his office, leaving Lily Jordan to hold back the tide. He went directly to No. 1 shaft where he was welcomed like the prodigal son by Dimitri and his old Line Managers. They were all anxious to know who would be replacing him as Underground Manager. Rod promised to find out that afternoon when he visited Head Office, and changed into his overalls and helmet.

At the spot where Davy Delange had died, Rod found a gang fixing a screen of wire mesh over the hanging wall to protect the fuses of his drop-blast. The electric cable that carried the blasting circuit to the surface was covered with a distinctive green plastic coating and securely pegged to the roof of the drive.

In the concrete blast room at the shaft head, his electrician had already set up a separate control for this circuit. It would be in readiness at all times. He could fire it within minutes. Rod felt as though a great weight had been lifted from his shoulders as he passed through the swinging ventilation doors and tramped on up the drive to speak to Johnny Delange.

Half-way to the face he met the gigantic figure of Big King coming back towards him with a small gang of lashing boys under his command. Rod greeted him, and Big King stopped and let his gang go on out of earshot before he spoke.

'I wish to speak.'

'Speak then.' Rod noticed suddenly that Big King's face was gaunt, his eyes appeared sunken and his skin had the dusty greyish look of sickness so evident in an ailing Bantu.

'I wish to return to my wives in Portuguese Mozambique,' said Big King.

'Why?' Rod was dismayed at the prospect of losing such a valuable boss boy.

'My blood is thin.' This was as non-committal an answer as any man has ever received. In essence it meant, 'My reasons are my own, and I have no intention of disclosing them.'

'When your blood is thick again, will you return to work here?' Rod asked.

'That is with the gods.' An answer signifying no more than the one preceding it.

'I cannot stop you if you wish to go, Big King, you know that,' Rod told him. 'Report to the Compound Manager and he will mark your notice.'

'I have told the Compound Manager. He wants me to work out my ticket, thirty-three more days.'

'Of course,' Rod nodded. 'You know that it is a contract. You must work it out.'

'I wish to leave at once,' Big King replied stubbornly.

'Then you must give me your reason. I cannot let you break contract except if there is some good reason.' Rod knew better than to set a dangerous precedent like that.

'There is no reason.' Big King admitted defeat. 'I will work out the ticket.'

He left Rod and followed his gang down the drive. Since the night he killed the Portuguese, Big King had slept little and eaten less. Worry had kept his stomach in a turmoil of dysentry, he had neither danced nor sung. Nothing that Crooked Leg nor the Shangaan Induna could say comforted him. He waited for the police to come. As the days passed, so the flesh melted from his body, he knew that they could come before the thirty-three days of his contract expired.

His approach to Rod had been a last despairing effort. Now he was resigned. He knew that the police were inexorable. One day soon they would come. They would lock the silver chains on his wrists and lead him to the closed van. He had seen many men led away like that and he had heard what happened to them after that. The white man's law was the same as the tribal law of the Shangaans. The taking of life must be paid for with life.

They would break his neck with the rope. His ancestors would have crushed his skull with a war club, it was the same in the end.

Rod found Johnny Delange drinking cold tea from his canteen while his gang barred down the face.

'How's it going?' he asked.

'Now we have finished messing about, it has started moving again.' Johnny wiped cold tea from his lips and recorked the canteen. 'We have broken almost fifteen hundred feet since Davy died.'

'That's good going.' Rod ignored the reference to the methane explosion and the drop-blast matt.

'Would have been better if Davy were still alive.' Johnny disliked Campbell, the miner who had replaced Davy on the night shift. 'The night shift aren't breaking their fair ground.'

'I'll chase them up,' Rod promised.

'You do that.' Johnny turned away to shout an order at his gang.

Rod stood and stared at the end of the drive. Less than a thousand feet ahead lay the dark hard rock of the Big Dipper – and beyond it . . .? Rod felt his skin creep as he remembered his nightmare. That cold green translucent thing waiting for them beyond the dyke.

'All right, Johnny, you are getting close now.' Rod tore his imagination away from that green horror. 'As soon as you hit the Serpentine rock you are to stop work immediately and report to me. Is that understood?'

'You'd better tell that to Campbell also,' said Johnny. 'The night shift may hit the Big Dipper.'

'I'll tell him,' Rod agreed. 'But you make sure you remember. I want to be down here when we hole through the dyke.'

Rod glanced at his watch. It was almost two o'clock. He had an hour to get to the consultant's meeting at Head Office.

'You are late, Mr Ironsides.' Dr Manfred Steyner looked up from the head of the board-room table.

'My apologies, gentlemen.' Rod took his seat at the long oak table. 'Just one of those days.'

The men about the table murmured sympathetic acknowledgement, and Dr Steyner studied him for a moment without expression before remarking.

'I would be obliged for a few minutes of your time after this meeting, Mr Ironsides.'

'Of course, Dr Steyner.'

'Good.' Manfred nodded. 'Now that Mr Ironsides has graced the table with his presence, the meeting can come to order.' It was the closest any of them had every heard Dr Steyner come to making a joke.

It was dark outside when the meeting ended. The participants shrugged on their coats, made their farewells and left Manfred and Rod sitting at the table with its overflowing ash trays and littered pencils and note pads.

Manfred Steyner waited for fully three minutes after the door had closed on the last person to leave. Rod was accustomed to these long intent silences, yet he was uneasy. He sensed a new hostility in the man's attitude. He covered his awkwardness by lighting another cigarette and blowing a series of smoke rings at the portrait of Norman Hradsky, the original chairman of the company. Flanking Hradsky's portrait were two others. One of a slim blond man, with ravaged good looks and laughing blue eyes. The captain read: 'Dufford Charleywood. Director of C.R.C. from 1867–1872.' The other portrait in its heavy gilt frame depicted an impressively build man with mutton-chop whiskers and black Irish features. 'Sean Courtney' said the caption, and the dates were the same as Charleywood's.

These three had founded the Company, and Rod knew a little of their story. They had been as pretty a bunch of rogues as would be found in any convict settlement. Hradsky had ruined the other two in an ingenious bear raid on the stock exchange, and had virtually stolen their shares in the Company.*

We have become a lot more sophisticated since then, thought

*Read *When the Lion Feeds*

565

Rod. He looked instinctively towards the head of the long table and met Dr Steyner's level, unblinking stare. *Or have we?* he wondered. Just what devilment has our friend in mind?

Manfred Steyner was examining Rod with detached curiosity. So remote from any emotional rancour was Manfred, that he intended using the relationship that had developed between this man and his wife to further the instructions he had received that morning.

'How far is the end of the drive from the dyke?' he asked suddenly.

'Less than a thousand feet.'

'How much longer before you reach it?'

'Ten days. No more, possibly less.'

'As soon as the dyke is reached, all work on it must cease immediately. The timing of this is important, do you understand?'

'I have already instructed my miners not to hole through without my specific orders.'

'Good.' Manfred lapsed into silence for another full minute. Andrew had called him that morning with instructions from the man. Ironsides was to be well away from the Sonder Ditch when they pierced the dyke. It was left to Manfred to engineer his absence.

'I must inform you, Mr Ironsides, that it will be at least three weeks before I give the order to drill through. When you reach the dyke, it will be necessary for me to proceed to Europe to make certain arrangements there. I will be away for at least ten days during which time no work of any type must be allowed in the drive to the Big Dipper.'

'You will be away over Christmas?' Rod asked with surprise.

'Yes,' Manfred nodded, and could read Rod's mind.

Terry will be alone, Rod thought quickly, she will be alone over Christmas. The Sonder Ditch goes onto *essential services only* for a full seven days over Christmas. Just a skeleton crew to keep her going. I could get away for a week, a whole week away together.

Manfred waited until he knew that Rod had reached the decision to which he had been steered, then he asked: 'You understand? You will await my order to hole through. You need not expect that order until the middle of January.'

'I understand.'

'You may go.' Manfred dismissed him.

'Thanks,' Rod acknowledged drily.

There was a coffee bar in the ground-floor shopping centre of Reef Building. Rod beat a bearded hippie to the telephone booth, and dialled the Sandown number. It was safe enough, he had just left Manfred upstairs.

'Therese Steyner,' she answered his call.

'We've got a week to ourselves,' he told her. 'One whole glorious week.'

'When?' she demanded joyously.

And he told her.

'Where shall we go?' she asked.

'We'll think of somewhere.'

57

At 11.26 a.m. on December 16th, Johnny Delange blasted the face of the drive, and went forward in the fumes and dust.

In the beam of his lantern, the new rock blown from the face was completely different from the blueish Ventersdorp quartzite. It was a glassy, blackish green, veined with tiny white lines, more like marble than country rock.

'We are on the dyke.' He spoke to Big King, and stooped to pick up a lump of the Serpentine rock. He weighed it in his hand.

'We've done it, we've beaten the bastard!'

Big King stood silently beside him. He did not share Johnny's elation.

'Right!' Johnny tossed the lump of rock back onto the pile. 'Bar down, and make safe. Then pull them out of the drive. We are finished here until further orders.'

'Well done, Johnny,' applauded Rod. 'Clean her up and pull out of the drive. I don't know how much longer it will be till we get the order to hole through the dyke. But take a holiday in the meantime. I'll pay you four fathoms of bonus a day while you are waiting.' He broke the connection with his finger, keeping the receiver to his ear. He dialled and spoke to the switchboard girl at Head Office. 'Get me Dr Steyner, please. This is Rodney Ironsides.' He waited a few seconds and then Manfred came on the line.

'We've hit the Big Dipper,' Rod told him.

'I will leave for Europe on tomorrow morning's Boeing,' said Manfred. 'You are to do nothing until I return,' Manfred cradled the receiver and depressed the button on his intercom.

'Cancel all my appointments,' he told his secretary. 'I am unavailable.'

'Very well, Dr Steyner.'

Manfred picked up the receiver of his unlisted, direct-line telephone. He dialled.

'Hello, Andrew. Will you tell him that I am ready to discharge my obligations. We have intersected the Big Dipper.' He listened for a few seconds, then spoke again. 'Very well, I will wait for your reply.'

Andrew replaced the telephone and went out through the sliding glass doors onto the terrace. It was a lazy summer's day, hushed with heat, and the sun sparkled on the crystal clear waters of the swimming-pool. Insects murmured languidly in the massed banks of blooms that surrounded the terrace.

The fat man stood before an artist's easel. He wore a blue beret and a white smock that hung like a maternity dress over his jutting stomach.

His model lay face down on an air mattress by the edge of the pool. She was a dainty, dark-haired girl with a pixy face and a doll-like body. Her discarded bikini lay in a damp bundle on the flags of the terrace. Drops of water caught the sun and bejewelled her creamy buttocks, giving her a paradoxical air of innocence and oriental eroticism.

'That was Steyner,' said Andrew. 'He reports that they have hit the Big Dipper.'

The fat man did not look up. He went on laying paint upon the canvas with complete concentration.

'Please lift your right shoulder, my dear, you are covering that utterly delightful bosom of yours,' he instructed, and the girl obeyed him immediately.

Finally he stepped back and regarded his own work critically.

'You may have a break now.' He wiped his brushes while the naked girl stood up, stretched like a cat and then dived into the pool. She surfaced with the water slicking her short dark hair against her head like the pelt of an otter, and swam slowly to the far end of the pool.

'Cable New York, Paris, London, Tokyo and Berlin the code word "Gothic",' he instructed Andrew. This was the word which would unleash the bear offensive on the financial markets of the world. On receipt of those cables, agents in the major cities would begin to sell the shares of the companies mining the Kitchenerville field, sell them by the millions.

'Then instruct Steyner to get Ironsides out of the way, and hole through the dyke.'

Manfred answered Andrew's return call on the unlisted line. He listened to, and acknowledged, his instructions. Afterwards he sat still as a lizard, running over his preparations. Reviewing them minutely, examining them for flaws. There were none.

It was time to begin the purchase of Sonder Ditch shares. He called his secretary on the intercom and instructed her to place calls to numbers in Cape Town, Durban and Johannesburg itself. He wanted the purchase orders to come through a number of different brokers, so that it would not be obvious that there was only one buyer in the market. There was also the question of credit; he was not covering the purchase orders with Banker's guarantee. The stock brokers were buying for him simply on his name and reputation and position with C.R.C. Manfred could not place too large a buying order with any one firm lest they ask him to provide surety. Dr Manfred Steyner had no surety to offer.

So, instead, he placed moderate orders with dozens of different firms. By three o'clock that afternoon Manfred had ordered the purchase of three quarters of a million Rands' worth of shares. He had no means of paying for those shares but he knew he would never be called upon to do so. When he sold them again in a few weeks' time they would have doubled in value.

A few minutes after his final conversation with the firm of Swerling and Wright in Cape Town, his secretary came through on the intercom.

'S.A.A. have confirmed your reservation on the Boeing to Salisbury. Flight 126 at nine a.m. tomorrow. You are booked to return to Johannesburg on the Rhodesian Airways Viking at 6 p.m. tomorrow evening.'

'Thank you.' Manfred grudged this wasted day but it was imperative that Theresa believed he had left for Europe. She must see him depart on the S.A.A. flight. 'Please get my wife on the phone for me.'

'Theresa,' he told her, 'something important has come up. I have to fly to London tomorrow morning. I am afraid I will be away over Christmas.'

Her display of surprise and regret was unconvincing. She and

Ironsides had made their own arrangements for the time he was away, Manfred was convinced of this.

It was all working out very well, he thought, as he cradled the receiver, very well indeed.

58

The Daimler drew up under the portico of Jan Smuts Airport and the chauffeur opened the door for Terry and then for Manfred.

While the porter removed his luggage from the boot of the Daimler, Manfred swept the car park with a quick scrutiny. So early in the morning it was less than half filled. There was a cream Volkswagen with a Kitchenerville number plate parked near the far end. All the line and senior members of the Sonder Ditch had cream Volkswagens as their official vehicles.

'The bee has come to the honeypot,' thought Manfred, and smiled bleakly. He took Terry's elbow into the main concourse of the airport.

Terry waited while Manfred went through his ticket and immigration formalities. On the outside she was a demure and dutiful wife, but she also had seen the Volkswagen and inside she was itching and bubbling with excitement. Darting surreptitious glances from behind her sunglasses, looking for that tall broad-shouldered figure among the crowds.

It seemed a lifetime until she stood alone on the observation balcony with the wind whipping her piebald calf-skin coat around her legs, and blowing her hair into a snapping, dancing tangle. The long shark-like shape of the Boeing jet crouched at the far end of the runway and as it started forward Terry turned from the balcony rail and ran back into the main building.

Rod was waiting for her just inside the doors, and he swung her off her feet.

'Gottcha!'

With her feet dangling, she put her arms around his neck and kissed him.

The watchers paused and then smiled, and there was a minor traffic jam at the head of the stairs.

'Come on,' she entreated, 'let's not waste a minute of it.'

He put her on her feet, and they ran down the staircase hand in hand. Terry paused only to dismiss the chauffeur, and then they ran through the car park like children let out of school, and clambered into the Volkswagen. Their luggage was on the back seat.

'Go,' she said, 'go as fast as you can!'

Twenty minutes later Rod pulled the Volkswagen to a tyre-squealing halt in front of the hangars at the private airfield.

The twin-engined Cessna stood on the tarmac. Both engines were ticking over in readiness, and the mechanic climbed down from the cockpit when he recognized Terry.

'Hello, Terry, right on time,' he greeted her.

'Hello, Hank. You've got her warmed up already. You are a sweety!'

'Filed your flight plan also. Nothing too good for my most favourite customer.' The mechanic was a chunky grizzled little man, and he looked at Rod curiously.

'Give you a hand with the bags,' he said.

By the time they had the luggage stowed away in its compartment, Terry was in the cockpit speaking to the control tower.

Rod climbed up into the passenger seat beside her.

Terry switched off her radio and leaned over Rod's lap to speak to Hank.

'Thanks, Hank.' She paused delicately, and then went on with a rush. 'Hank, if anyone asks you, I was on my own today, okay?'

'Okay.' Hank grinned at her. 'Happy landings.' And he closed the cockpit door, and Terry taxied out onto the runway.

'Is this yours? Rod asked. It was a hundred thousand Rands' worth of aircraft.

'Pops gave it to me for my birthday,' Terry replied. 'Do you like it?'

'Not bad,' Rod admitted.

Terry turned upwind and applied the wheel brakes while she ran the engines up to peak revs, testing their response.

Suddenly Rod realized that he was in the hands of a woman pilot. He fell silent and his nerves began to tighten up.

'Let's go,' said Terry and kicked off the brakes. The Cessna surged forward, and Rod gripped the arm rests and froze with his gaze fixed dead ahead.

'Relax, Ironsides,' Terry advised him without taking her eyes off the runway, 'I've been flying since I was sixteen.'

At three thousand feed she levelled out and banked gently onto an easterly heading.

'Now that didn't hurt too much did it?' She smiled sideways at him.

'You are quite a girl,' he told her. 'You can do all sorts of tricks.'

'You just wait,' she warned him. 'You ain't seen nothing yet!'

They flew in silence until the Highveld had fallen away behind them, and they were over the dense green mattress of the Bushveld.

'I'm going to divorce him.' She broke the silence, and Rod was not surprised that they were experiencing the mental telepathy of closely attunded minds. He had been thinking about her husband also.

'Good,' he said.

'You think I'd have a chance with you if I did?'

'If you played your cards right, you might get that lucky.'

'Conceited swine,' she said. 'I don't know why I love you.'

'Do you?' he asked.

'Yes.'

'And I you.'

They relapsed into a contented silence, until Terry put the Cessna in a shallow dive.

'What's wrong?' Rod asked with alarm.

'Going down to have a look for game.'

They flew low over thick olive-green bush broken by veils of golden brown grass.

'There,' said Rod, pointing ahead. A line of fat black bugs moving across one of the open places. 'Buffalo!'

'And over there.' Terry pointed left.

'Zebra and wildebeeste,' Rod identified them. 'And there is a giraffe.' Its long stalk of a neck stuck up like a periscope. It broke into an awkward stiff-legged run as the aircraft roared overhead.

'We have arrived.' Terry indicated a pair of round granite koppies on the horizon ahead. They were as symmetrical as a young girl's breasts, and as they drew nearer Rod made out the thatched roof of a large building standing in the hollow between the koppies. Beyond it a long straight landing-strip had been cut from the trees, and the fat white sausage of a wind sock flew from its pole.

Terry throttled back and circled the homestead. On the lawns half a dozen tiny figures waved up at the Cessna, and as they watched, two of the figures climbed into a toy Landrover and set off for the landing-strip. A ribbon of white dust blew out from behind it.

'That's Hans,' Terry explained. 'We can go down now.'

She lined the Cessna up for its approach, and then let it sink down with the motors bumbling softly. The ground came up and jarred the undercarriage, then they were taxiing to meet the racing Landrover.

The man who piled out of the Landrover was white-haired, and sunburned like old leather.

'Mrs Steyner!' He was making no attempt to conceal his pleasure. 'Its been much too long. Where have you been?'

'I've been busy, Hans.'

'New York? What the hell for?' said Hans surprisingly.

'This is Mr Ironsides.' Terry introduced them. 'Rod, this is Hans Kruger.'

'Van Breda?' asked Hans as they shook hands. 'You related to the van Bredas from Caledon?'

'I don't think so,' Rod muttered weakly and looked at Terry appealingly.

'He is stone deaf,' Terry explained. 'Both his ear drums blown out by a hangfire in the 1930s. He won't admit it though.'

'I'm glad to hear it,' Hans nodded, happily. 'You always were a healthy girl. I remember when you were a little piccanin.'

'He is an absolute darling though, so is his wife. They look after the shooting lodge for Pops,' Terry told Rod.

'Good idea!' Hans agreed heartily. 'Let's get your bags in the Landrover and go up to the house. I bet Mr van Breda could use a drink also.' And he winked at Rod.

The lodge had thatch and rough-hewn timber roofing, stone-flagged floors covered with cured animal skins and Kelim rugs. There was a walk-in fireplace flanked by gun racks on which were displayed fifty fine examples of the gunsmith's art. The furniture was massive and masculine, leather-cushioned and low. The Spanish plaster walls were hung with trophies, horned heads and native weapons.

A vast wooden staircase led up to the bedrooms that opened off the gallery above the main room. The bedrooms were air-conditioned and after they had got rid of Hans and his fat wife, Rod and Terry tested the bed to see if it was suitable.

An hour and a half later the bed had been judged eminently satisfactory, and as they went down to pass further judgement on the gargantuan lunch that fat Mrs Hans had spread for them, Terry remarked, 'Has it ever occurred to you, Mr Ironsides, that there are parts of your anatomy other than your flanks which are ferrous in character?' Then she giggled and added softly, 'And thank the Lord for that!'

Lunch was an exhausting experience and Terry pointed out that there was little sense in going out before four o'clock as the game would still be in thick cover avoiding the midday heat, so they went back upstairs.

After four o'clock Rod selected a .375 magnum Holland and Holland rifle from the rack, filled a cartridge belt with ammunition from one of the drawers, and they went out to the Landrover.

'How big is this place?' Rod asked as he turned the Landrover away from the gardens and took the track out into the virgin bush.

'You can drive for twenty miles in any direction and it's all ours. Over there our boundary runs against the Kruger National Park,' Terry answered.

They drove along the banks of the river, skirting sandbanks on which grew fluffy-headed reeds. The water ran fast between glistening black rocks, then spread into slow lazy pools.

They saw a dozen varieties of big game, stopping every few hundred yards to watch some lovely animal.

'Pops obviously doesn't allow shooting here,' Rod remarked, as a kudu bull with long spiral horns and trumpet-shaped ears studied them with big wet eyes from a range of thirty feet. 'The game is as tame as domestic cattle.'

'Only family are allowed to shoot,' Terry agreed. 'You qualify as family, however.'

Rod shook his head. 'It would be murder.' Rod indicated the kudu. 'That old fellow would eat out of your hand.'

'I'm glad you feel like that,' Terry said, and they drove on slowly.

The evening was not cool enough to warrant a log fire in the cavernous fireplace of the lodge. They lit one anyway because

Rod decided it would be pleasant to sit in front of a big, leaping fire, drink whisky and hold the girl you love.

59

When Inspector Grobbelaar lowered his teacup, there was a white scum of cream on the tips of his moustache. He licked it off carefully, and looked across at Sergeant Hugo.

'Who have we got next?' he asked.

Hugo consulted his notebook.

'Philemon N'gabai.' He read out the name, and Grobbelaar sighed.

'Number forty-eight, only sixteen more.' The single smeary fingerprint on the fragment of glass from the cold container had been examined by the fingerprint department. They had provided a list of sixty-four names anyone of which might be the owner of that print. Each of them had to be interrogated, it was a lengthy and so far unrewarding labour.

'What do we know about friend Philemon?' Grobbelaar asked.

'He is approximately forty years old. A Shangaan from Mozambique. Height 5' 7½", weight 146 lb. Crippled right leg. Two previous convictions. 1956: 60 days for bicycle theft. 1962: 90 days for stealing a camera from a parked car,' Hugo read from the file.

'At one hundred and forty-six pounds I don't see him breaking many necks. But send him in, let's talk to him,' Grobbelaar suggested and dunked his moustache in the tea cup again. Hugo nodded to the African Sergeant and he opened the door to admit Crooked Leg and his escort of an African constable.

They advanced to the desk at which the two detectives sat in their shirt sleeves. No one spoke. The two interrogators subjected him to a calculated and silent scrutiny to set him at as great a disadvantage as possible.

Grobbelaar prided himself on being able to sniff out a guilty conscience at fifty paces, and Philemon N'gabai reeked of guilt. He could not stand still, he was sweating heavily, and his eyes darted from floor to ceiling. He was guilty as hell, but not necessarily of murder. Grobbelaar did not feel the slightest confidence as he shook his head sorrowfully and asked, 'Why did you do it, Philemon? We have found the marks of your hand on the gold bottle.'

The effect on Crooked Leg was instantaneous and dramatic. His lips parted and began to tremble, saliva dripped onto his chin. His eyes for the first time fixed on Grobbelaar's face, wide and staring.

'Hello! Hello!' Grobbelaar thought, straightening in his chair, coming completely alert. He sensed Hugo's quickening interest beside him.

'You know what they do to people who kill, Philemon? They take them away to . . .' Grobbelaar did not have an opportunity to finish.

With a howl Crooked Leg darted for the door. His crippled gait was deceptive, he was fast as a ferret. He had the door open before the Bantu Sergeant collared him and dragged him gibbering and struggling back into the room.

'The gold, but not the man! I did not kill the Portuguese,' he babbled, and Grobbelaar and Hugo exchanged glances.

'Pay dirt!' Hugo exclaimed with deep satisfaction.

'Bull's eye!' agreed Grobbelaar, and smiled, a rare and fleeting occurrence.

60

'You see it has a little light that comes on to show you where the keyhole is,' said the salesman pointing to the ignition switch on the dashboard.

'Ooh! Johnny, see that!' Hettie gushed, but Johnny Delange had his head under the bonnet of the big glossy Ford Mustang.

'Why don't you sit in her?' the salesman suggested. He was very cute really, Hattie decided, with dreamy eyes and the most *fabulous* side burns.

'Ooh! Yes, I'd love to.' She manoeuvred her bottom into the leather bucket seat of the sports car. Her skirt pulled up, and the salesman's dreamy eyes followed the hem all the way.

'Can you adjust the seat?' Hettie asked innocently looking up at him.

'Here, I'll show you.' He leaned into the interior of the Mustang and reached across Hettie's lap. His hand brushed over her thigh, and Hettie pretended not to notice his touch. He smelled of Old Spice after-shave lotion.

'That's better!' Hettie murmured, and wriggled into a more comfortable position, contriving to make the movement provocative and revealing.

The salesman was encouraged, he lingered with his wrist just touching a sleek thigh.

'What's the compression ratio on this model?' Johnny Delange demanded as he emerged from the engine, and the salesman straightened up quickly and hurried to join him.

An hour later Johnny signed the purchase contract, and both he and Hettie shook the salesman's hand.

'Let me give you my card,' the salesman insisted, but Johnny had returned to his new toy, and Hettie took the cardboard business card.

'Call me if you need anything, anything at all,' said the salesman with heavy significance.

'Dennis Langley. Sales Manager,' Hettie read out aloud. 'My! You're very young to be Sales Manager.'

'Not all that young!'

'I'll bet,' Hettie murmured, and her eyes were suddenly bold. She ran the tip of a pink tongue over her lips. 'I won't lose it,' she promised, and placing the card in her handbag, walked to the Mustang, leaving him with a tantalizing promise and a memory of swaying hips and clicking heels.

They raced the new Mustang as far as Potchefstroom; Hettie encouraging Johnny to overtake slower vehicles with inches to spare for oncoming traffic. With horn blaring he tore over blind rises, forking ringed fingers at the protesting toots of other drivers. They had the speedometer registering 120 m.p.h. on the return run, and it was dark as they pulled into the driveway and Johnny hit the brakes hard to avoid running into the back of a big black Daimler that was parked outside their front door.

'Jesus,' gasped Johnny. 'That's Dr Steyner's bus!'

'Who is Dr Steyner?' Hettie demanded.

'Hell, he's one of the big shots from Head Office.'

'You're kidding!' Hettie challenged him.

'Truth!' Johnny affirmed. 'One of the real big shots.'

'Bigger than Mr Ironsides?' The General Manager of the Sonder Ditch was as high up the social ladder as Hettie had ever looked.

'Tin Ribs is chicken feed compared to this joker. Just look at his bus, its five times better than Tin Ribs's clapped-out old Maserati.'

'Gee!' Hettie could follow the logic of this line of argument. 'What's he want with us?'

'I don't know,' Johnny admitted with a twinge of anxiety. 'Let's go and find out.'

The lounge of the Delange home was not the setting which showed Dr Manfred Steyner to best advantage.

He sat on the edge of a scarlet and gold plastic-covered armchair as stiff and awkward as the packs of china dogs that stood on every table and shelf of the show cabinet, or the porcelain wild ducks which flew in diminishing perspective along the pale pink painted wall. In contrast to the tinsel Christmas decorations that festooned the ceiling and the gay greeting cards that Hettie had pinned to strips of green ribbon, Manfred's black homburg and Astrakhan-collared overcoat were unnecessarily severe.

'You will forgive my presumption,' he greeted them without rising. 'You were not at home and your maid let me in.'

'Your welcome, I'm sure,' Hettie simpered.

'Of course you are, Dr Steyner,' Johnny supported her.

'Ah! So you know who I am?' Manfred asked with satisfaction. This would make his task so much easier.

'Of course we do.' Hettie went to him and offered her hand. 'I am Hettie Delange, how do you do?'

With horror Manfred saw that her armpit was unshaven, filled with damp ginger curls. Hettie had not bathed since the previous evening. Manfred's nostrils twitched and he fought down a queasy wave of nausea.

'Delange, I want to speak to you alone.' He cowered away from Hettie's overwhelming physical presence.

'Sure.' Johnny was eager to please. 'How about you making us some coffee, honey,' he asked Hettie.

Ten minutes later Manfred sank with relief into the lush upholstery of the Daimler's rear seat. He ignored the two Delanges waving their farewells, and closed his eyes. It was done. Tomorrow morning Johnny Delange would be on shift and drilling into the glassy green rock of the Big Dipper.

By noon Manfred would own quarter of a million shares in the Sonder Ditch.

In a week he would be a rich man.

In a month he would be divorced from Theresa Steyner. He would sue with all possible notoriety on the grounds of adultery. He no longer needed her.

The chauffeur drove him back to Johannesburg.

61

It began on the floor of the Johannesburg Stock Exchange.

For some months nearly all the activity had been in the industrial counters, centring about the Alex Sagov group of companies and their merger negotiations.

The only spark of life in the mining and mining financials had been Anglo American Corporation and De Beers Deferred rights issues, but this was now old news and the prices had settled at their new levels. So it was that nobody was expecting fireworks when the call over of the gold mining counters began. The brokers' clerks crowding the floor were quietly spoken and behaved, when the first squib popped.

'Buy Sonder Ditch,' from one end of the hall.

'Buy Sonder Ditch,' a voice raised.

'Buy!' The throng stirred, heads turned.

'Buy.' The brokers suddenly agitated swirled in little knots, broke and reformed as transactions were completed. The price jumped fifty cents, and a broker ran from the floor to confer with his principal.

Here a broker thumped another on the back to gain his attention, and his urgency was infectious.

'Buy! Buy!'

'What the hell's happening?'

'Where is the buying coming from?'

'It's local!'

The price hit ten Rand a share, and then the panic began in earnest.

'It's overseas buying.'

'Eleven Rand!'

Brokers rushed to telephone warnings to favoured clients that a bull run was developing.

'Twelve fifty. It's only local buying.'

'Buy at best. Buy five thousand.'

Clerks raced back onto the floor carrying the hastily tele-phoned instructions, and plunged into the hysterical trading.

'Jesus Christ! Thirteen Rand, sell now. Take your profit! It can't go much higher.'

'Thirteen seventy-five, it's overseas buying. Buy at best.'

In fifty brokers' offices around the country, the professionals who spent their lives hovering over the tickers regained their balance and, cursing themselves for having been taken unawares, they scrambled onto the bull wagon. Others, the more canny ones, recognized the makings of a sick run and off-loaded their holdings, selling industrial shares as well as mining shares. Prices ran amok.

At ten-fifteen there was a priority call from the offices of the Minister of Finance in Pretoria to the office of the President of the Johannesburg Stock Exchange.

'What are you going to do?'

'We haven't decided. We won't close the floor if we can pos-sibly help it.'

'Don't let it go too far. Keep me informed.'

Sixteen Rand and still spiralling when at eleven o'clock South African time, the London Stock Exchange came in. For the first fifteen wild minutes the price of Sonder Ditch gold mining rocketed in sympathy with the Johannesburg market.

Then suddenly and unexpectedly the Sonder Ditch shares ran head-on into massive selling pressure. Not only the Sonder Ditch, but all the Kitchenerville gold mining companies stag-gered as the pressure increased. The prices wavered, rallied a few shillings and then fell back, wavered again, and then crashed downwards, plummeting far below their opening prices.

'Sell!' was the cry. 'Sell at best!' Within minutes freshly-made paper fortunes were wiped away.

When the price of the Sonder Ditch gold mining shares fell to five Rand seventy-five cents, the committee of the Johannesburg Stock Exchange closed the door in the interests of the national welfare, preventing further trading.

But in New York, Paris and London the investing public con-tinued to beat South African gold mining shares to death.

In the air-conditioned office of a skyscraper building, the little bald-headed man was smashing his balled fist onto the desk top of his superior officer.

'I told you not to trust him,' he was almost sobbing with anger. 'The fat greedy slug. One million dollars wasn't enough for him! No, he had to blow the whole deal!'

'Please, Colonel,' his chief intervened. 'Control yourself. Let us make a fair and objective appraisal of this financial activity.'

The bald-headed man sank back into his chair, and tried to light a cigarette with hands that trembled so violently as to extinguish the flame of his lighter.

'It sticks out a mile.' He flicked the lighter again, and puffed quickly. 'The first activity on the Johannesburg Exchange was Dr Steyner being clever. Buying up shares on the strength of our dummy report. That was quite natural and we expected it, in fact we wanted that to happen. It took suspicion away from us.' His cigarette had gone out, the tip was wet with spit. He threw it away and lit another.

'Fine! Everything was fine up to then. Doctor Steyner had committed financial suicide, and we were on the pig's back.' He sucked at his new cigarette. 'Then! Then our fat friend pulls the big double-cross and starts selling the Kitchenerville shares short. He must have gone into the market for millions.'

'Can we abort the operation at this late date?' his chief asked.

'Not a chance.' The bald head shook vigorously. 'I have sent a cable to our fat friend, ordering him to freeze the work on the tunnel but can you imagine him obeying that order? He is financially committed for millions of dollars and he will protect that investment with every means at his disposal.'

'Could we not warn the management of the Sonder Ditch company?'

'That would put the finger squarely on us, would it not?'

'Hmm!' the chief nodded. 'We could send them an anonymous warning.'

'Who would put any credence on that?'

'You're right,' the chief sighed. 'We will just have to batten down our hatches and ride out the storm. Sit tight and deny everything.'

'That is all we can do.' The cigarette had gone out again, and there were bits of tobacco in his moustache. The little man flicked his lighter.

'The bastard, the fat, greedy bastard!' he muttered.

Johnny and Big King rode up shoulder to shoulder in the cage. It had been a good shift. Despite the hardness of the Serpentine rock that cut down the drilling rate by fifty per cent, they had been able to get in five blasts that day. Johnny reckoned they had driven more than half-way through the Big Dipper. There was no night shift working now. Campbell had gone back to the stopes, so the honour of holing through would be Johnny's. He was excited at the prospect. Tomorrow he would be through into the unknown.

'Until tomorrow, Big King,' he said as they reached the surface and stepped out of the cage.

They separated, Big King heading for the Bantu hostel, Johnny to the glistening new Mustang in the car park.

Big King went straight to the Shangaan Induna's cottage without changing from his working clothes. He stood in the doorway and the Induna looked up from the letter he was writing.

'What news, my father?' Big King asked.

'The worst,' the Induna told him softly. 'The police have taken Crooked Leg.'

'Crooked Leg would not betray me,' Big King declared, but without conviction.

'Would you expect him to die in your place?' asked the Induna. 'He must protect himself.'

'I did not mean to kill him,' Big King explained miserably. 'I did not mean to kill the Portuguese, it was the gun.'

'I know, my son.' The Induna's voice was husky with helpless pity.

Big King turned from the doorway and walked down across the lawns to the ablution block. The spring and swagger had gone from his step. He walked listlessly, slouching, dragging his feet.

Manfred Steyner sat at his desk. His hands lay on the blotter before him, one thumb wearing a turban of crisp white bandage. His only movement was the steady beat of a pulse in his throat and a nerve that fluttered in one eyelid. He was deathly pale, and a light sheen of perspiration gave his features the look of having been sculptured from washed marble.

The volume of the radio was turned high, so the voice of the announcer boomed and reverberated from the panelled walls.

'The climax of the drama was reached at eleven forty-five South African time when the President of the Johannesburg Stock Exchange declared the floor closed and all further trading suspended.

'Latest reports from the Tokyo Stock Exchange are that Sonder Ditch gold mining shares were being traded at the equivalent of four Rand forty cents. This compares with the morning's opening price of the same share on the Johannesburg Stock Exchange of nine Rand forty-five cents.

'A spokesman for the South African Government stated that although no reason for these extraordinary price fluctuations was apparent, the Minister of Mines, Doctor Carel De Wet, had ordered a full-scale commission of enquiry.'

Manfred Steyner stood up from his desk and went through into the bathroom. With his flair for figures he did not need pen and paper to compute that the shares he had purchased that morning had depreciated in value by well over one million Rand at the close of business that evening.

He knelt on the tiled floor in front of the toilet bowl and vomited.

64

The sky was darkening rapidly, for the sun had long ago sunk below a blazing horizon.

Rod heard the whisper of wings, and strained his eyes upwards into the gloom. They came in fast, in vee-formation, slanting down towards the pool of the river. He stood up from the blind and swung the shotgun on them, leading well ahead of the line of flight.

He squeezed off both barrels, Wham! Wham! And the duck broke formation and rocketed upwards, whirring aloft on noisy wings.

'Damn it!' said Rod.

'What's wrong, dead-eye Dick, did you miss?' asked Terry.

'The light's too bad.'

'Excuses! Excuses!' Terry stood up beside him, and Rod pushed a balled fist lightly against her cheek.

'That's enough from you, woman. Let's go home.'

Carrying the shotguns and bunches of dead duck, they trudged along the bank in the dusk to the waiting Landrover.

It was completely dark as they drove back to the lodge.

'What a wonderful day it's been,' Terry murmured dreamily. 'If for nothing else, I will always be grateful to you for teaching me how to enjoy my life.'

Back at the lodge, they bathed and changed into fresh clothes. For dinner they had wild duck and pineapple, with salads from Mrs Fat Hans' vegetable garden. Afterwards, they sprawled on the leopard-skin rugs in front of the fireplace and watched the log fire without talking, relaxed and happy and tired.

'My God, it's almost nine o'clock,' Terry checked her wristwatch. 'I fancy a bit of bed myself, how about you, Mr Ironsides?'

'Let's hear the nine o'clock news first.'

'Oh, Rod! Nobody ever listens to the news here. This is fairyland!'

Rod switched on the radio and the first word froze them both. It was 'Sonder Ditch'.

In horrified silence they listened to the report. Rod's expression was granite hard, his mouth a tight grim line. When the news report ended, Rod switched off the radio set and lit a cigarette.

'There is trouble,' he said. 'Big trouble. I'm sorry, Terry, we must go back. As soon as possible. I have to get back to the mine.'

'I know,' Terry agreed immediately. 'But Rod, I can't take off from this landing-strip in the dark. There is no flare path.'

'We'll leave at first light.'

Rod slept very little that night. Whenever she woke, Terry sensed him lying unsleeping, worrying. Twice she heard him get up and go to the bathroom.

In the very early hours of the morning she woke from her own troubled sleep and saw him silhouetted against the starlit window. He was smoking a cigarette and staring out into the darkness. It was the first night they had spent together without making love. In the dawn Rod was haggard and puffy-eyed.

They were airborne at eight o'clock and they landed in Johannesburg a little after ten.

Rod went straight to the telephone in Hank's office and Lily Jordan answered his call.

'Miss Jordan, what the hell is happening? Is everything all right?'

'Is that you, Mr Ironsides. Oh! Thank God! Thank God you've come, something terrible has happened!'

65

Johnny Delange blew the face of the drive twice before nine o'clock, cutting thirty feet further into the glassy green dyke.

He had found that by drilling his cutter blast holes an additional three feet deeper, he could achieve a shatter effect on the serpentine rock which more than compensated for the additional drilling time. This next blast he was going to flout standard regulations and experiment with double charging his cutter holes. He would need additional explosives.

'Big King,' he shouted to make himself heard above the roar of drills. 'Take a gang back to the shaft station. Pick up six cases of Dynagel.'

He watched Big King and his gang retreat back down the drive, and then he lit a cigarette and turned his attention to his machine boys. They were poised before the rock face, sweating behind their drills. The dark rock of the dyke absorbed the light from the overhead electric bulbs. It made the end of the drive a gloomy place, filled with a sense of foreboding.

Johnny began to think about Davy. He was aware suddenly of a sense of disquiet, and he moved restlessly. He felt the hair on his forearms come slowly erect, each on a separate goose pimple. *Davy is here.* He knew it suddenly, and surely. His flesh crawled and he went cold with dread. He turned quickly and looked over his shoulder. The tunnel behind him was deserted, and Johnny gave a sickly grin.

'Shaya, madoda,' he called loudly and unnecessarily to his gang. They could not hear him above the roar of the drills, but the sound of his own voice helped reassure him.

Yet the creepy sensation was still with him. He felt that Davy was still there, trying to tell him something.

Johnny fought the sensation. He walked quickly forward, standing close to his machine boys, as though to draw comfort from their physical presence. It did not help. His nerves were shrieking now, and he felt himself beginning to sweat.

Suddenly the machine boy who was drilling the cutter hole in the centre of the face staggered backwards.

'Hey!' Johnny shouted at him, then he saw that water was spurting in fine needle jets from around the drill steel. Something was squeezing the drill steel out of its hole, like toothpaste out of a tube. It was pushing the machine boy backwards.

'Hey!' Johnny started forward and at that instant the heavy metal drill was fired out of the rock with the force of a cannon ball. It decapitated the machine boy, tearing his head from his body with such savagery that his carcass was thrown far back down the drive, his blood spraying the dark rock walls.

From the drill hole shot a solid jet of water. It came out under such pressure that when it caught the machine boy's assistant in the chest it stove in his ribs as though he had been hit by a speeding automobile.

'Out!' yelled Johnny. 'Get out!' And the rock face exploded. It blew outwards with greater force than if it had been blasted with Dynagel. It killed Johnny Delange instantly. He was smashed to a bloody pulp by the flying rock. It killed every man in his gang with him, and immediately afterwards the monstrous burst of water that poured from the face picked up their mutilated remains and swept them down the drive.

Big King was at the shaft station when they heard the water coming. It sounded like an express train in a tunnel, a dull bellow of irresistible power. The water was pushing the air from the drive ahead of it, so that a hurricane of wind came roaring from the mouth of the drive, blowing out a cloud of dust and loose rubbish.

Big King and his gang stood and stared in uncomprehending terror until the head of the column of water shot from the drive, frothing solid, carrying with it a plug of debris and human remains.

Bursting into the T-junction of the main 66 level haulage, the strength of the flood was reduced, yet still it swept down towards the lift station in a waist deep wall.

'This way!' Big King was the first to move. He leapt for the steel emergency ladder that led up to the level above. The rest of his gang were not fast enough, the water picked them up and crushed them against the steel-mesh barrier that guarded the shaft. The crest of the wave burst around Big King's legs, sucking at him, but he tore himself from its grip and climbed to safety.

Beneath him the water poured into the shaft like bath water into a plug hole, forming a spinning whirlpool about the collar as it roared down to flood the workings below 66 level.

66

Leaving Terry at the airfield to solicit transport from Hank, the mechanic, Rod drove directly to the head of No. 1 shaft of the Sonder Ditch. He jumped from the Volkswagen into the clamouring crowd clustered above the shaft head.

Dimitri was wide-eyed and distracted, beside him Big King towered like a black colossus.

'What happened?' Rod demanded.

'Tell him,' Dimitri instructed Big King.

'I was at the shaft with my gang. A river leaped from the mouth of the drive, a great river of water running faster than the Zambesi in flood; roaring like a lion the water ate all the men with me. I alone climbed above it.'

'We've hit a big one, Rod,' Dimitri interrupted. 'It's pouring in fast. We calculate it will flood the entire workings up to 66 level in four hours from now.'

'Have you cleared the mine?' Rod demanded.

'All the men are out except Delange and his gang. They were in the drive. They've been chopped, I'm afraid,' Dimitri answered.

'Have you warned the other mines we could have a burst through into their workings?'

'Yes, they are pulling all their shifts out.'

'Right.' Rod set off for the blast control room with Dimitri trotting to keep up with him. 'Give me your keys, and find the foreman electrician.'

Within minutes the three of them were crowded into the tiny concrete control room.

'Check in the special circuit,' Rod instructed. 'I'm going to shoot the drop-blast matt and seal off the drive.'

The foreman electrician worked quickly at the control panel. He looked up at Rod.

'Ready!' he said.

'Check her in,' Rod nodded.

The foreman threw the switch. The three of them caught their breath together.

Dimitri said it for them: 'Red!'

On the control panel of the special circuit the red bulb glared balefully at them, the Cyclops eye of the god of despair.

'Christ!' swore the foreman. 'The circuit is shot. The water must have torn the wires out.'

'It may be a fault in the board.'

'No.' The foreman shook his head with certainty.

'We've had it,' whispered Dimitri. 'Goodbye the Sonder Ditch!'

Rod burst out of the control room into the expectant crowd outside.

'Johnson!' He singled out one of his mine captains. 'Go down to the Yacht Club at the dam, get me the rubber rescue dinghy. Quick as you can, man.'

The man scurried away, and Rod turned on the electrician foreman as he emerged from the control room.

'Get me a battery hand-operated blaster, a reel of wire, pliers, gloves, two coils of nylon rope. Hurry!'

The foreman went.

'Rod.' Dimitri caught his arm. 'What are you going to do?'

'I'm going down there. I'm going to find the break in the circuit and I'm going to blast her by hand.'

'Jesus!' Dimitri gasped. 'You are crazy, Rod. You'll kill yourself for sure!'

Rod completely ignored his protest.

'I want one man with me. A strong man. The strongest there is, we will have to drag the dinghy against the flood.' Rod looked about him. Big King was standing by the banksman's office. The two of them were tall enough to face each other over the heads of the men between them.

'Will you come with me, Big King?' Rod asked.

'Yes,' said Big King.

67

In less than twenty minutes they were ready. Rod and Big King were stripped down to singlets and bathing-trunks. They wore canvas tennis shoes to protect their feet, and the hard helmets on their heads were incongruous against the rest of their attire.

The rubber dinghy was ex-naval disposal. A nine-foot air-filled mattress, so light that a man could lift it with one hand. Into it was packed the equipment they would need for the task ahead. A water-proof bag contained the battery blaster, the reel of insulated wire, the pliers, gloves and a spare lantern. Lashed to the eyelets along the sides of the dinghy were two coils of light nylon rope, a small crowbar, an axe and a razor-sharp machete in a leather sheath. To the bows of the dinghy were fastened a pair of looped nylon towing lines.

'What else will you need, Rod?' Dimitri asked.

Rod shook his head thoughtfully. 'That's it, Dimitri. That should do it.'

'Right!' Dimitri beckoned and four men came forward and carried the dinghy into the waiting cage.

'Let's go,' said Dimitri and followed the dinghy into the cage. Big King went next and Rod paused a second to look up at the sky. It was very blue and bright.

Before the onsetter could close the shutter door, a Silver Cloud Rolls-Royce came gliding onto the bank. From the rear door emerged first Hurry Hirschfeld and then Terry Steyner.

'Ironsides!' roared Hurry. 'What the hell is going on?'

'We've hit water,' Rod answered him from the cage.

'Water? Where did it come from?'

'Beyond the Big Dipper.'

'You drove through the Big Dipper?'

'Yes.'

'You bastard, you've drowned the Sonder Ditch,' roared Hurry, advancing on the cage.

'Not yet, I haven't,' Rod contradicted.

'Rod.' Terry was white-faced beside her grandfather. 'You can't go down there.' She started forward.

Rod pushed the onsetter aside and pulled down the steel shutter door of the cage. Terry threw herself against the steel mesh of the guard barrier, but the cage was gone into the earth.

'Rod,' she whispered, and Hurry Hirschfeld put his arm around her shoulders and led her to the Rolls-Royce.

From the back seat of the Rolls, Hurry Hirschfeld was conducting a Kangaroo Court Trial of Rodney Ironsides. One by one he called for the line managers of the Sonder Ditch and questioned them. Even those who were loyal to Rod could say little in his defence, and there were others who took the opportunity to level old scores with Rodney Ironsides.

Sitting beside her grandfather, Terry heard such a condemnation of the man she loved as to chill her to the depths of her soul. There was no doubt that Rodney Ironsides, without Head Office sanction, had instituted a new development so risky and contrary to company policy as to be criminal in concept.

'Why did he do it?' muttered Hurry Hirschfeld. He seemed bewildered. 'What could he possibly achieve by driving through the Big Dipper. It looks like a deliberate attempt to sabotage the Sonder Ditch.' Hurry's anger began to seethe within him. 'The bastard! He has drowned the Sonder Ditch and killed dozens of men.' He punched his fist into the palm of his hand. 'I'll make him pay for this. I'll break him, so help me God, I'll smash him! I'll bring criminal charges against him. Malicious damage to property. Manslaughter. Culpable homicide! By Jesus, I'll have his guts for this!'

Listening to Hurry ranting and threatening, Terry could keep silent no longer.

'It wasn't his fault, Pops. Truly it wasn't. He was forced to do it.'

'Ha!' snorted Hurry. 'I heard you at the pithead a few minutes ago. Just what is this man to you, Missy, that you spring to his defence so nobly?'

'Pops, please believe me.' Her eyes were enormous in her pale face.

'Why should I believe you? The two of you are obviously up to mischief together. Naturally you will try and protect him.'

596

'Listen to me at least,' she pleaded, and Hurry checked the run of his tongue and breathing heavily he turned to face her.

'This better be good, young lady,' he warned her.

In her agitation she told it badly, and half-way through she realized that she wasn't even convincing herself. Hurry's expression became more and more bleak, until he interrupted her impatiently.

'Good God, Theresa, this isn't like you. To try and put the blame for this onto your own husband! That's despicable! To try and switch the blame for this . . .'

'It's true! As God is my witness.' Terry was almost in tears, she was tugging at Hurry's sleeve in her agitation. 'Rod was forced to do it. He had no option.'

'You have proof of this?' Hurry asked drily, and Terry fell silent, staring at him dumbly. What proof was there?

68

The cage checked and slowed as it approached 65 level. The lights were still burning, but the workings were deserted. They lugged the dinghy out onto the station.

They could hear the dull waterfall roar of the flood on the level below them. The displacement of huge volumes of water disturbed the air so that a strong cool breeze was blowing up the shaft.

'Big King and I will go down the emergency ladder. You will lower the dinghy to us afterwards,' Rod told Dimitri. 'Make sure all the equipment is tied into it.'

'Right.' Dimitri nodded.

All was in readiness. The men who had come down with them in the cage were waiting expectantly. Rod could find no reason for further delay. He felt something cold and heavy settle in his guts.

'Come on, Big King.' And he went to the steel ladder.

'Good luck, Rod,' Dimitri's voice floated down to him, but Rod saved his breath for that cold dark climb downwards.

All the lights had fused on 66 level, and in the beam of his lamp the water below him was black and agitated. It poured into the mouth of the shaft, bending the mesh barrier inwards. The mesh acted as a gigantic sieve, straining the floating rubbish from the flood. Amongst the timber and planking, the sodden sacking and unrecognizable objects, Rod made out the water-logged corpses of the dead pressed against the wire.

He climbed down and gingerly lowered himself into the water. Instantly it dragged at his lower body, shocking in its power. It was waist deep here, but he found that by bracing his body against the steel ladder he could maintain his footing.

Big King climbed down beside him, and Rod had to raise his voice above the hissing thunder of water.

'All right?'

'Yes. Let them send down the boat.'

Rod flashed his lamp up the shaft, and within minutes the dinghy was swaying slowly down to them. They reached up and guided it right side up to the surface of the water, before untying the rope.

The dinghy was sucked firmly against the wire mesh, and Rod checked its contents quickly. All was secure.

'Right.' Rod tied a bight of the nylon ripe around his waist, and climbed up the wire mesh barrier until he could reach the roof of the tunnel. Behind him Big King was paying out the nylon line.

Rod leaned out until he could get his hands on the compressed air pipes that ran along the roof of the tunnel. The pipes were as thick as a man's wrist, bolted securely into the hanging wall of the drive they would support a man's weight with ease. Rod settled his grip firmly on the piping and then kicked his feet free from the barrier. He hung above the rushing waters, his feet just brushing the surface.

Hand over hand, swinging forward with feet dangling, he started up the tunnel. The nylon rope hung down behind him like a long white tail. It was three hundred feet to where the water boiled from the drive into the main haulage, and Rod's shoulder muscles were shrieking in protest before he reached it. It seemed that his arms were being wrenched from their sockets, for the weight of the nylon rope that was dragging in the water was fast becoming intolerable.

There was a back eddy in the angle formed by the drive and the haulage. Here the flood swirled in a vortex, and Rod lowered himself slowly into it. The water buffeted him, but again he was able to cower against the side wall of the haulage and hold his footing. Quickly he began tying the rope onto the rawlbolts that were driven into the sidewall to consolidate the rock. Within minutes he had established a secure base from which to operate, and when he flashed his lamp back down the haulage he saw Big King following him along the compressed air piping.

Big King dropped into the waist deep water beside Rod, and they gripped the nylon rope and rested their burning arm muscles.

'Ready?' asked Rod at last, and Big King nodded.

They laid hold of the rope that led back to the dinghy and

599

hauled upon it. For a moment nothing happened, the other end might just as well have been anchored to a mountain.

'Together!' grunted Rod, and they recovered a foot of rope.

'Again!' And they drew the dinghy inch by inch up the haulage against the rush of water.

Their hands were bleeding when they at last pulled the laden dinghy up to their own position and anchored it to the rawbolts beside them. It bounched and bobbed with the water drumming against its underside.

Neither Rod nor Big King could talk. They hung exhausted on the body lines with the water ripping at their skin and gasped for breath.

At last Rod looked up at Big King, and in the lamp light he saw his own doubts reflected in Big King's eyes. The drop-blast matt was a thousand feet up the drive. The strength and speed of the water in the drive was almost double what it was in the haulage. Could they ever fight their way against such primeval forces as these that were now unleashed about them?

'I will go next,' Big King said and Rod nodded his agreement.

The huge Bantu drew himself up the rope until he could reach the compressed air pipe. His skin in the lamplight glistened like that of a porpoise. Hand over hand he disappeared into the gaping black maw of the drive. His lamp threw deformed and monstrous shadows upon the walls of rock.

When Big King's lamp flashed the signal to him, Rod climbed up to the pipe and followed him into the drive. Three hundred feet later he found Big King had established another base. But here they were exposed to the full force of the flood, and they were pulled so violently against the body lines that the harsh nylon smeared the skin from their bodies. Together they dragged the dinghy up to them and anchored it.

Rod was sobbing softly as he held his torn hands to his chest and wondered if he could do it again.

'Ready?' Big King asked beside him, and Rod nodded. He reached up and placed the raw flesh of his palms onto the metal piping, and felt the tears of pain flood his eyes. He blinked them back and dragged himself forward.

Vaguely he realized that should he fall, he was a dead man. The flood would sweep him away, dragging him along the jagged side walls of the drive, ripping his flesh from the bone, and finally hurling him against the mesh surrounding the shaft to crush the life from his body.

He went on until he knew he could go no farther. Then he selected a raw bolt in the side wall and looped the rope through it. And they repeated the whole heart-breaking procedure. Twice as he strained against the dinghy rope Rod saw his vision explode into stars and pinwheels. Each time he dragged himself back from the brink of unconsciousness by sheer force of will.

The example that Big King was setting was the inspiration which kept Rod from failing. Big King worked without change of expression, but his eyes were bloodshot with exertion. Only once Rod heard him grunt like a gut-shot lion, and there was bright blood on the rope where he touched it.

Rod knew he could not give in while Big King held on.

Reality dissolved slowly into a dark roaring nightmare of pain, wherein muscles and bone were loaded beyond all endurance, and yet continued to function. It seemed that for all time Rod had hung on arms that were leadened and slow with exhaustion. He was inching his way along the compressed air pipe for yet another advance up the drive. Sweat running into his eyes was blurring his vision, so at first he did not credit what he saw ahead of him in the darkness.

He shook his head to clear his eyes, and then squinted along the beam of his lamp. A heavy timber structure was hanging drunkenly from the roof of the drive. The bolts that held it were resisting the efforts of the water to tear it loose.

Rod realized abruptly that this was what remained of the frame which had held the ventilation doors. The doors were gone, ripped away, but the frame was still in position. He knew that just beyond the ventilation doors the drop-blast matt began. They had reached it!

New strength flowed into his body and he swung forward along the pipe. The timber frame made a fine anchor point and Rod secured the rope to it, and flashed back the signal to Big King. He hung in the loop of rope and rested awhile, then he forced himself to take an interest in his surroundings. He played the beam over the distorted timber frame and saw instantly why the blasting circuit had been broken.

In the lamp light the distinctive green plastic-coated blasting cable hung in festoons from the roof of the drive, clearly it had become entangled in the ventilation doors and been severed when they were ripped away. The loose end of the cable dangled to the surface of the racing water. Rod fastened his eyes on it, drawing comfort and strength from the knowledge that they would not have to continue their agonized journey down the drive.

When Big King came up out of the gloom, Rod indicated the dangling cable.

'There!' he gasped, and Big King narrowed his eyes in acknowledgement; he was unable to speak.

It was five minutes before they could commence the excruciating business of hauling the dinghy up and securing it to the door frame.

Again they rested. Their movements were slowing up drastically. Neither of them had much strength left to draw upon.

'Get hold of the end of the cable,' Rod instructed Big King, and he dragged himself over the side of the dinghy and lay sprawled full-length on the floor boards.

His weight forced the dinghy deeper, increasing its resistance to the racing water, and the rope strained against the wooden frame. Rod began clumsily to unpack the battery blaster. Big King stood waist-deep clinging with one arm to the wooden frame, reaching forward with the other towards the end of the green-coated cable. It danced just beyond his finger tips, and he edged forward against the current, steadying himself against the timber frame, placing a greater strain on the retaining bolts.

His fingers closed on the cable and with a grunt of satisfaction he passed it back to Rod.

Working with painstaking deliberation, Rod connected the crocodile clips from the reel of wire to the loose end of the green cable. Rod's plan was for both he and Big King to climb aboard the dinghy, and, paying out the nylon rope, let themselves be carried back down the drive. At the same time they would be letting the wire run from its reel. At a safe distance they would fire the drop-blast matt.

Rod's fingers were swollen and numbed. The minutes passed as he completed his preparations and all that while the strain on the wooden frame was heavy and consistent.

Rod looked up from his task, and crawled to his knees.

'All right, Big King,' he wheezed as he knelt in the bows of the dinghy and gripped the wooden frame to steady the dinghy. 'Come aboard. We are ready.'

Big King waded forward and at that instant the retaining bolts on one side of the heavy timber frame gave way. With a rending, tearing sound the frame slewed across the tunnel. The beams of timber crossed each other like the blades of a pair of gigantic scissors. Both Rod's arms were between the beams. The bones in his forearms snapped with the loud crackle of breaking sticks.

With a scream of pain Rod collapsed onto the floorboards of the dinghy, his arms useless, sticking out at absurd angles from their shattered bones. Three feet away Big King was still in the water. His mouth was wide open, but no sound issued from his throat. He stood still as a black statue and his eyes bulged from their sockets. Even through his own suffering Rod was horrified by the expression on Big King's contorted features.

Below the surface of the water the bottom timber beams had performed the same scissor movement, but this time they had caught Big King's lower body between them. They had closed across his pelvis and crushed it. Now they held him in a vicelike grip from which it was not possible to shake them.

The white face and the black face were but a few feet apart. The two stricken companions in disaster, looked into each other's eyes and knew that there was no escape. They were doomed.

'My arms,' whispered Rod huskily. 'I cannot use them.' Big King's bulging eyes held Rod's gaze.

'Can you reach the blaster?' Rod whispered urgently. 'Take it and turn the handle. Burn it, Big King, burn it!'

Slow comprehension showed in Big King's pain-glazed eyes.

'We are finished, Big King. Let us go like men. Burn it, bring down the rock!'

Above them the rock was sown with explosive. The blaster was connected. In his agitation Rod tried to reach out for the blaster. His forearm swung loosely, the fingers hanging open like the petals of a dead flower, and the pain checked him.

'Get it, Big King,' Rod urged him, and Big King picked up the blaster and held it against his chest with one arm.

'The handle!' Rod encouraged him. 'Turn the handle!'

But instead Big King reached into the dinghy once more and drew the machete from its sheath.

'What are you doing?' Rod demanded, and in reply Big King swung the blade back over his shoulder and then brought it forward in a gleaming arc aimed at the nylon rope that held the

603

dinghy anchored to the wooden frame. Clunk! The blade bit into the wood, severing the rope that was bound around it.

Freed by the stroke of the machete, the dinghy was whisked away by the current. Lying in the dancing rubber dinghy, Rod heard a bull voice bellow above the rush of the water.

'Go in peace, my friend.'

Then Rod was careening back along the drive, a hell ride during which the dinghy spun like a top and in the beam of his lamp the roof and walls melted into a dark racing blur as Rod lay maimed on the floor of the dinghy.

Then suddenly the air jarred against his ear drums, a long rolling concussion in the confines of the drive and he knew that Big King had fired the drop-blast matt. Rodney Ironsides slipped over the edge of consciousness into a soft warm dark place from which he hoped never to return.

69

Dimitri squatted on his haunches above the shaft at 65 level. He was smoking his tenth cigarette. The rest of the men waited as impatiently as he did, every few minutes Dimitri would cross to the shaft and flash his lamp down the hundred foot hole to 66 level.

'How long have they been gone,' he asked, and they all glanced at their watches.

'An hour and ten minutes.'

'No, an hour and fourteen minutes.'

'Christ, call me a liar for four minutes!'

And they lapsed into silence once more. Suddenly the station telephone shrilled, and Dimitri jumped up and ran to it.

'No, Mr Hirschfeld, nothing yet!'

He listened a moment.

'All right, send him down then.'

He hung up the telephone, and his men looked at him enquiringly.

'They are sending down a policeman,' he explained.

'What the hell for?'

'They want Big King.'

'Why?'

'Warrant of arrest for murder.'

'Murder?'

'Ja, they reckon he murdered the Portuguese storekeeper.'

'Jeez!'

'Big King, is that so!' Delighted to have found something to pass the time, they fell into an animated debate.

The police inspector arrived in the cage at 65 level, but he was disappointing. He looked like a down-at-heel undertaker, and he replied to their eager questions with a sorrowful stare that left them stuttering.

For the fifteenth time Dimitri went to the shaft and peered

down into it. The blast shook the earth around them, a long rumbling that persisted for many seconds.

'They've done it!' yelled Dimitri, and began to caper wildly. His men leapt to their feet and began beating each other on the back, shouting and laughing. The police inspector alone took no part in the celebrations.

'Wait,' yelled Dimitri at last. 'Shut up all of you! Shut up! Damn it! Listen!'

They fell silent.

'What is it?' someone asked. 'I can't hear anything.'

'That's just it!' exulted Dimitri. 'The water! It has stopped!'

Only then did they become aware that the dull roar of water to which their ears had become resigned was now ended. It was quiet; a cathedral hush lay upon the workings. They began to cheer, their voices thin in the silence, and Dimitri ran to the steel ladder and swarmed down it like a monkey.

From thirty feet up Dimitri saw the dinghy marooned amongst the filth and debris around the shaft. He recognized the crumpled figure lying in the bottom of it.

'Rod!' he was shouting before he reached the station at 66 level. 'Rod, are you all right?'

The floor of the haulage was wet, and here and there a trickle of water still snaked towards the shaft. Dimitri ran to the stranded dinghy and started to turn Rod onto his back. Then he saw his arms.

'Oh, Christ!' he gasped in horror, then he was yelling up the ladder. 'Get a stretcher down here.'

Rod regained consciousness to find himself covered with blankets and strapped securely into a mine stretcher. His arms were splinted and bandaged, and from the familiar rattle and rush of air he knew he was in the cage on the way to the surface.

He recognized Dimitri's voice raised argumentatively.

'Damn it! The man is unconscious and badly injured, can't you leave him alone?'

'I have my duty to perform,' a strange voice answered.

'What's he want, Dimitri?' Rod croaked.

'Rod, how are you?' At the sound of his voice Dimitri was kneeling beside the stretcher anxiously.

'Bloody awful,' Rod whispered. 'What does this joker want?'

'He's a police officer. He wants to arrest Big King for murder,' Dimitri explained.

'Well, he's a bit bloody late,' whispered Rod, and even through his pain this seemed to Rod to be terribly funny. He began to laugh. He sobbed with laughter, each convulsion sending bright bursts of pain along his arms. He was shaking uncontrollably with shock, sweat pouring from his face, and he was laughing wildly.

'He's a bit bloody late,' he repeated through his hysterical laughter as Dr Dan Stander pushed the hypodermic needle into his arm and shot him full of morphine.

70

Hurry Hirschfeld stood in the main haulage on 66 level. There was bustle all around him. Already the crews from the cementation company were manhandling their equipment up towards the blocked drive.

These were specialists from an independent contracting company. They were about to begin pumping thousands of tons of liquid cement into the rock jam that sealed the drive. They would pump it in at pressures in excess of 3000 pounds per square inch, and when that concrete set it would form a plug that would effectively seal off the drive for all time. It would also form a burial vault for the body of Big King, thought Hurry, a fitting monument to the man who had saved the Sonder Ditch.

He would arrange to have a commemorative plaque placed on the outer wall of the cement plug with a suitable inscription describing the man and the deed.

The man's dependants must be properly taken care of, perhaps they could be flown down for the unveiling of the plaque. Anyway he could leave that to Public Relations and Personnel.

The haulage stank of wetness and mud. It was dank and clammy cool, and it would not improve his lumbago. Hurry had seen enough; he started back towards the shaft. Faintly he was aware of the muted clangour of the mighty pumps which in a few days would free the Sonder Ditch of the water that filled her lower levels.

The laden stretchers with their grisly blanket-covered burdens stood in a row under the hastily rigged electric lights along one wall of the tunnel. Hurry's expression hardened as he passed them.

'I'll have the guts of the man responsible for this,' he vowed silently as he waited for the cage.

Terry Steyner rode in the rear of the ambulance with Rod. She wiped the mud from his face.

'How bad is it, Dan?' she asked.

'Hell, Terry, he'll be up and about in a few days. The arms of course are not very pretty, that's why I'm taking him directly to Johannesburg. I want a specialist orthopaedic surgeon to set them. Apart from that he is suffering from shock pretty badly and his hands are superficially lacerated. But he will be fine.'

Dan watched curiously as Terry fussed ineffectually with the damp hair of the drugged man.

'You want a smoke?' he asked.

'Light me one, please Dan.'

He passed her the cigarette.

'I didn't know that you and Rod were so friendly,' he ventured.

Terry looked up at him quickly.

'How very delicate you are, Dr Stander,' she mocked him.

'None of my business, of course.' Hurriedly Dan withdrew.

'Don't be silly, Dan. You're a good friend of Rod's and Joy is mine. You two are entitled to know. I am desperately, crazily in love with this big hunk. I intend divorcing Manfred just as soon as possible.'

'Is Rod going to marry you?'

'He hasn't said anything about marriage but I'll sure as hell start working on him,' Terry grinned, and Dan laughed.

'Good luck to you both, then. I'm sure Rod will be able to get another job.'

'What do you mean?' Terry demanded.

'They say your grandfather is threatening to fire him so high he'll be the first man on the moon.'

Terry relapsed into silence. Proof was what Pops had asked for, but what proof was there?

'They'll be waiting on the X-Ray reports.' Joy Allbright gave her opinion. Since her engagement to Dan, Joy had suddenly become something of a medical expert. She had rushed down to the Johannesburg Central Hospital at Dan's hurried telephonic request. Dan wanted her to keep Terry company while she waited for Rod to come out of emergency. They sat together in the waiting-room.

'I expect so,' Terry agreed. Something Joy had just said had jolted in her mind, something she must remember.

'It takes them twenty minutes or so to expose the plates and develop them. Then the radiologist has to examine the plates and make his report to the surgeon.'

There, Joy had said it again. Terry sat up straight and concentrated on what Joy had said. Which word had disturbed her?

Suddenly she had it.

'The report!' she exclaimed. 'That's it. The report, that's the proof.'

She leapt out of her chair.

'Joy! Give me the keys of your car,' she demanded.

'What on earth?' Joy looked startled.

'I can't explain now. I have to get home to Sandown urgently, give me your keys. I'll explain later.'

Joy fished in her handbag and produced a leather key folder. Terry snatched it from her.

'Where are you parked?' Terry demanded.

'In the car park, near the main gate.'

'Thanks, Joy.' Terry dashed from the waiting-room, her high heels clattered down the passage.

'Crazy woman.' Joy looked after her bewildered.

Ten minutes later Dan looked into the waiting-room.

'Rod's fine now. Where's Terry?'

'She went mad—' And Joy explained her abrupt departure. Dan looked grave.

'I think we'd better follow her, Joy.'

'I think you're right, darling.'

'I'll just grab my coat,' said Dan.

There was only one place where Manfred would keep the geological report on the Big Dipper that Rod had told her about. That was in the safe deposit behind the panelling in his study. Because her jewellery was kept in the same safe, Terry had a key and the combination to the lock.

Even in Joy's Alfa Romeo, taking liberties with the traffic regulations, it was a thirty-five minute drive out to Sandown. It was after five in the evening when Terry coasted down the long driveway and parked before the garages.

The extensive grounds were deserted, for the gardeners finished at five, and there was no sign of life from the house. This was as it should be, for she knew Manfred was still in Europe. He was not due back for at least another four days.

Leaving the ignition keys in the Alfa, Terry ran up the pathway and onto the stoep. She fumbled in her handbag and found the keys to the front door. She let herself in, and went directly to Manfred's study. She slid the concealing panel aside and set about the lengthy business of opening the steel safe. It required both key and combination to activate the mechanism, and Terry had never developed much expertise at tumbling the combination.

Finally, however, the door swung open and she was confronted by the voluminous contents. Terry began removing the various documents and files, examining each one and then stacking them neatly on the floor beside her.

She had no idea of the shape, size nor colour of the report for which she was searching, it was ten minutes before she selected an unmarked folder and flicked open the cover. 'Confidential Report on the geological formations of the Kitchenerville gold fields, with special reference to those areas lying to the east of the Big Dipper Dyke.'

Terry felt a wonderful lift of relief as she read the titling for she had begun doubting that the report was here. Quickly she thumbed through the pages and began reading at random. There was no doubt.

'This is it!' she exclaimed aloud.

'I'll take that, thank you.' The dreaded familiar voice cut into her preoccupation, and Terry spun around and came to her feet in one movement, clutching the file protectively to her breast. She backed away from the man who stood in the doorway.

She hardly recognized her own husband. She had never seen him like this. Manfred was coatless, and his shirt was without collar or stud. He appeared to have slept in his trousers, for they were rumpled and baggy. There was a yellow stain down the front of his white shirt.

His scanty brown hair was dishevelled, hanging forward wispily onto his forehead. He had not shaved, and the skin around his eyes was discoloured and puffy.

'Give that to me.' He came towards her with hand outstretched.

'Manfred.' She kept moving away from him. 'What are you doing here? When did you get back?'

'Give it to me, you slut.'

'Why do you call me that?' She asked, trying for time.

'Slut!' he repeated, and lunged towards her. Terry whirled away from him lightly.

She ran for the study door, with Manfred close behind her. She beat him into the passage and raced for the front door. Her heel caught in one of the persian carpets that covered the floor of the passage, and she staggered and fell against the wall.

'Whore!' He was on her instantly trying to wrestle the report out of her hands, but she clung to it with all her strength. Face to face they were almost of a height, and she saw the madness in his eyes.

Suddenly Manfred released her. He stepped back, bunched his fist and swung it round-armed into her cheek. Her head jerked back and cracked against the wall. He drew back his fist and hit her again. She felt the quick warm burst of blood spurt from her nose, and staggered through the door beside her into the dining-room. She was dizzy from the blows and she fell against the heavy stinkwood table.

Manfred was close behind her. He charged her, sending her sprawling backwards onto the table. He was on top of her, both his hands at her throat.

'I'm going to kill you, you whore,' he wheezed. His thumbs hooked and pressed deep into the flesh of her throat. With the frenzied strength of despair, Terry clawed at his eyes with both hands. Her nails scored his face, raking long red lines into his flesh. With a cry Manfred released her, and backed away holding both hands to his injured face, leaving Terry lying gasping across the table.

He stood for a moment, then uncovered his face and inspected the blood on his hands.

'I'll kill you for that!'

But as he advanced towards her, Terry rolled over the table.

'Whore! Slut! Bitch!' he screamed at her, following her around the table. Terry kept ahead of him.

There were a matched pair of heavy Stuart crystal decanters on the sideboard, one containing port, the other sherry. Terry snatched up one of them and turned to face Manfred. She hurled the decanter with all her remaining strength at his head.

Manfred did not have time to duck. The decanter cracked against his forehead, and he fell backwards, stunned. Terry snatched up the report and ran out of the dining-room, down the passage, out of the front door and into the garden. She was running weakly, following the driveway towards the main road.

Then behind her she heard the engine of an automobile roar into life. Panting wildly, holding the report, she stopped and looked back. Manfred had followed her out of the house. He was behind the steering wheel of Joy's Alfa Romeo. As she watched he threw the car into gear and howled towards her, blue smoke burning from the rear tyres with the speed of the acceleration. His face behind the windscreen was white and streaked with the marks of her nails, his eyes were staring, insane, and she knew he was going to ride her down.

She kicked off her shoes and ran off the driveway onto the lawns.

Crouched forward in the driver's seat of the Alfa, Manfred watched the fleeing figure ahead of him.

Terry ran with the full-hipped sway of the mature woman, her long legs were tanned and her hair flew out loosely behind her.

Manfred was not concerned with the return of the geological report, its existence was no longer of significance to him. What he wanted was to completely destroy this woman. In his crazed state, she had become the symbol and the figurehead of all his woes. His humiliation and fall were all linked to her, he could exact his vengeance by destroying her, crushing that revolting warm and clinging body, bruising it, ripping it with the steel of the Alfa Romeo's chassis.

He hit second gear and spun the steering-wheel. The Alfa swerved from the driveway, and as its rear wheels left the tarmac, they skidded on the thick grass. Deftly Manfred checked the skid and lined up on Terry's running back.

Already she was among the protea bushes on the lower terrace. The Alfa buck-jumped the slope, flying bird-free before crashing down heavily on its suspension. Wheels spun and bit, and the sleek vehicle shot forward again.

Terry looked back over her shoulder, her face was white and her eyes very big and fear-filled. Manfred giggled. He was aware of a sense of power, the ability to dispense life or death. He steered for her, reckless of all consequences, intent on destroying her.

There was a six-foot tall protea bush ahead of him, and

Manfred roared through it, bursting it asunder. Scattering branches and leaves, giggling again, he saw Terry directly ahead of him. She was still looking back at him, and at that moment she stumbled and fell onto her knees.

She was helpless. Her face streaked with tears and blood, her hair falling forward in wild disorder, kneeling as though for the headsman's stroke. Manfred felt a flood of disappointment. He did not want it to end so soon, he wanted to savour this sadistic elation, this sense of power.

At the last possible moment he yanked the wheel over and the car slewed violently. It shot past Terry with six inches to spare, and its rear wheels pelted her with clods of turf and thrown dirt.

Laughing aloud, wild-eyed, Manfred held the wheel hard over, bringing the Alfa around in a tight skidding circle, crackling sideways through another protea bush.

Terry was up and running again. He saw immediately that she was heading for the change rooms of the swimming-pool among the trees on the bottom lawn and she was far enough ahead to elude him, perhaps.

'Bitch!' he snarled, and crash-changed into third gear, with engine revs peaking. The Alfa howled in pursuit of the running girl.

Had Terry thrown the bulky report aside, she might have reached the brick change rooms ahead of the racing sports car, but the report hampered and slowed her. She still had twenty yards to cover, she was running along the paved edge of the swimming-pool, and she sensed that the car was right on top of her.

Terry dived sideways, hitting the water flat on her side, and the Alfa roared past. Manfred trod heavily on the brakes, the Michelin metallic tyres screeched against the paving stones, and Manfred out of the driver's seat the moment the Alfa stopped.

He ran back to the pool side. Terry was floundering towards the far steps. She was exhausted, weak with exertion and terror. Her sodden hair streamed down over her face, and she was gasping open-mouthed for air.

Manfred laughed again, a high-pitched, almost girlish giggle, and he dived after her, landing squarely between Terry's shoulder blades with his full weight. She went under, sucking water agonizingly into already aching lungs, and when she surfaced she was coughing and gagging, blinded with water and her own wet hair.

Almost immediately she felt herself seized from behind and forced face down into the water. For half a minute she struggled fiercely, then her movements slowed and became weaker.

Manfred stood over her, chest deep in the clear water, gripping her around the waist and by a handful of her sodden hair, forcing her face deep below the surface. He had lost his spectacles, and he blinked owlishly. The wet silk of his shirt clung to his upper body, and the water had slicked his hair down.

As he felt the life going out of her, and her movements becoming sluggish and slow, he began to laugh again. The broken, incoherent laughter of a madman.

'Dan!' Joy pointed off through the trees. 'That's my car down there, parked by the swimming-pool!'

'What the hell is it doing there?'

'There's something wrong, Terry wouldn't drive through her beloved garden, unless there was!'

Dan braked sharply and pulled his Jaguar to the side of the driveway.

'I'm going to take a look.' He slid out of the car and started off across the lawns. Joy opened her own door and trotted after him.

Dan saw the man in the water, fully dressed, intent on what he was doing. He recognized Manfred Steyner.

'What the hell is he up to?' Dan started running. He reached the edge of the pool, and suddenly he realized what was happening.

'Christ! He's drowning her,' he shouted aloud, and he sprang into the water.

He did not waste time struggling with Manfred. He hit him a great open-handed, round-armed blow, that cracked against the side of Manfred's head like a pistol shot and sent him lurching sideways, releasing his grip on Terry.

Ignoring Manfred, Dan picked Terry from the water like a drowned kitten and waded to the steps. He carried her out and laid her face down on the paving. He knelt over her and began applying artificial respiration. He felt Terry stir under his hands, then cough and retch weakly.

Joy came up at the run and dropped on her knees beside him.

'My God, Dan, what happened?'

'That little bastard was trying to drown her.'

Dan looked up from his labours without interrupting the rhythm of his movement over Terry. She spluttered and retched again.

On the far side of the pool Manfred Steyner had dragged himself from the pool. He was sitting on the edge with his feet still dangling into the water, his head was hanging and he was fingering the side of his face where Dan had hit him. On his lap he held a wet pulpy mess that had been the geological report.

'Joy, can you take over here? Terry's not too far gone, and I want to get my hands on that little Hun.'

Joy took Dan's place over Terry's prostrate form, and Dan stood up.

'What are you going to do to him?' Joy asked.

'I'm going to beat him to a pulp.'

'Good show!' Joy encouraged him.' 'Give him one for me.'

Manfred had heard the exchange and as Dan ran around the edge of the pool he scrambled to his feet, and staggered to the parked Alfa. He slammed the door and whirred the engine to life. Dan was just too late to stop him. The car shot forward across the lawns, leaving Dan running, futile, behind it.

'Look after her, Joy!' Dan shouted back.

By the time Dan had run up the terrace to his Jaguar and reversed it to point in the opposite direction, the Alfa had disappeared through the white gates with a musical flutter of its exhaust.

'Come on, girlie,' Dan spoke to his Jaguar. 'Let's go get him.'

The rear wheels spun as he pulled away.

Without his spectacles Manfred Steyner's vision was blurred and milky. The outlines of all objects on which he looked were softened and indistinct.

He instinctively checked the Alfa at the stop street at the bottom of the lane. He sat undecided, water still streaming from his clothing, squelching in his shoes. Beside him on the passenger seat lay the sodden report, its pages beginning to disintegrate from its soaking and the rough handling it had received.

He had to get rid of it. It was the shred of incriminating evidence. That was the only clear thought Manfred had. For the first time in his life the crystalline clarity of his thought processes was interrupted. He was confused, his mind jerking abruptly from one subject to another, the intense pleasure of inflicting hurt on Terry mingled with the sting and smart of his own injuries. He could not concentrate on either sensation for overlying it all was a sense of fear, of uncertainty. He felt vulnerable, hunted, hurt and shaken. His brain flickered and wavered as though a computer had developed an electrical fault. The answers it produced were nonsensical.

He looked in the rear view mirror, saw the Jaguar glide out between the white gates and turn towards him.

'Christ!' he panicked. He rammed his foot down on the accelerator and engaged the clutch. The Alfa screeched out into the main highway, swerved into the path of a heavy truck, bounded over the far kerb and swung back into the road.

Dan watched it tear away towards Kyalami.

He let the truck pass and then swung into the traffic behind it. He had to wait until the road was clear ahead before he could overtake the truck, and by that time the Alfa was a dwindling cream speck ahead of him.

Dan settled back in the leather bucket seat, and gave the Jaguar its head. He was furious, outraged by the treatment he had seen Manfred meeting out to Terry. Her swollen and bruised face had shocked him and his feet were firmly set upon the path of vengeance.

His hands gripped the steering-wheel fiercely, he was muttering threats of violence as the speedometer moved up over the hundred mile per hour mark and he began relentlessly overhauling the cream sports car.

Steadily he moved up behind the Alfa until he was driving almost on its rear bumper. The Alfa was held up by a green school bus. Dan could not pass, however, for there was a steady stream of traffic coming in the opposite direction.

He fastened his attention on the back of Manfred's head, still fuming with anger.

Dan dropped down a gear, ready to pull out and overtake the Alfa when the opportunity arose. At that moment Manfred looked up into his rear view mirror. Dan saw the reflection of his white face with disordered damp hair hanging onto the forehead, saw his expression change immediately he recognized Dan and the Alfa shot out into the face of the approaching traffic.

There was a howl and blare of horns, vehicles swerved to make way for Manfred's wild rush. Dan glimpsed frightened faces flicking past, but the Alfa had squeezed around the green bus and was speeding away.

Dan dropped back, then sent the Jaguar like a thrown javelin through the gap between bus and kerb, overtaking on the wrong side and ignoring the bus driver's yell of protest.

The Jaguar had a higher top speed, and on the long straight Pretoria highway Dan crept up steadily on the cream Alfa.

He could see Manfred glancing repeatedly into his driving-mirror, and he grinned mirthlessly.

Ahead of them the highway rose and then dipped over a low rounded ridge. A double avenue of tall blue gum trees flanked each side of the road.

Travelling in the same direction as the two high performance sports cars was a mini of a good vintage year. Its elderly driver was triumphantly about to overtake an overloaded vegetable truck. Neck and neck they approached the blind rise at twenty-five miles per hour, between them they effectively blocked half the road.

The horn of the Alfa wailed a high-pitched warning, and Manfred pulled out to overtake both slower vehicles. He was level with them, well out over the white dividing line, when a cement truck popped up over the blind rise.

Dan stood on his brake pedal with all the strength of his right leg, and watched it happen.

The cement truck and the Alfa came head on towards each other at a combined speed of well over a hundred miles per hour. At the last moment the Alfa began to turn away but it was too late by many seconds.

It caught the heavy cement truck a glancing blow and was hurled across the path of the two slower vehicles, miraculously touching neither of them; it skidded sideways leaving reeking black smears of rubber on the tarmac, and hurdled the low bank. It struck one of the blue gums full on, with a force that shivered the giant tree trunk and brought down a rain of leaves.

Dan pulled the Jaguar into the side of the road, parked it, and walked back.

He knew there was no hurry. The drivers of the mini and the vegetable truck were there before him. They were attempting to talk each other down, both of them excited and relieved by their own escapes.

'I'm a doctor,' said Dan, and they fell back respectfully.

'He doesn't need a doctor,' said one of them. 'He needs an undertaker.'

One look was sufficient. Dr Manfred Steyner was as dead as Dan had ever seen anybody. His crushed head was thrust through the windscreen. Dan picked up the sodden bundle of paper from the seat beside the huddled body. He was aware that some particular importance was attached to it.

Dan's anger had evaporated entirely, and he felt a twinge of pity as he looked into the wreckage at the corpse. It appeared so frail and small – of such little consequence.

The sunlight was sparkling bright, broken into a myriad eyestinging fragments by the rippling surface of the bay.

The breeze was strong enough for the Arrow class yachts to fly their spinnakers as they came down on the wind. The sails bulged out blue and yellow and bright scarlet against the sombre green of the great whale-black bluff above Durban Bay.

Under the awning on the afterdeck of the motor yacht it was cool, but the fat man wore only a pair of white linen slacks with his feet thrust into dark blue cloth espadrilles.

Sprawled in a deck-chair, his belly bulged smooth and hard over the waistband of his slacks; he was tanned a dark mahogany colour and his body-hair grew thick and curly from chest to navel.

'Thank you, Andrew.' He extended his empty glass, and the younger man carried it to the open-air bar. The fat man watched him as he mixed another Pimms No. 1 cup.

A white-clad crew member clambered down the companion way from the bridge. He touched his cap respectfully to the fat man.

'Captain's respects, sir, and we are ready to sail when you give the order.'

'Thank you. Please tell the captain we will sail as soon as Miss du Maine comes aboard.' And the crew man ran back to the bridge.

'Ah!' The fat man sighed happily as Andrew placed the Pimms in his out-stretched hand. 'I have really earned this break. The last few weeks have been nerve-racking, to say the least.'

'Yes, sir,' Andrew agreed dutifully. 'But, as usual, you snatched victory from the ashes.'

'It was close,' the fat man agreed. 'Young Ironsides gave us all a nasty fright with his drop-blast matt. I was only just able to make good my personal commitments before the price shot up again. The profit was not as high as I had anticipated, but then I have never made a habit of peering into the mouths of gift-horses.'

'It was a pity that our associates lost all that money,' Andrew ventured.

'Yes, yes. A great pity. But rather them than us, Andrew.'

'Indeed, sir.'

'In a way I am glad it worked out as it did. I am a patriotic man, at heart. I am relieved that it was not necessary to disrupt the economy of the country to make our little profit.'

He stood up suddenly, his interest quickening as a taxi cab came down onto the Yacht Club jetty. The cabby opened a rear door and from it emerged a very beautiful young lady.

'Ah, Andrew! Our guest has arrived. You may warn the captain that we will be sailing within minutes; and send a man to fetch her luggage.'

He went to the entry port to welcome the young lady.

72

In mid-summer in the Zambesi Valley the heat is a solid white shimmering thing. In the noon day nothing moves in the merciless sunlight.

At the centre of the native village grew a baobab tree. A monstrous bloated trunk with malformed branches like the limbs of a polio victim. The carrion crows sat in it, black and shiny as cockroaches. A score of grass huts ringed the tree, and beyond them lay the tilled fields. The millet stood tall and green in the sun.

Along the rude track towards the village came a Landrover. It came slowly, lurching and jolting over the rough ground, its motor growling in low gear. Printed in black on its sides were the letters A.R.C., African Recruiting Corporation.

The children heard it first, and crawled from the grass huts. Naked black bodies, and shrill excited voices in the sunlight.

They ran to meet the Landrover and danced beside it, shrieking and laughing. The Landrover came to a halt in the meagre shade under the baobab tree. An elderly white man climbed from the cab. He wore khaki safari clothes and a wide-brimmed hat. Complete silence fell, and one of the oldest boys fetched a carved stool and placed it in the shade.

The white man sat on the stool. A girl came forward, knelt before him and offered a gourd of millet beer. The white man drank from the gourd. No one spoke, none would disturb an honoured guest until he had taken refreshment, but from the grass huts the adult members of the village came. Blinking into the sunlight, winding their loin clothes about their waists. They came and squatted in a semi-circle before the white man on his stool.

He lowered the gourd and set it aside. He looked at them.

'I see you, my friends,' he greeted them, and the response was warm.

'We see you, old one,' they chorused, but the expression of their visitor remained grave.

'Let the wives of King Nkulu come forward,' he called. 'Let them bring each their first-born son with them.'

Four women and four adolescent boys left the crowd and came shyly into the open. For a moment the white man studied them compassionately, then he stood and stepped forward. He placed a hand on the shoulder of each of the two eldest lads.

'Your father has gone to *his* fathers,' he told them. There was a stirring, an intake of breath, a startled cry, and then, as was proper, the eldest wife let out the first sobbing wail of mourning.

One by one each wife sank down onto the dry musty earth and covered her head with her shawl.

'He is dead,' the white man repeated against the background of their keening lament. 'But he died in such honour as to let his name live on forever. So great was his dying that for all their lives money will each month be paid to his wives, and for each of his sons there is already set aside a place at the University that each may grow as strong in learning as his father was in body. Of Big King there will be raised up an image in stone.

'The wives of Big King and his sons will travel in a flying machine to I'Goldi, that their eyes also may look upon the stone image of the man who was their husband and their father.' The white man paused for breath, it was a lengthy speech in the midday heat of the valley. He wiped his face and then tucked the handkerchief into his pocket.

'He was a lion!'

'Ngwenyama!' whispered the sturdy twelve-year-old boy standing beside the white man. The tears started from his eyes and greased down his cheeks. He turned away and ran alone into the millet fields.

73

Dennis Langley, the Sales Manager of Kitchenerville Motors who were the local Ford agents, stretched his arms over his head luxuriously. He sighed with deep contentment. What a lovely way to spend a working day morning.

'Happy?' asked Hettie Delange beside him in the double bed. In reply Dennis grinned and sighed again.

Hettie sat up and let the sheet fall to her waist. Her breasts were big and white, and damp with perspiration. She looked down on his naked chest and arm muscles approvingly.

'Gee, you're built nicely.'

'So are you,' Dennis smiled up at her.

'You're different from the other chaps I've gone out with,' Hettie told him. 'You speak so nicely – like a gentleman, you know.'

Before Dennis Langley could decide on a suitable reply, the front door bell shrilled, the sound of it echoing through the house. Dennis shot into an upright position with a fearful expression on his face.

'Who's that?' he demanded.

'It's probably the butcher delivering the meat.'

'It may be my wife!' Dennis cautioned her. 'Don't answer it.'

'Of course I've got to answer it, silly.' Hettie threw back the sheet, and rose in her white and golden glory to find her dressing-gown. The sight was enough to momentarily quiet Dennis Langley's misgivings, but as she belted her gown and hid it from view he urged her again.

'Be careful! Make sure it's not her before you open the door.'

Hettie opened the front door, and immediately drew her gown more closely around her with one hand, while the other she tried to pat her hair into a semblance of order.

'Hello,' she breathed.

The tall young man in the doorway was really rather dreamy.

624

He wore a dark business suit and carried an expensive leather briefcase.

'Mrs Delange?' he inquired. He had a nice soft dreamy voice.

'Yes, I'm Mrs Delange.' Hettie fluttered her eyelashes. 'Won't you come in?'

She led him through to the lounge, and she was pleasantly aware of his eyes on the opening of her gown.

'What can I do for you?' she asked archly.

'I am your local representative of the Sanlam Insurance Company, Mrs Delange. I have come to express my company's condolences on your recent sad bereavement. I would have called sooner, but I did not wish to intrude on your sorrow.'

'Oh!' Hettie dropped her eyes, immediately adopting the role of the widow.

'However, we hope we can bring a little light to disperse the darkness that surrounds you. You may know that your husband was a policy-holder with our Company?'

Hettie shook her head, but watched with interest while the visitor opened his briefcase.

'Yes, he was. Two months ago he took out a straight life policy with double indemnity. The policy was ceded to you.' The Insurance man extracted a sheaf of papers from his case. 'I have here my company's cheque in full settlement of all claims under the policy. If you will just sign for it, please.'

'How much?' Hettie abandoned the role of the bereaved.

'With the double indemnity, the cheque is for forty-eight thousand Rand.'

Hettie's eyes flew wide with delight.

'Gee!' she gasped. 'That's *fabulous*!'

74

Hurry's original intentions had expanded considerably. Instead of a plaque on the cement plug at 66 level, the monument to Big King had become a life-sized statue in bronze. He sited it on the lawns in front of the Adminstrative offices of the Sonder Ditch on a base of black marble.

It was effective. The artist had captured a sense of urgency, of vibrant power. The inscription was simple, just the name of the man – 'King Nkulu' – and the date of his death.

Hurry attended the unveiling in person, even though he hated ceremonies and avoided them whenever possible. In the front row of guests facing him his granddaughter sat beside Doctor Stander and his very new blonde wife. She winked at him and Hurry frowned lovingly back at her.

From the seat beside Hurry, young Ironsides stood up to introduce the Chairman. Hurry noted the expression on his granddaughter's face as she transferred all her attention to the tall young man with both his arms encased in plaster of Paris and supported by slings.

'Perhaps I should have fired him, after all,' thought Hurry. 'He is going to cut one out of my herd.'

Hurry glanced sideways at his General Manager, and decided with resignation, 'Too late'. Then he went on to cheer himself. 'Anyway he looks like good breeding stock.'

His line of thought switched again. 'Better start making arrangements to transfer him up to Head Office. He will need a lot of grooming and polishing.'

Without thinking he fished a powerful-looking cigar from his breast pocket. He had it half-way to his mouth when he caught Terry's scandalized glare. Silently her lips formed the words: 'Your doctor!'

Guiltily Hurry Hirschfeld stuffed the cigar back into his pocket.